THE WORLD OF ICE & FIRE

THE UNTOLD HISTORY OF WESTEROS AND THE GAME OF THRONES

GEORGE R. R. MARTIN

ELIO M. GARCÍA, JR. AND LINDA ANTONSSON

THE WORLD OF ICE & FIRE

THE UNTOLD HISTORY OF WESTEROS AND THE GAME OF THRONES

GEORGE R. R. MARTIN

ELIO M. GARCÍA, JR. AND LINDA ANTONSSON

HARPER
Voyager

FANTASY FLIGHT GAMES (FFG) IS ONE OF THE WORLD'S LEADING PUBLISHERS OF HOBBY GAMES. KNOWN FOR THE QUALITY OF ITS COMPONENTS AND ITS INNOVATIVE GAMEPLAY, FFG IMMERSES PLAYERS IN THE WORLD OF GEORGE R.R. MARTIN'S A SONG OF ICE AND FIRE WITH SUCH TITLES AS A GAME OF THRONES: THE BOARD GAME SECOND EDITION AND A GAME OF THRONES: THE CARD GAME.

WWW.FANTASYFLIGHTGAMES.COM

FACEBOOK: WWW.FACEBOOK.COM/FANTASYFLIGHTGAMES

FOLLOW US ON TWITTER: @FFGAMES

HarperCollins*Publishers*
1 London Bridge Street,
London, SE1 9GF

www.harpervoyagerbooks.co.uk

Published by Harper*Voyager*,
an Imprint of HarperCollins*Publishers* 2014

8

Copyright © George R.R. Martin 2014

George R.R. Martin asserts the moral right to be identified as the author of this work

Images on pages 38, 92, 116, 136, 181, 188-189, 230-231, 248, and 293 are © Fantasy Flight Publishing Inc.
Book design by Rosebud Eustace.

A catalogue record for this book is available from the British Library

ISBN: 978-0-00-758091-0

MIX
Paper from
responsible sources
FSC **FSC® C007454**
www.fsc.org

FSC is a non-profit international organisation established
to promote the responsible management of the world's forests.
Products carrying the FSC label are independently certified
to assure consumers that they come from forests that are managed
to meet the social, economic and ecological needs
of present and future generations.

Find out more about HarperCollins and the environment at
www.harpercollins.co.uk/green

GEORGE R.R. MARTIN'S A WORLD OF ICE & FIRE—A GAME OF THRONES GUIDE

GET THE ONLY OFFICIAL A SONG OF ICE AND FIRE APP FROM GEORGE R.R. MARTIN WITH HUNDREDS OF DETAILED CHARACTER BIOS, PLACE PROFILES, HOUSE LISTINGS, INTERACTIVE MAPS, AND ANTI-SPOILER PROTECTION. SEARCH FOR "WORLD OF ICE AND FIRE" ON YOUR APP STORE.

Apple and the Apple logo are trademarks of Apple Inc., registered in the U.S. and other countries.
App Store is a service mark of Apple Inc.

END PAPER | *Dragonstone.*   RIGHT | *Storm's End.*

Contents

Preface ix

ANCIENT HISTORY 03

   The Dawn Age 05

   The Coming of the First Men 08

   The Age of Heroes 10

   The Long Night 11

   The Rise of Valyria 13

   Valyria's Children 15

   The Arrival of the Andals 17

   Ten Thousand Ships 21

   The Doom of Valyria 26

THE REIGN OF THE DRAGONS 29

   The Conquest 31

THE TARGARYEN KINGS 47

   Aegon I 49

   Aenys I 52

   Maegor I 55

   Jaehaerys I 60

   Viserys I 66

   Aegon II 73

   Aegon III 82

   Daeron I 87

   Baelor I 89

   Viserys II 94

   Aegon IV 95

Daeron II 100

Aerys I 104

Maekar I 106

Aegon V 107

Jaehaerys II 111

Aerys II 113

THE FALL OF THE DRAGONS 122

   The Year of the False Spring 124

   Robert's Rebellion 127

   The End 129

THE GLORIOUS REIGN 131

THE SEVEN KINGDOMS 133

   The North 135

      The Kings of Winter 137

      The Mountain Clans 139

      The Stoneborn of Skagos 139

      The Crannogmen of the Neck 140

      The Lords of Winterfell 141

      Winterfell 142

   The Wall and Beyond 145

      The Night's Watch 145

      The Wildlings 146

   The Riverlands 151

      House Tully 156

      Riverrun 160

   The Vale 163

      House Arryn 169

      The Eyrie 170

   The Iron Islands 175

      Driftwood Crowns 178

      The Iron Kings 182

The Black Blood 183

The Greyjoys of Pyke 187

The Red Kraken 188

The Old Way and the New 190

Pyke 195

The Westerlands 195

House Lannister Under the Dragons . 198

Casterly Rock 204

The Reach 207

Garth Greenhand 207

The Gardener Kings 209

Andals in the Reach 211

Oldtown 213

House Tyrell 217

Highgarden 218

The Stormlands 221

The Coming of the First Men 222

House Durrandon 223

Andals in the Stormlands 225

House Baratheon 227

The Men of the Stormlands 231

Storm's End 233

Dorne 235

The Breaking 237

Kingdoms of the First Men 238

The Andals Arrive 238

The Coming of the Rhoynar 240

Queer Customs of the South 241

Dorne Against the Dragons 243

Sunspear 248

BEYOND THE SUNSET KINGDOM 251

Other Lands 252

The Free Cities 253

Lorath 253

Norvos 256

Qohor 259

The Quarrelsome Daughters:
Myr, Lys, and Tyrosh 261

Pentos 266

Volantis 267

Braavos 271

Beyond the Free Cities 277

The Summer Isles 277

Naath 282

The Basilisk Isles 282

Sothoryos 284

The Grasslands 287

The Shivering Sea 294

Ib 295

East of Ib 298

The Bones and Beyond 299

Yi Ti 300

The Plains of the Jogos Nhai 304

Leng 306

Asshai-by-the-Shadow 308

Afterword 311

Appendix: Targaryen Lineage 312

Appendix: Stark Lineage 314

Appendix: Lannister Lineage 316

Appendix: Reign of the Kings 319

Index 320

Art Credits 326

To his most esteemed and gracious

lord, Tommen

the First of His Name, King of the

Audals and the Rhoynar and the First Men,

Lord of the Seven Kingdoms and

Protector of the Realm, Yandel,

humble Maester of the Citadel,

wishes thousandfold prosperity,

now and forever, and wisdom unmatched.

Preface

IT IS SAID with truth that every building is constructed stone by stone, and the same may be said of knowledge, extracted and compiled by many learned men, each of whom builds upon the works of those who preceded him. What one of them does not know is known to another, and little remains truly unknown if one seeks far enough. Now I, Maester Yandel, take my turn as mason, carving what I know to place one more stone in the great bastion of knowledge that has been built over the centuries both within and without the confines of the Citadel—a bastion raised by countless hands that came before, and which will, no doubt, continue to rise with the aid of countless hands yet to come.

I was a foundling from my birth in the tenth year of the reign of the last Targaryen king, left on a morning in an empty stall in the Scribe's Hearth, where acolytes practiced the art of letters for those who had need. The course of my life was set that day, when I was found by an acolyte who took me to the Seneschal of that year, Archmaester Edgerran. Edgerran, whose ring and rod and mask were silver, looked upon my squalling face and announced that I might prove of use. When first told this as a boy, I took it to mean he foresaw my destiny as a maester; only much later did I come to learn from Archmaester Ebrose that Edgerran was writing a treatise on the swaddling of infants and wished to test certain theories.

But inauspicious as that may seem, the result was that I was given to the care of servants and received the occasional attention of maesters. I was raised as a servant myself amongst the halls and chambers and libraries, but I was given the gift of letters by Archmaester Walgrave. Thus did I come to know and love the Citadel and the knights of the mind who guarded its precious wisdom. I desired nothing more than to become one of them—to read of far places and long-dead men, to gaze at the stars and measure the passing of the seasons.

And so I did. I forged the first link in my chain at three-and-ten, and other links followed. I completed my chain and took my oaths in the ninth year of the reign of King Robert, the First of His Name, and found myself blessed to continue at the Citadel, to serve the archmaesters and aid them in all that they did. It was a great honor, but my greatest desire was to create a work of mine own, a work that humble but lettered men might read—and read to their wives and children—so that they would learn of things both good and wicked, just and unjust, great and small, and grow wiser as I had grown wiser amidst the learning of the Citadel. And so I set myself to work once more at my forge, to make new and notable matter around the masterworks of the long-dead maesters who came before me. What follows herein sprang from that desire: a history of deeds gallant and wicked, peoples familiar and strange, and lands near and far.

ABOVE | *Aegon the Conqueror upon Balerion, the Black Dread.*

THE WORLD OF
ICE & FIRE

THE UNTOLD HISTORY OF WESTEROS AND
THE GAME OF THRONES

Ancient History

THE
KNOWN
WORLD

WESTEROS

ESSOS

SOTHORYOS

THERE ARE NONE who can say with certain knowledge when the world began, yet this has not stopped many maesters and learned men from seeking the answer. Is it forty thousand years old, as some hold, or perhaps a number as large as five hundred thousand—or even more? It is not written in any book that we know, for in the first age of the world, the Dawn Age, men were not lettered.

We can be certain that the world was far more primitive, however—a barbarous place of tribes living directly from the land with no knowledge of the working of metal or the taming of beasts. What little is known to us of those days is contained in the oldest of texts: the tales written down by the Andals, by the Valyrians, and by the Ghiscari, and even by those distant people of fabled Asshai. Yet however ancient those lettered races, they were not even children during the Dawn Age. So what truths their tales contain are difficult to find, like seeds among chaff.

What can most accurately be told about the Dawn Age? The eastern lands were awash with many peoples—uncivilized, as all the world was uncivilized, but numerous. But on Westeros, from the Lands of Always Winter to the shores of the Summer Sea, only two peoples existed: the children of the forest and the race of creatures known as the giants.

Of the giants in the Dawn Age, little and less can be said, for no one has gathered their tales, their legends, their histories. Men of the Watch say the wildlings have tales of the giants living uneasily alongside the children, ranging where they would and taking what they wanted. All the accounts claim that they were huge and powerful creatures, but simple. Reliable accounts from the rangers of the Night's Watch, who were the last men to see the giants while they still lived, state that they were covered in a thick fur rather than simply being very large men as the nursery tales hold.

There is considerable evidence of burials among the giants, as recorded in Maester Kennet's *Passages of the Dead*—a study of the barrow fields and graves and tombs of the North in his time of service at Winterfell, during the long reign of Cregan Stark. From bones that have been found in the North and sent to the Citadel, some maesters estimate that the largest of the giants could reach fourteen feet, though others say twelve feet is nearer the truth. The tales of long-dead rangers written down by maesters of the Watch all agree that the giants did not make homes or garments, and knew of no better tools or weapons than branches pulled from trees.

The giants had no kings and no lords, made no homes save in caverns or beneath tall trees, and they worked neither metal nor fields. They remained creatures of the Dawn Age even as the ages passed them by, men grew ever more numerous, and the forests were tamed and dwindled. Now the giants are gone even in the lands beyond the Wall, and the last reports of them are more than a hundred years old. And even those are dubious—tales that rangers of the Watch might tell over a warm fire.

The children of the forest were, in many ways, the opposites of the giants. As small as children but dark and beautiful, they lived in a manner we might call crude today, yet they were still less barbarous than the giants. They worked no metal, but they had great art in working obsidian (what the smallfolk call dragonglass, while the Valyrians knew it by a word meaning "frozen fire") to make tools and weapons for hunting. They wove no cloths but were skilled in making garments of leaves and bark. They learned to make bows of weirwood and to construct flying snares of grass, and both of the sexes hunted with these.

Their song and music was said to be as beautiful as they were, but what they sang of is not remembered save in small fragments handed down from ancient days. Maester Childer's *Winter's Kings, or the Legends and Lineages of the Starks of Winterfell* contains a part of a ballad alleged to tell of the time Brandon the Builder sought the aid of the children while raising the Wall. He was taken to a secret

The archives of the Citadel contain a letter from Maester Aemon, sent in the early years of the reign of Aegon V, which reports on an account from a ranger named Redwyn, written in the days of King Dorren Stark. It recounts a journey to Lorn Point and the Frozen Shore, in which it is claimed that the ranger and his companions fought giants and traded with the children of the forest. Aemon's letter claimed that he had found many such accounts in his examinations of the archives of the Watch at Castle Black, and considered them credible.

PREVIOUS PAGES | *Constructing the Wall.*

place to meet with them, but could not at first understand their speech, which was described as sounding like the song of stones in a brook, or the wind through leaves, or the rain upon the water. The manner in which Brandon learned to comprehend the speech of the children is a tale in itself, and not worth repeating here. But it seems clear that their speech originated, or drew inspiration from, the sounds they heard every day.

The gods the children worshipped were the nameless ones that would one day become the gods of the First Men—the innumerable gods of the streams and forests and stones. It was the children who carved the weirwoods with faces, perhaps to give eyes to their gods so that they might watch their worshippers at their devotions. Others, with little evidence, claim that the greenseers—the wise men of the children—were able to see through the eyes of the carved weirwoods. The supposed proof is the fact that the First Men themselves believed this; it was their fear of the weirwoods spying upon them that drove them to cut down many of the carved trees and weirwood groves, to deny the children such an advantage. Yet the First Men were less learned than we are now, and credited things that their descendants today do not; consider Maester Yorrick's *Wed to the Sea, Being an Account of the History of White Harbor from Its Earliest Days*, which recounts the practice of blood sacrifice to the old gods. Such sacrifices persisted as recently as five centuries ago, according to accounts from Maester Yorrick's predecessors at White Harbor.

This is not to say that the greenseers did not know lost arts that belong to the higher mysteries, such as seeing events at a great distance or communicating across half a realm (as the Valyrians, who came long after them, did). But mayhaps some of the feats of the greenseers have more to do with foolish tales than truth. They could not change their forms into those of beasts, as some would have it, but it seems true that they were capable of communicating with animals in a way that we cannot now achieve; it is from this that legends of skinchangers, or beastlings, arose.

In truth, the legends of the skinchangers are many, but the most common—brought from beyond the Wall by men of the Night's Watch, and recorded at the Wall by septons and maesters of centuries past—hold that the skinchangers not only communicated with beasts, but could control them by having their spirits mingle. Even among the wildlings, these skinchangers were feared as unnatural men who could call on animals as allies. Some tales speak of skinchangers losing themselves in their beasts, and others say that the animals could speak with a human voice when a skinchanger controlled them. But all the tales agree that the most common skinchangers were men who controlled wolves—even direwolves—and these had a special name among the wildlings: wargs.

Legend further holds that the greenseers could also delve into the past and see far into the future. But as all our learning has shown us, the higher mysteries that claim this power also claim that their visions of the things to come are unclear and often misleading—a useful thing to say when seeking to

Though considered disreputable in this, our present day, a fragment of Septon Barth's *Unnatural History* has proved a source of controversy in the halls of the Citadel. Claiming to have consulted with texts said to be preserved at Castle Black, Septon Barth put forth that the children of the forest could speak with ravens and could make them repeat their words. According to Barth, this higher mystery was taught to the First Men by the children so that ravens could spread messages at a great distance. It was passed, in degraded form, down to the maesters today, who no longer know how to speak to the birds. It is true that our order understands the speech of ravens . . . but this means the basic purposes of their cawing and rasping, their signs of fear and anger, and the means by which they display their readiness to mate or their lack of health.

Ravens are amongst the cleverest of birds, but they are no wiser than infant children, and considerably less capable of true speech, whatever Septon Barth might have believed. A few maesters, devoted to the link of Valyrian steel, have argued that Barth was correct, but not a one has been able to prove his claims regarding speech between men and ravens.

fool the unwary with fortune-telling. Though the children had arts of their own, the truth must always be separated from superstition, and knowledge must be tested and made sure. The higher mysteries, the arts of magic, were and are beyond the boundaries of our mortal ability to examine.

Yet no matter the truths of their arts, the children were led by their greenseers, and there is no doubt that they could once be found from the Lands of Always Winter to the shores of the Summer Sea. They made their homes simply, constructing no holdfasts or castles or cities. Instead they resided in the woods, in crannogs, in bogs and marshes, and even in caverns and hollow hills. It is said that, in the woods, they made shelters of leaves and withes up in the branches of trees—secret tree "towns."

It has long been held that they did this for protection from predators such as direwolves or shadowcats, which their simple stone weapons—and even their vaunted greenseers—were not proof against. But other sources dispute this, stating that their greatest foes were the giants, as hinted at in tales told in the North, and as possibly proved by Maester Kennet in the study of a barrow near the Long Lake—a giant's burial with obsidian arrowheads found amidst the extant ribs. It brings to mind a transcription of a wildling song in Maester Herryk's *History of the Kings-Beyond-the-Wall*, regarding the brothers Gendel and Gorne. They were called upon to mediate

a dispute between a clan of children and a family of giants over the possession of a cavern. Gendel and Gorne, it is said, ultimately resolved the matter through trickery, making both sides disavow any desire for the cavern, after the brothers discovered it was a part of a greater chain of caverns that eventually passed beneath the Wall. But considering that the wildlings have no letters, their traditions must be looked at with a jaundiced eye.

The beasts of the woods and the giants were eventually joined by other, greater dangers, however.

A possibility arises for a third race to have inhabited the Seven Kingdoms in the Dawn Age, but it is so speculative that it need only be dealt with briefly.

Among the ironborn, it is said that the first of the First Men to come to the Iron Isles found the famous Seastone Chair on Old Wyk, but that the isles were uninhabited. If true, the nature and origins of the chair's makers are a mystery. Maester Kirth in his collection of ironborn legends, *Songs the Drowned Men Sing*, has suggested that the chair was left by visitors from across the Sunset Sea, but there is no evidence for this, only speculation.

LEFT | *A giant.* ABOVE | *A child of the forest.*

THE COMING OF THE FIRST MEN

ACCORDING TO THE most well-regarded accounts from the Citadel, anywhere from eight thousand to twelve thousand years ago, in the southernmost reaches of Westeros, a new people crossed the strip of land that bridged the narrow sea and connected the eastern lands with the land in which the children and giants lived. It was here that the First Men came into Dorne via the Broken Arm, which was not yet broken. Why these people left their homelands is lost to all knowing, but when they came, they came in force. Thousands entered and began to settle the lands, and as the decades passed, they pushed farther and farther north. Such tales as we have of those migratory days are not to be trusted, for they suggest that, within a few short years, the First Men had moved beyond the Neck and into the North. Yet, in truth, it would have taken decades, even centuries, for this to occur.

What does seem to be accurate from all the tales, however, is that the First Men soon came to war with the children of the forest. Unlike the children, the First Men farmed the land and raised up ringforts and villages. And in so doing, they took to chopping down the weirwood trees, including those with carved faces, and for this, the children attacked them, leading to hundreds of years of war. The First Men—who had brought with them strange gods, horses, cattle, and weapons of bronze—were also larger and stronger than the children, and so they were a significant threat.

The hunters among the children—their wood dancers—became their warriors as well, but for all their secret arts of tree and leaf, they could only slow the First Men in their advance. The greenseers employed their arts, and tales say that they could call the beasts of marsh, forest, and air to fight on their behalf: direwolves and monstrous snowbears, cave lions and eagles, mammoths and serpents, and more. But the First Men proved too powerful, and the children are said to have been driven to a desperate act.

Legend says that the great floods that broke the land bridge that is now the Broken Arm and made the Neck a swamp were the work of the greenseers, who gathered at Moat Cailin to work dark magic. Some contest this, however: the First Men were already in Westeros when this occurred, and stemming the tide from the east would do little more than slow their progress. Moreover, such power is beyond even what the greenseers are traditionally said to have been capable of . . . and even those accounts appear exaggerated. It is likelier that the inundation of the Neck and the breaking of the Arm were natural events, possibly caused by a natural sinking of the land. What became of Valyria is well-known, and in the Iron Islands, the castle of Pyke sits on stacks of stone that were once part of the greater island before segments of it crumbled into the sea.

Regardless, the children of the forest fought as fiercely as the First Men to defend their lives. Inexorably, the war ground on across generations, until at last the children understood that they could not win. The First Men, perhaps tired of war, also wished to see an end to the fighting. The wisest of both races prevailed, and the chief heroes and rulers of both sides met upon the isle in the Gods Eye to form the Pact. Giving up all the lands of Westeros save for

ABOVE | *A carved weirwood.*   RIGHT | *The children of the forest and the First Men forming the Pact.*

the deep forests, the children won from the First Men the promise that they would no longer cut down the weirwoods. All the weirwoods of the isle on which the Pact was forged were then carved with faces so that the gods could witness the Pact, and the order of green men was made afterward to tend to the weirwoods and protect the isle.

With the Pact, the Dawn Age of the world drew to a close, and the Age of Heroes followed.

Whether the green men still survive on their isle is not clear although there is the occasional account of some foolhardy young riverlord taking a boat to the isle and catching sight of them before winds rise up or a flock of ravens drives him away. The nursery tales claiming that they are horned and have dark, green skin is a corruption of the likely truth, which is that the green men wore green garments and horned headdresses.

THE AGE OF HEROES

THE AGE OF HEROES lasted for thousands of years, in which kingdoms rose and fell, noble houses were founded and withered away, and great deeds were accomplished. Yet what we truly know of those ancient days is hardly more than what we know of the Dawn Age. The tales we have now are the work of septons and maesters writing thousands of years after the fact—yet unlike the children of the forest and the giants, the First Men of this Age of Heroes left behind some ruins and ancient castles that can corroborate parts of the legends, and there are stone monuments in the barrow fields and elsewhere marked with their runes. It is through these remnants that we can begin to ferret out the truth behind the tales.

What is commonly accepted is that the Age of Heroes began with the Pact and extended through the thousands of years in which the First Men and the children lived in peace with one another. With so much land ceded to them, the First Men at last had room to increase. From the Land of Always Winter to the shores of the Summer Sea, the First Men ruled from their ringforts. Petty kings and powerful lords proliferated, but in time some few proved to be stronger than the rest, forging the seeds of the kingdoms that are the ancestors of the Seven Kingdoms we know today. The names of the kings of these earliest realms are caught up in legend, and the tales that claim their individual rules lasted hundreds of years are to be understood as errors and fantasies introduced by others in later days.

Names such as Brandon the Builder, Garth Greenhand, Lann the Clever, and Durran Godsgrief are names to conjure with, but it is likely that their legends hold less truth than fancy. Elsewhere, I shall endeavor to sift what grain can be found from the chaff, but for now it is enough to acknowledge the tales.

And besides the legendary kings and the hundreds of kingdoms from which the Seven Kingdoms were born, stories of such as Symeon Star-Eyes, Serwyn of the Mirror Shield, and other heroes have become fodder for septons and singers alike. Did such heroes once exist? It may be so. But when the singers number Serwyn of the Mirror Shield as one of the Kingsguard—an institution that was only formed during the reign of Aegon the Conqueror—we can see why it is that few of these tales can ever be trusted. The septons who first wrote them down took what details suited them and added others, and the singers changed them—sometimes beyond all recognition—for the sake of a warm place in some lord's hall. In such a way does some long-dead First Man become a knight who follows the Seven and guards the Targaryen kings thousands of years after he lived (if he ever did). The legion of boys and youths made ignorant of the past history of Westeros by these foolish tales cannot be numbered.

It is best to remember that when we speak of these legendary founders of realms, we speak merely of some early domains—generally centered on a high seat, such as Casterly Rock or Winterfell—that in time incorporated more and more land and power into their grasp. If Garth Greenhand ever ruled what he claimed was the Kingdom of the Reach, it is doubtful its writ was anything more than notional beyond a fortnight's ride from his halls. But from such petty domains arose the mightier kingdoms that came to dominate Westeros in the millennia to come.

THE LONG NIGHT

AS THE FIRST MEN established their realms following the Pact, little troubled them save their own feuds and wars, or so the histories tell us. It is also from these histories that we learn of the Long Night, when a season of winter came that lasted a generation—a generation in which children were born, grew into adulthood, and in many cases died without ever seeing the spring. Indeed, some of the old wives' tales say that they never even beheld the light of day, so complete was the winter that fell on the world. While this last may well be no more than fancy, the fact that some cataclysm took place many thousands of years ago seems certain. Lomas Longstrider, in his *Wonders Made by Man*, recounts meeting descendants of the Rhoynar in the ruins of the festival city of Chroyane who have tales of a darkness that made the Rhoyne dwindle and disappear, her waters frozen as far south as the joining of the Selhoru. According to these tales, the return of the sun came only when a hero convinced Mother Rhoyne's many children—lesser gods such as the Crab King and the Old Man of the River—to put aside their bickering and join together to sing a secret song that brought back the day.

It is also written that there are annals in Asshai of such a darkness, and of a hero who fought against it with a red sword. His deeds are said to have been performed before the rise of Valyria, in the earliest age when Old Ghis was first forming its empire. This legend has spread west from Asshai, and the followers of R'hllor claim that this hero was named Azor Ahai, and prophesy his return. In the *Jade Compendium*, Colloquo Votar recounts a curious legend from Yi Ti, which states that the sun hid its face from the earth for a lifetime, ashamed at something none could discover, and that disaster was averted only by the deeds of a woman with a monkey's tail.

However, if this fell winter did take place, as the tales say, the privation would have been terrible to behold. During the hardest winters, it is customary for the oldest and most infirm amongst the northmen to claim they are going out hunting—knowing full well they will never return and thus leaving a little more food for those likelier to survive. Doubtless this practice was common during the Long Night.

Yet there are other tales—harder to credit and yet more central to the old histories—about creatures known as the Others. According to these tales, they came from the frozen Land of Always Winter, bringing the cold and darkness with them as they sought to extinguish all light and warmth. The tales go on to say they rode monstrous ice spiders and the horses of the dead, resurrected to serve them, just as they resurrected dead men to fight on their behalf.

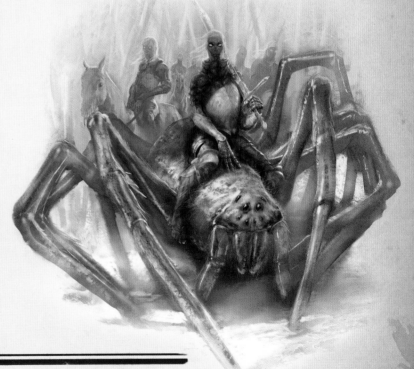

Though the Citadel has long sought to learn the manner by which it may predict the length and change of seasons, all efforts have been confounded. Septon Barth appeared to argue, in a fragmentary treatise, that the inconstancy of the seasons was a matter of magical art rather than trustworthy knowledge. Maester Nicol's *The Measure of the Days*—otherwise a laudable work containing much of use—seems influenced by this argument. Based upon his work on the movement of stars in the firmament, Nicol argues unconvincingly that the seasons might once have been of a regular length, determined solely by the way in which the globe faces the sun in its heavenly course. The notion behind it seems true enough—that the lengthening and shortening of days, if more regular, would have led to more regular seasons—but he could find no evidence that such was ever the case, beyond the most ancient of tales.

LEFT | *A ruined ringfort of the First Men.* ABOVE | *The Others mounted on ice spiders and dead horses, as the legends claim.*

How the Long Night came to an end is a matter of legend, as all such matters of the distant past have become. In the North, they tell of a last hero who sought out the intercession of the children of the forest, his companions abandoning him or dying one by one as they faced ravenous giants, cold servants, and the Others themselves. Alone he finally reached the children, despite the efforts of the white walkers, and all the tales agree this was a turning point. Thanks to the children, the first men of the Night's Watch banded together and were able to fight—and win—the Battle for the Dawn: the last battle that broke the endless winter and sent the Others fleeing to the icy north. Now, six thousand years later (or eight thousand as *True History* puts forward), the Wall made to defend the realms of men is still manned by the sworn brothers of the Night's Watch, and neither the Others nor the children have been seen in many centuries.

Archmaester Fomas's *Lies of the Ancients*—though little regarded these days for its erroneous claims regarding the founding of Valyria and certain lineal claims in the Reach and westerlands—does speculate that the Others of legend were nothing more than a tribe of the First Men, ancestors of the wildlings, that had established itself in the far north. Because of the Long Night, these early wildlings were then pressured to begin a wave of conquests to the south. That they became monstrous in the tales told thereafter, according to Fomas, reflects the desire of the Night's Watch and the Starks to give themselves a more heroic identity as saviors of mankind, and not merely the beneficiaries of a struggle over dominion.

THE RISE OF VALYRIA

AS WESTEROS RECOVERED from the Long Night, a new power was rising in Essos. The vast continent, stretching from the narrow sea to the fabled Jade Sea and faraway Ulthos, seems to be the place where civilization as we know it developed. The first of these (not withstanding the dubious claims of Qarth, the YiTish legends of the Great Empire of the Dawn, and the difficulties of finding any truth in the tales of legendary Asshai) was rooted in Old Ghis: a city built upon slavery. The legendary founder of the city, Grazdan the Great, remains so revered that men of the slaver families are still often given his name. It was he who, according to the oldest histories of the Ghiscari, founded the lockstep legions with their tall shields and three spears, which were the first to fight as disciplined bodies. Old Ghis and its army proceeded to colonize its surroundings, then, pressing on, to subjugate its neighbors. Thus was the first empire born, and for centuries it reigned supreme.

It was on the great peninsula across from Slaver's Bay that those who brought an end to the empire of Old Ghis—though not to all of their ways—originated. Sheltered there, amidst the great volcanic mountains known as the Fourteen Flames, were the Valyrians, who learned to tame dragons and make them the most fearsome weapon of war that the world ever saw. The tales the Valyrians told of themselves claimed they were descended from dragons and were kin to the ones they now controlled.

The great beauty of the Valyrians—with their hair of palest silver or gold and eyes in shades of purple not found amongst any other peoples of the world—is well-known, and often held up as proof that the Valyrians are not entirely of the same blood as other men. Yet there are maesters who point out that, by careful breeding of animals, one can achieve a desirable result, and that populations in isolation can often show quite remarkable variations from what might be regarded as common. This may be a likelier answer to the mystery of the Valyrian origins although it does not explain the affinity with dragons that those with the blood of Valyria clearly had.

The Valyrians had no kings but instead called themselves the Freehold because all the citizenry who held land had a voice. Archons might be chosen to help lead, but they were elected by the lords freeholder from amongst their number, and only for a limited time. It was rare for Valyria to be swayed by one freeholding family alone although it was not entirely unknown either.

The five great wars between the Freehold and Old Ghis when the world was young are the stuff of legend—conflagrations that ended each time in the victory of the Valyrians over the Ghiscari. It was during the fifth and final war that the Freehold chose to make sure there would be no sixth war. The ancient brick walls of Old Ghis, first erected by Grazdan the Great in ancient days, were razed.

In such fragments of Barth's *Unnatural History* as remain, the septon appears to have considered various legends examining the origins of dragons and how they came to be controlled by the Valyrians. The Valyrians themselves claimed that dragons sprang forth as the children of the Fourteen Flames, while in Qarth the tales state that there was once a second moon in the sky. One day this moon was scalded by the sun and cracked like an egg, and a million dragons poured forth. In Asshai, the tales are many and confused, but certain texts—all impossibly ancient—claim that dragons first came from the Shadow, a place where all of our learning fails us. These Asshai'i histories say that a people so ancient they had no name first tamed dragons in the Shadow and brought them to Valyria, teaching the Valyrians their arts before departing from the annals.

Yet if men in the Shadow had tamed dragons first, why did they not conquer as the Valyrians did? It seems likelier that the Valyrian tale is the truest. But there were dragons in Westeros, once, long before the Targaryens came, as our own legends and histories tell us. If dragons did first spring from the Fourteen Flames, they must have been spread across much of the known world before they were tamed. And, in fact, there is evidence for this, as dragon bones have been found as far north as Ib, and even in the jungles of Sothoryos. But the Valyrians harnessed and subjugated them as no one else could.

LEFT | *The dragonlords of Valyria.*

What now remains of the once-proud empire of Old Ghis is a paltry thing—a few cities clinging like sores to Slaver's Bay and another that pretends to be Old Ghis come again. For after the Doom came to Valyria, the cities of Slaver's Bay were able to throw off the last of the Valyrian shackles, ruling themselves in truth rather than playing at it. And what remained of the Ghiscari swiftly reestablished their trade in slaves—though where once they won them by conquest, now they purchased and bred them.

"Bricks and blood built Astapor, and bricks and blood her people," an old rhyme says, referring to the red-bricked walls of the city and of the blood shed by the thousands of slaves who would live, labor, and die constructing them. Ruled by men who name themselves the Good Masters, Astapor is best known for the creation of the eunuch slave-soldiers called the Unsullied—men raised from boyhood to be fearless warriors who feel no pain. The Astapori pretend that they are the lockstep legions of the Old Empire come again, but those men were free, and the Unsullied are not.

Of Yunkai, the yellow city, little needs be said, for it is a most disreputable place. The men who rule it, calling themselves the Wise Masters, are steeped in corruption, selling bed slaves and boy-whores and worse.

The most formidable of the cities along Slaver's Bay is ancient Meereen, but like the rest, it is a crumbling place, its population a fraction of what it once supported at the height of the Old Empire. Its walls of many-colored bricks contain endless suffering, for the Great Masters of Meereen train slaves to fight and die at their pleasure in the blood-soaked fighting pits.

All three cities have been known to pay tribute to passing *khalasars* rather than face them in open battle, but the Dothraki provide many of the slaves that the Ghiscari train and sell—slaves taken from their conquests and sold in the flesh marts of Meereen, Yunkai, and Astapor.

The most vital of the Ghiscari cities is also the smallest and the newest, and no less a pretender to greatness: New Ghis, left to its own devices on its isle. There, its masters have formed iron legions in mimicry of the legions of the Old Empire, but unlike the Unsullied, these are free men, as the soldiers of the Old Empire were.

The colossal pyramids and temples and homes were given over to dragonflame. The fields were sown with salt, lime, and skulls. Many of the Ghiscari were slain, and still others were enslaved and died laboring for their conquerors. Thus the Ghiscari became but another part of the new Valyrian empire, and in time they forgot the tongue that Grazdan spoke, learning instead High Valyrian. So do empires end and others arise.

VALYRIA'S CHILDREN

THE VALYRIANS LEARNED one deplorable thing from the Ghiscari: slavery. The Ghiscari whom they conquered were the first to be thus enslaved, but not the last. The burning mountains of the Fourteen Flames were rich with ore, and the Valyrians hungered for it: copper and tin for the bronze of their weapons and monuments; later iron for the steel of their legendary blades; and always gold and silver to pay for it all.

from the Freehold, or political marriages used to better bind these cities to Valyria. Yet most of the histories that recount this take as their source Gessio Haratis's *Before the Dragons*. Haratis was himself from Pentos, and at the time, Volantis was threatening to restore the Valyrian empire under its control, so the notion of an independent Pentos with origins distinct from Valyria was a most politic convenience.

The properties of Valyrian steel are well-known, and are the result of both folding iron many times to balance and remove impurities, and the use of spells—or at least arts we do not know—to give unnatural strength to the resulting steel. Those arts are now lost, though the smiths of Qohor claim to still know magics for reworking Valyrian steel without losing its strength or unsurpassed ability to hold an edge. The Valyrian steel blades that remain in the world might number in the thousands, but in the Seven Kingdoms there are only 227 such weapons according to Archmaester Thurgood's *Inventories*, some of which have since been lost or have disappeared from the annals of history.

None can say how many perished, toiling in the Valyrian mines, but the number was so large as to surely defy comprehension. As Valyria grew, its need for ore increased, which led to ever more conquests to keep the mines stocked with slaves. The Valyrians expanded in all directions, stretching out east beyond the Ghiscari cities and west to the very shores of Essos, where even the Ghiscari had not made inroads.

It was this first bursting forth of the new empire that was of paramount importance to Westeros and the future Seven Kingdoms. As Valyria sought to conquer more and more lands and peoples, some fled for safety, retreating before the Valyrian tide. On the shores of Essos, the Valyrians raised cities, which we know today as the Free Cities. Their origins were diverse.

Qohor and Norvos were founded following religious schisms. Others, such as Old Volantis and Lys, were trading colonies first and foremost, founded by wealthy merchants and nobles who purchased the right to rule themselves as clients of the Freehold rather than subjects. These cities chose their own leaders rather than receiving archons dispatched from Valyria (often on dragonback) to oversee them. It is claimed in some histories that Pentos and Lorath were of a third type—cities already extant before the Valyrians came whose rulers paid homage to Valyria and thus retained their right to native rule. In these cities, what influx of Valyrian blood there was came from migrants

However, it is clear that Braavos is unique among all the Free Cities, as it was founded not by the will of the Freehold, nor by its citizens, but instead by its slaves. According to the tales of the Braavosi, a huge slaver fleet that had been out collecting tributes in human flesh from the lands of the Summer and Jade Seas became victim to a slave uprising instead; the success of this uprising was doubtless dependent on the fact that the Valyrians were wont to use slaves as oarsmen and even sailors, and that these men then joined the uprising. Seizing control of the fleet but realizing there was no place nearby to hide from the Freehold, the slaves instead elected to seek out some land far from Valyria and its subjects, and founded their own city in hiding. Legend says that the moonsingers prophesied that the fleet must travel far north to a forlorn corner of Essos—a place of mudflats and brackish water and fogs. There, the slaves first laid the foundation of their city.

For centuries, the Braavosi remained hidden from the world in their remote lagoon. And even after it unveiled itself, Braavos continued to be known as the Secret City. The Braavosi were a people who were no people: scores of races, a hundred tongues, and hundreds of gods. All they had in common was the Valyrian that formed the common trade language of Essos—and the fact that they were now free where once they had been slaves. The moonsingers were honored for leading them to their city, but the wisest among

the freed slaves determined that, to unify themselves, they must accept all the gods the slaves had brought with them, holding none higher than any other.

In short, the names and numbers of the peoples who fell to Valyria are unknown to us today. What records the Valyrians kept of their conquests were largely destroyed by the Doom, and few if any of these peoples documented their own histories in a way that survived the Freehold's dominion.

A few, such as the Rhoynar, lasted against the tide for centuries, or even millennia. The Rhoynar, who founded great cities along the Rhoyne, were said to be the first to learn the art of iron-making. Also, the confederation of cities later called the Kingdom of Sarnor survived the Valyrian expansion thanks to the great plain that separated one from the other . . . only for that plain and the people who occupied it—the Dothraki horselords—to be the source of Sarnor's downfall after the Doom.

And those who would not be slaves but were unable to withstand the might of Valyria fled. Many failed and are forgotten. But one people, tall and fair-haired, made courageous and indomitable by their faith, succeeded in their escape from Valyria. And those men are the Andals.

Of the history of Valyria as it is known today, many volumes have been written over the centuries, and the details of their conquests, their colonizations, the feuds of the dragonlords, the gods they worshipped, and more could fill libraries and still not be complete. Galendro's *The Fires of the Freehold* is widely considered the most definitive history, and even there the Citadel lacks twenty-seven of the scrolls.

THE ARRIVAL OF THE ANDALS

THE ANDALS ORIGINATED in the lands of the Axe, east and north of where Pentos now lies, though they were for many centuries a migratory people who did not remain in one place for long. From the heartlands of the Axe—a great spur of land surrounded on all sides by the Shivering Sea—they traveled south and west to carve out Andalos: the ancient realm the Andals ruled before they crossed the narrow sea.

Andalos stretched from the Axe to what is now the Braavosian Coastlands, and south as far as the Flatlands and the Velvet Hills. The Andals brought iron weapons with them and suits of iron plates, against which the tribes that inhabited those lands could do little. One such tribe was the hairy men; their name is lost, but they are still remembered in certain Pentoshi histories. (The Pentoshi believe them to be akin to the men of Ib, and the histories of the Citadel largely agree, though some argue that the hairy men settled Ib, and others that the hairy men came first from Ib.)

The fact that the Andals forged iron has been taken by some as proof that the Seven guided them—that the Smith himself taught them this art—and so do the holy texts teach.

But the Rhoynar were already an advanced civilization at this time, and they too knew of iron, so it takes only the study of a map to realize that the earliest Andals must have had contact with the Rhoynar. The Darkwash and the Noyne lay directly in the path of the Andals' migration, and there are remnants of Rhoynish outposts in Andalos, according to the Norvoshi historian Doro Golathis. And it would not be the first time that men learned of the working of iron from the Rhoynar; it is said that the Valyrians learned the art from them as well, although the Valyrians eventually surpassed them.

For thousands of years the Andals abided in Andalos, growing in number. In the oldest of the holy books, *The Seven-Pointed Star*, it is said that the Seven themselves walked among their people in the hills of Andalos, and it was they who crowned Hugor of the Hill and promised him and his descendants great kingdoms in a foreign land. This is what the septons and septas teach as the reason why the Andals left Essos and struck west to Westeros, but the history that the Citadel has uncovered over the centuries may provide a better reason.

LEFT | *The fires of the Fourteen Flames coursing through Valyria, fuel for the pyromancer's magic.*

An old legend told in Pentos claims that the Andals slew the swan maidens who lured travelers to their deaths in the Velvet Hills that lie to the east of the Free City. A hero whom the Pentoshi singers call Hukko led the Andals at that time, and it is said that he slew the seven maids not for their crimes but instead as sacrifice to his gods. There are some maesters who have noted that Hukko may well be a rendering of the name of Hugor. But even more so than in the Seven Kingdoms, ancient legends from the east must be distrusted. Too many peoples have traveled back and forth, and too many legends and tales have mingled.

For a few centuries, as the Andals prospered in the Hills of Andalos, they were left more or less to themselves. But with the fall of Old Ghis came the great surge of conquest and colonization from the Freehold of Valyria, as they expanded their domains and sought more slaves. At first, the Rhoyne and the Rhoynar served as a buffer. By the time the Valyrians reached that great river, they found it difficult to make a crossing in force. The dragonlords might not be troubled, but the foot- and horsemen found it daunting in the face of Rhoynish resistance, given that the Rhoynish were by now as powerful as Ghis at its height. There was a truce for years between the Valyrians and the Rhoynar, but it only protected the Andals so far.

At the mouth of the Rhoyne, the Valyrians founded the first of their colonies. There, Volantis was raised by some of the wealthiest men of the Freehold in order to gather up the wealth that flowed down the Rhoyne, and from Volantis their conquering forces crossed the river in great strength. The Andals might have fought against them at first, and the Rhoynar might even have aided them, but the tide was unstoppable. So it is likely the Andals chose to flee rather than face the inevitable slavery that came with Valyrian conquest. They retreated to the Axe—the lands from which they had sprung—and when that did not protect them, they retreated farther north and west until they came to the sea. Some might have given up there and surrendered to their fate, and others still might have made their last stand, but many and more made ships and sailed in great numbers across the narrow sea to the lands of the First Men in Westeros.

The Valyrians had denied the Andals the promise of the Seven on Essos, but in Westeros they were free. Made zealous by the conflict and flight, the warriors of the Andals carved the seven-pointed star upon their bodies and swore by their blood and the Seven not to rest until they had hewn their kingdoms from the Sunset Lands. Their success gave Westeros a new name: *Rhaesh Andahli*—the Land of the Andals, as the Dothraki now name it.

It's agreed by the septons, the singers, and the maesters alike that the first place where the Andals landed was on the

ABOVE | *Andal adventurers in the Vale, with the Mountains of the Moon in the distance.*

Fingers in the Vale of Arryn. Carvings of the seven-pointed star are scattered upon the rocks and stones throughout that area—a practice that eventually fell out of use as the Andal conquests progressed.

Sweeping through the Vale with fire and sword, the Andals began their conquest of Westeros. Their iron weapons and armor surpassed the bronze with which the First Men still fought, and many First Men perished in this war. It was a war—or a series of many wars—which likely lasted for decades. Eventually some of the First Men submitted, and, as I noted earlier, there are still houses in the Vale who proudly proclaim their descent from the First Men, such as the Redforts and the Royces.

The singers say that the Andal hero Ser Artys Arryn rode upon a falcon to slay the Griffon King upon the Giant's Lance, thereby founding the kingly line of House Arryn. This is foolishness, however, a corruption of the true history of the Arryns with legends out of the Age of Heroes. Instead, the Arryn kings supplanted the High Kings of House Royce.

When the Vale was secured, the Andals turned their attention to the rest of Westeros and poured forth through the Bloody Gate. In the wars that followed, Andal adventurers carved out small kingdoms from the old realms of the First Men and fought one another as often as they fought their enemies.

In the wars over the Trident, it's said that as many as seven Andal kings joined forces against the last true King of the Rivers and Hills, Tristifer the Fourth, who was descended from the First Men, and defeated him in what the singers claim was his hundredth battle. His heir, Tristifer the Fifth, proved unable to defend his father's legacy, and so the kingdom fell to the Andals.

In this same era one Andal, remembered in legend as Erreg the Kinslayer, came across the great hill of High Heart. There, while under the protection of the kings of the First Men, the children of the forest had tended to the mighty carved weirwoods that crowned it (thirty-one, according to Archmaester Laurent in his manuscript *Old Places of the Trident*). When Erreg's warriors sought to cut down

the trees, the First Men are said to have fought beside the children, but the might of the Andals was too great. Though the children and First Men made a valiant effort to defend their holy grove, all were slain. The tale-tellers now claim that the ghosts of the children still haunt the hill by night. To this day, rivermen shun the place.

As with the First Men before them, the Andals proved bitter enemies to the remaining children. To their eyes, the children worshipped strange gods and had strange customs, and so the Andals drove them out of all the deep woods the Pact had once given them. Weakened and grown insular over the years, the children lacked whatever advantages they had once had over the First Men. And what the First Men could never succeed in doing—eradicating the children entirely—the Andals managed to achieve in short order. Some few children may have fled to the Neck, where there was safety amidst the bogs and crannogs, but if they did, no trace of them remains. It is possible that a few survived on the Isle of Faces, as some have written, under the protection of the green men, whom the Andals never succeeded in destroying. But again, no definitive proof has ever been found.

Regardless, the few children remaining fled or died, and the First Men found themselves losing war after war,

The clans of the Mountains of the Moon are clearly descendants of the First Men who did not bend the knee to the Andals and so were driven into the mountains. Furthermore, there are similarities in their customs to the customs of the wildlings beyond the Wall—such as bride-stealing, a stubborn desire to rule themselves, and the like—and the wildlings are indisputably descended from the First Men.

ABOVE | *The slaughter of the children of the forest by the Andal warrior, Erreg the Kinslayer.*

and kingdom after kingdom, to the Andal invaders. The battles and wars were endless, but eventually all the southron kingdoms fell. As with the Valemen, some submitted to the Andals, even taking up the faith of the Seven. In many cases, the Andals took the wives and daughters of the defeated kings to wife, as a means of solidifying their right to rule. For, despite everything, the First Men were far more numerous than the Andals and could not simply be forced aside. The fact that many southron castles still have godswoods with carved weirwoods at their hearts is said to be thanks to the early Andal kings, who shifted from conquest to consolidation, thus avoiding any conflict based on differing faiths.

Even the ironborn—the fierce, sea-roving warriors who must have at first thought themselves safe upon their isles—fell to the wave of Andal conquest. For though it took a thousand years for the Andals to turn their attention to the Iron Islands, when they did, they did so with renewed zeal. The Andals swept over the islands, extinguishing the line of Urron Redhand, which had ruled by axe and sword for a thousand years.

Haereg writes that, at first, the new Andal kings sought to force worship of the Seven on the ironborn, but the ironborn would not have it. Instead they allowed it to co-exist with their worship of the Drowned God. As on the mainland, the Andals married the wives and daughters of the ironborn and had children by them. But unlike on the mainland, the Faith never took root; more, it did not hold firm even among the families of Andal blood. In time, only the Drowned God came to rule over the Iron Islands, with only a few houses remembering the Seven.

It was the North and the North alone that was able to keep the Andals at bay, thanks to the impenetrable swamps of the Neck and the ancient keep of Moat Cailin. The number of Andal armies that were destroyed in the Neck cannot be easily reckoned, and so the Kings of Winter preserved their independent rule for many centuries to come.

TEN THOUSAND SHIPS

THE LAST OF the great migrations into Westeros happened long after the coming of the First Men and the Andals. Once the Ghiscari wars had ended, the dragonlords of Valyria turned their gaze toward the west, where the growth of Valyrian power brought the Freehold and its colonies into conflict with the peoples of the Rhoyne.

The mightiest river in the world, the Rhoyne's many tributaries stretched across much of western Essos. Along their banks had arisen a civilization and culture as storied and ancient as the Old Empire of Ghis. The Rhoynar had grown rich off the bounty of their river; Mother Rhoyne, they named her.

Fishers, traders, teachers, scholars, workers in wood and stone and metal, they raised their elegant towns and cities from the headwaters of the Rhoyne down to her mouth, each lovelier than the last. There was Ghoyan Drohe in the Velvet Hills, with its groves and waterfalls; Ny Sar, the city of fountains, alive with song; Ar Noy on the Qhoyne, with its halls of green marble; pale Sar Mell of the flowers; sea-girt Sarhoy with its canals and saltwater gardens; and Chroyane, greatest of all, the festival city with its great Palace of Love.

Art and music flourished in the cities of the Rhoyne, and it is said their people had their own magic—a water magic very different from the sorceries of Valyria, which were woven of blood and fire. Though united by blood and culture and the river that had given them birth, the Rhoynish cities were elsewise fiercely independent, each with its own prince . . . or princess, for amongst these river folk, women were regarded as the equals of men.

By and large a peaceful people, the Rhoynar could be formidable when roused to wroth, as many a would-be Andal conqueror learned to his sorrow. The Rhoynish warrior with his silver-scaled armor, fish-head helm, tall spear, and turtle-shell shield was esteemed and feared by all those who faced him in battle. It was said the Mother Rhoyne herself whispered to her children of every threat, that the Rhoynar princes wielded strange, uncanny powers, that Rhoynish women fought as fiercely as Rhoynish men, and that their cities were protected by "watery walls" that would rise to drown any foe.

For many centuries the Rhoynar lived in peace. Though many a savage people dwelt in the hills and forests around Mother Rhoyne, all knew better than to molest the river folk. And the Rhoynar themselves showed little interest in expansion; the river was their home, their mother, and their god, and few of them wished to dwell beyond the sound of her eternal song.

When adventurers, exiles, and traders from the Freehold of Valyria began to expand beyond the Lands of the Long Summer in the centuries after the fall of the Old Empire of Ghis, the Rhoynish princes embraced them at first, and their priests declared that all men were welcome to share the bounty of Mother Rhoyne.

As those first Valyrian outposts grew into towns, and those towns into cities, however, some Rhoynar came to regret the forbearance of their fathers. Amity gave way to enmity, particularly upon the lower river, where the ancient city of Sar Mell and the walled Valyrian town Volon Therys faced each other across the waters, and on the shores of the Summer Sea, where the Free City of Volantis soon rivaled the storied port of Sarhoy, each of them commanding one of Mother Rhoyne's four mouths.

Disputes between the citizens of the rival cities became ever more common and ever more rancorous, finally giving birth to a series of short but bloody wars. Sar Mell and Volon Therys were the first cities to meet in battle. Legend claims that the clash began when the Valyrians netted and butchered one of the gigantic turtles the Rhoynar called the Old Men of the River and held sacred as the consorts of Mother Rhoyne herself. The First Turtle War lasted less than a moon's turn. Sar Mell was raided and burned, yet emerged victorious when Rhoynish water wizards called up the power of the river and flooded Volon Therys. Half the city was washed away, if the tales can be believed.

Other wars followed, however: the War of Three Princes, the Second Turtle War, the Fisherman's War, the Salt War,

the Third Turtle War, the War on Dagger Lake, the Spice War, and many more, too numerous to recount here. Cities and towns were burned, drowned, and rebuilt. Thousands were killed or enslaved. In these conflicts, the Valyrians emerged as victors more oft than not. The princes of the Rhoyne, fiercely proud of their independence, fought alone, whilst the Valyrian colonies aided one another, and when hard-pressed, called upon the power of the Freehold itself. Beldecar's *History of the Rhoynish Wars* is without equal in describing these conflicts, which stretched over the best part of two and a half centuries.

This series of conflicts reached a bloody climax a thousand years ago in the Second Spice War, when three Valyrian dragonlords joined with their kin and cousins in Volantis to overwhelm, sack, and destroy Sarhoy, the great Rhoynar port city upon the Summer Sea. The warriors of Sarhoy were slaughtered savagely, their children carried off into slavery, and their proud pink city put to the torch. Afterward the Volantenes sowed the smoking ruins with salt so that Sarhoy might never rise again.

The utter destruction of one of the richest and most beautiful of the cities of the Rhoyne, and the enslavement of her people, shocked and dismayed the remaining Rhoynar princes. "We shall all be slaves unless we join together to end this threat," declared the greatest of them, Garin of Chroyane. This warrior prince called upon his fellows to join with him in a great alliance, to wash away every Valyrian city on the river.

Only Princess Nymeria of Ny Sar spoke against him. "This is a war we cannot hope to win," she warned, but the other princes shouted her down and pledged their swords to Garin. Even the warriors of her own Ny Sar were eager to fight, and Nymeria had no choice but to join the great alliance.

The largest army that Essos had ever seen soon assembled at Chroyane, under the command of Prince Garin. According to Beldecar, it was a quarter of a million strong. From the headwaters of the Rhoyne down to her many mouths, every man of fighting age took up sword and shield and made his way to the festival city to join this great campaign. So long as the army remained beside Mother Rhoyne, the prince declared, they need not fear the dragons of Valyria; their own water wizards would protect them against the fires of the Freehold.

Garin divided his enormous host into three parts; one marched down the east bank of the Rhoyne, one along the west, whilst a huge fleet of war galleys kept pace on the waters between, sweeping the river clean of enemy ships. From Chroyane, Prince Garin led his gathered might downriver, destroying every village, town, and outpost in his path and smashing all opposition.

At Selhorys he won his first battle, overwhelming a Valyrian army thirty thousand strong and taking the city by storm. Valysar met the same fate. At Volon Therys, Garin found himself facing a hundred thousand foes, a hundred war elephants, and three dragonlords. Here too he prevailed, though at great cost. Thousands burned, but thousands more sheltered in the shallows of the river, whilst their wizards raised enormous waterspouts against the foe's dragons. Rhoynish archers brought down two of the dragons, whilst the third fled, wounded. In the aftermath, Mother Rhoyne rose in rage to swallow Volon Therys. Thereafter men began to name the victorious prince Garin the Great, and it is said that, in Volantis, great lords trembled in terror as his host advanced. Rather than face him in the field, the Volantenes retreated back behind their Black Walls and appealed to the Freehold for help.

And the dragons came. Not three, as Prince Garin had faced at Volon Therys, but three hundred or more, if the tales that have come down to us can be believed. Against their fires, the Rhoynar could not stand. Tens of thousands burned whilst others rushed into the river, hoping that the embrace of Mother Rhoyne would offer them protection against dragonflame . . . only to drown in their mother's embrace. Some chroniclers insist that the fires burned so hot that the very waters of the river boiled and turned to steam. Garin the Great was captured alive and made to watch his people suffer for their defiance. His warriors were shown no such mercy. The Volantenes and their Valyrian kin put them to the sword—so many that it was said that their blood turned the great harbor of Volantis red as far as the eye could see. Thereafter the victors gathered their own forces and moved north along the river, sacking Sar Mell savagely before advancing on Chroyane, Prince Garin's own city. Locked in a golden cage at the command of the dragonlords, Garin was carried back to the festival city to witness its destruction.

At Chroyane, the cage was hung from the walls, so that the prince might witness the enslavement of the women and children whose fathers and brothers had died in his gallant, hopeless war . . . but the prince, it is said, called down a curse upon the conquerors, entreating Mother Rhoyne to avenge her children. And so, that very night, the Rhoyne flooded out of season and with greater force than was known in living memory. A thick fog full of evil humors fell, and the Valyrian conquerors began to die of greyscale. (There is, at least, this much truth to the tale: in later centuries, Lomas Longstrider wrote of the drowned ruins of Chroyane, its foul fogs and waters, and the fact that wayward travelers infected with greyscale now haunt the ruins—a hazard for those who travel the river beneath the broken span of the Bridge of Dream.)

Higher on the Rhoyne, in Ny Sar, Princess Nymeria soon received the news of Garin's shattering defeat and the enslavement of the people of Chroyane and Sar Mell. The same fate awaited her own city, she saw. Accordingly, she gathered every ship that remained upon the Rhoyne, large or small, and filled them full of as many women and children as they could carry (for almost all the men of fighting age had marched with Garin, and died). Down the river Nymeria led this ragged fleet, past ruined and smoking towns and fields of the dead, through waters choked with bloated, floating corpses. To avoid Volantis and its hosts, she chose the older channel and emerged into the Summer Sea where once Sarhoy had stood.

Legend tells us that Nymeria took ten thousand ships to sea, searching for a new home for her people beyond the long reach of Valyria and its dragonlords. Beldecar argues that this number was vastly inflated, perhaps as much as tenfold. Other chroniclers offer other numbers, but in truth no true count was ever made. We can safely say there were a great many ships. Most were river craft, skiffs and poleboats, trading galleys, fishing boats, pleasure barges, even rafts, their decks and holds crammed full of women and

the glistening green waters of the Zamoyos, amongst quicksands, crocodiles, and rotting, half-drowned trees. Princess Nymeria herself remained with the ships at Zamettar, a Ghiscari colony abandoned for a thousand years, whilst others made their way upriver to the cyclopean ruins of Yeen, haunt of ghouls and spiders.

There were riches to be found in Sothoryos—gold, gems, rare woods, exotic pelts, queer fruits, and strange spices—but the Rhoynar did not thrive there. The sullen wet heat oppressed their spirits, and swarms of stinging flies spread one disease after another: green fever, the dancing plague, blood boils, weeping sores, sweetrot. The young and very old proved especially vulnerable to such contagions. Even to splash in the river was to court death, for the Zamoyos was infested with schools of carnivorous fish, and tiny worms that laid their eggs in the flesh of swimmers. Two of the new towns on Basilisk Point were raided by slavers, their populaces put to the sword or carried off in chains, whilst Yeen had to contend with attacks from the brindled ghouls of the jungle deeps.

For more than a year the Rhoynar struggled to survive in Sothoryos, until the day when a boat from Zamettar arrived at Yeen to find that every man, woman, and child in that haunted, ruined city had vanished overnight. Then Nymeria summoned her people back to the ships and set sail once again.

For the next three years the Rhoynar wandered the southern seas, seeking a new home. On Naath, the Isle of Butterflies, the peaceful people gave them welcome, but the god that protects that strange land began to strike down the newcomers by the score with a nameless mortal illness, driving them back to their ships. In the Summer Isles, they settled on an uninhabited rock off the eastern shore of Walano, which soon became known as the Isle of Women, but its thin stony soil yielded little food, and many starved. When the sails were raised again, some of the Rhoynar abandoned Nymeria to follow a priestess named Druselka, who claimed to have heard Mother Rhoyne calling her children home . . . but when Druselka and her followers returned to their old cities, they found their enemies waiting, and most were soon hunted down, slain, or enslaved.

The battered, tattered remainder of the ten thousand ships sailed west with Princess Nymeria. This time she made for Westeros. After so much wandering, her ships were even

children and old men. Only one in ten was remotely seaworthy, Beldecar insists. Nymeria's voyage was long and terrible. More than a hundred ships foundered and sank in the first storm her fleet encountered. As many or more turned back in fear, and were taken by slavers out of Volantis. Others fell behind or drifted away, never to be seen again.

The remainder of the fleet limped across the Summer Sea to the Basilisk Isles, where they paused to take on fresh water and provisions, only to fall afoul of the corsair kings of Ax Isle, Talon, and the Howling Mountain, who put aside their own quarrels long enough to descend upon the Rhoynar with fire and sword, putting twoscore ships to the torch and carrying off hundreds into slavery. In the aftermath, the corsairs offered to allow the Rhoynar to settle upon the Isle of Toads, provided they gave up their boats and sent each king thirty virgin girls and pretty boys each year as tribute.

Nymeria refused and took her fleet to sea once again, hoping to find refuge amongst the steaming jungles of Sothoryos. Some settled on Basilisk Point, others beside

ABOVE | *Princess Nymeria leading the ten thousand ships.*

less seaworthy than when they had first departed Mother Rhoyne. The fleet did not arrive in Dorne complete. Even now there are isolated pockets of Rhoynar on the Stepstones, claiming descent from those who were shipwrecked. Other ships, blown off course by storms, made for Lys or Tyrosh, giving themselves up to slavery in preference to a watery grave. The remaining ships made landfall on the coast of Dorne near the mouth of the river Greenblood, not far from the ancient sandstone walls of The Sandship, seat of House Martell.

Dry, desolate, and thinly peopled, Dorne at this time was a poor land where a score of quarrelsome lords and petty kings warred endlessly over every river, stream, well, and scrap of fertile land. Most of these Dornish lords viewed the Rhoynar as unwelcome interlopers, invaders with queer foreign ways and strange gods, who should be driven back into the sea whence they'd come. But Mors Martell, the Lord of the Sandship, saw in the newcomers an opportunity . . . and if the singers can be believed, his lordship also lost his heart to Nymeria, the fierce and beautiful warrior queen who had led her people across the world to keep them free.

It is said that, amongst the Rhoynar who came to Dorne with Nymeria, eight of every ten were women . . . but a quarter of those were warriors, in the Rhoynish tradition, and even those who did not fight had been hardened during their travels and travails. As well, thousands who had been boys when fleeing the Rhoyne had grown into manhood and taken up the spear during their years of wandering. By joining with the newcomers, the Martells increased the size of their host by tenfold.

When Mors Martell took Nymeria to wife, hundreds of his knights, squires, and lords bannermen also wed Rhoynish women, and many of those who were already wed took them for their paramours. Thus were the two peoples united by blood. These unions enriched and strengthened House Martell and its Dornish allies. The Rhoynar brought considerable wealth with them; their artisans, metalworkers, and stonemasons brought skills far in advance of those achieved by their Westerosi counterparts, and their armorers were soon producing swords and spears and suits of scale and plate no Westerosi smith could hope to match. Even more crucially, it is said the Rhoynish water witches knew secret spells that made dry streams flow again and deserts bloom.

To celebrate these unions, and make certain her people could not again retreat to the sea, Nymeria burned the Rhoynish ships. "Our wanderings are at an end," she declared. "We have found a new home, and here we shall live and die."

(Some of the Rhoynar mourned the loss of the ships, and rather than embracing their new land, they took to plying the waters of the Greenblood, finding it a pale shadow of Mother Rhoyne, whom they continued to worship. They still exist to this day, known as the orphans of the Greenblood).

The flames lit the coast for fifty leagues as hundreds of leaking, listing hulks were put to the torch and turned to ash; in the light of their burning, Princess Nymeria named Mors Martell the Prince of Dorne, in the Rhoynish style, asserting his dominion over "the red sands and the white, and all the lands and rivers from the mountains to the great salt sea."

Such supremacy was easier to declare than to achieve, however. Years of war followed, as the Martells and their Rhoynar partners met and subdued one petty king after another. No fewer than six conquered kings were sent to the Wall in golden fetters by Nymeria and her prince, until only the greatest of their foes remained: Yorick Yronwood, the Bloodroyal, Fifth of His Name, Lord of Yronwood, Warden of the Stone Way, Knight of the Wells, King of Redmarch, King of the Greenbelt, and King of the Dornish.

For nine years Mors Martell and his allies (amongst them House Fowler of Skyreach, House Toland of Ghost Hill, House Dayne of Starfall, and House Uller of the Hellholt) struggled against Yronwood and his bannermen (the Jordaynes of the Tor, the Wyls of the Stone Way, together with the Blackmonts, the Qorgyles, and many more), in battles too numerous to mention. When Mors Martell fell to Yorick Yronwood's sword in the Third Battle of the Boneway, Princess Nymeria assumed sole command of his armies. Two more years of battle were required, but in the end it was Nymeria that Yorick Yronwood bent the knee to, and Nymeria who ruled thereafter from Sunspear.

Though she married twice more (first to the aged Lord Uller of Hellholt, and later to the dashing Ser Davos Dayne of Starfall, the Sword of the Morning), Nymeria herself remained the unquestioned ruler of Dorne for almost twenty-seven years, her husbands serving only as counselors and consorts. She survived a dozen attempts upon her life, put down two rebellions, and threw back two invasions by the Storm King Durran the Third and one by King Greydon of the Reach.

When at last she died, it was the eldest of her four daughters by Mors Martell who succeeded her, not her son by Davos Dayne, for by then the Dornish had come to adopt many of the laws and customs of the Rhoynar, though the memories of Mother Rhoyne and the ten thousand ships were fading into legend.

THE DOOM OF VALYRIA

WITH THE DESTRUCTION of the Rhoynar, Valyria soon achieved complete domination of the western half of Essos, from the narrow sea to Slaver's Bay, and from the Summer Sea to the Shivering Sea. Slaves poured into the Freehold and were quickly dispatched beneath the Fourteen Flames to mine the precious gold and silver the freeholders loved so well. Perhaps in preparation for their crossing of the narrow sea, the Valyrians also established their westernmost outpost on the isle that would come to be known as Dragonstone some two hundred years before the Doom. No king opposed them—and though the local lords of the narrow sea made some effort to resist it, the strength of Valyria was too great. With their arcane arts, the Valyrians raised the Citadel at Dragonstone.

Two centuries passed—centuries in which the coveted Valyrian steel began to trickle into the Seven Kingdoms more swiftly than before—though not swiftly enough for all the lords and kings who desired it. And although the sight of a dragonlord flying high above Blackwater Bay was not unknown, it occurred more frequently as time passed. Valyria felt its outpost was secured, and the dragonlords thus continued their schemes and intrigues on their native continent.

And then, unexpected to all (save perhaps Aenar Targaryen and his maiden daughter Daenys the Dreamer), the Doom came to Valyria.

To this day, no one knows what caused the Doom. Most say that it was a natural cataclysm—a catastrophic explosion caused by the eruption of all Fourteen Flames together. Some septons, less wise, claim that the Valyrians brought the disaster on themselves for their promiscuous belief in a hundred gods and more, and in their godlessness they delved too deep and unleashed the fires of the Seven hells on the Freehold. A handful of maesters, influenced by fragments of the work of Septon Barth, hold that Valyria had used spells to tame the Fourteen Flames for thousands of years, that their ceaseless hunger for slaves and wealth was as much to sustain these spells as to expand their power, and that when at last those spells faltered, the cataclysm became inevitable.

Of these, some argue that it was the curse of Garin the Great at last coming to fruition. Others speak of the priests of R'hllor calling down the fire of their god in queer rituals. Some, wedding the fanciful notion of Valyrian magic to the reality of the ambitious great houses of Valyria, have argued that it was the constant whirl of conflict and deception amongst the great houses that might have led to the assassinations of too many of the reputed mages who renewed and maintained the rituals that banked the fires of the Fourteen Flames.

The one thing that can be said for certain is that it was a cataclysm such as the world had never seen. The ancient, mighty Freehold—home to dragons and to sorcerers of unrivaled skill—was shattered and destroyed within hours. It was written that every hill for five hundred miles split asunder to fill the air with ash and smoke and fire so hot and hungry that even the dragons in the sky were engulfed and consumed. Great rents opened in the earth, swallowing palaces, temples, and entire towns. Lakes boiled or turned to acid, mountains burst, fiery fountains spewed molten rock a thousand feet into the air, and red clouds rained down dragonglass and the black blood of demons. To the north, the ground splintered and collapsed and fell in on itself, and an angry sea came boiling in.

The proudest city in all the world was gone in an instant, the fabled empire vanished in a day. The Lands of the Long Summer—once the most fertile in all the world—were scorched and drowned and blighted, and the toll in blood would not be fully realized for a century to come.

What followed in the sudden vacuum was chaos. The dragonlords had been gathered in Valyria as was their wont . . . except for Aenar Targaryen, his children, and his dragons, who had fled to Dragonstone and so escaped the Doom. Some accounts claim that a few others survived, too . . . for a time. It is said that some Valyrian dragonlords in Tyrosh and Lys were spared, but that in the immediate political upheaval following the Doom, they and their dragons were killed by the citizens of those Free Cities. The histories of Qohor likewise claim that a visiting dragonlord, Aurion, raised forces from the Qohorik colonists and proclaimed himself the first Emperor of Valyria. He flew away on the back of his great dragon, with thirty thousand men following behind afoot, to lay claim to what remained of Valyria and to reestablish the Freehold. But neither Emperor Aurion nor his host were ever seen again.

The time of the dragons in Essos was at an end.

Volantis, the mightiest of the Free Cities, quickly laid claim to Valyria's mantle. Men and women of noble Valyrian

In the wake of all the conflicts, and the struggles that continue to this day over the Disputed Lands, the plague of the Free Companies was born and took root. At first, these bands of sellswords merely fought for whoever paid them. But there are those who say that, whenever peace threatened, the captains of these Free Companies acted to instigate new wars to sustain themselves, and so grew fat on the spoils.

blood, though not dragonlords, called for war upon the other cities. The tigers, as those who advocated conquest came to be known, led Volantis into a great conflict with the other Free Cities. They had great success at first, their fleets and armies controlling Lys and Myr and commanding the southern reaches of the Rhoyne. It was only when they overreached and attempted to seize Tyrosh, as well, that their burgeoning empire collapsed. Unnerved by the Volantene aggression, Pentos joined the Tyroshi in resistance, Myr and Lys rebelled, and the Sealord of Braavos provided a fleet of a hundred ships to aid Lys. Also, the Westerosi Storm King, Argilac the Arrogant, led a host into the Disputed Lands—in return for the promise of gold and glory—that defeated a Volantene host attempting to retake Myr.

Near the end, even the future Conqueror, the still-young Aegon Targaryen, became involved in the struggle. His ancestors had long looked east, but his attention from an early age had been turned westward. Still, when Pentos and Tyrosh approached him, inviting him to join a grand alliance against Volantis, he listened. And for reasons unknown to this day, he chose to heed their call . . . to a point. Mounting the Black Dread, it is said that he flew to the east, meeting with the Prince of Pentos and the magisters of the Free City, and from there flew Balerion to Lys in time to set ablaze a Volantene fleet that was preparing to invade that Free City.

Volantis suffered further defeats—at Dagger Lake, where the fire galleys of Qohor and Norvos destroyed much of the Volantene fleet that controlled the Rhoyne; and in the east when the Dothraki began to swarm out of the Dothraki sea, leaving ruined towns and cities in their wake as they fell on the weakened Volantis. At last, the elephants—the Volantene faction who favored peace, and who were largely drawn from the wealthy tradesmen and merchants who suffered most in the war—took power from the tigers, who favored conquest, and put an end to the fighting.

As for Aegon Targaryen, shortly after his role in defeating Volantis it is written that he lost all interest in the affairs of the east. Believing Volantis's rule at an end, he flew back to Dragonstone. And now, no longer distracted by the wars of Essos, he turned his gaze west.

The Freehold of Valyria and its empire were destroyed by the Doom, but the shattered peninsula remains. Strange tales are told of it today, and of the demons that haunt the Smoking Sea where the Fourteen Flames once stood. In fact, the road that joins Volantis to Slaver's Bay has become known as the "demon road," and is best avoided by all sensible travelers. And men who have dared the Smoking Sea do not return, as Volantis learned during the Century of Blood when a fleet it sent to claim the peninsula vanished. There are queer rumors of men living still among the ruins of Valyria and its neighboring cities of Oros and Tyria. Yet others dispute this, saying that the Doom still holds Valyria in its grip.

A few of the cities away from the heart of Valyria remain inhabited, however—places founded by the Freehold or subject to it. The most sinister of these is Mantarys, a place where the men are said to be born twisted and monstrous; some attribute this to the city's presence on the demon road. The reputations of Tolos, where the finest slingers in the world can be found, and of the city of Elyria on its isle, are less sinister, and less noteworthy as well, for they have made ties to the Ghiscari cities on Slaver's Bay and otherwise avoid involvement in any efforts to reclaim the burning heart of Valyria.

ABOVE | *A dragon burning during the Doom.*

The Reign of the Dragons

HERE FOLLOWS AN account of the reign of House Targaryen, from Aegon the Conqueror to Aerys the Mad King. Many are the maesters who have written on these matters, and the knowledge they have fashioned informs much of what will follow. But in one thing, I have taken a liberty: the account of Aegon's Conquest is not my own work but something lately discovered in the archives of the Citadel, forgotten since the sad end of Aegon, the Fifth of His Name. This fragment—part of a greater work that seemed intended as a history of the Targaryen kings—was found gathering dust among papers belonging to the Archmaester Gerold, the historian whose writings on the history of Oldtown were well regarded in his day. But it was not written by him. The style alone gives it away, but certain notes found with these papers indicate they were written by Archmaester Gyldayn, the last maester to serve at Summerhall before its

destruction in the reign of Aegon the Fortunate, the Fifth of his Name, who may have sent them to Gerold for his commentary and approval.

The history of the Conquest is as complete as any, and that is why I have placed it here, so that—at last—more eyes than mine and the late Archmaester Gerold's may appreciate and learn from it. There are other manuscripts by this same hand that I have discovered, but many pages have been misplaced or destroyed, and still others have been damaged by neglect and by fire. It may be that one day, more will be found, and this lost masterwork will be fit to be copied and bound, for what I have found has stirred great excitement in the Citadel.

Until then, however, its fragments serve as one among many sources for the reigns of the Targaryen kings, from the Conqueror to the late Aerys II—the last Targaryen king to sit the Iron Throne.

The Conquest

The maesters of the Citadel who keep the histories of Westeros have used Aegon's Conquest as their touchstone for the past three hundred years. Births, deaths, battles, and other events are dated either AC (After the Conquest) or BC (Before the Conquest).

True scholars know that such dating is far from precise. Aegon Targaryen's conquest of the Seven Kingdoms did not take place in a single day. More than two years passed between Aegon's landing and his Oldtown coronation . . . and even then the Conquest remained incomplete since Dorne remained unsubdued. Sporadic attempts to bring the Dornishmen into the realm continued all through King Aegon's reign and well into the reigns of his sons, making it impossible to fix a precise end date for the Wars of Conquest.

Even the start date is a matter of some misconception. Many assume, wrongly, that the reign of King Aegon I Targaryen began on the day he landed at the mouth of the Blackwater Rush, beneath the three hills where the city of King's Landing eventually stood. Not so. The day of Aegon's Landing was celebrated

by the king and his descendants, but the Conqueror actually dated the start of his reign from the day he was crowned and anointed in the Starry Sept of Oldtown by the High Septon of the Faith. This coronation took place two years after Aegon's Landing, well after all three of the major battles of the Wars of Conquest had been fought and won. Thus it can be seen that most of Aegon's actual conquering took place from 2–1 BC, Before the Conquest.

The Targaryens were of pure Valyrian blood, dragonlords of ancient lineage. Twelve years before the Doom of Valyria (114 BC), Aenar Targaryen sold his holdings in the Freehold and the Lands of the Long Summer and moved with all his wives, wealth, slaves, dragons, siblings, kin, and children to Dragonstone, a bleak island citadel beneath a smoking mountain in the narrow sea.

PREVIOUS PAGES | *Aegon the Conqueror upon Balerion, the Black Dread.* LEFT | *Dragonstone.*

At its apex Valyria was the greatest city in the known world, the center of civilization. Within its shining walls, twoscore rival houses vied for power and glory in court and council, rising and falling in an endless, subtle, oft-savage struggle for dominance. The Targaryens were far from the most powerful of the dragonlords, and their rivals saw their flight to Dragonstone as an act of surrender, as cowardice. But Lord Aenar's maiden daughter Daenys, known forever afterward as Daenys the Dreamer, had foreseen the destruction of Valyria by fire. And when the Doom came twelve years later, the Targaryens were the only dragonlords to survive.

Dragonstone had been the westernmost outpost of Valyrian power for two centuries. Its location athwart the Gullet gave its lords a stranglehold on Blackwater Bay, and enabled both the Targaryens and their close allies, the Velaryons of Driftmark (a lesser house of Valyrian descent), to fill their coffers off the passing trade. Velaryon ships, along with those of another allied Valyrian house, the Celtigars of Claw Isle, dominated the middle reaches of the narrow sea, whilst the Targaryens ruled the skies with their dragons.

Yet even so, for the best part of a hundred years after the Doom of Valyria (the rightly named Century of Blood), House Targaryen looked east, not west, and took little interest in the affairs of Westeros. Gaemon Targaryen, brother and husband to Daenys the Dreamer, followed Aenar the Exile as Lord of Dragonstone, and became known as Gaemon the Glorious. Gaemon's son Aegon and his daughter Elaena ruled together after his death. After them the lordship

ABOVE | *Aegon the Conqueror in battle.*

passed to their son Maegon, his brother Aerys, and Aerys's sons, Aelyx, Baelon, and Daemion. The last of the three brothers was Daemion, whose son Aerion then succeeded to Dragonstone.

The Aegon who is known to history as Aegon the Conqueror and Aegon the Dragon was born on Dragonstone in 27 BC. He was the only son, and second child, of Aerion, Lord of Dragonstone, and Lady Valaena of House Velaryon, herself half-Targaryen on her mother's side. Aegon had two trueborn siblings; an elder sister, Visenya, and a younger sister, Rhaenys. It had long been the custom amongst the dragonlords of Valyria to wed brother to sister, to keep the bloodlines pure, but Aegon took both his sisters to bride. By tradition, he was expected to wed only his older sister, Visenya; the inclusion of Rhaenys as a second wife was unusual, though not without precedent. It was said by some that Aegon wed Visenya out of duty and Rhaenys out of desire.

All three siblings had shown themselves to be dragonlords before they wed. Of the five dragons who had flown with Aenar the Exile from Valyria, only one survived to Aegon's day: the great beast called Balerion, the Black Dread. The remaining two dragons—Vhagar and Meraxes—were younger, hatched on Dragonstone itself.

A common myth, oft heard amongst the ignorant, claims that Aegon Targaryen had never set foot upon the soil of Westeros until the day he set sail to conquer it, but this cannot be true. Years before that voyage, the Painted Table had been carved and decorated at Lord Aegon's command: a massive slab of wood, some fifty feet long, carved in the shape of Westeros and painted to show all the woods and rivers and towns and castles of the Seven Kingdoms. Plainly, Aegon's interest in Westeros long predated the events that drove him to war. As well, there are reliable reports of Aegon and his sister Visenya visiting the Citadel of Oldtown in their youth, and hawking on the Arbor as guests of Lord Redwyne. He may have visited Lannisport as well; accounts differ.

The Westeros of Aegon's youth was divided into seven quarrelsome kingdoms, and there was hardly a time when two or three of these kingdoms were not at war with one another. The vast, cold, stony North was ruled by the Starks of Winterfell. In the deserts of Dorne, the Martell princes held sway. The gold-rich westerlands were ruled by the Lannisters of Casterly Rock, the fertile Reach by the Gardeners of Highgarden. The Vale, the Fingers, and the Mountains of the Moon belonged to House Arryn . . . but the most belligerent kings of Aegon's time were the two whose realms lay closest to Dragonstone, Harren the Black and Argilac the Arrogant.

From their great citadel Storm's End, the Storm Kings of House Durrandon had once ruled the eastern half of Westeros from Cape Wrath to the Bay of Crabs, but their powers had been dwindling for centuries. The Kings of the Reach had nibbled at their domains from the west, the Dornishmen harassed them from the south, and Harren the Black and his ironmen had pushed them from the Trident and the lands north of the Blackwater Rush. King Argilac, last of the Durrandon, had arrested this decline for a time, turning back a Dornish invasion whilst still a boy, crossing the narrow sea to join the great alliance against the imperialist "tigers" of Volantis, and slaying Garse VII Gardener, King of the Reach, in the Battle of Summerfield twenty years later. But Argilac had grown older; his famous mane of black hair had gone grey, and his prowess at arms had faded.

North of the Blackwater, the riverlands were ruled by the bloody hand of Harren the Black of House Hoare, King of the Isles and the Rivers. Harren's ironborn grandsire, Harwyn Hardhand, had taken the Trident from Argilac's grandsire, Arrec, whose own forebears had thrown down the last of the river kings centuries earlier. Harren's father had extended his domains east to Duskendale and Rosby. Harren himself had devoted most of his long reign, close on forty years, to building a gigantic castle beside the Gods Eye, but with Harrenhal at last nearing completion, the ironborn were soon free to seek fresh conquests.

No king in Westeros was more feared than Black Harren, whose cruelty had become legendary all through the Seven Kingdoms. And no king in Westeros felt more threatened than Argilac the Storm King, last of the Durrandon—an aging warrior whose only heir was his maiden daughter. Thus it was that King Argilac reached out to the Targaryens on Dragonstone, offering Lord Aegon his daughter in marriage, with all the lands east of the Gods Eye from the Trident to the Blackwater Rush as her dowry.

Aegon Targaryen spurned the Storm King's proposal. He had two wives, he pointed out; he did not need a third. And the dower lands being offered had belonged to Harrenhal for more than a generation. They were not Argilac's to give. Plainly, the aging Storm King meant to establish the Targaryens along the Blackwater as a buffer between his own lands and those of Harren the Black.

The Lord of Dragonstone countered with an offer of his own. He would take the dower lands being offered if Argilac would also cede Massey's Hook and the woods and plains from the Blackwater south to the river Wendwater and the headwaters of the Mander. The pact would be sealed by the marriage of King Argilac's daughter to Orys Baratheon, Lord Aegon's childhood friend and champion.

These terms Argilac the Arrogant rejected angrily. Orys Baratheon was a baseborn half brother to Lord Aegon, it was whispered, and the Storm King would not dishonor his daughter by giving her hand to a bastard. The very suggestion enraged him. Argilac had the hands of Aegon's envoy cut off and returned to him in a box. "These are the only hands your bastard shall have of me," he wrote.

Aegon made no reply. Instead he summoned his friends, bannermen, and principal allies to attend him on Dragonstone. Their numbers were small. The Velaryons on Driftmark were sworn to House Targaryen, as were the Celtigars of Claw Isle. From Massey's Hook came Lord Bar Emmon of Sharp Point and Lord Massey of Stonedance, both sworn

to Storm's End, but with closer ties to Dragonstone. Lord Aegon and his sisters took counsel with them and visited the castle sept to pray to the Seven of Westeros as well, though he had never before been accounted a pious man.

On the seventh day, a cloud of ravens burst from the towers of Dragonstone to bring Lord Aegon's word to the Seven Kingdoms of Westeros. To the seven kings they flew, to the Citadel of Oldtown, to lords both great and small. All carried the same message: from this day forth there would be but one king in Westeros. Those who bent the knee to Aegon of House Targaryen would keep their lands and titles. Those who took up arms against him would be thrown down, humbled, and destroyed.

Accounts differ on how many swords set sail from Dragonstone with Aegon and his sisters. Some say three thousand; others number them only in the hundreds. This modest Targaryen host put ashore at the mouth of the Blackwater Rush, on the northern bank where three wooded hills rose above a small fishing village.

In the days of the Hundred Kingdoms, many petty kings had claimed dominion over the river mouth, amongst them the Darklyn kings of Duskendale, the Masseys of Stonedance, and the river kings of old, be they Mudds, Fishers, Brackens, Blackwoods, or Hooks. Towers and forts had crowned the three hills at various times, only to be thrown down in one war or another. Now only broken stones and overgrown ruins remained to welcome the Targaryens. Though claimed by both Storm's End and Harrenhal, the river mouth was undefended, and the closest castles were held by lesser lords of no great power or military prowess, and lords moreover who had little reason to love their nominal overlord, Harren the Black.

Aegon Targaryen quickly threw up a log-and-earth palisade around the highest of the three hills and dispatched his sisters to secure the submission of the nearest castles. Rosby yielded to Rhaenys and golden-eyed Meraxes without a fight. At Stokeworth a few crossbowmen loosed bolts at Visenya, until Vhagar's flames set the roofs of the castle keep ablaze. Then they too submitted.

The conquerors' first true test came from Lord Darklyn of Duskendale and Lord Mooton of Maidenpool, who joined their power and marched south with three thousand men to drive the invaders back

ABOVE | *Argilac the Arrogant's response to Aegon's offer.*

into the sea. Aegon sent Orys Baratheon out to attack them on the march, whilst he descended on them from above with the Black Dread. Both lords were slain in the one-sided battle that followed; Darklyn's son and Mooton's brother thereafter yielded up their castles and swore their swords to House Targaryen. At that time Duskendale was the principal Westerosi port on the narrow sea and had grown fat and wealthy from the trade that passed through its harbor. Visenya Targaryen did not allow the town to be sacked, but she did not hesitate to claim its riches, greatly swelling the coffers of the conquerors.

This perhaps would be an apt place to discuss the differing characters of Aegon Targaryen and his sisters and queens.

Visenya, eldest of the three siblings, was as much a warrior as Aegon himself, as comfortable in ringmail as in silk. She carried the Valyrian longsword Dark Sister, and was skilled in its use, having trained beside her brother since childhood. Though possessed of the silver-gold hair and purple eyes of Valyria, hers was a harsh, austere beauty. Even those who loved her best found Visenya stern, serious, unforgiving, and some said that she played with poisons and dabbled in dark sorceries.

Rhaenys, youngest of the three Targaryens, was all her sister was not: playful, curious, impulsive, given to flights of fancy. No true warrior, Rhaenys loved music, dancing, and poetry, and supported many a singer, mummer, and puppeteer. Yet it was said that Rhaenys spent more time on dragonback than her brother and sister combined, for above all things she loved to fly. She once was heard to say that before she died she meant to fly Meraxes across the Sunset Sea to see what lay upon its western shores. Whilst no one ever questioned Visenya's fidelity to her brother/husband, Rhaenys surrounded herself with comely young men, and (it was whispered) even entertained some in her bedchambers on the nights when Aegon was with her elder sister. Yet despite these rumors, observers at court could not fail to note that the king spent ten nights with Rhaenys for every night with Visenya.

Aegon Targaryen himself, strangely, was as much an enigma to his contemporaries as to us. Armed with the Valyrian steel blade Blackfyre, he was counted amongst the greatest warriors of his age, yet he took no pleasure in feats of arms and never rode in tourney or mêlée. His mount was Balerion the Black Dread, but he flew only to battle, or to travel swiftly across land and sea. His commanding presence drew men to his banners, yet he had no close friends, save Orys Baratheon, the companion of his youth. Women were drawn to him, but Aegon remained ever faithful to his sisters. As king, he put great trust in his small council and his sisters, leaving much of the day-to-day governance of the realm to them . . . yet did not hesitate to take command when he found it necessary. Though he dealt harshly with rebels and traitors, he was open-handed with former foes who bent the knee.

This he showed for the first time at the Aegonfort, the crude wood-and-earth castle he had raised atop what was henceforth and forever known as Aegon's High Hill. Having taken a dozen castles and secured the mouth of the Blackwater Rush on both sides of the river, he commanded the lords he had defeated to attend him. There they laid their swords at his feet, and Aegon raised them up and confirmed them in their lands and titles. To his oldest supporters he gave new honors. Daemon Velaryon, Lord of the Tides, was made master of ships, in command of the royal fleet. Triston Massey, Lord of Stonedance, was named master of laws, Crispian Celtigar master of coin. And Orys Baratheon he proclaimed to be "my shield, my

ABOVE | *Ravens bearing Aegon's proclamation to all corners of Westeros.*

stalwart, my strong right hand." Thus Baratheon is reckoned by the maesters the first King's Hand.

Heraldic banners had long been a tradition amongst the lords of Westeros, but such had never been used by the dragonlords of old Valyria. When Aegon's knights unfurled his great silken battle standard, with a red three-headed dragon breathing fire upon a black field, the lords took it for a sign that he was now truly one of them, a worthy high king for Westeros. When Queen Visenya placed a Valyrian steel circlet, studded with rubies, on her brother's head and Queen Rhaenys hailed him as, "Aegon, First of His Name, King of All Westeros, and Shield of His People," the dragons roared and the lords and knights sent up a cheer . . . but the smallfolk, the fisherman and field hands and goodwives, shouted loudest of all.

The seven kings that Aegon the Dragon meant to uncrown were not cheering, however. In Harrenhal and Storm's End, Harren the Black and Argilac the Arrogant had already called their banners. In the west, King Mern of the Reach rode the Ocean Road north to Casterly Rock to meet with King Loren of House Lannister. The Princess of Dorne dispatched a raven to Dragonstone, offering to join Aegon against Argilac the Storm King . . . but as an equal and ally, not a subject. Another offer of alliance came from the boy king of the Eyrie, Ronnel Arryn, whose mother asked for all the lands east of the Green Fork of the Trident for the Vale's support against Black Harren. Even in the North, King Torrhen Stark of Winterfell sat with his lords bannermen and counselors late into the night, discussing what was to be done about this would-be conqueror. The whole realm waited anxiously to see where Aegon would move next.

Within days of his coronation, Aegon's armies were on the march again. The greater part of his host crossed the Blackwater Rush, making south for Storm's End under the command of Orys Baratheon. Queen Rhaenys accompanied him, astride Meraxes of the golden eyes and silver scales. The Targaryen fleet, under Daemon Velaryon, left Blackwater Bay and turned north, for Gulltown and the Vale. With them went Queen Visenya and Vhagar. The king himself marched northeast, to the Gods Eye and Harrenhal, the gargantuan fortress that was the pride and obsession of King Harren the Black and which he had completed

and occupied on the very day Aegon landed in what would one day become King's Landing.

All three of the Targaryen thrusts faced fierce opposition. Lords Errol, Fell, and Buckler, bannermen to Storm's End, surprised the advance elements of Orys Baratheon's host as they were crossing the Wendwater, cutting down more than a thousand men before fading back into the trees. A hastily assembled Arryn fleet, augmented by a dozen Braavosi warships, met and defeated the Targaryen fleet in the waters off Gulltown. Amongst the dead was Aegon's admiral, Daemon Velaryon. Aegon himself was attacked on the south shore of the Gods Eye, not once but twice. The Battle of the Reeds was a Targaryen victory, but they suffered heavy losses at the Wailing Willows when two of King Harren's sons crossed the lake in longboats with muffled oars and fell upon their rear.

Such defeats proved no more than setbacks, however, and in the end, Aegon's enemies had no answer for his dragons. The men of the Vale sank a third of the Targaryen ships and captured near as many, but when Queen Visenya descended upon them from the sky, their own ships burned. Lords Errol, Fell, and Buckler hid in their familiar forests until Queen Rhaenys unleashed Meraxes and a wall of fire swept through the woods, turning the trees to torches. And the victors at the Wailing Willows, returning across the lake to Harrenhal, were ill prepared when Balerion fell upon them out of the morning sky. Harren's longboats burned. So did Harren's sons.

Aegon's foes also found themselves plagued by other enemies. As Argilac the Arrogant gathered his swords at Storm's End, pirates from the Stepstones descended on the shores of Cape Wrath to take advantage of their absence, and Dornish raiding parties came boiling out of the Red Mountains to sweep across the marches. In the Vale, young King Ronnel had to contend with a rebellion on the Three Sisters, when the Sistermen renounced all allegiance to the Eyrie and proclaimed Lady Marla Sunderland their queen.

Yet these were but minor vexations compared to what befell Harren the Black. Though House Hoare had ruled the riverlands for three generations, the men of the Trident had no love for their ironborn overlords. Harren the Black had driven thousands to their deaths in the building of his great castle of

RIGHT | *Visenya and Vhagar burning the Arryn fleet.*

Harrenhal, plundering the riverlands for materials and beggaring lords and smallfolk alike with his appetite for gold. So now the riverlands rose against him, led by Lord Edmyn Tully of Riverrun. Summoned to the defense of Harrenhal, Tully declared for House Targaryen instead, raised the dragon banner over his castle, and rode forth with his knights and archers to join his strength to Aegon's. His defiance gave heart to the other riverlords. One by one, the lords of the Trident renounced Harren and declared for Aegon the Dragon. Blackwoods, Mallisters, Vances, Brackens, Pipers, Freys, Strongs . . . summoning their levies, they descended on Harrenhal.

Suddenly outnumbered, King Harren the Black took refuge in his supposedly impregnable stronghold. The largest castle ever raised in Westeros, Harrenhal boasted five gargantuan towers, an inexhaustible source of fresh water, huge, subterranean vaults well stocked with provisions, and massive walls of black stone higher than any ladder and too thick to be broken by any ram or shattered by a trebuchet. Harren barred his gates and settled down with his remaining sons and supporters to withstand a siege.

Aegon of Dragonstone was of a different mind. Once he had joined his power with that of Edmyn Tully and the other riverlords to ring the castle, he sent a maester to the gates under a peace banner, to parley. Harren emerged to meet him—an old man and grey, yet still fierce in his black armor. Each king had his banner-bearer and his maester in attendance, so the words that they exchanged are still remembered.

"Yield now," Aegon began, "and you may remain as Lord of the Iron Islands. Yield now, and your sons will live to rule after you. I have eight thousand men outside your walls."

"What is outside my walls is of no concern to me," said Harren. "Those walls are strong and thick."

"But not so high as to keep out dragons. Dragons fly."

"I built in stone," said Harren. "Stone does not burn."

To which Aegon said, "When the sun sets, your line shall end."

It is said that Harren spat at that and returned to his castle. Once inside, he sent every man of his to the parapets, armed with spears and bows and crossbows, promising lands and riches to whichever of them could bring the dragon down. "Had I a daughter, the dragonslayer could claim her hand as well," Harren the Black proclaimed. "Instead I will give him one of Tully's daughters, or all three if he likes. Or he may pick one of Blackwood's whelps, or Strong's, or any girl born of these traitors of the Trident, these lords of yellow mud." Then Harren the Black retired to his tower, surrounded by his household guard, to sup with his remaining sons.

As the last light of the sun faded, Black Harren's men stared into the gathering darkness, clutching their spears and crossbows. When no dragon appeared, some may have thought that Aegon's threats had been hollow. But Aegon Targaryen took Balerion up high, through the clouds, up and up until the dragon was no bigger than a fly upon the moon. Only then did he descend, well inside the castle walls. On wings as black as pitch, Balerion plunged through the night, and when the great towers of Harrenhal appeared beneath him, the dragon roared his fury and bathed them in black fire, shot through with swirls of red.

Stone does not burn, Harren had boasted, but his castle was not made of stone alone. Wood and wool, hemp and straw, bread and salted beef and grain, all took fire. Nor were Harren's ironmen made of stone. Smoking, screaming, shrouded in flames, they ran across the yards and tumbled from the wallwalks to die upon the ground below. And even stone will crack and melt if a fire is hot enough. The riverlords outside the castle walls said later that the towers of Harrenhal glowed red against the night, like five great candles . . . and like candles, they began to twist and melt, as runnels of molten stone ran down their sides.

Harren and his last sons died in the fires that engulfed his monstrous fortress that night. House Hoare died with him, and so too did the Iron Islands' hold on the riverlands. The next day, outside the smoking ruins of Harrenhal, King Aegon accepted an oath of fealty

from Edmyn Tully, Lord of Riverrun, and named him Lord Paramount of the Trident. The other riverlords did homage as well—to Aegon as king and to Edmyn Tully as their liege lord. When the ashes had cooled enough to allow men to enter the castle safely, the swords of the fallen, many shattered or melted or twisted into ribbons of steel by dragonfire, were gathered up and sent back to the Aegonfort in wagons.

South and east, the Storm King's bannermen proved considerably more loyal than King Harren's. Argilac the Arrogant gathered a great host about him at Storm's End. The seat of the Durrandons was a mighty fastness, its great curtain wall even thicker than the walls of Harrenhal. It too was thought to be impregnable to assault. Word of King Harren's end soon reached the ears of his old enemy King Argilac, however. Lords Fell and Buckler, falling back before the approaching host (Lord Errol had been killed), had sent him word of Queen Rhaenys and her dragon. The old warrior king roared that he did not intend to die as Harren had, cooked inside his own castle like a suckling pig with an apple in his mouth. No stranger to battle, he would decide his own fate, sword in hand. So Argilac the Arrogant rode forth from Storm's End one last time, to meet his foes in the open field.

The Storm King's approach was no surprise to Orys Baratheon and his men; Queen Rhaenys, flying Meraxes, had witnessed Argilac's departure from Storm's End and was able to give the Hand a full accounting of the enemy's numbers and dispositions. Orys took up a strong position on the hills south of Bronzegate, and dug in there on the high ground to await the coming of the stormlanders.

As the armies came together, the stormlands proved true to their name. A steady rain began to fall that morning, and by midday had turned into a howling gale. King Argilac's lords bannermen urged him to delay his attack until the next day, in hopes the rain would pass, but the Storm King outnumbered the conquerors almost two to one and had almost four times as many knights and heavy horse. The sight of the Targaryen banners flapping sodden above his own hills enraged him, and the battle-seasoned old warrior did not fail to note that the rain was blowing from the south, into the faces of the Targaryen men on their hills. So Argilac the Arrogant gave the command to attack, and the battle known to history as the Last Storm began.

The fighting lasted well into the night, a bloody business, and far less one-sided than Aegon's conquest of Harrenhal. Thrice Argilac the Arrogant led his knights against the Baratheon positions, but the slopes were steep and the rains had turned the ground soft and muddy, so the warhorses struggled and foundered, and the charges lost all cohesion and momentum. The stormlanders fared better when they sent their spearmen up the hills on foot. Blinded by the rain, the invaders did not see them climbing until it was too late, and the wet bowstrings of the archers made their bows useless. One hill fell, then another, and the third and final charge of the Storm King and his knights broke through the Baratheon center . . . only to come upon Queen Rhaenys and Meraxes. Even on the ground, the dragon proved formidable. Dickon Morrigen and the Bastard of Blackhaven, commanding the vanguard, were engulfed in dragonflame, along with the knights of King Argilac's personal guard. The warhorses panicked and fled in terror, crashing into riders behind them and turning the charge into chaos. The Storm King himself was thrown from his saddle.

Yet still Argilac continued to battle. When Orys Baratheon came down the muddy hill with his own men, he found the old king holding off half a dozen men, with as many corpses at his feet. "Stand aside," Baratheon commanded. He dismounted, so as to meet the king on equal footing, and offered the Storm King one last chance to yield. Argilac cursed him instead. And so they fought, the old warrior king with his streaming white hair and Aegon's fierce, black-bearded Hand. Each man took a wound from the other, it was said, but in the end the last of the Durrandon got his wish and died with a sword in his hand and a curse on his lips. The death of their king took all heart out of the stormlanders, and as the word spread that Argilac had fallen, his lords and knights threw down their swords and fled.

For a few days it was feared that Storm's End might suffer the same fate as Harrenhal, for Argilac's daughter Argella barred her gates at the approach of Orys Baratheon and the Targaryen host, and declared herself the Storm Queen. Rather than bend the knee, the defenders of Storm's End would die to the last man, she promised when Queen Rhaenys flew Meraxes

into the castle to parley. "You may take my castle, but you will win only bones and blood and ashes," she announced . . . but the soldiers of the garrison proved less eager to die. That night they raised a peace banner, threw open the castle gate, and delivered Lady Argella gagged, chained, and naked to the camp of Orys Baratheon.

It is said that Baratheon unchained her with his own hands, wrapped his cloak around her, poured her wine, and spoke to her gently, telling her of her father's courage and the manner of his death. And afterward, to honor the fallen king, he took the arms and words of the Durrandon for his own. The crowned stag became his sigil, Storm's End became his seat, and Lady Argella his wife.

With both the riverlands and stormlands now under the control of Aegon the Dragon and his allies, the remaining kings of Westeros saw plainly that their own turns were coming. At Winterfell, King Torrhen called his banners; given the vast distances in the North, he knew that assembling an army would take time. Queen Sharra of the Vale, regent for her son Ronnel, took refuge in the Eyrie, looked to her defenses, and sent an army to the Bloody Gate, gateway to the Vale of Arryn. In her youth Queen Sharra had been lauded as "the Flower of the Mountain," the fairest maid in all the Seven Kingdoms. Perhaps hoping to sway Aegon with her beauty, she sent him a portrait of herself and offered herself to him in marriage, provided he named her son Ronnel as his heir. Though the portrait did finally reach him, it is not known whether Aegon

Targaryen ever replied to her proposal; he had two queens already, and Sharra Arryn was by then a faded flower, ten years his elder.

Meanwhile, the two great western kings had made common cause and assembled their own armies, intent on putting an end to Aegon for good and all. From Highgarden marched Mern IX of House Gardener, King of the Reach, with a mighty host. Beneath the walls of Castle Goldengrove, seat of House Rowan, he met Loren I Lannister, King of the Rock, leading his own host down from the westerlands. Together the two kings commanded the mightiest host ever seen in Westeros: an army fifty-five thousand strong, including some six hundred lords great and small and more than five thousand mounted knights. "Our iron fist," boasted King Mern. His four sons rode beside him, and both of his young grandsons attended him as squires.

The two kings did not linger long at Goldengrove; a host of such size must remain on the march lest it eat the surrounding countryside bare. The allies set out at once, marching north by northeast through tall grasses and golden fields of wheat.

Advised of their coming in his camp beside the Gods Eye, Aegon gathered his own strength and advanced to meet these new foes. He commanded only a fifth as many men as the two kings, and much of his strength was made up of men sworn to the riverlords, whose loyalty to House Targaryen was of recent vintage and untested. With the smaller host, however, Aegon was able to move much more quickly than his foes. At the town of Stoney Sept, both his queens joined him with their dragons—Rhaenys from Storm's End, and Visenya from Crackclaw Point, where she had accepted many fervent pledges of fealty from the local lords. Together the three Targaryens watched from the sky as Aegon's army crossed the headwaters of the Blackwater Rush and raced south.

The two armies came together amongst the wide, open plains south of the Blackwater, near to where the Goldroad would run one day. The two kings rejoiced when their scouts returned to them to report Targaryen numbers and dispositions. They had five men for every one of Aegon's, it seemed, and the disparity in lords and knights was even greater. And the land was wide and open, all grass and wheat as far as the eye could see, ideal for heavy horse. Aegon Targaryen did not

ABOVE | *Orys Baratheon, the first Lord of Storm's End.*

command the high ground, as Orys Baratheon had at the Last Storm; the ground was firm, not muddy. Nor were they troubled by rain. The day was cloudless, though windy. There had been no rain for more than a fortnight.

King Mern had brought half again as many men to the battle as King Loren, and so demanded the honor of commanding the center. His son and heir, Edmund, was given the vanguard. King Loren and his knights formed the right, Lord Oakheart the left. With no natural barriers to anchor the Targaryen line, the two kings meant to sweep around Aegon on both flanks, then take him in the rear, whilst their "iron fist," a great wedge of armored knights and high lords, smashed through Aegon's center.

Aegon Targaryen drew his own men up in a rough crescent bristling with spears and pikes, with archers and crossbowmen just behind and light cavalry on either flank. He gave command of his host to Jon Mooton, Lord of Maidenpool, one of the first foes to come over to his cause. The king himself intended to do his fighting from the sky, beside his queens. Aegon had noted the absence of rain as well; the grass and wheat that surrounded the armies was tall and ripe for harvest . . . and very dry.

The Targaryens waited until the two kings sounded their trumpets and started forward beneath a sea of banners. King Mern himself led the charge against the center on his golden stallion, his son Gawen beside him with his banner, a great green hand upon a field of white. Roaring and screaming, urged on by horns and drums, the Gardeners and Lannisters charged through a storm of arrows down onto their foes, sweeping aside the Targaryen spearmen, shattering their ranks. But by then Aegon and his sisters were in the air.

Aegon flew above the ranks of his foes upon Balerion, through a storm of spears and stones and arrows, swooping down repeatedly to bathe his foes in flame. Rhaenys and Visenya set fires upwind of the enemy and behind them. The dry grasses and stands of wheat went up at once. The wind fanned the flames and blew the smoke into the faces of the advancing ranks of the two kings. The scent of fire sent their mounts into panic, and as the smoke thickened, horse and rider alike were blinded. Their ranks began to break as walls of fire rose on every side of them. Lord Mooton's men, safely upwind of the conflagration, waited with their bows

and spears and made short work of the burned and burning men who came staggering from the inferno.

The Field of Fire, the battle was named afterward.

More than four thousand men died in the flames. Another thousand perished from sword and spears and arrows. Tens of thousands suffered burns, some so bad that they remained scarred for life. King Mern IX was amongst the dead, together with his sons, grandsons, brothers, cousins, and other kin. One nephew survived for three days. When he died of his burns, House Gardener died with him. King Loren of the Rock lived, riding through a wall of flame and smoke to safety when he saw the battle lost.

The Targaryens lost fewer than a hundred men. Queen Visenya took an arrow in one shoulder but soon recovered. As his dragons gorged themselves on the dead, Aegon commanded that the swords of the slain be gathered up and sent downriver.

Loren Lannister was captured the next day. The King of the Rock laid his sword and crown at Aegon's feet, bent the knee, and did him homage. And Aegon, true to his promises, lifted his beaten foe back to his feet and confirmed him in his lands and lordship, naming him Lord of Casterly Rock and Warden of the West. Lord Loren's bannermen followed his example, and so too did many lords of the Reach, those who had survived the dragonfire.

Yet the conquest of the west remained incomplete, so King Aegon parted from his sisters and marched at once for Highgarden, hoping to secure its surrender before some other claimant could seize it for his own. He found the castle in the hands of its steward, Harlan Tyrell, whose forebears had served the Gardeners for centuries. Tyrell yielded up the keys to the castle without a fight and pledged his support to the conquering king. In reward Aegon granted him Highgarden and all its domains, naming him Warden of the South and Lord Paramount of the Mander, and giving him dominion over all House Gardener's former vassals.

It was King Aegon's intent to continue his march south and enforce the submission of Oldtown, the Arbor, and Dorne, but whilst at Highgarden the word of a new challenge came to his ears. Torrhen Stark, King in the North, had crossed the Neck and entered the riverlands, leading an army of savage Northmen thirty thousand strong. Aegon at once started north to meet him, racing ahead of his army on the wings of Balerion, the Black Dread. He sent word to his two queens as well, and to all the lords and knights who had bent the knee to him after Harrenhal and the Field of Fire.

When Torrhen Stark reached the banks of the Trident, he found a host half again the size of his own awaiting him south of the river. Riverlords, westermen, stormlanders, men of the Reach . . . all had come. And above their camp Balerion, Meraxes, and Vhagar prowled the sky in ever-widening circles.

Torrhen's scouts had seen the ruins of Harrenhal, where slow, red fires still burned beneath the rubble. The King in the North had heard many accounts of the Field of Fire as well. He knew that the same fate might await him if he tried to force a crossing of the river. Some of his lords bannermen urged him to attack all the same, insisting that Northern valor would carry the day. Others urged him to fall back to Moat Cailin and make his stand there on Northern soil. The king's bastard brother Brandon Snow offered to cross the Trident alone under cover of darkness, to slay the dragons whilst they slept.

King Torrhen did send Brandon Snow across the Trident. But he crossed with three maesters by his side, not to kill but to treat. All through the night messages went back and forth. The next morning, Torrhen Stark himself crossed the Trident. There upon the south bank of the Trident, he knelt, laid the ancient crown of the Kings of Winter at Aegon's feet, and swore to be his man. He rose as Lord of Winterfell and Warden of the North, a king no more. From that day to this day, Torrhen Stark is remembered as the King Who Knelt . . . but no Northman left his burned bones beside the Trident, and the swords Aegon collected from Lord Stark and his vassals were not twisted or melted or bent.

Now once again Aegon Targaryen and his queens parted company. Aegon turned south once more, marching toward Oldtown, whilst his two sisters mounted their dragons—Visenya for a second attempt at the Vale of Arryn, and Rhaenys for Sunspear and the deserts of Dorne.

Sharra Arryn had strengthened the defenses of Gulltown, moved a strong host to the Bloody Gate, and tripled the size of the garrisons in Stone, Snow, and Sky, the waycastles that guarded the approach to the Eyrie. All these defenses proved useless against Visenya Targaryen, who rode Vhagar's leathery wings above them all and landed in the Eyrie's inner courtyard. When the regent of the Vale rushed out to confront her, with a dozen guards at her back, she found Visenya with Ronnel Arryn seated on her knee, staring at the dragon, wonder-struck. "Mother, can I go flying with the lady?" the boy king asked. No threats were spoken, no angry words exchanged. The two queens smiled at one another and exchanged courtesies instead. Then Lady Sharra sent for the three crowns (her own regent's coronet, her son's small crown, and the Falcon Crown of Mountain and Vale that the Arryn kings had worn for a thousand years), and surrendered them to Queen Visenya, along with the swords of her garrison. And it was said afterward that the little king flew thrice about the summit of the Giant's Lance and landed to find himself a little lord. Thus did Visenya Targaryen bring the Vale of Arryn into her brother's realm.

Rhaenys Targaryen had no such easy conquest. A host of Dornish spearmen guarded the Prince's Pass, the gateway through the Red Mountains, but Rhaenys did not engage them. She flew above the pass, above the red sands and the white, and descended upon Vaith to demand its submission, only to find the castle empty and abandoned. In the town beneath its walls, only

women and children and old men remained. When asked where their lords had gone, they would only say, "Away." Rhaenys followed the river downstream to Godsgrace, seat of House Allyrion, but it too was deserted. On she flew. Where the Greenblood met the sea, Rhaenys came upon the Planky Town, where hundreds of poleboats, fishing skiffs, barges, houseboats, and hulks sat baking in the sun, joined together with ropes and chains and planks to make a floating city, yet only a few old women and small children appeared to peer up at her as Meraxes circled overhead.

Finally the queen's flight took her to Sunspear, the ancient seat of House Martell, where she found the Princess of Dorne waiting in her abandoned castle. Meria Martell was eighty years of age, the maesters tell us, and had ruled the Dornishmen for sixty of those years. She was very fat, blind, and almost bald, her skin sallow and sagging. Argilac the Arrogant had

PREVIOUS PAGES | *The submission of Torrhen Stark, the King Who Knelt.*
ABOVE | *The meeting between Meria Martell and Rhaenys Targaryen.*

named her "the Yellow Toad of Dorne," but neither age nor blindness had dulled her wits.

"I will not fight you," Princess Meria told Rhaenys, "nor will I kneel to you. Dorne has no king. Tell your brother that."

"I shall," Rhaenys replied, "but we will come again, Princess, and the next time we shall come with fire and blood."

"Your words," said Princess Meria. "Ours are Unbowed, Unbent, Unbroken. You may burn us, my lady . . . but you will not bend us, break us, or make us bow. This is Dorne. You are not wanted here. Return at your peril."

Thus queen and princess parted, and Dorne remained unconquered.

To the west, Aegon Targaryen met a warmer welcome. The greatest city in all of Westeros, Oldtown was ringed about with massive walls and ruled by the Hightowers of Hightower, the oldest, richest, and most powerful of the noble houses of the Reach. Oldtown was also the center of the Faith. There dwelt the High Septon, Father of the Faithful, the voice of the new gods on earth, who commanded the obedience of millions of the devout throughout the realms (save in the North, where the old gods still held sway), and the blades of the Faith Militant, the fighting orders the smallfolk called the Stars and Swords.

Yet when Aegon Targaryen and his host approached Oldtown, they found the city gates open, and Lord Hightower waiting to make his submission. As it happened, when word of Aegon's landing first reached Oldtown, the High Septon had locked himself within the Starry Sept for seven days and seven nights, seeking after the guidance of the gods. He took no nourishment but bread and water, it was said, and spent all his waking hours in prayer, moving from one altar to the next. And on the seventh day, the Crone had lifted her golden lamp to show him the path ahead. If Oldtown took up arms against Aegon the Dragon, His High Holiness saw, the city would surely burn, and the Hightower and the Citadel and the Starry Sept would be cast down and destroyed.

Manfred Hightower, Lord of Oldtown, was a cautious lord, and godly. One of his younger sons served with the Warrior's Sons, and another had only recently taken vows as a septon. When the High Septon told him of the vision vouchsafed him by the Crone, Lord Hightower determined that he would not oppose the Conqueror by force of arms. Thus it was that no men from Oldtown burned on the Field of Fire, though the Hightowers were bannermen to the Gardeners of Highgarden. And thus it was that Lord Manfred rode forth to greet Aegon the Dragon as he approached, and to offer up his sword, his city, and his oath. (Some say that Lord Hightower also offered up the hand of his youngest daughter, which Aegon declined politely, lest it offend his two queens).

Three days later, in the Starry Sept, His High Holiness himself anointed Aegon with the seven oils, placed a crown upon his head, and proclaimed him Aegon of House Targaryen, the First of His Name, King of the Andals, the Rhoynar, and the First Men, Lord of the Seven Kingdoms, and Protector of the Realm. ("Seven Kingdoms" was the style used, though Dorne had not submitted. Nor would it, for more than a century to come).

Only a handful of lords had been present for Aegon's first coronation at the mouth of the Blackwater, but hundreds were on hand to witness his second, and tens of thousands cheered him afterward in the streets of Oldtown as he rode through the city on Balerion's back. Amongst those at Aegon's second coronation were the maesters and archmaesters of the Citadel. Perhaps for that reason, it was this coronation, rather than the Aegonfort crowning or the day of Aegon's Landing, that became fixed as the start of Aegon's reign.

Thus were the Seven Kingdoms of Westeros hammered into one great realm, by the will of Aegon the Conqueror and his sisters.

Many thought that King Aegon would make Oldtown his royal seat after the wars were done, whilst others thought he would rule from Dragonstone, the ancient island citadel of House Targaryen. The king surprised them all by proclaiming his intent to make his court in the new town already rising beneath the three hills at the mouth of the Blackwater Rush, at the place where he and his sisters had first set foot on the soil of Westeros. King's Landing, the new town was called. From there Aegon the Dragon ruled his realm, holding court from a great metal seat made from the melted, twisted, beaten, and broken blades of all his fallen foes, a perilous seat that would soon be known through all the world as the Iron Throne of Westeros.

The Targaryen Kings

KING AEGON, THE First of His Name, might have conquered the Seven Kingdoms by the age of twenty-seven, but now he faced the formidable challenge of ruling his newly forged realm. The seven warring kingdoms had rarely been at peace within their own borders let alone without them, and uniting them under one rule required a truly remarkable man. So it was fortunate for the realm that Aegon was such a man—a man with vision and determination aplenty. And though his vision of a united Westeros proved harder to realize than Aegon might have believed—not to mention far costlier—it was a vision that shaped the course of history for hundreds of years to come.

It was Aegon who saw a great royal city to rival and surpass Lannisport and Oldtown spring up around his crude Aegonfort. And while King's Landing might have been a crowded, muddy, and stinking place at its outset, it was always full of activity. A makeshift sept constructed out of the hulk of a cog on the Blackwater served the common people, and soon a much grander sept was raised on Visenya's Hill with money sent by the High Septon. (This would be later joined by the Sept of Remembrance on the Hill of Rhaenys as a memorial to the queen.) Where once only fishing boats were seen, now cogs and galleys from Oldtown, Lannisport, the Free Cities, and even the Summer Isles began to appear as the flow of trade shifted from Duskendale and Maidenpool to King's Landing. The Aegonfort itself grew larger, bursting past its initial palisade to encompass more of Aegon's High Hill, and a new wooden keep was raised, its walls fifty feet high. It stood until 35 AC, when Aegon tore it down so that the Red Keep could be raised as a castle fit for the Targaryens and their heirs.

By 10 AC, King's Landing had become a true city, and by 25 AC it had surpassed White Harbor and Gulltown to become the realm's third largest city. And yet, for much of this time, it was a city without walls. It may be that Aegon and his sisters thought that no one would dare assault a city

that held dragons, but in 19 AC word came of a pirate fleet sacking Tall Trees Town in the Summer Isles, carrying off thousands into slavery and a fortune in wealth. Troubled by this—and realizing that he and Visenya were not always at King's Landing—Aegon at last commanded that walls be raised. Grand Maester Gawen and the Hand, Ser Osmund Strong, were given charge of the project. Aegon decreed there should be room enough for the city to expand within those walls, and that seven great gatehouses would defend seven gates, in honor of the Seven. Construction began the next year, and by 26 AC it was completed.

As the city and its prosperity grew, so did that of the realm. This was in part due to the Conqueror's efforts to win the respect of his vassals and that of the smallfolk. In this, he was often aided by Queen Rhaenys (whilst she lived), for whom the smallfolk were of special concern. She was likewise a patron to singers and bards—something her sister, Queen Visenya, thought a waste, but those singers made songs of praise for the Targaryens and carried them throughout the realm. And if those songs also contained bold lies that made Aegon and his sisters seem all the more glorious, the queen did not rue it . . . although the maesters might.

The queen also did much to bring the realm together through the marriages she arranged between far-flung houses. Thus, Rhaenys's death in Dorne in 10 AC, and the wrath that followed it, was felt by much of the realm, who had loved the beautiful, kindhearted queen.

Yet despite a reign covered in glory, the First Dornish War stood out as Aegon's one great defeat. The First Dornish War began boldly in 4 AC, and ended in 13 AC after years of tragedy and spilled blood. Many were the calamities of that war. The death of Rhaenys, the years of the Dragon's Wroth, the murdered lords, the would-be assassins in King's Landing and the Red Keep itself; it was a black time.

But out of all the tragedy was born one glorious thing: the Sworn Brotherhood of the Kingsguard. When Aegon

According to the history of Archmaester Gyldayn, it was suggested at court that Aegon left Queen Visenya in charge of building the Red Keep so that he would not have to endure her presence on Dragonstone. In their later years, their relationship—never a warm one to begin with—had grown even more distant.

PREVIOUS PAGES | *The Iron Throne.* LEFT | *Aegon the Conqueror crowned by the High Septon.*

and Visenya placed prices on the heads of the Dornish lords, many were murdered, and in retaliation the Dornishmen hired their own catspaws and killers. On one occasion in 10 AC, Aegon and Visenya were both attacked in the streets of King's Landing, and if not for Visenya and Dark Sister, the king might not have survived. Despite this, the king still believed that his guards were sufficient to his defense; Visenya convinced him otherwise. (It is recorded that when Aegon pointed out his guardsmen, Visenya drew Dark Sister and cut his cheek before his guards could react. "Your guards are slow and lazy," Visenya is reported to have said, and the king was forced to agree.)

It was Visenya, not Aegon, who decided the nature of the Kingsguard. Seven champions for the Lord of the Seven Kingdoms, who would all be knights. She modeled their vows upon those of the Night's Watch, so that they would forfeit all things save their duty to the king. And when Aegon spoke of a grand tourney to choose the first Kingsguard, Visenya dissuaded him, saying he needed more than skill in arms to protect him; he also needed unwavering loyalty. The king entrusted Visenya with selecting the first members of the order, and history shows he was wise to do so: two died defending him, and all served to the end of their days with honor. *The White Book* recounts their names, as it has recorded

The "rule of six," now part of the common law, was established by Rhaenys as she sat the Iron Throne while the king was upon one of his progresses. A petition was made by the brothers of a woman who had been beaten to death by her husband after he caught her with another. He defended himself by rightly noting that it was lawful for a man to chastise an adulterous wife (which was true enough, though in Dorne, matters are elsewise) so long as he used a rod no thicker than a thumb. However, he had struck her a hundred times, according to the brothers, and this he did not deny. After deliberating with the maesters and septons, Rhaenys declared that, whilst the gods made women to be dutiful to their husbands and so could be lawfully beaten, only six blows might ever be struck—one for each of the Seven, save the Stranger, who was death. For this reason, she declared that ninety-four of the husband's blows had been unlawful and agreed that the dead woman's brothers could match those blows upon the husband.

the name and deeds of every knight who swore the vows: Ser Corlys Velaryon, the first Lord Commander; Ser Richard Roote; Ser Addison Hill, Bastard of Cornfield; Ser Gregor Goode and Ser Griffith Goode, brothers; Ser Humfrey the Mummer, a hedge knight; and Ser Robin Darklyn, called Darkrobin, the first of many Darklyns to wear the white cloak.

Having established councillors early on—who in Jaehaerys I's day formed the small council that would advise the kings thereafter—Aegon the Conqueror often left the day-to-day governance of the realm to his sisters and these trusted councillors. And instead, he worked to knit the realm together with his presence—to awe his subjects and (when needed) frighten them. For half the year the king flew between King's Landing and Dragonstone by turns, for whilst the city was his royal seat, the isle that smelled of sulfur and brimstone and the salt sea was the place he loved the best. But the other half of the year he dedicated to the royal progress. He traveled throughout the realm for the rest of his life, until his final progress in 33 AC—making a point of paying his respects to the High Septon in the Starry Sept each time he visited Oldtown, guesting beneath the roofs of the lords of the great houses (even Winterfell, on that last progress), and beneath the roofs of many lesser lords, knights, and common innkeepers. The king brought a glittering train with him wherever he went; in one progress, fully a thousand knights followed him, and many lords and ladies of the court besides.

In these progresses, the king was accompanied not only by his courtiers but by maesters and septons as well. Six maesters were often in his company to advise him upon the local laws and traditions of the former realms, so that he might rule in judgment at the courts he held. Rather than attempting to unify the realm under one set of laws, he respected the differing customs of each region and sought to judge as their past kings might have. (It would be left for a later king to bring the laws of the realm into accord.) From the conclusion of the First Dornish War until Aegon's death in 37 AC, the realm was at peace, and Aegon ruled with wisdom and forbearance. He had given the realm both "an heir and a spare" by his two wives: the elder Prince Aenys by Rhaenys (long dead) and the younger Prince Maegor by Visenya.

He died where he had been born, on his beloved Dragonstone. The accounts agree that he was in the Chamber of the Painted Table, recounting to his grandsons Aegon and Viserys the tales of his conquests, when he stumbled in his speech and collapsed. It was a stroke, the maesters said, and the Dragon passed quickly and in peace. His body was burned in the yard of Dragonstone's citadel, as was the custom of the Targaryens and the Valyrians before them. Aenys, the Prince of Dragonstone and heir to the Iron Throne, was at Highgarden when he learned of his father's death and swiftly flew on his dragon to receive his crown. But all who followed Aegon the Conqueror on the Iron Throne found the realm far less amenable to their rule.

LEFT | *Early King's Landing and the Aegonfort.*   ABOVE | *The crown of Aegon the Conqueror.*

WHEN THE DRAGON passed at the age of four-and-sixty, his reign had been uncontested by all save the Dornishmen. He had ruled wisely: showing himself well during his royal progresses, displaying due deference to the High Septons, rewarding those who served well, and aiding those who required it. Yet beneath the surface of this largely peaceful rule was a roiling cauldron of dissent. In their hearts, many of his subjects still cherished the old days, when the great houses ruled their own domains with unquestioned sovereignty. Others wished vengeance, for loved ones killed in the wars. And still others saw the Targaryens as abominations: brothers wed to sisters, with their incestuous couplings producing misbegotten heirs. The strength of Aegon and his sisters—and their dragons—had been enough to subdue those who opposed them, but the same could not be said for their heirs.

It was Aenys, Aegon's firstborn son by his beloved Rhaenys, who came to the throne in the year 37 AC at the age of thirty. He was crowned with great ceremony in the Red Keep in the midst of its construction, donning an ornate golden crown rather than his father's circlet of Valyrian steel.

But though his father and brother, Maegor (who was Visenya's child), were both warriors born, Aenys was made of different stuff. He had begun life as a weak and sickly infant and remained so throughout his earliest years. Rumors abounded that this could be no true son of Aegon the Conqueror, who had been a warrior without peer. In fact, it was well-known

that Queen Rhaenys delighted in handsome singers and witty mummers; perhaps one of these might have fathered the child. But the rumors dampened and eventually died when the sickly child was given a young hatchling who was named Quicksilver. And as the dragon grew, so too did Aenys.

Still, Aenys remained a dreamer, a dabbler in alchemy, a patron of singers and mummers and mimes. Moreover, he hungered too much for approval, and this led him to dither and hesitate over his decisions for fear of disappointing one side or another. It was this flaw that most marred his reign and brought him to an early and ignominious end.

After the Conqueror's death, it did not take long before challenges to the Targaryen rule emerged. The first of these was the bandit and outlaw named Harren the Red, who claimed to be a grandson of Harren the Black. With the help of a castle servant, Harren the Red seized both Harrenhal and its current ruler, the infamous Lord Gargon (remembered as Gargon the Guest for his custom of attending every wedding in his domain to exercise his right to First Night). Lord Gargon was gelded in the castle's godswood and left to bleed to death while Red Harren proclaimed himself Lord of Harrenhal and King of the Rivers.

All this took place while the king guested at Riverrun, the seat of the Tullys. But by the time Aenys and Lord Tully moved to deal with this threat, they found Harrenhal empty, Gargon's loyal men put to the sword, and Harren the Red and his followers returned to banditry.

More rebels soon appeared in the Vale and the Iron Islands, while a Dornishman naming himself the Vulture King gathered thousands of followers to stand against the Targaryens. Grand Maester Gawen wrote that the king was stunned by this news, for Aenys fancied himself beloved of the commons. And the king again acted indecisively: at first commanding that a host sail for the Vale to deal with the usurper Jonos Arryn, who had imprisoned his own brother Lord Ronnel, then suddenly recalling the order for fear that Harren the Red and his men might infiltrate King's Landing. The king even determined to call a Great Council to discuss how to deal with these matters. Fortunately for the realm, others acted more swiftly.

Lord Royce of Runestone gathered forces that swept away the rebels under Jonos Arryn, penning him and his followers in the Eyrie—although this led directly to the murder of the imprisoned Lord Ronnel, when Jonos sent his brother flying

LEFT | *King Aenys I upon the Iron Throne.*

out the Moon Door to his death. Yet the Eyrie proved no safe haven when Prince Maegor came calling on the back of Balerion, the Black Dread—the dragon that he had always desired and could finally claim following his father's death. Jonos and his followers all died by the noose, at Maegor's hand.

Meanwhile, in the Iron Islands, the man who claimed to be King Lodos reborn was swiftly dispatched by Lord Goren Greyjoy, who sent his pickled head to King Aenys. In return, Aenys granted Goren a boon—a boon that Lord Goren used to oust the Faith from the Iron Islands, to the dismay of the rest of the realm.

As for the Vulture King, the Martells largely ignored this little insurrection within their own borders. Although Princess Deria assured Aenys that the Martells only desired peace and were doing what they could to put down the rebellion, it was left mostly to the Marcher lords to resolve it. And at first, the so-called Vulture King seemed more than their match. His early victories led to swelling support, until his followers numbered some thirty thousand strong. It was only when he split this great host—both for lack of supplies to feed them and his confidence that each could defeat any foe that went against them—that his troubles began. Now they could be defeated piecemeal by the former Hand Orys Baratheon and the might of the Marcher lords—especially Savage Sam Tarly, whose sword, Heartsbane, was said to be red from hilt to point after the dozens of Dornishmen he cut down in the course of the Vulture Hunt, as the chase after the Vulture King became known.

The first rebel was also the last. Harren the Red, who was still at large, was finally cornered by Aenys's Hand, Lord Alyn Stokeworth. In the fighting that ensued, Harren killed Lord Alyn, only to be killed by the Hand's squire in turn.

With peace reestablished, the king thanked the chief lords and champions who had put down these rebels and enemies of the throne—and the foremost reward went to

his brother, Prince Maegor, whom Aenys named as the new Hand of the King. It seemed, at the time, the wisest choice. And yet, it sowed the seeds that sealed Aenys's doom.

It had long been the Valyrian custom to marry within the family, thus preserving the royal bloodlines. Yet this was not a custom native to Westeros, and was viewed as an abomination by the Faith. The Dragon and his sisters had been accepted without comment, and the issue had not arisen when Prince Aenys was wed in 22 AC to Alyssa Velaryon, the daughter of the king's master of ships and lord admiral; though she was a Targaryen upon her mother's side, this made her only a cousin. But when the tradition looked to continue yet again, matters came to a sudden head.

Queen Visenya proposed that Maegor be wed to Aenys's first child, Rhaena, but the High Septon mounted a vigorous protest, and Maegor was wed instead to the High Septon's own niece, Lady Ceryse of House Hightower. But that proved a barren marriage, while Aenys's bore more fruit, as Rhaena was followed by his son and heir, Aegon, and later Viserys, Jaehaerys, and Alysanne. Perhaps envious, after two years as Hand—and the birth to his brother of yet another daughter, Vaella, who died as an infant—Maegor shocked the realm in 39 AC by announcing that he had taken a second wife—Alys of House Harroway—in secret. He had wed her in a Valyrian ceremony officiated by Queen Visenya for want of a septon willing to wed them. The public outcry was such that Aenys was finally forced to exile his brother.

Aenys seemed content to let the matter lie with Maegor's exile, but the High Septon was still not satisfied. Not even the appointment of the reputed miracle-worker, Septon Murmison, as Aenys's new Hand could wholly repair the breach with the Faith. And in 41 AC, Aenys made matters worse when he chose to wed his eldest daughter, Rhaena, to his son and heir, Aegon, whom he named Prince of Dragonstone in Maegor's place. From the Starry Sept came

---

FROM THE HISTORY OF ARCHMAESTER GYLDAYN

The tradition amongst the Targaryens had always been to marry kin to kin. Wedding brother to sister was thought to be ideal. Failing that, a girl might wed an uncle, a cousin, or a nephew; a boy, a cousin, aunt, or niece. This practice went back to Old Valyria, where it was common amongst many of the ancient families, particularly those who bred and rode dragons. "The blood of the dragon must remain pure," the wisdom went. Some of the sorcerer princes also took more than one wife when it pleased them, though this was less common than incestuous marriage. In Valryia before the Doom, wise men wrote, a thousand gods were honored, but none were feared, so few dared to speak against these customs.

This was not true in Westeros, where the power of the Faith went unquestioned. Incest was denounced as vile sin, whether between father and daughter, mother and son, or brother and sister, and the fruits of such unions were considered abominations in the sight of gods and men. With hindsight, it can be seen that conflict between the Faith and House Targaryen was inevitable.

a denunciation such as no king had ever received before, addressed to "King Abomination"—and suddenly pious lords and even the smallfolk who had once loved Aenys turned against him.

Septon Murmison was expelled from the Faith for performing the ceremony, and zealous Poor Fellows took up arms, hacking Murmison to pieces a fortnight later as he was carried by litter across the city. The Warrior's Sons began to fortify the Hill of Rhaenys, making the Sept of Remembrance into a citadel that could stand against the king. In addition, some Poor Fellows attempted to murder the king and his family in the castle itself, scaling its walls and slipping into the royal apartments. It was only thanks to a knight of the Kingsguard that the royal family survived.

In the face of all this, Aenys abandoned the city with his family and fled to the safety of Dragonstone. There, Visenya counseled him to take his dragons and bring fire and blood to both the Starry Sept and the Sept of Remembrance. Instead, the king, who was incapable of making a firm decision, fell ill, with painful cramps wracking his stomach and loose bowels. By the end of 41 AC, most of the realm had turned against him. Thousands of Poor Fellows prowled the roads, threatening the king's supporters, and dozens of lords took up arms against the Iron Throne. Though Aenys was only five-and-thirty, it was said that he looked more like a man of sixty, and Grand Maester Gawen despaired of improving his condition.

The dowager Queen Visenya took over his care, and for a time he improved. And then, quite suddenly, he suffered a collapse when he learned that his son and daughter were besieged in Crakehall Castle, where they had taken refuge when their yearly progress was interrupted by the uprising against the throne. He died three days later, and like his father before him, was burned on Dragonstone, after the fashion of the Valyrians of old.

In later days, after Visenya's death, it was suggested that King Aenys's sudden demise was Visenya's doing, and some spoke of her as a kinslayer and kingslayer. Did she not prefer Maegor over Aenys in all things? Did she not have the ambition that her son should rule? Why, then, did she tend to her stepson and nephew when she seemed disgusted with him? Visenya was many things, but a woman capable of pity never seemed to be one of them. It is a question that cannot be readily dismissed . . . nor readily answered.

MAEGOR I

MAEGOR, THE FIRST of His Name, came to the throne after the sudden death of his brother, King Aenys, in the year 42 AC. He is better remembered as Maegor the Cruel, and it was a well-earned sobriquet, for no crueler king ever sat the Iron Throne. His reign began with blood and ended in blood as well. The histories tell us he enjoyed war and battle, but it is clear that it was violence he most craved—violence and death and absolute mastery over all he deemed his. What demon possessed him none could say. Even today, some give thanks that his tyranny was a short one, for who knows how many noble houses might have vanished forever simply to sate his desire?

Visenya then challenged any who denied Maegor's right to rule to prove themselves, and the captain of the Warrior's Sons accepted the challenge. Ser Damon Morrigen, called Damon the Devout, agreed to a trial of seven after the ancient fashion: Ser Damon and six Warrior's Sons against the king and his six champions. It was a contest in which the kingdom itself was at stake, and the accounts and tales are many—and often contradictory. What we do know is that King Maegor was the last man left standing, but that he took a grievous blow to the head at the very end and fell senseless to the ground just moments after the last of the Warrior's Sons died.

It was said Aenys was an adequate sword and lance—capable enough not to disgrace himself, but little more. Maegor, on the other hand, was defeating hardened knights in the mêlée when he was all of three-and-ten, and quickly won renown in the royal tourney of 28 AC when he defeated three knights of the Kingsguard in succession in the lists, and went on to win the mêlée. He was knighted by King Aegon at six-and-ten, the youngest knight in the realm at that time.

No sooner had Aenys been buried than Visenya mounted Vhagar and flew east to Pentos, to recall her son Maegor to the Seven Kingdoms following his exile. Maegor flew back across the narrow sea with Balerion, staying at Dragonstone for long enough to be crowned with his father's Valyrian steel crown instead of his brother's more ornate one.

Grand Maester Gawen protested, noting that, by the laws of inheritance, Prince Aegon, Aenys's eldest son, should be king. Maegor's response was to declare the maester a traitor, sentence him to death, and take his head with a single swing of Blackfyre. After that, few others dared to support Aegon's claim. Ravens flew, declaring that a new king had been crowned—one who would treat his loyal supporters justly and bring a traitor's death to those who opposed him.

Chief among Maegor's foes were the Faith Militant—the orders of the Warrior's Son and the Poor Fellows—and his war against them provided a constant backdrop to his reign. In King's Landing, the militant orders had seized hold of the Sept of Remembrance and the half-built Red Keep. But Maegor flew straight into the city, fearless upon Balerion, and raised the red dragon of House Targaryen on Visenya's Hill to rally men to him. Thousands joined him.

For twenty-seven days, Maegor was dead to the world. On the twenty-eighth, Queen Alys arrived from Pentos (Maegor was still without issue), and with her came a Pentoshi beauty called Tyanna of the Tower. She had become Maegor's lover during his exile, it was clear, and some whispered Queen Alys's as well. The Dowager Queen, after meeting with Tyanna, gave the king over to her care alone—a fact that troubled Maegor's supporters.

On the thirtieth day since the trial of seven, the king awoke with the sunrise and walked out onto the walls. Thousands cheered—though not at the Sept of Remembrance, where hundreds of the Warrior's Sons had gathered for their morning prayers. Then Maegor mounted Balerion and flew from Aegon's High Hill to the Hill of Rhaenys and, without warning, unleashed the Black Dread's fire. As the Sept of Remembrance was set alight, some tried to flee, only to be cut down by the archers and spearmen that Maegor had made ready. The screams of the burning and dying men were said to echo throughout the city, and scholars claim that a pall hung over King's Landing for seven days.

This was only the beginning of Maegor's war against the Faith Militant, however. The High Septon remained staunchly opposed to his rule, and Maegor continued to

LEFT | *The burning of the Sept of Remembrance.*

gather more and more lords to his side. At the battle at Stonebridge, the Poor Fellows fell in droves and it is said that the Mander ran red with blood for twenty leagues. Afterward, the bridge and the castle that commanded it became known as Bitterbridge.

An even greater battle was joined at the Great Fork of the Blackwater, where thirteen thousand Poor Fellows—as well as hundreds of knights from the chapter of the Warrior's Sons at Stoney Sept, and hundreds more besides from rebel lords of the riverlands and westerlands who joined them—fought against the king. It was a savage battle that lasted until nightfall, but it was a decisive victory for King Maegor. The king flew on Balerion's back in the battle, and though rains dampened the Black Dread's flames, the dragon still left death in its wake.

The Faith Militant remained Maegor's bitterest enemy for all of his reign, and he remained theirs. Even the mysterious death of the High Septon in 44 AC, followed by a High Septon far more genial and biddable who attempted to disband the Stars and Swords, did little to reduce the constant violence. Maegor's wars against them were further compounded by his many marriages, as he strove to produce an heir. Yet no matter how many women he wedded—or bedded—he found himself childless. He made brides of women whom he had widowed—women of proved fertility—but the only children born of his seed proved monstrosities: misshapen, eyeless, limbless, or having the parts of man and woman both. His descent into true madness, some say, began with the first of these abominations.

Maegor does hold one distinction in his reign: the completion of the Red Keep in the year 45 AC. It was a project begun by King Aegon and continued by King Aenys, but it was Maegor who saw it finished. He went beyond the plans of both his father and brother, raising a moated castle within the larger castle, which in later days was known as Maegor's Holdfast. More notably, he was the first to command that secret tunnels and passages be made. False walls were introduced, and trapdoors—and riddled throughout Aegon's High Hill were more and more tunnels. Maegor's lack of heirs seemed to matter little as he threw himself into overseeing the construction. He appointed his good-father, Lord Harroway, as his new Hand, and left him to govern the realm for a time while he saw the castle completed.

But, as was typical of Maegor's reign, even this great achievement was turned to horror. When the keep was at last completed, the king threw a riotous feast for the masons and carvers and other craftsmen who had helped to construct the castle. But after three days of revelry at the king's expense, they were all put to the sword so that the secrets of the Red Keep would be Maegor's alone.

In the end, it was a confluence of the Faith and his own family that proved Maegor's undoing. In 43 AC, his nephew, Prince Aegon, attempted to win back the throne that by law should have been his, in what came to be known as the great Battle Beneath the Gods Eye. Aegon died in that battle, leaving behind his wife and sister Rhaena, and their two twin daughters; his dragon, Quicksilver, was lost as well.

FROM THE HISTORY OF ARCHMAESTER GYLDAYN

Hardly had the last stone been set on the Red Keep than Maegor commanded that the ruins of the Sept of Remembrance be cleared from the top of Rhaenys's Hill, and with them the bones and ashes of the Warrior's Sons who had perished there. In their place, he decreed, a great stone "stable for dragons" would be erected, a lair worthy of Balerion, Vhagar, and their get. Thus commenced the building of the Dragonpit. Perhaps unsurprisingly, it proved difficult to find builders, stonemasons, and laborers to work on the project. So many men ran off that the king was finally forced to use prisoners from the city's dungeons as his workforce, under the supervision of builders brought in from Myr and Volantis.

Then, late in 45 AC, King Maegor entered a new campaign against the rebellious Faith Militant, who had not put down their swords at the new High Septon's behest. According to an inventory from that time, the next year the king brought back two thousand skulls as trophies from his campaign, which he claimed to be from outlawed Warrior's Sons and Poor Fellows, though many thought they were more likely the heads of smallfolk who just happened to be in the wrong place at the wrong time. Day by day, the realm turned against the king.

The death of the Dowager Queen Visenya in 44 AC was a notable event although Maegor seemed to take it in his stride. She had been his greatest ally and supporter from birth, seeking his advancement over his elder brother Aenys, and doing what she could to secure his legacy. In the confusion after her death, Aenys's widow, Queen Alyssa, slipped away from Dragonstone with her children, as well as with Dark Sister, Visenya's Valyrian steel sword. Alyssa and Aenys's next eldest son after Aegon, Prince Viserys, had been kept at the Red Keep as the king's squire, however, and he suffered for her flight. He died after nine days of questioning at the hands of Tyanna of the Tower. The king left his body in the castle courtyard, like so much offal, for a fortnight, hoping that word of it would force Queen Alyssa to claim her son's body, but she did not return. Viserys was fifteen at his death.

BELOW | *The Battle at Stonebridge.*

In 48 AC, Septon Moon and Ser Joffrey Doggett—also known as the Red Dog of the Hills—led the Poor Fellows against the king, and Riverrun stood with them. When Lord Daemon Velaryon, the admiral of the king's fleets, turned against Maegor as well, many of the great houses joined with him. Maegor's tyrannical reign could no longer be borne, and the realm rose up to end it. Unifying them all was the claim put forward by the young Prince Jaehaerys—Aenys

and Alyssa's only remaining son, now all of fourteen years of age—and supported by the Lord of Storm's End whom Jaehaerys had named as Protector of the Realm and Hand of the King. When Queen Rhaena—whom Maegor had married after Aegon's death—learned of her brother's proclamation, she fled on her dragon, Dreamfyre, stealing Blackfyre away as her king and husband slept. Even two of the Kingsguard abandoned Maegor, joining Jaehaerys instead.

Maegor's response to this was slow and confused, and it seems that this series of betrayals—and perhaps even the loss of his mother's guidance—had left him, in his own way, as broken as Aenys. He called his loyal lords to King's Landing, but all that came were minor lords of the crownlands, who had little to marshal against the king's many enemies. It was late at night, during the hour of the wolf, when the remaining lords departed the council chamber, leaving Maegor to brood alone. Early the next morning, he was found dead on the throne, his robes sodden with blood, his arms slashed open by the barbs of the Iron Throne.

Thus ended Maegor the Cruel. How he came to die is a matter of much speculation. Though the singers would have us believe that the Iron Throne itself killed him, some suspect his Kingsguard, and others some mason whom the king had failed to kill and who knew the secrets of the Red Keep. But perhaps even likelier is the suggestion that the king killed himself rather than suffer defeat. Whatever the truth, it was a reign that ended in the only way it could after the six years of terror that Maegor had visited upon the realm. But his nephew's reign would do much to mend the deep wounds he had made in the Seven Kingdoms.

ABOVE | *Maegor I, dead upon the Iron Throne.* RIGHT | *The brides of Maegor the Cruel (l. top to bottom: Ceryse Hightower, Tyanna of the Tower, Alys Harroway; r. top to bottom: Elinor Costayne, Jeyne Westerling, Rhaena Targaryen).*

The Brides of Maegor the Cruel

⤙ Ceryse of House Hightower ⤚

Ceryse was the daughter of Martyn Hightower, the Lord of Oldtown. She was advanced by her uncle, the High Septon, after he protested the betrothal of the thirteen-year-old Prince Maegor to Maegor's newborn niece, Princess Rhaena. Ceryse and Maegor were married in 25 AC. The prince claimed to have consummated their marriage a dozen times on their wedding night, but no sons ever came of it. He soon grew tired of Ceryse's failure to bear him an heir and began taking other brides. Ceryse died in 45 AC, taken by a sudden illness, though it is also rumored that she was killed at the king's command.

⤙ Alys of House Harroway ⤚

Alys was the daughter of Lucas Harroway, the new Lord of Harrenhal. A secret marriage took place in 39 AC, while Maegor was Hand, leading to Maegor's exile to Pentos. Alys became queen after Maegor brought her back from Pentos. She was the first woman to become pregnant by the king in the year 48 AC, but she lost the babe soon after. What was expelled from her womb was a monstrosity, eyeless and twisted, and in his fury Maegor blamed and executed her midwives, septas, and the Grand Maester Desmond. Tyanna of the Tower convinced the king that the child was the product of Alys's secret affairs, however, leading to the death of Queen Alys, her companions, her father and his Hand, the Lord Lucas, and every Harroway or Harroway kinsman King Maegor could discover between King's Landing and Harrenhal. Lord Edwell Celtigar was named Hand afterward.

⤙ Tyanna of the Tower ⤚

Tyanna was the most feared of the brides of King Maegor. Rumored to have been the natural daughter of a Pentoshi magister, she had been a tavern dancer who rose up to become a courtesan. She was said to practice sorcery and alchemy. She was wed to the king in 42 AC, but their marriage bed was as barren as the rest. Called the king's raven by some, she was feared for her ability to ferret out secrets and served as his mistress of whisperers. She eventually confessed her responsibility for the abominations that were born of Maegor's seed, claiming she had poisoned his other brides. She was killed by Maegor's own hand in 48 AC, her heart cut out with Blackfyre and thrown to his dogs.

⤙ The Black Brides ⤚

In 47 AC, Maegor took three women to wife in a single ceremony—all women of proven fertility, and all widows who had lost their husbands to Maegor's wars or at his command. They were:

⤙ Elinor of House Costayne ⤚

Elinor was the youngest of the Black Brides, but though she was nine-and-ten at her marriage, she had already given her husband, Ser Theo Bolling, three children. Ser Theo was arrested by knights of the Kingsguard, accused of conspiring with Queen Alyssa to place her son, Prince Jaehaerys, on the throne, and was then executed—all on the same day. After seven days of mourning, Elinor was summoned to wed Maegor. She, too, became pregnant, and like Alys before her, she gave birth to a stillborn abomination said to have been born eyeless and with small wings. She survived that monstrous labor, however, and was one of the two wives who survived the king.

⤙ Rhaena of House Targaryen ⤚

When Prince Aegon was killed by Maegor in the Battle Beneath the Gods Eye, Rhaena took refuge on Fair Isle under the protection of Lord Farman, who hid her and her twin daughters. Tyanna found the twin girls, however, and Rhaena was then forced to wed Maegor. Maegor named her daughter, Aerea, as his heir while disinheriting Queen Alyssa's surviving son, Jaehaerys. Along with Elinor, Rhaena was the only other queen to survive Maegor.

⤙ Jeyne of House Westerling ⤚

Tall and slender, Lady Jeyne had been wed to Lord Alyn Tarbeck, who died with the rebels at the Battle Beneath the Gods Eye. Having given him a posthumous son, her fecundity was proven and she was being courted by the son of the Lord of Casterly Rock when the king sent for her. In 47 AC she was with child, but three moons before the child was due, her labor began, and from her womb came another stillborn monster. She did not survive the child for long.

JAEHAERYS I

JAEHAERYS CAME TO the throne in 48 AC, in a time when the realm had been torn asunder by the ambitions of rebellious lords, the fury of the High Septon, and the cruelty of his uncle, Maegor I. Crowned at four-and-ten by the High Septon with his father's own crown, he began his reign under the regency of his mother, the Dowager Queen Alyssa, and the guidance of Lord Robar of House Baratheon, Lord Protector of the Realm and Hand of the King in those early years. Once in his majority, the king wed his sister Alysanne, and theirs was a fruitful marriage.

Though young to the throne, Jaehaerys revealed himself from an early age to be a true king. He was a fine warrior, skilled with lance and bow, and a gifted horseman. He was a dragonrider as well, riding upon Vermithor—a great beast of bronze and tan who was the largest of the living dragons after Balerion and Vhagar. Decisive in thought and deed, Jaehaerys was wise beyond his years, always seeking the most peaceable ends.

His queen, Alysanne, was also well loved throughout the realm, being both beautiful and high-spirited, as well as charming and keenly intelligent. Some said that she ruled the realm as much as the king did, and there was some truth to that. It was at her behest that King Jaehaerys at last forbade the right of the First Night, despite the many lords who jealously guarded it. And the Night's Watch came to rename the castle of Snowgate in her honor, dubbing it Queensgate instead. They did this in thanks for the treasure in jewels she gave them to pay for the construction of a new castle, Deep Lake, to replace the huge and ruinously costly Nightfort, and for her role in winning them the New Gift that bolstered their flagging strength.

For forty-six years, the Old King and Good Queen Alysanne were wed, and for the most part it was a happy marriage, with children and grandchildren aplenty.

Two estrangements are recorded, but they did not last more than a year or two before the pair resumed their customary friendship. The Second Quarrel, however, is of note, as it was due to Jaehaerys's decision in 92 AC to pass over his granddaughter Rhaenys—the daughter of his deceased eldest son and heir, Prince Aemon—in favor of bestowing Dragonstone and the place of heir apparent on his next eldest son, Baelon the Brave. Alysanne saw no reason why a man should be favored over a woman . . . and if Jaehaerys thought women of less use, then he would have no need of her. They reconciled in time, but the Old King outlived his beloved queen, and in his last years it was said that the grief of their parting hung over his court like a pall.

Yet if Alysanne was Jaehaerys's great love, his greatest friend was Septon Barth. No man of humble birth ever rose so high as the plainspoken but brilliant septon. He was the son of a common blacksmith and had been given to the Faith while young. But his brilliance made itself known, and in time he came to serve in the library at the Red Keep, tending the king's books and records. There King Jaehaerys became acquainted with him, and soon named him Hand of the King. Many lords of great lineage looked askance at this—and the High Septon and Most Devout were said to be even more concerned over questions of his orthodoxy—but Barth more than proved himself.

With Barth's aid and advice, King Jaehaerys did more to reform the realm than any other king who lived before or after. Where his grandsire, King Aegon, had left the laws

---

FROM THE HISTORY OF ARCHMAESTER GYLDAYN

The great tourney held at King's Landing in 98 AC to celebrate the fiftieth year of King Jaehaerys's reign surely gladdened the queen's heart as well, for all her surviving children, grandchildren, and her great-granddaughter returned to share in the feasts and celebrations.

Not since the Doom of Valyria had so many dragons been seen in one place at one time, it was truly said. The final tilt, wherein the Kingsguard knights Ser Ryam Redwyne and Ser Clement Crabb broke thirty lances against each other before King Jaehaerys proclaimed them cochampions, was declared to be the finest display of jousting ever seen in Westeros.

RIGHT | *The great tourney of 98 AC.*

of the Seven Kingdoms to the vagaries of local tradition and custom, Jaehaerys created the first unified code, so that from the North to the Dornish Marches, the realm shared a single rule of law. Great works to improve King's Landing were also implemented—drains and sewers and wells, especially, for Barth believed that fresh water and the flushing away of offal and waste were important to a city's health. Furthermore, the Conciliator began the construction of the great network of roads that would one day join King's Landing to the Reach, the stormlands, the westerlands, the riverlands, and even the North—understanding that to knit together the realm it must be easier to travel among its regions. The kingsroad was the greatest of these roads, reaching hundreds of leagues to Castle Black and the Wall.

Yet some say the most important achievement of the rule of Jaehaerys and Septon Barth was a reconciliation with the Faith. The Poor Fellows and Warrior's Sons, no longer hunted as they had been in Maegor's day, were much reduced and officially outlawed thanks to Maegor, but they were still present. And still restless, in their eagerness to restore their orders. More pressingly, the Faith's traditional right to judge its own had begun to prove troublesome, and many lords complained of unscrupulous septries and septons making free with the wealth and property of their neighbors and those they preached to.

Some counselors urged the Old King to deal with the remnants of the Faith Militant harshly—to stamp them out once and for all before their zealotry could return the realm to chaos. Others cared more for ensuring that the septons were answerable to the same justice as the rest of the realm. But Jaehaerys instead dispatched Septon Barth to Oldtown, to speak with the High Septon, and there they began to

forge a lasting agreement. In return for the last few Stars and Swords putting down their weapons, and for agreeing to accept outside justice, the High Septon received King Jaehaerys's sworn oath that the Iron Throne would always protect and defend the Faith. In this way, the great schism between crown and Faith was forever healed.

And so the greatest problem of the later years of Jaehaerys's reign was the fact that there were simply too many Targaryens, and too many possible successors. Ill fate had left Jaehaerys lacking a clear heir not once but twice, following the death of Baelon the Brave in 101 AC. To resolve the matter of his heir once and for all, Jaehaerys called the first Great Council in the year 101 AC, to put the matter before the lords of the realm. And from all corners of the realm the lords came. No castle could hold so many save for Harrenhal, so it was there that they gathered. The

lords, great and small, came with their trains of bannermen, knights, squires, grooms, and servants. And behind them came yet more—the camp followers and washerwomen, the hawkers and smiths and carters. Thousands of tents sprang up over the moons, until the castle town of Harrenton was accounted the fourth largest city of the Realm.

At this council, nine lesser claimants were heard and dismissed, leaving only two primary claimants to the throne: Laenor Velaryon, son of Princess Rhaenys—who was the eldest daughter of Jaehaerys's eldest son, Aemon—and Prince Viserys, eldest son of Baelon the Brave and Princess Alyssa. Each had their merits, for primogeniture favored Laenor, while proximity favored Viserys, who was also the last Targaryen prince to ride Balerion before the dragon's death in 94 AC. Laenor himself had recently acquired a dragon, a splendid creature that he named Seasmoke. But

The children of Jaehaerys I, the Conciliator, and Good Queen Alysanne, who lived to adulthood

PRINCE AEMON
Killed in battle against Myrish pirates who had seized the eastern side of Tarth.

PRINCE BAELON (*called the Spring Prince for the season of his birth, and Baelon the Brave*)
When Septon Barth passed away in his sleep in 99 AC, the famed Kingsguard knight Ser Ryam Redwyne was made Hand. But his valor and prowess with sword and lance proved to not be matched by his ability to rule. Baelon followed him as Hand less than a year after, and served admirably. But while hunting in 101 AC, Prince Baelon complained of a stitch in his side, and died within days of a burst belly.

ARCHMAESTER VAEGON
Called the Dragonless, Vaegon was given to the Citadel from an early age and held the ring and rod and mask of yellow gold when he became an archmaester.

PRINCESS DAELLA
Wed to Lord Rodrik Arryn in 80 AC, Daella died in childbed after delivering to him a daughter, Aemma.

PRINCESS ALYSSA
Alyssa was wife to her brother Baelon the Brave; two of her sons would come to wear crowns.

PRINCESS VISERRA
Viserra was betrothed to Lord Manderly of White Harbor only to die by mishap shortly afterward. A wild, high-spirited maid, she fell from a horse while racing drunkenly through the streets of King's Landing.

SEPTA MAEGELLE
Given to the Faith, Maegelle grew to be a septa known for her compassion and her gift for healing. She was the chief cause of the reconciliation of the Old King and Queen Alysanne in 94 AC, following the Second Quarrel. She nursed children afflicted with greyscale, but she became afflicted with the same illness and died in 96 AC.

PRINCESS SAERA
Though given to the Faith as Maegelle was, Saera did not have Maegelle's temperament. She ran away from the motherhouse where she was a novice and crossed the narrow sea. She was at Lys for a time, then Old Volantis, where she ended her days as the proprietor of a famous pleasure house.

PRINCESS GAEL (*called the Winter Child*)
Simple-minded but sweet, Gael was most beloved of the queen. She disappeared from court in 99 AC, allegedly dying of a summer fever, but in fact she had drowned herself in the Blackwater after having been seduced and abandoned by a traveling singer, leaving her with nothing but a growing belly. †

† In her grief, Queen Alysanne followed her to the grave less than a year afterward.

for many lords of the realm, what mattered most was that the male line take precedence over the female line—not to mention that Viserys was a prince of four-and-twenty while Laenor was just a boy of seven.

But against all this, Laenor had one shining advantage: he was the son of Lord Corlys Velaryon, the Sea Snake, the wealthiest man in the Seven Kingdoms. The Sea Snake was named for Ser Corlys Velaryon, the first Lord Commander of the Kingsguard, but his fame did not come from his skill with sword and lance and shield but for his voyages across the seas of the world, seeking new horizons. He was a scion of House Velaryon: a family of old and storied Valyrian heritage who had come to Westeros before the Targaryens, as the histories agree, and who often provided the bulk of the royal fleet. So many Velaryons served as lord admiral and master of ships that it was, at times, almost considered a hereditary office.

Lord Corlys traveled widely, both to the south and to the north, and once sought for a rumored passage around the top of Westeros—though he turned back his ship, the *Ice Wolf,* when he found only frozen seas and giant icebergs. But his greatest voyages were upon the *Sea Snake,* by which name he would later be known. Many ships of Westeros had sailed as far as Qarth to trade for spices and silk, but he dared to go farther, reaching the fabled lands of Yi Ti and Leng, whose wealth doubled that of House Velaryon in a single voyage.

Nine great voyages were made upon the *Sea Snake,* and on the last, Corlys filled the ship's hold with gold and bought twenty more ships at Qarth, loading them with spices, elephants, and the finest silk. Some were lost, and the elephants died at sea, according to Maester Mathis's *The Nine Voyages,* but the wealth that remained made House Velaryon the richest in the realm—richer even than the Lannisters and Hightowers, for a time.

Corlys Velaryon became a lord after his grandsire's death and used his wealth to raise a new seat, High Tide, to replace the damp, cramped castle Driftmark and house the ancient Driftwood Throne—the high seat of the Velaryons, which legend claims was given to them by the Merling King to conclude a pact. So much trade came to flow to and from Driftmark that the towns of Hull and Spicetown sprang up, becoming the chief ports of trade in Blackwater Bay for a time, surpassing even King's Landing.

His fame, his reputation, and his wealth did much to support his son Laenor's claim. Boremund Baratheon also supported Laenor's claim, as did Lord Ellard Stark. So, too, did Lord Blackwood, Lord Bar Emmon, and Lord Celtigar. But they were too few. The tide was against them, and though the maesters who counted the results never gave numbers, it was rumored that the Great Council had voted twenty to one in favor of Prince Viserys. The king, not present for final deliberations, named Viserys the Prince of Dragonstone.

In his last years, King Jaehaerys named Ser Otto Hightower as his Hand, and Ser Otto brought his family to King's Landing with him. Among them was young Alicent—a clever girl of fifteen years, who became Jaehaerys's companion in his age. She read to him, fetched his meals, and even helped to bathe and dress him. It is said that, at times, the king thought her to be one of his own daughters. Unkinder rumors claimed that she was his lover.

King Jaehaerys, the First of His Name—known as the Conciliator, and the Old King (being the only Targaryen ruler who lived to such an advanced age)—died peacefully in his bed in 103 AC, while Lady Alicent read to him from his friend Barth's *Unnatural History.* He was nine-and-sixty at his death, and had ruled wisely and well for five-and-fifty years. Westeros mourned, and it was claimed that even in Dorne men wept and women tore their garments in lament for a king who had been so just and good. His ashes were interred with that of his beloved, the Good Queen Alysanne, beneath the Red Keep. And the realm never saw their like again.

FROM THE HISTORY OF ARCHMAESTER GYLDAYN

In the eyes of many, the Great Council of 101 AC thereby established an iron precedent on matters of succession: regardless of seniority, the Iron Throne of Westeros could not pass to a woman, nor through a woman to her male descendents.

PREVIOUS PAGES | *The Great Council of 101 AC.* LEFT | *King Jaehaerys I and Good Queen Alysanne with their son, Prince Aemon.*

— 65 —

VISERYS I

AFTER THE LONG and peaceful reign of Jaehaerys I, Viserys inherited a secure throne, a full treasury, and a legacy of goodwill that his grandfather had cultivated over fifty years. House Targaryen was never again so powerful as it was in Viserys's reign. More princes and princesses of the blood existed than at any other time since the Doom, and there were never so many dragons at one time as there were in the years 103 AC to 129 AC.

the Valyrian steel blade Dark Sister for his prowess. He had been among the brashest of Viserys's supporters prior to the Great Council and had even gathered a small army of sworn swords and men-at-arms when rumors claimed that Corlys Velaryon was readying a fleet to defend the rights of his son, Laenor. King Jaehaerys avoided bloodshed, but many remembered that Daemon had been ready to come to blows over the matter.

But the great upheaval of the Dance of the Dragons had its roots in Viserys's reign, and it was chiefly due to the blood royals. In the early part of his reign, Viserys I's chief annoyance was his own brother, Prince Daemon Targaryen. Daemon was mercurial and quick to take offense, but he was dashing, daring, and dangerous. He was knighted at six-and-ten, like Maegor I, and Jaehaerys I himself gave Daemon

Daemon had been wed to Rhea Royce in 97 AC when she was heir to the ancient seat of Runestone in the Vale. It was a fine, rich match, but Daemon found the Vale little to his liking, and liked his wife even less, and they were soon estranged.

It had likewise proved a barren union, and though Viserys I refused his brother's entreaties to set aside the

---

FROM THE HISTORY OF ARCHMAESTER GYLDAYN

Though he had wed the Lady of Runestone in 97 AC, during the Old King's reign, the marriage had not been a success. Prince Daemon found the Vale of Arryn boring ("In the Vale, the men fuck sheep," he wrote. "You cannot fault them. Their sheep are prettier than their women."), and soon developed a mislike of his lady wife, whom he called "my bronze bitch," after the runic bronze armor worn by the lords of House Royce.

---

marriage, he did recall him to court to take up the burden of rule. Daemon served first as master of coins, then master of law, but it was his chief rival, the Hand Ser Otto Hightower, who finally convinced Viserys to remove him from these offices. So in 104 AC, Viserys made his brother commander of the City Watch.

Prince Daemon improved the armaments and training of the watch and gave them the golden cloaks that led them to be known as the "gold cloaks" to this day. He often joined his men in patrolling the city, swiftly becoming known to both the meanest urchin and the wealthiest tradesman, and earned a certain dark reputation in the stews and brothels where he was wont to make free of the wares on offer. Crime fell sharply, though some said it was because Daemon delighted in meting out harsh punishments. Yet those who benefited from his rule loved him well, and Daemon soon became known as "Lord Flea Bottom." Later still, after Viserys refused him the title of Prince of Dragonstone, he came to be called "the Prince of the City." It was in the brothels of the city that he found a favorite, a paramour—a very pale Lysene dancer named Mysaria, whose looks and reputation led the prostitutes who knew her to call her Misery, the White Worm. Later, she became Daemon's mistress of whisperers

Some said that Daemon's support for his brother in the Great Council was motivated by the belief he would be his brother's heir. But in Viserys's mind, he already had an heir: Rhaenyra, his sole daughter by his cousin, Queen Aemma of House Arryn. Rhaenyra was born in 97 AC, and as a child her father doted upon her, and took her everywhere with him—even to the council chamber, where he encouraged her to watch and listen intently. For these reasons, the court doted on her as well, and many paid homage to her. The singers dubbed her the Realm's Delight, for she was bright and precocious—a beautiful child who was already a drag- onrider at the age of seven as she flew on the back of her she-dragon Syrax, named for one of the old gods of Valyria.

In 105 AC, her mother finally delivered the son that the king and queen had both longed for, but the queen died in childbirth, and the boy—named Baelon—only survived her by a day. By this time, Viserys I was heartily sick of being hectored over the succession, and disregarding the precedents of 92 AC and the Great Council of 101 AC, he officially declared that Rhaenyra was Princess of Dragonstone and his heir. A grand ceremony was arranged in which hundreds of lords knelt to do homage to the princess while she sat at her father's feet. Prince Daemon was not among them.

The year 105 AC holds one more event of note: the induction of Ser Criston Cole into the Kingsguard. Born in 82 AC, as the son of a steward in the service of the Dondarrions of Blackhaven, Criston had risen to the attention of the court at a tourney in Maidenpool to cele- brate Viserys's ascension to the throne, where he won the mêlée and was the last but one in the jousting.

Black-haired, green-eyed, and comely, he proved a de- light to the ladies of the court—and to Princess Rhaenyra most of all. She took a childish fancy to him, naming him "my white knight" and begging her father to make him her sworn shield, which he did. After that, Cole was always by her side and carried her favor in the lists. It was said in later years that the princess only had eyes for Ser Criston, but there is reason to doubt that this was wholly true.

Matters became more complicated when, with Ser Otto Hightower's encouragement, King Viserys announced his intention to wed the Lady Alicent, Ser Otto's daughter and the Old King's former nursemaid. For the most part, the realm celebrated this union. Rhaenyra, secure in her place as heir, welcomed her father's new bride, for they had long known one another at court. Not all was so joy- ous in the Vale, however, where Prince Daemon was said to have whipped the servant who brought him tidings of the marriage, nor at Driftmark, where Lord Corlys and

LEFT | *King Viserys I upon the Iron Throne.* ABOVE | *Daemon Targaryen, the Prince of the City, with his gold cloaks.*

Princess Rhaenys had seen their daughter, Laena, rejected by the king as well.

Among the fruits of King Viserys's marriage to Alicent was the alliance between Prince Daemon and the Sea Snake. Tired of waiting for a crown that seemed increasingly more distant, Daemon was determined to carve out his own kingdom. In this, he and Corlys Velaryon could make common cause, thanks to the predations of the Kingdom of the Three Daughters—or the Triarchy, as it was sometimes called—which was the union between Lys, Myr, and Tyrosh that had been born out of a successful alliance against Volantis. At first, this alliance was applauded in the Seven Kingdoms, but soon they grew worse than the pirates and corsairs they had defeated.

The fighting began in 106 AC, with the Sea Snake providing the fleet and Daemon providing Caraxes and his skill in commanding men to lead the second sons and landless knights who flocked to Daemon's banner. King Viserys contributed to their war, sending gold for the hire of men and supplies.

They won many victories over the next two years, culminating in Prince Daemon killing the Myrish prince—Admiral Craghas Drahar, called Crabfeeder—in single combat. (When he learned that Daemon had declared himself King of the Narrow Sea in 109 AC, King Viserys was heard to say that his brother could keep his crown if it "kept him out of trouble".) It proved a premature claim to victory, however. The Triarchy dispatched a new fleet and army the following year, and Dorne joined the Triarchy in the war against Daemon's fledgling, petty kingdom.

In 107 AC, Alicent bore Viserys the boy Aegon, and the king finally had a son. Aegon was followed by a sister, Helaena, his future bride, and by another son named Aemond. But the birth of a son meant that the succession was once more called into question—and not least by the queen herself, as well as her father the Hand, who were anxious to see their blood set over Aemma's. Ser Otto overstepped himself, however, and in 109 AC he was replaced by Lord Lyonel Strong, who had served ably as master of laws. For King Viserys, the matter was long settled; Rhaenyra was his heir, and he did not wish to hear arguments otherwise—despite the decrees of the Great Council of 101, which always placed a man above a woman.

The accounts and letters preserved from this time begin to speak of a "queen's party" and the "party of the princess." Thanks to the tourney of 111 AC, they were soon known by simpler names: the greens and the blacks. At this tourney, we are told, Queen Alicent was beautifully clad in a gown of green, while Rhaenyra left no one in doubt of her inheritance by wearing black embellished with red, for the banners of House Targaryen. This same tourney saw the return of Daemon Targaryen, King of the Narrow Sea, from his wars. He wore his crown when Caraxes alighted, but he knelt before his brother and removed the crown, offering it up in a token of fealty. Viserys raised him back up, returned the crown, and kissed him upon both cheeks; for all the turmoil between them, Viserys truly loved his brother. Those at the tourney cheered—but none more loudly than Rhaenyra, who loved her dashing uncle well. More than well, perhaps . . . though our sources are contradictory.

It was only a few moons later that Daemon was exiled. As for the reason? Our sources differ greatly. Some, such as Runciter and Munkun, suggest that King Viserys and King Daemon quarreled (for brotherly love rarely stands in the way of disagreements), and that is why Daemon left. Others say that it was Alicent (at Ser Otto's prompting, possibly) who convinced Viserys that Daemon must leave. But two speak more fully on the matter.

Septon Eustace's *The Reign of King Viserys, First of His Name, and the Dance of the Dragons That Came After* was written by the septon after the war came to its end. Though dry and ponderous in his writing, Eustace was clearly a confidant of the Targaryens, and speaks accurately of many things. Mushroom's *The Testimony of Mushroom* is another matter, however. A dwarf three feet tall, with an enormous head (and an enormous member to go with it, if he is to be believed), Mushroom was the court jester, and was thought to be a lackwit. Therefore, the worthies of the court spoke freely around him. His *Testimony* alleges to be his account of the events of the years when he was at court, set down by a scribe whose name we do not know, and it is filled with Mushroom's tales of plots, murders, trysts, debaucheries, and more—and all in the most explicit detail. Septon Eustace's and Mushroom's accounts are often at odds with one another, but at times there are some surprising areas of agreement between them.

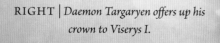

RIGHT | *Daemon Targaryen offers up his crown to Viserys I.*

Strong, who was called Breakbones and was accounted the strongest knight in the realm), showering her with gifts (as the twins Ser Jason and Ser Tyland Lannister did at Casterly Rock), composing songs to her beauty, and even fighting duels for her favor (as sons of Lord Blackwood and Lord Bracken had done). There was even talk of wedding her to the Prince of Dorne, to unite the two realms at last. Queen Alicent (and Ser Otto, her father) naturally advanced the suit of her son Prince Aegon, though he was much younger. But the two siblings had never gotten along, and Viserys knew his queen desired the match more out of ambition for her son than out of Aegon's love for Rhaenyra.

Ignoring all of these suits, Viserys turned instead to the Sea Snake and Princess Rhaenys, whose son Laenor had once been his rival at the Great Council of 101. Laenor had the blood of the dragon on both sides, and even a dragon of his own—the splendid grey-and-white dragon he called Seasmoke. Better, the match would unite the two factions that had once stood opposed at the Great Council of 101. Yet there was one problem: at the age of nine-and-ten, Laenor preferred the company of squires of his own age, and was said never to have known a woman intimately, nor to have any bastards. But to this, Grand Maester Mellos was said to have remarked, "What of it? I am not fond of fish, but when fish is served, I eat it."

Rhaenyra was of a different mind entirely. Perhaps she harbored hopes of wedding Prince Daemon, as Eustace claims, or of seducing Criston Cole to her bed, as Mushroom cheerfully suggests. But Viserys would hear none of it, and against all her objections he needed only to note that, if she refused the marriage, he would reconsider the succession. And then came the final break between Ser Criston Cole and Rhaenyra, though to this day we do not know if it was instigated by Ser Criston or Rhaenyra. Did she try to seduce him once more? Did he finally admit his love, now that it seemed she'd be wed, and tried to persuade her to run away with him?

We cannot say. Nor can we say if there is any truth to the claim that, after Cole left her, she instead gave up her maidenhood (if, indeed, she still had it) to Ser Harwin Strong—a much less scrupulous sort of knight. Mushroom claims that he himself found them abed, but half of what he says cannot be trusted—and the other half one sometimes wishes not to trust. What we can say for certain is that in 114 AC, Princess Rhaenyra and the newly knighted Ser Laenor were wed and, as is the custom, a tourney was held in celebration. At this tourney, Rhaenyra had a new champion

Eustace claims that Daemon and Princess Rhaenyra were caught abed together by Ser Arryk Cargyll, and it was this that made Viserys exile his brother from the court. Mushroom tells a different tale, however: that Rhaenyra had eyes only for Ser Criston Cole, but that the knight had declined her overtures. It was then that her uncle offered to school her in the arts of love, so that she might move the virtuous Ser Criston to break his vows. But when she finally thought herself ready to approach him, the knight—whom Mushroom swears was as chaste and virtuous as an aged septa—reacted in horror and disgust. Viserys soon heard of it. And whatever version of the tale was true, we do know that Daemon asked for Rhaenyra's hand, if only Viserys would set aside his marriage to Lady Rhea. Viserys refused, and instead exiled Daemon from the Seven Kingdoms, never to return upon pain of death. Daemon departed, returning to the Stepstones to continue with his war.

In 112 AC, Ser Harrold Westerling passed away and Ser Criston Cole was made the Lord Commander of the Kingsguard in his place. And in 113 AC, Princess Rhaenyra came of age. In the years before this, many men had paid court to her (among them the heir to Harrenhal, Ser Harwin

in Breakbones, while Ser Criston for the first time wore the favor of Queen Alicent. Accounts of the tourney all agree that Cole fought in a black fury and defeated all challengers. He shattered Breakbone's collarbone and elbow, leading Mushroom to dub him Brokenbones, but the worst injuries he meted out were to Laenor's favorite, the handsome knight Ser Joffrey Lonmouth, who was called the Knight of Kisses. Ser Joffrey was borne from the field senseless and bloody, and lingered for six days before dying, leaving Laenor to weep bitter tears of grief.

Afterward, Ser Laenor departed for Driftmark, and some wondered if the marriage had even been consummated. Rhaenyra and her husband largely spent their time apart, she on Dragonstone and he on Driftmark. Yet if the realm worried about her heirs, they need not wait long. Near the end of 114 AC, Rhaenyra delivered a healthy boy whom she named Jacaerys (not Joffrey, as Ser Laenor had hoped), called Jace by friends and family. And yet . . . Rhaenyra was of the blood of the dragon, and Ser Laenor likewise had the aquiline nose, fine features, silver-white hair, and purple eyes that bespoke his own Valyrian heritage. Why, then, did Jacaerys have brown hair and eyes, and a pug nose? Many looked at them, and then at the hulking Ser Harwin Strong—now chief of the blacks, and Rhaenyra's constant companion—and wondered.

Rhaenyra bore two more sons—Lucerys (called Luke) and Joffrey—during her marriage to Ser Laenor Velaryon, and each one was born healthy and strapping, with the brown hair and pug nose that neither Rhaenyra nor Laenor possessed. Among the greens, it was said that they were ob-viously the sons of Breakbones, and many doubted whether they could be dragonriders. But at Viserys's command, each had a dragon's egg placed in his cradle, and each egg hatched, producing the dragons Vermax, Arrax, and Tyraxes. The king, for his part, ignored the rumors, for he clearly meant to keep Rhaenyra as his heir.

Four tragedies in 120 AC caused it to be remembered as the Year of the Red Spring (not to be confused with the Red Spring of 236 AC), for it laid the foundation for the Dance of the Dragons. The first of these tragedies was the death of Laena Velaryon, Laenor's sister. Once considered as a bride for Viserys, she had wed Prince Daemon in 115 AC after his wife, Lady Rhea, died while hunting in the Vale. (Daemon, meanwhile, had grown tired of the Stepstones and had given up his crown; five other men would follow him as Kings of the Narrow Sea, until that sellsword "kingdom" ended for good and all.)

Laena gave Daemon two twin daughters, Baela and Rhaena. Though King Viserys had at first been angered by the marriage, which took place without his leave, he allowed Daemon to present his daughters at court in 117 AC, against the objections of his small council; he still loved his brother and perhaps thought that fatherhood would temper him. In 120 AC, Laena was brought to bed again with child, and delivered the son that Daemon had always desired. What was drawn from her womb was twisted and deformed, however, and died shortly after birth. Laena, too, soon expired.

But it was her parents, Lord Corlys and Princess Rhaenys, who had the greater cause to lament that year. They still mourned their daughter when their son was taken. All accounts agree that Laenor was attending a market fair at Spicetown when he was murdered. Eustace named his friend and companion (and lover, as some would have it) Ser Qarl Correy, saying they quarreled because Laenor meant to put him aside for a new favorite. Blades were drawn, and Laenor was killed. Ser Qarl fled, never to be seen again. Mushroom, however, suggests a blacker tale: that Prince Daemon had paid Correy to murder Laenor, to free Rhaenyra for himself.

The third tragedy was the ugly squabble between the sons of Alicent and the sons of Rhaenyra, caused when the dragonless Aemond Targaryen attempted to claim the late Laena's dragon, Vhagar, for himself. Pushes and shoves were followed by fists after Aemond mocked Rhaenyra's boys as the "Strongs"—until young Prince Lucerys took a knife and plunged it into Aemond's eye. Afterward, Aemond was known as Aemond One-eye—though he did manage

Before her marriage to Daemon, Laena had been betrothed for almost a decade to the son of a former Sealord of Braavos, but the youth had squandered his father's fortune and influence and had become nothing but a hanger-on at High Tide and an embarrassment to Lord Corlys. It was no great surprise when Daemon, paying a visit after his wife's death, saw Laena (who was said to be surpassingly lovely) and spoke in private with the Sea Snake about a marriage. Soon after, Prince Daemon provoked her Braavosi betrothed so mercilessly that the youth challenged him to a single combat.

So ended the Sealord's wastrel son.

to win Vhagar. (He had opportunity to avenge the loss of his eye in the years to come, though the realm would bleed because of it.)

In the end, Viserys attempted to make peace, and he did so by proclaiming that any man or woman who questioned the paternity of Rhaenyra's children would have his or her tongue torn out. He then commanded Alicent and his sons to return to King's Landing, while Rhaenyra was to remain with her sons at Dragonstone, so that they might not quarrel again. Ser Erryk Cargyll remained at Dragonstone as Rhaenyra's sworn shield, taking the place of Ser Harwin Strong, who returned to Harrenhal.

The last tragedy—and some might say the least—was the fire at Harrenhal that took the lives of Lord Lyonel and his son and heir, Ser Harwin. But those who speak so are ignorant. Viserys, now old and weary, and increasingly disinterested in the governance of the realm, was left without a Hand, while Rhaenyra was left without both a husband and, as some claimed, a paramour. Some accounts see it as an accident, no more. But others suggest more wicked possibilities. Some believe that Larys Clubfoot—one of the king's inquisitors and Lord Lyonel's youngest son—might have arranged it so that he might rule Harrenhal. Other histories even hint that Prince Daemon himself was behind it.

Rather than bring in a new Hand, the king recalled Ser Otto from Oldtown at Alicent's urging and named him Hand again. And rather than mourn her late husband, Rhaenyra at last wed her uncle, Prince Daemon. In the last days of 120 AC, she even delivered to him his first son, whom she named Aegon, after the Conqueror. (When she learned of

it, Queen Alicent was said to be enraged, for her own eldest son also bore the Conqueror's name. The two Aegons came to be known as Aegon the Elder and Aegon the Younger.) The year 122 AC saw Rhaenyra and Daemon delivered of a second son, Viserys. Viserys was not so robust as Aegon the Younger or his Velaryon half siblings, but he proved precocious. Some took it as an omen, however, when the dragon egg placed in his cradle did not hatch.

And so matters progressed, until the fateful day in 129 AC when Viserys I at last died. His son, Aegon the Elder, had wed his daughter, Helaena, and Helaena had borne to Aegon the twins Jaehaerys and Jaehaera (the latter of whom was a strange child, slow to grow, never weeping or smiling as children do), and another son named Maelor in 127 AC. On Driftmark, the Sea Snake began to fail and took to his bed. Viserys, now in the winter of his years but still hearty, injured himself on the Iron Throne in 128 AC after rendering a judgment. The wound became dangerously infected, and in the end Maester Orwyle (who had succeeded Maester Mellos in the previous year) was forced to amputate two fingers. That measure was not stringent enough, however, and as 128 ended and 129 began, Viserys was growing increasingly ill.

On the third day of the third moon of 129 AC, while entertaining Jaehaerys and Jaehaera from his bed with a tale of their great-great-grandsire and his queen battling giants, mammoths, and wildlings beyond the Wall, the king grew tired. He sent his grandchildren away when the tale was done and fell

into a sleep from which he never awoke. He had ruled for six-and-twenty years, reigning over the most prosperous era in the history of the Seven Kingdoms but seeding within it the disastrous decline of his house and the death of the last of the dragons.

ABOVE LEFT | *The sons of Princess Rhaenyra (l. to r.): Jacaerys, Joffrey, and Lucerys.*
ABOVE RIGHT | *The sons of King Viserys (l. to r.): Aegon, Daeron, and Aemond.*

NO WAR WAS ever bloodier or crueler than the Dance of the Dragons, as the singers and Munkun have chosen to name it. It was the worst kind of war—a war between siblings. Despite Viserys's unwavering preference for Rhaenyra, Prince Aegon was convinced to take up his father's crown, by his mother and the small council, before Viserys I's corpse was cold. When Rhaenyra, the Princess of Dragonstone, learned of it, she fell into a rage. She was, at the time, in confinement at Dragonstone, awaiting the birth of her third child to Prince Daemon.

with his dagger there at the table. Mushroom disagrees, suggesting Cole threw Beesbury out a window—though it should be remembered that Mushroom was on Dragonstone at this time, with Rhaenyra. But that was far from the last murder in the early days of the Dance. However, the most lamentable were the murders of the young princes Lucerys Velaryon, the son of Rhaenyra, and Jaehaerys, the son and heir of Aegon.

Luke Velaryon's death was witnessed by many eyes at the court of Storm's End, and the accounts largely agree.

FROM THE HISTORY OF ARCHMAESTER GYLDAYN

On Dragonstone, no cheers were heard. Instead, screams echoed through the halls and stairwells of Sea Dragon Tower, and down from the queen's apartments where Rhaenyra Targaryen strained and shuddered in her third day of labor. The child had not been due for another turn of the moon, but the tidings from King's Landing had driven the princess into a black fury, and her rage seemed to bring on the birth, as if the babe inside her were angry too, and fighting to get out. The princess shrieked curses all through her labor, calling down the wroth of the gods upon her half brothers and their mother, the queen, and detailing the torments she would inflict upon them before she would let them die. She cursed the child inside her too, Mushroom tells us. "*Get out,*" she screamed, clawing at her swollen belly as her maester and her midwife tried to restrain her. "*Monster, monster, get out, get out, GET OUT!*"

When the babe at last came forth, she proved indeed a monster: a stillborn girl, twisted and malformed, with a hole in her chest where her heart should have been, and a stubby, scaled tail. Or so Mushroom describes her. The dwarf tells us that it was he who carried the little thing to the yard for burning. The dead girl had been named Visenya, Princess Rhaenyra announced the next day, when milk of the poppy had blunted the edge of her pain. "She was my only daughter, and they killed her. They stole my crown and murdered my daughter, and they shall answer for it."

Once past the birth, Rhaenyra prepared for war. Both she and Alicent had their supporters among their kin—and among the great lords of the realm. And each side had dragons. It was a recipe for disaster, and so it proved. The realm bled as it never had before, and it would be years before all the scars were healed.

Mushroom's claim that Queen Alicent had hurried her husband's demise with a "pinch of poison" in his wine we may, perhaps, dismiss. But none can doubt that the first blood to be spilled in the Dance was that of the aged master of coin, Lord Beesbury, when he insisted that Viserys's true heir was Rhaenyra, and that she must be crowned. The accounts differ as to how this dissenter was removed. Some say he died of a chill after being thrown into the black cells, and some that Ser Criston Cole—the Lord Commander who would soon be called the Kingmaker—opened his throat

Dispatched by his mother to Storm's End to enlist Lord Borros's support, he arrived to find Prince Aemond Targaryen there before him. Aemond was older, stronger, and crueler than Lucerys—and he hated Lucerys with a passion, for it was Lucerys who had cost him his eye nine years earlier. Lord Borros denied Aemond his desire for revenge inside his hall—but stated that he had no care whatever for what happened without. So Prince Aemond, upon Vhagar, chased down the fleeing Lucerys and his young dragon Arrax. The prince and his dragon—hampered by the storm raging outside the castle walls—both died within sight of Storm's End, plummeting into the sea.

Rhaenyra, the accounts all say, collapsed at the news. Not so, Lucerys's stepfather, Prince Daemon Targaryen. The words Prince Daemon sent to Dragonstone after having learned of the news of Lucerys's death were, "An eye

At the outset of the war, Aegon II's chief supporters were Lord Hightower, Lord Lannister, and eventually Lord Baratheon. Lord Tully desired to fight for the king, but was old and bedridden, and his grandson defied him. Rhaenyra's chief supporters were her good-father Lord Velaryon, her cousin Lady Jeyne Arryn, and Lord Stark (though his help was slow in coming, as he kept every man to harvest what they could before winter fell on the North). Lord Greyjoy attacked the westerlands in her name, as well, to the shock of King Aegon, who had courted his support. The Tullys eventually joined Rhaenyra's cause, in defiance of the late Lord Tully's wishes. The Tyrells, however, remained uninvolved in the war, as did the Dornishmen.

for an eye, a son for a son. Lucerys shall be avenged." He was the Prince of the City, and he still had many friends in the stews and brothels of King's Landing. Chief of them was his once-paramour, Mysaria, the White Worm. She arranged his vengeance, hiring a brute and a rat-catcher known to history as Blood and Cheese. Thanks to his pro-

fession, the rat-catcher knew all the secrets of Maegor's tunnels. Slipping into the Red Keep, Blood and Cheese seized hold of Queen Helaena and her children . . . and then offered Aegon II's wife a brutal choice: which of her sons would die? She wept and pled and offered her own life to no avail. In the end, she named Maelor—the youngest,

ABOVE | *The deaths of Prince Lucerys and his dragon, Arrax.*

and deemed too young to understand. Blood and Cheese killed Prince Jaehaerys instead, as his mother screamed her horror. Then Blood and Cheese fled with the prince's head; true to their word that they were only after one of Aegon's sons.

These were not the only murders in that long and brutal war. As piteous as Jaehaerys's death was, that of little Prince Maelor, who did not long survive his brother, was worse. Ser Rickard Thorne of the Kingsguard was dispatched to carry Maelor away in secret to Oldtown, where he would be secure in the Hightower, but at Bitterbridge he was stopped and brought down by a mob. Maelor himself was torn apart at Bitterbridge as the men and women of the mob each struggled to claim the infant as their own prize. When Lord Hightower razed Bitterbridge in revenge and came to exact justice on Lady Caswell, she begged mercy for her children before hanging herself from her castle walls.

Even the Kingsguard were enlisted into the strife. Ser Criston Cole dispatched Ser Arryk Cargyll to Dragonstone with the intention of having him infiltrate the citadel in the guise of his twin, Ser Erryk. There, he was to kill Rhaenyra (or her children; accounts differ). Yet as chance would have it, Ser Erryk and Ser Arryk met by happenstance in one of the halls of the citadel. The singers tell us that they professed their love for one another before the steel clashed, and fought with love and duty in their hearts for an hour before they died weeping in one another's arms. The account of Mushroom, who claims to have witnessed the duel, says the reality was far more brutal: they condemned one another for traitors, and within moments had mortally wounded each other.

While this took place, Ser Criston Cole decided to punish the "black lords"—those bannermen of the crownlands who remained loyal to Rhaenyra. Rosby, Stokeworth, and Duskendale fell before him, but at Rook's Rest, Lord Staunton had already received word of Cole's arrival. Instead of fighting, he barricaded himself in his castle, then dispatched a raven to Dragonstone, begging for aid.

That aid arrived in the form of Princess Rhaenys—then five-and-fifty, but as fearless and determined as she had been in her youth—and her dragon Meleys, the Red Queen. But Cole had brought dragons too—for Aegon II himself arrived on the field upon Sunfyre, and his brother Aemond One-eye rode Vhagar, the greatest living dragon.

It is recounted that Princess Rhaenys, the Queen Who Never Was, did not shrink from her foe. With a glad cry and a crack of her whip, she sent Meleys flying up to face them. Only Vhagar and Aemond came out of that battle unscathed; Sunfyre was crippled, and King Aegon II barely survived, suffering broken ribs, a broken hip, and burns that covered half his body. Worst was his left arm, where the dragonfire melted the king's armor into his flesh. Rhaenys's body was found several days later amidst the ruin of the Red Queen's corpse, but so burned as to be unrecognizable.

Aegon spent the next year of his reign in isolation, healing from his terrible wounds, but the war raged on. And while King Aegon had many advantages in the war with his elder sister, his strength in dragons was not among them. At the war's outset, Aegon counted only four dragons large enough to fight, while his sister had eight and access to still more. First were three older dragons that had yet to be claimed by new riders: Silverwing, Queen Alysanne's old mount; Seasmoke, who had been the pride of Ser Laenor Velaryon; and Vermithor, unridden since the death of King Jaehaerys. Then there were three wild dragons that might be tamed if riders could be found: the Cannibal, said by the smallfolk to have lurked on Dragonstone even before the Targaryens came (though Munkun and Barth are dubious of this claim); Grey Ghost, shy of people, gorging on fish it plucked from the sea; and the Sheepstealer, brown and plain, preferring to feed on what sheep it could steal from the sheepfolds. Prince Jacaerys announced (with the prompting of Mushroom, if his *Testimony* is to be believed) that any man or woman who could ride one of these dragons would be ennobled.

On Dragonstone, where the Targaryens had long ruled, the common folk had seen their beautiful, foreign rulers almost as gods. Many maids deflowered by Targaryen lords accounted themselves blessed if a "dragonseed" was planted in their womb, and for this reason there were many on Dragonstone who could rightly claim—or at least suspect—that some Targaryen blood ran in their veins.

Netty—outlived her prince as well as his wife. Nettles and the Sheepstealer vanished before the war's end, and none could say where they went until years after. But of all the new dragonriders, the worst were the drunkard named Ulf the Sot, who took the name Ulf the White once knighted, and the huge and powerful blacksmith's bastard Hugh the Hammer, also called Hard Hugh, who became known as Hugh Hammer when he received his knighthood. Not satisfied with the honor of riding upon the dragons Silverwing and Vermithor, they desired lordships and wealth. After first fighting for Rhaenyra, they turned their cloaks at the First Battle of Tumbleton in return for lordships, and were cursed as the Two Betrayers ever after. Both died miserable deaths, killed by the men they thought beholden to them—the one by poisoned wine, the other slain by Bold Jon Roxton with Orphan-Maker.

Many attempted to mount the dragons that were still available on Dragonstone. The most perilous of these were the wild dragons, so it was no wonder that the dragons who had previously accepted riders were the first to find new riders. Among these new dragonriders was Addam of Hull—a brave and noble youth who was brought by his mother, Marilda of Hull, to try for a dragon along with his brother Alyn. She revealed that the boys were the sons of Laenor Velaryon—a fact that many found remarkable, but which Lord Corlys did not question when he adopted them both into House Velaryon.

The battles during the Dance cannot be readily counted, for they were almost beyond number, and much of the realm

Mushroom puts forward a more plausible possibility on Addam and Alyn's parentage: that it was Lord Corlys himself who fathered both boys, back when he spent many of his days at the shipyards of Hull where Marilda's father was a shipwright. The boys had gone unacknowledged, kept far from court, while the fiery-tempered Queen Who Never Was lived. But after her death, Lord Corlys took the opportunity to acknowledge them . . . after a fashion.

Addam claimed Laenor's dragon, Seasmoke. His brother, Alyn, had less success with Sheepstealer, and for the rest of his days bore the marks of the dragon's flames on his back and legs.

Sheepstealer was eventually tamed by Nettles—a plain, baseborn, disreputable girl who fed the dragon mutton day by day until it became used to her. The dragon and its rider played their part in the war, but Nettles's loyalties were not so clear as brave Ser Addam's. When she and Prince Daemon became lovers, it drove a final wedge between Rhaenyra and her lord husband. Nettles—whom the prince fondly called

was torn asunder in the conflict. Men raised the banner of the king, bearing the golden three-headed dragon that Aegon had taken for his sigil, only to find their neighbor had taken up Rhaenyra's red dragon quartered with the moon-and-falcon of her Arryn mother and the seahorse of her late husband. Brother fought brother, father fought son, and the whole realm bled.

Many of the hosts were gathered by various lords on behalf of the king or queen they supported, but if any could be said to have held command of all the loyal forces on each

ABOVE AND RIGHT | *Princess Rhaenys upon Meleys attacking King Aegon II upon Sunfyre.*

When Rhaenyra learned of the betrayal of Hugh Hammer and Ulf the White at First Tumbleton, where they turned their dragons against her forces, her rage was such that she tried to arrest the other dragonseed who had taken dragons at her behest. Among them was Addam Velaryon, but he was forewarned by the Sea Snake, and so escaped. Young Ser Addam died bravely at the Second Battle of Tumbleton, proving his faithfulness with his life after it had been called into question by the deeds of the Two Betrayers. When his bones were returned to Driftmark from Raventree Hall in 138 AC, the epitaph Lord Alyn put on his tomb consisted of one word: "LOYAL."

side, they were Prince Daemon Targaryen and Prince Aemond Targaryen respectively. Aemond took up the mantle of Protector of the Realm and Prince Regent after both Aegon II and Sunfyre were gravely injured at Rook's Rest in the battle with Rhaenys and Meleys. He even donned his brother's crown—Aegon the Conqueror's crown of rubies and Valyrian steel—though he did not call himself king.

Sadly for the greens, this proved to be unfortunate. Aemond was too inexperienced and too bold to take effective command. Prince Daemon was, at the time, in control of Harrenhal. So Aemond brashly planned an assault to take Harrenhal from his rival, denuding King's Landing of defenders in the process. He arrived to find the castle empty and was jubilant—until he learned the real reason for the desertion. For while Aemond had been marching on Harrenhal, Daemon had met Queen Rhaenyra and her dragonriders over King's Landing, their dragons wheeling above the city. The gold cloaks—many of whom still considered themselves loyal to Daemon—betrayed the officers Aegon had put in charge and surrendered the city with little bloodshed, though blood was spilled in the executions that followed as Ser Otto Hightower, Lord Jasper Wylde (the master of laws, called Ironrod for his sternness), and Lords Rosby and Stokeworth (who had once been of Rhaenyra's party before turning their cloaks) were beheaded. The Dowager Queen Alicent was imprisoned, but Aegon II (still recovering from the injuries he received at Rook's Rest) and his remaining children—as well as Lord Larys Strong—had been spirited out of the castle by secret ways.

The realm truly went mad during the Dance of the Dragons, but it was at King's Landing where most of the dragons lost their lives. King's Landing had fallen bloodlessly to Rhaenyra, thanks to Prince Daemon's cunning, but after the First Battle of Tumbleton, unrest spread

throughout the city. Only sixty leagues away, Tumbleton had been sacked in the most savage fashion: thousands burned, thousands more drowned attempting to swim across the river to safety, girls and women were ravished until they died, and dragons feeding among the ruins. The victory Lord Hightower had won with the aid of Prince Daeron and the Two Betrayers sent terror through the city, as the Kingslanders were sure they would be next. Rhaenyra's own strength was scattered and spent, so that there were only dragons left to defend the city.

It was the fear of dragons, and of their presence, that gave birth to the Shepherd. Who he was we cannot say, as his name is lost to history. Some suppose he was a poor beggar, others that he might have been one of the Poor Fellows who, though outlawed, still stubbornly haunted the realm. Whoever he was, he began to preach in the Cobbler's Square, saying that the dragons were demons, the spawn of godless Valyria, and the doom of men. Scores listened—then hundreds, then thousands. Fear begat anger, and anger begat a thirst for blood. And when the Shepherd announced that the city would be saved only when the city was cleansed of dragons, people listened.

On the twenty-second day of the fifth moon of the year 130 AC, Aemond One-eye and Daemon Targaryen entered their last battle. On that same day, chaos and death seized King's Landing. Queen Rhaenyra had imprisoned Lord Corlys for helping his grandson, Ser Addam Velaryon, escape arrest when he was accused of treason. Some of the Sea Snake's sworn swords joined the riotous mob

THE MOST NOTABLE BATTLES OF THE DANCE

THE BATTLES OF 129 AC

BATTLE OF THE BURNING MILL, where Prince Daemon and the Blackwoods defeated the Brackens and took the Stone Hedge.

BATTLE OF THE GULLET, where Corlys Velaryon's fleet was defeated by the ships of the Triarchy, Aegon's allies. This battle resulted in the death of Jacaerys, Prince of Dragonstone, and Vermax, his dragon—and the death of Prince Aegon the Younger's dragon, Stormcloud.

BATTLE OF THE HONEYWINE, where Aegon the Elder's youngest brother Prince Daeron won his spurs saving Lord Hightower's host from lords Rowan, Tarly, and Costayne.

THE BATTLES OF 130 AC

BATTLE AT THE RED FORK, where the westermen broke the riverlords and swarmed into the riverlands, but not before Lord Jason Lannister was mortally wounded by the squire Pate of Longleaf.

BATTLE OF THE LAKESHORE (called the Fishfeed)—the bloodiest land battle of the war on the shores of the Gods Eye—where the Lannister host was driven into the lake by the riverlords and died in the thousands.

BUTCHER'S BALL, where Aegon II's Hand, Ser Criston Cole, challenged Ser Garibald Grey, Lord Roderick Dustin (called the Ruin), and Ser Pate of Longleaf (called the Lionslayer) and was refused. Cole was killed ingloriously by arrows rather than by the sword, and his host was destroyed thereafter.

FIRST BATTLE OF TUMBLETON, where the Two Betrayers (dragonriders Ulf the White and Hugh Hammer) turned their cloaks, and the remaining Winter Wolves (the grizzled Northmen who followed Lord Dustin to war) cut their way through ten times their number. This resulted in the deaths of Lord Ormund Hightower, who led the forces of the greens, and his famous cousin Ser Brynden at the hands of Lord Roderick Dustin, who was also slain. The savage sack of Tumbleton followed.

STORMING OF THE DRAGONPIT, no true battle, where an unruly mob, under the leadership of a man known as the Shepherd, went mad. This resulted in the death of five dragons; the loss of both Ser Willum Royce and the Valyrian sword Lamentation that he bore; and the deaths of Ser Glendon Goode, who was Lord Commander of the Queensguard for one day, and Joffrey, Prince of Dragonstone.

BATTLE ABOVE THE GODS EYE, where the infamous duel between Prince Aemond One-eye and Prince Daemon Targaryen—and between Vhagar and Caraxes—took place. It is said that Daemon leapt from Caraxes to Vhagar, and slew Prince Aemond with Dark Sister as the dragons fell to the waters below. Vhagar and Caraxes died in turn, as did Daemon Targaryen, though his bones were never recovered.

SECOND BATTLE OF TUMBLETON, where the dragons truly danced. This resulted in the mysterious death of Prince Daeron the Daring, the brave death of Ser Addam Velaryon, and the deaths of Seasmoke, Tessarion, and Vermithor.

THE BATTLE OF 131 AC

BATTLE OF THE KINGSROAD, dubbed by those who fought in it "the Muddy Mess," which was the last battle of the war. This resulted in the death of Lord Borros Baratheon at the hands of young Lord Tully.

in Cobbler's Square, and some scaled the walls to try to free the Sea Snake, only to be hanged when they were caught. Queen Helaena then fell to her death, impaled on the spikes surrounding Maegor's Holdfast—a suicide some said, and others a murder. And that night, the city burned as the Shepherd's mob marched on the Dragonpit, attempting to slay all the dragons within.

Young Joffrey Velaryon, the Prince of Dragonstone, plummeted to his death when trying to ride his mother's dragon, Syrax, to the Dragonpit in order to save his own dragon, Tyraxes. Neither dragon survived. Wild tales and rumors followed about the deaths of the dragons: that some were hewn down by men, others by the Shepherd, others by the Warrior himself. Whatever the truth, five dragons died that bloody night as the mobs broke into the huge dome and found the dragons chained, and people perished in droves. Half the dragons that began the Dance were already dead, and the war was not yet over. Rhaenyra fled the city shortly after.

An end did come at last, but it was not the deaths of dragons or of princes that brought it about, but instead the

ABOVE | *Dark Sister.*

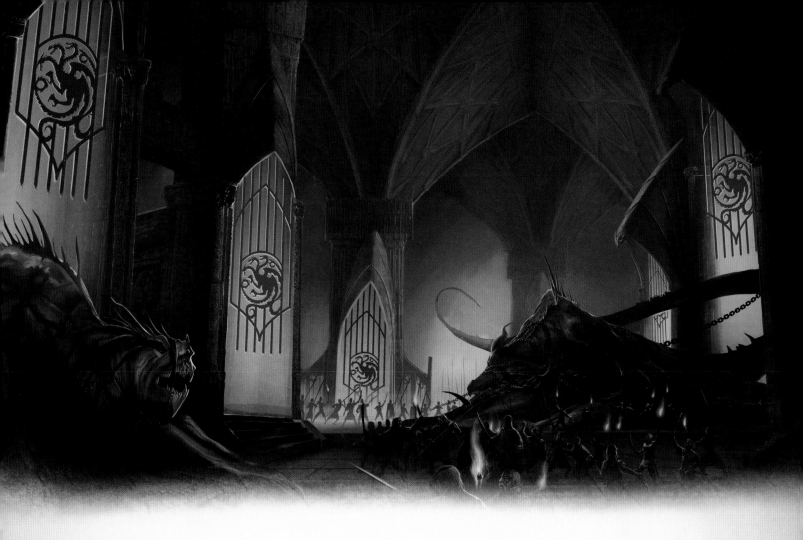

death of the queen and the king for whom they (and tens of thousands more) had perished. Rhaenyra died first. When her husband Prince Daemon fell, House Velaryon turned against her. With her enemies once more in possession of King's Landing, she fled practically penniless, and was forced to sell her crown to find passage to Dragonstone. But when she arrived, she found a freshly injured Aegon II there before her, with his dying dragon, Sunfyre.

Munkun's *True Telling*, based upon Orwyle's account, reveals that when King's Landing fell, Larys Strong saw to it that the king was spirited away to hide. Cunningly, Strong sent him to Dragonstone, rightly believing that Rhaenyra would never think to look for her brother at her own stronghold. For half a year he recovered from his wounds in a remote fishing village whilst Rhaenyra and much of her court were in King's Landing, and during

Madness gripped the city after Rhaenyra fled, and it showed itself in many ways. Strangest of all was the rise of two pretender kings who reigned during the time remembered as the Moon of the Three Kings.

The first was Trystane Truefyre, a squire to a disreputable hedge knight named Ser Perkin the Flea, who Ser Perkin declared was the natural son of Viserys I. After the storming of the Dragonpit and Rhaenyra's flight, the Shepherd and his mob ruled much of the city, but Ser Perkin installed Trystane in the abandoned Red Keep and began to issue edicts. When Aegon II eventually retook the city, Trystane begged the boon of knighthood before he was executed, and this he received.

The other king was curiouser still—a child who became known as Gaemon Palehair. The son of a whore, this four-year-old boy was claimed to be a bastard of Aegon II (which was not improbable, given the king's bawdy ways in his youth). From his seat in the House of Kisses atop Visenya's Hill, he gathered followers by the thousands and issued a series of edicts. His mother later was hanged, having confessed he was the son of a silver-haired oarsman from Lys, but Gaemon was spared and taken into the king's household. In time he befriended Aegon III, becoming his constant companion and food taster for some years, before dying of poison that might have been intended for the king himself.

ABOVE | *The Storming of the Dragonpit.*

that time Sunfyre arrived from Crackclaw Point, despite the dragon's crippled wing, which made it ungainly in the air. Thus hidden, they were able to recover their strength. (Sunfyre went on to kill the shy, wild dragon called the Grey Ghost, leading to confused reports claiming that it was the Cannibal that did it.)

King Aegon found many around Dragonstone who had grievances against Rhaenyra—for the loss of sons, husbands, and brothers in her war, or for slights they imagined—and with their aid he conquered Dragonstone. It took no more than an hour, largely unopposed as it was . . . except for Prince Daemon's daughter, the fourteen-year-old Baela Targaryen and her young dragon, Moondancer. Baela had escaped the men who tried to seize her and had made her way to her dragon. And as Aegon II sought to land in the courtyard of the castle on Sunfyre, thinking himself triumphant, the dragon and the princess rose to meet him.

Moondancer was much smaller than Sunfyre, but also much swifter and far more nimble, and neither the dragon nor the princess on her back lacked courage. The dragon swooped and clawed and snapped at Sunfyre, raking and tearing until at last a blast of flame blinded the beast. Tangled together, the two dragons fell, and their riders with them. Aegon II leapt at the last moment from Sunfyre's back, both legs shattering, while Baela remained with Moondancer to the bitter end. When Alfred Broome drew his sword to kill her where she lay broken and unconscious, Ser Marston

Waters tore the sword from his grasp and carried her to the maester, saving her life.

Of this great battle, Rhaenyra knew nothing, but it did not matter. Aegon II, ever spiteful of his sister and enraged at the agony of his shattered legs and the impending death of his dragon, fed Rhaeynra to Sunfyre before the eyes of her sole surviving son (so far as any man or woman in the Seven Kingdoms knew), Aegon the Younger. So passed the Realm's Delight, the Half-Year Queen, on the twenty-second day of the tenth moon of 130 AC.

Her half-brother did not long survive her. Though Rhaenyra was dead and Aegon the Younger was in his hands, Aegon II still had many enemies who continued to fight against him. They fought as much out of fear of his reprisals as they did for Rhaenyra, but they fought, and they proved the greater foe. When Lord Borros Baratheon at last stirred with his strength, marching against what remained of Rhaenyra's forces, there might have been a chance to turn the tide. But Lord Borros fell at the Battle of the Kingsroad, his host shattered. And the young riverlords known as the Lads, whose host had defeated him, were within a stone's throw of the city—while Lord Stark was coming down the kingsroad with a host of his own.

It was at this time that Lord Corlys Velaryon—freed from the dungeons and pardoned, and now serving on the king's small council—advised Aegon to surrender and take the black. The king refused, however, and planned to give

ABOVE | *Rhaenyra facing her death.*

orders to have his young nephew's ear removed as a warning to Aegon the Younger's supporters. He climbed into his litter to be carried to his apartments, and was given a cup of wine on the way.

When his escort arrived with the litter and lifted the curtain, they found the king dead with blood on his lips.

And so ended King Aegon II, poisoned by the men who served him—for they had seen the end even if he had not.

The broken, shattered realm suffered for a while yet, but the Dance of the Dragons was done. Now what awaited the realm was the False Dawn, the Hour of the Wolf, the rule of the regents, and the Broken King.

THE DRAGONS IN THE DANCE

KING AEGON II'S DRAGONS

SUNFYRE (King Aegon): Splendid but young, crippled for much of the war after Rook's Rest, then slain in battle with the dragon Moondancer at Dragonstone.

VHAGAR (Prince Aemond One-eye): The last of Aegon the Conqueror's three dragons, old but huge and powerful, killed in battle with Caraxes above the Gods Eye.

DREAMFYRE (Queen Helaena): Once the dragon of Jaehaerys I's sister Rhaena, crushed beneath the collapsing dome at the Storming of the Dragonpit.

TESSARION (Prince Daeron): The Blue Queen, the youngest of the dragons of fighting weight belonging to Aegon's supporters, killed at Second Tumbleton.

MORGHUL (Princess Jaehaera): Too young for war, killed at the Storming of the Dragonpit by the Burning Knight.

SHRYKOS (Prince Jaehaerys): Too young for war, killed at the Storming of the Dragonpit by Hobb the Hewer.

QUEEN RHAENYRA'S DRAGONS

SYRAX (Queen Rhaenyra): Huge and formidable, killed at the Storming of the Dragonpit.

CARAXES (Prince Daemon): The Blood Wyrm, huge and formidable, killed in battle with Vhagar above the Gods Eye.

VERMAX (Prince Jacaerys): Young but strong, killed with his rider at the Battle of the Gullet.

ARRAX (Prince Lucerys): Young but strong, killed with his rider by Vhagar above Shipbreaker Bay.

TYRAXES (Prince Joffrey): Young but strong, killed at the Storming of the Dragonpit.

STORMCLOUD (Prince Aegon the Younger): Killed by arrow and bolt at the Battle of the Gullet.

MELEYS (Princess Rhaenys): The Red Queen, old and cunning, lazy, but fearsome when roused, killed at Rook's Roost with her rider, the Queen Who Never Was.

MOONDANCER (Lady Baela): Slender and beautiful, just large enough to carry a girl, killed by Sunfyre at Dragonstone, but not before dealing a mortal wound.

SILVERWING (Ser Ulf the White): Good Queen Alysanne's dragon, mounted by a dragonseed and betrayer, survived him and the Dance both, but became wild and made her lair in an isle in Red Lake.

SEASMOKE (Ser Addam of Hull): Once Ser Laenor Velaryon's dragon, mounted by a dragonseed, killed by Vermithor at Second Tumbleton.

VERMITHOR (Ser Hugh Hammer): Old and hoary, the Old King's mount, mounted by a dragonseed and betrayer, killed in battle with Seasmoke and Tessarion at Second Tumbleton.

SHEEPSTEALER (Nettles): A wild dragon tamed by a dragonseed, vanished at war's end.

GREY GHOST: A wild dragon, shy of people, never tamed, killed by Sunfyre at Dragonstone.

THE CANNIBAL: A wild dragon, a scavenger and killer of hatchlings, never tamed and vanished at war's end.

MORNING (Lady Rhaena): Too young for war, survived the Dance.

WHEN AEGON THE Younger came to the Iron Throne in 131 AC as Aegon III, after the death of his uncle Aegon II, the realm may well have thought that its troubles were done. Aegon III's supporters had defeated the last of Aegon II's host at the Battle of the Kingsroad and had full control of King's Landing. The Velaryon fleet once more served the Iron Throne, and the Sea Snake would surely help to guide the young king. But these hopes were built on sand, and this period was soon known as the False Dawn. Aegon II had sent men across the narrow sea in search of sellswords, and none knew when or if those would return to avenge their king. In the west, the Red Kraken and his reavers ravished Fair Isle and the western coast. And a terrible, hard winter—first declared by the Conclave in Oldtown in 130 AC,

on Maiden's Day—had taken a firm grip on the realm, and would last for six cruel years.

Nowhere in the Seven Kingdoms did the winter matter more than in the North—and the fear of such a winter had driven the Winter Wolves to gather beneath the banner of Lord Roderick Dustin and die fighting for queen Rhaenyra. But behind them came a greater army of childless and homeless men, unwed men, old men, and younger sons, under the banner of Lord Cregan Stark. They had come for a war, for adventure and plunder, and for a glorious death to spare their kin beyond the Neck one more mouth to feed.

The poisoning of King Aegon II had denied them that chance. Lord Stark still marched his army into King's Landing, but to a much different outcome. He had planned to punish Storm's End, Oldtown, and Casterly Rock for having supported the king. But Lord Corlys had already sent envoys to the Rock and Storm's End and Oldtown, suing for peace. For six days, while the court waited for news of Lord Corlys's success or failure and the realm trembled at the thought of more war, Lord Cregan Stark held sway at court. This came to be known as the Hour of the Wolf.

Yet in one thing, Lord Stark would not be dissuaded: the betrayers and poisoners of King Aegon II must pay the price. To kill a cruel and unjust king in lawful battle was one thing. But foul murder, and the use of poison, was a betrayal against the very gods who had anointed him. Cregan had twenty-two men arrested in Aegon III's name—among them Larys Clubfoot and Corlys Velaryon. Cowed, the young Aegon III—who was eleven at the time—agreed to make Lord Stark his Hand.

Cregan Stark served in that office for a single day, presiding over the trials and executions. Most of the accused took the black (led by the cunning Ser Perkin the Flea). Two alone chose death—Ser Gyles Belgrave of the Kingsguard, who did not wish to outlive his king, and Larys the Clubfoot, the last of the ancient line of House Strong.

Lord Corlys was spared a trial by the machinations of Baela and Rhaena Targaryen, who convinced Aegon to issue an edict restoring to him his offices and honors, then by Black Aly Blackwood when she gave Lord Stark her hand in marriage in return for the boon of allowing Aegon's edict to stand.

ABOVE | *Young King Aegon III.*

The day after the executions, Lord Stark resigned as Hand. No man ever held the office so briefly, and few left it as gladly. He returned to the North, leaving many of his fierce Northmen behind in the south. Some wed widows in the riverlands, others sold their swords or swore them in service, and a few turned to banditry. But the Hour of the Wolf was done, and it was time for the regents.

The period of Aegon's regency—which stretched from 131 AC, when he inherited the throne, to 136 AC when he came of age—was presided over by a council of seven. Only one of those regents—Grand Maester Munkun—lasted for the whole of the term; the others died and resigned and were replaced as needed. Of these, the greatest was the Sea Snake, who passed from this veil of tears in 132 AC at the age of seventy-nine; for seven days his body lay in state beneath the Iron Throne, and the realm wept.

he refused to divulge where he had hidden much of Aegon II's royal treasury. But the Winter Fever took him in 133.

Matters deteriorated further when Unwin Peake, Lord of Starpike, Dunstonbury, and Whitegrove, became first a regent, then the Hand. He had played a significant role at First and Second Tumbleton, and had felt slighted when he was not chosen to be among the first regents. But he soon made up for that, acquiring more and more power. He saw his kin hold many high offices, attempted to wed his own daughter to King Aegon III following the apparent suicide of Queen Jaehaera, and endeavored to weaken his rivals by any means at hand.

Lord Alyn, the Sea Snake's grandson, was chief among the Hand's rivals. He was refused his father's place as a regent, then was made to sail against the Stepstones. There he won the name of Oakenfist following a great victory at

THE REGENTS OF KING AEGON III

THE FIRST COUNCIL OF SEVEN

LADY JEYNE ARRYN, THE MAIDEN OF THE VALE
Dead of illness in Gulltown in 134 AC.

LORD CORLYS VELARYON, THE SEA SNAKE
Dead of old age in 132 AC, aged seventy-nine.

LORD ROLAND WESTERLING OF THE CRAG
Dead of the Winter Fever in 133 AC.

LORD ROYCE CARON OF NIGHTSONG
Gave up his place in 132 AC.

LORD MANFRYD MOOTON OF MAIDENPOOL
Dead of age and illness in 134 AC.

SER TORRHEN MANDERLY OF WHITE HARBOR
Gave up his place in 132 AC, following the death of his father and brother from the Winter Fever.

GRAND MAESTER MUNKUN
The only man to hold the office from 131 AC to 136 AC.

THE REST

LORD UNWIN PEAKE
Given Lord Corlys's seat in 132 AC, resigned in 134 AC.

LORD THADDEUS ROWAN
Given a place in 133 AC, following the death of Lord Westerling, and relieved of his office in 136 AC.

SER CORWYN CORBRAY
Husband to Rhaena Targaryen, replaced Lord Mooton in 134 AC, and killed by a crossbowman at Runestone that same year.

WILLAM STACKSPEAR
Chosen by lot in the Great Council of 136 AC.

MARQ MERRYWEATHER
Chosen by lot in the Great Council of 136 AC.

LORENT GRANDISON
Chosen by lot in the Great Council of 136 AC.

The years of Aegon's regency were marked by turmoil. Ser Tyland Lannister—one of the men who had returned empty-handed from the Free Cities (for the free companies were richly paid during the wars that followed the collapse of the Kingdom of the Three Daughters)—served ably as Hand of the King, despite the blinding and mutilations he suffered at the hands of Queen Rhaenyra's torturers when

sea, but his newborn fame proved divisive when he returned to King's Landing. The Hand had intended to seize control of the Stepstones and put an end to the pirate kingdom of Racallio Ryndoon, but Velaryon's swift action meant that the greater part of the fleet could not land the forces needed to accomplish this. Oakenfist's fame and reputation only increased in the wake of his victory, winning him honors

The last living offspring of Aegon II, Jaehaera Targaryen was eight when she wed her cousin Aegon III, and ten when she threw herself from Maegor's Holdfast to the spikes of the dry moat below. She lived on for half an hour, in agony, before she died.

Yet some question the manner of her death. Was it truly by her own hand? Some whispered that she was murdered, and many suspects were named. Among them was Ser Mervyn Flowers of the Kingsguard, the bastard brother of Lord Unwin Peake, who had been at her door when she died. Yet even Mushroom thinks it unlikely that Flowers was the kind of man to push his charge—a child—to such an ugly death. He suggests a different possibility: that Flowers did not kill her but stepped aside to let someone else do the deed—someone like the unscrupulous Free Cities sellsword Tessario the Tiger, whom Lord Unwin had brought into his service.

Though we will never know the truth of the events that day, it now seems likely that Jaehaera's death was somehow instigated by Lord Peake.

and rewards from the regents despite Lord Peake's protests. In the end, the Hand convinced the regents to dispatch Oakenfist to the westerlands to deal with the Red Kraken's longships when Lord Dalton Greyjoy refused to give up his prizes and cease his reaving. This was a perilous journey, intended almost certainly to result in Lord Alyn's defeat or death. Instead, Oakenfist turned it into the first of his six great voyages.

In all this, Aegon III—too young to rule—was but a pawn. He was a melancholy youth, and sullen, interested in very little. He always wore black, and might go for days without speaking a word to anyone. His only companion in these first years was Gaemon Palehair, the boy pretender, now his servant and friend. After Lord Peake came to power, Gaemon was given a new role as the king's whipping boy, to suffer the punishments that could not be meted out against the royal person. Later Gaemon Palehair died in the attempted poisoning of the king and his young, beautiful queen Daenaera Velaryon.

Lady Daenaera was a cousin to Alyn Oakenfist, fathered by his cousin Daeron, who died fighting for him in the Stepstones. A surpassingly beautiful child, Daenaera was but six when the princesses Rhaena and Baela presented her to the king—the last of a thousand maids who had been presented him at the great ball of 133 AC. This ball had been declared by the Hand, Lord Peake, after the regents stopped his efforts to betroth his own daughter to the king—though he did not give up that aspiration and was greatly frustrated by the king's ultimate choice.

His efforts to have the choice put aside were opposed by both Aegon and the other regents. Outraged, Lord Unwin threatened to resign the Handship to bend the regents to his will, only to find the others delighted to oblige him. They

appointed one of their number, Lord Thaddeus Rowan, to take his place as Hand.

Aegon had only one true joy during these years: the return of his younger brother, Prince Viserys. The realm had thought Viserys slain at the Battle of the Gullet, and the king had never forgiven himself for abandoning his brother when he fled on the back of his dragon, Stormcloud. But Viserys was eventually recovered from Lys by Oakenfist, where he had been held in secret by merchant princes who thought to profit from his ransom or his death. The price that Lord Velaryon agreed to for his release was enormous, and soon proved a matter of contention. But his release—with his new Lyseni bride, the beautiful Larra Rogare, seven years his elder—was a joy regardless, and for the rest of his days he was the only person Aegon ever fully trusted.

In the end, it was Larra Rogare and her wealthy, ambitious family who helped break the power of the regents and, almost certainly, that of Lord Peake. It was an inadvertent role they played, however, caught up as they were in the Lyseni Spring. This was a time when the Rogare Bank waxed greater than the Iron Bank, and so fell prey to the plots to control the king; they were blamed for many more acts than they were actually guilty of. Lord Rowan, then the Hand and one of the last regents, was accused of being complicit in their crimes and was tortured for information. Ser Marston Waters, now somehow Hand of the King in his place (Munkun, the only regent at this time besides Rowan, is reticent to discuss this in the *True Telling*), dispatched men to seize Lady Larra after having arrested her brothers. But the king and his brother refused to give her up, and were besieged in Maegor's Holdfast by Waters and his supporters for eighteen days. The conspiracy eventually unraveled as Ser Marston—perhaps recalling his duty—attempted to

RIGHT | *Aegon III's dismissal of both the regents and the Hand, Lord Manderly.*

fulfill his king's command to arrest those who had falsely implicated the Rogares and Lord Rowan. Waters himself was killed by his own sworn brother, Ser Mervyn Flowers, when he attempted to arrest him.

Order reestablished itself, with Munkun serving as Hand and regent for the rest of the remaining year until new regents were appointed and a new Hand was found. The time of the regency finally ended on the sixteenth nameday of the king, when he entered the small council chamber, dismissed his regents, and relieved his then-Hand, Lord Manderly, of his office.

It was a broken reign that followed, for Aegon himself was broken. He was melancholy to the end of his days, found pleasure in almost nothing, and locked himself in his chambers to brood for days on end. He likewise came to dislike being touched—even by the hand of his beautiful queen. Even after she had flowered, he was long in calling

her to his bed . . . but ultimately their marriage was blessed with two sons and three daughters. The eldest, Daeron, was named the Prince of Dragonstone and heir apparent.

Though he strove to give the realm peace and plenty in the wake of the Dance, Aegon III proved unwilling to court his own people, or his lords. His might have been a very different reign were it not for that one flaw in him—his coldness when it came to those he ruled. His brother, Prince Viserys—who in his last years served as his Hand—had the gift of charm, but he himself grew stern after his wife abandoned him and their children for her native Lys.

Yet together, Aegon and Viserys ably dealt with the remaining turmoil in the realm. One such incident was the troublesome appearance of several pretenders claiming to be Prince Daeron the Daring—the youngest brother of Aegon II who was killed at Second Tumbleton but whose body was never identified—leaving the door open for

FROM THE ACCOUNT OF GRAND MAESTER MUNKUN OF THE KING'S WORDS TO LORD MANDERLY WHEN HE ENDED THE REGENCY

I mean to give the smallfolk peace and food and justice. If that will not suffice to win their love, let Mushroom make a progress. Or perhaps we might send a dancing bear. Someone once told me that the commons love nothing half so much as dancing bears. You may call a halt to this feast tonight as well. Send the lords home to their own keeps and give the food to the hungry. Full bellies and dancing bears shall be my policy.

unscrupulous men to make their false claims. (But those feigned princes have since been conclusively shown to be imposters.) They even attempted to restore the Targaryen dragons, despite Aegon's fears—for which none could blame him after witnessing his mother being eaten alive. He dreaded the sight of dragons—and had even less desire to ride upon one—but he was convinced that they would cow those who sought to oppose him. At Viserys's suggestion, he sent away for nine mages from Essos, attempting to use their arts to kindle a clutch of eggs. This proved both a debacle and a failure.

There were four dragons still living at the start of his reign—Silverwing, Morning, Sheepstealer, and the Cannibal. Yet Aegon III will always be remembered as the Dragon-bane, for the last Targaryen dragon died during his reign in the year 153 AC.

The reign of the Broken King—also known as Aegon the Unlucky—ended with the king's death at thirty-six years of age, from consumption. Many of his subjects thought him far older, for his boyhood was cut too short. The melancholy king is not remembered fondly, and his legacy would pale before that of his sons.

DAERON I

WHEN AEGON III died in the twenty-sixth year of his reign, 157 years after the Conqueror was crowned, he left behind two sons and three daughters. The eldest of his sons, Daeron, was a mere boy of fourteen years when he assumed the throne. Perhaps because of Daeron's charm and genius, or perhaps because of his memory of what transpired during the regency of Daeron's father, Prince Viserys chose not to insist on a regency while the young king was in his minority. Instead, Viserys continued to serve as Hand while King Daeron ruled ably and capably.

Few foresaw that Daeron, the First of His Name, would cover himself in glory as did his ancestor Aegon the Conqueror, whose crown he wore. (His father had preferred a simple circlet.) Yet that glory turned to ashes almost as swiftly. A youth of rare brilliance and forcefulness, Daeron at first met resistance from his uncle, his councillors, and many great lords when he first proposed to "complete the Conquest" by bringing Dorne into the realm at last. His lords reminded him that, unlike the Conqueror and his sisters, he had no more dragons fit for war. To this Daeron famously responded: "You have a dragon. He stands before you."

In the end, the king could not be gainsaid, and when he revealed his plans—plans formulated, it is said, with the help and advice of Alyn Velaryon, the Oakenfist—some began to think it could indeed be done, for the proposed campaign improved upon that of Aegon's own.

Daeron I amply proved his prowess on the field of Dorne, which for hundreds of years had defied the Reach, the stormlords, and even the dragons of House Targaryen. Daeron divided his host into three forces: one led by Lord Tyrell, who came down the Prince's Pass at the western end of the Red Mountains of Dorne; one led by the king's cousin and master of ships, Alyn Velaryon, traveling by sea; and one led by the king himself, marching down the treacherous pass called the Boneway, where he made use of goat tracks that others considered too dangerous, to go around the Dornish watchtowers and avoid the same traps that had caught Orys Baratheon. The young king then swept away every force that sought to stop him. The Prince's Pass was won, and, most importantly, the royal fleet broke the Planky Town and then was able to drive upriver.

With Dorne effectively divided in half by Lord Alyn's control of the Greenblood, the Dornish forces in the east and west could not aid one another directly. And from this

stemmed a series of bold battles that would take a volume entire to relate in full. Many accounts of this war can be found, but the best of them is *The Conquest of Dorne*, King Daeron's own account of his campaign, which is rightly considered a marvel of elegant simplicity in both its prose and its strategies.

LEFT | *All that remains of the Targaryen dragons today: the skull of Balerion the Black Dread.*
ABOVE | *King Daeron I, the Young Dragon.*

Within a year, the invaders were at the gates of Sunspear and battling their way through the so-called shadow city. In 158 AC, the Prince of Dorne and twoscore of the most powerful Dornish lords bent their knees to Daeron at the Submission of Sunspear. The Young Dragon had accomplished what Aegon the Conqueror never had. There were rebels still in the deserts and mountains—men swiftly branded as outlaws—but they were few in number to begin with.

The king quickly consolidated his control of Dorne, dealing with these rebels when he found them . . . though not without difficulty. In one infamous episode, a poisoned

charge of Dorne, valiantly attempted to quell the fires of rebellion, traveling from castle to castle with each turn of the moon—punishing any supporters of the rebels with the noose, burning down the villages that harbored the outlaws, and so on. But the smallfolk struck back, and each new day found supplies stolen or destroyed, camps burned, horses killed, and slowly the count of dead soldiers and men-at-arms rose—killed in the alleyways of the shadow city, ambushed amidst the dunes, murdered in their camps.

But the true rebellion began when Lord Tyrell and his train traveled to Sandstone, where his lordship was murdered

---

Dornish letters recorded in Maester Gareth's *Red Sands* suggest that Lord Qorgyle, the Lord of Sandstone, himself arranged for Lord Tyrell's murder. However, his motives were the subject of speculation in later years. Some say he grew angry that his early show of loyalty—by putting an end to the rabble-rousing of one of the more notorious rebel lords—was given such little consideration by Lord Tyrell, whilst others claim that his initial aid was all part of a treacherous plan he made with his castellan to lull the king and Lord Tyrell into trusting him.

---

arrow meant for the king was taken instead by his cousin Prince Aemon (the younger son of Prince Viserys), who had to be sent home by ship to recover. Yet by 159 AC the hinterlands were pacified, and the Young Dragon was free to return in triumph to King's Landing, leaving Lord Tyrell in Dorne to keep the peace. As assurance for Dorne's future loyalty and good behavior, fourteen highborn hostages were carried back with him to King's Landing, the sons and daughters of almost all the great houses of Dorne.

This tactic proved less effective than Daeron might have hoped, however. Whilst the hostages helped ensure the continued loyalty of their own blood, the king had not anticipated the tenacity of Dorne's smallfolk, over whom he had no hold. Ten thousand men, it is said, died in the battle for Dorne; forty thousand more died over the course of the following three years, as common Dornishmen fought on stubbornly against the king's men.

Lord Tyrell, whom Daeron had left in

in a bed of scorpions. As word spread of his demise, open rebellion swept Dorne from one end to the other.

In 160 AC the Young Dragon himself was forced to return to Dorne to put down the rebels. He won several small victories as he fought through the Boneway while Lord Alyn Oakenfist descended once again upon the Planky Town and the Greenblood. Apparently broken, in 161 AC the Dornishmen agreed to meet to renew their fealty and discuss terms . . . but it was treachery and murder they plotted, not peace. In a bloody betrayal, the Dornish attacked the Young Dragon and his retinue beneath the peace banner. Three knights of the Kingsguard were slain attempting to protect the king (a fourth, to his eternal shame, threw down his sword and yielded). Prince Aemon the Dragonknight was wounded and captured, but not before cutting down two of the betrayers. The Young Dragon himself died with Blackfyre in his hand, surrounded by a dozen enemies.

King Daeron I's reign was thus four short years in length; his ambition had proved too great. Glory may be everlasting, yet it is fleeting as well—soon forgotten in the aftermath of even the most famous of victories if they lead to greater disasters.

ABOVE | *Skulls of the dead in Dorne.* RIGHT | *King Baelor I's penance through the deserts of Dorne.*

BAELOR I

NEWS SOON REACHED King's Landing of King Daeron's death and the rout of his remaining forces. The outrage that followed was swiftly directed at the Dornish hostages. At the command of the King's Hand, Prince Viserys, they were thrown into the dungeons to await hanging. The Hand's eldest son, Prince Aegon, even delivered the Dornish girl he had made his paramour to his father to await execution.

The Young Dragon had never married, nor fathered children. Accordingly, upon his death, the Iron Throne passed to his brother Baelor, a youth of ten-and-seven. Baelor proved to be the most pious king in the Targaryen dynasty, and some say in the history of all the Seven Kingdoms. His first act as king was to grant pardon to the Dornish hostages. Many similar acts of piety and forgiveness followed throughout Baelor's ten-year reign. Even as his lords and council cried for vengeance, Baelor publicly forgave his brother's killers and declared that he meant to "bind up the wounds" of his brother's war and make peace with Dorne. As an act of piety, he declared, he would go to Dorne "with neither sword nor army," to return their hostages and sue for peace. And so he did, walking barefoot from King's Landing to Sunspear, clad only in sackcloth, while the hostages rode fine horses behind him.

There are many songs of Baelor's journey to Dorne that found their way out of septries and motherhouses to spill from the tongues of singers. Mounting the Stone Way, Baelor soon came to the place where the Wyls had imprisoned his cousin Prince Aemon. He found the Dragonknight naked in a cage. It is said that Baelor pleaded, but Lord Wyl refused to free Aemon, forcing His Grace instead to offer a prayer for his cousin and swear that he would return. Many generations since have wondered just what Prince Aemon must have thought of this, seeing his reedy-voiced, slender kinsman—haggard and with bare, bleeding feet—making this promise. And yet Baelor pressed on and survived the Boneway, which had proved the undoing for many thousands before him.

The crossing of the desert between the northern foothills and the Scourge on foot, practically alone, nearly undid him. And yet he persevered. It was an arduous journey, but he survived to meet with the Prince of Dorne in what some consider to be the first miracle of Blessed Baelor's reign. And the second miracle might well be that he succeeded in forging a peace with Dorne that lasted throughout his reign. As part of the terms of the agreement, Baelor agreed that his young cousin Daeron—grandson of his Hand, Viserys, and the son of Viserys's eldest son Prince Aegon—should be betrothed to Princess Mariah, eldest child of the Prince of Dorne. Both were children at the time, so the marriage was to take place when they were of age.

After a sojourn in the Old Palace of Sunspear, the Prince of Dorne offered Baelor a galley to take him back to King's Landing. However, the young king insisted that the Seven had commanded him to walk. Some in the Dornish court feared that Prince Viserys would take it as a new cause for

war when (not if) Baelor died upon the road, so the prince made every effort to make certain that the Dornish lords along the route would be hospitable. When he mounted the Boneway, Baelor turned his attention to recovering Prince Aemon from his imprisonment. He had asked the Dornish prince to explicitly command the Dragonknight's release, and this Lord Wyl accepted. Yet instead of freeing Aemon himself, he gave Baelor the key to Aemon's cage, and an invitation to use it. But now, not only was Aemon naked in a cage, exposed to the hot sun by day and the cold

wind by night, but also a pit had been dug beneath the cage, and within it were many vipers. The Dragonknight is said to have begged for the king to leave him, to go and seek aid in the Dornish Marches instead, but Baelor is said to have smiled and told him that the gods would protect him. Then he stepped into the pit.

Later, the singers claimed that the vipers bowed their heads to Baelor as he passed, but the truth is otherwise. Baelor was bitten half a dozen times while crossing to the cage, and though he opened it, he nearly collapsed before the Dragonknight was able to thrust open the door and pull his cousin from the pit. The Wyls are said to have laid wagers as Prince Aemon struggled to climb out of the cage with Baelor flung across his back, and perhaps it was their cruelty that spurred him to climb to the top of the cage and leap to safety.

Prince Aemon carried Baelor halfway down the Boneway before a village septon in the Dornish mountains gave him clothing and an ass on which to carry the comatose king. Eventually Aemon reached the watchtowers of the Dondarrions, and then was conducted to Blackhaven, where the local maester cared for the king as best he could before sending them on to Storm's End for further treatment. And all the while, it is said, Baelor was wasting away, still lost to the world.

He only regained consciousness on the way to Storm's End, and then only to mutter prayers. It was half a year and more before he was well enough to travel on to King's Landing; and in all that time, Prince Viserys managed the realm as King's Hand, maintaining Baelor's peace treaty with the Dornish.

The realm celebrated when Baelor at last regained the Iron Throne. Yet Baelor's interests remained firmly on the Seven, and his first new edicts must have caused consternation among those who had been used to Aegon III's sober rule, Daeron's benign neglect, and Viserys's shrewd stewardship. Having been wed in 160 AC to his sister Daena, the king proceeded to convince the High Septon to dissolve the marriage. It was contracted before he was king, he argued, and had never been consummated.

After the union was dissolved, Baelor went further by placing Daena and her younger sisters Rhaena and Elaena into their own "Court of Beauty" within the Red Keep, in what came to be called the Maidenvault. The king announced that he wished to preserve their innocence from the wickedness of the world and the lusts of impious men,

ABOVE | *Baelor braving the vipers to rescue Prince Aemon the Dragonknight.*
RIGHT | *The sisters of King Baelor I (l. to r.): Elaena, Rhaena, and Daena.*

The Sisters of Baelor I

Daena is the most famed of the three sisters, and was the most loved—for her beauty as much as her fierce courage. She was known as a skilled horsewoman, a fearsome archer with the Dornish bow her brother Daeron had brought back from his conquests, and she was practiced at riding at rings (though she was never allowed to ride in a tourney, despite her efforts to the contrary). Daena quickly became known as the Defiant, for she was the most restless of the three sisters in her imprisonment, and on three separate occasions escaped disguised as a servant or one of the smallfolk. She even contrived, toward the end of Baelor's reign, to get herself with child—though some might say it would have been better had she been less defiant, for all the trouble that son brought to the realm.

Of Baelor's other sisters, Rhaena was almost as pious as her brother, and in time became a septa. Elaena, the youngest, was more willful than Rhaena, but not as beautiful as either of her sisters. While in the Maidenvault, it is said she cut her "crowning glory"—her long hair, platinum-pale with a streak of gold running through it—and sent it to her brother, pleading for her freedom with the promise that, shorn as she was, she would now be too ugly to tempt any man. Her pleas fell on deaf ears, however.

Elaena outlived her siblings and led a tumultuous life once freed from the Maidenvault. Following in Daena's footsteps, she bore the bastard twins Jon and Jeyne Waters to Alyn Velaryon, Lord Oakenfist. She hoped to wed him, it is written, but a year after his disappearance at sea, she gave up hope and agreed to marry elsewhere.

She was thrice wed. Her first marriage was in 176 AC, to the wealthy but aged Ossifer Plumm, who is said to have died while consummating the marriage. She conceived, however, for Lord Plumm did his duty before he died. Later, scurrilous rumors came to suggest that Lord Plumm, in fact, died at the sight of his new bride in her nakedness (this rumor was put in the lewdest terms—terms which might have amused Mushroom but which we need not repeat), and that the child she conceived that night was by her cousin Aegon—he who later became King Aegon the Unworthy.

Her second marriage was at the behest of Aegon the Unworthy's successor, King Daeron the Good. Daeron wed her to his master of coin, and this union led to four more children . . . and to Elaena becoming known to be the true master of coin, for her husband was said to be a good and noble lord but one without a great facility for numbers. She swiftly grew influential, and was trusted by King Daeron in all things as she labored on his behalf and on that of the realm.

The third marriage was one of her own choice, after she fell in love with Ser Michael Manwoody, a Dornishman who had attended Princess Mariah at her court. Manwoody, who in early life had studied at the Citadel, was a cultured man of great wit and learning who had become a trusted servant to King Daeron after Daeron's marriage to Queen Mariah. He was sent to Braavos to negotiate with the Iron Bank on several occasions, and there is record of a correspondence between him and the keyholders of the Iron Bank (sealed with his seal and signed with his name, but apparently in the hand of Elaena) regarding these negotiations.

Elaena wed Ser Michael, apparently with Daeron's blessing, not long after her second husband died. Elaena said, in her later years, that it wasn't his intelligence that made her love Ser Manwoody, but his love of music. He was known to play the harp for her, and when he died, Elaena commanded that his effigy be carved holding a harp, and not the sword and spurs of knighthood as is common.

but some wondered if he did not fear the temptation of their beauty on his own behalf.

Though Viserys, the princesses themselves, and other members of the court protested, the deed was done, and the princesses were cloistered away in the heart of the Red Keep, accompanied only by maidens that lords and knights sent to the Red Keep to curry favor with Baelor.

More protest came when Baelor went on to outlaw prostitution within King's Landing, and no one could impress on him how much trouble that would cause. More than a thousand whores and their children, it is said, were rounded up and put out of the city. The unrest that followed was something that King Baelor chose not to acknowledge as he busied himself with his newest project: a great sept that would be built on top of Visenya's Hill—a sept that he said he had seen in a vision. So was the Great Sept first envisioned, though it was not completed until many years after his death.

Ultimately, some have wondered if the king's near death in Dorne did not affect his mind in some way, for as the years of his reign progressed, his decisions grew ever more zealous and erratic. Though the smallfolk loved him—he emptied the treasury regularly to fund his charitable acts,

including the year when he donated a loaf of bread daily to every man and woman in the city—the lords of the realm were beginning to grow uneasy. The king had not only ended his marriage to Daena, but he had made sure he would never wed again by taking a septon's vows, aided and abetted by a High Septon who was becoming increasingly influential in the kingdom. The king's edicts were becoming more concerned with spiritual matters at the expense of the

Or perhaps not, for Baelor had by then become convinced that the gods had given an eight-year-old boy—a street urchin, some later claimed, but more likely a draper's son—the power to perform miracles. Baelor claimed to have seen the boy speaking with doves that answered him in the voice of men and women—the voices of the Seven, according to Baelor. This, he declared, should be the next High Septon. Again the Most Devout did as the king desired,

One unfortunate aspect of King Baelor's zealotry was his insistence on burning books. Though some books might hold little that is worth knowing, and some might even hold matter that is dangerous, destroying knowledge is a painful thing. That Baelor had the *Testimony of Mushroom* burned is no great surprise, given its ribald and scandalous content. But Septon Barth's *Unnatural History*, however mistaken some of its proposals, was the work of one of the brightest minds in the Seven Kingdoms. Barth's study and alleged practice of the higher arts proved enough to win Baelor's enmity and the destruction of his work, even though *Unnatural History* contains much that is neither controversial nor wicked. It is only fortunate that fragments have survived, so that the lore within was not wholly lost.

material as well—including his effort to require the Citadel to use doves, not ravens, to carry their messages (a debacle discussed at length in Walgrave's *Black Wings, Swift Words*), and his attempt to provide exemptions from taxation for those who ensured the virtue of their daughters through the judicious use of chastity belts.

Toward the end of the reign, Baelor began to spend more and more time fasting and praying, attempting to make up for all the sins and offenses he believed he and his subjects were committing against the Seven on a daily basis. When the High Septon died, Baelor informed the Most Devout that the gods had revealed the identity of the future High Septon to him, and they promptly elected Baelor's choice to the office—a common man named Pate who was a gifted worker in stone, but without letters, simple-minded, and unable to recall even a simple prayer. It was a blessing, perhaps, that this lackwit High Septon only survived a year before a fever took him.

and so the youngest High Septon to ever wear the crystal crown was chosen.

The eventual birth of Daemon Waters, the natural child of Daena Targaryen by a father she refused to name (but whom the realm later learned was none other than her cousin, Aegon, while he was still a prince), led to another fit of fasting by the king. He had already nearly killed himself some years before, when he fasted for a moon's turn following the deaths of his cousin Princess Naerys's twins shortly after their delivery. This time Baelor took it yet further, refusing anything but water and taking only enough bread to still the cries of his stomach. For forty days he kept his regimen. On the forty-first day, he was found collapsed before the altar of the Mother.

Grand Maester Munkun did what he could to heal the king. So, too, did the boy High Septon, but his miracles were at an end. The king joined the Seven in the tenth year of his reign, in 171 AC.

Malicious rumors that followed in the wake of Viserys's ascension—begun, some say, by the pen of the Lady Maia of House Stokeworth—suggested that Viserys poisoned the king in order to finally gain the throne after a decade and more of waiting. Others have suggested that Viserys poisoned Baelor for the good of the realm, since the septon-king had come to believe that the Seven called on him to convert all the unbelievers in his realm. This would have led to a war with the North and the Iron Islands that would have caused great turmoil.

LEFT | *The Great Sept of Baelor.*

VISERYS II

THOUGH BOTH OF the sons of King Aegon III were dead, his three daughters yet survived, and there were some amongst the smallfolk—and even some lords—who felt that the Iron Throne should by rights now pass to Princess Daena. They were few, however; a decade of isolation in the Maidenvault had left Daena and her sisters without powerful allies, and memories of the woes that had befallen the realm when last a woman sat the Iron Throne were still fresh. Daena the Defiant was seen by many lords as being wild and unmanageable besides . . . and wanton as well, for a year earlier she had given birth to a bastard son she named Daemon, whose sire she steadfastly refused to name.

The precedents of the Great Council of 101 and the Dance of the Dragons were therefore cited, and the claims of Baelor's sisters were set aside. Instead the crown passed to his uncle, the King's Hand, Prince Viserys.

It has been written that while Daeron warred and Baelor prayed, Viserys ruled. For fourteen years he served as Hand to his nephews, and before them he served his brother, King Aegon III. It is said he was the shrewdest Hand since Septon Barth, though his good efforts were diminished in the reign of the Broken King, who lacked any desire to please his subjects or win their love. In his *Lives of Four Kings,* Grand Maester Kaeth seems to hold little opinion, good or bad, of Viserys . . . but there are those who say that, by rights, the book should be about five kings, Viserys included. And yet Viserys is passed over for a discussion of his son, Aegon the Unworthy, instead.

After his years as a hostage in Lys following the Dance, Viserys returned to King's Landing with a beautiful Lyseni bride, Larra Rogare, the daughter of a wealthy and influential noble house. Tall and willowy, with the silver-gold hair and purple eyes of Valyria (for the blood still runs strong in Lys), she was seven years Viserys's elder. She was also a woman who never felt a part of the court and was never truly happy there. Yet she gave him three children before she at last returned to her native Lys.

The eldest was Aegon, born in the Red Keep in 135 AC after Viserys's return from Lys. He was a robust lad who grew to be handsome and charming, and also irresponsible and capricious, devoted to his pleasures. He caused his father much trouble and toil, and the realm much pain.

In 136 AC, Aemon followed. He was as robust as Aegon as an infant, and as beautiful to look upon, but his brother's faults were not in him. He proved the greatest jouster and swordsman of his age—a knight worthy to bear Dark Sister. He became known as the Dragonknight for the three-headed dragon crest wrought in white gold upon his helm. To this very day some call him the noblest knight who ever lived and one of the most storied names to ever serve in the Kingsguard.

The last of Viserys's children was his only daughter, Naerys, born in 138 AC. She had skin so pale that it seemed almost translucent, men said. She was small of frame (and made smaller by having little appetite), with very fine features, and singers wrote songs in praise of her eyes—a deep violet in hue and very large, framed by pale lashes.

She loved Aemon best of her brothers, for he knew how to make her laugh—and he had something of the same piety that she possessed, while Aegon did not. She loved the Seven as dearly as she loved her brother, if not more so, and might have been a septa if her lord father had allowed it. But he did not, and Viserys instead wed her to his son Aegon in 153 AC, with King Aegon III's blessing. The singers say that Aemon and Naerys both wept during the ceremony, though the histories tell us Aemon quarreled with Aegon at the wedding feast, and that Naerys wept during the bedding rather than the wedding.

There are those who write that many of the follies of the Young Dragon and Baelor the Blessed originated in Prince Viserys, while others argue that Viserys moderated the worst of their obsessions as best he could. Though his reign lasted little more than a year, it is instructive to consider his reforms of the royal household and its functions; the establishment of a new royal mint; his efforts to increase trade across the narrow sea; and his revisions of the code of laws that Jaehaerys the Conciliator had established during his long reign.

Viserys II had within him the capacity to be a new Conciliator, for no king had ever been shrewder or more capable. Tragically, a sudden illness carried him away in 172 AC.

It need not be said that some found the illness and its swiftness suspicious, but none dared speak their suspicion at the time. It would be more than a decade before the first accusation was put to paper that Viserys had been poisoned by none other than his successor, his son Aegon.

Is there truth to this suspicion? We cannot say for certain. But given all the infamous and corrupt deeds of Aegon the Unworthy, both before and after he assumed the crown, it cannot be discounted.

AEGON IV

WITH HIS FATHER'S death in 172 AC, Aegon, the Fourth of his Name, came at last to the throne that he had coveted as a boy. He had been comely in his youth, skilled with lance and sword, a man who loved to hunt and hawk and dance. He was the brightest prince at court in his generation and was admired for his wit. But he had one great flaw: he could not rule himself. His lusts, his gluttony, his desires—they all controlled him utterly. Seated upon the Iron Throne, his misrule began with small acts of pleasure, but in time his appetites knew no bounds, and his corruption led to acts that haunted the realm for generations. "Aenys was weak and Maegor was cruel," Kaeth writes, "and Aegon II was grasping, but no king before or after would practice so much willful misrule."

Aegon soon filled his court with men chosen not for their nobility, honesty, or wisdom, but for their ability to amuse and flatter him. And the women of his court were largely those who did the same, letting him slake his lusts upon their bodies. On a whim, he often took from one noble house to give to another, as he did when he casually appropriated the great hills called the Teats from the Brackens and gifted them to the Blackwoods. For the sake of his desires, he gave away priceless treasures, as he did when he granted his Hand, Lord Butterwell, a dragon's egg in return for access to all three of his daughters. He deprived men of their rightful inheritance when he desired their wealth, as rumors claim he did following the death of Lord Plumm upon his wedding day.

For the smallfolk, his reign might have been a source of gossip and amusement. To the lords of the realm who did not stay at court, and who did not wish to have Aegon make free with their daughters, he might have seemed strong and decisive, frivolous, but largely harmless. But to those who dared enter his circle, he was too mercurial, too greedy, and too cruel to be anything but dangerous.

It was said of Aegon that he never slept alone and did not count a night complete until he had spent himself in a woman. His carnal lusts were satiated by all manner of women, from the highest born of princesses to the meanest whore, and he seemed to make no difference between them. In his last years, Aegon claimed he had slept with at least nine hundred women (the exact number eluded him), but that he only truly loved nine. (Queen Naerys, his sister, was not counted among them). The nine mistresses came from near and far, and some gave him natural children, but each and every one (save the last) was dismissed when he grew weary of her. However, one of those natural children came from a woman not accounted his mistress: Princess Daena, the Defiant.

Daemon was the name Daena gave to this child, for Prince Daemon had been the wonder and the terror of his age, and in later days that was seen as a warning of what the boy would become. Daemon Waters was his full name when he was born in 170 AC. At that time, Daena refused to name the father, but even then Aegon's involvement was suspected. Raised at the Red Keep, this handsome youth was given the instruction of the wisest maesters and the best masters-at-arms at court, including Ser Quentyn Ball, the fiery knight called Fireball. He loved nothing better than deeds of arms and excelled at them, and many saw in him a warrior who would one day be another Dragonknight. King Aegon knighted Daemon in his twelfth year when he won a squires' tourney (thereby making him the youngest

ABOVE | *The young Prince Aegon, with his parents, Prince Viserys II and Larra Rogare.*

knight ever made in the time of the Targaryens, surpassing Maegor I) and shocked his court, kin, and council by bestowing upon him the sword of Aegon the Conqueror, Blackfyre, as well as lands and other honors. Daemon took the name Blackfyre thereafter.

Queen Naerys—the one woman Aegon IV bedded in whom he took no pleasure—was pious and gentle and frail, and all these things the king misliked. Childbirth also proved a trial to Naerys, for she was small and delicate. When Prince Daeron was born on the last day of 153 AC, Grand Maester Alford warned that another pregnancy might kill her. Naerys was said to address her brother thus: "I have done my duty by you, and given you an heir. I beg you, let us live henceforth as brother and sister." We are told that Aegon replied: "That is what we are doing." Aegon continued to insist his sister perform her wifely duties for the rest of her life.

Matters between them were inflamed further by Prince Aemon, their brother, who had been inseparable from Naerys when they were young. Aegon's resentment of his noble, celebrated brother was plain to all, for the king delighted in slighting Aemon and Naerys both at every turn. Even after the Dragonknight died in his defense, and Queen Naerys perished in childbed the year after, Aegon IV did little to honor their memory.

The king's quarrels with his close kin became all the worse after his son Daeron grew old enough to voice his opinions. Kaeth's *Lives of Four Kings* makes it plain that the false accusations of the queen's adultery made by Ser Morgil Hastwyck were instigated by the king himself, though at the time Aegon denied it. These claims were disproved by Ser Morgil's death in a trial by combat against the Dragonknight. That these accusations came at the same time as Aegon and Prince Daeron were quarreling over the king's plans to launch an unprovoked war against Dorne was surely no coincidence. It was also the first (but not the last) time that Aegon threatened to name one of his bastards as his heir instead of Daeron.

After the deaths of his siblings, the king began to make barely veiled references to his son's alleged illegitimacy—something he dared only because the Dragonknight was dead. His courtiers and hangers-on aped the king, and this calumny spread.

In the last years of his reign, Prince Daeron proved the chief obstacle to Aegon's misrule. Some lords of the realm clearly saw opportunity in the increasingly corpulent, gluttonous king who could be convinced to part with honors, offices, and lands for the promise of pleasures.

Others, who condemned the king's behavior, began to flock to Prince Daeron; despite all his threats and calumnies and tasteless japes, the king never formally disowned his son. Accounts differ as to why: some suggest that some shriveled part of Aegon still knew honor, or at least shame. The likeliest cause, however, was that he knew that such an act would bring war to the realm, for Daeron's allies—chief among them the Prince of Dorne, whose sister Daeron had wed—would defend his rights. Perhaps it was for this reason that Aegon turned his attention to Dorne, using the hatred for the Dornishmen that still burned in the marches, the stormlands, and the Reach to suborn some of Daeron's allies and use them against his most powerful supporters.

Fortunately for the realm, the king's plans to invade Dorne in 174 AC proved a complete failure. Though His Grace built a huge fleet, thinking to succeed as Daeron the Young Dragon had done, it was broken and scattered by storms on its way to Dorne.

This was far from the greatest folly of Aegon IV's stillborn invasion of Dorne, however, for His Grace had also turned to the dubious pyromancers of the ancient Guild of Alchemists, commanding them to "build me dragons." These wood-and-iron monstrosities, fitted with pumps that shot jets of wildfire, might perhaps have been of some use in a siege. But Aegon proposed to drag these devices up and through the Boneway, where there are places so steep that the Dornishmen have carved steps.

They did not come even that far, however, for the first of the dragons went up in flames in the kingswood, far from the Boneway. Soon all

ABOVE | *Blackfyre, the sword of the Targaryen kings.*
RIGHT | *The knighting of Daemon Blackfyre by his father, King Aegon IV.*

seven were burning. Hundreds of men burned in those fires, along with almost a quarter of the kingswood. After that, the king gave up his ambitions and never spoke of Dorne again.

The reign of this unworthy monarch came to an end in 184 AC, when King Aegon was nine-and-forty years of age. He was grossly fat, barely able to walk, and some wondered how his last mistress—Serenei of Lys, the mother of Shiera Seastar—could ever have withstood his embraces. The king himself died a horrible death, his body so swollen and obese that he could no longer lift himself from his couch, his limbs rotting and crawling with fleshworms. The maesters claimed they had never seen its like, whilst

septons declared it a judgment of the gods. Aegon was given milk of the poppy to dull his pain, but elsewise little could be done for him.

His last act before his death, all accounts agree, was to set out his will. And in it, he left the bitterest poison the realm ever knew: he legitimized all of his natural children, from the most baseborn to the Great Bastards—the sons and daughters born to him by women of noble birth. Scores of his natural children had never been acknowledged; Aegon's dying declaration meant naught to them. For his acknowledged bastards, however, it meant a great deal. And for the realm, it meant blood and fire for five generations.

The nine mistresses of Aegon IV, the Unworthy

LADY FALENA STOKEWORTH
Ten years older than the king

Lady Falena "made him a man" in 149, when Aegon was fourteen. When a Kingsguard found them abed together in 151, his father wed Falena to his master-at-arms, Lucas Lothston, and persuaded the king to name Lothston Lord of Harrenhal in order to remove Falena from court. However, over the next two years, Aegon paid frequent visits to Harrenhal.

⌁ Children by Falena Stokeworth: None acknowledged.

MEGETTE (MERRY MEG)
The young and buxom wife of a blacksmith

While riding near Fairmarket in 155, Aegon's horse threw a shoe, and when he sought out the local smith, he came to notice the man's young wife. He went on to buy her for seven gold dragons (and the threat of Ser Joffrey Staunton of the Kingsguard). Megette was installed in a house in King's Landing; she and Aegon were even "wed" in a secret ceremony conducted by a mummer playing a septon. Megette gave her prince four

children in as many years. Prince Viserys put an end to it, returning Megette to her husband and placing the daughters with the Faith to be trained as septas. Megette was beaten to death within a year by the blacksmith.

⌁ Children by Merry Meg: Alysanne, Lily, Willow, Rosey.

LADY CASSELLA VAITH
Daughter of a Dornish lord

After the Submission of Sunspear, Aegon escorted the hostages that the king had gathered from the lords of Dorne back to King's Landing. Among them was Cassella Vaith, a willowy maid with green eyes and pale white-blond hair, whom Aegon ended up keeping "hostage" in his own chambers. When the Dornishmen revolted and murdered King Daeron, all the hostages were to be killed, and Aegon—by then bored of her—returned Cassella to her place with the other prisoners. However, the new king, Baelor, pardoned all the hostages and personally took them back to Dorne. Cassella never wed, and in her old age she was consumed by the delusion that she had been Aegon's one true love and that he would soon send for her.

⌁ Children by Cassella Vaith: None.

BELLEGERE OTHERYS
(THE BLACK PEARL OF BRAAVOS)
Smuggler, trader, sometime pirate, captain of the Widow Wind, *born of a union between a Braavosi merchant's daughter and an envoy from the Summer Isles*

After Naerys fell pregnant and almost died in 161, King Baelor sent Aegon to Braavos on a diplomatic mission. Accounts of the time suggest it was an excuse to make certain Aegon left Naerys alone as she recovered from a failed child-birth. There he met Bellegere Otherys. His affair with the Black Pearl continued for ten years, though it was said that Bellegere had a husband in every port and that Aegon was but one of many. She gave birth to three children during the decade, two girls and a boy of doubtful paternity.

⌁ Children by the Black Pearl: Bellenora, Narha, Balerion.

LADY BARBA BRACKEN
The vivacious dark-haired daughter of Lord Bracken of Stone Hedge, and a companion to the three princesses in Maidenvault

With Baelor's death in 171 and Viserys II's ascension to the throne, the princesses were once again permitted male company. Aegon (now Prince of Dragonstone and heir apparent) became entranced with sixteen-year-old Barba. On his own ascent in 172, he named her father as his Hand and openly took her for his mistress. She bore him a bastard only a fortnight before another set of twins—a stillborn boy and a girl, Daenerys, who survived—

were delivered by Queen Naerys. With the queen lingering near death, the Hand—Barba's father—talked openly of wedding his daughter to the King. After the queen's recovery, the scandal proved Barba's undoing, as young Prince Daeron and his uncle, the Dragonknight, forced Aegon to send her and the bastard away. The boy, raised at Stone Hedge by the Brackens, was called Aegor Rivers, but in time became known as Bittersteel.

⤙ Children by Barba Bracken: Aegor Rivers (Bittersteel).

LADY MELISSA (MISSY) BLACKWOOD
The best loved of the king's mistresses

Both younger and prettier than Lady Barba (albeit far less buxom), as well as more modest, Missy had a kind heart and generous nature that led even Queen Naerys herself—as well as the Dragonknight and Prince Daeron—to befriend her. During the five years of her "reign," Missy bore the king three bastards, most notably the boy Brynden Rivers (born 175), later called Bloodraven.

⤙ Children by Melissa Blackwood: Mya, Gwenys, Brynden (Bloodraven).

LADY BETHANY BRACKEN
Lady Barba's younger sister

Bethany was groomed by her father and sister expressly to win the king's favor and displace Missy Blackwood. In 177, she caught Aegon's eye as he visited at Stone Hedge to see his bastard son, Aegor. By now, the king was fat and foul-tempered, but Bethany delighted him, and he took her back with him to King's Landing. However, Bethany found his royal embraces distressing. For comfort, she turned to a knight of the Kingsguard, Ser Terrence Toyne. The pair was discovered abed by Aegon himself in 178. Ser Terrence was tortured to death and both Lady Bethany and her father were executed. When Ser Terrence's brothers sought to avenge his death, Prince Aemon the Dragonknight was slain while defending his brother, King Aegon.

⤙ Children by Bethany Bracken: None.

LADY JEYNE LOTHSTON
Daughter of Lady Falena, the king's first mistress, by either Lord Lucas Lothston or the king himself

Jeyne was brought to court by her mother in 178, when she was fourteen. Aegon made Lord Lothston his new Hand, and it was said (but never proved) that he enjoyed mother and daughter together in the same bed. He soon gave Jeyne a pox he'd caught from the whores he'd been seeing after Lady Bethany's execution, and the Lothstons were then all sent from court again.

⤙ Children by Jeyne Lothston: None.

SERENEI OF LYS (SWEET SERENEI)
A Lysene beauty from an ancient but impoverished line, brought to court by Lord Jon Hightower, the new Hand

Serenei was the most beautiful of Aegon's mistresses, but she was also reputed to be a sorceress. She died giving birth to the last of the king's bastard children, a girl called Shiera Seastar who became the greatest beauty in the Seven Kingdoms, beloved of both her half brothers, Bittersteel and Bloodraven, whose rivalry would ripen to hatred.

⤙ Children by Serenei: Shiera.

LEFT | (l. to r.): Lady Melissa Blackwood, Serenei of Lys, Lady Falena Stokeworth, Bellegere Otherys

ABOVE | (l. to r.): Lady Bethany Bracken, Lady Barba Bracken, Megette (Merry Meg), Lady Cassella Vaith, Lady Jeyne Lothston

DAERON II

IN THE 184TH year since Aegon's Conquest, Aegon IV, the Unworthy, at last let go of life.

His son and heir, Prince Daeron, departed Dragonstone within the fortnight after learning of his father's demise and was swiftly crowned by the High Septon in the Red Keep. He chose to be crowned with his father's crown—a decision likely intended to quell any remaining doubts about his legitimacy. Daeron then acted swiftly to put right many of the things that Aegon had put wrong, beginning by removing all the members of the king's small council and replacing them with men of his own choosing, most of whom proved wise and capable councillors. It was a year and more before the City Watch was similarly repaired, for King Aegon had often used promotion to the Watch as a way to shower largesse on those he most favored, and they in turn made sure that the brothels—and even the decent women of the city—were available for Aegon's lusts.

Daeron did not stop there, however, in his efforts to improve those things that his father had corrupted or had left to rot through malign neglect. He was conscientious in his duties to the realm and sought to stabilize it in the wake of Aegon's deathbed decree, which legitimized all his bastard half siblings. Although he could not—and would not—rescind his father's last wishes, he did what he could to keep the Great Bastards close, treating them honorably

and continuing the incomes that the king had bestowed on them. He paid the dowry that Aegon had promised to the Archon of Tyrosh, thereby seeing his half brother Daemon Blackfyre wed to Rohanne of Tyrosh as Aegon had desired, for all that Ser Daemon was only four-and-ten. On their wedding day, he granted Daemon a tract of land near the Blackwater, with the right to raise a castle. Some said he did such things to assert his rule and legitimacy over the Great Bastards, and others because he was kind and just. But whatever the truth, such efforts sadly proved in vain.

Yet his realm was not marked solely by the question of the Great Bastards, or even Aegon's misrule. His marriage to Mariah of Dorne—now Queen of the Seven Kingdoms—had been happy and fruitful, and one of his earliest significant acts after assuming the throne was to begin negotiations with his good-brother, Prince Maron, to unify Dorne under Targaryen rule. Two years of negotiation later, an agreement was reached in which Prince Maron agreed to be betrothed to Daeron's sister, Daenerys, once she was of age. They were wed the following year, and with that marriage, Prince Maron knelt and swore his oaths of fealty before the Iron Throne.

King Daeron raised up the Dornish prince to great acclaim, and together they departed the Red Keep and rode to the Great Sept to lay a golden wreath at the foot of the statue of Baelor the Blessed while proclaiming, "Baelor, your work is done." It was a great moment, at last unifying the realm from the Wall to the Summer Sea as Aegon the Conqueror had once dreamed—and doing so without the terrible cost of life that Daeron II's namesake, the Young Dragon, had paid.

In the following year, Daeron raised a great seat in the Dornish Marches, near to where the boundaries of the Reach, the stormlands, and Dorne met. Calling it Summerhall to mark the peace he had created, it was more palace than castle and lightly fortified at best; in the years to come, many sons of House Targaryen would hold the seat as Prince of Summerhall.

However, Prince Maron had won a few concessions in the accord, and the lords of Dorne held significant rights and privileges that the other great houses did not—the right to keep their royal title first among them, but also the autonomy to maintain their own laws, the right to assess and gather the taxes due to the Iron Throne with only irregular oversight from the Red Keep, and other such

It has been said in the years after Daemon Blackfyre proved a traitor that his hatred of Daeron began to grow early. It was Aegon's desire—not Daemon's—that he be wed to Rohanne of Tyrosh. Instead, Daemon had developed a passion for Daeron's sister, young Princess Daenerys. Only two years younger than Daemon, the princess supposedly loved the bastard prince in turn, if the singers can be believed, but neither Aegon IV nor Daeron II were willing to let such feelings rule in matters of state. Aegon saw more profit in a tie to Tyrosh, perhaps because its fleet would be of use if he made another attempt to conquer Dorne.

This seems plausible enough, but a different tale claims that Daemon was not so much opposed to wedding Rohanne of Tyrosh as he was convinced that he could follow in the footsteps of Aegon the Conqueror and Maegor the Cruel and have more than one bride. Aegon might even have promised to indulge him in this (some of Blackfyre's partisans later claimed this was the case) but Daeron was of a different mind entirely. Not only did Daeron refuse to permit his brother more than one wife, but he also gave Daenerys's hand to Maron Martell, as part of the bargain to finally unite the Seven Kingdoms with Dorne.

Whether Daenerys loved Daemon, as those who rose for the Black Dragon later claimed, who could say? In the years afterward, Daenerys was never aught but a loyal wife to Prince Maron, and if she mourned Daemon Blackfyre, she left no record of it.

matters. Dissatisfaction at these concessions was one of the seeds from which the first Blackfyre Rebellion sprang, as was the belief that Dorne held too much influence over the king—for Daeron II brought many Dornishmen to his court, some of whom were granted offices of note.

Still, Daeron's reign quickly stabilized the realm, and he soon came to be called Daeron the Good by the smallfolk and noble lords alike. He was widely seen as just and good-hearted, even if some questioned the influence of his Dornish wife. And though he was no warrior—descriptions of the era note that he was small of frame, with thin arms, round shoulders, and a scholarly disposition—two of his four sons seemed all that could be wished in a knight, lord, or heir. The eldest, Prince Baelor, won the name Breakspear at the age of seventeen, following his famous victory at Princess Daenerys's wedding tourney; he defeated Daemon Blackfyre in the final tilt. And his youngest son, Prince Maekar, seemed like to show a similar prowess.

Yet too many men looked upon Baelor's dark hair and eyes and muttered that he was more Martell than Targaryen, even though he proved a man who could win respect with ease and was as open-handed and just as his father. Knights and lords of the Dornish Marches came to mistrust Daeron, and Baelor as well, and began to look more and more to the old days, when Dornishmen were the enemy to fight, not rivals for the king's attention or largesse. And then they would look at Daemon Blackfyre—grown tall and powerful, half a god among mortal men, and with the Conqueror's sword in his possession—and wonder.

The seeds of rebellion had been planted, but it took years for them to bear fruit. There was no final insult, no great wrong, that led Daemon Blackfyre to turn against King Daeron. If it was truly all for the love of Daenerys, how is it that eight years passed before the rebellion bloomed? That was a long time to harbor thwarted love, especially when Rohanne had already given him seven sons and daughters besides, and Daenerys had also borne Prince Maron several heirs.

In truth, the seeds found fertile ground because of Aegon the Unworthy. Aegon had hated the Dornish and warred against them, and those lords who desired the return of those days—despite all the associated misrule—would never be happy with this peaceable king. Many famed warriors who looked with dismay on the peace in the realm and the Dornish in the king's court began to seek Daemon out.

Perhaps at first, Daemon Blackfyre merely indulged such talk for the sake of his vanity. After all, years had passed between the first men approaching Daemon and the actual rebellion. What, then, tipped Daemon over into proclaiming for the throne? It seems likely it was another of the Great Bastards: Ser Aegor Rivers, called Bittersteel. Perhaps it was his Bracken blood that made Aegor so choleric and so quick to take offense. Perhaps it was the ignominious fall of the Brackens in King Aegon's esteem, leading to his exile from Aegon's court. Or perhaps it was only his rivalry with his half brother and fellow bastard Brynden Rivers, who had been able to maintain his close relations at court—for Bloodraven's mother had been well loved during her life, and was fondly remembered, so the

LEFT | *Daeron II and Prince Maron Martell at the monument to King Baelor.*

Blackwoods did not suffer as the Brackens did when the king cast off his respective mistresses.

Whatever the case may be, Aegor Rivers soon began to press Daemon Blackfyre to proclaim for the throne, and all the more so after Daemon agreed to wed his eldest daughter, Calla, to Aegor. Bitter his steel may have been, but worse was his tongue. He spilled poison in Daemon's ear, and with him came the clamoring of other knights and lords with grievances.

In the end, years of such talk bore their fruit, and Daemon Blackfyre made his decision. Yet it was a decision he made rashly, for word soon reached King Daeron that Blackfyre meant to declare himself king within the turn of the moon. (We do not know how word came to Daeron, though Merion's unfinished *The Red Dragon and the Black* suggests that another of the Great Bastards, Brynden Rivers, was involved.) The king sent the Kingsguard to arrest Daemon before he could take his plans for treason any further. Daemon was forewarned, and with the help of the famously hot-tempered knight Ser Quentyn Ball, called Fireball, he was able to escape the Red Keep safely. Daemon Blackfyre's allies used this attempted arrest as a cause for war, claiming that Daeron had acted against Daemon out of no more than baseless fear. Others still named him Daeron Falseborn, repeating the calumny that Aegon the Unworthy himself was said to have circulated in the later years of his reign: that he had been sired not by the king but by his brother, the Dragonknight.

In this manner did the First Blackfyre Rebellion begin, in the year 196 AC. Reversing the colors of the traditional Targaryen arms to show a black dragon on a red field, the rebels declared for Princess Daena's bastard son Daemon Blackfyre, First of His Name, proclaiming him the eldest true son of King Aegon IV, and his half brother Daeron the bastard. Subsequently many battles were fought between the black and red dragons in the Vale, the westerlands, the riverlands, and elsewhere.

The rebellion ended at the Redgrass Field, nigh on a year later. Some have written of the boldness of the men who fought with Daemon, and others of their treason. But for all their valor in the field and their enmity against Daeron, theirs was a lost cause. Daemon and his eldest sons, Aegon and Aemon, were brought down beneath the withering fall of arrows sent by Brynden Rivers and his private guards, the Raven's Teeth. This was followed by Bittersteel's mad charge, with Blackfyre in his hand, as he attempted to rally Daemon's forces. Meeting with Bloodraven in the midst of the charge, a mighty duel ensued, which left Bloodraven blinded in one eye and sent Bittersteel fleeing.

But the battle came to an end when Prince Baelor Breakspear appeared with a host of stormlords and Dornishmen, falling on the rebel rear, while the young Prince Maekar rallied what remained of Lord Arryn's van and made an implacable anvil against which the rebels were hammered and destroyed. Ten thousand men had died for Daemon Blackfyre's vanity, and many more were wounded and maimed. King Daeron's efforts at peace had been shattered, through no fault of his own save perhaps too much mercy for his envious half brother.

In the aftermath, King Daeron showed a sternness that few expected. Many lords and knights who had supported the Black Dragon had lands and seats and privileges stripped from them and were forced to give over hostages. Daeron had trusted them, had done all he could to rule justly, and still they turned against him. Daemon Blackfyre's surviving sons fled to Tyrosh, their mother's home, and with them went Bittersteel. The realm would continue to be troubled by the claims of the Blackfyre Pretenders for four more generations, until the last of the descendants of Daemon Blackfyre through the male line was sent to the grave.

With his half brothers dealt with and the strength of his sons and heirs supporting him, many thought that King Daeron had now ensured that the realm would be under Targaryen rule for centuries to come. Few could doubt that Baelor Breakspear would be a great king, for he was the heart of chivalry and the soul of wisdom, and came to serve his father most ably as Hand. But no man can know the will of the gods. Baelor Breakspear was cut down in his prime by his own

brother Maekar at the tourney at Ashford in the year 209 AC. It was not in the tilt, or the mêlée, but in a trial of seven—the first in a century—in which Baelor fought on behalf of a lowly hedge knight of no parentage of note. His death was a mishap, almost certainly, and it is written that Prince Maekar always bitterly regretted Baelor's passing and marked its anniversary every year. Yet Baelor died, and doubtless Maekar and the realm wondered if one hedge knight was worth the loss of the Prince of Dragonstone and the Hand of the King. (But then, they did not know how high that hedge knight would rise—though that is a different history.)

Baelor had sons—the young princes Valarr and Matarys—and so too did Maekar, and the king had two other sons besides (though the realm was less certain about Aerys, bookish and obsessed with arcane matters,

and Rhaegel, a sweet boy touched by madness). But then the Great Spring Sickness swept the Seven Kingdoms, affecting all save the Vale and Dorne, where they closed the ports and mountain passes. Worst hit of all was King's Landing. The High Septon, the Seven's voice on earth, died, as did a third of the Most Devout, and nearly all the silent sisters in the city. Corpses were piled in the ruins of the Dragonpit until they stood ten feet high and, in the end, Bloodraven had the pyromancers burn the corpses where they lay. A quarter of the city went up in flames along with them, but there was nothing else to be done.

Worse still, the sons of Baelor Breakspear were amongst those carried away, as was Daeron II, whom many called the Good. He had reigned for five-and-twenty years, and most of those years saw peace and plenty for the realm.

In Essos, Bittersteel gathered exiled lords and knights, and their descendants, to him. He formed the Golden Company in 212 AC, and soon established it as the foremost free company of the Disputed Lands. "Beneath the gold, the bitter steel" became their battle cry, renowned across Essos. After Bittersteel, the company was led by descendants of Daemon Blackfyre until the last of them, Maelys the Monstrous, was slain in the Stepstones.

LEFT | *Bittersteel leading the Golden Company.*
ABOVE | *Daemon Blackfyre leading the charge at the Redgrass Field.*

ASSUMING THE THRONE in 209 AC, Daeron's second son, Aerys, had never imagined he would be king, and was singularly ill suited to sit the Iron Throne. Aerys was learned, in his way, though his interests were largely to do with dusty tomes concerned with ancient prophecy and the higher mysteries. Wed to Aelinor Penrose, he never showed an interest in getting her with child, and rumor had it that he had even failed to consummate the marriage. His small council, at their wits' ends, hoped it was simply some dislike of her that moved him, and thus they urged him to put her aside to take another wife. But he would not hear of it.

Donning the crown during the Great Spring Sickness, Aerys I faced a realm in turmoil from the first. Hardly had the plague begun to ebb when Dagon Greyjoy, Lord of the Iron Islands, sent ironborn ships reaving all up and down the shores of the Sunset Sea, whilst across the narrow sea Bittersteel plotted with the sons of Daemon Blackfyre. Perhaps it was because of these difficulties that Aerys turned to Brynden Rivers to serve as his Hand.

that the Black Dragon must return from across the narrow sea and take his rightful place.

Lord Gormon Peake was at the center of an attempt to bring about a new uprising. For his role in the First Blackfyre Rebellion, Peake had been stripped of two of the three castles his house had held for centuries. After the drought and the Great Spring Sickness, Lord Gormon convinced Daemon Blackfyre's eldest surviving son, Daemon the Younger, to cross the narrow sea and make a play for the throne.

The conspiracy came to a head in 211 AC at the wedding tourney at Whitewalls, the great seat that Lord Butterwell had raised near the Gods Eye. This was the same Butterwell who had once been Daeron's Hand, until the king had dismissed him in favor of Lord Hayford because of his suspicious failure to act successfully against Daemon Blackfyre in the early days of his rebellion. At Whitewalls, under pretense of celebrating Lord Butterwell's marriage and competing in the tournament, many lords and knights had gathered, all of whom shared a desire to place a Blackfyre on the throne.

It has been suggested by some that a likelier cause for Bloodraven's rise to power was the fact that Aerys's interest in arcane lore and ancient history matched that of Rivers, whose studies of the higher mysteries were an open secret at the time. Bloodraven had already risen to prominence at the court, but few expected that Aerys would name him Hand. When he did, it kindled a quarrel between the king and his brother, Prince Maekar, who had expected the Handship to come to him. Thereafter Prince Maekar departed King's Landing for Summerhall for years to come.

Bloodraven proved to be a capable Hand, but also a master of whisperers who rivaled Lady Misery, and there were those who thought he and his half sister and paramour, Shiera Seastar, used sorcery to ferret out secrets. It became common to refer to his "thousand eyes and one," and men both high and low began to distrust their neighbor for fear of their being a spy in Bloodraven's employ. Yet Aerys had need of spies, given the trouble that followed the Great Spring Sickness. Summer came, and with it a drought that lasted more than two years. Many blamed the king, and many more accused Bloodraven. There were poor brothers who preached treason, and knights and lords as well. And amongst those were some who whispered a specific treason:

Were it not for the fact that Bloodraven had informants among the conspirators, Daemon the Younger could have launched a troubling rebellion from within the heart of the riverlands, but even before the tourney had concluded, the Hand turned up

RIGHT | *The arrest of Daemon II Blackfyre.*

That Daemon the Younger dreamed of becoming king is well-known, as is the fact that Bittersteel did not support him in his effort to claim the throne. But why Bittersteel supported the father but refused the son remains a question that is sometimes argued over in the halls of the Citadel. Many will claim that Young Daemon and Lord Gormon could not convince Bittersteel that their plan was sound, and truth be told, it seems a fair argument; Peake was blind to reason in his thirst for revenge and the recovery of his seats, and Daemon was convinced that he would succeed no matter the odds. Yet others suggest that Bittersteel was a hard man who had little use for anything beyond war and mistrusted Daemon's dreams and his love of music and fine things. And others still raise an eyebrow at Daemon's close relationship to the young Lord Cockshaw, and suggest that this would have troubled Aegor Rivers enough to deny the young man his aid.

outside Whitewalls with a host of his own, and the Second Blackfyre Rebellion ended before it could truly be said to have begun. Gormon Peake was among the conspirators executed in the wake of the thwarted rebellion, while others such as Lord Butterwell suffered the loss of land and seats. As for Daemon, he lived on for several more years, a hostage in the Red Keep. Some wondered at his imprisonment, but the wisdom of it was plain: his next eldest brother, Haegon, could not claim the throne if Daemon were still alive.

The Second Blackfyre Rebellion proved a debacle, but that was not always to be the case. In 219 AC, Haegon Blackfyre and Bittersteel launched the Third Blackfyre Rebellion. Of the deeds done then, both good and ill—of the leadership of Maekar, the actions of Aerion Brightflame, the courage of Maekar's youngest son, and the second duel between Bloodraven and Bittersteel—we know well. The pretender Haegon I Blackfyre died in the aftermath of battle, slain treacherously after he had given up his sword, but Ser Aegor Rivers, Bittersteel, was taken alive and returned to the Red Keep in chains. Many still insist that if he had been put to the sword then and there, as Prince Aerion and Bloodraven urged, it might have meant an early end to the Blackfyre ambitions.

But that was not to be. Though Bittersteel was tried and found guilty of high treason, King Aerys spared his life, instead commanding that he be sent to the Wall to live out his days as a man of the Night's Watch. That proved a

foolish mercy, for the Blackfyres still had many friends at court, some of them only too willing to play the informer. The ship carrying Bittersteel and a dozen other captives was taken in the narrow sea on the way to Eastwatch-by-the-Sea, and Aegor Rivers was freed and returned to the Golden Company. Before the year was out, he crowned Haegon's eldest son as King Daemon III Blackfyre in Tyrosh, and resumed his plotting against the king who had spared him.

King Aerys sat the Iron Throne for the better part of two more years, before dying in 221 AC of natural causes.

In the course of that reign, His Grace had recognized a series of heirs, though none were children of his body; Aerys died without issue, his marriage still unconsummated. His brother Rhaegel, third son of Daeron the Good, had predeceased him, choking to death upon a lamprey pie in 215 AC during a feast. Rhaegel's son, Aelor, then became the new Prince of Dragonstone and heir to the throne, only to die two years after, slain in a grotesque mishap by the hand of his own twin sister and wife, Aelora, under circumstances that left her mad with grief. (Sadly, Aelora eventually took her own life after being attacked at a masked ball by three men known to history as the Rat, the Hawk, and the Pig.)

The last of the heirs Aerys recognized before his death would be the one to succeed him to the throne: the king's sole surviving brother, Prince Maekar.

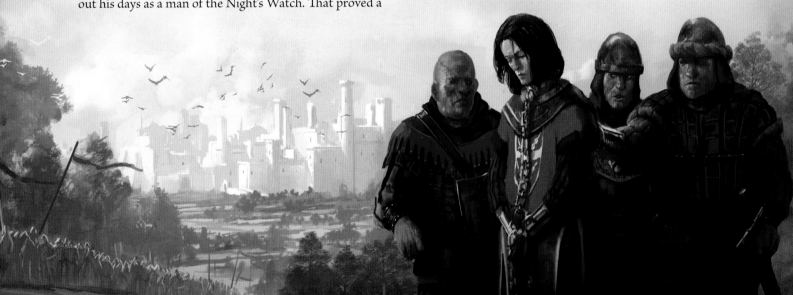

MAEKAR I

MAEKAR WAS AN energetic king and a warrior of note, but also a harsh man, quick to judge and to condemn. He had never possessed his brother Baelor's gifts that made friends and allies come easily, and after his brother's death at his hands—however inadvertent—he became even more stern and unforgiving. Such was his desire to split from the past that he had a new crown made—a warlike crown with black iron points in a band of red gold, since Aegon the Conqueror's crown had been lost after Daeron I's death in Dorne. Yet Maekar ruled in a time of relative peace, between two of the Blackfyre Rebellions, and what turmoil there was in his reign was largely sparked by his own sons.

The chief issue of Maekar's reign was the question of his heirs. He had a number of sons and daughters, but there were those who had reason to doubt their fitness to rule. The eldest, Prince Daeron, was known as the Drunken, and preferred to be styled Prince of Summerhall because he found Dragonstone such a gloomy abode. Next after him was Prince Aerion, known as Brightflame or Brightfire—a most puissant knight but cruel and capricious, and a dabbler in the black arts. Both of these princes died before their father, though both had issue. Prince Daeron sired a daughter, Vaella, in 222 AC, but the girl sadly proved simple. Aerion Brightfire's son was born in 232 AC, and given the ominous name of Maegor by his sire, but the Bright Prince himself died that same year when he drank a cup of wildfire in the belief that it would allow him to transform himself into a dragon.

Maekar's third son, Aemon, was a bookish boy who had been sent to the Citadel in his youth and emerged as a sworn and chained maester. Youngest of the king's sons was Prince Aegon, who had served as squire to a hedge knight—the same hedge knight in whose defense Baelor Breakspear died—whilst a boy, and earned the name "Egg." "Daeron is a jape and Aerion is a fright, but Aegon is more than half a peasant" one court wit was heard to remark.

When King Maekar died in battle in 233 AC, whilst leading his army against a rebellious lord on the Dornish Marches, considerable confusion arose as to the succession.

Rather than risk another Dance of the Dragons, the King's Hand, Bloodraven, elected to call a Great Council to decide the matter.

In 233 AC, hundred of lords great and small assembled in King's Landing. With both of Maekar's elder sons deceased, there were four possible claimants. The Great Council dismissed Prince Daeron's sweet but simple-minded daughter Vaella immediately. Only a few spoke up for Aerion Brightflame's son Maegor; an infant king would have meant a long, contentious regency, and there were also fears that the boy might have inherited his father's cruelty and madness. Prince Aegon was the obvious choice, but some lords distrusted him as well, for his wanderings with his hedge knight had left him "half a peasant," according to many. Enough hated him, in fact, that an effort was made to determine whether his elder brother Maester Aemon might be released from his vows, but Aemon refused, and nothing came of it.

Even as the Great Council was debating, however, another claimant appeared in King's Landing: none other than Aenys Blackfyre, the fifth of the Black Dragon's seven sons. When the Great Council had first been announced, Aenys had written from exile in Tyrosh, putting forward his case in the hope that his words might win him the Iron Throne that his forebears had thrice failed to win with their swords. Bloodraven, the King's Hand, had responded by offering him a safe conduct, so the pretender might come to King's Landing and present his claim in person.

Unwisely, Aenys accepted. Yet hardly had he entered the city when the gold cloaks seized hold of him and dragged him to the Red Keep, where his head was struck off forthwith and presented to the lords of the Great Council, as a warning to any who might still have Blackfyre sympathies.

Soon thereafter, the "Prince Who Was An Egg" was chosen by a majority of the Great Council. The fourth son of a fourth son, Aegon V would become widely known as Aegon the Unlikely for having stood so far out of the succession in his youth.

ABOVE | *The crown of King Maekar I.* RIGHT | *King Aegon the Unlikely (standing at back) and his sons (l. to r.) Duncan, Jaehaerys, and Daeron.*

THE FIRST ACT of Aegon's reign was the arrest of Brynden Rivers, the King's Hand, for the murder of Aenys Blackfyre. Bloodraven did not deny that he had lured the pretender into his power by the offer of a safe conduct, but contended that he had sacrificed his own personal honor for the good of the realm.

Though many agreed, and were pleased to see another Blackfyre pretender removed, King Aegon felt he had no choice but to condemn the Hand, lest the word of the Iron Throne be seen as worthless. Yet after the sentence of death was pronounced, Aegon offered Bloodraven the chance to take the black and join the Night's Watch. This he did. Ser Brynden Rivers set sail for the Wall late in the year of 233 AC. (No one intercepted his ship). Two hundred men went with him, many of them archers from Bloodraven's personal guard, the Raven's Teeth. The king's brother, Maester Aemon, was also amongst them.

long winter that reigned from 130 to 135 AC. King Aegon, always concerned for the welfare of the poor and weak, did what he could to increase the flow of grain and other food to the North, but some felt he did too much in this regard.

His rule was also quickly tested by those whose affairs he had meddled in too often as a prince, attempting to reduce their rights and privileges. Nor had the Blackfyre threat ended with the death of Aenys Blackfyre; Bloodraven's infamous betrayal had only hardened the enmity of the exiles across the narrow sea. In 236 AC, as a cruel six-year-long winter drew to a close, the Fourth Blackfyre Rebellion saw the self-styled King Daemon III Blackfyre, son of Haegon and grandson of Daemon I, cross the narrow sea with Bittersteel and the Golden Company at his back, in a fresh attempt to seize the Iron Throne.

The invaders landed on Massey's Hook, south of Blackwater Bay, but few rallied to their banners. King Aegon V

Bloodraven would rise to become Lord Commander of the Night's Watch in 239 AC, serving until his disappearance during a ranging beyond the Wall in 252 AC.

Aegon's reign was a challenging one, starting as it did in the midst of a winter that had lasted three years and showed no signs of abating. There was starvation and suffering in the North, as there had been a hundred years before, in the

himself rode out to meet them, with his three sons by his side. In the Battle of Wendwater Bridge, the Blackfyres suffered a shattering defeat, and Daemon III was slain by the Kingsguard knight Ser Duncan the Tall, the hedge

knight for whom "Egg" had served as a squire. Bittersteel eluded capture and escaped once again, only to emerge a few years later in the Disputed Lands, fighting with his sellswords in a meaningful skirmish between Tyrosh and Myr. Ser Aegor Rivers was sixty-nine years of age when he fell, and it is said he died as he had lived, with a sword in his hand and defiance upon his lips. Yet his legacy would live on in the Golden Company and the Blackfyre line he had served and protected.

There were other battles during the time of Aegon V, for the unlikely king was forced to spend much of his reign in armor, quelling one rising or another. Though beloved by the smallfolk, King Aegon made many enemies amongst the lords of the realm, whose powers he wished to curtail. He enacted numerous reforms and granted rights and protections to the commons that they had never known before, but each of these measures provoked fierce opposition and sometimes open defiance amongst the lords. The most outspoken of his foes went so far as to denounce Aegon V as a "bloody-handed tyrant intent on depriving us of our gods-given rights and liberties."

It was well-known that the resistance against him taxed Aegon's patience—especially as the compromises a king must make to rule well often left his greatest hopes receding further and further into the future. As one defiance followed another, His Grace found himself forced to bow to the recalcitrant lords more often than he wished. A student of history and lover of books, Aegon V was oft heard to say that had he only had dragons, as the first Aegon had, he could have remade the realm anew, with peace and prosperity and justice for all.

Even his sons proved a trial to this good-hearted king, when they might have been a strength. Aegon V had married for love, taking to wife the Lady Betha Blackwood, the spirited (some say willful) daughter of the Lord of Raventree Hall, who became known as Black Betha for her dark eyes and raven hair. When they wed, in 220 AC, the bride was nineteen and Aegon twenty, so far down in the line of succession that the match provoked no opposition. In the years that followed, Black Betha gave Aegon three sons (Duncan, Jaehaerys, and Daeron) and two daughters (Shaera and Rhaelle).

It had long been the custom of House Targaryen to wed brother to sister to keep the blood of the dragon pure, but for whatever cause, Aegon V had become convinced that such incestuous unions did more harm than good. Instead he resolved to join his children in marriage with the sons and daughters of some of the greatest lords of the Seven Kingdoms, in the hopes of winning their support for his reforms and strengthening his rule.

With the help of Black Betha, a number of advantageous betrothals were made and celebrated in 237 AC whilst Aegon's children were still young. Had the marriages taken place, much good might have come of them . . . but His Grace had failed to account for the willfulness of his own blood. Betha Blackwood's children proved to be as stubborn as their mother, and like their father, chose to follow their hearts when choosing mates.

Aegon's eldest son Duncan, Prince of Dragonstone and heir to the throne, was the first to defy him. Though betrothed to a daughter of House Baratheon of Storm's End, Duncan became enamored of a strange, lovely, and mysterious girl who called herself Jenny of Oldstones in 239 AC, whilst traveling in the riverlands. Though she dwelt half-wild amidst ruins and claimed descent from the long-vanished kings of the First Men, the smallfolk of surrounding villages mocked such tales, insisting that she was only some half-mad peasant girl, and perhaps even a witch.

It was true that Aegon had been a friend to the smallfolk, had practically grown up among them, but to countenance the marriage of the heir to the throne to a commoner of uncertain birth was beyond him. His Grace did all he could to have the marriage undone, demanding that Duncan put Jenny aside. The prince shared his father's stubbornness, however, and refused him. Even when the High Septon, Grand Maester, and small council joined together to insist King Aegon force his son to choose between the Iron Throne and this wild woman of the woods, Duncan would not budge. Rather than give up Jenny, he foreswore his claim to the crown in favor of his brother Jaehaerys, and abdicated as Prince of Dragonstone.

Even that could not restore the peace, nor win back the friendship of Storm's End, however. The father of the spurned girl, Lord Lyonel Baratheon of Storm's End—known as the Laughing Storm and famed for his prowess in battle—was not a man easily appeased when his pride was wounded. A short, bloody rebellion ensued, ending only when Ser Duncan of the Kingsguard defeated Lord Lyonel in single combat, and King Aegon gave his solemn word that his youngest daughter, Rhaelle, would wed Lord Lyonel's heir. To seal the bargain, Princess Rhaelle was sent to Storm's End to serve as Lord Lyonel's cupbearer and companion to his lady wife. Jenny of Oldstones—Lady Jenny, as she was called by courtesy—was eventually accepted at court, and throughout the Seven Kingdoms the smallfolk held her especially dear. She and her prince, forever after known as the Prince of Dragonflies, were a favorite subject of singers for many years.

Next was Prince Jaehaerys, now Prince of Dragonstone. Though King Aegon had acquired a distaste for the Valyrian custom of incestuous marriage during his years amongst the smallfolk, Prince Jaehaerys was of a more traditional bent, for from a very early age he had loved his sister Shaera and dreamed of wedding her in the old Targaryen fashion. Once aware of his desires, King Aegon and Queen Betha had done their best to separate the two, yet somehow distance only seemed to inflame the mutual passion of this prince and princess.

Prince Jaehaerys was not as forceful as his brother, but when Duncan defied his father to follow his own heart, and the king and court yielded to his desire, the younger prince did not fail to take note. In 240 AC, a year after Prince Duncan's marriage, Prince Jaehaerys and Princess Shaera each eluded their guardians and were secretly married. Jaehaerys was fifteen and Shaera fourteen at the time of their wedding. By the time the king and queen learned what had happened, the marriage had already been consummated. Aegon felt he had no choice but to accept it. Once again the king had to deal with the wounded pride and anger of the noble houses thus affronted, for Jaehaerys had been betrothed to Celia Tully, daughter of the Lord of Riverrun, and Shaera to Luthor Tyrell, the heir to Highgarden.

for Daeron remained unwed throughout the remainder of his short life. A born soldier who rejoiced in tournament and battle, he preferred the companionship of Ser Jeremy Norridge, a dashing young knight who had been with the prince since the two of them were squires together at Highgarden. Prince Daeron brought to his father, Aegon, an altogether deeper sort of grief when he was killed in battle in 251 AC, leading an army against the Rat, the Hawk, and the Pig. Ser Jeremy died at his side, but the rebellion was quashed, and the rebels slain or hanged.

In 258 AC on Essos, another challenge rose to Aegon's reign, when nine outlaws, exiles, pirates, and sellsword captains met in the Disputed Lands beneath the Tree of Crowns to form an unholy alliance. The Band of Nine swore their oath of mutual aid and support in carving out kingdoms for each of their members. Amongst them was the last Blackfyre, Maelys the Monstrous, who had command of the Golden Company, and the kingdom they pledged to win for him was the Seven Kingdoms. Prince Duncan, when told of the pact, famously remarked that crowns were being sold nine a penny; thereafter the Band of Nine became known as the Ninepenny Kings in Westeros. It was thought at first that the Free Cities of Essos would surely bring their power against them and put an end to their pretensions, but nonetheless preparations were made, should Maelys and his allies turn on the Seven Kingdoms. But there was no great urgency to them, and King Aegon remained intent on his reign.

Corrupted by the example of his brothers, even King Aegon's youngest son Prince Daeron vexed his father in like manner. Though betrothed to Lady Olenna Redwyne of the Arbor when both of them were nine, Prince Daeron repudiated the match in 246 AC, when he was eighteen . . . though in his case, there appears to have been no other woman,

And intent on one more thing: dragons. As he grew older, Aegon V had come to dream of dragons flying once more above the Seven Kingdoms of Westeros. In this, he was not unlike his predecessors, who brought septons to pray over the last eggs, mages to work spells over them, and maesters to pore over them. Though friends and counselors sought to dissuade him, King Aegon grew ever more convinced that only with dragons would he ever wield sufficient power to make the changes he wished to make in the realm and force the proud and stubborn lords of the Seven Kingdoms to accept his decrees.

The last years of Aegon's reign were consumed by a search for ancient lore about the dragon breeding of Valyria, and it was said that Aegon commissioned journeys to places as far away as Asshai-by-the-Shadow with the hopes of finding texts and knowledge that had not been preserved in Westeros.

What became of the dream of dragons was a grievous tragedy born in a moment of joy. In the fateful year 259 AC, the king summoned many of those closest to him to Summerhall, his favorite castle, there to celebrate the impending birth of his first great-grandchild, a boy later named Rhaegar, to his grandson Aerys and granddaughter Rhaella, the children of Prince Jaehaerys.

It is unfortunate that the tragedy that transpired at Summerhall left very few witnesses alive, and those who survived would not speak of it. A tantalizing page of Gyldayn's history—surely one of the very last written before his own death—hints at much, but the ink that was spilled over it in some mishap blotted out too much.

FROM THE HISTORY OF ARCHMAESTER GYLDAYN

. . . the blood of the dragon gathered in one . . .

. . . seven eggs, to honor the seven gods, though the king's own septon had warned . . .

. . . pyromancers . . .

. . . wild fire . . .

. . . flames grew out of control . . . towering . . . burned so hot that . . .

. . . died, but for the valor of the Lord Comman . . .

THE TRAGEDY OF Summerhall brought Jaehaerys, the Second of His Name, to the Iron Throne in 259 AC. Scarcely had he donned the crown than the Seven Kingdoms found themselves plunged into war, for the Ninepenny Kings had taken and sacked the Free City of Tyrosh and seized the Stepstones; from there, they stood poised to attack Westeros.

them rather than awaiting their landing on the shores of the Seven Kingdoms.

King Jaehaerys had intended to lead the attack upon the Ninepenny Kings himself, but his Hand, Lord Ormund Baratheon, persuaded him that would be unwise. The king was unused to the rigors of campaign and not skilled in arms, the Hand pointed out, and it would be folly to risk

---

THE NAMES AND STYLES OF THE BAND OF NINE, WHO CAUSED GREAT TURMOIL IN ESSOS AND THE STEPSTONES

THE OLD MOTHER: A pirate queen.

SAMARRO SAAN, THE LAST VALYRIAN: A notorious pirate from a notorious family of pirates from Lys, with the blood of Valyria in his veins.

XHOBAR QHOQUA, THE EBON PRINCE: An exile prince from the Summer Isle, he had found his fortunes in the Disputed Lands and led a sellsword company.

LIOMOND LASHARE, THE LORD OF BATTLES: A famed sellsword captain.

SPOTTED TOM THE BUTCHER: Hailing from Westeros, he was captain of a free company in the Disputed Lands.

SER DERRICK FOSSOWAY, THE BAD APPLE: An exile from Westeros, and a knight with a black reputation.

NINE EYES: Captain of the *Jolly Fellows*.

ALEQUO ADARYS, THE SILVERTONGUE: A Tyroshi merchant prince who was wealthy and ambitious.

MAELYS BLACKFYRE, THE MONSTROUS: Captain of the Golden Company, named for his grotesquely huge torso and arms, fearsome strength, and savage nature. A second head grew from his neck, no bigger than a fist. He won command of the Golden Company by fighting his cousin, Daemon Blackfyre, for it, killing his cousin's destrier with a single punch and then twisting Daemon's head until it was torn from his shoulders.

Jaehaerys had known that the Band of Nine meant to win the Seven Kingdoms for Maelys the Monstrous, who had declared himself King Maelys I Blackfyre, but like his father, Aegon, Jaehaerys had hoped the alliance of rogues would founder in Essos, or fall at the hands of some alliance amongst the Free Cities. Now the moment was at hand, and King Aegon V was gone, as was the Prince of Dragonflies. Prince Daeron, that splendid knight, had died years before, leaving only Jaehaerys, the least martial of Aegon's three sons.

The new king was four-and-thirty years of age as he ascended the Iron Throne. No one would have called him formidable. Unlike his brothers, Jaehaerys II Targaryen was thin and scrawny, and had battled various ailments all his life. Yet he did not lack for courage, or intelligence. Drawing on his father's plans, His Grace put aside his grief, called his lords bannermen, and resolved to meet the Ninepenny Kings upon the Stepstones, choosing to take the war to

losing him in battle so soon after the tragedy of Summerhall. Jaehaerys finally allowed himself to be persuaded to remain at King's Landing with his queen. Command of the host was given to Lord Ormund, as King's Hand.

In 260 AC, his lordship landed Targaryen armies upon three of the Stepstones, and the War of the Ninepenny Kings turned bloody. Battle raged across the islands and the channels between for most of that year. Maester Eon's *Account of the War of the Ninepenny Kings*, one of the finest works of its kind, is a splendid source for the details of the fighting, with its many battles on land and sea and notable feats of arms. Lord Ormund Baratheon, the Westerosi commander, was amongst the first to perish. Cut down by the hand of Maelys the Monstrous, he died in the arms of his son and heir, Steffon Baratheon.

Command of the Targaryen host passed to the new young Lord Commander of the Kingsguard, Ser Gerold

LEFT | *The destruction of Summerhall.*

Hightower, the White Bull. Hightower and his men were hard-pressed for a time, but as the war hung in the balance, a young knight named Ser Barristan Selmy slew Maelys in single combat, winning undying renown and deciding the issue in a stroke, for the remainder of the Ninepenny Kings had little or no interest in Westeros and soon fell back to their own domains. Maelys the Monstrous was the fifth and last of the Blackfyre Pretenders; with his death, the curse that Aegon the Unworthy had inflicted on the Seven Kingdoms by giving his sword to his bastard son was finally ended.

Half a year of hard fighting remained before the Stepstones and the Disputed Lands were freed from the remaining Band of Nine, and it would be six years before Alequo Adarys, the Tyrant of Tyrosh, was poisoned by his queen and the Archon of Tyrosh was restored. For the Seven Kingdoms, it had been a grand victory, though not without cost in lives or suffering.

The realm thereafter returned to peace. Though never strong, Jaehaerys II proved to be a capable king, restoring order to the Seven Kingdoms and reconciling many of the great houses who had grown unhappy with the Iron Throne because of King Aegon V's attempted reforms. But his reign proved to be a short one. In 262 AC, King Jaehaerys II sickened and died abed after a short illness, complaining of a sudden shortness of breath. He was but thirty-seven years of age at his passing, and had sat the Iron Throne for scarce three years.

AERYS TARGARYEN, the Second of His Name, was but eighteen years of age when he ascended the Iron Throne in 262 AC, upon the death of his father, Jaehaerys, after little more than three years of rule. A handsome youth, Aerys had fought gallantly in the Stepstones during the War of the Ninepenny Kings. Though not the most diligent of princes, nor the most intelligent, he had an undeniable charm that won him many friends. He was also vain, proud, and changeable, traits that made him easy prey for flatterers and lickspittles, but these flaws were not immediately apparent to most at the time of his ascension.

Not even the wisest could have known that Aerys II would in time be known as the Mad King, nor that his reign would ultimately put an end to near three centuries of Targaryen rule in Westeros. Yet even as Aerys donned his crown, in that fateful year of 262 AC, a lusty black-haired son named Robert had just been born to his cousin Steffon Baratheon and his lady wife at Storm's End, whilst far to the north at Winterfell, Lord Rickard Stark celebrated the birth of his own son, Brandon. Another Stark, Eddard, followed within a year. All three of these infants, would, in the fullness of time, play crucial roles in the downfall of the dragons.

The new king had already provided the realm with an heir in the person of his son Rhaegar, born amongst the flames of Summerhall. Aerys and his queen, his sister Rhaella, were young, and it was anticipated that they would have many more children. This was a vital question at the time, for the tragedies of Aegon the Unlikely's reign had trimmed the noble tree of House Targaryen down to just a pair of lonely branches.

Aerys II did not lack for ambition. Upon his coronation, he declared that it was his wish to be the greatest king in the history of the Seven Kingdoms, a conceit certain of his friends encouraged by suggesting that one day he might be remembered as Aerys the Wise or even Aerys the Great.

His father's court had been made up largely of older, seasoned men, many of whom had also served during the reign of King Aegon V. Aerys II dismissed them one and all, replacing them with lords of his own generation. Most notably, he retired the aged and exceedingly cautious Hand, Edgar Sloane, and named in his place Ser Tywin Lannister, the heir to Casterly Rock. At twenty years of age, Ser Tywin thus became the youngest Hand in the history of the Seven Kingdoms. Many maesters to this day insist that his appointment was the wisest thing that "Aerys the Wise" ever did.

Aerys and Tywin had known each other since childhood. As a boy, Tywin Lannister had served as a royal page at King's Landing. He and Prince Aerys, together with a younger page, the prince's cousin Steffon Baratheon of Storm's End, had become inseparable. During the War of the Ninepenny Kings, the three friends had fought together, Tywin as a new-made knight, Steffon and Prince Aerys as squires. When Prince Aerys won his spurs at six-and-ten, it was to Ser Tywin he granted the signal honor of dubbing him a knight. In 261 AC, Tywin Lannister had proved his prowess as a commander when he put down an uprising by two of his father's most powerful vassals, the Lords Tarbeck and Reyne, extinguishing both of their ancient houses in the process. Though the brutality of his methods drew censure from some, none could dispute that Ser Tywin restored order to the westerlands after the chaos and conflict of his father's rule.

Aerys Targaryen and Tywin Lannister made for an unlikely partnership, it must be said. The young king was lively and active in the early years of his reign. He loved music, dancing, and masked balls, and was exceedingly fond of young women, filling his court with fair maidens from every corner of the realm. Some say he had as many mistresses as his ancestor Aegon the Unworthy (a most unlikely assertion given all we know of that monarch). Unlike Aegon IV, however, Aerys II always seemed to lose interest in his lovers quickly. Many lasted no longer than a fortnight and few as long as half a year.

His Grace was full of grand schemes as well. Not long after his coronation, he announced his intent to conquer the Stepstones and make them a part of his realm for all time. In 264 AC, a visit to King's Landing by Lord Rickard Stark of Winterfell awakened his interest in the North, and he hatched a plan to build a new Wall a hundred leagues north of the existing one and claim all the lands between. In 265 AC, offended by "the stink of King's Landing," he spoke of building a "white city" entirely of marble on the south bank of the Blackwater Rush. In 267 AC, after a dispute with the Iron Bank of Braavos regarding certain monies borrowed by his father, he announced that he would build the largest war fleet in the history of the world "to bring the Titan to

LEFT | *Ser Barristan Selmy and Maelys the Monstrous locked in combat.*

his knees." In 270 AC, during a visit to Sunspear, he told the Princess of Dorne that he would "make the Dornish deserts bloom" by digging a great underground canal beneath the mountains to bring water down from the rainwood.

None of these grandiose plans ever came to fruition; most, indeed, were forgotten within a moon's turn, for Aerys II seemed to grow bored with his royal enthusiasms as quickly as he did his royal paramours. And yet the Seven Kingdoms prospered greatly during the first decade of his reign, for the King's Hand was all that the king himself was not—diligent, decisive, tireless, fiercely intelligent, just, and stern. "The gods made and shaped this man to rule," Grand Maester Pycelle wrote of Tywin Lannister in a letter to the Citadel after serving with him on the small council for two years.

And rule he did. As the king's own behavior grew increasingly erratic, more and more the day-to-day running of the realm fell to his Hand. The realm prospered under Tywin Lannister's stewardship—so much so that King Aerys's endless caprices did not seem so portentous. Many Targaryens before him had exhibited similar behavior without great cause for concern. From Oldtown to the Wall, men began to say that Aerys might wear the crown, but it was Tywin Lannister who ruled the realm.

It was Tywin Lannister who settled the crown's dispute with the Braavosi (though without "making the Titan kneel," to the king's displeasure), by repaying the monies lent to Jaehaerys II with gold from Casterly Rock, thereby taking the debts upon himself. Tywin won the approbation of many great lords by repealing what remained of the laws Aegon V had enacted to curb their powers. Tywin reduced tariffs and taxes on shipping going in and out of the cities of King's Landing, Lannisport, and Oldtown, winning the support of many wealthy merchants. Tywin built new roads and repaired old ones, held many splendid tournaments about the realm to the delight of knights and commons both, cultivated trade with the Free Cities, and sternly punished bakers found guilty of adding sawdust to their bread and butchers selling horsemeat as beef. In all these efforts he was greatly aided by Grand Maester Pycelle, whose accounts of the reign of Aerys II give us our best portrait of these times.

Yet despite these accomplishments, Tywin Lannister was little loved. His rivals charged that he was humorless, unforgiving, unbending, proud, and cruel. His lords bannermen respected him and followed him loyally in war and peace, but none could truly be named his friends. Tywin despised his father, the weak-willed, fat, and ineffectual

ABOVE | *King Aerys, the Second of His Name.*

Lord Tytos Lannister, and his relations with his brothers Tygett and Gerion were notoriously stormy. He showed more regard for his brother Kevan, a close confidant and constant companion since childhood, and his sister Genna, but yet even in those cases, Tywin Lannister appeared more dutiful than affectionate.

In 263 AC, after a year as the King's Hand, Ser Tywin married his beautiful young cousin Joanna Lannister, who had come to King's Landing in 259 AC for the coronation of King Jaehaerys II and remained thereafter as a lady-in-waiting to Princess (later Queen) Rhaella. The bride and groom had known each other since they were children together at Casterly Rock. Though Tywin Lannister was not a man given to public display, it is said that his love for his lady wife was deep and long-abiding. "Only Lady Joanna truly knows the man beneath the armor," Grand Maester Pycelle wrote the Citadel, "and all his smiles belong to her and her alone. I do avow that I have even observed her make him laugh, not once, but upon three separate occasions!"

Sadly, the marriage between Aerys II Targaryen and his sister, Rhaella, was not as happy; though she turned a

to him. "The gods will not suffer a bastard to sit the Iron Throne," he told his small council; none of Rhaella's stillbirths, miscarriages, or dead princes had been his, the king proclaimed. Thereafter, he forbade the queen to leave the confines of Maegor's Holdfast and decreed that two septas would henceforth share her bed every night, "to see that she remains true to her vows."

What Tywin Lannister made of this is not recorded, but in 266 AC, at Casterly Rock, Lady Joanna gave birth to a pair of twins, a girl and a boy, "healthy and beautiful, with hair like beaten gold." This birth only exacerbated the tension between Aerys II Targaryen and his Hand. "I appear to have married the wrong woman," His Grace was reported to have said, when informed of the happy event. Nonetheless, he sent each child its weight in gold as a nameday gift and commanded Tywin to bring them to court when they were old enough to travel. "And bring their mother, too, for it has been too long since I gazed upon that fair face," he insisted.

The following year, 267 AC, saw the death of Lord Tytos Lannister at the age of six-and-forty. Reportedly, his lordship's heart burst as he was climbing a steep turnpike

---

The scurrilous rumor that Joanna Lannister gave up her maidenhead to Prince Aerys the night of his father's coronation and enjoyed a brief reign as his paramour after he ascended the Iron Throne can safely be discounted. As Pycelle insists in his letters, Tywin Lannister would scarce have taken his cousin to wife if that had been true, "for he was ever a proud man and not one accustomed to feasting upon another man's leavings."

It has been reliably reported, however, that King Aerys took unwonted liberties with Lady Joanna's person during her bedding ceremony, to Tywin's displeasure. Not long thereafter, Queen Rhaella dismissed Joanna Lannister from her service. No reason for this was ever given, but Lady Joanna departed at once for Casterly Rock and seldom visited King's Landing thereafter.

---

blind eye to most of the king's infidelities, the queen did not approve of his "turning my ladies into his whores." (Joanna Lannister was not the first lady to be dismissed abruptly from Her Grace's service, nor was she the last). Relations between the king and queen grew even more strained when Rhaella proved unable to give Aerys any further children. Miscarriages in 263 and 264 were followed by a stillborn daughter born in 267. Prince Daeron, born in 269, survived for only half a year. Then came another stillbirth in 270, another miscarriage in 271, and Prince Aegon, born two turns premature in 272, dead in 273.

At first His Grace comforted Rhaella in her grief, but over time his compassion turned to suspicion. By 270 AC, he had decided that the queen was being unfaithful

stair to the bedchambers of his mistress. With his passing, Ser Tywin Lannister became the Lord of Casterly Rock and Warden of the West. When he returned to the west to attend his father's funeral and set the westerlands in order, King Aerys decided to accompany him. Though His Grace left the queen behind in King's Landing (Her Grace was pregnant with the child who proved to be the stillborn Princess Shaena), he took their eight-year-old son Rhaegar, Prince of Dragonstone, and more than half the court. For the better part of the next year, the Seven Kingdoms were ruled from Lannisport and Casterly Rock, where both the king and his Hand were in residence.

The court returned to King's Landing in 268 AC, and governance resumed as before . . . but it was plain to all that the friendship between the king and his Hand was fraying. Where previously Aerys had sided with Tywin Lannister on most matters of substance, now the two men began to disagree. During a trade war between the Free Cities of Myr and Tyrosh on the one hand and Volantis on the other, Lord Tywin advocated a policy of neutrality; King Aerys saw more advantage in providing gold and arms to the Volantenes. When Lord Tywin adjudicated a border dispute between House Blackwood and House Bracken in favor of the Blackwoods, His Grace overruled him and gave the disputed mill to Lord Bracken.

Over his Hand's strenuous objections, the king doubled the port fees at King's Landing and Oldtown, and tripled them for Lannisport and the realm's other ports and harbors. When a delegation of small lords and rich merchants came before the Iron Throne to complain, however, Aerys blamed the Hand for the exactions, saying, "Lord Tywin shits gold, but of late he has been constipated and had to find some other way to fill our coffers." Whereupon His Grace restored port fees and tariffs to their previous levels, earning much acclaim for himself and leaving Tywin Lannister the opprobrium.

The growing rift between the king and the King's Hand was also apparent in the matter of appointments. Whereas previously His Grace had always heeded his Hand's counsel, bestowing offices, honors, and inheritances as Lord Tywin recommended, after 270 AC he began to disregard the men put forward by his lordship in favor of his own choices. Many westermen found themselves dismissed from the king's service for no better cause than the suspicion that they might be "Hand's men." In their places, King Aerys appointed his own favorites . . . but the king's favor had become a chancy thing, his mistrust easy to awaken. Even the Hand's own kin were not exempt from royal displeasure. When Lord Tywin wished to name his brother Ser Tygett Lannister as the Red Keep's master-at-arms, King Aerys gave the post to Ser Willem Darry instead.

By this time, King Aerys had become aware of the widespread belief that he himself was but a hollow figurehead and Tywin Lannister the true master of the Seven Kingdoms. These sentiments greatly angered the king, and His Grace became determined to disprove them and to humble his "overmighty servant" and "put him back into his place."

At the great Anniversary Tourney of 272 AC, held to commemorate Aerys's tenth year upon the Iron Throne, Joanna Lannister brought her six-year-old twins Jaime and Cersei from Casterly Rock to present before the court. The king (very much in his cups) asked her if giving suck to them had "ruined your breasts, which were so high and proud." The question greatly amused Lord Tywin's rivals, who were always pleased to see the Hand slighted or made mock of, but Lady Joanna was humiliated. Tywin Lannister attempted to return his chain of office the next morning, but the king refused to accept his resignation.

Aerys II could, of course, have dismissed Tywin Lannister at any time and named his own man as Hand of the King, but instead, for whatever reason, the king chose to keep his boyhood friend close by him, laboring on his behalf, even as he began to undermine him in ways both great and small. Slights and gibes became ever more numerous; courtiers hoping for advancement soon learned that the quickest way to catch the king's eye was by making mock of his solemn, humorless Hand. Yet through all this, Tywin Lannister suffered in silence.

In 273 AC, however, Lady Joanna was taken to childbed once again at Casterly Rock, where she died delivering Lord Tywin's second son. Tyrion, as the babe was named, was a malformed, dwarfish babe born with stunted legs, an oversized head, and mismatched, demonic eyes (some reports also suggested he had a tail, which was lopped off at his lord father's command). Lord Tywin's Doom, the smallfolk called this ill-made creature, and Lord Tywin's Bane. Upon hearing of his birth, King Aerys infamously said, "The gods cannot abide such arrogance. They have plucked a fair flower from his hand and given him a monster in her place, to teach him some humility at last."

It was not long before reports of the king's remarks reached Lord Tywin as he grieved at Casterly Rock. Thereafter, no shred of the old affection between the two men endured. Never a man to make a show of his emotion, Lord Tywin continued on as Hand of the King, dealing with the daily tedium of the Seven Kingdoms, while the king grew ever more erratic, violent, and suspicious. Aerys began to surround himself with informers, paying handsome rewards to men of dubious repute for whispers, lies, and tales of treasons, real and imagined. When one such reported that the captain of the Hand's personal guard, a knight named Ser Ilyn Payne, had been heard boasting it was Lord Tywin who truly ruled the Seven Kingdoms, His Grace sent the Kingsguard to arrest the man and had his tongue ripped out with red-hot pincers.

The march of the king's madness seemed to abate for a time in 274 AC, when Queen Rhaella gave birth to a son. So profound was His Grace's joy that it seemed to restore him to his old self once again . . . but Prince Jaehaerys died later that same year, plunging Aerys into despair. In his black rage, he decided the babe's wet nurse was to blame and had the woman beheaded. Not long after, in a change of heart, Aerys announced that Jaehaerys had been poisoned by his own mistress, the pretty young daughter of one of his household knights. The king had the girl and all her kin tortured to death. During the course of their torment, it is recorded, all confessed to the murder, though the details of their confessions were greatly at odds.

Afterward, King Aerys fasted for a fortnight and made a walk of repentance across the city to the Great Sept, to pray with the High Septon. On his return, His Grace announced that henceforth he would sleep only with his lawful wife, Queen Rhaella. If the chronicles can be believed, Aerys remained true to this vow, losing all interest in the charms of women from that day in 275 AC.

His Grace's new fidelity was apparently pleasing to the Mother Above, it must be said, for the following year, Queen Rhaella gave the king the second son that he had prayed for. Prince Viserys, born in 276 AC, was small but robust, and as beautiful a child as King's Landing had ever seen. Though Prince Rhaegar at seventeen was everything that could be wanted in an heir apparent, all Westeros rejoiced to know that at last he had a brother, another Targaryen to secure the succession.

The birth of Prince Viserys only seemed to make Aerys II more fearful and obsessive, however. Though the new young princeling seemed healthy enough, the king was terrified lest he suffer the same fate as his brothers. Kingsguard knights were commanded to stand over him night and day to see that no one touched the boy without the king's leave. Even the queen herself was forbidden to be alone with the infant. When her milk dried up, Aerys insisted on having his own food taster suckle at the teats of the prince's wet nurse, to ascertain that the woman had not smeared poison on her nipples. As gifts for the young prince arrived from all the lords of the Seven Kingdoms, the king had them piled in the yard and burned, for fear that some of them might have been ensorcelled or cursed.

Later that same year, Lord Tywin Lannister, perhaps unwisely, held a great tournament at Lannisport in honor of Viserys's birth. Mayhaps it was meant to be a gesture toward reconciliation. There the wealth and power of House Lannister was displayed for all the realm to see. King Aerys at first refused to attend, then relented, but the queen and her new son were kept under confinement back at King's Landing.

There, seated on his throne amongst hundreds of notables in the shadow of Casterly Rock, the king cheered lustily as his son Prince Rhaegar, newly knighted, unhorsed both Tygett and Gerion Lannister, and even overcame the gallant Ser Barristan Selmy, before falling in the champion's tilt to the renowned Kingsguard knight Ser Arthur Dayne, the Sword of the Morning.

Perhaps seeking to gain advantage of His Grace's high spirits, Lord Tywin chose that very night to suggest that it was past time the king's heir wed and produced an heir of his own; he proposed his own daughter, Cersei, as wife for the crown prince. Aerys II rejected this proposal brusquely, informing Lord Tywin that he was a good and valuable servant, yet a servant nonetheless. Nor did His Grace agree to appoint Lord Tywin's son Jaime as squire to Prince Rhaegar; that honor he granted instead to the sons of several of his own favorites, men known to be no friends of House Lannister or the Hand.

By this time it was plain to see that Aerys II Targaryen was already sliding rapidly into madness, but it was in the year 277 AC that His Grace plunged irrevocably into the abyss, with the Defiance of Duskendale.

The ancient harbor town of Duskendale had been a seat of kings of old, in the days of the Hundred Kingdoms. Once the most important port on Blackwater Bay, the town had seen its trade dwindle and its wealth shrink as King's Landing grew and burgeoned, a decline that its young lord, Denys Darklyn, wished to halt. Many have long debated why Lord Darklyn chose to do what he did, but most agree that his Myrish wife, the Lady Serala, played some part. Her detractors blame her entirely for what transpired; the Lace Serpent, as they name her, poisoned Lord Darklyn against his king with her pillow talk. Her defenders insist that the folly lay with Lord Denys himself; his wife is hated simply because she was a woman of foreign birth who prayed to gods alien to Westeros.

It was Lord Denys's desire to win a charter for Duskendale that would give it more autonomy from the crown, much as had been done for Dorne many years before, that began the trouble. This did not seem to him such a vast demand; such charters were common across the narrow sea, as Lady Serala most certainly had told him. Yet it was understandable that Lord Tywin, as Hand, firmly rejected his proposals, for fear it might set a dangerous precedent. Infuriated at the refusal, Lord Darklyn then devised a new plan to win his charter (and with it, lower port fees and tariffs to allow Duskendale once more to vie for trade with King's Landing)—a plan that was pure folly.

The Defiance of Duskendale began quietly enough. Lord Denys, seeing that Aerys's erratic behavior had begun to strain his relations with Lord Tywin, refused to pay the taxes expected of him and instead invited the king to come to Duskendale and hear his petition. It seems most unlikely that King Aerys would ever have considered accepting this invitation . . . until Lord Tywin advised him to refuse in the strongest possible terms, whereupon the king decided

to accept, informing Grand Maester Pycelle and the small council that he meant to settle this matter himself and bring the defiant Darklyn to heel.

Against Lord Tywin's advice, the king traveled to Duskendale with a small escort led by Ser Gwayne Gaunt of the Kingsguard. The invitation proved to be a trap, however—and one that the Targaryen king walked into blindly. He was seized with his escort, and some of the men—most notably Ser Gwayne—were killed while attempting to defend their king.

The immediate response to the news from Duskendale was shock, then outrage. There were those who urged a sudden assault upon the town to free the king and punish the rebels for this enormity. But Duskendale was surrounded by strong walls, and the Dun Fort, the ancient seat of House Darklyn, which overlooked the harbor, was even more formidable. Taking it by storm would be no easy task.

Lord Tywin thus sent out riders and ravens, gathering forces while commanding the Darklyns to give up the king. Lord Denys instead sent word that, if any attempt was made to break his walls, he would put His Grace to death. Some in the small council questioned this, declaring that no son of Westeros would ever dare commit such a heinous crime, but Lord Tywin would not chance it. Instead, with a sizable host, he moved to surround Duskendale, blockading it by land and by sea.

With a royal host massed outside of his walls and his supply chain cut off, Lord Darklyn's determination began

to falter. He made several efforts to parley, but Lord Tywin refused to hear him, instead repeating his demand for the complete and unconditional surrender of the town and castle and the release of the king.

The Defiance lasted for half a year. Within the walls of Duskendale, the mood soon began to sour as the stores and larders ran dry. Yet, huddled within the ancient Dun Fort, Lord Denys was convinced that it was only a matter of time before Lord Tywin would weaken and offer better terms.

Those who knew the resolve of Tywin Lannister knew better. Instead, the Hand's heart grew harder, and he sent Duskendale's lord one final demand for surrender. Should he refuse again, Lord Tywin promised, he would take the town by storm and put every man, woman, and child within to the sword. (The tale, oft told, that Lord Tywin sent his bard to deliver the ultimatum, and commanded him to sing "The Rains of Castamere" for Lord Denys and the Lace Serpent is a colorful detail that is, alas, unsupported by the records).

Most of the small council were with the Hand outside Duskendale at this juncture, and several of them argued against Lord Tywin's plan on the grounds that such an attack would almost certainly goad Lord Darklyn into putting King Aerys to death. "He may or he may not," Tywin Lannister reportedly replied, "but if he does, we have a better king right here." Whereupon he raised a hand to indicate Prince Rhaegar.

Scholars have debated ever since as to Lord Tywin's intent. Did he believe Lord Darklyn would back down? Or was he, in truth, willing, and perhaps even eager, to see Aerys die so that Prince Rhaegar might take the Iron Throne?

None will ever know for certain, thanks to the courage of Ser Barristan Selmy of the Kingsguard. Ser Barristan offered to enter the town in secret, find his way to the Dun Fort, and spirit the king to safety. Selmy had been known as Barristan the Bold since his youth, but this was a boldness that Tywin Lannister felt bordered on madness. Yet such was his respect for the prowess and courage of Ser Barristan that he gave him a day to attempt his plan before storming Duskendale.

The songs of Ser Barristan's daring rescue of the king are many, and, for a rarity, the singers hardly had to embroider it. Ser Barristan did indeed scale the walls unseen in the dark of the night, using nothing but his bare hands, and he did disguise himself as a hooded beggar as he made his way to the Dun Fort. It is true, as well, that he managed to scale the walls of the Dun Fort in turn, killing a guard on the wallwalk before he could raise the alarm. Then, by stealth and courage, he found his way to the dungeon where the king

was being kept. By the time he had Aerys Targaryen out of the dungeon, however, the king's absence had been noted, and the hue and cry went up. And then the true breadth of Ser Barristan's heroism was revealed, for he stood and fought rather than surrender himself or his king.

And not only did he fight, but he struck first, taking Lord Darklyn's good-brother and master-at-arms, Ser Symon Hollard, and a pair of guards unawares, slaying them all—and so avenging the death of his Sworn Brother, Ser Gwayne Gaunt of the Kingsguard, who had been killed at Hollard's hand. He hurried with the king to the stables, fighting his way through those who tried to intervene, and the two were able to ride out of Dun Fort before the castle's gates could be closed. Then there was the wild ride through the streets of Duskendale, while horns and trumpets sounded the alarm, and the race up to the walls as Lord Tywin's archers attempted to clear it of defenders.

With the king escaped and safe, there was nothing left for Lord Darklyn save surrender, but it is doubtful he knew the terrible revenge that the king intended. When Darklyn and his family were presented to him in chains, Aerys demanded their deaths—and not only Darklyn's immediate kin but his uncles and aunts and even distant kinsmen in Duskendale. Even his good-kin, the Hollards, were attainted and destroyed. Only Ser Symon's young nephew, Dontos Hollard, was spared—and only then because Ser Barristan begged that mercy as a boon, and the king he had saved could not refuse him. As to Lady Serala, hers was a crueler death. Aerys had the Lace Serpent's tongue and her womanly parts torn out before she was burned alive (yet her enemies say that she should have suffered more and worse for the ruin she brought down upon the town).

Captivity at Duskendale had shattered whatever sanity had remained to Aerys II Targaryen. From that day forth, the king's madness reigned unchecked, growing worse with every passing year. The Darklyns had dared lay hands upon his person, shoving him roughly, stripping him of his royal raiment, even daring to strike him. After his release, King Aerys would no longer allow himself to be touched, even by his own servants. Uncut and unwashed, his hair grew ever longer and more tangled, whilst his fingernails lengthened and thickened into grotesque yellow talons. He forbade any blade in his presence save for the swords carried by the knights of his Kingsguard, sworn to protect him. His judgments became ever harsher and crueler.

Once safely returned to King's Landing, His Grace refused to leave the Red Keep for any cause and remained

LEFT | *The blockade of Duskendale.*

a virtual prisoner in his own castle for the next four years, during which time he grew ever more wary of those around him, Tywin Lannister in particular. His suspicions extended even to his own son and heir. Prince Rhaegar, he was convinced, had conspired with Tywin Lannister to have him slain at Duskendale. They had planned to storm the town walls so that Lord Darklyn would put him to death, opening the way for Rhaegar to mount the Iron Throne and marry Lord Tywin's daughter.

Determined to prevent that from happening, King Aerys turned to another friend of his childhood, summoning Steffon Baratheon from Storm's End and naming him to the small council. In 278 AC, the king sent Lord Steffon across the narrow sea on a mission to Old Volantis, to seek a suitable bride for Prince Rhaegar, "a maid of noble birth from an old Valyrian bloodline." That His Grace entrusted this task to the Lord of Storm's End rather than his Hand, or Rhaegar himself, speaks volumes. The rumors were rife that Aerys meant to make Lord Steffon his new Hand upon the successful completion of this mission, that Tywin Lannister was about to be removed from office, arrested, and tried for high treason. And there was many a lord who took delight in that prospect.

The gods had other notions, however. Steffon Baratheon's mission ended in failure, and on his return from Volantis, his ship foundered and sank in Shipbreaker Bay, within sight of Storm's End. Lord Steffon and his wife were both drowned as their two elder sons watched from the castle walls. When word of their deaths reached King's Landing, King Aerys flew into a rage and told Grand Maester Pycelle that Tywin Lannister had somehow divined his royal intentions and arranged for Lord Baratheon's murder. "If I dismiss him as Hand, he will kill me, too," the king told the grand maester.

In the years that followed, the king's madness deepened. Though Tywin Lannister continued as Hand, Aerys no longer met with him save in the presence of all seven Kingsguard. Convinced that the smallfolk and lords were plotting against his life and fearing that even Queen Rhaella and Prince Rhaegar might be part of these plots, he reached across the narrow sea to Pentos and imported a eunuch named Varys to serve as his spymaster, reasoning that only a man without friends, family, or ties in Westeros could be relied upon for the truth. The Spider, as he soon became known to the smallfolk of his realm, used the crown's gold to create a vast web of informers. For the rest of Aerys's reign, he would crouch at the king's side, whispering in his ear.

In the wake of Duskendale, the king also began to display signs of an ever-increasing obsession with dragonfire, similar to that which had haunted several of his forebears. Lord Darklyn would never have dared defy him if he had been a dragonrider, Aerys reasoned. His attempts to bring forth dragons from eggs found in the depths of Dragonstone (some so old that they had turned to stone) yielded naught, however.

Frustrated, Aerys turned to the Wisdoms of the ancient Guild of Alchemists, who knew the secret of producing the volatile jade green substance known as wildfire, said to be a close cousin to dragonflame. The pyromancers became a regular fixture at his court as the king's fascination with fire grew. By 280 AC, Aerys II had taken to burning traitors, murderers, and plotters, rather than hanging or beheading them. The king seemed to take great pleasure in these fiery executions, which were presided over by Wisdom Rossart, the grand master of the Guild of Alchemists . . . so much so that he granted Rossart the title of Lord and gave him a seat upon the small council.

His Grace's growing madness had become unmistakable by that time. From Dorne to the Wall, men had begun to refer to Aerys II as the Mad King. In King's Landing, he was called King Scab, for the many times he had cut himself upon the Iron Throne. Yet with Varys the Spider and his whisperers listening, it had become very dangerous to voice any of these sentiments aloud.

Meanwhile, King Aerys was becoming ever more estranged from his own son and heir. Early in the year 279 AC, Rhaegar Targaryen, Prince of Dragonstone, was formally betrothed to Princess Elia Martell, the delicate young sister of Doran Martell, Prince of Dorne. They were wed the following year, in a lavish ceremony at the Great Sept of Baelor in King's Landing, but Aerys II did not attend. He told the small council that he feared an attempt upon his life if he left the confines of the Red Keep, even with his Kingsguard to protect him. Nor would he allow his younger son, Viserys, to attend his brother's wedding.

When Prince Rhaegar and his new wife chose to take up residence on Dragonstone instead of the Red Keep, rumors flew thick and fast across the Seven Kingdoms. Some claimed that the crown prince was planning to depose his father and seize the Iron Throne for himself, whilst others said that King Aerys meant to disinherit Rhaegar and name Viserys heir in his place. Nor did the birth of King Aerys's first grandchild, a girl named Rhaenys, born on Dragonstone in 280 AC, do aught to reconcile father and son. When Prince Rhaegar returned to the Red Keep to present his daughter

RIGHT | *King Aerys II condemns the Darklyns.*

to his own mother and father, Queen Rhaella embraced the babe warmly, but King Aerys refused to touch or hold the child and complained that she "smells Dornish."

Amidst all this, Lord Tywin Lannister continued to serve as Hand of the King. "Lord Tywin looms as large as Casterly Rock," wrote Grand Maester Pycelle, "and no king has ever had so diligent or capable a Hand." Seemingly secure in his office after the death of Steffon Baratheon, Lord Tywin even went so far as to bring his beautiful young daughter, Cersei, to court.

In 281 AC, however, the aged Kingsguard knight Ser Harlan Grandison passed away in his sleep, and the uneasy accord between Aerys II and his Hand finally snapped, when His Grace chose to offer a white cloak to Lord Tywin's eldest son.

At five-and-ten, Ser Jaime Lannister was already a knight—an honor he had received from the hand of Ser Arthur Dayne, the Sword of the Morning, whom many considered to be the realm's most chivalrous warrior. Jaime's knighthood had been won during Ser Arthur's campaign against the outlaws known as the Kingswood Brotherhood, and none could doubt his prowess.

Ser Jaime was also Lord Tywin's heir, however, and carried all his hopes for the perpetuation of House Lannister, as his lordship's other son was the malformed dwarf, Tyrion. Moreover, the Hand had been in the midst of negotiating an advantageous marriage pact for Ser Jaime when the king informed him of his choice. At a stroke, King Aerys had deprived Lord Tywin of his chosen heir and made him look foolish and false.

Yet Grand Maester Pycelle tells us that when Aerys II announced Ser Jaime's appointment from the Iron Throne, his lordship went to one knee and thanked the king for the great honor shown to his house. Then, pleading illness, Lord Tywin asked the king's leave to retire as Hand.

King Aerys was delighted to oblige him. Lord Tywin accordingly surrendered his chain of office and retired from court, returning to Casterly Rock with his daughter. The king replaced him as Hand with Lord Owen Merryweather, an aged and amiable lickspittle famed for laughing loudest at every jape and witticism uttered by the king, no matter how feeble.

Henceforth, His Grace told Pycelle, the realm would know for a certainty that the man who wore the crown also ruled the Seven Kingdoms.

Aerys Targaryen and Tywin Lannister had met as boys, had fought and bled together in the War of the Ninepenny Kings, and had ruled the Seven Kingdoms together for close to twenty years, but in 281 AC this long partnership, which had proved so fruitful to the realm, came to a bitter end.

Shortly thereafter, Lord Walter Whent announced plans for a great tourney to be held at his seat at Harrenhal, to celebrate his maiden daughter's nameday. King Aerys II chose this event for the formal investiture of Ser Jaime Lannister as a knight of the Kingsguard . . . thus setting in motion the events that would end the Mad King's reign and write an end to the long rule of House Targaryen in the Seven Kingdoms.

IN THE ANNALS of Westeros, 281 AC is known as the Year of the False Spring. Winter had held the land in its icy grip for close on two years, but now at last the snows were melting, the woods were greening, the days were growing longer. Though the white ravens had not yet flown, there were many even at the Citadel of Oldtown who believed that winter's end was nigh.

As warm winds blew from the south, lords and knights from throughout the Seven Kingdoms made their way toward Harrenhal to compete in Lord Whent's great tournament on the shore of the Gods Eye, which promised to be the largest and most magnificent competition since the time of Aegon the Unlikely.

We know a great deal about that tourney, for the things that transpired beneath the walls of Harrenhal were set down by a score of chroniclers and recorded in many a letter and testament. Yet there is much and more that we shall never know, for even whilst the greatest knights of the Seven Kingdoms vied in the lists, other and more dangerous games were being played in the halls of Black Harren's accursed castle and the tents and pavilions of the lords assembled.

Many tales have grown up around Lord Whent's tournament: tales of plots and conspiracies, betrayals and rebellions, infidelities and assignations, secrets and mysteries, almost all of it conjecture. The truth is known only to a few, some of whom have long passed beyond this mortal vale and must forever hold their tongues. In writing of this fateful gathering, therefore, the conscientious scholar must take care to separate fact from fancy, to draw a sharp line between what is known and what is simply suspected, believed, or rumored.

This is known: The tourney was first announced by Walter Whent, Lord of Harrenhal, late in the year 280 AC, not long after a visit from his younger brother, Ser Oswell Whent, a knight of the Kingsguard. That this would be an event of unrivaled magnificence was clear from the first, for Lord Whent was offering prizes thrice as large as those given at the great Lannisport tourney of 272 AC, hosted by Lord Tywin Lannister in celebration of Aerys II's tenth year upon the Iron Throne.

Most took this simply as an attempt by Whent to outdo the former Hand and demonstrate the wealth and splendor of his house. There were those, however, who believed this no more than a ruse, and Lord Whent no more

than a catspaw. His lordship lacked the funds to pay such munificent prizes, they argued; someone else must surely have stood behind him, someone who did not lack for gold but preferred to remain in the shadows whilst allowing the Lord of Harrenhal to claim the glory for hosting this magnificent event. We have no shred of evidence that such a "shadow host" ever existed, but the notion was widely believed at the time and remains so today.

But if indeed there was a shadow, who was he, and why did he choose to keep his role a secret? A dozen names have been put forward over the years, but only one seems truly compelling: Rhaegar Targaryen, Prince of Dragonstone.

If this tale be believed, 'twas Prince Rhaegar who urged Lord Walter to hold the tourney, using his lordship's brother Ser Oswell as a go-between. Rhaegar provided Whent with gold sufficient for splendid prizes in order to bring as many lords and knights to Harrenhal as possible. The prince, it is said, had no interest in the tourney as a tourney; his intent was to gather the great lords of the realm together in what amounted to an informal Great Council, in order to discuss ways and means of dealing with the madness of his father, King Aerys II, possibly by means of a regency or a forced abdication.

If indeed this was the purpose behind the tourney, it was a perilous game that Rhaegar Targaryen was playing. Though few doubted that Aerys had taken leave of his senses, many still had good reason to oppose his removal from the Iron Throne, for certain courtiers and councillors had gained great wealth and power through the king's caprice and knew that they stood to lose all should Prince Rhaegar come to power.

The Mad King could be savagely cruel, as seen most plainly when he burned those he perceived to be his enemies, but he could also be extravagant, showering men who pleased him with honors, offices, and lands. The lickspittle lords who surrounded Aerys II had gained much and more from the king's madness and eagerly seized upon any opportunity to speak ill of Prince Rhaegar and inflame the father's suspicions of the son.

Chief amongst the Mad King's supporters were three lords of his small council: Qarlton Chelsted, master of coin, Lucerys Velaryon, master of ships, and Symond Staunton, master of laws. The eunuch Varys, master of whisperers, and Wisdom Rossart, grand master of the Guild of Alchemists,

PREVIOUS PAGES | *Prince Rhaegar presenting the crown of winter roses to Lyanna Stark.*
RIGHT | *The Mad King, Aerys II.*

also enjoyed the king's trust. Prince Rhaegar's support came from the younger men at court, including Lord Jon Connington, Ser Myles Mooton of Maidenpool, and Ser Richard Lonmouth. The Dornishmen who had come to court with the Princess Elia were in the prince's confidence as well, particularly Prince Lewyn Martell, Elia's uncle and a Sworn Brother of the Kingsguard. But the most formidable of all Rhaegar's friends and allies in King's Landing was surely Ser Arthur Dayne, the Sword of the Morning.

To Grand Maester Pycelle and Lord Owen Merryweather, the King's Hand, fell the unenviable task of keeping peace between these factions, even as their rivalry grew ever more venomous. In a letter to the Citadel, Pycelle wrote that the divisions within the Red Keep reminded him uncomfortably of the situation before the Dance of the Dragons a century before, when the enmity between Queen Alicent and Princess Rhaenyra had split the realm in two, to grievous cost. A similarly bloody conflict might await the Seven Kingdoms once again, he warned, unless some accord could be reached that would satisfy both Prince Rhaegar's supporters and the king's.

Had any whiff of proof come into their hands to show that Prince Rhaegar was conspiring against his father, King Aerys's loyalists would most certainly have used it to bring about the prince's downfall. Indeed, certain of the king's men had even gone so far as to suggest that Aerys should disinherit his "disloyal" son, and name his younger brother heir to the Iron Throne in his stead. Prince Viserys was but seven years of age, and his eventual ascension would certainly mean a regency, wherein they themselves would rule as regents.

In such a climate, it was scarce surprising that Lord Whent's great tournament excited much suspicion. Lord Chelsted urged His Grace to forbid it, and Lord Staunton went even further, suggesting a prohibition against all tourneys.

Such events were widely popular with the commons, however, and when Lord Merryweather warned Aerys that forbidding the tournament would only serve to make him even more unpopular, the king chose another course and announced his intention to attend. It would mark the first time that Aerys II had left the safety of the Red Keep since the Defiance of Duskendale. No doubt His Grace reasoned that his enemies would not dare conspire against him under his very nose. Grand Maester Pycelle tells us that Aerys hoped that his presence at such a grand event would help him win back the love of his people.

If that was indeed the king's intent, it was a grievous miscalculation. Whilst his attendance made the Harrenhal tourney even grander and more prestigious than it already was, drawing lords and knights from every corner of the realm, many of those who came were shocked and appalled when they saw what had become of their monarch. His long yellow fingernails, tangled beard, and ropes of unwashed, matted hair made the extent of the king's madness plain to all. Nor was his behavior that of a sane man, for Aerys could go from mirth to melancholy in the blink of an eye, and many of the accounts written of Harrenhal speak of his hysterical laughter, long silences, bouts of weeping, and sudden rages.

Above all, King Aerys II was suspicious: suspicious of his own son and heir, Prince Rhaegar; suspicious of his host, Lord Whent; suspicious of every lord and knight who had come to Harrenhal to compete . . . and even more suspicious of those who chose to absent themselves, the most notable of whom was his former Hand, Tywin Lannister, Lord of Casterly Rock.

At the tourney's opening ceremonies, King Aerys made a great public show of Ser Jaime Lannister's investiture as a Sworn Brother of his Kingsguard. The young knight said his vows before the royal pavilion, kneeling on the

green grass in his white armor as half the lords of the realm looked on. When Ser Gerold Hightower raised him up and clasped his white cloak about his shoulders, a roar went up from the crowd, for Ser Jaime was much admired for his courage, gallantry, and prowess with a sword, especially in the westerlands.

Though Tywin Lannister did not himself deign to attend the tourney at Harrenhal, dozens of his lords bannermen and hundreds of knights were on hand, and they raised a loud and lusty cheer for the newest and youngest Sworn Brother of the Kingsguard. The king was pleased. In his madness, we are told, His Grace believed that they were cheering for him.

Scarce had the thing been done, however, than King Aerys II began to nurse grave doubts about his new protector. The king had seized upon the notion of bringing Ser Jaime into his Kingsguard as a way of humbling his old friend, Grand Maester Pycelle tells us. Only now, belatedly, did His Grace come to the realization that he would henceforth have Lord Tywin's son beside him day and night . . . with a sword at his side.

The thought frightened him so badly that he could hardly eat at that night's feast, Pycelle avows. Accordingly, Aerys II summoned Ser Jaime to attend him (whilst squatting over his chamberpot, some say, but this ugly detail may have been a later addition to the tale), and commanded him to return to King's Landing to guard and protect Queen Rhaella and Prince Viserys, who had not accompanied His Grace to the tourney. The lord commander, Ser Gerold Hightower, offered to go in Ser Jaime's stead, but Aerys refused him.

For the young knight, who had no doubt hoped to distinguish himself in the tourney, this abrupt exile came as a bitter disappointment. Nonetheless, Ser Jaime remained true to his vows. He set off for the Red Keep at once and played no further part in the events at Harrenhal . . . save perhaps in the mind of the Mad King.

For seven days the finest knights and noblest lords of the Seven Kingdoms contended with lance and sword in the fields beneath the towering walls of Harrenhal. At night, victors and vanquished alike repaired to the castle's cavernous Hall of a Hundred Hearths, for feasting and celebration. Many songs and stories are told of those days and nights beside the Gods Eye. Some are even true. To recount every joust and jape is far outside our purpose here. That task we gladly leave to the singers. Two incidents must not be passed over, however, for they would prove to have grave consequences.

The first was the appearance of a mystery knight, a slight young man in ill-fitting armor whose device was a carved white weirwood tree, its features twisted in mirth. The Knight of the Laughing Tree, as this challenger was called, unhorsed three men in successive tilts, to the delight of the commons.

King Aerys II was not a man to take any joy in mysteries, however. His Grace became convinced that the tree on the mystery knight's shield was laughing at him, and—with no more proof than that—decided that the mystery knight was Ser Jaime Lannister. His newest Kingsguard had defied him and returned to the tourney, he told every man who would listen.

Furious, he commanded his own knights to defeat the Knight of the Laughing Tree when the jousts resumed the next morning, so that he might be unmasked and his perfidy exposed for all to see. But the mystery knight vanished during the night, never to be seen again. This too the king took ill, certain that someone close to him had given warning to "this traitor who will not show his face."

Prince Rhaegar emerged as the ultimate victor at the end of the competition. The crown prince, who did not normally compete in tourneys, surprised all by donning his armor and defeating every foe he faced, including four knights of the Kingsguard. In the final tilt, he unhorsed Ser Barristan Selmy, generally regarded as the finest lance in all the Seven Kingdoms, to win the champion's laurels.

The cheers of the crowd were said to be deafening, but King Aerys did not join them. Far from being proud and pleased by his heir's skill at arms, His Grace saw it as a threat. Lords Chelsted and Staunton inflamed his suspicions further, declaring that Prince Rhaegar had entered the lists to curry favor with the commons and remind the assembled lords that he was a puissant warrior, a true heir to Aegon the Conqueror.

And when the triumphant Prince of Dragonstone named Lyanna Stark, daughter of the Lord of Winterfell, the queen of love and beauty, placing a garland of blue roses in her lap with the tip of his lance, the lickspittle lords gathered around the king declared that further proof of his perfidy. Why would the prince have thus given insult to his own wife, the Princess Elia Martell of Dorne (who was present), unless it was to help him gain the Iron Throne? The crowning of the Stark girl, who was by all reports a wild and boyish young thing with none of the Princess Elia's delicate beauty, could only have been meant to win the allegiance of Winterfell to Prince Rhaegar's cause, Symond Staunton suggested to the king.

Yet if this were true, why did Lady Lyanna's brothers seem so distraught at the honor the prince had bestowed upon her? Brandon Stark, the heir to Winterfell, had to be restrained from confronting Rhaegar at what he took as a slight upon his sister's honor, for Lyanna Stark had long been betrothed to Robert Baratheon, Lord of Storm's End. Eddard Stark, Brandon's younger brother and a close friend to Lord Robert, was calmer but no more pleased. As for Robert Baratheon himself, some say he laughed at the prince's gesture, claiming that Rhaegar had done no more than pay Lyanna her due . . . but those who knew him better say the young lord brooded on the insult, and that his heart hardened toward the Prince of Dragonstone from that day forth.

And well it might, for with that simple garland of pale blue roses, Rhaegar Targaryen had begun the dance that would rip the Seven Kingdoms apart, bring about his own death and thousands more, and put a welcome new king upon the Iron Throne.

The False Spring of 281 AC lasted less than two turns. As the year drew to a close, winter returned to Westeros with a vengeance. On the last day of the year, snow began to fall upon King's Landing, and a crust of ice formed atop the Blackwater Rush. The snowfall continued off and on for the best part of a fortnight, by which time the Blackwater was hard frozen, and icicles draped the roofs and gutters of every tower in the city.

As cold winds hammered the city, King Aerys II turned to his pyromancers, charging them to drive the winter off with their magics. Huge green fires burned along the walls of the Red Keep for a moon's turn. Prince Rhaegar was

not in the city to observe them, however. Nor could he be found in Dragonstone with Princess Elia and their young son, Aegon. With the coming of the new year, the crown prince had taken to the road with half a dozen of his closest friends and confidants, on a journey that would ultimately lead him back to the riverlands. Not ten leagues from Harrenhal, Rhaegar fell upon Lyanna Stark of Winterfell, and carried her off, lighting a fire that would consume his house and kin and all those he loved—and half the realm besides.

But that tale is too well-known to warrant repeating here.

ROBERT'S REBELLION

WHAT FOLLOWED PRINCE Rhaegar's infamous abduction of Lyanna Stark was the ruin of House Targaryen. The full depth of King Aerys's madness was subsequently revealed in his depraved actions against Lord Stark, his heir, and their supporters after they demanded redress for Rhaegar's wrongs. Instead of granting them fair hearing, King Aerys had them brutally slain, then followed these murders by demanding that Lord Jon Arryn execute his former wards,

Robert Baratheon and Eddard Stark. Many now agree that the true start of Robert's Rebellion began with Lord Arryn's refusal and his courageous calling of his banners in the defense of justice. Yet not all the lords of the Vale agreed with Lord Jon's decision, and soon fighting broke out as loyalists to the crown attempted to bring Lord Arryn down.

The fighting then spread across the Seven Kingdoms like wildfire, as lords and knights took sides. Many alive

ABOVE | *Rhaegar Targaryen, the Prince of Dragonstone.*

famed is Robert's grand victory at Stoney Sept, also called the Battle of the Bells, where he slew the famous Ser Myles Mooton—once Prince Rhaegar's squire—and five men besides, and might well have killed the new Hand, Lord Connington, had the battle brought them together. The victory sealed the entry of the riverlands into the conflict, following the marriage of Lord Tully's daughters to Lords Arryn and Stark.

The royalist forces were left reeling and scattered by such victories though they did their best to rally. The Kingsguard were dispatched to recover the remnant of Lord Connington's force, and Prince Rhaegar returned from the south to take command of the new levies being raised in the crownlands. And after a partial victory at Ashford, which led to Robert's withdrawal, the Stormlands were left open to Lord Tyrell. Bringing the might of the Reach to bear, the reachlords swept away all resistance and settled in to besiege Storm's End. Shortly afterward, the host was joined by Lord Paxter Redwyne's mighty fleet from the Arbor, completing the siege by land and sea. That siege wore on until the conclusion of the war.

From Dorne, in defense of Princess Elia, ten thousand spears came over the Boneway and marched to King's Landing to bolster the host that Rhaegar was raising. Those who were there at court during this time have recounted that Aerys's behavior was erratic. He was untrusting of any save his Kingsguard—and then only imperfectly, for he kept Ser Jaime Lannister close at all hours to serve as a hostage against his father.

When Prince Rhaegar at last marched up the kingsroad to the Trident, with him were all but one of the Kingsguard who had remained in King's Landing: Ser Barristan the Bold, Ser Jonothor Darry, and Prince Lewyn of Dorne. Prince Lewyn took command of the Dornish troop sent by his nephew, the Prince Doran, but it is said that he did so only after threats from the Mad King, who feared that the Dornishmen looked to betray him. Only the young Ser Jaime Lannister remained in King's Landing.

Of the famous battle on the Trident, much has been written and said. But all know that the two armies clashed at the crossing that would ever after be called the Ruby Ford for the scattered rubies on Prince Rhaegar's armor. The opponents were well matched. Rhaegar's forces numbered some forty thousand, a tenth part of which were anointed knights, while the rebels had somewhat fewer men, but those they possessed were tested in battle, while much of Rhaegar's force was raw and new.

today fought in these battles, and so can speak with greater knowledge of them than I, who was not there. I therefore leave it to such men to write the true and detailed history of Robert's Rebellion; far be it for me to offend those who yet live by presenting an imperfect summary of events, or mistakenly praising those who have since proved unworthy. So instead, I will look only to the lord and knight who ascended the Iron Throne at the end, repairing a realm nearly destroyed by madness.

Robert Baratheon proved himself a fearless, indomitable warrior as more and more men flocked to his banner. Robert was the first over the walls at Gulltown, when Lord Grafton raised his banner for Targaryens, and from there he sailed to Storm's End—risking capture by the royal fleet—to call his banners. Not all came willing: Aerys's Hand, Lord Merryweather, encouraged certain stormlords to rise up against Lord Robert. Yet it was an effort that proved fruitless following Lord Robert's victories at Summerhall, where he won three battles in a single day. His hastily gathered forces defeated Lords Grandison and Cafferen in turn, and Robert went on to kill Lord Fell in single combat before taking his famous son Silveraxe captive.

More victories were to come for Lord Robert and the stormlords as they marched to join forces with Lord Arryn and the Northmen who supported their cause. Rightly

ABOVE | *King Robert Baratheon, the First of His Name.*

The battle at the ford was fierce, and many lives were lost in the fray. Ser Jonothor Darry was cut down in the midst of the conflict, as was Prince Lewyn of Dorne. But the most important death was yet to come.

The battle screamed about Lord Robert and Prince Rhaegar both, and by the will of the gods, or by chance—or perhaps by design—they met amidst the shallows of the ford. The two knights fought valiantly upon their destriers, according to all accounts. For despite his crimes, Prince Rhaegar was no coward. Lord Robert was wounded by the dragon prince in the combat, yet in the end, Baratheon's ferocious strength and his thirst to avenge the shame brought upon his stolen betrothed proved the greater. His warhammer found its mark, and Robert drove the spike through Rhaegar's chest, scattering the costly rubies that blazed upon the prince's breastplate.

Some men on both sides stopped fighting at once, leaping instead into the river to recover the precious stones. And a general rout quickly began as the royalists started fleeing the field.

Lord Robert's wounds prevented him from taking up the pursuit, so he gave that into the hands of Lord Eddard Stark. But Robert proved his chivalry when he refused to allow the gravely wounded Ser Barristan to be killed. Instead, he sent his own maester to tend the great knight. In such fashion did the future king win the fierce devotion of his friends and allies—for few men were ever so open-handed and merciful as Robert Baratheon.

THE END

BIRDS FLEW AND couriers raced to bear word of the victory at the Ruby Ford. When the news reached the Red Keep, it was said that Aerys cursed the Dornish, certain that Lewyn had betrayed Rhaegar. He sent his pregnant queen, Rhaella, and his younger son and new heir, Viserys, away to Dragonstone, but Princess Elia was forced to remain in King's Landing with Rhaegar's children as a hostage against Dorne. Having burned his previous Hand, Lord Chelsted, alive for bad counsel during the war, Aerys now appointed another to the position: the alchemist Rossart—a man of low birth, with little to recommend him but his flames and trickery.

Ser Jaime Lannister was meanwhile left in charge of the Red Keep's defenses. The walls were manned by knights and watchmen, awaiting the enemy. When the first army that arrived flew the lion of Casterly Rock, with Lord Tywin at its head, King Aerys anxiously ordered the gates to be opened, thinking that at last his old friend and former Hand had come to his rescue, as he had done at the Defiance of Duskendale. But Lord Tywin had not come to save the Mad King.

This time, Lord Tywin's cause was that of the realm's, and he was determined to bring an end to the reign that madness had brought low. Once within the walls of the city, his soldiers assaulted the defenders of King's Landing, and blood ran red in the streets. A handpicked cadre of men raced to the Red Keep to storm its walls and seek out King Aerys, so that justice might be done.

The Red Keep was soon breached, but in the chaos, misfortune soon fell upon Elia of Dorne and her children, Rhaenys and Aegon. It is tragic that the blood spilled in war may as readily be innocent as it is guilty, and that those who ravished and murdered Princess Elia escaped justice. It is not known who murdered Princess Rhaenys in her bed, or smashed the infant Prince Aegon's head against a wall. Some whisper it was done at Aerys's own command when he learned that Lord Lannister had taken up Robert's cause, while others suggest that Elia did it herself for fear of what would happen to her children in the hands of her dead husband's enemies.

Aerys's Hand, Rossart, was killed at a postern gate after cravenly attempting to flee the castle. And last of all to die was King Aerys himself, at the hand of his remaining Kingsguard knight, Ser Jaime Lannister. Like his father, Ser Jaime did as he thought best for the realm, bringing an end to the Mad King.

And so ended both the reign of House Targaryen and Robert's Rebellion—the war that put an end to nearly three hundred years of Targaryen rule and ushered in a new golden era under the auspices of House Baratheon.

The Glorious Reign

SINCE THE FALL of House Targaryen, the realm has prospered greatly. Robert, the First of His Name, took charge of a fractured Westeros and swiftly healed it of the many ills inflicted by the Mad King and his son. As his first act, the unwed king took to wife the most beautiful woman in the realm, Cersei of House Lannister—thereby granting to House Lannister all the honors that Aerys had denied it. And though all know Lord Tywin might well have become Hand again, the king, in his graciousness, gave that office to his old friend and protector, Lord Jon Arryn, instead. The wise and just Lord Arryn has indeed helped the king shepherd the realm to prosperity since.

But this is not to say that Robert's reign has been completely untroubled. Six years after he was crowned, Balon Greyjoy unlawfully rose against his king—not for any harm done to him or to his people but merely out of wanton ambition. Lord Stannis Baratheon, Robert's middle brother, led the royal fleet against Lord Greyjoy, while King Robert himself rode at the head of a mighty host. Great feats of arms were performed by King Robert when Pyke was eventually taken and subdued. The king then made Balon Greyjoy—the pretender to the crown of the Iron Isles—bend the knee to the Iron Throne. And as assurance of his fealty, his only surviving son was taken hostage.

Now the realm is at peace, and all that Robert's ascension to the throne once promised has come to pass. Our noble king has overseen one of the longest summers in many years, filled with prosperity and good harvests. Moreover, the king and his beloved queen have given the realm three golden heirs to ensure that House Baratheon will long reign supreme. And though a false King-beyond-the-Wall has recently declared himself, Mance Rayder is an oathbreaker fled from the Night's Watch, and the Night's Watch has always brought swift justice to those who have betrayed it. This king will amount to nothing, as have all the other wildling kings before him.

It may not always be so. As this history has shown, the world has seen many ages. Many thousands of years have passed from the Dawn Age to today. Castles have risen and fallen, as have kingdoms. Crofters have been born, grown to work the fields, and died of age or mishap or illness, leaving behind children to do the same. Princes have been born, grown to wear a crown, and died in war or bed or tourney, leaving behind reigns great, forgettable, or reviled. The world has known ice in the Long Night, and it has known fire in the Doom. From the Frozen Shore to Asshai-by-the-Shadow, this world of ice and fire has revealed a rich and glorious history—although there is much yet to be discovered. If more fragments of Maester Gyldayn's manuscript are located—or if other such incomparable treasures (at least to the maesters' eyes) are uncovered—more of our ignorance may be sponged away. But one thing can be said with certainty. As the next thousand years unfold—and the thousands beyond that—many more will be born, and live, and die. And history will continue to unfold, as strange and complex and compelling as what my humble pen was able to lay before you here.

No man can say with certainty what the future may hold. But perhaps, in knowing what has already transpired, we can all do our part to avoid the mistakes of our forebears, to emulate their successes, and to create a world more harmonious for our children and their children, for generations to come.

In the name of the glorious King Robert, First of His Name, I humbly conclude this history of the kings of the Seven Kingdoms.

LEFT | *The Red Keep and King's Landing.*

THE VAST AND frigid realm of the Kings of Winter, the Starks of Winterfell, is generally considered the first and oldest of the Seven Kingdoms, in that it has endured, unconquered, for the longest. The vagaries of geography and history set the North apart from their southron neighbors.

It is often said that the North is as large as the other six kingdoms put together, but the truth is somewhat less grand: the North, as ruled today by House Stark of Winterfell and Barrowton in the Barrowlands. The former is largely empty in spring and summer but filled to bursting in autumn and winter with those seeking the protection and patronage of Winterfell to help them survive the lean times. Not only do townsmen arrive from the outlying villages and crofts, but many a son and daughter of the mountain clans have been known to make their way to the winter town when the snows begin to fall in earnest.

For centuries it has been the custom to speak of the Seven Kingdoms of Westeros. This familiar usage derives from the seven great kingdoms that held sway over most of Westeros below the Wall during years immediately preceding Aegon's Conquest. Yet even then, the term was far from exact, for one of those "kingdoms" was ruled by a princess rather than a king (Dorne), and Aegon Targaryen's own "kingdom" of Dragonstone was never included in the count.

Nonetheless, the term endures. Just as we speak of the Hundred Kingdoms of yore, though there was never a time when Westeros was actually divided into a hundred independent states, we must bow to common usage and talk of the Seven Kingdoms, despite the imprecision.

Winterfell, comprises little more than a third of the realm. Beginning at the southern edge of the Neck, the domains of the Starks extend as far north as the New Gift (itself part of their realm until King Jaehaerys I convinced Winterfell to cede those lands to the Night's Watch). Within the North are great forests, windswept plains, hills and valleys, rocky shores, and snow-crowned mountains. The North is a cold land—much of it rising moorlands and high plains giving way to mountains in its northern reaches—and this makes it far less fertile than the reaches of the south. Snow has been known to fall there even in summer, and it is deadly in winter.

White Harbor, the North's sole true city, is the smallest city in the Seven Kingdoms. The most prominent towns in the North are the "winter town" beneath the walls of Barrowton, too, is somewhat of a curiosity—a gathering place built at the foot of the reputed barrow of the First King, who once ruled supreme over all the First Men, if the legends can be believed. Rising from the midst of a wide and empty plain, it has prospered thanks to the shrewd stewardship of the Dustins, loyal bannermen to the Starks, who have ruled the Barrowlands in their name since the fall of the last of the Barrow Kings.

The men of the North are descendants of the First Men, their blood only slowly mingling with that of the Andals who overwhelmed the kingdoms to the south. The original language of the First Men—known as the Old Tongue—has come to be spoken only by the wildlings beyond the Wall, and many other aspects of their culture have faded away (such as the grislier aspects of their worship, when criminals

---

The rusted crown upon the arms of House Dustin derives from their claim that they are themselves descended from the First King and the Barrow Kings who ruled after him. The old tales recorded in Kennet's *Passages of the Dead* claim that a curse was placed on the Great Barrow that would allow no living man to rival the First King. This curse made these pretenders to the title grow corpselike in their appearance as it sucked away their vitality and life. This is no more than legend, to be sure, but that the Dustins share blood and descent from the Barrow Kings of old seems sure enough.

PREVIOUS PAGES | *The Vale of Arryn.*

As knighthood is rare in the North, the knightly tourney and its pageantry and chivalry are as rare as hen's teeth beyond the Neck. Northmen fight ahorse with war lances but seldom tilt for sport, preferring mêlées that are only just this side of battles. There are accounts of contests that have lasted half a day and left fields trampled and villages half-torn down. Serious injuries are common in such a mêlée, and deaths are not unheard of. In the great mêlée at Last Hearth in 170 AC, it is said that no fewer than eighteen men died, and half again that number were sorely maimed before the day was done.

and traitors were killed and their bodies and entrails hung from the branches of weirwoods.)

But the Northmen still retain something of the old ways in their customs and their manner. Their life is harder, and so they are hardened by it, and the pleasures that in the south are considered noble are thought childish and less worthy than the hunting and brawling that the Northmen love best.

Even their house names mark them out, for the First Men bore names that were short and blunt and to the point; names like Stark, Wull, Umber, and Stout all stem from the days when the Andals had no influence on the North.

One notable custom that the Northmen hold dearer than any other is guest right, the tradition of hospitality by which a man may offer no harm to a guest beneath his roof, nor a guest to his host. The Andals held to something like it as well, but it looms less large in southron minds. In his text *Justice and Injustice in the North: Judgments of Three Stark Lords*, Maester Egbert notes that crimes in the North in which guest right was violated were rare but were invariably treated as harshly as the direst of treasons. Only kinslaying is deemed as sinful as the violations of these laws of hospitality.

In the North, they tell the tale of the Rat Cook, who served an Andal king—identified by some as King Tywell II of the Rock, and by others as King Oswell I of the Vale and Mountain—the flesh of the king's own son, baked into a pie. For this, he was punished by being turned into a monstrous rat that ate its own young. Yet the punishment was incurred not for killing the king's son, or for feeding him to the king, but for the breaking of guest right.

THE KINGS OF WINTER

Song and story tell us that the Starks of Winterfell have ruled large portions of the lands beyond the Neck for eight thousand years, styling themselves the Kings of Winter (the more ancient usage) and (in more recent centuries) the Kings in the North. Their rule was not an uncontested one. Many were the wars in which the Starks expanded their rule or were forced to win back lands that rebels had carved away. The Kings of Winter were hard men in hard times.

Ancient ballads, amongst the oldest to be found in the archives of the Citadel of Oldtown, tell of how one King of Winter drove the giants from the North, whilst another felled the skinchanger Gaven Greywolf and his kin in "the savage War of the Wolves," but we have only the word of singers that such kings and such battles ever existed.

More historical proof exists for the war between the Kings of Winter and the Barrow Kings to their south, who styled themselves the Kings of the First Men and claimed supremacy over all First Men everywhere, even the Starks themselves. Runic records suggest that their struggle, dubbed the Thousand Years War by the singers, was actually a series of wars that lasted closer to two hundred years than a thousand, ending when the last Barrow King bent his knee to the King of Winter, and gave him the hand of his daughter in marriage.

Even this did not give Winterfell dominion over all the North. Many other petty kings remained, ruling over realms great and small, and it would require thousands of years and many more wars before the last of them was conquered. Yet one by one, the Starks subdued them all, and during these struggles, many proud houses and ancient lines were extinguished forever.

Amongst the houses reduced from royals to vassals we can count the Flints of Breakstone Hill, the Slates of Blackpool, the Umbers of Last Hearth, the Lockes of Oldcastle, the Glovers of Deepwood Motte, the Fishers of the Stony Shore, the Ryders of the Rills . . . and mayhaps even the Blackwoods of Raventree, whose own family traditions insist they once ruled most of the wolfswood before being driven from their lands by the Kings of Winter (certain runic records support this claim, if Maester Barneby's translations can be trusted).

Chronicles found in the archives of the Night's Watch at the Nightfort (before it was abandoned) speak of the war for Sea Dragon Point, wherein the Starks brought down the Warg King and his inhuman allies, the children of the forest. When the Warg King's last redoubt fell, his sons were put to the sword, along with his beasts and greenseers, whilst his daughters were taken as prizes by their conquerors.

House Greenwood, House Towers, House Amber, and House Frost met similar ends, together with a score of lesser houses and petty kings whose very names are lost to history. Yet the bitterest foes of Winterfell were undoubtedly the Red Kings of the Dreadfort, those grim lords of House Bolton whose domains of old stretched from the Last River to the White Knife, and as far south as the Sheepshead Hills.

The enmity between the Starks and Boltons went back to the Long Night itself, it is claimed. The wars between these two ancient families were legion, and not all ended in victory for House Stark. King Royce Bolton, Second of His Name, is said to have taken and burned Winterfell itself; his namesake and descendant Royce IV (remembered by history as Royce Redarm, for his habit of plunging his arm into the bellies of captive foes to pull out their entrails with his bare hand) did the same three centuries later. Other Red Kings were reputed to wear cloaks made from the skins of Stark princes they had captured and flayed.

Yet in the end, even the Dreadfort fell before the might of Winterfell, and the last Red King, known to history as Rogar the Huntsman, swore fealty to the King of Winter and sent his sons to Winterfell as hostages, even as the first Andals were crossing the narrow sea in their longships.

LEFT | *Moat Cailin* ABOVE | *The arms of House Stark (center) and some of its vassals (clockwise from top): Glover, Ryswell, Manderly, Dustin, Bolton, Tallhart, Reed, Umber, Karstark, Hornwood, and Mormont.*

After the defeat of the Boltons, the last of their Northern rivals, the greatest threats to the dominion of House Stark came by sea. The northern boundary of the Stark domains was protected by the Wall and the men of the Night's Watch, whilst to the south, the only way through the swamps of the Neck passed below the ruined towers and sinking walls of the great fortress called Moat Cailin. Even when the Marsh Kings held the Moat, their crannogmen stood staunch against any invaders from the south, allying with the Barrow Kings, Red Kings, and Kings of Winter as need be to turn back any southron lord who sought to attack the North. And once King Rickard Stark added the Neck to his domain, Moat Cailin proved even more imposing—a bulwark against the powers of the south. Few sought to push past it, and the histories say that none ever succeeded.

The North's long, ragged coastlines, both to the east and the west, remained vulnerable, however; it would be there where the rule of Winterfell would be most oft threatened . . . by ironborn in the west and Andals in the east.

Crossing the narrow sea in their hundreds and thousands, the longships of the Andals made landings in the North just as they did to the south, but wherever they came ashore, the Starks and their bannermen fell upon them and drove them back into the sea. King Theon Stark, known to history as the Hungry Wolf, turned back the greatest of these threats, making common cause with the Boltons to smash the Andal warlord Argos Sevenstar at the Battle of the Weeping Water.

In the aftermath of his victory, King Theon raised his own fleet and crossed the narrow sea to the shores of Andalos, with Argos's corpse lashed to the prow of his flagship. There, it is said, he took a bloody vengeance, burning a score of villages, capturing three tower houses and a fortified sept, and putting hundreds to the sword. The heads of the slain the Hungry Wolf claimed as prizes, carrying them back to Westeros and planting them on spikes along his own coasts as a warning to other would-be conquerors. (Later in his blood-drenched reign, he himself conquered the Three Sisters and landed an army on the Fingers, but these conquests did not long endure. King Theon also fought the ironborn in the west, driving them from Cape Kraken and

Bear Island, put down a rebellion in the Rills, and joined the Night's Watch in an incursion beyond the Wall that broke the power of the wildlings for a generation).

Even before the coming of the Andals, the Wolf's Den had been raised by King Jon Stark, built to defend the mouth of the White Knife against raiders and slavers from across the narrow sea (some scholars suggest these were early Andal incursions, whilst others argue they were the forebears of the men of Ib, or even slavers out of Valyria and Volantis).

Held for centuries by a succession of houses (including the Greystarks, an offshoot of House Stark itself, as well as Flints, Slates, Longs, Holts, Lockes, and Ashwoods), the ancient fortress would be the focus of a succession of conflicts. During the wars between Winterfell and the Andal Kings of Mountain and Vale, the Old Falcon, Osgood Arryn, laid siege to the Wolf's Den. His son, King Oswin the Talon, captured it and put it to the torch. Later, it fell under attack from the pirate lords of the Three Sisters and slavers out of the Stepstones. It was not until some thousand years before the Conquest, when the fugitive Manderlys came to the North and swore their oaths at the Wolf's Den, that the problem of the defense of the White Knife—the river that provides access into the very heart of the North—was resolved with the creation of White Harbor.

The west coast of the North has also oft been beset by reavers, and several of the Hungry Wolf's wars were forced upon him when longships out of Great Wyk, Old Wyk, Pyke, and Orkmont descended upon his western coasts beneath the banners of Harrag Hoare, King of the Iron Islands. For a time the Stony Shore did fealty to Harrag and his ironmen, swathes of the wolfswood were nothing but ashes, and Bear Island was a base for reaving, ruled by Harrag's black-hearted son, Ravos the Raper. Though Theon Stark slew Ravos with his own hand, and expelled the ironmen from his shores, they would return under Harrag's grandson, Erich the Eagle, and again under the Old Kraken, Loron Greyjoy, who retook both Bear Island and Cape Kraken (King Rodrik Stark reclaimed the first of those after the Old Kraken's death, whilst his sons and grandsons battled for the latter). The wars between the North and the ironborn would continue thereafter, but less decisively.

Until King's Landing rose beside the Blackwater, White Harbor was the newest city in the Seven Kingdoms. Built with the wealth that the Manderlys had brought with them from the Reach after having been driven into exile by Lord Lorimar Peake at the behest of King Perceon III Gardener, who feared their swelling power in the Reach, White Harbor has more in common with the fine castles and towers of the Reach than with the castles of the North; it is said that the New Keep was built to reflect the castle of Dunstonbury, which the Manderlys had lost in their exile.

THE MOUNTAIN CLANS

The clans of the Northern mountains are especially famed for their adherence to the laws of hospitality, and the petty lords who rule these clans often vie with one another to be the most open-handed of hosts. These clans—located largely in the mountainous regions beyond the wolfswood, in the high valleys and meadows, and along the Bay of Ice and certain rivers of the North—owe their allegiance to the Starks, but their disputes have oft created difficulties for the Lords of Winterfell and the Kings of Winter before them, forcing them to send men into the mountains to quell the bloodshed (commemorated in such songs as "Black Pines" and "Wolves in the Hills"), or to summon the chiefs to Winterfell to argue their cases.

The mightiest of the Northern clans are the Wulls, the fisherfolk who dwell along the shores of the Bay of Ice. Their hatred of the wildlings is matched only by their hatred of the men of the Iron Islands, who have often raided along the shore of the bay, burning their halls, carrying off their crops, and taking their wives and daughters as thralls and salt wives. Large tracts of the Stony Shore, Bear Island, Sea Dragon Point, and Cape Kraken have all been held by ironmen at times. Indeed, Cape Kraken, closest to the Iron Islands, has changed hands so many times that many maesters believe its populace to be closer in blood to the ironmen than to Northmen.

The histories of the North claim that Rodrik Stark won Bear Island back from the ironborn in a wrestling match, and perhaps there is truth to this tale; the kings of the Iron Isles were often moved to prove their prowess and their right to wear the driftwood crown with feats of strength. More sober scholars call this into question, suggesting that if there was "wrestling," it was with words.

THE STONEBORN OF SKAGOS

Despite centuries of feuds, the mountain clans have traditionally remained loyal to the Starks through war and peace. The same cannot be said of the savage denizens of Skagos, the mountainous island east of the Bay of Seals.

The Skagosi who reside there are little regarded by the other Northmen, who consider them no better than wildlings and name them Skaggs. The Skagosi call themselves the stoneborn, referring to the fact that Skagos means "stone" in the Old Tongue. A huge, hairy, foul-smelling folk (some maesters believe the Skagosi to have a strong admixture of Ibbenese blood; others suggest that they may be descended from giants), clad in skins and furs and untanned hides, and said to ride on unicorns, the Skagosi are the subject of many a dark rumor. It is claimed that they still offer human sacrifice to their weirwoods, lure passing ships to destruction with false lights, and feed upon the flesh of men during winter.

Like as not, the Skagosi surely did once practice cannibalism, though whether this custom still lingers to this day is a matter of much dispute. *The Edge of the World*—a collection of tales and legends compiled by Maester Balder, who served the commander of Eastwatch-by-the-Sea during the sixty-year rule of Lord Commander Osric Stark—is our chief source for much of what we know of the Skagosi, including the Feast of Skane, wherein a Skagosi war fleet descended upon the smaller nearby isle of Skane, raping and carrying off the Skanish women whilst slaying the Skanish men and consuming their flesh in a feast that lasted a fortnight. Whether

ABOVE | *A warrior of Skagos.*

The "unicorns" of Skagos were once scoffed at by maesters at the Citadel. The occasional "unicorn horn" offered by disreputable merchants has never been more than the horn of a kind of whale hunted by the whalers of Ib. However, horns of quite a different kind—reputed to be from Skagos—have been seen by the maesters at Eastwatch upon occasion. It is also said that those seafarers brave enough to trade on Skagos have glimpsed the stoneborn lords riding great, shaggy, horned beasts, monstrous mounts so sure-footed they have been known to climb the sides of mountains. A living example of such a creature—or even a skeleton—has long been sought for study, but none has ever been brought to Oldtown.

this be true or not, Skane remains uninhabited to this day, though tumbled stones and overgrown foundations testify that men did once dwell amongst its windswept hills and stony shores.

Though rarely seen off their island, the stoneborn once were accustomed to crossing the Bay of Seals to trade or, more oft, raid—until King Brandon Stark, Ninth of His Name, broke their power once and for all, destroyed their ships, and forbade them the sea. For most of recorded history, they have remained an isolated, backward, savage folk, as like to murder those who land upon their isle as to trade with them. When they do consent to trade, the Skagosi offer pelts, obsidian blades and arrowheads, and "unicorn horns" for goods they desire.

Some Skagosi have served in the Night's Watch as well. More than a thousand years ago, a Crowl (a member of a clan that passes for nobility on Skagos) was even Lord Commander for a time, and the *Annals of the Black Centaur* speak of a Stane (a member of another Skagosi family) who rose to become First Ranger but died shortly thereafter.

Skagos has often been a source of trouble for the Starks—both as kings when they sought to conquer it and as lords when they fought to keep its fealty. Indeed, as recently as the reign of King Daeron II Targaryen (Daeron the Good), the isle rose up against the Lord of Winterfell—a rebellion that lasted years and claimed the lives of thousands of others, including that of Barthogan Stark, Lord of Winterfell (called Barth Blacksword), before finally being put down.

THE CRANNOGMEN OF THE NECK

Last (and some might say the least) of the peoples of the North are the swamp-dwellers of the Neck, known as crannogmen for the floating islands on which they raise their halls and hovels. A small, sly people (some say they are small in stature because they intermarried with the children of the forest, but more likely it results from inadequate nourishment, for grains do not flourish amidst the fens and swamps and salt marshes of the Neck, and the crannogmen subsist largely upon a diet of fish, frogs, and lizards), they are quite secretive, preferring to keep to themselves.

South of the Neck, the riverfolk whose lands adjoin their own say that the crannogmen breathe water, have webbed hands and feet like frogs, and use poisons on their frog spears and their arrows. That last, it must be said, is true enough; many a merchant has brought rare herbs and plants with many queer properties to the Citadel, for the maesters seek such things out to better understand their properties and their value. But of the rest, there is no truth to it: crannogmen are men, albeit smaller than most, even if they live in a fashion unique in the Seven Kingdoms.

Long ago, the histories claim, the crannogmen were ruled by the Marsh Kings. Singers tell of them riding on lizard lions and using great frog spears like lances, but that is clearly fancy. Were these Marsh Kings even truly kings, as we understand it? Archmaester Eyron writes that the crannogmen saw their kings as the first among equals, who were often thought to be touched by the old gods—a fact

LEFT | *A crannogman of the Neck.*

that was said to show itself in eyes of strange hues, or even in speaking with animals as the children are said to have done.

Whatever the truth, the last man to be called Marsh King was killed by King Rickard Stark (sometimes called the Laughing Wolf in the North, for his good nature), who took the man's daughter to wife, whereupon the crannogmen bent their knees and accepted the dominion of Winterfell. In the centuries since, the crannogmen have become stout allies of the Starks, under the leadership of the Reeds of Greywater Watch.

THE LORDS OF WINTERFELL

After the Conquest and the unification of the Seven Kingdoms, the Starks became Wardens of the North rather than kings, swearing their fealty to the Iron Throne, yet remained supreme within their own domains in all but name. Though Torrhen Stark had given up the ancient crown of the Kings of Winter, his sons were less glad of the Targaryen yoke, and some among them entertained talk of rebelling, and of raising the Stark banner whether Lord Torrhen consented or not.

Fire made when the doomed prince Jacaerys Velaryon had flown to Winterfell upon his dragon.

After the Dance of the Dragons, the Starks were more overtly loyal to the Targaryens than previously. Indeed, Lord Cregan Stark's son and heir fought beneath the Targaryen banner when the Young Dragon sought to conquer Dorne. Rickon Stark fought bravely, his deeds sometimes reported by King Daeron in his *Conquest of Dorne*, and Rickon's death

Whether anti-Targaryen feelings were made worse by Queen Rhaenys Targaryen's efforts to knit together the new, single realm with marriages between the great houses is left to the reader to consider. That Torrhen Stark's daughter was wed to the young and ill-fated Lord of the Vale is well-known; it was one of the many peace-binding marriages forged by Rhaenys. But there are letters preserved at the Citadel suggesting that Stark accepted these arrangements only after much protest, and that the bride's brothers refused to attend the wedding entirely.

Later still, it was said that the Starks were bitter at the Old King and Queen Alysanne for having forced them to carve away the New Gift and give it the Night's Watch; this may be one reason for why Lord Ellard Stark sided with Corlys Velaryon and Princess Rhaenys at the Great Council of 101 AC.

We have earlier discussed House Stark's role in the Dance of the Dragons. Let it be added that Lord Cregan Stark reaped many rewards for his loyal support of King Aegon III . . . even if it was not a royal princess marrying into his family, as had been agreed in the Pact of Ice and

outside of Sunspear in one of the final battles was lamented in the North for years to come because of the troubles that dogged the reigns of his half brothers.

In the decades that followed, the North saw the Starks dealing with the rebellion of Skagos, a renewed onslaught of reaving by the ironborn under Dagon Greyjoy, and a wildling invasion led by Raymun Redbeard, the King-Beyond-the-Wall in 226 AC. In each of these, Starks died. Yet the house continued with its fortunes mostly unchanged—likely because of the firm resolve of most Lords of Winterfell not to become embroiled in the intrigues of the southron

Though in these days it is said that Lord Ellard Stark was glad to aid the Night's Watch with the Gift, and took little convincing, the truth is otherwise. Letters from Lord Stark's brother to the Citadel, asking the maesters to provide precedents against the forced donation of property, made it plain that the Starks were not eager to do as King Jaehaerys bid. It may be that the Starks feared that, under the control of the Castle Black, the New Gift would inevitably decline—for the Night's Watch would always look northward and never give much thought to their new tenants to the south. And as it happens, that soon came to pass, and the New Gift is now said to be largely unpopulated thanks to the decline of the Watch and the rising toll taken by raiders from beyond the Wall.

court. When the Stark line was nearly obliterated by Mad King Aerys after Rhaegar's abduction of Lyanna, some misguided men laid the blame at the feet of the late Lord Rickard, whose alliances by blood and friendship tied the great houses together and ensured that they would act together in response to the Mad King's crimes.

WINTERFELL

The greatest castle of the North is Winterfell, the seat of the Starks since the Dawn Age. Legend says that Brandon the Builder raised Winterfell after the generation-long winter known as the Long Night to become the stronghold of his descendants, the Kings of Winter. As Brandon the Builder is connected with an improbable number of great works (Storm's End and the Wall, to name but two prominent examples) over a span of numerous lifetimes, the tales have likely turned some ancient king, or a number of different kings of House Stark (for there have been many Brandons in the long reign of that family) into something more legendary.

The castle itself is peculiar in that the Starks did not level the ground when laying down the foundations and walls of the castle. Very likely, this reveals that the castle was built in pieces over the years rather than being planned as a single structure. Some scholars suspect that it was once a complex of linked ringforts, though the centuries have eradicated almost all evidence of this.

The outer walls of Winterfell were raised during the last two decades of the reign of King Edrick Snowbeard. Though Edrick is famed for a reign that lasted nearly a century, his rule in his dotage was increasingly erratic. Seeing this, many different factions tried to seize control of his faltering realm. The most obvious threats were from his own numerous—and fractious—descendants, but others took their chances as well, including ironmen, slavers from across the narrow sea, wildlings, and Northern rivals such as the Boltons.

The inner walls, which were once the only defensive walls, are estimated to be some two thousand years old, and perhaps some sections are older still. In later years, a defensive moat was dug around them, then a second wall was raised beyond the moat, giving the castle a formidable defense. The inner walls stand a hundred feet high, the outer walls eighty; any attacker who succeeded in capturing the outer wall would still find defenders on the inner walls loosing spears and stones and arrows down at him.

To the trained eye, the architecture of Winterfell is an amalgam of many different eras. And its vastness not only encompasses buildings but open areas as well. In fact, three acres alone are given over to an ancient godswood, where legend tells us Brandon the Builder once prayed to his gods. Whether this is true or not, the antiquity of the grove cannot be contested. And the godswood no doubt benefits from the hot springs that are contained within it, protecting the trees from the worst of the winter's chill.

We can dismiss Mushroom's claim in his *Testimony* that the dragon Vermax left a clutch of eggs somewhere in the depths of Winterfell's crypts, where the waters of the hot springs run close to the walls, while his rider treated with Cregan Stark at the start of the Dance of the Dragons. As Archmaester Gyldayn notes in his fragmentary history, there is no record that Vermax ever laid so much as a single egg, suggesting the dragon was male. The belief that dragons could change sex at need is erroneous, according to Maester Anson's *Truth*, rooted in a misunderstanding of the esoteric metaphor that Barth preferred when discussing the higher mysteries.

Within its walls, the castle sprawls across several acres of land, encompassing many freestanding buildings. The oldest of these—a long-abandoned tower, round and squat and covered with gargoyles—has become known as the First Keep. Some take this to mean that it was built by the First Men, but Maester Kennet has definitively proved that it could not have existed before the arrival of the Andals since the First Men and the early Andals raised square towers and keeps. Round towers came sometime later.

Indeed, the presence of the hot springs—which pepper the land around Winterfell—may be the chief reason why the First Men initially settled there. One can easily imagine the value that a ready source of water—and hot water, at that—would have had in the depths of a Northern winter. In recent centuries, the Starks have raised structures that have made direct use of these springs for the purpose of heating their dwellings.

Hot springs such as the one beneath Winterfell have been shown to be heated by the furnaces of the world—the same fires that made the Fourteen Flames or the smoking mountain of Dragonstone. Yet the smallfolk of Winterfell and the winter town have been known to claim that the springs are heated by the breath of a dragon that sleeps beneath the castle. This is even more foolish than Mushroom's claims and need not be given any consideration.

LEFT | *Winterfell, with the winter town outside its walls.*

THE WALL AND BEYOND

THE NIGHT'S WATCH

Unique in the Seven Kingdoms is the Night's Watch, the sworn brotherhood that has defended the Wall over centuries and millennia, born in the aftermath of the Long Night, the generation-long winter that brought the Others down on the realms of men and nearly put an end to them.

The history of the Night's Watch is a long one. Tales still tell of the black knights of the Wall and their noble calling. But the Age of Heroes is long done, and the Others have not shown themselves in thousands of years, if indeed they ever existed.

And so, year by year, the Watch has dwindled. Their own records prove that this decline has been in progress even before the age of Aegon the Conqueror and his sisters. Though the black brothers of the Watch still guard the realms of men as nobly as they may, the threats they face no longer come from Others, wights, giants, greenseers, wargs, skinchangers, and other monsters from children's tales and legend, but rather, barbaric wildlings armed with stone axes and clubs; savages to be sure, but only men, and no match for disciplined warriors.

It was not always so. Whether the legends are true or not, it is plain that the First Men and the children of the forest (and even the giants, if we take the word of the singers) feared something enough that it drove them to begin raising the Wall. And this great construction, as simple as it is, is justly accounted among the wonders of the world. It may be that its earliest foundations were of stone—the maesters differ in this—but now all that can be seen for a distance of a hundred leagues is ice. Nearby lakes provided the material, which the First Men cut into huge blocks and hauled upon sledges to the Wall, and worked into place one by one. Now, thousands of years later, the Wall stands more than seven hundred feet tall at its highest point (though its height varies considerably over the hundred leagues of its length, as it follows the contours of the land).

Beneath the shadow of that wall of ice, the Night's Watch raised nineteen strongholds—though they are unlike any other castles in the Seven Kingdoms, for they have no curtain walls or other defensive fortifications to protect them (the Wall itself being more than ample against any threat coming from the north, and the Watch insists it has no foes to the south).

The greatest and oldest of these is the Nightfort, which has been abandoned for the past two hundred years; as the Watch shrunk, its size made it too large and too costly to maintain. Maesters who served at the Nightfort whilst it was still in use made it plain that the castle had been expanded upon many times over the centuries and that little remained of its original structure save for some of the deepest vaults chiseled out of the rock beneath the castle's feet.

Yet over the thousands of years of its existence as the chief seat of the Watch, the Nightfort has accrued many legends of its own, some of which have been recounted in Archmaester Harmune's *Watchers on the Wall*. The oldest of these tales concern the legendary Night's King, the thirteenth Lord Commander of the Night's Watch, who was alleged to have bedded a sorceress pale as a corpse and declared himself a king. For thirteen years the Night's King and his "corpse queen" ruled together, before King of Winter, Brandon the Breaker, (in alliance, it is said, with the King-Beyond-the-Wall, Joramun) brought them down. Thereafter, he obliterated the Night's King's very name from memory.

In the Citadel, the archmaesters largely dismiss these tales—though some allow that there may have been a Lord Commander who attempted to carve out a kingdom for himself in the earliest days of the Watch. Some suggest that perhaps the corpse queen was a woman of the Barrowlands, a daughter of the Barrow King who was then a power in his own right, and oft associated with graves. The Night's King has been said to have been variously a Bolton, a Woodfoot,

---

Legend has it that the giants helped raise the Wall, using their great strength to wrestle the blocks of ice into place. There may be some truth to this though the stories make the giants out to be far larger and more powerful than they truly were. These same legends also say that the children of the forest—who did not themselves build walls of either ice or stone—would contribute their magic to the construction. But the legends, as always, are of dubious value.

LEFT | *Castle Black and the Wall.*

CASTLES OF THE NIGHT'S WATCH

ACTIVE

The Shadow Tower

Castle Black (*now the seat of the Lord Commander of the Watch*)

Eastwatch-by-the-Sea

ABANDONED

Westwatch-by-the-Bridge

Sentinel Stand

Greyguard

Stonedoor

Hoarfrost Hill

Icemark

The Nightfort

Deep Lake

Queensgate (*which was once named Snowgate
before being renamed in honor
of Good Queen Alysanne*)

Oakenshield

Woodswatch-by-the-Pool

Sable Hall

Rimegate

Long Barrow

Torches

Greenguard

an Umber, a Flint, a Norrey, or even a Stark, depending on where the tale is told. Like all tales, it takes on the attributes that make it most appealing to those who tell it.

The Night's Watch, which might well be called the first militant order in the Seven Kingdoms (for the first duty of all its members is to defend the Wall, and all are trained at arms to this end), has divided its sworn brothers into three groups:

1) the stewards, who supply the Watch with food, clothing, and all the other things they need to make war,

2) the builders, who tend to the Wall and the castles,

3) the rangers, who venture into the wilds beyond to make war upon the wildlings.

Leading them are the senior officers of the Watch, the chief of whom is the Lord Commander. He himself is appointed by election: the men of the Watch, each and every one—from the unlettered former poachers to the scions of the great houses—will cast a vote for the man he believes should lead them. Once one man has the greater part of the votes, he will lead the Watch until his death. It is a custom that has largely served the Watch well, and efforts to subvert it (as when Lord Commander Runcel Hightower attempted to leave the Watch to his bastard son some five hundred years ago) have never lasted.

Sadly, the most important truth about the Night's Watch today is its decline. It may once have served a great purpose. But if the Others ever existed, they have not been seen in thousands of years and are of no threat to men. It is the wildlings beyond the Wall who are the danger the Night's Watch now face. Yet only when there are kings-beyond-the-Wall have the wildlings ever truly presented a threat to the realms of men.

The vast expense in sustaining the Wall and the men who man it has become increasingly intolerable. Only three of the castles of the Night's Watch are now manned, and the order is a tenth of the size that it was when Aegon and his sisters landed, yet even at this size, the Watch remains a burden.

Some argue that the Wall serves as a useful way of ridding the realm of murderers, rapers, poachers, and their ilk, whilst others question the wisdom of putting weapons in the hands of such and training them in the arts of war. Wildling raids may rightly be considered more of a nuisance than a menace; many wise men suggest that they might be better dealt with by allowing the lords of the North to extend their rule beyond the Wall so that they can drive the wildlings back.

Only the fact that the Northmen themselves greatly honor the Watch has kept it functioning, and a great part of the food that keeps the black brothers of Castle Black, the Shadow Tower, and Eastwatch-by-the-Sea from starving comes not from the Gift but from the yearly gifts these Northern lords deliver to the Wall in token of their support.

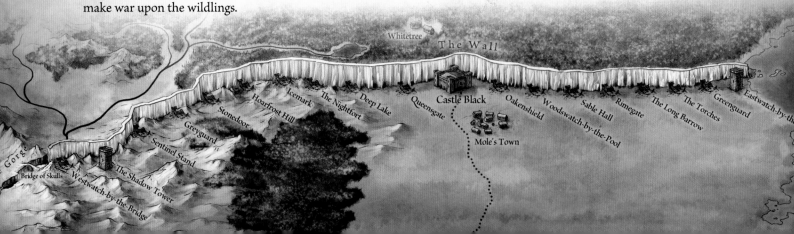

THE WILDLINGS

In the lands beyond the Wall live the diverse people—all descended from the First Men—that we of the more civilized south name wildlings.

This is not a term they use themselves. The largest and most numerous of the various peoples beyond the Wall named themselves the free folk, in their belief that their savage customs allow them lives of greater freedom than the kneelers of the south. And it is true that they live with neither lords nor kings and need bow to neither man nor priest, regardless of their birth or blood or station.

But they also live meanly, and are not free from starvation, from the extremities of cold, from barbaric warfare, or from the depredations of their own kind. The lawlessness beyond the Wall is nothing to envy, as any man who has seen wildlings can attest. (And many have so attested, in a number of works based on accounts from the rangers of the Night's Watch). Their pride in their poverty, in their stone axes and wicker-wood shields, and in their flea-infested pelts, is part of the reason they are set apart from the people in the Seven Kingdoms.

The countless tribes and clans of the free folk remain worshippers of the old gods of the First Men and children of the forest, the gods of the weirwood trees (some accounts say that there are those who worship different gods: dark gods beneath the ground in the Frostfangs, gods of snow and ice on the Frozen Shore, or crab gods at Storrold's Point, but such has never been reliably confirmed).

Rangers of the Night's Watch speak of still stranger peoples who dwell in the more distant corners of the lands beyond the Wall, of bronze-clad warriors from a hidden vale far to the north, and Hornfoots who go barefoot even over ice and snow. We know of the wild people of the Frozen Shore who live in huts of ice and ride sleds pulled by hounds. There are half a dozen tribes who make their homes in caverns, and rumors tell of cannibals in the upper reaches of the icy rivers beyond the Wall. But few rangers have penetrated more than half a hundred leagues into the haunted forest, and doubtless there are more kinds of wildlings than even they can imagine.

The threat posed to the realm by these savage peoples can safely be discounted, save for the times, once in a great while, when they united beneath the leadership of a king-beyond-the-Wall. Though many wildling raiders and war chiefs have aspired to this title, few have ever achieved it. None of the wildlings who have risen up to become King-Beyond-the-Wall have

done aught to build a true kingdom or care for their people; in truth, such men are warlords, not monarchs, and though elsewise much different one from the other, each has led his peoples against the Wall, in hopes of breaching it and conquering the Seven Kingdoms to the south.

The first King-Beyond-the-Wall, according to legend, was Joramun, who claimed to have a horn that would bring down the Wall when it woke "the giants from the earth." (That the Wall

The wildling raiders trouble the realm largely for iron and steel—things they lack the skill to make themselves. Many raiders are armed with weapons of wood and stone, even of horn in some cases. Some carry bronze axes and knives, but even these are considered valuable. The famous war leaders amongst them often sport stolen steel, sometimes taken from rangers of the Watch whom they have killed.

LEFT | *The castles of the Night's Watch.* ABOVE | *A wildling raider.*

Hardhome was once the only settlement approaching a town in the lands beyond the Wall, sheltered on Storrold's Point and commanding a deepwater harbor. But six hundred years ago, it was burned and its people destroyed, though the Watch cannot say for a certainty what happened. Some say that cannibals from Skagos fell on them, others that slavers from across the narrow sea were at fault. The strangest stories, from a ship of the Watch sent to investigate, tell of hideous screams echoing down from the cliffs above Hardhome, where no living man or woman could be found. A most fascinating account of Hardhome can be found in Maester Wyllis's *Hardhome: An Account of Three Years Spent Beyond-the-Wall among Savages, Raiders, and Woods-witches*. Wyllis journeyed to Hardhome on a Pentoshi trader and established himself there as a healer and counselor so that he might write of their customs. He was given the protection of Gorm the Wolf—a chieftain who shared control of Hardhome with three other chiefs. When Gorm was murdered in a drunken brawl, however, Wyllis found himself in mortal danger and made his way back to Oldtown. There he set down his account, only to vanish the year after the illuminations were done. It was said in the Citadel that he was last seen at the docks, looking for a ship that would take him to Eastwatch-by-the-Sea.

still stands says something of his claim, and perhaps even of his existence.)

The brothers Gendel and Gorne were joint kings three thousand years ago. Leading their host down beneath the earth into a labyrinth of twisting subterranean caverns, they passed beneath the Wall unseen to attack the North. Gorne slew the Stark king in battle, then was killed in turn by the king's heir, and Gendel and his remaining wildlings fled back to their caverns, never to been seen again.

The Horned Lord would follow them, a thousand years after (or perhaps two). His name is lost to history, but he was said to have used sorcery to pass the Wall. After him, centuries later, came Bael the Bard, whose songs are still sung beyond the Wall . . . but there are questions as to

Among the wildlings, it is said that Gendel and his people became lost and trapped in the caverns and still wander there today. Among the histories of the rangers, however, it is said that Gendel was slain as well, and that only a handful of his followers lived to flee back into the ground.

whether he truly existed or not. The wildlings say he did and credit many songs to his name, but the old chronicles of Winterfell say nothing of him. Whether this was due to the defeats and humiliations he was said to have visited upon them (including, according to one improbable story, deflowering a Stark maid and getting her with child) or because he never existed, we cannot truly say.

The last King-Beyond-the-Wall to cross the Wall was Raymun Redbeard, who brought the wildlings together in 212 or 213 AC. It was not until 226 AC that he and the wildlings would breach the Wall by climbing in their hundreds and thousands up the slick ice and down the other side.

Raymun's host numbered in the thousands, by all accounts, and they fought their way as far south as Long Lake. There, Lord Willam Stark and the Drunken Giant, Lord Harmond of House Umber, brought their armies against them. With two hosts surrounding him, and the lake to his back, Redbeard fought and died, but not before slaying Lord Willam.

When the Night's Watch appeared at last, led by its Lord Commander Jack Musgood (called Jolly Jack Musgood before the invasion, and Sleepy Jack Musgood forever after), the battle was done and the angry Artos Stark (the late Lord Willam's brother, accounted the most fearsome warrior of his age) gave the black brothers the duty of burying the dead. This task, at the least, they performed admirably.

BELOW | *A wildling host gathering at the Wall.*

RIVERLANDS

Greywater Watch

The Twins

CAPE of EAGLES

Seagard

IRON ISLANDS

IRONMAN'S BAY

GREEN FORK

KINGSROAD

Oldstones

BLUE FORK

Fairmarket

Bloody Gate

ROAD

RIVER

RED FORK

Inn
of the
Kneeling Man

Stone Hedge

Inn at the
Crossroads

Saltpans

TUMBLESTONE

Riverrun

RIVER ROAD

TRIDENT

Quiet Isle

BAY of CRABS

Lord
harroway's
Town

high heart

RED FORK ROAD

harrenhal

Maidenpool

Acorn hall

GOD'S EYE

Antlers

hornvale

Pinkmaiden

Isle
of
Faces

Stoney
Sept

KINGSROAD

WESTERLAND

BLACKWATER RUSH

King's
Landing

CROWNLANDS

LEGEND

♜	MAJOR CASTLE
♜	CASTLES
⌂	TOWN
🏠	INN
⛰	RUINS
🐂	CATTLE
✝	HILL
- - -	ROAD

REACH

THE RIVERLANDS

MUCH HISTORY—RIFE with both glory and tragedy—has been made in the lands watered by the river Trident and its three great vassal streams.

Stretching from the Neck to the banks of the Blackwater, and east to the borders of the Vale, the riverlands are the beating heart of Westeros. No other land in the Seven Kingdoms has seen so many battles, nor so many petty kings and royal houses rising and falling. The causes of this are clear. Rich and fertile, the riverlands border on every other realm in the Seven Kingdoms save Dorne, yet have few natural boundaries to deter invasion. The waters of the Trident make the lands ripe for settlement, farming, and conquest, whilst the river's three branches stimulate trade and travel during peacetime, and serve as both roads and barriers in times of war.

on weathered stones in runes whose meanings are even now disputed at the Citadel. Thus, whilst singers and storytellers may regale us with colorful tales of Artos the Strong, Florian the Fool, Nine-Finger Jack, Sharra the Witch Queen, and the Green King of the Gods Eye, the very existence of such personages must be questioned by the serious scholar.

The true history of the riverlands begins with the coming of the Andals. After crossing the narrow sea and sweeping over the Vale, these conquerors from the east moved to make it their own, sailing their longships up the Trident and its three great branches. In those days, it seems the Andals fought in bands behind chieftains who the later septons would name kings. Piece by piece, they encroached upon the many petty kings whose realms the rivers watered.

The importance of the Trident to the region was never made clearer then when King Harwyn Hoare, the grandfather of Harren the Black, fought over the riverlands with the Storm King Arrec. The ironborn reavers were able to achieve dominance on the rivers and use them as a means to transport forces swiftly between far-flung strongholds and battlefields. The Storm King suffered his worst defeat at the crossing of the Blue Fork near Fairmarket, where the longships proved decisive in allowing the ironborn to seize the crossing despite Arrec's superior numbers.

The three branches of the Trident give the riverlands their name: the Red Fork, colored by the mud and silt that tumbles down from the western mountains; the Green Fork, whose mossy waters emerge from the swamps of the Neck; and the Blue Fork, named for the purity of its sparkling, spring-fed flow. Their wide waters are the roads by which goods pass through the riverlands, and it is not unknown to see lines of poleboats stretching a mile or more. There has never been a city in the riverlands, strange as that might seem (though large market towns are common), likely because of the fractious history of the region and a tendency for the kings of the past to refuse the charters that might have given some Saltpans or Lord Harroway's Town or Fairmarket leave to expand.

During the long centuries when the First Men reigned supreme in Westeros, countless petty kingdoms rose and fell in the riverlands. Their histories, entwined and embroidered with myth and song, are largely forgotten, save for the names of a few legendary kings and heroes whose deeds are recorded

Songs speak to us through the years of the Fall of Maidenpool and the death of its boy king, Florian the Brave, Fifth of That Name; of the Widow's Ford, where three sons of Lord Darry held back the Andal warlord Vorian Vypren and his knights for a day and a night, slaying hundreds before they fell themselves; of the night in the White Wood, where supposedly the children of the forest emerged from beneath a hollow hill to send hundreds of wolves against an Andal camp, tearing hundreds of men apart beneath the light of a crescent moon; of the great Battle of Bitter River, where the Brackens of Stone Hedge and the Blackwoods of Raventree Hall made common cause against the invaders, only to be shattered by the charge of 777 Andal knights and seven septons, bearing the seven-pointed star of the Faith upon their shields.

The seven-pointed star went everywhere the Andals went, borne before them on shields and banners, embroidered on their surcoats, sometimes incised into their very flesh. In their zeal for the Seven, the conquerors looked upon the old gods of the First Men and the children of the forest as little more than demons, and fell upon the weirwood groves sacred to them with steel and fire, destroying the great white trees wherever they found them and hacking out their carved faces.

The great hill called High Heart was especially holy to the First Men, as it had been to the children of the forest before them. Crowned by a grove of giant weirwoods, ancient as any that had been seen in the Seven Kingdoms, High Heart was still the abode of the children and their greenseers. When the Andal king Erreg the Kinslayer surrounded the hill, the children emerged to defend it, calling down clouds of ravens and armies of wolves . . . or so the legend tells us. Yet neither tooth nor talon was a match for the steel axes of the Andals, who slaughtered the greenseers, the beasts, and the First Men alike, and raised beside the High Heart a hill of corpses half again as high . . . or so the singers would have us believe.

True History suggests otherwise, insisting that the children had abandoned the riverlands long before the Andals crossed the narrow sea. But however it happened, the grove was destroyed. Today only stumps remain where once the weirwoods stood.

suggests they were third). The Blackwoods and Brackens both claim to have ruled the riverlands at various times during the Age of Heroes.

The Mudds succeeded in unifying more of the riverlands than any of their predecessors, but their reign was not to last. The Hammer of Justice was succeeded by his son, Tristifer V, or Tristifer the Last, who proved unable to stem the Andal tide and failed even to hold his own people together.

The Andal kings who brought down Oldstones and slew Tristifer the Last intermarried with remaining nobility of the First Men and butchered those who would not bend the knee. A quarrelsome, warlike folk, the Andals divided up the riverlands amongst themselves. The blood of the last kings of the First Men had scarce dried before their Andal conquerors began to war each upon the others for dominance. Though many a lord would name himself King of the Rivers and Hills or King of the Trident, centuries would pass before any of these petty monarchs held sway over enough of the riverlands to be worthy of these titles.

The first of the Andal kings to bring all the riverlands under his sway was a bastard born of a tryst between two ancient enemies, the Blackwoods and the Brackens. As a boy, he was Benedict Rivers, despised by all, but he grew to

Though Erreg's name is one of the blackest in the ancient histories, one may wonder if he ever existed in truth. Archmaester Perestan has suggested that Erreg might, in fact, be a corruption of an Andal title and not a name at all. Perestan goes further in his *A Consideration on History*, suggesting this nameless Andal chieftain had cut down the trees at the behest of a rival of the river king, who used the Andals as sellswords.

The penultimate and greatest of the river kings to stand before the Andals was Tristifer IV of House Mudd, the Hammer of Justice, who ruled from a great castle called Oldstones, on a hill by the banks of the Blue Fork. The singers tell us he fought a hundred battles against the invaders and won nine-and-ninety of them, only to fall in the hundredth, when he rode to war against an alliance of seven Andal kings. Yet it seems convenient that there are seven kings in the songs; likely this is another tale concocted by the septons as a lesson in piety.

Before the Mudds, there had been other kings near as powerful. The Fishers are said in some chronicles to have been the first and oldest line of river kings (in others, they are accounted the second dynasty, and the fragmentary *Annals of the Rivers* from the ancient septry at Peasedale

be the greatest warrior of his age, Ser Benedict the Bold. His prowess in battle won him the support of both his mother's house and his father's, and soon other riverlords bent their knees to him as well. It required more than thirty years for Benedict to throw down the last of the petty kings of the Trident. Only when the last had yielded did he don a crown himself.

As king, he became known as Benedict the Just, a name that pleased him so much that he set aside his bastard surname and took Justman as the name of his house. As wise as he was stern, he reigned for three-and-twenty years, extending his domains as far as Maidenpool and the Neck. His son, another Benedict, reigned for sixty years and added Duskendale, Rosby, and the mouth of the Blackwater to the river realm.

House Justman ruled the riverlands for close on three centuries, the chronicles tell us. Their line was ended when Qhored Hoare, King of the Iron Islands, murdered the sons of King Bernarr II whilst they were held captive in Pyke. Their father did not long survive them, provoked into a hopeless war for vengeance against the ironborn.

Another period of anarchy and bloodshed followed. The realm that Benedict the Bold had knitted together was torn asunder once again, and a hundred years of conflict saw petty kings from the Houses Blackwood, Bracken, Vance, Mallister, and Charlton contending with one another for supremacy.

The unlikely victor in these struggles was Lord Torrence Teague, an adventurer of uncertain birth who seized a fortune in gold in a daring attack upon the westerlands and used the wealth to bring sellswords across the narrow sea in great numbers. Seasoned warriors all, their blades proved the difference, and Teague was crowned King of the Trident at Maidenpool after six long years of war.

It is said, however, that neither King Torrence nor his heirs ever sat securely on their thrones. The Teagues were so little loved by those they ruled that they were forced to keep the sons and daughters of all the great houses of the Trident at their court as hostages, in case of treason. Even so, the fourth Teague monarch, King Theo the Saddle-Sore, spent his entire reign ahorse, leading his knights from one rebellion to the next whilst hanging hostages from every tree.

As with the First Men, the dynasties of the Andal river kings oft proved short-lived, for enemies surrounded their realms on every side. Ironmen from the isles raided their coasts to the west, whilst pirates from the Stepstones and Three Sisters did the same to the east. Westermen rode down from the hills across the Red Fork to pillage and conquer, and the wild hill tribes emerged from the Mountains of the Moon to burn, plunder, and carry off women. From the southwest, the lords of the Reach sent iron columns of knights across the Blackwater whenever it pleased them; to the southeast lay the domains of the Storm Kings, ever eager for gold and glory.

In all the long history of the Trident, under hundreds of rulers, there was hardly ever a time when the riverfolk were not at war with at least one of their neighbors. Sometimes they were forced to fight upon two or even three fronts at once.

Worse, few of the river kings ever enjoyed the full support of his own lords bannermen. Memories of ancient wrongs and bygone betrayals were not oft put aside by the lords of the Trident, whose enmities ran as deep as the rivers that watered their lands. Time and time again, one or more of

these riverlords would join with some invader against their own king; indeed, in some cases, it was these very lords who brought the outsiders into the riverlands, offering them lands or gold or daughters for their help against familiar foes.

Many a river king was toppled by such alliances, and each new battle only served to set the stage for another to follow. With hindsight, it is plain to see that it was only a matter of time until one of the invaders chose to stay and claim the riverlands for his own.

The first to do so was the Storm King, Arlan III Durrandon.

Humfrey of House Teague was King of the Rivers and the Hills in those days. A pious ruler, he founded many septs and motherhouses across the riverlands and attempted to repress the worship of the old gods within his realm.

This led Raventree to rise against him, for the Blackwoods had never accepted the Seven. The Vances of Atranta and the Tullys of Riverrun joined them in rebellion. King Humfrey and his loyalists, supported by the Swords and Stars of the Faith Militant, were on the point of crushing them when Lord Roderick Blackwood sent to Storm's End for aid. His lordship was tied to House Durrandon by marriage, as King Arlan had taken one of Lord Roderick's daughters to wife, wedding her by the old rites beneath the great dead weirwood in Raventree's godswood.

Arlan III was quick to respond. Calling all his banners, the Storm King led a great host across the Blackwater Rush,

ABOVE | *King Benedict of House Justman.*

smashing King Humfrey and his loyalists in a series of bloody battles and lifting the siege of Raventree. Roderick Blackwood and Elston Tully both fell in the fighting, along with Lords Bracken, Darry, Smallwood, and both Lords Vance. King Humfrey, his brother and champion, Ser Damon, and his sons Humfrey, Hollis, and Tyler all perished in the campaign's final battle, a bloody affray fought beneath two hills called the Mother's Teats on land claimed by both the Blackwoods and the Brackens.

King Humfrey was the first to die that day, it is written. His heir, Prince Humfrey, took up his crown and sword, but died a short time later, whereupon the second son, Hollis, did the same, only to be killed in turn. And so it went, the bloody crown of the last river king passing from son to son, and finally to King Humfrey's brother, all within the space of a single afternoon. By the time the sun went down, House Teague had been entirely extinguished, along with the Kingdom of Rivers and Hills. The fight in which they died has hereafter been known as the Battle of Six Kings, in honor of Arlan III the Storm King and the five river kings his stormlanders slew, some of whom reigned for minutes, not even hours.

Certain letters found by maesters in service at Storm's End and Raventree Hall in later centuries suggest that Arlan III did not intend to claim the riverlands for himself when he marched north but rather planned to restore the crown to House Blackwood, in the person of his good-father Lord Roderick. His lordship's death in battle twisted those plans awry, however, for the heir to Raventree was a boy of eight, and the Storm King neither liked nor trusted Lord Blackwood's surviving brothers. It appears that King Arlan briefly considered crowning his good-daughter Shiera, Roderick Blackwood's eldest child, with his own son ruling at her side, but the riverlords spoke out against being ruled by a woman, and His Grace decided to add the riverlands to his own domains.

And so they would remain for more than three centuries, though the riverlords rose against Storm's End at least once each generation. A dozen pretenders from as many houses would adopt the style of River King or King of the Trident and vow to throw off the yoke of the stormlanders. Some even succeeded . . . for a fortnight, a moon's turn, even a year. But their thrones were built on mud and sand, and in the end a fresh host would march from Storm's End to topple them and hang the men who'd presumed to sit upon them. Thus ended the brief inglorious reigns of Lucifer Justman (Lucifer the Liar), Marq Mudd (the Mad Bard), Lord Robert Vance, Lord Petyr Mallister, Lady Jeyne Nutt,

the bastard king Ser Addam Rivers, the peasant king Pate of Fairmarket, and Ser Lymond Fisher, Knight of Oldstones, along with a dozen more.

When Storm's End's grasp upon the riverlands was finally shattered, it was no riverlord who broke it but a rival conqueror from beyond the lands of the Trident: Harwyn Hoare, called the Hardhand, King of the Iron Islands. Crossing Ironman's Bay with a hundred longships, Harwyn's force landed forty leagues south of Seagard and marched inland to the Blue Fork, carrying their ships with them on their shoulders in a feat the singers of the isles still celebrate.

As the ironborn moved up and down the rivers, reaving and raiding as they pleased, the riverlords fell back before them or took shelter in their castles, unwilling to risk battle in the name of a king many of them reviled. Those who did take up arms were savagely punished. A bold young knight named Samwell Rivers, a natural son of Tommen Tully, Lord of Riverrun, assembled a small host and met King Harwyn on the Tumblestone, but his lines shattered when the Hardhand charged. Hundreds drowned attempting to flee. Rivers himself was hacked in two, so that half his body might be delivered to each of his parents.

Lord Tully abandoned Riverrun without a fight, fleeing with all his strength to join the host gathering at Raventree Hall under Lady Agnes Blackwood and her sons. But when Lady Agnes advanced upon the ironborn, her belligerent neighbor Lord Lothar Bracken fell upon her rear with all his strength and put her men to flight. Lady Agnes herself and two of her sons were captured and delivered to King Harwyn, who forced the mother to watch as he strangled her boys with his bare hands. Yet Lady Agnes did not weep if the tales are true. "I have other sons," she told the King of the Iron Isles. "Raventree shall endure long after you and yours are cast down and destroyed. Your line shall end in blood and fire."

Likely this prophetic speech is a later invention, added to the tale by some singer or storyteller. What we do know is that Harwyn Hardhand was so impressed by his captive's defiance that he offered to spare her life and take her as a salt wife. "I would sooner have your sword inside me than your cock," Lady Agnes replied. Harwyn Hardhand granted her wish.

The rout of Lady Blackwood's host spelled the end of the riverlords' resistance to the ironborn, but not the end of the fighting, for word of the invasion had finally reached King Arrec Durrandon at distant Storm's End. Assembling a mighty host, the Storm King raced north to meet the foe.

So eager was this young king to come to grips with the ironmen that he soon outpaced his own baggage train—a

RIGHT | *The Storm King Arrec overlooking the battle at Fairmarket.*

grievous mistake, as Arrec learned when he crossed the Blackwater and found every castle shut against him and neither food nor fodder to be found, only burning towns and blackened fields.

Many of the riverlords had joined the ironmen by then. Under the command of the Lords Goodbrook, Paege, and Vypren, they slipped across the Blackwater and fell upon the slow-moving baggage train before it reached the river, putting King Arrec's rear guard to flight and seizing his supplies.

Thus it was a stumbling, starving host of stormlanders who finally faced Harwyn Hardhand at Fairmarket, where Lothar Bracken, Theo Charlton, and a score of other riverlords had joined him. King Arrec had half again as many fighters as his foes, but his men were weary from days of marching, confused and dispirited, and their king soon showed himself to be both headstrong and indecisive. When battle was joined, the result was a shattering defeat for the stormlanders. Arrec himself escaped the carnage, but two of his brothers died in the fighting, and the rule of Storm's End over the lands of the Trident came to a sudden, bloody end.

Across the riverlands, it is said, many smallfolk rejoiced to hear the tidings, whilst their lords, emboldened, rose against the few small garrisons of stormlanders that remained scattered across the region, casting them out or putting them to the sword. The bells at Stoney Sept rang for a day and a night, the chroniclers tell us, and singers and begging brothers went from town to town to proclaim that the men of the Trident were their own masters once again.

These celebrations proved short-lived, however. It has been said, particularly about Stone Hedge, that Lord Lothar Bracken had made common cause with the ironborn in the belief that the Hardhand would make him king once the stormlanders had been expelled, but there is no written evidence that supports this claim. It seems unlikely: Harwyn

Hoare was not the sort of man to give away crowns. Just as Arlan III Durrandon had done three centuries earlier, Harwyn claimed the riverlands for himself. Those riverlords who had fought beside him had done naught but exchange one master for another . . . and their new master was harsher, crueler, and more exacting than the old one.

Lothar Bracken himself was amongst the first to learn that lesson when he sought to rise against the Hardhand half a year later. Only a few minor lords rallied to his banners, and King Harwyn crushed him utterly, sacking, then slighting Stone Hedge and hanging Lord Bracken from a crow cage for the best part of a year whilst he slowly starved to death.

In later life, King Arrec twice attempted to cross the Blackwater and take back what he had lost, but without success. His eldest son and successor, King Arlan V, tried as well, and died in the attempt.

Harwyn Hardhand would rule the riverlands until his own death (he died abed at the age of sixty-four, whilst taking carnal pleasure of one of his many salt wives), and his son and grandson would succeed him each in turn, continuing the brutal domination of the ironborn over the peoples of the Trident. Harwyn's grandson, King Harren the Black, spent most of his life in the riverlands building the gigantic fortress that would bear his name, returning to the Iron Islands only infrequently.

Such was the state of affairs when Aegon the Conqueror came ashore and put an end to Harren and House Hoare. The rule of the ironborn over the riverlands ended in the holocaust that engulfed Harrenhal. Afterward, Aegon named Edmyn Tully of Riverrun, first of the riverlords to declare for the Targaryens, the Lord Paramount of the Trident, reducing the other riverlords to vassals. Kingship he retained for himself; there would be no kings in Westeros but Aegon.

HOUSE TULLY

The Tullys of Riverrun were never kings, though the books of lineages will show any number of connections to the dynasties of the past. It may have been these old connections that started House Tully on its path to becoming Lords Paramount of the Trident under Aegon I.

Tully names appear in many chronicles and annals of the Trident, back unto the days of the First Men, when the first Edmure Tully and his sons fought beside the Hammer of Justice, Tristifer IV Mudd, in many of his ninety-nine victories. After Tristifer's death, Ser Edmure went over to the mightiest of the Andal conquerors, Armistead Vance. It was from him that Edmure's son Axel received a grant of lands at the juncture of the Red Fork and its swift-running vassal the Tumblestone. There Lord Axel established his seat, in a red castle he named Riverrun.

Placed as it was, Riverrun soon proved to have great strategic value, and the petty kings contending during the age of anarchy soon began to vie for the support of House Tully. Axel and his descendants grew wealthy and powerful, and in time became the bulwark of many a river king, for they defended the Trident's western marches against the Kingdom of the Rock.

The Tullys were accounted amongst the foremost lords of the riverlands by the time that the Storm Kings won their final war against the last King of the Rivers and Hills. Some noble houses were destroyed in those wars, but most bent the knee to the Storm Kings once the Teagues were dispossessed, and the Tullys were amongst them. Soon Tullys began to appear in prominent offices and trusted positions.

Riverrun weathered the reigns of the Storm Kings and survived the subsequent ironborn conquest largely intact. Other powerful houses of the riverlands were not so fortunate. A decade before Aegon's Conquest, the Blackwoods and Brackens had entered into a new private war in their ancient feud. Previously their ironborn overlords had largely ignored such conflicts amongst their vassals—indeed, if the *Iron Chronicle* can be believed, Harwyn Hardhand oft seemed to pit his bannermen against one another to keep them weak.

But this time the feuding disrupted the construction of Harrenhal, and that was enough reason for Harren the Black to deal with them harshly. So it was that, when Aegon the Conqueror marched upon Harrenhal, the Tullys of Riverrun were the most powerful of riverlords still remaining.

HEREWITH A LIST OF HOUSES THAT HAVE AT ONE TIME OR ANOTHER RULED THE RIVERLANDS, AS ASSERTED IN THE HISTORIES

HOUSE FISHER, of the Misty Isle

HOUSE BLACKWOOD, of Raventree

HOUSE BRACKEN, of Stone Hedge

HOUSE MUDD, of Oldstones (last dynasty of the First Men to rule the riverlands)

HOUSE JUSTMAN

HOUSE TEAGUE (last of the Kings of the Rivers and Hills native to the riverlands)

HOUSE DURRANDON, of Storm's End

HOUSE HOARE, of the Iron Islands

ABOVE | *The arms of House Tully (center) and some houses of note, past and present, (clockwise from top): Mallister, Mooton, Darry, Mudd, Piper, Strong, Vance, Bracken, Blackwood, Whent, Lothston, and Frey.* RIGHT | *The deaths of Prince Aegon and his dragon, Quicksilver.*

The feud of the Blackwoods and Brackens is infamous, and rightly so, for it stretches back thousands of years to before the coming of the Andals. The origins of it are contested and shrouded in legend. The Blackwoods say they were kings and the Brackens little more than petty lords set on betraying and deposing them, while the Brackens say much the same about the Blackwoods. That they were both royal houses on the Trident seems true enough, and none can doubt that their enmity sprang from some cause, so entrenched that it has become legendary. Powerful as they were, they have maintained their feud despite the many kings who have attempted to make a peace between them. Even the Old King, Jaehaerys the Conciliator, failed in his attempt to halt this ceaseless war, for the peace he forged did not long outlast the end of his reign.

Forty years of Black Harren's rule, which brought penury and the deaths of thousands, had won him no love in the riverlands. Consequently, Aegon's arrival was heralded by lords great and small flocking to his banner, keen to overthrow their cruel foreign king—and chief amongst them was Edmyn Tully. When Harrenhal burned and Harren the Black's line was ended, Aegon gave the rule of the riverlands to Lord Edmyn. Some even proposed that Lord Tully be granted dominion over the Iron Islands as well, though that did not come to pass.

Lord Edmyn did much to repair the damage that Harren had left behind him. New ties were forged, as when the new-made Lord Quenton Qoherys—once master-at-arms at Dragonstone, and by then lord of ruined Harrenhal and its sizable lands—took Lord Tully's daughter to wife. (Though in later years this would prove a troublesome connection, alleviated only by the swift, sad end of House Qoherys). It was in 7 AC, as well, that Lord Edmyn began his two years as Hand of the King, ending when he resigned the office and returned to Riverrun and his family.

In the years to come, men of House Tully would play a role in many of the chief events of the early Targaryen kings. When King Aenys I guested at Riverrun and Harren the Red slew Gargon the Guest, it was to the Tullys and their bannermen that His Grace turned to try to wrest Harrenhal away from the outlaw king. In later years, the Tullys—together with the Harroways, who at that time ruled Harrenhal—fielded part of the army that surrounded and defeated Prince Aegon and his dragon, Quicksilver, in his war against his uncle, Maegor the Cruel.

The Lords of Harrenhal

Lord Gargon, the second and last Qoherys lord of Harrenhal, was the grandson of Lord Quenton. He was notorious for his appetite for women and became known as the Guest for his habit of attending every wedding within his domains, so that he might take advantage of the lord's right to the first night. It is no surprise that the father of a maid Lord Gargon deflowered opened a sally port for Harren the Red and his band of outlaws, or that Gargon was gelded before he died. Harrenhal would earn a reputation as cursed in the years that followed, as many of its ruling houses would meet unhappy ends:

HOUSE HARROWAY

Raised to Harrenhal in the reign of Aenys I, following the death of Gargon Qoherys, Lord Lucas Harroway saw his daughter Alys wed to Maegor. She became one of Maegor's queens, and he became Hand, until Maegor the Cruel had them and all their line killed.

HOUSE TOWERS

After destroying House Harroway, King Maegor decreed that the strongest of his knights would have the castle, though not all of its lands. Twenty-three knights of his household fought in the blood-soaked streets of Lord Harroway's Town for the prize. Ser Walton Towers was the victor and was granted the seat, though he died soon thereafter of his wounds. His line faltered two generations later when the last Lord Towers died without heirs.

HOUSE STRONG

Lyonel Strong, famed as a warrior but also a man of great natural gifts who had earned six links in his chain at the Citadel, was granted the lordship in the reign of Jaehaerys I. He served as master of laws, then Hand to Viserys I, while his sons became deeply entangled in the court. He and his heir, Ser Harwin, were killed in a fire that broke out in Harrenhal, leaving the younger son Larys Strong to become Lord of Harrenhal. Larys survived the Dance of the Dragons but not the Judgment of the Wolf.

HOUSE LOTHSTON

Ser Lucas Lothston—master-at-arms at the Red Keep— was given the seat as a gift from King Aegon III in 151 AC. Newly wed to the Lady Falena Stokeworth, following the scandal of her relations with Prince Aegon, the future Aegon the Unworthy, Lothston soon departed court with his bride. He returned to King's Landing in Aegon's reign, serving as Hand for less than a year before Aegon again banished him from court along with his wife and daughter. Their line was ended in madness and chaos when Lady Danelle Lothston turned to the black arts during the reign of King Maekar I.

HOUSE WHENT

Knights in the service of the Lothstons, they were given Harrenhal as a reward for their service in bringing the Lothstons down. They hold the seat to this day, but tragedy has marked them.

It was during the early days of the Dance that Prince Daemon Targaryen led Queen Rhaenyra's forces to a bloodless victory at Harrenhal, seizing the castle and making it a rallying place for her supporters. There were many such supporters in the riverlands, who rose in their thousands and joined the prince's host in Rhaenyra's name. Notable amongst them was the puissant knight, Lord Forrest Frey, who had once been a suitor for Rhaenyra's hand. The Freys were not an old house. They had risen to prominence some six hundred years ago, their line originating from a petty lord who raised a rickety wooden bridge across the narrowest part of the Green Fork. But as their wealth and influence grew, so did the Crossing. And soon the castle grew from a single tower that overlooked the bridge to two formidable towers that bracketed the river between them. These two keeps, now called the Twins, are amongst the strongest in the realm.

Lord Forrest fought gallantly for the queen he had loved, until the Fishfeed, where he was amongst many lords and knights killed in the war's bloodiest battle. His widow, the Lady Sabitha of House Vypren, proved redoubtable for her courage and notorious for her lack of mercy. According to Mushroom, she was a "sharp-featured, sharp-tongued harridan of House Vypren, who would sooner ride than dance, wore mail instead of silk, and was fond of killing men and kissing women."

But it was not long before Riverrun, too, began to chafe beneath King Maegor's heel. As his enemies rose around him, the Tullys rallied to the banners of Prince Jaehaerys Targaryen, brother of the slain Prince Aegon, in the final year of his cruel uncle's reign.

Through the years that followed, the Tullys continued to leave their mark on history. Lord Grover Tully spoke for Prince Viserys Targaryen over Laenor Velaryon as the successor to Jaehaerys I in the Great Council of 101 AC. When the Dance of the Dragons erupted in 129 AC, the

LEFT | *The great castle of Harrenhal.*   ABOVE | *Lord Forrest Frey riding to war.*

old lord proved loyal to his principles and King Aegon II. . . but he was aged then, and bedridden, and his grandson Ser Elmo defied him and had the gates barred and the banners kept close.

Later during the Dance, Ser Elmo Tully led the riverlords into battle at Second Tumbleton, but on the side of Queen Rhaenyra rather than King Aegon II, whom his grandsire had favored. The battle proved a victory—at least in part—and soon after, his grandfather finally died, and Ser Elmo became Lord of Riverrun. But he did not long enjoy his station; he died on the march forty-nine days later, leaving his young son, Ser Kermit, to succeed him.

Lord Kermit brought the Tullys to the height of their power. Vital and bold, he fought tirelessly for Queen Rhaenyra, and her son, Prince Aegon, later King Aegon III. Lord Kermit was the chief commander of the host that descended on King's Landing in the last days of the war, and he personally slew Lord Borros Baratheon in the final battle of the Dance of the Dragons.

His successors ruled as best they could after him, but Riverrun was never again as prominent as during those years. Loyal to House Targaryen through all the Blackfyre Rebellions, House Tully finally soured on the dragon kings during the madness of King Aerys II Targaryen, and Lord Hoster Tully joined Robert Baratheon and his rebels and helped bind together the alliance that brought Robert to the Iron Throne by granting the hands of his daughters to Lord Jon Arryn of the Eyrie and Lord Eddard Stark of Winterfell.

RIVERRUN

The seat of House Tully is small when compared to the great fortress castles of other great houses. It is not even the largest castle in the riverlands, for Harren the Black's ruined immensity of Harrenhal could contain ten Riverruns.

Yet Riverrun is stout and well constructed, and its position at the juncture of two rivers, surrounded by deep waters on two sides, makes it exceedingly difficult to assault. Though besieged many times over the centuries, Riverrun has seldom been taken, and never by storm. Key to the castle's strength is the moat dug beneath its western wall, where the main gate stands. Many castles in the Seven Kingdoms have moats, but few are created with complicated sluice gates that allow them to be flooded at need. This gives Riverrun's moat a depth and breadth few others can achieve. With its moat fully flooded, Riverrun becomes an island, all but invulnerable to assault.

ABOVE | *Ser Elmo Tully.* RIGHT | *Riverrun.*

THE VALE

THE VALE OF ARRYN—a long, wide, fertile valley entirely ringed by the great grey-green peaks of the mighty Mountains of the Moon—is as rich as it is beautiful. Perhaps that was why the first Andal invaders chose to land there when they crossed the narrow sea beneath the banners of their gods. The proof of that claim lies in the stones carved all about the Fingers, which bear images of stars, swords, and axes (or hammers, as some have argued). The sacred book of the Faith, *The Seven-Pointed Star*, speaks of a "golden land amidst towering mountains" when Hugor of the Hill received his vision of the bounty that would one day belong to the Andals.

Isolated from the rest of Westeros by its towering mountains, the Vale proved the perfect ground for the Andals to carve out their first kingdoms in this new land. The First Men, who were there before the Andals, fought these seaborne conquerors stubbornly, but the Vale was but thinly peopled in those days, and they soon found themselves outnumbered in every fight. No sooner was one longship set aflame or driven back into the sea, the singers say, than ten more rose from the dawn. Nor could the First Men match the zeal of the invaders, and their bronze axes and byrnies of bronze scales proved less than equal to the steel swords and iron ringmail of the Andals.

Moreover, the Vale and its surrounding peaks were divided into a score of petty kingdoms when the first Andals began wading ashore, with the seven-pointed star painted (or carved, in some cases) on their chests. Riven by ancient enmities, the kings of the First Men did not unite against the invaders when first they appeared but rather made pacts and alliances with them, seeking to use the newcomers in their wars against one another. (A familiar folly that was to be repeated time and time again as the Andals spread out across Westeros).

Dywen Shell and Jon Brightstone, both of whom claimed the title King of the Fingers, went so far as to pay Andal warlords to cross the sea, each thinking to use their swords against the other. Instead the warlords turned upon their hosts. Within a year Brightstone had been taken, tortured, and beheaded, and Shell roasted alive inside his wooden longhall. An Andal knight named Corwyn Corbray took the daughter of the former for his bride and the wife of the latter for his bedwarmer, and claimed the Fingers for his own (though Corbray, unlike many of his fellows, never

named himself a king, preferring the more modest style of Lord of the Five Fingers).

Farther south, the wealthy harbor town of Gulltown on the Bay of Crabs was ruled by Osgood Shett, Third of His Name, a grizzled old warrior who claimed the ancient, vainglorious title King of the True Men, a style that supposedly went back ten thousand years to the Dawn Age. Though Gulltown itself was seemingly secure behind its thick stone walls, King Osgood and his forebears had long been waging an intermittent war against the Bronze Kings of Runestone, a more powerful neighbor from a house as old and storied as their own. Yorwyck Royce, Sixth of That Name, had claimed the Runic Crown when his sire died in battle three years previous, and had proved to be a most redoubtable foe, defeating the Shetts in several battles and driving them back inside their town walls.

Unwisely, King Osgood turned to Andalos for help in recovering all he had lost. Thinking to avoid the fate of Shell and Brightstone, he sought to bind his allies to him with blood in place of gold; he gave his daughter in marriage to the Andal knight Gerold Grafton, took Ser Gerold's eldest daughter for his own bride, and married a younger daughter to his son and heir. All the marriages were performed by septons, according to the rites of the Seven From Across the Sea. Shett even went so far as to convert to the Faith himself, swearing to build a great sept in Gulltown should the Seven grant him victory. Then he sallied forth with his Andal allies to meet the Bronze King.

King Osgood won his victory, as it happened, but he himself did not survive the battle, and afterward it was whispered amongst the Gulltowners and other First Men that it was Ser Gerold himself who struck him down. Upon his return to the town, the Andal warlord claimed his goodfather's crown for his own, dispossessing the younger Shett and confining him to his bedchamber until such time as he had gotten Ser Gerold's daughter with child (after which the father vanishes from the pages of history).

When Gulltown rose against him, King Gerold put down the protests brutally, and soon the gutters of the town ran red with the blood of the First Men . . . and women and children as well. The dead were thrown in the bay to feed the crabs. In the years that followed, the rule of House Grafton remained uncontested, for (surprisingly) Ser Gerold proved a sage and clever ruler, and the town prospered greatly under him and his successors, growing to be the first and only city of the Vale.

Not all the lords and kings of the First Men were so foolish as to invite their conquerors into their halls and homes. Many chose to fight instead. Chief amongst these was the aforementioned Bronze King, Yorwyck VI of Runestone, who led the Royces to several notable victories over the Andals, at one point smashing seven longships that had dared to land upon his shores and decorating the walls of Runestone with the heads of their captains and crews. His heirs carried on the fight after him, for the wars between the First Men and the Andals lasted for generations.

The last of the Bronze Kings was Yorwyck's grandson, Robar II, who inherited Runestone from his sire less than a fortnight before his sixteenth nameday yet proved to be a warrior of such ferocity and cunning and charm that he almost succeeded in stemming the Andal tide.

By that time the Andals controlled three-quarters of the Vale and had begun to fight amongst themselves, as had the First Men before them. Robar Royce saw opportunity in their disunity. Across the Vale, a handful of First Men still held out against the Andals; the Redforts of Redfort, the Hunters of Longbow Hall, the Belmores of Strongsong, and the Coldwaters of Coldwater Burn chief amongst them. One by one, Robar made alliance with each of them, and many smaller clans and houses besides, bringing them to his cause with marriages, grants of land, gold, and (in one celebrated case) by outshooting the Lord Hunter in an archery contest (legend claims that King Robar cheated). So honeyed was his tongue that he even won the allegiance of Ursula Upcliff, a reputed sorceress who called herself bride of the Merling King.

Many of the lords who gathered beneath his banners had been petty kings, but now they set aside their crowns, bending the knee before Robar Royce and proclaiming him High King of the Vale, the Fingers, and the Mountains of the Moon.

Finally united as one people under a single ruler, the First Men went on to win a series of smashing victories against their divided, quarrelsome conquerors. Wisely, King Robar did not attempt to attack all Andals everywhere to drive them from his shores. Instead he warred upon one enemy at a time, often making common cause with one Andal chief to bring down another.

The King of the Fingers was first to fall. Legend tells us that King Robar slew Qyle Corbray himself, after striking Corbray's famous blade, Lady Forlorn, from his hand. Gulltown was retaken by storm when Robar sent his own sister inside the walls to persuade the Shetts to rise against the Graftons and open the city gates. The Hammer of the Hills, the Andal king who held the eastern end of the Vale, was next to face the resurgent First Men and fell before King Robar's host beneath the walls of Ironoaks. For one brief, shining moment, it appeared as if the First Men might yet retake their lands under the leadership of this brave young king.

But it was not to be. Robar had won his last victory, for the remaining Andal lords and petty kings had finally come to realize their peril. And now it was the Andals who put aside their differences to make common cause and unite beneath the banners of a single warlord. The man they chose to lead them was neither king nor prince, nor even lord, but a knight named Ser Artys Arryn. A young man,

of an age with King Robar, he was esteemed amongst his peers as the finest warrior of his day, a champion with sword and lance and morningstar, and a cunning and resourceful leader of men, beloved by all who fought beside him. Though of pure Andal blood, Ser Artys had been born in the Vale in the shadow of the Giant's Lance, where falcons soared amongst the mountain's jagged peaks. On his shield he bore the moon-and-falcon, whilst a pair of falcon's wings decorated his silver warhelm. The Falcon Knight, men called him, then as now.

To speak of what happened next, we must return to the realm of song and legend. The singers say the two hosts came together at the foot of the Giant's Lance, within a league of the house where Ser Artys had been born. Though the armies were roughly equal in number, Robar Royce held the high ground with the mountain at his back, a strong defensive position.

Having arrived days before the Andals, the First Men had dug trenches in front of their ranks and lined them with sharpened stakes (smeared with offal and excrement, says Septon Mallow's account of the battle). Most of the First Men were afoot; the Andals had a ten-to-one advantage in mounted knights and were better armed and armored as well. They came late to the battle, if the tales are true; King Robar had looked for them three days earlier and every day since.

It was dusk when the Andal army finally appeared, to raise their tents half a league from their foes. But even in that fading light, Robar Royce did not fail to mark their leader. His silvered armor and winged helm made the Falcon Knight unmistakable, even from afar.

No doubt the night that followed was a restless one in both camps, for every man there knew that battle would be joined at the break of day, with the Vale itself hanging in the balance. Clouds blew in from the east, hiding the moon and stars, so the night was dark indeed. The only light came from hundreds of campfires burning in the camps, with a river of darkness between them. From time to time, the singers say, archers on one side or another lofted an arrow in the air, hoping that it might find a foe, but whether any of the blind shafts drew blood, the tales do not tell.

As the east began to lighten, men rose from their stony beds, donned their armor, and prepared for the battle. Then a shout rang through the Andal camp. There to the west, a sign had been seen: seven stars, gleaming in the grey dawn sky. *"The gods are with us,"* went up the cry from a thousand throats. *"Victory is ours."* As trumpets blew, the vanguard of the Andals charged up the slope, banners streaming. Yet the First Men showed no dismay at the sign that had appeared in the sky; they held their ground and battle was joined, as savage and bloody a fight as any in the long history of the Vale.

Seven times the Andals charged, the singers say; six times the First Men threw them back. But the seventh attack, led by a fearsome giant of a man named Torgold Tollett, broke through. Torgold the Grim, this man was called, but even his name was a jape, for it is written that he went into battle laughing, naked above the waist, with a bloody seven-pointed star carved across his chest and an axe in each hand.

The songs say that Torgold knew no fear and felt no pain. Though bleeding from a score of wounds, he cut a red swathe through Lord Redfort's staunchest warriors, then took his lordship's arm off at the shoulder with a single cut. Nor was he dismayed when the sorceress Ursula Upcliff appeared upon a bloodred horse to curse him. By then he was bare-handed, having left both of his axes buried in a foe's chest, but the singers say he leapt upon the witch's horse, grasped her face between two bloody hands, and tore her head from her shoulders as she screamed for succor.

Then chaos ensued, as the Andals came pouring through the gap in the ranks of the First Men. Victory seemed within their grasp, but Robar Royce was not so easily defeated. Where another man might have fallen back to regroup, or

fled the field, the High King commanded a counterattack. He led the charge himself, smashing through the confusion with his champions by his side. In his hand was Lady Forlorn, that dread blade he had plucked from the dead hands of the King of the Fingers. Slaying men right and left, the king fought his way to Torgold the Grim. As Robar slashed at his head, Tollett grabbed for his blade, still laughing . . . but Lady Forlorn sliced through his hands and buried herself in Torgold's skull.

The giant died choking on his last laugh, the singers say. Whereupon the High King spied the Falcon Knight across the field and spurred toward him; should their leader fall, the Andals would lose heart and break, he hoped.

They came together as the battle raged around them, the king in bronze armor, the hero in silvered steel. Though the Falcon Knight's armor flashed brilliantly in the morning sun, his sword was no Lady Forlorn. The duel was done almost before it began, as the Valyrian steel sheared through the winged helm and laid the Andal low. For an instant, as his foe toppled from the saddle, Robar Royce must surely have thought his battle won.

Then he heard the trumpets, ringing through the dawn air, the sound coming from behind him. And turning in his saddle, the High King beheld in dismay five hundred fresh Andal knights pouring down the slopes of the Giant's Lance to take his own host in the rear. Leading the attack was a champion in silvered steel, with a moon-and-falcon on his shield and wings upon his warhelm. Ser Artys Arryn had clad one of his knights retainer in his spare suit of armor, leaving him in camp whilst he himself took his best horsemen up and around a goat track that he remembered from his childhood, so they might reappear behind the First Men and descend on them from above.

The rest was a rout. Attacked from front and rear, the last great host of the First Men of the Vale was cut to pieces. Thirty lords had come to fight for Robar Royce that day. Not a one survived. And though the singers say the High King slew foes by the score, in the end he, too, was slain. Some say Ser Artys killed him, whilst others name Lord Ruthermont, or Luceon Templeton, the Knight of Ninestars. The Corbrays of Heart's Home have always insisted that it was Ser Jaime Corbray who dealt the mortal blow, and for proof they point to Lady Forlorn, reclaimed for House Corbray after the battle.

Such is the tale of the Battle of the Seven Stars as it is told by the singers and the septons. A stirring story to be sure, but the scholar must ask, how much of it is true? We

PREVIOUS PAGES | *The Battle of Seven Stars.*

shall never know. All that is certain is that King Robar II of House Royce met Ser Artys Arryn in a great battle at the foot of the Giant's Lance, where the king died and the Falcon Knight dealt the First Men a blow from which they never recovered.

No fewer than fourteen of the oldest and noblest houses of the Vale ended that day. Those whose lines endured—the Redforts, the Hunters, the Coldwaters, the Belmores, and the Royces themselves amongst them—did so only by the dint of yielding up gold and land and hostages to their conquerors and bending their knees to swear fealty to Artys Arryn, the First of His Name, new-crowned King of Mountain and Vale.

In time some of these fallen houses would regain much of the pride and wealth and power lost on the battlefield that day, but that would require the passage of centuries. As for the victors, the Arryns would rule the Vale as kings until the coming of Aegon the Conqueror and his sisters, and thereafter served as the Lords of the Eyrie, Protectors of the Vale, and Wardens of the East. And from that day forth, the Vale itself has been known as the Vale of Arryn.

The fate of the defeated was far crueler. As word of the victory spread across the narrow sea, more and more longships set sail from Andalos, and more and more Andals poured into the Vale and the surrounding mountains. All of them required land—land the Andal lords were pleased to give them. Wherever the First Men sought to resist, they were ground underfoot, reduced to thralls, or driven out. Their own lords, beaten, were powerless to protect them.

Some of the First Men surely survived by joining their own blood with that of the Andals, but many more fled westward to the high valleys and stony passes of the Mountains of the Moon. There the descendants of this once-proud people dwell to this very day, leading short, savage, brutal lives amongst the peaks as bandits and outlaws, preying upon any man fool enough to enter their mountains without a strong escort. Little better than the free folk beyond the Wall, these mountain clans, too, are called wildlings by the civilized.

Though the Vale is guarded by mountains, that has not prevented outside attacks. The high road from the riverlands through the Mountains of the Moon has seen much blood spilled, for steep and stony as it is, it provides the most likely way for an army to enter the Vale. Its eastern end is guarded by the Bloody Gate, once merely a rough-hewn, unmortared wall after the fashion of the ringforts of the First Men. But in the reign of King Osric V Arryn, this fortress was constructed anew. Over the centuries, a dozen invading armies have smashed themselves to pieces attempting to breach the Bloody Gates.

The coast of the Vale—rocky and full of treacherous shallows and reefs—provides poor anchorage, which again

---

Here are the names of the most notable clans of the Mountains of the Moon, as reported by the Archmaester Arnel in his *Mountain and Vale*:

STONE CROWS	SONS OF THE TREE
MILK SNAKES	BURNED MEN
SONS OF THE MIST	HOWLERS
MOON BROTHERS	REDSMITHS
BLACK EARS	PAINTED DOGS

Lesser clans exist as well, often being formed after some feud splinters one clan, but these usually last only a short time before they are swallowed up by rivals or wiped out by the knights of the Vale.

Most of these clan names have some meaning, however obscure those meanings might be to us. The Black Ears take the ears of men they defeat in battle as trophies, we know. Amongst the Burned Men, a youth must give some part of his body to the fire to prove his courage before he can be deemed a man. This practice might have originated in the years after the Dance of the Dragons, some maesters believe, when an offshoot clan of the Painted Dogs were said to have worshipped a fire-witch in the mountains, sending their boys to bring her gifts and risk the flames of the dragon she commanded to prove their manhood.

has added to their defense, but the Arryn kings, well aware that their own ancestors came to Westeros from across the sea, have never neglected their coastal defenses. Strong castles and forts guard the most vulnerable coastlines, and even the stony, windswept Fingers are studded with watchtowers, each with its own beacon to warn against raiders from the sea.

The Andals were ever a warlike folk, for one of the Seven that they worship is the Warrior himself. Though secure in their own domains, some Kings of the Vale have from time to time sought conquest beyond their own borders. In such wars they had the advantage of knowing that, should the fighting go against them, they could always fall back behind the great natural walls of their mountains.

Nor did the Kings of the Mountain and Vale neglect their fleets. In Gulltown they possessed a fine and formidable natural harbor, and under the Arryns it grew into one of the foremost cities of the Seven Kingdoms. Though the Vale itself is famously fertile, it is small compared to the domains of other kings (and even some great lords), and the Mountains of the Moon are bleak, stony, and inhospitable. Trade is therefore of paramount importance to the rulers of the Vale, and the wiser of the Arryn kings always took care to protect it by building warships of their own.

In the waters off their eastern and northern coasts lie threescore islands, some no more than crab-infested rocks and roosts for seabirds, others quite large and oft inhabited. With their fleets, the Arryn kings were able to extend their rule to these isles. Pebble was taken by King Hugh Arryn (the Fat) after a short struggle, the Paps by his grandson, King Hugo Arryn (the Hopeful) after a long one. The Witch Isle, seat of House Upcliff with its sinister reputation, was brought into the realm by marriage, when King Alester Arryn, the Second of His Name, took Arwen Upcliff for his bride.

The last isles to be wedded to the Vale were the Three Sisters. For thousands of years, these islands had boasted their own cruel kings, pirates and raiders whose longships sailed the Bite, the narrow sea, and even the Shivering Sea with impunity, plundering and reaving as they would and returning to the Sisters laden with gold and slaves.

These depredations finally led the Kings of Winter to send their own war fleets to seek dominion over the Sisters—for whoever holds the Three Sisters holds the Bite.

The Rape of the Three Sisters is the name by which the Northern conquest of the islands is best known. *The Chronicles of Longsister* ascribe many horrors to that conquest: wild Northmen killing children to fill their cooking pots,

soldiers drawing the entrails from living men to wind them about spits, the executions of three thousand warriors in a single day at the Headman's Mount, Belthasar Bolton's Pink Pavilion made from the flayed skins of a hundred Sistermen . . .

How far these tales can be trusted is uncertain, but it is worth noting that these atrocities, whilst oft mentioned in accounts of the war written by men from the Vale, go largely unmentioned in Northern chronicles. It cannot be denied, however, that the rule of the Northmen was onerous enough to the Sistermen for them to send their surviving lords scurrying to the Eyrie to plead for help from the King of Mountain and Vale.

This help King Mathos Arryn, Second of His Name, was pleased to provide, upon the condition that the Sistermen agreed to do fealty to him and his descendants thereafter, and acknowledge the right of the Eyrie to rule over them. When his lady wife questioned the wisdom of involving the Vale in this War Across the Water, His Grace famously replied that he would sooner have a pirate than a wolf for his neighbor. The king set sail for Sisterton with a hundred warships.

He never returned, but his sons carried on the war after him. For a thousand years, Winterfell and the Eyrie contested for the rule of the Three Sisters. The Worthless War, some dubbed it. Time and time again the fighting seemed at an end, only to flare up once more a generation later. The islands changed hands more than a dozen times. Thrice the Northmen landed on the Fingers. The Arryns sent a fleet up the White Knife to burn the Wolf's Den, and the Starks replied by attacking Gulltown and burning hundreds of ships in their wroth when the city walls proved too strong for them.

In the end the Arryns emerged victorious, and the Three Sisters have remained part of the Vale ever since, save for the brief reign of Queen Marla Sunderland in the immediate aftermath of Aegon's Conquest; she was deposed at the sight of the approaching Braavosi fleet that the Northmen had hired at King Aegon's command. Her brother swore homage to the Targaryens, and she herself ended her days as a silent sister.

"This was not a case of the Eyrie winning so much as Winterfell losing interest," Archmaester Perestan observes in *A Consideration of History*. "For ten long centuries the direwolf and the falcon had fought and bled over three rocks, until one day the wolf awoke as from a dream and realized it was only stone between his teeth, whence he spat it out and walked away."

HOUSE ARRYN

House Arryn derives from the oldest and purest line of Andal nobility. The Arryn kings can proudly trace back their lineage to Andalos itself, and some of them have gone so far as to claim descent from Hugor of the Hill.

In any discussion of the origins of House Arryn, however, it is crucial to distinguish between history and legend.

There is abundant historical evidence for the existence of Ser Artys Arryn, the Falcon Knight, the first Arryn king to rule over Mountain and Vale. His victory over King Robar II at the Battle of the Seven Stars is well attested to, even though the details of that victory might have been somewhat embroidered in the centuries that followed. King Artys was undoubtedly a real man, albeit an extraordinary one.

In the Vale, however, the deeds of this real historical personage have become utterly confused with those of his legendary namesake, another Artys Arryn, who lived many thousands of years earlier during the Age of Heroes, and is remembered in song and story as the Winged Knight.

The first Ser Artys Arryn supposedly rode upon a huge falcon (possibly a distorted memory of dragonriders seen from afar, Archmaester Perestan suggests). Armies of eagles fought at his command. To win the Vale, he flew to the top of the Giant's Lance and slew the Griffin King. He counted giants and merlings amongst his friends, and wed a woman of the children of the forest, though she died giving birth to his son.

A hundred other tales are told of him, most of them just as fanciful. It is highly unlikely that such a man ever existed; like Lann the Clever in the westerlands, and Brandon the Builder in the North, the Winged Knight is made of legend, not of flesh and blood. If such a hero ever walked the Mountains and Vale, far back in the dim mists of the Dawn Age, his name was certainly not Artys Arryn, for the Arryns came from pure Andal stock, and this Winged Knight lived and flew and fought many thousands of years before the first Andals came to Westeros.

Like as not, it was the singers of the Vale who conflated these two figures, attributing the deeds of the legendary Winged Knight to the historic Falcon Knight, perhaps in order to curry favor with the real Artys Arryn's successors by placing this great hero of the First Men amongst their forebears.

The true tale of House Arryn contains neither giants nor griffins nor huge falcons, yet from the day Ser Artys first donned the Falcon Crown to the present, they have rightly held a storied place in the history of the Seven Kingdoms. Since the days of Aegon's Conquest, the Lords of the Eyrie have served the Iron Throne as Wardens of the East, defending the coasts of Westeros against enemies from beyond the sea. Before that, the chronicles tell of countless battles with the savage mountain clans; the thousand-year struggle with the North over the Three Sisters; bloody sea battles wherein the Arryn fleets turned back slavers from Volantis, ironborn reavers, and pirates from the Stepstones and Basilisk Isles. The Starks may well be older, but their legends came before the First Men had letters, while the Arryns fostered learning amongst the septries and septs, and their good works and great deeds were soon chronicled and remarked on in the devotional works of the Faith.

With the unification of the realm and the establishment of the boy Ronnel Arryn (the King Who Flew) as the first Lord of the Eyrie, there were new opportunities for the house. It was no great surprise when Queen Rhaenys Targaryen arranged the betrothal of young Ronnel to the daughter of Torrhen Stark, for that was but one of the many such marriages she made in the name of peace. Sadly, Lord Ronnel later died a violent death at the hands of his brother Jonos the Kinslayer, but the Arryn line continued through a kinsman and has remained deeply involved in many of the great matters of the Seven Kingdoms.

House Arryn can even boast the rare distinction of twice being deemed worthy of marriage with the blood of the dragon. Rodrik Arryn, Lord of the Eyrie, was honored

ABOVE | *The arms of House Arryn (center) and some of its vassals (clockwise from top): Waynwood, Royce, Corbray, Baelish, Belmore, Grafton, Hunter, Redfort, and Templeton.*

by King Jaehaerys I Targaryen and his wife, the Good Queen Alysanne, with the hand of their daughter, Princess Daella, and a child of that union, the Lady Aemma Arryn, in turn became the first wife of King Viserys I Targaryen and mother to his firstborn child, Princess Rhaenyra, who contended with her half brother Aegon II for the Iron Throne. In that struggle, Jeyne Arryn, Lady of the Eyrie and Maiden of the Vale, proved a staunch friend to Rhaenyra Targaryen and her sons, ultimately serving as one of the regents for King Aegon III. From that day, every Targaryen to sit the Iron Throne had a bit of Arryn blood.

The Arryns played their part in the wars of the Targaryen kings, and in the Blackfyre rebellions, standing stoutly with the Iron Throne against the Blackfyre Pretenders. During the First Blackfyre Rebellion, Lord Donnel Arryn boldly led the vanguard of the royalist host, though his lines were shattered by Daemon Blackfyre, and his lordship in peril for his life until Ser Gwayne Corbray of the Kingsguard appeared with reinforcements.

Lord Arryn survived to fight another day, and years later shut the Vale to traffic from the high road and by sea when the Great Spring Sickness swept over the Seven Kingdoms; thus, the Vale and Dorne alone were unaffected by that terrible plague.

In more recent years, the importance of the role played by Lord Jon Arryn in Robert's Rebellion cannot be gainsaid. Indeed, it was Lord Jon's refusal to deliver the heads of his wards, Eddard Stark and Robert Baratheon, that began the revolt. Had he done as he was commanded, the Mad King might yet sit the Iron Throne. Despite his advanced years, Lord Arryn fought valiantly beside Robert on the Trident. After the war, the new king proved his wisdom when he made Lord Jon Arryn his first Hand. His lordship's sagacity has helped King Robert rule the Seven Kingdoms wisely and justly ever since. It is a joy to the realm when a great man serves as Hand to a great king, for peace and plenty will surely come of it.

At the Great Council of 101 AC, the Arryns played little role, as Lady Jeyne was in her minority. To the Council in her stead came the Lord Protector of the Vale, Yorbert Royce of Runestone. One of the mightiest houses of the Vale, the Royces still boast proudly of their descent from the First Men and their last great king, Robar II. Even to this day, the Lords of Runestone go into battle clad in the bronze armor of their forebears, etched with runes that are said to ward the armor's wearer from harm. Alas, the number of Royces who have died whilst wearing this runic armor is daunting. Furthermore, Maester Denestan in his *Questions* speculates that the armor is far less ancient than it appears.

THE EYRIE

Many have claimed that the Eyrie of the Arryns is the most beautiful castle in all the Seven Kingdoms, and it is hard to deny the truth of this (though the Tyrells surely do). Seven slim white towers crown the Eyrie where it sits high upon a shoulder of the Giant's Lance, and no castle in Westeros boasts more marble in its walls or upon its floors.

And yet the Arryns and the men of the Vale will tell you that the Eyrie is impregnable as well, for its position high atop the mountainside makes it all but impossible to assault.

The smallest of the royal seats of Westeros, the Eyrie was not originally the seat of House Arryn. That honor belongs to the Gates of the Moon, a much larger castle that stands at the foot of the Giant's Lance, on the very site where Ser Artys Arryn and his Andals made their camp on the night

before the Battle of the Seven Stars. Still uncertain on his throne in the early years of his realm, King Artys wanted a seat strong enough to withstand siege and storm should the First Men rise against him. The Gates of the Moon served well enough in that regard, but there was more of fort than palace about it, and those seeing it for the first time have been known to remark that it is a fine castle for a lesser lord but no fit abode for a king.

This did not trouble King Artys overmuch, as it happens, for he was seldom there. The first Arryn king spent most of his reign on horseback, riding from one end of his domains to the next in an unending royal progress. "My throne is made of saddle leather," he was wont to say, "and my castle is a tent."

King Artys was succeeded by his two eldest sons, who reigned in turn as the second and third Kings of Mountain and Vale. Unlike their sire, they spent considerable portions of their reigns at the Gates of the Moon and seemed content there, though each of them commanded certain additions to the castle. It was the fourth Arryn king, the grandson of Artys I, who began the process that resulted in the building of the Eyrie. Roland Arryn had been fostered with an Andal king in the riverlands as a boy and had traveled widely after winning his spurs, visiting Oldtown and Lannisport before returning to the Vale upon his father's death to don the Falcon Crown. Having seen the wonders of the Hightower and Casterly Rock, and the great castles of the First Men that still dotted the lands of the Trident, he felt the Gates of the Moon looked mean and ugly by comparison. King Roland's first impulse was to tear down the Gates and build his new seat upon the same site, but that winter thousands of wildlings descended from the mountains in search of food and shelter, for the high valleys had been buried by deep falls of snow. Their depredations brought home to the king how vulnerable his seat was at its present site.

Legend claims it was his future wife, Lord Hunter's daughter Teora, who reminded him of how his grandfather had defeated Robar Royce, by attacking from the high ground. Much taken by the girl's words, and by the girl herself, Lord Roland resolved to seize the highest ground of all and decreed the building of the castle that would become the Eyrie.

He did not live to see it completed. The task His Grace had set his builders was a daunting one, for the lower slopes of the Giant's Lance were steep and overgrown, and up higher the bare stone of the mountain became precipitous and icy. More than a decade was spent just clearing a winding switch-back road up the mountain's side. Beyond the trees, a small army of stonemasons were set to work with hammers and chisel to carve out steps to ease the ascent where the slope grew steeper. Meanwhile, Roland sent his builders across the Seven Kingdoms in search of stone, for His Grace was not pleased with the look of the marble available in the Vale.

In time there came another winter and another attack upon the Vale by the wild clans of the Mountains of the Moon. Taken unawares by a band of Painted Dogs, King Roland I Arryn was pulled from his horse and murdered, his skull smashed in by a stone maul as he tried to free his longsword from its scabbard. He had reigned for six-and-twenty years, just long enough to see the first stones laid for the castle he had decreed.

Building continued through the reigns of his son and his son's son, but progress was painfully slow, for all the marble had to be brought in by ship from Tarth, then carried up the side of the Giant's Lance by mules. Dozens of the mules died whilst making the ascent, along with four common workmen and a master stonemason. Slowly the castle walls began to rise, foot by foot . . . until the Falcon Crown passed to the great-grandson of the king who had first dreamed the dream of a castle in the sky. War and wenching were the passions of King Roland II, not building; the cost of the Eyrie had become prohibitive, and the new king needed gold to pay for the campaign in the riverlands that he was planning. Hardly had his father been laid to rest than King Roland II commanded a halt to all work on the castle.

Thus it came to pass that the Eyrie was abandoned to the skies for the better part of four years. Falcons roosted amongst its half-completed towers whilst King Roland II fought the First Men in the riverlands in search of gold and glory.

Conquests proved harder to achieve than he had antic-ipated, however. After several small, meaningless victories over petty kings, he found himself facing Tristifer IV, the Hammer of Justice. The last truly great king of the First Men handed Roland Arryn a shattering defeat, then served him a worse one the following year. In peril of his life, His Grace fled to the castle of one of his erstwhile allies, an Andal lord, only to be betrayed and delivered back to Tristifer in chains. Four years after riding forth from the Vale in splendor, King Roland II was beheaded at Oldstones by the Hammer of Justice himself.

Few mourned his passing in the Vale, where his bellig-erence and vainglory had won him no friends. When his brother Robin Arryn succeeded him, work on the Eyrie was resumed. Yet it was forty-three years and four kings later before the castle was finally completed and fit for habitation. Maester Quince, the first man of his order to serve there, declared the Eyrie to be "the most splendid work ever built by the hands of men, a palace worthy of the gods themselves. Surely even the Father Above does not have such a seat."

From that time to this, the Eyrie has remained the seat of House Arryn in spring, summer, and autumn. In winter, ice and snow and howling winds make the ascent impossible, and the castle itself uninhabitable, but in summer the castle is bathed by cool, fresh mountain breezes, a welcome refuge from the sweltering heat on the valley floor below. There is no other castle like it in all the world, or at least none has been recorded that matches it.

RIGHT | *The Gates of the Moon.*

It is worth remarking on the statue that stands in the Eyrie's godswood, a fine likeness of the weeping Alyssa Arryn. Legend holds that six thousand years ago, Alyssa saw her husband, brothers, and sons all slain, and that she never shed a tear. Therefore, the gods punished her by not allowing her to rest until her tears fell upon the Vale below. The great waterfall that tumbles from the Giant's Lance is known as Alyssa's Tears, for the waters pour from such a height that they turn to mist long before they ever reach the ground.

How true is the tale? Alyssa Arryn did live, of that we may be reasonably sure, but it is unlikely that she lived six thousand years ago. *True History* suggests four thousand years whilst Denestan halves that number in *Questions*.

The Eyrie has never fallen by force. To assault it, an attacker first must take the Gates of the Moon at the mountain's base, a formidable castle in its own right. Should that be done, the long ascent remains, and as he climbs, the attacker must assault no less than three waycastles that protect the winding way up the mountain: Stone, Snow, and Sky.

This series of defenses makes the approach to the Eyrie difficult enough, but even should the attacker overcome each of these waycastles in turn, he would then find himself at the base of a sheer cliff, with the Eyrie itself still perched six hundred feet above him, reachable only by winch or ladder.

Small wonder then that few serious efforts have ever been made to besiege the Eyrie. Since its completion, the Arryn kings have always known that they had an impregnable redoubt in which to take refuge if hard-pressed. The maesters who have served House Arryn, students of the art of warfare all, have been unanimous in the belief that the castle cannot be taken . . .

. . . save perhaps with dragons, as Visenya Targaryen once proved when she landed in the Eyrie's inner yard on her dragon, Vhagar, and persuaded the mother of the last Arryn king to submit to House Targaryen and yield up the Falcon Crown.

Almost three hundred years have come and gone since that day, however, and the last dragon perished long ago in King's Landing, so the future Lords of the Eyrie may once again sleep secure in the knowledge that their splendid seat remains forever invulnerable and impregnable.

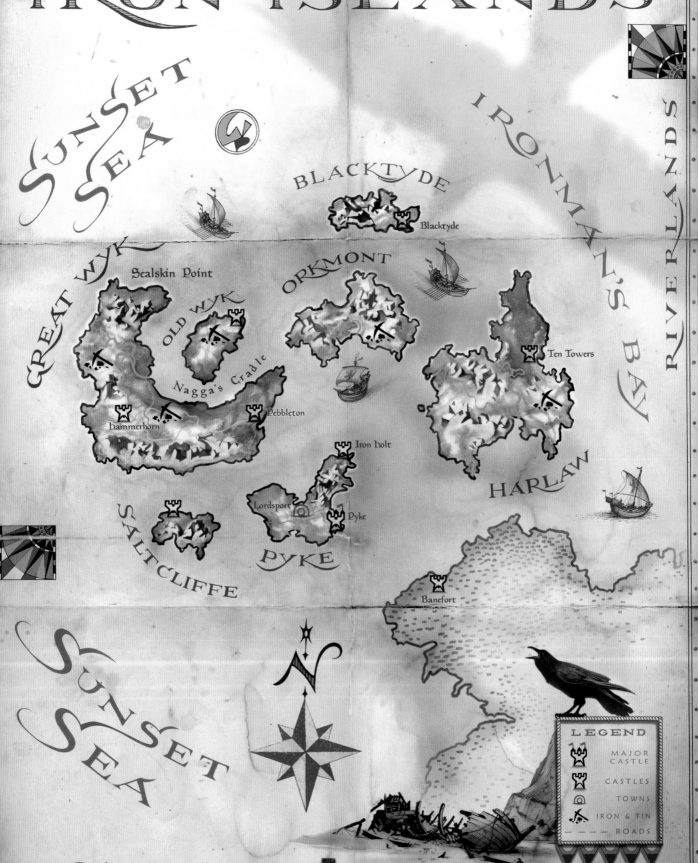

THE NORTH

IRON ISLANDS

SUNSET SEA

IRONMAN'S BAY

RIVERLANDS

BLACKTYDE

Blacktyde

GREAT WYK

Sealskin Point

OLD WYK

ORKMONT

Ten Towers

Nagga's Cradle

HARLAW

hammerhorn

Pebbleton

Iron holt

Lordsport

Pyke

SALTCLIFFE

PYKE

Banefort

SUNSET SEA

WESTERLANDS

LEGEND

MAJOR CASTLE

CASTLES

TOWNS

IRON & TIN

ROADS

THE *IRON ISLANDS*

WERE THE FIRST MEN truly first?

Most scholars believe they were. Before their coming, it is thought, Westeros belonged to the giants, the children of the forest, and the beasts of the field. But on the Iron Islands, the priests of the Drowned God tell a different tale.

According to their faith, the ironborn are a race apart from the common run of mankind. "We did not come to these holy islands from godless lands across the seas," the priest Sauron Salt-Tongue once said. "We came from beneath those seas, from the watery halls of the Drowned God who made us in his likeness and gave to us dominion over all the waters of the earth."

Even among the ironborn there are some who doubt this and acknowledge the more widely accepted view of an ancient descent from the First Men—even though the First Men, unlike the later Andals, were never a seafaring people. Certainly, we cannot seriously accept the assertions of the ironborn priests, who would have us believe that the ironmen are closer kin to fish and merlings than the other races of mankind.

here either, for another god had come before the Seven: the Drowned God, creator of the seas and father of the ironborn.

The Drowned God has no temples, no holy books, no idols carved in his likeness, but he has priests aplenty. Since long before recorded history these itinerant holy men have infested the Iron Islands, preaching his word and denouncing all other gods and those who follow them. Ill clad, unkempt, oft barefoot, the priests of the Drowned God have no permanent abode but wander the islands as they will, seldom straying far from the sea. Most are illiterate; theirs is an oral tradition, and younger priests learn the prayers and rituals from the elder. Wherever they might wander, lords and peasants are obliged to give them food and shelter in the name of the Drowned God. Some priests eat only fish. Most do not bathe, save in the sea itself. Men from other lands often think them mad, and so they may appear, but it cannot be denied that they wield great power.

Though most ironborn have naught but scorn for the Seven of the south and the old gods of the North, they do recognize a second deity. In their theology, the Drowned

---

Archmaester Haereg once advanced the interesting notion that the ancestors of the ironborn came from some unknown land west of the Sunset Sea, citing the legend of the Seastone Chair. The throne of the Greyjoys, carved into the shape of a kraken from an oily black stone, was said to have been found by the First Men when they first came to Old Wyk. Haereg argued that the chair was a product of the first inhabitants of the islands, and only the later histories of maesters and septons alike began to claim that they were in fact descended of the First Men. But this is the purest speculation and, in the end, Haereg himself dismissed the idea, and so must we.

Yet however the ironborn arose, it cannot be denied that they stand apart, with customs, beliefs, and ways of governance quite unlike those common elsewhere in the Seven Kingdoms.

All these differences, Archmaester Haereg asserts in his *History of the Ironborn*, are rooted in religion. These cold, wet, windswept islands were never well forested, and their thin soil did not support the growth of weirwoods. No giants ever made their homes here, nor did the children of the forest walk what woods there were. The old gods worshipped by these elder races were likewise absent. And though the Andals did reach the islands eventually, their Faith never took root

God is opposed by the Storm God, a malignant deity who dwells in the sky and hates men and all their works. He sends cruel winds, lashing rains, and the thunder and lightning that bespeak his endless wroth.

Some say that the Iron Islands are named for the ore that is found there in such abundance, but the ironborn themselves insist that the name derives from their nature, for they are a hard people, as unbending as their god. Mapmakers tell us that there are thirty-one Iron Islands in the main grouping off Ironman's Bay west of the Cape of Eagles, and thirteen more clustered around the Lonely Light, far out in the vastness of the Sunset Sea. The major islands of the

say they lie with seals to bring forth half-human children, whilst others whisper that they are skinchangers who can take the forms of sea lions, walrus, even spotted whales, the wolves of the western seas.

Strange tales like this are common at the edges of the world, however, and the Lonely Light stands farthest west of all the lands known to us. Many a bold mariner has sailed beyond the light of its beacon over the centuries, seeking the fabled paradise said to lie over the horizon, but the sailors who return (many do not) speak only of boundless grey oceans stretching on and on forever.

Such riches as the Iron Islands possess lie under the hills of Great Wyk, Harlaw, and Orkmont, where lead, tin, and iron can be found in abundance. These ores are the chief export of the islands. There are many fine metalworkers amongst the ironborn, as might be expected; the forges of Lordsport produce swords, axes, ringmail, and plate second to none.

The soil of the Iron Islands is thin and stony, more suitable for the grazing of goats than the raising of crops. The ironborn would surely suffer famine every winter but for the endless bounty of the sea and the fisherfolk who reap it.

The waters of Ironman's Bay are home to great schools of cod, black cod, monkfish, skate, icefish, sardines, and mackerel. Crabs and lobsters are found along the shores of all the islands, and west of Great Wyk swordfish, seals, and whales roam the Sunset Sea. Archmaester Hake, born and raised on Harlaw, estimates that seven of every ten families on the Iron Islands are fisherfolk. However mean and poor these men might be on land, upon the sea they are their own masters. "The man who owns a boat need never be a thrall," Hake writes, "for every captain is a king upon the deck of his own ship." It is their catch that feeds the islands.

Yet even more than the fisherman, ironborn esteem their reavers. "Wolves of the sea," the men of the westerlands and riverlands named them in days of yore, and rightly. Like wolves, they oft hunted in packs, crossing stormy seas in their swift longships and descending on peaceful villages and towns up and down the shores of the Sunset Sea to raid, rob, and rape. Fearless sailors and fearsome fighters, they would appear out of the morning mists to do their bloody work and be back at sea before the sun had reached its zenith, their longships laden with plunder and crowded with wailing children and frightened women.

Archmaester Haereg has argued that it was a need for wood that first set the ironborn on this bloody path. In the dawn of days, there were extensive forests on Great Wyk, Harlaw, and Orkmont, but the shipwrights of the isles had

chain number seven: Old Wyk, Great Wyk, Pyke, Harlaw, Saltcliffe, Blacktyde, and Orkmont.

Harlaw is the most populous of the isles, Great Wyk the largest and the richest in ore, and Old Wyk the holiest, the place where the kings of salt and rock gathered in the Grey King's Hall of old to choose who would reign over them. Rugged, mountainous Orkmont was home to the Iron Kings of House Greyiron in centuries gone by. Pyke boasts Lordsport, the largest town in the islands, and is the seat of House Greyjoy, rulers over the islands since Aegon's Conquest. Blacktyde and Saltcliffe are less notable. The tower keeps of lesser lords stand on some of the smaller islets, beside miniscule fishing villages. Others are used for the grazing of sheep, while many more remain uninhabited.

A secondary island grouping lies eight days' sail to the northwest in the Sunset Sea. There, seals and sea lions make their rookeries on windswept rocks too small to support even a single household. On the largest rock stands the keep of House Farwynd, named the Lonely Light for the beacon that blazes atop its roof day and night. Queer things are said of the Farwynds and the smallfolk they rule. Some

ABOVE | *The Grey King upon his throne made from Nagga's jaws.*

such a voracious need for timber that one by one the woods vanished. So the ironborn had no choice but to turn to the vast forests of the green lands, the mainland of Westeros.

All that the islands lacked the reavers found in the green lands. Little and less was taken in trade; much and more was bought in blood, with the point of a sword or the edge of an axe. And when the reavers returned to the islands with such plunder, they would say that they had "paid the iron price" for it; those who stayed behind "paid the gold price" to acquire these treasures, or went without. And thusly, Haereg tells us, were the reavers and their deeds exalted above all by singers, smallfolk, and priests alike.

Many legends have come down to us through the millennia of the salt kings and reavers who made the Sunset Sea their own, men as wild and cruel and fearless as any who have ever lived. Thus we hear of the likes of Torgon the Terrible, Jorl the Whale, Dagon Drumm the necromancer, Hrothgar of Pyke and his kraken-summoning horn, and Ragged Ralf of Old Wyk.

Most infamous of all was Balon Blackskin, who fought with an axe in his left hand and a hammer in his right. No weapon made of man could harm him, it was said; swords glanced off and left no mark, and axes shattered against his skin.

Did such men ever truly walk the earth? It is hard to know since most supposedly lived and died thousands of years before the ironmen learned to write; literacy remains rare in the Iron Islands to this day, and those who have the skill are oft mocked as weaklings or feared as sorcerers. So much of what we know of these demigods of the dawn comes to us from the peoples they plundered and preyed upon, written in the Old Tongue and the runes of the First Men.

The lands the reavers plundered were densely wooded but thinly peopled in those days. Then as now, the ironborn were loath to go too far from the salt waters that sustained them, but they ruled the Sunset Sea from Bear Island and the Frozen Shore down to the Arbor. The feeble fishing boats and trading cogs of the First Men, which seldom ventured out of sight of land, were no match for the swift longships of the ironmen with their great sails and banks of oars. And when battle was joined upon the shores, mighty kings and famous warriors fell before the reavers like wheat before a scythe, in such numbers that the men of the green lands told each other that the ironborn were demons risen from some watery hell, protected by fell sorceries and possessed of foul black weapons that drank the very souls of those they slew.

Whenever autumn waned and winter threatened, the longships would come raiding after food. And so the Iron Islands ate, even in the depths of winter, whilst oft as not the men who had planted, tended, and harvested the crops starved. "We do not sow," became the boast of the Greyjoys, whose rulers began to style themselves Lords Reaper of Pyke.

The reavers brought more than gold and grain back to the Iron Islands; they brought captives as well, who would henceforth serve their captors as thralls. Amongst the ironborn, only reaving and fishing were considered worthy work for free men. The endless stoop labor of farm and field was suitable only for thralls. The same was true for mining. Yet those thralls who were set to field work counted themselves fortunate, Haereg writes, for many and more of them lived to grow old and were even allowed to marry and have children. Such could not be said of those condemned to work the mines—those dark, dangerous pits beneath the hills where the masters were brutal, the air was dank and foul, and life was short.

Most of the male captives brought back to the Iron Islands spent the remainder of their lives at hard labor in the fields or mines. Some few, the sons of lords and knights and rich merchants, were ransomed for gold. Thralls who could read, write, and do sums served their masters as stewards, tutors, and scribes. Stonemasons, cordwainers,

Thralldom was a common practice amongst the First Men during their long dominion over Westeros—further support for the ironborn having descended from the First Men.

Further, thralldom should not be conflated with chattel slavery as it exists in certain of the Free Cities and lands farther east. Unlike slaves, thralls retain certain important rights. A thrall belongs to his captor, and owes him service and obedience, but he is still a man, not property. Thralls cannot be bought or sold. They may own property, marry as they wish, have children. The children of slaves are born into bondage, but the children of thralls are born free; any babe born on one of the islands is considered ironborn, even when both his parents are thralls. Nor may such children be taken from their parents until the age of seven, when most begin an apprenticeship or join a ship's crew.

coopers, chandlers, carpenters, and other skilled craftsmen were even more valuable.

It was young women the reavers prized most, however. Older women were sometimes carried off by those captains in need of scullions, cooks, seamstresses, weavers, midwives, and the like, but fair maids and girls near their first flowering were taken on every raid. Most ended their days upon the islands as serving girls, whores, household drudges, or wives to other thralls, but the fairest and strongest and most nubile would be kept as salt wives by their captors.

In their marriage customs, as in their gods, the ironborn differ from mainland Westeros. Wherever the Faith prevails in the Seven Kingdoms, a man joins himself for life to a single wife, and a maid to but one husband. On the Iron Islands, however, a man may have only one "rock wife" (unless she should die, whereupon he may take another), but any number of "salt wives." A rock wife must be a freeborn woman of the Iron Islands. Her place is at her man's side in board and bed, and her children come before all others. Salt

wives are almost always women and girls captured during raids. The number of salt wives that a man can support speaks to his power, wealth, and virility.

Still, it must not be thought that salt wives of the ironborn are no more than concubines, whores, or bed slaves. Salt marriages, like rock marriages, were customarily performed by priests of the Drowned God (albeit in ceremonies considerably less solemn than those that bind a man to his rock wife), and the children of such unions were considered legitimate. "Salt sons" may even inherit, when a man has no trueborn sons by his rock wife.

Salt marriage has declined notably on the Iron Islands since the Conquest, for Aegon the Dragon made the stealing of women a crime throughout the Seven Kingdoms (at the urging of Queen Rhaenys, it is said). The Conqueror also forbade the reavers to prey upon his own domains. These prohibitions have only been sporadically enforced under his successors, however, and many ironborn still yearn to return to what they call the Old Way.

DRIFTWOOD CROWNS

In the Age of Heroes, the legends say, the ironborn were ruled by a mighty monarch known simply as the Grey King. The Grey King ruled the sea itself and took a mermaid to wife, so his sons and daughters might live above the waves or beneath them as they chose. His hair and beard and eyes were as grey as a winter sea, and from these he took his name. The crown he wore was made of driftwood, so all who knelt before him might know that his kingship came from the sea and the Drowned God who dwells beneath it.

The deeds attributed to the Grey King by the priests and singers of the Iron Islands are many and marvelous. It was the Grey King who brought fire to the earth by taunting the Storm God until he lashed down with a thunderbolt, setting a tree ablaze. The Grey King also taught men to weave nets and sails and carved the first longship from the hard pale wood of Ygg, a demon tree who fed on human flesh.

The Grey King's greatest feat, however, was the slaying of Nagga, largest of the sea dragons, a beast so colossal that

ABOVE | *An ironborn reaver takes his prize.*

she was said to feed on leviathans and giant krakens and drown whole islands in her wroth. The Grey King built a mighty longhall about her bones, using her ribs as beams and rafters. From there he ruled the Iron Islands for a thousand years, until his very skin had turned as grey as his hair and beard. Only then did he cast aside his driftwood crown and walk into the sea, descending to the Drowned God's watery halls to take his rightful place at his right hand.

The Grey King was king over all the Iron Islands, but he left a hundred sons behind him, and upon his death they began to quarrel over who would succeed him. Brother killed brother in an orgy of kinslaying until only sixteen remained. These last survivors divided up the islands between them. All the great houses of the ironborn claim descent from the Grey King and his sons save, curiously, the Goodbrothers of Old Wyk and Great Wyk, who supposedly derive from the Grey King's leal eldest brother.

kings and salt kings who would rule over them. Whenever a king died, the priests of the Drowned God would call a kingsmoot to choose his successor. Every man who owned and captained a boat was allowed a voice at these unruly gatherings, which oft went on for days, and in a few instances far longer. The ironborn also tell of occasions when the priests called "the captains and the kings" together to *remove* an unworthy ruler.

The power wielded by these prophets of the Drowned God over the ironborn should not be underestimated. Only they could summon kingsmoots, and woe to the man, be he lord or king, who dared defy them. The greatest of the priests was the towering prophet Galon Whitestaff, so-called for the tall carved staff he carried everywhere to smite the ungodly. (In some tales his staff was made of weirwood, in others from one of Nagga's bones.)

It was Galon who decreed that ironborn must not

The petrified bones of some gigantic sea creature do indeed stand on Nagga's Hill on Old Wyk, but whether they are actually the bones of a sea dragon remains open to dispute. The ribs are huge, but nowise near large enough to have belonged to a dragon capable of feasting on leviathans and giant krakens. In truth, the very existence of sea dragons has been called into question by some. If such monsters do exist, they must surely dwell in the deepest, darkest reaches of the Sunset Sea, for none has been seen in the known world for thousands of years.

So say the legends and the priests of the Drowned God.

History tells a different tale. The oldest surviving records at the Citadel reveal that each of the Iron Islands was once a separate kingdom, ruled by not one but two kings, a rock king and a salt king. The former ruled the island itself, dispensing justice, making laws, and settling disputes. The latter commanded at sea, whenever and wherever the island's longships sailed.

Surviving records suggest that the rock kings were almost always older than the salt kings; in some cases the two were father and son, which has led some to argue that the salt kings were no more than heirs, crown princes to their fathers. Yet there are other instances known to us where the rock king and salt king were of different houses, sometimes even rival houses known to be inimical to one another.

Elsewhere in Westeros, petty kings claimed crowns of gold by virtue of their birth and blood, but the driftwood crowns of the ironborn were not so easily won. Here alone in all of Westeros men made their own kings, assembling in great councils called kingsmoots to choose the rock

make war on other ironborn, who forbade them to carry off each other's women or raid each other's shores, and who forged the Iron Islands into a single kingdom, summoning the captains and the kings to Old Wyk to choose a high king to reign supreme over salt kings and rock kings alike. They chose Urras Greyiron, called Ironfoot, the salt king of Orkmont and most fearsome reaver of that age. Galon himself placed a driftwood crown upon the high king's head, and Urras Ironfoot became the first man since the Grey King to rule over all the ironborn.

Many years later, when Urras Ironfoot died of wounds sustained whilst reaving, his eldest son seized his crown and proclaimed himself King Erich I. Though half-blind and feeble with age by that time, Galon nonetheless arose in fury at these tidings, declaring that only the kingsmoot could make a king. The "captains and the kings" assembled once more on Old Wyk and Erich the Ugly was unmade and condemned to death, a fate he avoided by breaking up his father's crown and casting it into the sea as a sign of his submission to the Drowned God. In his place the kingsmoot raised up Regnar Drumm, called Raven-feeder, the rock king of Old Wyk.

The centuries that followed were a golden age for the Iron Islands, and a dark age for such First Men as lived beside the sea. Once the reavers had gone forth seeking food to sustain them during hard winters, wood to build their longships, salt wives to give them sons, and the riches the Iron Islands lacked, but they had always returned home with their plunder. Under the driftwood kings the practice gave way to something far more difficult and dangerous: conquest, colonization, and rule.

But after Qhored, a slow decline began. The kings who followed Qhored played a part in that, yet the men of the green lands were likewise growing stronger. The First Men were building longships of their own, their towns defended by stone walls in place of wooden palisades and spiked ditches.

The Gardeners and the Hightowers were the first to cease paying tribute. When King Theon III Greyjoy sailed against them, he was defeated and slain by Lord Lymond Hightower, the Sea Lion, who revived the practice of thralldom in Oldtown just long enough to set the ironmen captured during the battle to hard labor strengthening the city's walls.

By tradition, the driftwood crown itself was broken up and returned to the sea upon the death of its wearer. His successor would don a new crown made from driftwood freshly washed up upon the shore of his home island. Thus every driftwood crown was different from those that had gone before. Some were small and simple, others huge, unwieldy, and magnificent.

Archmaester Haereg's exhaustive *History of the Ironborn* lists 111 men who wore a driftwood crown as High King of the Iron Islands. The list is admittedly incomplete and rife with contradictions, yet none can doubt that the driftwood kings reached the zenith of their power under Qhored I Hoare (given as Greyiron in some accounts, and as Blacktyde in others), who wrote his name in blood in the histories of Westeros as Qhored the Cruel. King Qhored ruled over the ironborn for three-quarters of a century, living to the ripe old age of ninety. By his day, the First Men of the green lands had largely abandoned the shores of the Sunset Sea for fear of the reavers. And those who remained, chiefly lords in stout castles, paid tribute to the ironborn.

It was Qhored who famously boasted that his writ ran "wherever men could smell salt water or hear the crash of waves." In his youth, he captured and sacked Oldtown, bringing thousands of women and girls back to the Iron Islands in chains. At thirty, he defeated the Lords of the Trident in battle, forcing the river king Bernarr II to bend the knee and yield up his three young sons as hostages. Three years later, he put the boys to death with his own hand, cutting out their hearts when their father's annual tribute was late in coming. When their grieving sire went to war to avenge them, King Qhored and his ironmen destroyed Bernarr's host and had him drowned as a sacrifice to the Drowned God, putting an end to House Justman and throwing the riverlands into bloody anarchy.

The growing strength of the westerlands posed an even more acute threat to the dominion of the driftwood kings. Fair Isle was the first to fall, when its smallfolk rose up under Gylbert Farman to expel their ironborn overlords. A generation later, the Lannisters captured the town of Kayce when Herrock the Whoreson blew his great gold-banded horn and the town whores opened a postern gate to his men. Three successive ironborn kings attempted to retake the prize and failed, two of them dying on the point of Herrock's sword.

The ultimate indignity came courtesy of Gerold Lannister, King of the Rock. Gerold the Great, as he is remembered in the west, sailed his own fleet to the Iron Islands themselves in a daring raid, taking a hundred ironborn hostages. He kept them in Casterly Rock thereafter, hanging one every time his shores were raided.

In the century that followed, a succession of weaker kings lost the Arbor, Bear Island, Flint's Finger, and most of the ironborn enclaves along the Sunset Sea, until only a handful remained.

It must not be thought that the ironborn won no victories during these years. Balon V Greyjoy, called Coldwind, destroyed the feeble fleets of the King in the North. Erich V Harlaw retook Fair Isle in his youth, only to lose it again in his old age. His son Harron slew Gareth the Grim of Highgarden beneath the walls of Oldtown. Half a century later, Joron I Blacktyde captured Gyles II Gardener when

their fleets clashed off the Misty Islands. After torturing him to death, Joron had his corpse cut into pieces so that he might bait his fishhooks with "a chunk of king." Later in his reign, Joron swept across the Arbor with steel and fire, and supposedly carried off every woman on the island under thirty years of age, thereby earning himself the name Maidensbane, by which he is best remembered.

Yet all these triumphs proved short-lived, along with many of the kings who won them. As the centuries passed, the kingdoms of the green lands grew stronger and the Iron Islands weaker. And late in the Age of Heroes, another crisis weakened and divided the ironborn further still.

Upon the death of King Urragon III Greyiron (Urragon the Bald), his younger sons hurriedly convened a kingsmoot whilst their elder brother Torgon was raiding up the Mander,

thinking that one of them would be chosen to wear the driftwood crown. To their dismay, the captains and kings chose Urrathon Goodbrother of Great Wyk instead. The first thing the new king did was command that the sons of the old king be put to death. For that, and for the savage cruelty he oft displayed during his two years as king, Urrathon IV Goodbrother is remembered in history as Badbrother.

When Torgon Greyiron returned at last to the Iron Islands, he declared the kingsmoot to be invalid because he had not been present to make a claim. The priests supported him in this, for they had grown weary of Badbrother's arrogance and impiety. Smallfolk and great lords alike arose at their call, rallying to Torgon's banners, until Urrathon's own captains hacked Urrathon into pieces. Torgon the

ABOVE | *An ironborn longship at sea.*

= 181 =

Latecomer became king in his stead, and ruled for forty years without ever having been chosen and proclaimed at a kingsmoot. He proved to be a strong king, just and wise and fair-minded . . . but he could do little to arrest the declining fortunes of the Iron Islands, for it was during Torgon's reign that most of the Cape of Eagles was lost to the Mallisters of Seagard.

Torgon had struck one blow against the institution of the kingsmoot in his youth, by throwing over its chosen king. In his old age he struck another, calling upon his own son Urragon to help him rule. At court and council, in war and peace, the son remained at his father's side for the best part of five years, so when Torgon finally died it seemed only natural for his chosen heir to succeed him as Urragon IV Greyiron. No kingsmoot was summoned, and this time no Galon Whitestaff arose in wroth to protest the succession.

The final, fatal blow against the power of the captains and the kings assembled was dealt when Urragon IV himself died, after a long but undistinguished reign. It had been the dying king's wish that the high kingship pass to his great-nephew Urron Greyiron, salt king of Orkmont, known as Urron Redhand. The priests of the Drowned God were determined not to allow the power of kingmaking to be taken from them for a third time, so word went forth that the captains and kings should assemble on Old Wyk for a kingsmoot.

Hundreds came, amongst them the salt kings and rock kings of the seven major isles, and even the Lonely Light. Yet scarcely had they gathered when Urron Redhand loosed his axemen on them, and Nagga's ribs ran red with blood. Thirteen kings died that day, and half a hundred priests and prophets. It was the end of the kingsmoots, and the Redhand ruled as high king for twenty-two years thereafter, and his descendants after him. The wandering holy men never again made and unmade kings as they once had.

THE IRON KINGS

The Greyirons were amongst the oldest and most renowned of the great houses of the Iron Islands. During the long age of the kingsmoot, the captains and kings bestowed driftwood crowns on no fewer than thirty-eight Greyirons, according to Haereg, giving them twice as many high kings as any other house.

That era ended with Urron Redhand and the slaughter on Old Wyk. Henceforth the crown of the Iron Islands would be made of black iron and would pass from father to son by right of primogeniture. Nor would the Greyirons suffer any other kings on the isles. There would be no more salt kings, no more rock kings. Urron Redhand and his heirs styled themselves simply King of the Iron Islands. The rulers of Great Wyk, Old Wyk, Pyke, Harlaw, and the lesser isles were reduced to lords, and several ancient lines were extinguished entirely when they refused to bend their knees.

But House Greyiron's grasp upon its iron crown did not go uncontested. Along with the kingsmoot, Galon White-staff's prohibition against the ironborn making war on other ironborn also perished amidst the slaughter on Old Wyk. Over the centuries that followed, Urron Redhand and his successors had to deal with half a dozen major rebellions, and at least two major thrall uprisings. Nor were the lords and kings of the mainland slow to take advantage of the disunity amongst the ironborn. One by one, all the remaining footholds in the green lands were lost. The most telling blow was struck by King Garth VII, the Goldenhand, King of the Reach, when he drove the ironmen from the Misty Islands, renamed them the Shield Islands, and resettled them with his own fiercest warriors and finest seamen to defend the mouth of the Mander.

The arrival of the Andals in the Seven Kingdoms only hastened the decline of the Iron Islands, for unlike the First Men who had gone before, the Andals were fearless seamen, with longships of their own as swift and seaworthy as any that the ironborn could build. As the Andals flooded into the riverlands, the westerlands, and the Reach, new villages sprang up along the coasts, walled towns and stout stone-and-timber castles rose over every cove and harbor, and great lords and petty kings alike began to build warships to defend their shores and shipping.

In due time, the Andals swept over the Iron Islands just as they had all Westeros below the Neck. Successive waves of Andal adventurers descended on the islands, oft in alliance with one or another faction of the ironborn them-selves. The Andals intermarried with some of the ancient families of the islands and brought others to a bloody end with sword and axe.

House Greyiron was amongst those destroyed. The last Iron King, Rognar II, was brought down when the

Orkwoods, Drumms, Hoares, and Greyjoys made common cause against him, supported by a host of Andal pirates, sellswords, and warlords.

Afterward the victors could not agree on who should succeed Rognar as king, so it was decided that they would settle the matter by dancing the finger dance, a game popular amongst the ironborn wherein players spin a throwing axe at one another and attempt to snatch it from the air. Harras Hoare emerged as victor, at the cost of two fingers. As Harras Stump-hand, he ruled the Iron Islands for thirty years.

Many believe the tale of Harras's winning his crown by catching an axe to be no more than a singer's fancy. In truth, Archmaester Haereg suggests that Harras was chosen because he had taken an Andal maiden for his wife, thereby winning the support of her father and many other powerful Andal lords.

THE BLACK BLOOD

Archmaester Hake tells us that the kings of House Hoare were, "black of hair, black of eye, and black of heart." Their foes claimed their blood was black as well, darkened by the "Andal taint," for many of the early Hoare kings took maidens of that ilk to wife. True ironborn had salt water in their veins, the priests of the Drowned God proclaimed; the black-blooded Hoares were false kings, ungodly usurpers who must be cast down.

Many tried to do just that over the centuries, as Haereg relates in some detail. None succeeded. What the Hoares lacked in valor they made up for in cunning and cruelty. Few of their subjects ever loved them, but many had good reason to fear their wroth. Their very names proclaim their nature to us, even after the passage of hundreds of years. Wulfgar the Widowmaker. Horgan Priestkiller. Fergon the Fierce. Othgar the Soulless. Othgar Demonlover.

ABOVE | *Harras Stump-hand victorious.*

Craghorn of the Red Smile. The priests of the Drowned God denounced them all.

Were the kings of House Hoare truly as ungodly as these holy men proclaimed? Hake believes they were, but Archmaester Haereg takes a very different view, suggesting that the true crime of the "black-blooded" kings was neither impiety nor demon-worship, but tolerance. For it was under the Hoares that the Faith of the Andals came to the Iron Islands for the first time.

Prompted by their Andal queens, these kings granted the septas and septons their protection and gave them leave to move about the islands, preaching of the Seven. The first sept on the Iron Islands was built on Great Wyk during the reign of Wulfgar Widowmaker. When his great-grandson Horgan permitted the building of another on Old Wyk, where the kingsmoots had been held of old, the entire island rose up in bloody rebellion, goaded by the priests. The sept was burned, the septon pulled to pieces, the worshippers dragged into the sea to drown, that they might regain their faith. It was in answer to this, Haereg alleges, that Horgan Hoare began to slaughter priests.

The Hoare kings also discouraged the practice of reaving. And as reaving declined, trade grew. There was still a wealth of iron ore to be found beneath the hills of Great Wyk, Orkmont, Harlaw, and Pyke, and lead and tin as well. The ironmen's need for wood to build their ships remained as great as ever, but they no longer had the strength to take it wherever they found it. Instead they traded iron for timber. And when winter came and the cold winds blew, iron ore became the coin the kings of House Hoare used to buy barley, wheat, and turnips to keep their smallfolk fed (and beef and pork for their own tables). "Paying the iron price" took on a whole new meaning . . . one many ironborn found humiliating and the priests decried as shameful.

The nadir of ironborn pride and power was reached during the reigns of the three Harmunds. On the isles, they are best remembered as Harmund the Host, Harmund the Haggler, and Harmund the Handsome. Harmund the Host was the first king of the Iron Islands known to be literate.

He welcomed travelers and traders from the far corners of the world to his castle on Great Wyk, treasured books, and gave septons and septas his protection.

His son Harmund the Haggler shared his love of reading, and became renowned as a great traveler. He was the first king of the Iron Islands to visit the green lands without a sword in his hand. Having spent his youth as a ward of House Lannister, the second Harmund returned to Casterly Rock as a king and took the Lady Lelia Lannister, a daughter of the King of the Rock and "the fairest flower of the west," for his queen. On a later voyage he visited Highgarden and Oldtown, to treat with their lords and kings and foster trade.

His own sons were raised in the Faith, or King Harmund's own peculiar version of it. Upon his death, the eldest of them ascended the throne. Harmund the Handsome (influenced, some say, by his Lannister mother, the Dowager Queen Lelia) announced that henceforth reavers would be hanged as pirates rather than celebrated, and formally outlawed the taking of salt wives, declaring the children of such unions to be bastards with no right of inheritance. He was considering a measure to end the practice of thralldom on the isles as well when a priest known as the Shrike began to preach against him.

Other priests took up the cry, and the lords of the isles took heed. Only the septons and their followers stood by King Harmund, and he was overthrown within a fortnight, almost bloodlessly. What followed was far from bloodless, however. The Shrike himself tore out the deposed king's tongue, so he might never again speak "lies and blasphemies." Harmund was blinded as well, and his nose was cut off, so "all men might see him for the monster he is."

In his place, the lords and priests crowned his younger brother Hagon. The new king denounced the Faith, rescinded Harmund's edicts, and expelled the septons and septas from his realm. Within a fortnight every sept in the Iron Islands was aflame.

King Hagon, soon to be known as Hagon the Heartless, even permitted the mutilation of his own mother, Queen Lelia, the Lannister "whore" who was blamed by the Shrike

---

Though Harmund II accepted the Seven as true gods, he continued to do honor to the Drowned God as well, and on his return to Great Wyk spoke openly of "the Eight Gods," and decreed that a statue of the Drowned God should be raised at the doors of every sept. This pleased neither the septons nor the priests and was denounced by both. In an attempt to placate them, the king rescinded his decree and declared that god had but seven faces . . . but the Drowned God was one of those, as an aspect of the Stranger.

for turning her husband and sons away from the true god. Her lips, ears, and eyelids were cut off and her tongue ripped out with hot pincers, after which she was bundled onto a longship and returned to Lannisport. The King of the Rock, her nephew, was so angered by this atrocity that he called his banners.

The war that followed left ten thousand dead, three-quarters of them ironborn. In its seventh year, the westermen landed on Great Wyk, smashed Hagon's host in battle, and captured his castle. Hagon the Heartless was mutilated in the same fashion as his mother before being hanged. Ser Aubrey Crakehall, commanding the Lannister armies, ordered that Hoare Castle be razed to the ground, but as his men were looting, they came upon Harmund the Handsome in a dungeon. Crakehall briefly considered restoring Harmund to his throne, Haereg claims, but the former king was blind, broken, and half-mad from long confinement. Ser Aubrey granted him "the gift of death" instead, serving Harmund a cup of wine laced with milk of the poppy. Then, in an act of mad folly, the knight decided to claim the kingship of the Iron Islands for himself.

This pleased neither the ironborn nor the Lannisters. When word reached Casterly Rock, the king called his warships home, leaving Crakehall to fend for himself. Without the power and wealth of House Lannister to prop him up, "King Aubrey" saw his power crumble quickly. His reign lasted less than half a year before he was captured and sacrificed to the sea by the Shrike himself.

The war between the ironborn and the westermen continued in a desultory fashion for five more years, finally ending in an exhausted peace that left the Iron Islands impoverished, burned, and broken. The winter that followed was long and harsh, and is remembered on the isles as the Famine Winter. Hake tells us that three times as many ironmen perished of starvation that winter than had died in the battles that preceded it.

It would be centuries before the Iron Islands recovered, a long slow climb back up to prosperity and power. Of the kings who reigned during this bleak age, we need not treat. Many were puppets of the lords or priests. A few were more like the reavers of the Age of Heroes, men such as Harrag Hoare and his son Ravos the Raper who savaged the North in the years of the Hungry Wolf's bloody reign, but they were rare and far between.

Both reaving and trade played a part in the restoration of the pride and prowess of the islands. Other lands now built larger and more formidable warships than the ironmen,

but nowhere were sailors any more daring. Merchants and traders sailing from Lordsport on Pyke and the harbors of Great Wyk, Harlaw, and Orkmont spread out across the seas, calling at Lannisport, Oldtown, and the Free Cities, and returning with treasures their forebears had never dreamed of.

Reaving continued as well . . . but the "wolves of the sea" no longer hunted close to home, for the green-land kings had grown too powerful to provoke. Instead they found their prey in more distant seas, in the Basilisk Isles and the Stepstones and along the shores of the Disputed Lands. Some took service as sellsails, fighting for one or another of the Free Cities in their endless trade wars.

One such was Harwyn Hoare, thirdborn son of King Qhorwyn the Cunning. A shrewd and avaricious king, Qhorwyn had spent his entire reign accumulating wealth and avoiding war. "War is bad for trade," he said, infamously, even as he was doubling, then tripling the size of his fleets and commanding his smiths to forge more armor, swords, and axes. "Weakness invites attack," Qhorwyn declared. "To have peace, we must be strong."

ABOVE | *King Harwyn Hoare.*

His son Harwyn had no use for peace, but much and more for the arms and armor that his father forged. A belligerent boy by all accounts, and third in the succession, Harwyn Hoare was sent to sea at an early age. He sailed with a succession of reavers in the Stepstones, visited Volantis, Tyrosh, and Braavos, became a man in the pleasure gardens of Lys, spent two years in the Basilisk Isles as a captive of a pirate king, sold his sword to a free company in the Disputed Lands, and fought in several battles as a Second Son.

When Harwyn returned to the Iron Islands, he found his father Qhorwyn dying, and his eldest brother two years dead from greyscale. A second brother still stood between Harwyn and the crown, and his sudden death even as the king was breathing his last remains a matter of dispute to this day. Those present at Prince Harlan's passing all declared his death accidental, the result of a fall from his horse, but of course it would have been worth their lives to suggest otherwise. Beyond the Iron Islands, it was widely assumed that Prince Harwyn was behind his brother's demise. Some claimed he had done the deed himself, others that Prince Harlan had been slain by a Faceless Man of Braavos.

King Qhorwyn expired six days after the crown prince, leaving his thirdborn son to inherit. As Harwyn Hardhand, he would soon write his name in blood across the histories of the Seven Kingdoms.

When the new king visited his father's shipyards, he declared that "longships are meant to be sailed." When he inspected the royal armories, he announced that, "swords are made to be blooded." King Qhorwyn had oft said that weakness invites attack. When his son gazed across Ironman's Bay, he saw only weakness and confusion in the riverlands, where the lords of the Trident chafed restlessly beneath the heel of the Storm King, Arrec Durrandon, in distant Storm's End.

Harwyn assembled a host and led it across the bay on a hundred of his father's longships. Landing unchallenged north of Seagard, they carried their ships overland to the Blue Fork of the Trident, then swept downstream with fire and sword. A few of the river lords took up arms against them; most did not, for they had little love and less loyalty for their liege lord in the stormlands. In those days, the ironborn were thought to be savage fighters at sea but easily put to rout on land. But Harwyn Hoare was not like other ironborn. Tempered in the Disputed Lands, he proved to be as fierce afoot as he was at sea, routing every foe. After he dealt the Blackwoods a crushing defeat, many lords of the Trident declared for him.

At Fairmarket, Harwyn found himself facing Arrec Durrandon, the young Storm King, leading a host half again the size of his own . . . but the stormlanders were ill led, weary, and far from home, and the ironmen and riverlords shattered them. King Arrec lost two brothers and half his men, and was lucky to escape with his own life. As he fled south, the smallfolk of the riverlands rose up, and his garrisons were driven out or slaughtered. The broad, fertile riverlands and all their wealth passed from the hands of Storm's End to those of the ironmen.

In one bold stroke, Harwyn Hardhand had increased his holdings tenfold and made the Iron Islands once more a power to be feared. Those lords of the Trident who had joined him in hopes of freeing themselves from the Durrandons soon learned that their new masters were far more brutal and demanding than their old ones. Harwyn would rule his conquest with a heavy hand until his death, spending far more time in the riverlands than on the islands, riding from one end of the Trident to the other at the head of a rapacious army, sniffing out any hint of rebellion whilst collecting taxes, tribute, and salt wives. "His palace was a tent, his throne a saddle," men said of him.

His son Halleck, who succeeded to the crown when the Hardhand died in his sixty-fourth year, was a man of the same stripe. Halleck visited the Iron Islands only thrice during his reign, spending less than two years there all told. Though he called himself ironborn, sacrificed to the Drowned God, and always kept three priests at his side, there was more of the Trident than of the salt sea in Halleck Hoare, and he seemed to look upon the islands only as a source of arms, ships, and men. His own reign was even bloodier than his father's, if less successful, marked by unsuccessful wars against the westermen and stormlanders, and no less than three failed attempts to conquer the Vale, all ending in disaster at the Bloody Gate.

Like his sire, King Halleck spent a great deal of his reign in camp tents, on campaign. When not at war, he ruled his broad domains from a modest tower house at Fairmarket in the heart of the riverlands, near the site of his father's greatest victory.

His own son desired a grander seat than that, and would spend most of his own reign building it. But the tale of Harren the Black, and the building of Harrenhal, has been touched upon elsewhere.

The dragonflame that destroyed Harrenhal put a fiery end to King Harren's dreams, the domination of the riverlands by the ironborn, and the "black line" of House Hoare.

THE GREYJOYS OF PYKE

The death of Harren the Black and his sons left the Iron Islands kingless and in chaos.

Many great lords and famous warriors had been serving with King Harren in the riverlands. Some died with him in the burning of Harrenhal, others when the riverlands rose against them. Only a few reached the coast alive, and fewer still found longships waiting, unburned, to carry them home.

Aegon Targaryen and his sisters paid little heed to the Iron Islands in the immediate aftermath of Harrenhal. They had more pressing concerns, and powerful foes to defeat on every hand. Left to fend for themselves, the ironborn immediately fell to fighting.

Qhorin Volmark, a minor lord on Harlaw, was the first man to claim the kingship. His grandmother had been a younger sister of Harwyn Hardhand. On the basis of that tie, Volmark declared himself the rightful heir of "the black line."

On Old Wyk, twoscore priests gathered beneath the bones of Nagga to place a driftwood crown on one of their own, a barefoot holy man called Lodos who claimed to be the living son of the Drowned God.

Other claimants soon arose on Great Wyk, Pyke, and Orkmont, and for a full year and more their followers fought each other by land and sea. Aegon the Conqueror put an end to the fighting in 2 AC when he and Balerion descended upon Great Wyk, accompanied by a vast war fleet. The ironmen collapsed before him. Qhorin Volmark died at the Conqueror's own hand, cut down by Aegon's Valyrian steel blade, Blackfyre. On Old Wyk, the priest-king Lodos turned to his god, calling on the krakens of the deep to drag down Aegon's warships. When the krakens failed to appear, Lodos filled his robes with stones and walked into the sea to "take counsel" with his father. Thousands followed him. Their bloated corpses washed up on the shores of the isles for years to come, though the priest's own body was not amongst them. On Great Wyk and Pyke, the surviving contenders (the king on Orkmont having been slain the previous year) were quick to bend the knee and do homage to House Targaryen.

But who would rule them? On the mainland, some urged Aegon to make the ironborn vassals to Lord Tully of Riverrun, whom he had named Lord Paramount of the Trident. Others suggested that the islands be given to Casterly Rock. A few went so far as to implore him to scour the isles clean with dragonflame, putting an end to the scourge of the ironborn for all time.

Aegon chose a different course. Gathering the remaining lords of the Iron Islands together, he announced that he would allow them to choose their own lord paramount. Unsurprisingly they chose one of their own: Vickon Greyjoy, Lord Reaper of Pyke, a famous captain descended of the Grey King. Though Pyke was smaller and poorer than Great Wyk, Harlaw, and Orkmont, the Greyjoys boasted a long and distinguished lineage. In the days of the kingsmoot, only the Greyirons and Goodbrothers had produced more kings, and the Greyirons were gone.

Exhausted and impoverished by years of war, the ironmen accepted their new overlord without demur.

It took the Iron Islands the best part of a generation to recover from the wounds inflicted by Harren's fall and the fratricidal war that followed. Vickon Greyjoy, enthroned on Pyke on the Seastone Chair, proved a stern but cautious ruler. Though he did not outlaw reaving, he commanded that the practice be confined to distant waters, far beyond the shores of Westeros, so as not to provoke the wroth of the Iron Throne. And since Aegon had accepted the Seven as his gods and been anointed by the High Septon in Oldtown, Lord Vickon allowed the septons to return to the islands once again to preach the Faith.

This angered many pious ironborn and provoked the wroth of the priests of the Drowned God, as it always had before. "Let them preach," Lord Vickon said, when told of the unrest. "We have need of winds to fill our sails." He was Aegon's man, he reminded his son Goren, and no

ABOVE | *The arms of House Greyjoy (center) and some houses of note, past and present, (clockwise from top): Greyiron, Goodbrother, Wynch, Botley, Drumm, Harlaw, Hoare, and Blacktyde.*

man but a fool would dare rise against Aegon Targaryen and his dragons.

These were words that Goren Greyjoy would remember. When Lord Vickon died in 33 AC, Goren succeeded him as Lord of the Iron Islands, putting down a clumsy conspiracy to restore the black line by crowning Qhorin Volmark's son in his stead. He faced a more serious test four years later, when Aegon the Conqueror died of a stroke on Dragonstone, and his son Aenys was crowned king in his stead. Though amiable and well-meaning, Aenys Targaryen was widely perceived as a weakling, unfit to sit the Iron Throne. The new king was still on his royal progress when rebellions began to break out all across the realm.

One such revolt convulsed the Iron Islands, led by a man claiming that he was the priest-king Lodos returned at last from visiting his father. But Goren Greyjoy dealt with it decisively, going so far as to send the priest-king's pickled head to Aenys Targaryen. His Grace was so pleased with the gift that he promised Lord Goren any boon that was within his power to grant. As sage as he was savage, Greyjoy asked the king to give him leave to expel the septons and septas from the Iron Islands. King Aenys was forced to agree. A century would pass before another sept was opened on the islands.

For long years afterward the ironborn remained quiescent under a succession of Greyjoy lords. Eschewing further thoughts of conquest, they lived by fishing, trade, and mining. All the width of Westeros lay between King's Landing and Pyke, and the ironborn had little and less to do with affairs at court. Life was hard upon the islands, especially in winter, but that was as it had always been. Some men still dreamed of a return to the Old Way, when the ironborn were a people to be feared, but the Stepstones and the Summer Sea were far away, and the Greyjoys on the Seastone Chair would allow no reaving closer to home.

THE RED KRAKEN

The better part of a century would pass before the kraken woke, yet the dreams never died, for the priests still stood knee deep in the salt sea preaching of the Old Way, whilst in a hundred wharfside brothels and sailor's taverns old men still told tales of days gone by, when the ironborn were rich and proud, and every oarsman had a dozen salt wives to warm his bed by night. Many a boy and young man grew drunk upon such stories, hungry for the glories of the reaver's life.

One such was Dalton Greyjoy, the wild young son of the heir to Pyke and the Iron Islands. Of him Hake writes,

"He loved three things: the sea, his sword, and women." A fearless child, headstrong and hot-tempered, he is said to have been rowing at five and reaving at ten, sailing with his uncle to the Basilisk Isles to raid the pirate towns for plunder.

By the age of ten-and-four, Dalton Greyjoy had sailed as far as Old Ghis, fought in a dozen actions, and claimed four salt wives. His men loved him (more than can be said of his wives, for he tired of women quickly). His own love was his blade, a Valyrian steel longsword he had taken off a dead corsair and named Nightfall. In his fifteenth year, whilst fighting in the Stepstones as a sellsail, he saw his uncle slain and avenged his death, but he took a dozen wounds and emerged from the fight drenched head to heel in blood. From that day forth, men called him the Red Kraken.

Later that same year, word of his father's death reached him in the Stepstones, and the Red Kraken claimed the Seastone Chair as the Lord of the Iron Islands. At once he began building longships, forging swords, and training fighters. When asked why, the young lord replied, "The storm is coming."

The storm he had foreseen broke the next year, when King Viserys I Targaryen died in his sleep in the Red Keep of King's Landing. His daughter Rhaenyra and her half brother Aegon both laid claim to the Iron Throne, and the orgy of bloodletting, battle, rapine, and murder known as the Dance of the Dragons began. When word reached Pyke, the Red Kraken is said to have laughed aloud.

Throughout the war, Princess Rhaenyra and her blacks enjoyed a great advantage at sea, for amongst her supporters was Corlys Velaryon, Lord of the Tides, the fabled Sea Snake, who commanded the fleets of House Velaryon of Driftmark. Hoping to counter that, the green council of King Aegon II reached out to Pyke, offering Lord Dalton a place on the small council as lord admiral of the realm if he would bring his longships around Westeros to do battle with the Sea Snake. It was a handsome offer, and most boys would have leapt at it, but Lord Dalton had a shrewdness rare in one so young and elected to wait to see what Princess Rhaenyra might offer.

When her missive came, it was much more to his liking. The blacks did not need him to sail his fleet around Westeros and give battle in the narrow sea, a chancy proposition at best. The princess asked only that he attack her enemies. Amongst those enemies were the Lannisters of Casterly Rock, whose lands were close to home and vulnerable. Lord Jason Lannister had taken most of his knights, archers, and seasoned fighters east with him to attack Rhaenyra's allies in the riverlands, leaving the westerlands thinly defended. Lord Dalton saw opportunity.

Whilst Lord Jason fell in battle in the riverlands and his host staggered from battle to battle under a succession of commanders, the Red Kraken and his ironborn fell upon the westerlands like wolves upon a flock of sheep. Casterly Rock itself proved too strong for them, once Lord Jason's

widow Johanna barred its gates, but the ironmen burned the Lannister fleet and sacked Lannisport, carrying off vast amounts of gold, grain, and trade goods, and seizing hundreds of women and girls as salt wives, including the late Lord Jason's favorite mistress and their natural daughters.

Further raids and depredations followed. All up and down the western coasts the longships sailed, raiding as they had in days of old. The Red Kraken himself led the attack that captured Kayce. Faircastle fell, and with it Fair Isle and all its wealth. Lord Dalton claimed four of Lord Farman's daughters as salt wives and gave the fifth—"the homely one"—to his brother Veron.

For the better part of two years, the Red Kraken ruled the Sunset Sea as his forebears had done of old, whilst elsewhere in Westeros great armies marched and clashed and dragons wheeled across the skies and met in bloody battle.

All wars must end, however, and so it was with the Dance of the Dragons. Princess Rhaenyra died, and then King Aegon II. By that time most of the Targaryen dragons were dead as well, along with scores of lords both great and small, hundreds of valiant knights, and tens of thousands of common men and smallfolk. The remaining blacks and greens agreed to terms, and Rhaenyra's young son was crowned as King Aegon III and wed to Aegon II's daughter, Jaehaera.

Peace in King's Landing did not mean peace in the west, however. The Red Kraken had not lost his appetite for battle. When the council of regents ruling in the name of the new boy king commanded him to cease his raiding, he continued as before.

In the end, it was a woman who would prove the Red Kraken's undoing. A girl known to us only as Tess opened Lord Dalton's throat with his own dagger as he slept in Lord Farman's bedchamber in Faircastle, then threw herself into the sea.

The Red Kraken had never taken a rock wife. His closest heirs were his salt sons, young boys fathered on various of his salt wives. Within hours of his death, a bloody struggle for succession broke out. And even before the battles began on Old Wyk and Pyke, the smallfolk of Fair Isle rose up and slaughtered those ironmen who still remained amongst them.

In 134 AC, Lady Johanna Lannister took her revenge for all that the Red Kraken had inflicted on her and hers. With her own fleets destroyed, she persuaded Ser Leo Costayne, the aged lord admiral of the Reach, to deliver her swordsmen to the Iron Islands. Embroiled in their own war of succession, the ironborn were taken unawares. Thousands of men, women, and children were put to the sword, scores of villages and hundreds of longships put to the torch. Ultimately Costayne was slain in battle, his host largely scattered and destroyed. Only a portion of his fleet (laden with the spoils of war, including many tons of grain and salt fish) returned to Lannisport . . . but amongst the highborn captives they brought back to Casterly Rock was one of the Red Kraken's salt sons. Lady Johanna had him gelded and made him her son's fool. "A fine fool he proved," Archmaester Haereg observes, "yet not half so foolish as his father."

In other lands, a lord who brought such a fate upon his house and people would be justly reviled, but such is the nature of the ironborn of the isles that the Red Kraken is revered amongst them to this day and counted as one of their great heroes.

THE OLD WAY AND THE NEW

From that day to this, the Lord Reapers of House Greyjoy have ruled the Iron Islands from the Seastone Chair on Pyke. None since the Red Kraken has posed a true threat to the Seven Kingdoms or the Iron Throne, but few can truly be described as leal and faithful servants of the crown. Kings they were in days gone by, and even the passage of a thousand years cannot erase the memory of a driftwood crown.

A full account of their reigns can be found in Archmaester Haereg's *History of the Ironborn*. Therein you may read of Dagon Greyjoy, the Last Reaver, whose longships harried the western coasts when Aerys I Targaryen sat the Iron Throne. Of Alton Greyjoy, the Holy Fool, who sought new lands to conquer beyond the Lonely Light. Of Torwyn Greyjoy, who swore a blood oath with Bittersteel, then betrayed him to his enemies. Of Loron Greyjoy, the Bard, and his great and tragic friendship with young Desmond Mallister, a knight of the green lands.

Near the end of Haereg's great work you will come to Lord Quellon Greyjoy, the wisest of the men to sit the Seastone Chair since Aegon's Conquest. A huge man, six and a half feet tall, he was said to be as strong as an ox and as quick as a cat. In his youth he earned renown as a warrior, fighting corsairs and slavers in the Summer Sea. A leal servant of the Iron Throne, he led a hundred longships around the bottom

PREVIOUS PAGES | *The Red Kraken's reavers.*

of Westeros during the War of the Ninepenny Kings and played a crucial role in the fighting around the Stepstones.

As lord, however, Quellon preferred to walk the road of peace. He forbade reaving, save by his leave. He brought maesters to the Iron Islands by the score, to serve as healers to the sick and tutors to the young; with them came their ravens, whose black wings would tie the isles to the green lands tighter than ever before.

It was Lord Quellon who freed the remaining thralls and outlawed the practice of thralldom on the Iron Islands (in this he was not wholly successful). And whilst he took no salt wives himself, he allowed other men to do so but taxed them heavily for the privilege. Quellon Greyjoy sired nine sons on three wives. His first and second wives were rock wives, joined to him with the old rites by a priest of the Drowned God, but his last bride was a woman of the green lands, a Piper of Pinkmaiden Castle, wed to him in her father's hall by a septon.

In this, as in much else, Lord Quellon turned away from the ancient and insular traditions of the ironborn, in hopes of forging stronger bonds between his own domains and the rest of the Seven Kingdoms. So strong a lord was Quellon Greyjoy that few dared speak openly against him, for he was known to be strong-willed and stubborn and fearsome in his wroth.

Quellon Greyjoy still sat the Seastone Chair when Robert Baratheon, Eddard Stark, and Jon Arryn raised their banners in rebellion. Age had only served to deepen his cautious nature, and as the fighting swept across the green lands, his lordship resolved to take no part in the war. But his sons were relentless in their hunger for gain and glory, and his own health and strength were failing. For some time his lordship had been troubled by stomach pains, which had grown so excruciating that he took a draught of milk of the poppy every night to sleep. Even so, he resisted all entreaties until a raven came to Pyke with word of Prince Rhaegar's death upon the Trident. These tidings united his three eldest sons: the Targaryen were done, they told him, and House Greyjoy must needs join the rebellion at once or lose any hope of sharing in the spoils of victory.

Lord Quellon gave way. It was decided that the iron-born would demonstrate their allegiance by attacking the nearest Targaryen loyalists. Despite his age and growing infirmity, his lordship insisted on commanding the fleet himself. Fifty longships assembled off Pyke and bent oars toward the Reach. The greater part of the ironborn fleets remained at home to guard against Lannister attack, for it was not yet known whether Casterly Rock would side with the rebels or the royalists.

Little and less need be said of Quellon Greyjoy's final voyage. In the histories of Robert's Rebellion, it is no more than an afterthought, a sad and bloody business that had no impact upon the final outcome of the war. The ironborn sank some fishing boats and captured a few fat merchantmen, burned some villages and sacked a few small towns. But at the mouth of the Mander, they met unexpected resistance from the Shield Islanders, who sallied forth in their own longships to give battle. A dozen ships were seized or sunk in the fight that followed, and though the ironborn gave worse than they got, amongst their dead was Lord Quellon Greyjoy.

By that time the war was all but done. Prudently, his heir Balon Greyjoy chose to return to his home waters and claim the Seastone Chair.

The new Lord of the Iron Islands was Lord Quellon's eldest surviving son, a child of his second marriage (the sons of his first marriage all having died in youth). In many ways, he was like his sire. At thirteen he could run a longship's oars and dance the finger dance. At fifteen he spent a summer in the Stepstones, reaving. At ten-and-seven he was captain of his own ship. Though he lacked his father's size and brute strength, Balon Greyjoy had all his quickness and skill at arms. And no man could question his courage.

Yet even as a child, Lord Balon had burned to free the ironborn from the yoke of the Iron Throne and restore them to a place of pride and power. Once seated on the Seastone Chair, he swept away many of his lord father's decrees, abolishing the taxes on salt wives and declaring that men taken captive in war could indeed be kept as thralls. Though he did not expel the septons, he increased the taxes on them tenfold. The maesters he kept, for they had proved themselves too useful to forsake. Whilst he did put Pyke's own maester to death for reasons that remain somewhat obscure, Lord Balon immediately petitioned the Citadel for another.

Lord Quellon had spent most of his long reign avoiding war; Lord Balon began at once preparing for it. For more than gold or glory, Balon Greyjoy lusted for a crown. This dream of crowns has seemed to haunt House Greyjoy throughout its long history. Oft as not, it ends in defeat, despair, and death, as it did for Balon Greyjoy. For five years he prepared, gathering men and longships, and building a great fleet of massive warships with reinforced hulls and iron rams, their decks bristling with scorpions and spitfires. The ships of this

Iron Fleet were more galleys than longships, larger than any that the ironmen had built before.

In 289 AC Lord Balon struck, declaring himself the King of the Iron Islands and dispatching his brothers Euron and Victarion to Lannisport to burn the Lannister fleet. "The sea shall be my moat," he declared, as Lord Tywin's ships went up in flames, "and woe to any man who dares to cross it."

King Robert dared. Robert Baratheon, the First of His Name, had won everlasting glory on the Trident. Swift to respond, the young king called his banners and sent his brother Stannis, Lord of Dragonstone, around Dorne with the royal fleet. Warships from Oldtown and the Arbor and the Reach joined their strength to his. Balon Greyjoy sent his own brother Victarion to meet them, but in the Straits of Fair Isle, Lord Stannis lured the ironborn into a trap and smashed the Iron Fleet.

With Balon's "moat" now undefended, King Robert had no difficulty bringing his host across Ironman's Bay from Seagard and Lannisport. With his Wardens of the West and North beside him, Robert forced landings on Pyke, Great Wyk, Harlaw, and Orkmont, and cut his way across the isles with steel and fire. Balon was forced to fall back to his stronghold at Pyke, but when Robert brought down his curtain wall and sent his knights storming through the breech, all resistance collapsed.

The reborn Kingdom of the Iron Isles had lasted less than a year. Yet when Balon Greyjoy was brought before King Robert in chains, the ironman remained defiant. "You may take my head," he told the king, "but you cannot name me traitor. No Greyjoy ever swore an oath to a Baratheon." Robert Baratheon, ever merciful, is said to have laughed at that, for he liked spirit in a man, even in his foes. "Swear one now," he replied, "or lose that stubborn head of yours." And so Balon Greyjoy bent his knee and was allowed to live, after giving up his last surviving son as a hostage to his loyalty.

The Iron Islands endure today as they always have. From the reign of the Red Kraken to our present day, the story of the ironborn is the story of a people caught between dreams of past glory and the poverty of the present. Set apart from Westeros proper by the grey-green waters of the sea, the islands remain a realm unto themselves. The sea is always moving, always changing, the ironborn like to say, and yet it remains, eternal, boundless, never the same and always the same. So it is with the ironborn themselves, the people of the sea.

"You may dress an ironman in silks and velvets, teach him to read and write and give him books, instruct him in chivalry and courtesy and the mysteries of the Faith," writes Archmaester Haereg, "but when you look into his eyes, the sea will still be there, cold and grey and cruel."

PYKE

Pyke is neither the largest nor the grandest castle on the Iron Islands, but it may well be the oldest, and it is from there that the lords of House Greyjoy rule the ironborn. It has long been their contention that the isle of Pyke takes its name from the castle; the smallfolk of the islands insist the opposite is true.

Pyke is so ancient that no one can say with certainty when it was built, nor name the lord who built it. Like the Seastone Chair, its origins are lost in mystery.

Once, centuries ago, Pyke was as other castles: built upon solid stone on a cliff overlooking the sea, with a wall and keeps and towers. But the cliffs it rested upon were not as solid as they seemed, and beneath the endless pounding of the waves, they began to crumble. Walls fell, the ground gave way, outer buildings were lost.

What remains of Pyke today is a complex of towers and keeps scattered across half a dozen islets and sea stacks above the booming waves. A section of curtain wall, with a great gatehouse and defensive towers, stretches across the headland, the only access to the castle, and is all that remains of the original fortress. A stone bridge from the headland leads to the first and largest islets and Great Keep of Pyke.

Beyond that, rope bridges connect the towers one to the other. The Greyjoys are fond of saying that any man who can walk one of these bridges when a storm is howling can as easily run the oars. Beneath the castle walls, the waves still smash against the remaining rock stacks day and night, and one day those too will doubtless crash into the sea.

THE WESTERLANDS

THE WESTERLANDS ARE a place of rugged hills and rolling plains, of misty dales and craggy shorelines, a place of blue lakes and sparkling rivers and fertile fields, of broadleaf forests that teem with game of every sort, where half-hidden doors in the sides of wooded hills open onto labyrinthine caves that wend their way through darkness to reveal unimaginable wonders and vast treasures deep beneath the earth.

These are rich lands, temperate and fruitful, shielded by high hills to the east and south and the endless blue waters of the Sunset Sea to the west. Once the children of the forest made their homes in the woods, whilst giants dwelt amongst the hills, where their bones can still occasionally be found. But then the First Men came with fire and bronze axes to cut down the forests, plow the fields, and drive roads through the hill country where the giants made their abodes. Soon, the First Men's farms and villages spread across the west "from salt to stone," protected by stout motte-and-bailey forts, and later great stone castles, until the giants were no more, and the children of the forest vanished into the deep woods, the hollow hills, and the far north.

Many and more great houses trace their roots back to this golden age of the First Men. Amongst these are the Hawthornes, the Footes, the Brooms, and the Plumms. On Fair Isle, the longships of the Farmans helped defend the western coast against ironborn reavers. The Greenfields raised a vast timber castle called the Bower (now simply Greenfield), built entirely of weirwood. The Reynes of Castamere made a rich system of mines, caves, and tunnels as their own subterranean seat, whilst the Westerlings built the Crag above the waves. Other houses sprang from the loins of legendary heroes, of whom tales are told to this very day: the Crakehalls from Crake the Boarkiller, the Baneforts from the Hooded Man, the Yews from the Blind Bowman Alan o' the Oak, the Morelands from Pate the Plowman.

Each of these families became powers, and some in time took on the styles of lords and even kings. Yet by far the greatest lords in the westerlands were the Casterlys of the Rock, who had their seat in a colossal stone that rose beside the Sunset Sea. Legend tells us the first Casterly lord was a huntsman, Corlos son of Caster, who lived in a village near to where Lannisport stands today. When a lion began preying upon the village's sheep, Corlos tracked it back to its den, a cave in the base of the Rock. Armed only with a spear, he slew the lion and his mate but spared her newborn cubs—an act of mercy that so pleased the old gods (for this was long before the Seven came to Westeros) that they sent a sudden shaft of sunlight deep into the cave, and there in the stony walls, Corlos beheld the gleam of yellow gold, a vein as thick as a man's waist.

The truth of that tale is lost in the mists of time, but we cannot doubt that Corlos, or some progenitor of what would become House Casterly, found gold inside the Rock and soon began to mine there. To defend his treasure against those who would make off with it, he moved inside the cave and fortified its entrance. As years and centuries passed, his descendants delved deeper and deeper into the earth, following the gold, whilst carving halls and galleries and stairways and tunnels into the Rock itself, transforming the gigantic stone into a mighty fastness that dwarfed every castle in Westeros.

Though never kings, the Casterlys became the richest lords in all of Westeros and the greatest power in the westerlands, and remained so for hundreds of years. By then the Dawn Age had given way to the Age of Heroes.

That was when the golden-haired rogue called Lann the Clever appeared from out of the east. Some say he was an Andal adventurer from across the narrow sea, though this was millennia before the coming of the Andals to Westeros. Regardless of his origins, the tales agree that somehow Lann the Clever winkled the Casterlys out of their Rock and took it for his own.

The precise method by which he accomplished this remains a matter of conjecture. In the most common version of the tale, Lann discovered a secret way inside the Rock, a cleft so narrow that he had to strip off his clothes and coat himself with butter in order to squeeze through. Once inside, however, he began to work his mischief, whispering threats in the ears of sleeping Casterlys, howling from the darkness like a demon, stealing treasures from one brother to plant in the bedchamber of another, rigging sundry snares and deadfalls. By such methods he set the Casterlys at odds with one another and convinced them that the Rock was haunted by some fell creature that would never let them live in peace.

Other tellers prefer other versions of the tale. In one, Lann uses the cleft to fill the Rock with mice, rats, and other vermin, thereby driving out the Casterlys. In another, he smuggles a pride of lions inside, and Lord Casterly and his sons are all devoured, after which Lann claims his lordship's wife and daughters for himself. The bawdiest of the stories has Lann stealing in night after night to have his way with the Casterly maidens whilst they sleep. In nine months time, these maids all give birth to golden-haired children whilst still insisting they had never had carnal knowledge of a man.

The last tale, ribald as it is, has certain intriguing aspects that might hint at the truth of what occurred. It is Archmaester Perestan's belief that Lann was a retainer of some sort in service to Lord Casterly (perhaps a household guard), who impregnated his lordship's daughter (or daughters, though that seems less likely), and persuaded her father to give him the girl's hand in marriage. If indeed this was what occurred, assuming (as we must) that Lord Casterly had no trueborn sons, then in the natural course of events the Rock would have passed to the daughter, and hence to Lann, upon the father's death.

There is, to be sure, no more historical evidence for this than for any of the other versions. All that is known for certain is that sometime during the Age of Heroes, the Casterlys vanish from the chronicles, and the hitherto-unknown Lannisters appear in their place, ruling large portions of the westerlands from beneath Casterly Rock.

Lann the Clever supposedly lived to the age of 312, and sired a hundred bold sons and a hundred lissome daughters, all fair of face, clean of limb, and blessed with hair "as golden as the sun." But such tales aside, the histories suggest that the early Lannisters were fertile as well as fair, for many names began to appear in the chronicles, and within a few generations Lann's descendants had grown so numerous that even Casterly Rock could not contain all of them. Rather than tunnel out new passages in the stone, some sons and daughters from lesser branches of the house left to make their homes in a village a scant mile away. The land was fertile, the sea teemed with fish, and the site they had chosen had an excellent natural harbor. Soon enough the village grew into a town, then a city: Lannisport.

By the time the Andals came, Lannisport had become the second biggest city in Westeros. Only Oldtown was larger and richer, and trading ships from every corner of the world were sailing up the western coasts to call upon the golden city on the Sunset Sea. Gold had made House Lannister rich; trade made it even richer. The Lannisters of Lannisport prospered, built great walls around their city to defend it from those (chiefly ironborn) who sought to steal their wealth, and soon became kings.

Lann the Clever never called himself a king, as best we know, though some tales told centuries later have conferred that styling on him posthumously. The first true Lannister king we know of is Loreon Lannister, also known as Loreon the Lion (a number of Lannisters through the centuries have been dubbed "the Lion" or "the Golden," for understandable reasons), who made the Reynes of Castamere his vassals by wedding a daughter of that house, and defeated the Hooded King, Morgon Banefort, and his thralls in a war that lasted twenty years. Loreon might have been the first Lannister to style himself King of the Rock, but it was a title his sons and grandsons and their successors continued to bear for thousands of years. However, the boundaries of their kingdom did not reach their full scope until the arrival of the Andal invaders. The Andals came late to the westerlands, long after they had taken the Vale and toppled the kingdoms of the First Men in the riverlands. The first Andal warlord to march an army through the hills met a bloody end at the hands of King Tybolt Lannister (called, unsurprisingly, the Thunderbolt). The second and third attacks were dealt with likewise, but as more and more Andals began moving west in bands large and small, King Tyrion III and his son Gerold II saw their doom ahead.

Rather than attempting to throw back the invaders, these sage kings arranged marriages for the more powerful of the Andal war chiefs with the daughters of the great houses of the west. Cautious men, and well aware of what had happened in the Vale, they took care to demand a price for this largesse; the sons and daughters of the Andal lords so ennobled were taken as wards and fosterlings, to serve as squires and pages and cupbearers in Casterly Rock . . . and as hostages, should their fathers prove treacherous.

In time, Lannister kings wed their children to Andals as well; indeed, when Gerold III died without male issues, a council crowned his only daughter's husband, Ser Joffery Lydden, who took the Lannister name and became the first Andal to rule the Rock. Other noble houses were also born in such unions—such as Jast, Lefford, Parren, Droxe, Marbrand, Braxe, Serrett, Sarsfield, and Kyndall. And thus revitalized, the Kings of the Rock expanded their realm still farther.

Cerion Lannister extended his rule as far east as the Golden Tooth and its surrounding hills, defeating three lesser kings when they made an alliance against him. Tommen Lannister, the First of His Name, built a great fleet and brought Fair Isle into the realm, taking the daughter of the last Farman king to wife. Loreon II held the first tourney ever seen in the westerlands, defeating every knight who rode against him. The first Lancel Lannister (known, of course, as Lancel the Lion) rode to war against the Gardener kings of Highgarden and conquered the Reach as far south as Old Oak before being felled in battle. (His son, Loreon III, lost all his father had gained and earned the mocking name Loreon the Limp). King Gerold Lannister, known as Gerold the Great, sailed to the Iron Islands and returned with a hundred ironborn hostages, promising to hang one every time the ironmen dared raid his shores. (True to his word, Gerold hanged more than twenty of the hostages). Lancel IV is said to have beheaded the ironborn king Harrald Halfdrowned and his heir with a single stroke of the Valyrian steel greatsword Brightroar at the Battle of Lann's Point; he later died in battle at Red Lake whilst attempting to invade the Reach.

Some of the Lannister kings were famed for their wisdom, some for their valor, all for their open-handedness . . . save perhaps for King Norwin Lannister, better known as Norwin the Niggardly. Yet Casterly Rock also housed many a weak, cruel, and feeble king. Loreon IV was better known as Loreon the Lackwit, and his grandson Loreon V was dubbed Queen Lorea, for he was fond of dressing in his wife's clothing and wandering the docks of Lannisport in the guise of a common prostitute. (After their reigns, the name Loreon became notably less common amongst Lannister princes.) A later monarch, Tyrion II, was known as the Tormentor. Though a strong king, famed for prowess with his battle-axe, his true delight was torture, and it was whispered of him that he desired no woman unless he first made her bleed.

Ultimately the Lannister domains extended from the western shore to the headwaters of the Red Fork and Tumblestone, marked by the pass beneath the Golden Tooth, and from the southern shore of Ironman's Bay to the borders of the Reach. The boundaries of the wester-lands today follow those of the Kingdom of the Rock as it was before the Field of Fire, when King Loren Lannister (Loren the Last) knelt as a king and rose as a lord. But in bygone days, the boundaries were more fluid, particularly to the south, where the Lannisters oft contended against the Gardeners in the Reach, and to the east, where they warred against the many kings of the Trident.

In addition, the Lannister coastline lay closer to the Iron Islands than did any other kingdom, and the wealth of Lannisport and its trade was a constant temptation to the reavers of those benighted isles. Wars between the westermen and the ironborn erupted every generation or so; even during periods of peace, the ironmen came raiding after wealth and salt wives. Fair Isle did help shield the coast farther south; for this reason the Farmans have become famous for their hatred of the ironborn.

The great wealth of the westerlands, of course, stems primarily from their gold and silver mines. The veins of ore run wide and deep, and there are mines, even now, that have been delved for a thousand years and more and are yet to be emptied. Lomas Longstrider reports that, even in far Asshai-by-the-Shadow, there were merchants who asked him if it was true that the "Lion Lord" lived in a palace of solid gold and that crofters collected a wealth of gold simply by plowing their fields. The gold of the west has traveled far, and the maesters know there are no mines in all the world as rich as those of Casterly Rock.

The sword Brightroar came into the possession of the Lannister kings in the century before the Doom, and it is said that the weight of gold they paid for it would have been enough to raise an army. But it was lost little more than a century later, when Tommen II carried it with him when he sailed with his great fleet to ruined Valyria, with the intention of plundering the wealth and sorcery he was sure still remained. The fleet never returned, nor Tommen, nor Brightroar.

The last report of them is found in a Volantene chronicle called *The Glory of Volantis*. There it stated that a "golden fleet" bearing the "Lion King" had stayed there for supplies, and that the triarchs lavished him with gifts. The chronicle claims that he swore that half of all he found would be given to the triarchs in return for their generosity—and a prom-ise to send their fleet to his aid when he requested it. After that, he sailed away. The year after, the chronicle claims that the Triarch Marqelo Tagaros dispatched a squadron of ships toward Valyria to see if any sign of the golden fleet could be found, but they returned empty-handed.

ABOVE | *Brightroar, the lost Valyrian steel sword of the Lannisters.*

The wealth of the westerlands was matched, in ancient times, with the hunger of the Freehold of Valyria for precious metals, yet there seems no evidence that the dragonlords ever made contact with the lords of the Rock, Casterly or Lannister. Septon Barth speculated on the matter, referring to a Valyrian text that has since been lost, suggesting that the Freehold's sorcerers foretold that the gold of Casterly Rock would destroy them. Archmaester Perestan has put forward a different, more plausible speculation, suggesting that the Valyrians had in ancient days reached as far as Oldtown but suffered some great reverse or tragedy there that caused them to shun all of Westeros thereafter.

HOUSE LANNISTER UNDER THE DRAGONS

Once Loren the Last gave up his crown, the Lannisters were reduced to lords. Though their vast wealth remained untouched, they did not have close ties to House Targaryen (unlike the Baratheons) and unlike the Tullys they were too proud to at once scrabble for a place of prominence beneath the Iron Throne.

It was not until a generation later, when Prince Aegon and Princess Rhaena sought refuge from King Maegor the Cruel, that the Lannisters once again began to make a greater mark on the realm. Lord Lyman Lannister protected the prince and princess under his roof, extending guest right and refusing all the king's demands to turn them over. Yet his lordship did not pledge his swords to the fugitive prince and princess, nor did he bestir himself until after Prince Aegon had perished at his uncle's hands during the Battle Beneath the Gods Eye. Yet when Aegon's youngest brother Jaehaerys put forward his own claim to the Iron Throne, the Lannisters rallied to his support.

King Maegor's death and King Jaehaerys's coronation moved House Lannister closer to the Iron Throne, though the Velaryons, the Arryns, the Hightowers, the Tullys, and the Baratheons still eclipsed them in influence. Lord Tymond Lannister was present at the Great Council of 101 AC that decided the succession, famously arriving with a huge retinue of three hundred bannermen, men-at-arms, and servants . . . only to be outdone by Lord Matthos Tyrell of Highgarden, who counted five hundred in his retinue. The Lannisters chose to side with Prince Viserys in the deliberations—a choice remembered and rewarded some years later, when Viserys ascended the Iron Throne and made Lord Jason Lannister's twin brother Ser Tyland his master of ships. Later, Ser Tyland became master of coin for King Aegon II, and his close association with the Iron Throne and favored position at court brought his brother, Lord Jason, into the Dance of the Dragons on Aegon's side.

As the struggle for succession continued, however, Ser Tyland suffered greatly for hiding the greater part of the crown's gold where Rhaenyra Targaryen could not reach it when she took King's Landing. And the Lannisters' association with the Iron Throne proved ill-fated when the Red Kraken and his reavers fell upon the undefended westerlands whilst Lord Jason marched east at King Aegon II's behest. Queen Rhaenyra's supporters met his host at the crossing of the Red Fork, where Lord Jason fell in battle, mortally wounded by the grizzled squire Pate of Longleaf (knighted after the battle, this lowborn warrior was known as the Lionslayer for the rest of his days). The Lannister host continued to march, winning victories under Ser Adrian Tarbeck, then under Lord Lefford, before he perished at the Fishfeed, where his westermen were slaughtered among three armies.

Ser Tyland Lannister, meanwhile, fell prisoner to Queen Rhaenyra after she seized King's Landing. Cruelly tortured to force him to reveal where he had hidden the bulk of the crown's gold, Ser Tyland steadfastly refused to talk. When Aegon II and his loyalists won back the city, he was found to have been blinded, mutilated, and gelded. Yet his wits remained intact, and King Aegon retained him as master of coin. In the last days of his rule, Aegon II even sent Ser Tyland to the Free Cities in search of sellswords to support his cause against Rhaenyra's son, the future Aegon III, and his supporters.

A regency followed the end of the fighting since the new king, Aegon III, was but eleven years of age when he ascended the Iron Throne. In hopes of binding up the deep wounds left by the Dance, Ser Tyland Lannister was made Hand of the King. Perhaps those who had been his enemies deemed him too blind and broken to be a threat to them, but Ser Tyland served ably for the better part of two years, before dying of the Winter Fever in 133 AC.

In the years that followed, the Lannisters stood with the Targaryens against Daemon Blackfyre, though the Black Dragon's rebels won victories of note in the westerlands—especially at Lannisport and the Golden Tooth, where Ser Quentyn Ball, the hot-tempered knight renowned as Fireball, slew Lord Lefford and sent Lord Damon Lannister (later famed as the Grey Lion) into retreat.

Following the Grey Lion's passing in 210 AC, his son Tybolt succeeded him as Lord of Casterly Rock, only to perish himself two years later under suspicious circumstances. A young man in his prime, Lord Tybolt left no heir of the body save for a daughter, Cerelle, three years of age, whose reign as Lady of Casterly Rock proved cruelly short. In less than a year, she too was dead, whereupon the Rock and the westerlands and all the wealth and power of House Lannister passed to her uncle, Gerold, the late Lord Tybolt's younger brother.

A genial man, known to be exceedingly clever, Gerold had served as regent for his young niece, but the suddenness of her death at such a tender age set tongues to wagging, and it was whispered widely in the west that both Lady Cerelle and Tybolt had died at his hands.

No man now living can say with certainly whether there was any truth to these whispers, for Gerold Lannister soon proved himself to be an exceptionally shrewd, able, and fair-minded lord, greatly increasing the wealth of House Lannister, the power of Casterly Rock, and the trade at Lannisport. He ruled the westerlands for thirty-one years, earning the sobriquet Gerold the Golden. Yet the tragedies that befell House Lannister in the years that followed were proof enough for Lord Gerold's enemies. His beloved second wife, Lady Rohanne, vanished under mysterious circumstances in 230 AC, less than a year after giving birth to his lordship's fourth and youngest son, Jason. Tywald, the eldest of his twin sons, died in battle in 233 AC whilst squiring for Lord Robert Reyne of Castamere during the Peake Uprising. Lord Robert likewise died, leaving Ser Roger Reyne (the Red Lion), his eldest son, as his heir.

The most significant death by far that stemmed from the Peake Uprising was that of King Maekar himself, but the chaos this caused has been abundantly chronicled elsewhere. Less well-known, but no less baleful, are the dire effects the battle had upon the history of the west. Tywald Lannister had long been betrothed to the Red Lion's spirited young sister, Lady Ellyn. This strong-willed and hot-tempered maiden, who had for years anticipated becoming the Lady of Casterly Rock, was unwilling to forsake that dream. In the aftermath of her betrothed's death, she persuaded his twin brother, Tion, to set aside his own betrothal to a daughter of Lord Rowan of Goldengrove and espouse her instead. Lord Gerold, it is said, opposed this match, but grief and age and illness had left him a pale shadow of his former self, and in the end he gave way. In 235 AC, in a double wedding at Casterly Rock, Ser Tion Lannister took Ellyn Reyne to wife, whilst his younger brother Tytos wed Jeyne Marbrand, a daughter of Lord Alyn Marbrand of Ashemark.

Twice a widower, and ailing, Lord Gerold did not wed again, so after her marriage, Ellyn of House Reyne became the Lady of Casterly Rock in all but name.

As her good-father retreated to his books and his bedchamber, Lady Ellyn held a splendid court, staging a series of magnificent tourneys and balls and filling the Rock with artists, mummers, musicians . . . and Reynes. Her brothers Roger and Reynard were ever at her side, and offices, honors, and lands were showered upon them, and upon her uncles, cousins, and nephews and nieces as well. Lord Gerold's aged fool, an acerbic hunchback called Lord Toad, was heard to say, "Lady Ellyn must surely be a sorceress, for she has made it rain inside the Rock all year."

In 236 AC, the pretender Daemon Blackfyre, Third of His Name, crossed the narrow sea and landed upon Massey's Hook with Bittersteel and the Golden Company, intent on taking the Iron Throne. King Aegon V summoned leal lords from all across the Seven Kingdoms to oppose him, and the Fourth Blackfyre Rebellion began.

ABOVE | *The arms of House Lannister (center) and some houses of note, past and present, (clockwise from top): Crakehall, Brax, Clegane, Farman, Lefford, Reyne, Westerling, Payne, Marbrand, Lydden, Prester, and Tarbeck.*

It ended far more quickly than the pretender might have wished, at the Battle of Wendwater Bridge. Afterward, the corpses of the Black Dragon's slain choked the Wendwater and sent it overflowing its banks. The royalists, in turn, lost fewer than a hundred men . . . but amongst them was Ser Tion Lannister, heir to Casterly Rock.

The loss of the second of his "glorious twins" might well have been expected to break their grieving father, Lord Gerold. But curiously, the opposite seemed to be the case. As Ser Tion's body was laid to rest within Casterly Rock, Gerold the Golden roused himself and took firm hold of the westerlands once more, intent on doing all he could to prepare his thirdborn son, the weak-willed and unpromising boy Tytos, to succeed him.

The "Reign of the Reynes" was at an end. Lady Ellyn's brothers soon departed Casterly Rock for Castamere, accompanied by many of the other Reynes.

Lady Ellyn remained, but her influence dwindled, while that of Lady Jeyne grew. Soon, the rivalry between Ser Tion's widow and Tytos's wife became truly ugly, if the rumors set down by Maester Beldon can be believed. Beldon tells us that in 239 AC, Ellyn Reyne was accused of bedding Tytos Lannister, urging him to set aside his wife and marry her instead. However, young Tytos (then nineteen) found his brother's widow so intimidating that he was unable to perform. Humiliated, he ran back to his wife to confess and beg her forgiveness.

Lady Jeyne was willing to pardon her young husband but was less forgiving of her good-sister, and did not hesitate to inform Lord Gerold of the incident. Furious, his lordship resolved to rid Casterly Rock of Ellyn Reyne for good and all by finding her a new husband. Ravens flew, and a hasty match was made. Within the fortnight, Ellyn Reyne was wed to Walderan Tarbeck, Lord of Tarbeck Hall, the florid fifty-five-year-old widowed lord of an ancient, honorable, but impoverished house.

Ellyn Reyne, now Lady Tarbeck, departed Casterly Rock with her husband, never to return, but the rivalry between her and Lady Jeyne was not at an end. If anything, it seemed to intensify through what Lord Toad came to call the War of the Wombs. Though Lady Ellyn had not been able to give Ser Tion an heir, she proved more fertile with Walderan Tarbeck (who, it should be noted, had a number of older sons from his first two marriages), giving him two daughters and a son. Lady Jeyne answered with children of her own, the first of whom was a son. He was given the name Tywin, and legend claims that when his grandsire Lord Gerold ruffled the babe's golden hair, the child bit his finger.

Other children followed in good course, but Tywin, the eldest, was the only grandchild his lordship ever knew. In 244 AC, Gerold the Golden died of a bad bladder, unable to pass water. At the age of four-and-twenty, Tytos Lannister, his eldest surviving son, became Lord of Casterly Rock, Shield of Lannisport, and Warden of the West.

ABOVE | *Lady Ellyn Reyne and Lady Jeyne Marbrand in the court of Lord Gerold Lannister.*

All were offices for which he was manifestly unsuited. Lord Tytos Lannister had many virtues. Slow to anger and quick to forgive, he saw good in every man, great or small, and was too trusting by half. He was dubbed the Laughing Lion for his jovial manner, and for a time the west laughed with him . . . but soon enough, more were laughing at him instead.

Where matters of state were concerned, Lord Tytos proved weak-willed and indecisive. He had no taste for war and laughed away insults that would have had most of his forebears shouting for their swords. Many saw in his weakness an opportunity to grasp power, wealth, and land for themselves. Some borrowed heavily from Casterly Rock, then failed to repay the loans. When it was seen that Lord Tytos was willing to extend such debts, even forgive them, common merchants from Lannisport and Kayce began to beg for loans as well.

Lord Tytos's edicts were widely ignored, and corruption became widespread.

At feasts and balls, guests felt free to make mock of his lordship, even to his face. Twisting the lion's tail, this was called, and young knights and even squires vied with one another to see who could twist the lion's tail the hardest. It is said that no one laughed louder at these japes than Lord Tytos himself.

Maester Beldon, in one of his letters to the Citadel, wrote, "His lordship wants only to be loved. So he laughs, and takes no offense, and forgives, and bestows honors and offices and lavish gifts on those who mock him and defy him, thinking thereby to win their loyalty. Yet the more he laughs and gives, the more they despise him."

As the power of House Lannister waned, other houses grew stronger, more defiant, and more disorderly. And by 254 AC, even lords beyond the borders of the westerlands had grown aware that the lion of Casterly Rock was no longer a beast to be feared.

Late that year, Lord Tytos agreed to wed his seven-year-old daughter, Genna, to a younger son of Walder Frey, Lord of the Crossing. Though but ten years of age, Tywin denounced the betrothal in scathing terms. Lord Tytos did not relent, yet still men could see that this iron-willed, fearless child was hard beyond his years and nothing like his amiable father.

Not long after, Lord Tytos dispatched his heir to King's Landing, to serve as a cupbearer at King Aegon's court. His lordship's second son, Kevan, was sent away as well, to serve as page and later squire to the Lord of Castamere.

Old, rich, and powerful, the Reynes had prospered greatly from Lord Tytos's misrule. Roger Reyne, the Red Lion, was widely feared for his skill at arms; many considered him the deadliest sword in the westerlands. His brother, Ser Reynard, was as charming and cunning as Ser Roger was swift and strong.

As the Reynes rose, so too did their close allies, the Tarbecks of Tarbeck Hall. After centuries of slow decline, this poor but ancient house had begun to flourish, thanks in large part to the new Lady Tarbeck, the former Ellyn Reyne.

Though she herself remained unwelcome at the Rock, Lady Ellyn had contrived to extract large sums of gold from House Lannister through her brothers, for Lord Tytos found it very hard to refuse the Red Lion. Those funds she had used to restore the crumbling ruin that was Tarbeck Hall, rebuilding its curtain wall, strengthening its towers, and furnishing its keep in splendor to rival any castle in the west.

In 255 AC, Lord Tytos celebrated the birth of his fourth son at Casterly Rock, but his joy soon turned to sorrow. His beloved wife, the Lady Jeyne, never recovered from her labor, and died within a moon's turn of Gerion Lannister's birth. Her loss was a shattering blow to his lordship. From that day forth, no one ever again called him the Laughing Lion.

The years that followed were as dismal as any in the long history of the westerlands. Conditions in the west grew so bad that the Iron Throne felt compelled to take a hand. Thrice King Aegon V sent forth his knights to restore order to the westerlands, but each time the conflicts flared up once again as soon as the king's men had taken their leave. When His Grace perished in the tragedy at Summerhall in 259 AC, matters in the west deteriorated even further, for the new king, Jaehaerys II Targaryen, lacked his sire's strength of will and was besides soon embroiled in the War of the Ninepenny Kings.

A thousand knights and ten thousand men-at-arms went forth from the westerlands at the king's call, but Lord Tytos was not amongst them. His lordship's brother was given command in his stead, but in 260 AC Ser Jason Lannister died on Bloodstone. After his death, Ser Roger Reyne seized command of the remaining westermen and led them to several notable victories.

Lord Tytos's three eldest sons also acquitted themselves well upon the Stepstones. Knighted on the eve of the conflict, Ser Tywin Lannister fought in the retinue of the king's young heir, Aerys, Prince of Dragonstone, and was given the honor of dubbing him a knight at war's end. Kevan Lannister, squiring for the Red Lion, also won his spurs, and was

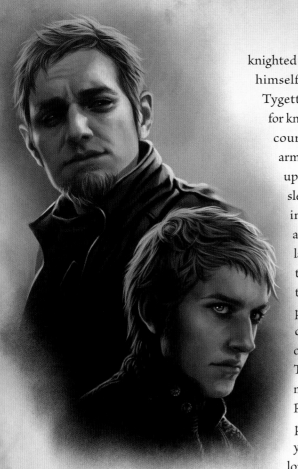

knighted by Roger Reyne himself. Their brother Tygett was too young for knighthood, but his courage and skill at arms were remarked upon by all, for he slew a grown man in his first battle and three more in later fights, one of them a knight of the Golden Company. Yet whilst his cubs were fighting on the Stepstones, Tytos Lannister remained at Casterly Rock, in the company of a certain young woman of low birth who had caught his eye whilst serving as a wet nurse to his youngest son.

The return of Lord Tytos's sons from war finally heralded change. Hardened by battle, and all too aware of the low regard in which the other lords of the realm held his father, Ser Tywin Lannister set out at once to restore the pride and power of Casterly Rock. His sire protested but feebly, we are told, then retreated back to the arms of his wet nurse whilst his heir took command.

Ser Tywin began by demanding repayment of all the gold Lord Tytos had lent out. Those who could not pay were required to send hostages to Casterly Rock. Five hundred knights, blooded and seasoned veterans of the Stepstones, were formed into a new company under the command of Ser Tywin's brother Ser Kevan, and charged with ridding the west of robber knights and outlaws.

Some hastened to obey. "The lion has awoken," said Ser Harys Swyft, the Knight of Cornfield, when the collectors arrived at his castle gates. Unable to repay his debt, he turned his daughter over to Ser Kevan as a hostage instead. But elsewhere, the collectors were met with sullen resistance and open defiance. Lord Reyne reportedly laughed when his maester read him Ser Tywin's edicts and counseled his friends and vassals to do nothing.

Lord Walderan Tarbeck unwisely chose a different course. He rode to Casterly Rock to protest, confident in his ability to cow Lord Tytos and force him to rescind his son's edicts. But he found himself facing Ser Tywin instead, who had him consigned to a dungeon.

With Lord Walderan in chains, Tywin Lannister no doubt expected the Tarbecks to yield. But Lady Tarbeck was quick to disabuse him of that notion. Instead that redoubtable woman sent forth her own knights and captured three Lannisters. Two of the captives were Lannisters of Lannisport, distant kin to the Lannisters of Casterly Rock, but the third was a young squire, Stafford Lannister, the eldest son and heir of Lord Tytos's late brother, Ser Jason.

The resulting crisis drew Lord Tytos away from his wet nurse long enough to overrule his strong-willed heir. His lordship not only commanded that Lord Tarbeck be released, unharmed, but also went so far as to apologize to him and forgive him his debts.

To safeguard the exchange of hostages, Lord Tytos turned to Lady Tarbeck's younger brother, Ser Reynard Reyne. The Red Lion's formidable seat at Castamere was chosen to host the meet. Ser Tywin refused to attend, so it was Ser Kevan who returned Lord Walderan, whilst Lady Tarbeck herself delivered Stafford and his cousins. Lord Reyne feasted all the parties, and a great show of amity was staged, with Lannisters and Tarbecks toasting one another, exchanging gifts and kisses, and vowing to remain each other's leal friends "through all eternity."

All eternity lasted not quite a year, Grand Maester Pycelle observed later. Tywin Lannister, who had not been present at the Red Lion's feast, had never weakened in his resolve to bring these overmighty vassals to heel. Late in the year 261 AC, he sent ravens to Castamere and Tarbeck Hall, demanding that Roger and Reynard Reyne and Lord and Lady Tarbeck present themselves at Casterly Rock "to answer for your crimes." The Reynes and Tarbecks chose defiance instead, as Ser Tywin surely knew they would. Both houses rose in open revolt, renouncing their fealty to Casterly Rock.

So Tywin Lannister called the banners. He did not seek his lord father's leave, nor even inform him of his intent, but rode forth himself with five hundred knights and three thousand men-at-arms and crossbowmen behind him.

House Tarbeck was the first to feel Ser Tywin's wroth. The Lannister host descended so quickly that Lord Walderan's vassals and supporters had no time to gather. Foolishly his lordship rode forth to meet Ser Tywin's host

ABOVE | *Lord Tytos Lannister and his heir, Ser Tywin.*

with only his household knights beside him. In a short, brutal battle, the Tarbecks were broken and butchered. Lord Walderan Tarbeck and his sons were beheaded, together with his nephews and cousins, his daughters' husbands, and any man who displayed the seven-pointed blue-and-silver star upon his shield or surcoat to boast of Tarbeck blood. And when the Lannister host resumed its march to Tarbeck Hall, the heads of Lord Walderan and his sons went before them, impaled on spears.

At their approach, Lady Ellyn Tarbeck closed her gates and sent forth ravens to Castamere, summoning her brothers. Trusting in her walls, Lady Tarbeck no doubt anticipated a long siege, but siege engines were readied within a day, and those walls proved little help when one great stone flew over them and brought down the castle's aged keep. Lady Ellyn and her son Tion the Red died in the keep's sudden collapse. All resistance at Tarbeck Hall ended soon after, and the gates were thrown open to the Lannister host. Tywin Lannister then ordered Tarbeck Hall put to the torch. The castle burned for a day and a night, until naught remained but a blackened shell. The Red Lion arrived in time to see the flames. Two thousand men rode with him—all he had been able to gather in the short time available.

Tywin Lannister had three times his strength, most accounts agree; some insist the Lannisters outnumbered the Reynes five to one. Hoping that surprise might carry the day, Roger Reyne commanded his trumpets to sound the attack and charged headlong toward Ser Tywin's camp. After the first shock, the Lannisters recovered quickly and their numbers soon began to tell. Lord Reyne had no choice but to wheel and flee, leaving near half his men dead upon the field. A rain of crossbow bolts chased his riders from the camp; one took Lord Reyne between the shoulders, punching through his backplate. The Red Lion rode on, only to fall from his horse less than a half a league farther on; he had to be carried back to Castamere.

The Lannister host arrived at Castamere three days later. Like Casterly Rock, the seat of House Reyne had begun as a mine. Rich veins of gold and silver had made the Reynes near as wealthy as the Lannisters during the Age of Heroes; to defend their riches, they had raised curtain walls about the entrance to their mine, closed it with an oak-and-iron gate, and flanked it with a pair of stout towers. Keeps and halls had followed, but all the while the mineshafts had gone deeper and deeper, and when at last the gold gave out, they had been widened into halls and galleries and snug bedchambers, a warren of tunnels and a vast, echoing ballroom. To the ignorant eye, Castamere seemed a modest holding, a fit seat for a landed knight or small lord, but those who knew its secrets knew that nine-tenths of the castle was beneath the ground.

It was to those deep chambers that the Reynes retreated now. Feverish and weak from loss of blood, the Red Lion was in no fit state to lead. Ser Reynard, his brother, assumed command in his stead. Less headstrong but more cunning than his brother, Reynard knew he did not have the men to defend the castle walls, so he abandoned the surface entirely to the foe and fell back beneath the earth. Once all his folk were safe inside the tunnels, Ser Reynard sent word to Ser Tywin above, offering terms. But Tywin Lannister did not honor Ser Reynard's offer with a reply. Instead he commanded that the mines be sealed. With pick and axe and torch, his own miners brought down tons of stone and soil, burying the great gates to the mines until there was no way in and no way out. Once that was done, he turned his attention to the small, swift stream that fed the crystalline blue pool beside the castle from which Castamere took its name. It took less than a day to dam the stream and only two to divert it to the nearest mine entrance.

The earth and stone that sealed the mine had no gaps large enough to allow a squirrel to pass, let alone a man ... but the water found its way down.

Ser Reynard had taken more than three hundred men, women, and children into the mines, it is said. Not a one emerged. A few of the guards assigned to the smallest and most distant of the mine entrances reported hearing faint screams and shouts coming from beneath the earth one night, but by daybreak the stones had gone silent once again.

No one has ever reopened the mines of Castamere. The halls and keeps above them, put to the torch by Tywin Lannister, stand empty to this day, a mute testament to the fate that awaits those foolish enough to take up arms against the lions of the Rock.

In 262 AC, King Jaehaerys II died in King's Landing, having sat the Iron Throne for only three years. His son Aerys, Prince of Dragonstone, succeeded him as King Aerys II. His first act as king—and his wisest, many say—was to summon his boyhood friend Tywin Lannister from Casterly Rock and name him the Hand of the King.

Ser Tywin was but twenty, the youngest man ever to serve as Hand, but the manner in which he had dealt with the rising of the Reynes and Tarbecks had made him well respected, even feared, throughout the Seven Kingdoms. His cousin Lady Joanna, the daughter of Lord Tytos's late brother Ser Jason, was already in King's Landing; she had been serving as a lady-in-waiting and companion to Rhaella since 259 AC. She and Ser Tywin were married a year after he became Hand of the King in a lavish ceremony at the Great Sept of Baelor, with King Aerys himself presiding over the wedding feast and bedding. In 266 AC, Lady Joanna gave birth to twins, a boy and a girl. Meanwhile, Ser Tywin's brother Ser Kevan had also wed, taking to bride the daughter of Ser Harys Swyft of Cornfield, who had once been given to him as a hostage for her father's debts.

In 267 AC, Lord Tytos Lannister's heart burst as he was climbing a steep flight of steps to the bedchamber of his mistress (his lordship had finally put aside his wet nurse, only to become besotted with the charms of a candlemaker's daughter). So at the age of five-and-twenty, Tywin Lannister became the Lord of Casterly Rock, Shield of Lannisport, and Warden of the West. With the Laughing Lion at last laid to rest, House Lannister had never been stronger nor more secure. The years that followed were golden ones, not only for the westerlands, but for all the Seven Kingdoms.

There was a worm inside the apple, though, for the growing madness of King Aerys II Targaryen soon imperiled all that Tywin Lannister sought to build. His lordship suffered great personal loss as well, for his beloved wife, Lady Joanna, died in 273 AC whilst giving birth to a hideously deformed child. With her death, Grand Maester Pycelle observes, the joy went out of Tywin Lannister, yet still he persisted in his duty.

Day by day and year by year, Aerys II turned ever more against his own Hand, the friend of his childhood, subjecting him to a succession of reproofs, reverses, and humiliations. All this Lord Tywin endured, but when the king made his son and heir, Ser Jaime, a knight of the Kingsguard, he could abide it no longer. Lord Tywin at last resigned the Handship in 281 AC.

Bereft of the counsel of the man he had relied upon so long, surrounded by lickspittles and schemers, King Aerys II was soon swallowed up entirely by his madness as the realm fell to pieces around him.

The events of Robert's Rebellion are revealed elsewhere and need no retelling save to note that Lord Tywin led a great Lannister host out of the west to capture King's Landing and the Red Keep for Robert Baratheon. Nigh unto three hundred years of Targaryen rule were brought to an end by the swords of Lord Tywin and his westermen. The following year, King Robert I Baratheon took Lord Tywin's daughter, the Lady Cersei, to wife, joining two of the greatest and noblest houses in all Westeros.

CASTERLY ROCK

Casterly Rock, the ancient seat of House Lannister, is no ordinary castle. Although crowned with towers and turrets and watchtowers, with stone walls and oaken gates and iron portcullises guarding its every means of egress, this ancient fortress is in truth a colossal rock beside the Sunset Sea, a rock that some say looks like a lion in repose when the sun sets and the shadows fall.

The Rock has been a habitation for men for thousands of years. Before the coming of the First Men it seems likely that the children of the forest and giants made their homes in the great sea-carved caverns at its base. Bears, lions, wolves, and bats have also been known to make their lairs within, along with countless lesser creatures.

Hundreds of mineshafts penetrate the lower parts of the Rock, where many veins of red and yellow gold gleam untouched in the stone even after millennia of mining. The Casterlys were the first to begin to carve halls and chambers from the mineshafts, and they established a ringfort on the Rock's peak, from which they could survey their domain.

The Rock has been measured as thrice the height of the Wall or the Hightower of Oldtown. Almost two leagues long from west to east, it is riddled throughout with tunnels, dungeons, storerooms, barracks, halls, stables, stairways, courtyards, balconies, and gardens. There is even a godswood of sorts, though the weirwood that grows there is a queer, twisted thing whose tangled roots have all but filled the cave where it stands, choking out all other growth.

The Rock even has a port inside it, complete with docks and wharves and shipyards, for the sea has carved great caves into its western face, natural gates deep and wide enough for longships and even cogs to enter and off-load their cargoes.

The Lion's Mouth—the huge natural cavern that forms the main entrance into the Rock—arches two hundred feet high from floor to ceiling. Over the centuries it has been widened and improved upon, and it is now said that twenty horsemen can ride abreast up its broad steps.

Casterly Rock has never been taken by storm or siege. No castle in the Seven Kingdoms is larger, richer, or better

RIGHT | *Casterly Rock.*

defended. Legends says that Visenya Targaryen, upon seeing it, thanked the gods that King Loren rode forth to face her brother Aegon on the Field of Fire, for if he had remained within the Rock, even dragonflame would not have daunted him.

The Lords of Casterly Rock have gathered many treasures over the centuries, and the sights of the Rock—especially the Golden Gallery, with its gilded ornaments and walls, and the Hall of Heroes where the costly armor worn by a hundred Lannister knights, lords, and kings stand eternal guard—are justly famed throughout the Seven Kingdoms, even in lands beyond the narrow sea.

THE LARGEST AND most populous of the six southern kingdoms (the North, vast in expanse though thinly peopled, being a land apart) is commonly referred to as the Reach, but this name is somewhat of a misnomer. The domains of House Tyrell, the Lords of Highgarden, now largely correspond with those of the Kingdom of the Reach as it existed for thousands of years before Aegon's Conquest, but that rich and fertile realm was, in fact, once comprised of four kingdoms:

Oldtown and its environs, bounded by the Red Mountains to the east and the headwaters of the Honeywine in the north.

The Arbor, the golden island beyond the Redwyne Strait, famed for wine and sunshine.

The western marches, from Horn Hill to Nightsong.

The Reach proper, a vast expanse of fields and farms, lakes and rivers, hills and woods and fragrant meadows, mills and mines, dotted with small villages, thriving market towns, and ancient castles, stretching from the Shield Islands in the Sunset Sea, up the mouth of the Mander, past Highgarden, to Red Lake, Goldengrove, and Bitterbridge, as far as Tumbleton and the Mander's headwaters.

This latter was the realm ruled by Gardeners of old, and in more recent days by the descendants of their stewards, the Tyrells of Highgarden. It was in these green fields that chivalry was born, history tells us; the gallant knights and fair maids of the Reach are celebrated throughout the Seven Kingdoms by the singers, whose own traditions first took root here as well.

Once and always a great realm, the Reach is many things to its inhabitants: the most populous, fertile, and powerful domain in the Seven Kingdoms, its wealth second only to the gold-rich west; a seat of learning; a center of music, culture, and all the arts, bright and dark; the breadbasket of Westeros; a nexus of trade; a home to great seafarers, wise and noble kings, dread sorcerers, and the most beautiful women in all Westeros. On a hill overlooking the Mander rises Highgarden, rightly hailed as the most beautiful castle in the realm. The Mander itself, which flows beneath its walls, is the longest and broadest river in the Seven Kingdoms. The great city of Oldtown is the equal of King's Landing in size, and it is superior in all other respects, being vastly older and more beautiful, with its cobbled streets, ornate guildhalls, stone houses, and three great monuments: the Starry Sept of the Faith, the Citadel of the Maesters, and the mighty Hightower, with its great beacon, the tallest tower in all the known world. Truly, the Reach is a land for superlatives.

GARTH GREENHAND

The story of the Reach begins with Garth Greenhand, the legendary progenitor not only of the Tyrells of Highgarden, but of the Gardener kings before them . . . and all the other great houses and noble families of the Green Realm as well.

A thousand tales are told of Garth, in the Reach and beyond. Most are implausible, and many contradictory. In some he is a contemporary of Bran the Builder, Lann the Clever, Durran Godsgrief, and the other colorful figures of the Age of Heroes. In others he stands as the ancestor of them all.

Garth was the High King of the First Men, it is written; it was he who led them out of the east and across the land bridge to Westeros. Yet other tales would have us believe that he preceded the arrival of the First Men by thousands of years, making him not only the First Man in Westeros, but the *only* man, wandering the length and breadth of the land alone and treating with the giants and the children of the forest. Some even say he was a god.

There is disagreement even on his name. Garth Greenhand, we call him, but in the oldest tales he is named Garth Greenhair, or simply Garth the Green. Some stories say he had green hands, green hair, or green skin overall. (A few even give him antlers, like a stag.) Others tell us that he dressed in green from head to foot, and certainly this is

A few of the very oldest tales of Garth Greenhand present us with a considerably darker deity, one who demanded blood sacrifice from his worshippers to ensure a bountiful harvest. In some stories the green god dies every autumn when the trees lose their leaves, only to be reborn with the coming of spring. This version of Garth is largely forgotten.

how he is most commonly depicted in paintings, tapestries, and sculptures. More likely, his sobriquet derived from his gifts as a gardener and a tiller of the soil—the one trait on which all the tales agree. "Garth made the corn ripen, the trees fruit, and the flowers bloom," the singers tell us.

Many of the more primitive peoples of the earth worship a fertility god or goddess, and Garth Greenhand has much and more in common with these deities. It was Garth who first taught men to farm, it is said. Before him, all men were hunters and gatherers, rootless wanderers forever in search

Some celebrated children of Garth Greenhand

John the Oak, the First Knight, who brought chivalry to Westeros (a huge man, all agree, eight feet tall in some tales, ten or twelve feet tall in others, sired by Garth Greenhand on a giantess). His own descendants became the Oakhearts of Old Oak.

Gilbert of the Vines, who taught the men of the Arbor to make sweet wine from the grapes that grew so fat and lush across their island, and who founded House Redwyne.

Florys the Fox, the cleverest of Garth's children, who kept three husbands, each ignorant of the existence of the others. (From their sons sprang House Florent, House Ball, and House Peake).

Maris the Maid, the Most Fair, whose beauty was so renowned that fifty lords vied for her hand at the first tourney ever to be held in Westeros. (The victor was the Grey Giant, Argoth Stone-Skin, but Maris wed King Uthor of the High Tower before he could claim her, and Argoth spent the rest of his days raging outside the walls of Oldtown, roaring for his bride.)

Foss the Archer, renowned for shooting apples off the head of any maid who took his fancy, from whom both the red apple and green apple Fossoways trace their descent.

Brandon of the Bloody Blade, who drove the giants from the Reach and warred against the children of the forest, slaying so many at Blue Lake that it has been known as Red Lake ever since.

Owen Oakenshield, who conquered the Shield Islands, driving the selkies and merlings back into the sea.

Harlon the Hunter and **Herndon of the Horn,** twin brothers who built their castle atop Horn Hill and took to wife the beautiful woods witch who dwelled there, sharing her favors for a hundred years (for the brothers did not age so long as they embraced her whenever the moon was full).

Bors the Breaker, who gained the strength of twenty men by drinking only bull's blood, and founded House Bulwer of Blackcrown. (Some tales claim Bors drank so much bull's blood he grew a pair of shiny black horns.)

Rose of Red Lake, a skinchanger, able to transform into a crane at will—a power some say still manifests from time to time in the women of House Crane, her descendants.

Ellyn Ever Sweet, the girl who loved honey so much she sought out the King of the Bees in his vast mountain hive and made a pact with him, to care for his children and his children's children for all time. She was the first beekeeper, and the mother to House Beesbury.

Rowan Gold-Tree, who was so bereft when her lover left her for a rich rival that she wrapped an apple in her golden hair, planted it upon a hill, and grew a tree whose bark and leaves and fruit were gleaming yellow gold, and to whose daughters the Rowans of Goldengrove trace their roots.

of sustenance, until Garth gave them the gift of seed and showed them how to plant and sow, how to raise crops and reap the harvest. (In some tales, he tried to teach the elder races as well, but the giants roared at him and pelted him with boulders, whilst the children laughed and told him that the gods of the wood provided for all their needs). Where he walked, farms and villages and orchards sprouted up behind him. About his shoulders was slung a canvas bag, heavy with seed, which he scattered as he went along. As befits a god, his bag was inexhaustible; within were seeds for all the world's trees and grains and fruits and flowers.

Garth Greenhand brought the gift of fertility with him. Nor was it only the earth that he made fecund, for the legends tell us that he could make barren women fruitful with a touch—even crones whose moon blood no longer flowed. Maidens ripened in his presence, mothers brought forth twins or even triplets when he blessed them, young girls flowered at his smile. Lords and common men alike offered up their virgin daughters to him wherever he went, that their crops might ripen and their trees grow heavy with fruit. There was never a maid that he deflowered who did not deliver a strong son or fair daughter nine moons later, or so the stories say.

These legends, though cherished by the smallfolk, are largely discounted by both the maesters of the Citadel and the septons of the Faith, who share the view that Garth Greenhand was a man, not a god. A hunter or war chief, most like, or perhaps a petty king, he might well have been the first lord of the First Men to lead his followers across the Arm of Dorne (as yet unbroken) and into the wilderness of Westeros, where only the elder races had previously trod.

God or man, Garth Greenhand fathered many children in this new land; on this all the tales agree. Many of those offspring grew to be heroes, kings, and great lords in their own right, founding mighty houses that endured for thousands of years.

Of all these, the greatest was his firstborn, Garth the Gardener, who made his home on the hill atop the Mander that in time became known as Highgarden, and wore a crown of flowers and vines. All of Garth Greenhand's other children did the Gardener homage as the rightful king of all men, everywhere. From his loins sprang House Gardener, whose kings ruled the Reach beneath the banner of a green hand for many thousands of years, until Aegon the Dragon and his sisters came to Westeros.

The list is long, and many are the legends, for there is scarce a noble house in all the Reach that does not boast of descent from one of Garth Greenhand's countless children. Even the heroes of other lands and kingdoms are sometimes numbered amongst the offspring of the Greenhand. Brandon the Builder was descended from Garth by way of Brandon of the Bloody Blade, these tales would have us believe, whilst Lann the Clever was a bastard born to Florys the Fox in some tales or Rowan Gold-Tree in others. However, Lann the Clever's descent from Garth Greenhand is a tale told in the Reach. In the westerlands, it is more oft said that Lann cozened Garth Greenhand himself by posing as one of his sons (Garth had so many that ofttimes he grew confused), thus making off with part of the inheritance that rightly belonged to Garth's true children.

That Garth Greenhand had many children cannot be denied, given how many in the Reach claim descent from him. But that all other lordly houses of Westeros were similarly descended seems most unlikely.

THE GARDENER KINGS

The history of the Reach in the days of the First Men is not unlike that of the other realms of Westeros. The bounty of these green and fertile lands did not make men more peaceful, nor less grasping. Here too the First Men strove against the children of the forest, rooting them out from their sacred groves and hollow hills, hewing down their weirwoods with great bronze axes. Here too kingdoms rose and fell and were forgotten, as petty kings and proud lords contended with one another for land and gold and glory, whilst towns burned and women wailed and sword rang against sword, century after century.

And yet there was a difference, in degree if not in kind, for almost all of the noble houses of the Reach shared a common ancestry, deriving as they did from Garth Greenhand and his many children. It was that kinship, many scholars have suggested, that gave House Gardener the primacy in the centuries that followed; no petty king could ever hope to rival the power of Highgarden, where Garth the Gardener's descendants sat upon a living throne (the Oakenseat) that grew from an oak that Garth Greenhand himself had

LEFT | *Garth Greenhand.*

the ironmen seldom ventured far inland, they controlled the Sunset Sea and exacted cruel tribute from the fisherfolk along the coasts. Having established themselves upon the Shield Islands by killing all the men they found there and claiming the women as their own, the ironborn even raided up the Mander with impunity.

King Qhored, the most fearsome of these ironborn overlords, boasted that his writ ran "wherever men can smell salt water or hear the crash of waves." He was known as Qhored the Cruel in the Reach, and the kings who succeeded him went by such bynames as Hagon the Terrible and Joron Maidensbane.

It was against these men and their followers that the kings of House Gardener contended for three centuries, sometimes in alliance with the Kings of the Rock and the Lords of Oldtown, and sometimes alone. No fewer than six of the Gardener kings died in battle, amongst them Gareth the Grim and Garth the Morningstar, whilst Gyles II was taken captive, tortured, and cut into small pieces to bait his captor's hooks. Yet the victory was at long last theirs, and each of them pushed the domains of House Gardener farther and brought more lands and lords beneath the rule of Highgarden.

That being said, many scholars still believe that the greatest of the Gardener kings were the peacemakers, not the fighters. Fewer songs are sung of them, it is true, but in the annals of history the names of Garth III (the Great), Garland II (the Bridegroom), Gwayne III (the Fat), and John II (the Tall) are writ large. Garth the Great extended the borders of his realm northward, winning Old Oak, Red Lake, and Goldengrove with pacts of friendship and mutual defense. Garland accomplished the same in the south, bringing Oldtown into his kingdom by wedding his daughter to Lymond (the Sea Lion) of House Hightower, whilst putting his own wives aside to marry Lord Lymond's daughter. Gwayne the Fat persuaded Lord Peake and Lord Manderly to accept his judgment on their quarrel, and do fealty for their lands, without fighting a single battle. John the Tall sailed his barge up the Mander to its very headwaters, planting the banner of the green hand wherever he went and receiving homage from the lords and petty kings whose lands lined that mighty river's banks.

Greatest of all the Gardeners was King Garth VII, the Goldenhand, a giant in both war and peace. As a boy, he turned back the Dornish when King Ferris Fowler led ten thousand men through the Wide Way (as the Prince's Pass was then called), intent on conquest. Soon after, he

planted, and wore crowns of vines and flowers when at peace, and crowns of bronze thorns (later iron) when they rode to war. Others might style themselves kings, but the Gardeners were the unquestioned High Kings, and lesser monarchs did them honor, if not obeisance.

In those centuries of trial and tumult, the Reach produced many a fearless warrior. From that day to this, the singers have celebrated the deeds of knights like Serwyn of the Mirror Shield, Davos the Dragonslayer, Roland of the Horn, and the Knight Without Armor—and the legendary kings who led them, among them Garth V (Hammer of the Dornish), Gwayne I (the Gallant), Gyles I (the Woe), Gareth II (the Grim), Garth VI (the Morningstar), and Gordan I (Grey-Eyes).

Many of these monarchs shared a common foe, for during these dark and bloody centuries, seaborne reavers from the Iron Islands dominated almost all of the western shore, from Bear Island to the Arbor. With their swift longships, the ironborn were able to strike and depart before any response came. Their raiders oft came ashore at unexpected places, taking their enemies unaware. Though

ABOVE | *King Garth VII Gardener, the Goldenhand.*

turned his attention to the sea and drove the last ironmen from their strongholds on the Shield Islands. Thereafter he resettled the islands with his fiercest fighters, granting them special dispensations for the purpose of turning them into a first defense against the ironborn, should they return. This proved a great success, and to this day the men of the Four Shields pride themselves on defending the mouth of the Mander and the heart of the Reach against any and all seaborne foes.

In his last and greatest war, Garth VII faced an alliance between the Storm King and the King of the Rock, intent on carving up the Reach between them, but he defeated them both, then with cunning words sowed such discord between them that they turned on one another with great slaughter at the Battle of Three Armies. In the aftermath he married his daughters to their heirs and signed a pact with each, fixing the borders between the three kingdoms.

Yet even that paled before his greatest accomplishment: three-quarters of a century of peace. Garth Goldenhand became King of the Reach at the age of twelve and died upon the Oakenseat when he was ninety-three, still sound of wits (if frail of body). During the eighty-one years of his reign, the Reach was at war for less than ten. Generations of boys were born and grew to manhood, sired children of their own, and died without ever knowing what it was to grasp a spear and shield and march away to war.

And with this long peace came an unprecedented prosperity. The Golden Reign, as this time came to be known, was when the Reach truly flowered.

Yet all golden ages end, and so it was in the Reach. Garth Goldenhand passed from this world. A great-grandson followed him upon the Oakenseat, then gave way to his own sons.

And then the Andals came.

ANDALS IN THE REACH

The Andals came late to the Reach.

Crossing the narrow sea in longships, they landed first upon the shores of the Vale, then later all along the eastern coasts. The fleets of Oldtown and the Arbor barred them from the Redwyne Straits and the Sunset Sea. Reports of the bounty of the Reach and the wealth and power of Highgarden and its kings undoubtedly reached the ears of many an Andal warlord, but other lands and other kings lay between them.

Thus, long before the Andals reached the Mander, the kings in Highgarden knew of their coming. They observed the fighting in the Vale, the stormlands, and the riverlands from afar, taking note of all that happened. Wiser perhaps than their counterparts from other regions, they did not make the error of allying with the Andals against local rivals. Gwayne IV (the Gods-fearing) sent his warriors searching out the children of the forest, in the hopes that the greenseers and their magic could halt the invaders. Mern II (the Mason) built a new curtain wall about Highgarden and commanded his lords bannermen to see to their own defenses. Mern III (the Madling) showered gold and honors on a woods witch who claimed that she could raise armies of the dead to throw the Andals back. Lord Redwyne built more ships, and Lord Hightower strengthened the walls of Oldtown.

Yet the great battles most of them had anticipated never came to pass. By the time the conquerors were done conquering the eastern shores, generations had passed and the Andals had raised up twoscore petty kings of their own, many of them at odds with one another. And in Highgarden, the Three Sage Kings followed one another upon the Oakenseat.

Garth IX Gardener, his son Merle I (the Meek), and his grandson Gwayne V were very different men, but they shared a common policy toward the Andals, one based on accord and assimilation rather than armed resistance. Garth IX brought a septon to his court and made him part of his councils, and built the first sept at Highgarden, though he himself continued to worship in the castle godswood. His son Merle I formally espoused the Faith, however, and helped fund the construction of septs, septries, and motherhouses all over the Reach. Gwayne V was the first Gardener born into the Faith, and the first to be made a knight by solemn rite and vigil. (Many of his noble forebears have had posthumous knighthood conveyed on them by singers and storytellers, but true knighthood only came to Westeros with the Andals).

Both Merle I and Gwayne V took Andal maidens as their wives, as a means of binding their brides' fathers to the realm. All three kings took Andals into their service as household knights and retainers. Amongst those so honored was an Andal knight named Ser Alester Tyrell, whose prowess at arms was such that he was made the king's champion and sworn shield under Gwayne V. Ser Alester's descendants in time became the hereditary stewards of Highgarden under the Gardeners.

The Three Sage Kings also found lands and lordships for the more powerful of the Andal kings descending on the Reach, in return for pledges of fealty. The Gardeners sought after Andal craftsmen as well and encouraged their lords bannermen to do the same. Blacksmiths and stonemasons in particular were handsomely rewarded. The former taught the First Men to arm and armor themselves in iron in place of bronze; the latter helped them strengthen the defenses of their castles and holdfasts.

And though some of these new-made lords foreswore their vows in later years, most did not. Rather, they joined with their liege lords to put down such rebels and defended the Reach against those Andal kings and warbands who came later. "When a wolf descends upon your flocks, all you gain by killing him is a short respite, for other wolves will come," King Garth IX said famously. "If instead you feed the wolf and tame him and turn his pups into your guard dogs, they will protect the flocks when the pack comes ravening." King Gwayne V said it more succinctly. "They gave us seven gods, we gave them dirt and daughters, and our sons and grandsons shall be as brothers."

Many noble houses of the Reach trace their ancestry back to Andal adventurers given lands and wives by Garth IX, Merle I, and Gwayne V, amongst them the Ormes, Parrens, Gracefords, Cuys, Roxtons, Ufferings, Leygoods, and Varners. As the centuries passed, the sons and daughters of these houses intermarried so freely with those descended from the First Men that it became impossible to tell them apart. Seldom has a conquest been achieved with less bloodshed.

The centuries that followed the Andal conquest were to prove less peaceful. The Gardeners who succeeded to the Oakenseat included strong men and weak, clever men and fools, and once even a woman, but few had the wisdom and cunning of the Three Sage Kings, so the golden peace of Garth Goldenhand did not come again. In that long epoch between the assimilation of the Andals and the coming of the dragons, the Kings of the Reach warred constantly with their neighbors in a perpetual struggle for land, power, and glory. The Kings of the Rock, the Storm Kings, the many quarrelsome kings of Dorne, and the Kings of the Rivers and Hills could all be counted amongst their foes (and ofttimes amongst their allies as well.)

Highgarden reached the apex of its power under King Gyles III Gardener, who led a glittering host of armored knights into the stormlands, smashed the armies of the aged Storm King, and conquered all the lands north of the rainwood save for Storm's End itself, which he besieged without result for two years. Gyles might well have completed his conquest had not the King of the Rock swept down upon the Reach in his absence, forcing him to lift his siege and hurry home to deal with the westermen. The broader war that followed involved three Dornish kings and two from the riverlands, and ended with Gyles III dead of a bloody flux and the borders between the realms restored to more or less where they had been before the bloodletting began.

The nadir of Gardener power came during the long reign of King Garth X, called Garth Greybeard, who succeeded to the crown at the age of seven and died at ninety-six—a reign even longer than that of his famous forebear Garth Goldenhand. Though vigorous in his youth, Garth X was a vain and frivolous king who surrounded himself with fools and flatterers. Neither wise nor clever, his wits abandoned him entirely in old age, and during the long years of his senility, he became the tool of first one faction, then another as those around him vied for wealth and power. His Grace had sired no sons, but Lord Peake had married one of his daughters, Lord Manderly another, and each was determined that his wife should succeed. The rivalry between them was marked by betrayal, conspiracy, and murder, finally escalating into open war. Others lords joined in on both sides.

With the lords of the Reach at swordpoint and the king too feeble to grasp what was occurring, much less stop it, the Storm King and the King of the Rock seized the moment, and large swathes of territory, whilst the Dornish raids grew bolder and more frequent. One Dornish king besieged Oldtown, whilst another crossed the Mander and sacked Highgarden. The Oakenseat, the living throne that had been the pride of House Gardener for years beyond count, was chopped to pieces and burned, and the senile King Garth X was found tied to his bed, whimpering and covered in his own filth. The Dornish cut his throat ("a mercy," one of them said later), then put Highgarden to the torch after stripping it of all its wealth.

Almost a decade of anarchy followed, but in the end twoscore of the great houses of the Reach, led by Ser Osmund Tyrell, the High Steward, made common cause, defeated both the Peakes and Manderlys, reclaimed the ruins of Highgarden, and placed a second cousin of the late and unlamented Garth Greybeard upon its new throne as King Mern VI Gardener.

Though a man of modest gifts, Mern VI had able counsel in his stewards. Ser Osmund Tyrell was succeeded in that office by his son, Ser Robert, and later by a grandson, Lorent. Relying on their acumen, Mern VI ruled well, rebuilding Highgarden and doing much and more to restore House Gardener and the Reach. His son, Garth XI, did the rest, taking such a terrible vengeance upon the Dornishmen that Lord Hightower said afterward that the Red Mountains had been green until Garth painted them with Dornish blood. For the remainder of his long reign, the king was known as Garth the Painter.

And so it went, king after king, in war and peace. Yet through it all the green hand flew proudly across the Reach, until King Mern IX rode out to meet Aegon Targaryen and his sisters upon the Field of Fire.

OLDTOWN

No history of the Reach is complete without a look at Oldtown, that most grand and ancient of cities, still the richest, largest, and most beautiful in all Westeros, even if King's Landing has eclipsed it as most populous.

How old is Oldtown, truly? Many a maester has pondered that question, but we simply do not know. The origins of the city are lost in the mists of time and clouded by legend. Some ignorant septons claim that the Seven themselves laid out its boundaries, other men that dragons once roosted on the Battle Isle until the first Hightower put an end to them. Many smallfolk believe the Hightower itself simply appeared one day. The full and true history of the founding of Oldtown will likely never be known.

We can state with certainty, however, that men have lived at the mouth of the Honeywine since the Dawn Age. The oldest runic records confirm this, as do certain fragmentary accounts that have come down to us from maesters who lived amongst the children of the forest. One such, Maester Jellicoe, suggests that the settlement at the top of Whispering Sound began as a trading post, where ships from Valyria,

LEFT | *The Oakenseat.*   ABOVE | *Dornish reavers in Oldtown.*

Old Ghis, and the Summer Isles put in to replenish their provisions, make repairs, and barter with the elder races, and that seems as likely a supposition as any.

Yet mysteries remain. The stony island where the Hightower stands is known as Battle Isle even in our oldest records, but why? What battle was fought there? When? Between which lords, which kings, which races? Even the singers are largely silent on these matters.

Even more enigmatic to scholars and historians is the great square fortress of black stone that dominates that isle. For most of recorded history, this monumental edifice has served as the foundation and lowest level of the Hightower, yet we know for a certainty that it predates the upper levels of the tower by thousands of years.

Who built it? When? Why? Most maesters accept the common wisdom that declares it to be of Valyrian construction, for its massive walls and labyrinthine interiors are all of solid rock, with no hint of joins or mortar, no chisel marks of any kind, a type of construction that is seen elsewhere, most notably in the dragonroads of the Freehold of Valyria, and the Black Walls that protect the heart of Old Volantis. The dragonlords of Valryia, as is well-known, possessed the art of turning stone to liquid with dragonflame, shaping it as they would, then fusing it harder than iron, steel, or granite.

If indeed this first fortress is Valyrian, it suggests that the dragonlords came to Westeros thousands of years before they carved out their outpost on Dragonstone, long before the coming of the Andals, or even the First Men. If so, did they come seeking trade? Were they slavers, mayhaps seeking after giants? Did they seek to learn the magic of the children of the forest, with their greenseers and their weirwoods? Or was there some darker purpose?

Such questions abound even to this day. Before the Doom of Valyria, maesters and archmaesters oft traveled to the Freehold in search of answers, but none were ever found. Septon Barth's claim that the Valyrians came to Westeros because their priests prophesied that the Doom of Man would come out of the land beyond the narrow sea can safely be dismissed as nonsense, as can many of Barth's queerer beliefs and suppositions.

More troubling, and more worthy of consideration, are the arguments put forth by those who claim that the first fortress is not Valyrian at all.

The fused black stone of which it is made suggests Valyria, but the plain, unadorned style of architecture does not, for the dragonlords loved little more than twisting stone into strange, fanciful, and ornate shapes. Within, the narrow, twisting, windowless passages strike many as being tunnels rather than halls; it is very easy to get lost amongst their turnings. Mayhaps this is no more than a defensive measure designed to confound attackers, but it too is singularly un-Valyrian. The labyrinthine nature of its interior architecture has led Archmaester Quillion to suggest that the fortress might have been the work of the mazemakers, a mysterious people who left remnants of their vanished civilization upon Lorath in the Shivering Sea. The notion is intriguing but raises more questions than it answers.

An even more fanciful possibility was put forth a century ago by Maester Theron. Born a bastard on the Iron Islands, Theron noted a certain likeness between the black stone of the ancient fortress and that of the Seastone Chair, the high seat of House Greyjoy of Pyke, whose origins are similarly ancient and mysterious. Theron's rather inchoate manuscript *Strange Stone* postulates that both fortress and seat might be the work of a queer, misshapen race of half men sired by creatures of the salt seas upon human women. These Deep Ones, as he names them, are the seed from which our legends of merlings have grown, he argues, whilst their terrible fathers are the truth behind the Drowned God of the ironborn.

The lavish, detailed, and somewhat disturbing illustrations included in *Strange Stone* make this rare volume fascinating to peruse, but the text is impenetrable in parts; Maester Theron had a gift for drawing but little skill with words. In any case, his thesis has no factual basis and may safely be dismissed. And thus we find ourselves back whence we began, forced to concede that the beginnings of Oldtown, Battle Isle, and its fortress must forever remain a mystery to us.

The reasons for the abandonment of the fortress and the fate of its builders, whoever they might have been, are likewise lost to us, but at some point we know that Battle Isle and its great stronghold came into the possession of the ancestors of House Hightower. Were they First Men, as most scholars believe today? Or did they mayhaps descend from the seafarers and traders who had settled at the top of Whispering Sound in earlier epochs, the men who came *before* the First Men? We cannot know.

When first glimpsed in the pages of history, the Hightowers are already kings, ruling Oldtown from Battle Isle. The first "high tower," the chroniclers tell us, was made of wood and rose some fifty feet above the ancient fortress that was its foundation. Neither it, nor the taller timber towers that followed in the centuries to come, were meant

RIGHT | *The Hightower on Battle Isle.*

to be a dwelling; they were purely beacon towers, built to light a path for trading ships up the fog-shrouded waters of Whispering Sound. The early Hightowers lived amidst the gloomy halls, vaults, and chambers of the strange stone below. It was only with the building of the fifth tower, the first to be made entirely of stone, that the Hightower became a seat worthy of a great house. That tower, we are told, rose two hundred feet above the harbor. Some say it was designed by Brandon the Builder, whilst others name his son, another Brandon; the king who demanded it, and paid for it, is remembered as Uthor of the High Tower.

For thousands of years thereafter, his descendants ruled Oldtown and the lands of the Honeywine as kings, and ships from the world over came to their growing city to trade. As Oldtown grew wealthy and powerful, neighboring lords and petty kings turned covetous eyes upon its riches, and pirates and reavers from beyond the seas heard tales of its splendors as well. Thrice in the space of a single century the city was taken and sacked, once by the Dornish king Samwell Dayne (the Starfire), once by Qhored the Cruel and his ironmen, and once by Gyles I Gardener (the Woe), who reportedly sold three-quarters of the city's inhabitants into slavery, but was unable to breach the defenses of the Hightower on Battle Isle.

The wooden palisades and ditch that had protected the city heretofore having so obviously been proved inadequate, the next King of the High Tower, Otho II, spent the best part of his reign surrounding Oldtown with massive stone walls, thicker and higher than any seen in Westeros to this point. This effort beggared the city for three generations, it is written, but such was their strength that later reavers and would-be conquerors were persuaded to seek for plunder elsewhere, and those who did presume to attack Oldtown did so to no avail.

It was not through war that the Hightowers were brought into the Kingdom of the Reach, however, but through long negotiations and marriage. When Lymond Hightower took to bride the daughter of King Garland II Gardener, whilst giving his own daughter's hand in marriage to her father, the Hightowers became bannermen to Highgarden, reduced from wealthy but relatively minor kings to the greatest lords of the Reach. (Oldtown was the last of the ancient realms to bend the knee to Highgarden, not long after the last King of the Arbor was lost

at sea, allowing his cousin, King Meryn III Gardener, to make the isle part of his domain).

By the terms of the marriage treaty, the Gardeners also undertook to defend the city against any assault by land, which freed Lord Lymond to turn his attention to his "great purpose," the building of ships and conquest of the seas. By the end of his reign, no lord or king in all of Westeros could match the strength of House Hightower at sea. A great statue of Lymond Hightower stands overlooking Oldtown's harbor to this day, gazing off down Whispering Sound. The last Hightower king is still remembered as the Sea Lion.

Lord Lymond's descendants shared his vision. With rare exceptions, they tended to their own gardens and their own city, avoiding entanglement in the endless wars of the petty kings, and later, of the Seven Kingdoms that emerged. "Highgarden defends our backs," Lord Jeremy Hightower said once, "so we are free to gaze outward, to the sea and the lands beyond." Gazing outward, and building ever more ships to protect his trade, Lord Jeremy doubled the city's wealth. His son Jason doubled it again, and rebuilt the Hightower a hundred feet taller.

The origins of the Citadel are almost as mysterious as those of the Hightower itself. Most credit its founding to the second son of Uthor of the High Tower, Prince Peremore the Twisted. A sickly boy, born with a withered arm and twisted back, Peremore was bedridden for much of his short life but had an insatiable curiosity about the world beyond his window, so he turned to wise men, teachers, priests, healers, and singers, along with a certain number of wizards, alchemists, and sorcerers. It is said the prince had no greater pleasure in life than listening to these scholars argue with one another. When Peremore died, his brother King Urrigon bequeathed a large tract of land beside the Honeywine to "Peremore's pets," that they might establish themselves and continue teaching, learning, and questing after truth. And so they did.

When the Andals came, the Hightowers were amongst the first lords of Westeros to welcome them. "Wars are bad for trade," said Lord Dorian Hightower, when he set aside his wife of twenty years, the mother of his children, to take an Andal princess as his bride. His grandson Lord Damon (the Devout) was the first to accept the Faith. To honor the new gods, he built the first sept in Oldtown and six more elsewhere in his realm. When he died prematurely of a bad belly, Septon Robeson became regent for his newborn son, ruling Oldtown in all but name for the next twenty years and ultimately becoming the first High Septon. The boy he raised and trained, Lord Triston Hightower, raised the Starry Sept in his honor after his passing.

In the centuries that followed, Oldtown became the unquestioned center of the Faith for all of Westeros. From the dark marble halls of the Starry Sept, a succession of High Septons donned the crystal crown (the first of which was given to the Faith by the Lord Triston's son Lord Barris) to become the voice of the Seven on earth, commanding the swords of the Faith Militant and the hearts of all the faithful from Dorne to the Neck. Oldtown became their holy city, and many devout men and women traveled there to pray at its septs and shrines and other holy places. Doubtless it was in part due to these ties to the Seven that the Hightowers were so often able to keep themselves separate from House Gardener's countless wars.

The Faith was not the only institution to flourish behind the massive walls of Oldtown, under the protection of the Hightower. Thousands of years before the first sept opened its doors, the city had been home to the Citadel, where boys and young men from all over Westeros came to study, learn, and forge their chains as maesters. No greater seat of knowledge exists anywhere in the world.

By the time of Aegon's Conquest, Oldtown was beyond question the greatest city in all of Westeros—the largest, richest, and most populous, and a center of both learning and faith. Even so, it might well have suffered the same fate as Harrenhal if not for the close ties between the Hightower and the Starry Sept, for it was the High Septon who persuaded Lord Manfred Hightower to offer no resistance to Aegon Targaryen and his dragons but instead to open his gates at the conqueror's approach and do him homage.

The conflict thus averted flared up again a generation later, however, during the bloody struggle between the Faith and the Conqueror's second son, the aptly named King Maegor the Cruel. The High Septon during the first years of Maegor's reign was kin by marriage to the Hightowers. His sudden death in 44 AC—shortly after King Maegor had threatened to incinerate the Starry Sept with dragonfire in his fury over His High Holiness's condemnation of his later marriages—is considered quite fortuitous, as it allowed Lord Martyn Hightower to open his gates before Balerion and Vhagar unleashed their flames.

The unexpected nature of the High Septon's death in 44 AC aroused much suspicion, however, and whispers of murder persist to this day. Some believe His High Holiness was removed by his own brother, Ser Morgan Hightower, commander of the Warrior's Sons in Oldtown (and it is undeniably true that Ser Morgan was the sole Warrior's Son pardoned by King Maegor). Others suspect Lord Martyn's maiden aunt, the Lady Patrice Hightower, though their argument seems to rest upon the belief that poison is a woman's weapon. It has even been suggested that the Citadel might have played a role in the removal of the High Septon, though this seems far-fetched at best.

HOUSE TYRELL

The Tyrells were never kings, though royal blood flows in their veins (as in half a hundred of the other great houses in the Reach). Ser Alester Tyrell, the founder of the line, was an Andal adventurer who became the champion and sworn shield to King Gwayne V Gardener, one of the Three Sage Kings. His eldest son became a notable knight as well, only to die in a tourney. His second son, Gareth, was of a more bookish bent and never achieved knighthood, choosing to serve as a royal steward instead. It is from him that today's Tyrells descend.

Gareth Tyrell and his son Leo performed their duties so ably that the Gardeners made the office of High Steward hereditary. Through the centuries, many generations of Tyrells served in that capacity. Many became close confidants and advisors to their kings; some also acted as castellans in times of war. At least one ruled the Reach as regent during the minority of King Garland VI. King Gyles III Gardener declared the Tyrells to be "my most leal servants," and King Mern VI was so pleased with them that he gave Ser Robert Tyrell the hand of his youngest daughter in marriage (thereby allowing their sons, grandsons, and all the generations to follow to claim descent from Garth Greenhand). That was the first marriage between House Gardener and House Tyrell, but nine more unions between the two houses followed in the centuries to come.

It was not their royal blood that made Aegon Targaryen choose to name the Tyrells as Lords of Highgarden, Wardens of the South, and Lords Paramount of the Reach after King Mern IX, the last of the Gardener kings, died, along with all his sons, upon the Field of Fire. Those honors were won by the prudence of Harlan Tyrell, who opened the gates of Highgarden at Aegon's approach and pledged himself and his family to House Targaryen.

Afterward, a number of the other great houses of the Reach complained bitterly about being made vassals of an "upjumped steward" and insisted that their own blood was far nobler than that of the Tyrells. It cannot be denied that the Oakhearts of Old Oak, the Florents of Brightwater Keep, the Rowans of Goldengrove, the Peakes of Starpike, and the Redwynes of the Arbor all had older and more distinguished lineages than the Tyrells, and closer blood ties to House Gardener as well. Their protests were of no avail, however ... mayhaps in part because all these houses had taken up arms against Aegon and his sisters on the Field of Fire, whereas the Tyrells had not.

Aegon Targaryen's judgment in this proved sound. Lord Harlan proved a capable steward for the Reach, though he only ruled until 5 AC, when he disappeared with his army in the deserts of Dorne during Aegon's First Dornish War.

His son, Theo Tyrell, was understandably reluctant to become involved in any further attempts to conquer Dorne, but eventually became embroiled when the conflict spilled out beyond the Red Mountains. When the Targaryens at last made peace with Dorne, Lord Theo turned his attention to consolidating Tyrell power by arranging a council of septons and maesters to examine and finally dismiss some of the more persistent of the claims to Highgarden by those who insisted that the seat was theirs.

As Lords of Highgarden and Wardens of the South, the descendants of these "upjumped stewards" rank amongst the most powerful lords of the realm, and they have been called on to fight beneath the Targaryen banner on many occasions. For most of those occasions, they have come as called—though, wisely, they played no part in the Dance of the Dragons, as the young Lord Tyrell was at the time a babe in swaddling clothes, and his mother and castellan chose to keep Highgarden out of that dreadful, fratricidal bloodbath.

Later, when King Daeron I Targaryen (the Young Dragon) marched on Dorne, the Tyrells proved their valor

---

ABOVE | *The arms of House Tyrell (center) and some houses of note, past and present, (clockwise from top), Caswell, Florent, Fossoway, Gardener, Hightower, Merryweather, Mullendore, Oakheart, Redwyne, Rowan, Tarly, and Ashford.*

by leading the main thrust over the Prince's Pass. Having served faithfully, if perhaps too boldly, Lord Lyonel Tyrell was given charge of Dorne after the Young Dragon returned in triumph to King's Landing. His lordship succeeded in keeping the Dornishmen pacified for a time, only to suffer a gruesome death in the infamous bed of scorpions. His murder ignited the rising that swept Dorne, eventually bringing about the death of the Young Dragon at the age of eight-and-ten.

Of the Tyrells who succeeded the ill-fated Lord Lyonel at Highgarden in the years since, the most notable is Lord Leo Tyrell, a tourney champion remembered to this day as Leo Longthorn. Many consider him the finest jouster ever

to couch a lance. Lord Leo also won distinction during the First Blackfyre Rebellion, winning notable victories against Daemon Blackfyre's adherents in the Reach, though his forces were unable to gather quickly enough to arrive in time for the Battle of the Redgrass Field.

The present Lord of Highgarden, Mace Tyrell, fought loyally for House Targaryen during Robert's Rebellion, defeating Robert Baratheon himself at the Battle of Ashford and later besieging his brother Stannis in Storm's End for the better part of a year. With the death of the Mad King Aerys II and his son Prince Rhaegar, however, Lord Mace laid down his sword, and is today once again Warden of the South and a leal servant of King Robert and the Iron Throne.

HIGHGARDEN

The great castle of Highgarden, the ancient seat of the Tyrell lords and the Gardener kings before them, sits atop a verdant hill overlooking the broad and tranquil waters of the Mander. Seen from afar, the castle "looks so much a part of the land one could think that it had grown there, rather than being built." Many consider Highgarden to be the most beautiful castle in all the Seven Kingdoms, a claim that only the men of the Vale see fit to dispute. (They prefer their own Eyrie).

The hill from which Highgarden rises is neither steep nor stony but broad in extent, with gentle slopes and a pleasing symmetry. From the castle's walls and towers, a man can see for leagues in all directions, across orchards and meadows and fields of flowers, including the golden roses of the Reach that have long been the sigil of House Tyrell.

Highgarden is girded by three concentric rings of crenellated curtain walls, made of finely dressed white stone and protected by towers as slender and graceful as maidens. Each wall is higher and thicker than the one below it. Between the outermost wall that girdles the foot of the hill and the middle wall above it can be found Highgarden's famed briar maze, a vast and complicated labyrinth of thorns and hedges maintained for centuries for the pleasure and delight of the castle's occupants and guests . . . and for defensive purposes, for intruders unfamiliar with the maze cannot easily find their way through its traps and dead ends to the castle gates.

Within the castle walls, greenery abounds, and the keeps are surrounded by gardens, arbors, pools, fountains, courtyards, and man-made waterfalls. Ivy covers the older buildings, and grapes and climbing roses snake up the sides

of statuary, walls, and towers. Flowers bloom everywhere. The keep is a palace like few others, filled with statues, colonnades, and fountains. Highgarden's tallest towers, round and slender, look down upon neighbors far more ancient, square and grim in appearance, the oldest of them dating from the Age of Heroes. The rest of the castle is of more recent construction, much of it built by King Mern VI after the destruction of the original structures by the Dornish during the reign of Garth Greybeard.

The gods, both old and new, are well served in Highgarden. The splendor of the castle sept, with its rows of stained-glass windows celebrating the Seven and the ubiquitous Garth Greenhand, is rivaled only by that of the Great Sept of Baelor in King's Landing and the Starry Sept of Oldtown. And Highgarden's lush green godswood is almost as renowned, for in the place of a single heart tree it boasts three towering, graceful, ancient weirwoods whose limbs have grown so entangled over the centuries that they appear to be almost a single tree with three trunks, reaching for each other above a tranquil pool. Legend has it these trees, known in the Reach as the Three Singers, were planted by Garth Greenhand himself.

No seat in the Seven Kingdoms has been more celebrated in song than Highgarden, and small wonder, for the Tyrells and the Gardeners before them have made their court a place of culture and music and high art. In the days before the Conquest, the Kings of the Reach and their queens presided over tourneys of love and beauty, where the greatest knights of the Reach competed for the love of the fairest maids not only with feats of arms, but with song, poetry,

RIGHT | *Highgarden.*

and demonstrations of virtue, piety, and chaste devotion. The greatest champions, men as pure and honorable and virtuous as they were skilled at arms, were honored with invitations to join the Order of the Green Hand.

Though the last members of that noble order perished beside their king on the Field of Fire (save in White Harbor, where the knights of House Manderly still profess membership), their traditions are still remembered in the Reach, where the Tyrells continue to uphold all that is best in knighthood and chivalry. Their Tourney of the Field of Roses in the reign of Jaehaerys I, the Old King, was famed far and wide as the greatest tourney in a generation, and many other great tourneys have been held in the Reach in more recent days.

CROWNLANDS

STORMLANDS

King's Landing

ROSEROAD

Grassy Vale

Bitterbridge

BLUEBURN

Longtable

Ashford

Felwood

Bronzegate

Haystack hall

Evenfall hall

Tarth

SHIPBREAKER BAY

Storm's End

Summerhall

Griffin's Roost

Crow's Nest

Rain house

Stonehelm

Mistwood

esTermont

Greenstone

THE RED MOUNTAINS

Blackhaven

BONEWAY

Weeping Town

CAPE WRATH

Nightsong

PRINCE'S PASS

Vulture's Roost

Wyl

SEA of DORNE

NARROW SEA

Skyreach

Yronwood

LEGEND

MAJOR CASTLE

CASTLES

CITIES

TOWNS

RUINS

LUMBER

AMBER

ROADS

R E A C H

DORNE

THE STORMLANDS

THE STORMS THAT blow up the narrow sea are infamous throughout the Seven Kingdoms, and in the Nine Free Cities as well. Though they may arise in any season, seafarers say that the worst of them come each autumn, forming in the warm waters of the Summer Sea south of the Stepstones, then roaring north across those bleak and stony islands. More than half continue north by northwest, according to the archives at the Citadel, sweeping over Cape Wrath and the rainwood, gathering strength (and moisture) as they cross the waters of Shipbreaker Bay before slamming into Storm's End on Durran's Point.

It is from these great gales that the stormlands take their name.

The heart of this ancient kingdom was Storm's End, the last and greatest of the castles raised by the hero king Durran Godsgrief in the Age of Heroes, which stands immense and immovable atop the towering cliffs of Durran's Point. South, beyond Shipbreaker Bay with its wild waters and treacherous rocks, lies Cape Wrath. The moist green tangle of the rainwood dominates the northern two-thirds of the cape. Farther south a broad plain opens up, rolling gently down to the Sea of Dorne, where numerous small fishing villages dot the shoreline. A thriving port and market, the Weeping Town (as it came to be known because it was where the body of the slain hero King Daeron I Targaryen returned to his kingdom after his murder in Dorne), stands here, and much of the region's trade passes through its harbor.

The great island of Tarth, with its waterfalls and lakes and soaring mountains, is considered part of the stormlands as well, as are Estermont and the myriad lesser isles found off Cape Wrath and the Weeping Town.

To the west the hills rise hard and wild, pushing against the sky until they give way to the Red Mountains, the border between the stormlands and Dorne. Deep dry valleys and great sandstone cliffs dominate the landscape here, and it is true that sometimes at sunset the peaks gleam scarlet and crimson against the clouds . . . yet there are those who say these mountains were named not for the color of their stone but for all the blood that has soaked into the ground.

Farther inland, beyond the foothills, lie the marches—a vast expanse of grasslands, moors, and windswept plains stretching westward and northward for hundreds of leagues. There in the sight of the Red Mountains, the great castles of the Marcher lords stand, built to guard the borders of the stormlands against Dornish incursions from the south and the steel-clad minions of the Kings of the Reach from the west. The greatest of the Marcher lords are the Swanns of Stonehelm, the Dondarrions of Blackhaven, the Selmys of Harvest Hall, and the Carons of Nightsong, whose Singing Towers marked the westernmost extent of the realm of the Storm Kings. All these remain sworn to Storm's End to this day, as they have been from time immemorial.

North of Storm's End, however, the borders of the kingdom have fluctuated greatly over the centuries, as Storm Kings strong and weak gained and lost lands in a succession of wars both great and small. Today, the writ of House Baratheon runs to the south bank of the Wendwater and lower reaches of the kingswood, and along the stony shores of the narrow sea up to the base of Massey's Hook . . . but before Aegon's Conquest, before even the coming of the Andals, the warrior kings of House Durrandon pushed their borders considerably farther.

Massey's Hook was part of their realm then, and all the kingswood as far as the Blackwater Rush. In certain epochs, the Storm Kings even ruled beyond the Blackwater. Towns as far-flung as Duskendale and Maidenpool once paid homage to Storm's End, and under the redoubtable warrior king Arlan III Durrandon, the stormlanders took dominion over the entire riverlands. They held them for more than three centuries.

Yet even at their greatest extent, the realms of the Durrandons and their successors have always been thinly peopled when compared to the Reach, the riverlands, and the west, and thus the might of the lords of Storm's End was diminished. Those who do choose to make their homes in the stormlands—whether along the stony shores of the narrow sea, amidst the dripping green forests of the rainwood, or on the windswept marches—are a special breed, however. The people of the stormlands are like unto their weather, it has oft been said: tumultuous, violent, implacable, unpredictable.

THE COMING OF THE FIRST MEN

The history of the stormlands stretches back to the Dawn Age. Long before the coming of the First Men, all Westeros belonged to the elder races—the children of the forest and the giants (and, some say, the Others, the terrifying "white walkers" of the Long Night).

The children made their homes in the vast primeval forest that once stretched from Cape Wrath to Cape Kraken, north of the Iron Islands (today all that remains of this great wood are the kingswood and the rainwood), and the giants in the foothills of the Red Mountains and along the rugged stony spine of Massey's Hook. Unlike the later Andals, who came to Westeros by sea, the First Men made their way from Essos across the great land bridge we now call the Broken Arm of Dorne, so Dorne itself and the stormlands to the north were the first parts of Westeros to know the steps of man.

The wet wild of the rainwood was a favored haunt of the children of the forest, the tales tell us, and there were giants in the hills that rose wild in the shadow of the Red Mountains, and amongst the defiles and ridges of the stony peninsula that came to be called Massey's Hook. Although the giants were a shy folk, and ever hostile to man, it is written that in the beginning, the children of the forest welcomed the newcomers to Westeros, in the belief that there was land enough for all.

The forest shaped the First Men, who made their homes beneath the ancient oaks, towering redwoods, sentinels, and soldier pines. By the banks of small streams rose rude villages where folk hunted and trapped as their lords permitted. The furs from the stormlands were well regarded, but the true riches of the rainwood were found in its timber and rare hardwoods. The harvesting of the trees soon brought

the First Men into conflict with the children of the forest, however, and for hundreds and thousands of years they made war upon one another, until the First Men took the old gods of the children for their own and divided up the lands in the Pact sealed on the Isle of Faces amidst the great lake called the Gods Eye.

The Pact came late in the history of man in Westeros, however; by the time it was signed, the giants (who were no part of it) were almost gone from the stormlands, and even the children were much diminished.

HOUSE DURRANDON

Much of the early history of Westeros is lost in the mists of time, where it becomes ever more difficult to separate fact from legend the further back one goes. This is particularly true of the stormlands, where the First Men were comparatively few and the elder races strong. Elsewhere in the Seven Kingdoms, the runes that tell their stories survive to this day, chiseled into cave walls and standing stones and the ruins of fallen strongholds, but in the stormlands oft as not the First Men carved the tales of their victories and defeats into the trunks of trees, long since rotted away.

Moreover, a tradition developed amongst the Storm Kings of old for naming the king's firstborn son and heir after Durran Godsgrief, founder of their line, further compounding the difficulties of the historian. The bewildering number of King Durrans has inevitably caused much confusion. The maesters of the Citadel of Oldtown have given numbers to

many of these monarchs, in order to distinguish one from the other, but that was not the practice of the singers (unreliable at the best of times) who are our chief source for these times.

The legends surrounding the founder of House Durrandon, Durran Godsgrief, all come to us through the singers. The songs tell us that Durran won the heart of Elenei, daughter of the sea god and the goddess of the wind. By yielding to a mortal's love, Elenei doomed herself to a mortal's death, and for this the gods who had given her birth hated the man she had taken for her lord husband. In their wroth, they sent howling winds and lashing rains to knock down every castle Durran dared to build, until a young boy helped him erect one so strong and cunningly made that it could defy their gales. The boy grew to be Brandon the Builder; Durran became the first Storm King. With Elenei at his side, he lived and reigned at Storm's End for a thousand years, or so the stories claim.

(Such a life span seems most unlikely, even for a hero married to the daughter of two gods. Archmaester Glaive, himself a stormlander by birth, once suggested that this King of a Thousand Years was in truth a succession of monarchs all bearing the same name, which seems plausible but must forever remain unproved.)

Whether he was one man or fifty, we know that in this time the kingdom extended its writ far beyond Storm's End and its hinterlands, absorbing neighboring kingdoms one by one over the centuries. Some were won by treaty, some by marriage, more by conquest—a process that was continued by Durran's descendants.

The Godsgrief himself was first to claim the rainwood, that wet wilderness that had hitherto belonged only to the children of the forest. His son Durran the Devout returned to the children most of what his father had seized, but a century later Durran Bronze-Axe took it back again, this time for good and all. The songs tell us that Durran the Dour slew Lun the Last, King of the Giants, at the Battle of Crookwater, but scholars still debate whether he was Durran V or Durran VI.

Maldon Massey built the castle Stonedance and established his lordship over Massey's Hook under another King Durran, called the Ravenfriend, but his dates and number remain in dispute as well. It was Durran the Young, also known as the Butcher Boy, who dammed the river Slayne with Dornish corpses, after turning back Yoren Yronwood and the warrior maid Wylla of Wyl in the Battle by the Bloody Pool . . . but was he the same king who became be-

sotted with his own niece in later life and died at the hands of his brother Erich Kin-Killer? These, and many similar questions, will most likely never be resolved.

Somewhat better sources exist for later centuries, however. We can say with fair certainty that the great island kingdom of Tarth fell under the sway of House Durrandon when Durran the Fair took to wife the daughter of its king, Edwyn Evenstar. Their grandson, Erich the Sailmaker (most likely Erich III), was the first to claim Estermont and the lesser isles farther south. It was another Durran (Durran X, most scholars agree) who extended the kingdom northward to the Blackwater Rush, and his son Monfryd I (the Mighty) who first crossed that great river, defeating the petty kings of House Darklyn and House Mooton in a series of wars, and seizing the prosperous port towns of Duskendale and Maidenpool.

Monfryd's son Durran XI (the Dim) and his own son Barron (the Beautiful) yielded up all he had gained and more besides. During the long years when Durwald I (the Fat) ruled in Storm's End, the Masseys broke away, Tarth thrice revolted, and even upon Cape Wrath a challenge arose, from a woods witch known only as the Green Queen, who held the rainwood against Storm's End for the best part of a generation. For a time it was said Durwald's rule extended no farther than a man could urinate off the walls of Storm's End.

The tide turned again when Morden II named his baseborn half brother Ronard as his castellan. A fearsome warrior, Ronard became the ruler of the stormlands in all but name and took King Morden's sister to wife. Within five years, he had claimed the kingship as well. It was Morden's own queen who placed Morden's crown on Ronard's head. If the songs be true, she shared his bed as well. Morden himself, deemed harmless, was confined to a cell in the tower.

His usurper ruled for nigh unto thirty years as Ronard the Bastard, smashing rebel bannerman and petty kings alike in battle after battle. Never a man to confine himself to a single woman, he claimed a daughter from every foe who bent the knee. By the time he died, he had supposedly fathered nine-and-ninety sons. Most were bastard born (though Ronard had three-and-twenty wives, the songs say) and did not share in their father's inheritance but had to make their own way in the world. For this reason, thousands of years later, many and more of the smallfolk of the stormlands, even the meanest and humblest amongst them, still boast of royal blood.

PREVIOUS PAGES | *Storm's End.* RIGHT | *Andals landing on the shores of the stormlands.*

ANDALS IN THE STORMLANDS

Erich VII Durrandon was king in the stormlands when the Andal longships first began to cross the narrow sea. History remembers him as Erich the Unready, for he took little note of these invaders, famously declaring that he had no interest in "the quarrels of strangers in a land far away." The Storm King was embroiled in his own wars at the time, attempting to reconquer Massey's Hook from its infamous pirate king, Justin Milk-Eye, whilst fending off the incursions of the Dornish king Olyvar Yronwood. Nor did Erich live to see the result of his inaction, for the Andals remained occupied with their conquest of the Vale for the rest of his lifetime.

His grandson, King Qarlton II Durrandon, was the first to face the Andals in battle. After four generations of war, that monarch—who styled himself Qarlton the Conqueror—finally completed the reconquest of Massey's

Hook, taking Stonedance after a year's siege and slaying the last king of House Massey, Josua (called Softspear).

The Storm King held his conquest for less than two years. An Andal warlord named Togarion Bar Emmon (called Togarion the Terrible) had established his own small kingdom north of the Blackwater but was being hard-pressed by the Darklyn king of Duskendale. Sensing weakness to the south, Togarion took to wife the daughter of Josua Softspear and crossed Blackwater Bay with all his power to establish a new kingdom on Massey's Hook. He built his own castle at Sharp Point, at the Hook's end, whilst driving the stormlanders from Stonedance and setting his wife's brother to rule there as a puppet dancing to his strings.

Qarlton the Conqueror soon had more serious woes to concern him than the loss of Massey's Hook. The eyes of the Andals had turned south, and longships had begun to

come ashore all up and down his coasts, full of hungry men with the seven-pointed stars painted on their shields and chests and brows, all of them bent on carving out kingdoms of their own. The rest of his reign, and that of his son and grandson (Qarlton III and Monfryd V) after him, were times of almost constant war.

Though the Storm Kings won half a dozen major battles—the greatest of these being the Battle of Bronzegate where Monfryd V Durrandon defeated the Holy Brotherhood of the Andals, an alliance of seven petty kings and war lords, at the cost of his own life—the longships kept coming. It was said that for every Andal who fell in battle, five more came wading ashore. Tarth was the first of the stormlands to be overwhelmed; Estermont soon followed.

The Andals established themselves on Cape Wrath as well and might well have taken all the rainwood if they had not proved as willing to make war on one another as upon the kingdoms of the First Men. But King Baldric I Durrandon (the Cunning) proved expert at setting them one against the other, and King Durran XXI took the unprecedented step of seeking out the remaining children of the forest in the caves and hollow hills where they had taken refuge and making common cause with them against the men from beyond the sea. In the battles fought at Black Bog, in the Misty Wood, and beneath the Howling Hill (the precise location of which has sadly been lost), this Weirwood Alliance dealt the Andals a series of stinging defeats and checked the decline of the Storm Kings for a time. An even more unlikely alliance, between King Cleoden I and three Dornish kings, won an even more telling victory over Drox the Corpse-Maker on the river Slayne near Stonehelm a generation later.

Yet it is an error to assert that the Storm Kings turned back the invaders. For all their victories, they never stemmed the Andal tide; though many an Andal king and warlord ended with his head impaled upon a spike above the gates of Storm's End, still the Andals kept coming. The reverse is also true; the Andals never truly conquered the line of Durrandon. Seven times they laid siege to Storm's End or sought to storm its mighty walls, history tells us; seven times they failed. The seventh failure was seen as a sign from the gods; after that, no further assaults were made.

In the end, the two sides simply came together. King Maldon IV took an Andal maiden as his wife, as did his son, Durran XXIV (Durran Half-Blood). Andal war chiefs became lords and petty kings, wed the daughters of stormlords and gave them their own daughters in return, did fealty for their lands, and swore their swords to the Storm Kings. Led by King Ormund III and his queen, the stormlanders put aside their old gods and took up the gods of the Andals, the Faith of the Seven. As the centuries passed, the two races of men became as one . . . and the children of the forest, all but forgotten, vanished entirely from the rainwood and the stormlands.

House Durrandon reached its greatest heights in the epoch that followed. During the Age of the Hundred Kingdoms, King Arlan I (the Avenger) swept all before him, extending the borders of his kingdom as far as the Blackwater Rush and the headwaters of the Mander. His great-grandson King Arlan III crossed both the Blackwater and the Trident and claimed the riverlands in their entirety, at one point planting his crowned stag banner on the shores of the Sunset Sea.

With the death of Arlan III, however, an inevitable decline began, for the stormlanders were stretched too thin to hold this vast kingdom together. Rebellion followed rebellion, petty kings sprang up like weeds, castles and keeps fell away . . . and then the ironborn came, led by Harwyn Hardhand, King of the Iron Islands, and it all befell as previously related. Even as the stormlanders reeled back before the ironmen in the north, the Dornish came swarming over the Boneway to press them in the south, and the Kings of the Reach sent their knights forth from Highgarden to reclaim all that had been lost in the west.

The Kingdom of the Storm shrank, king by king, battle by battle, year by year. The fall was halted briefly when a fierce warrior prince, Argilac (called the Arrogant), donned the stag's crown, but even a man as mighty as he could only stay the tide, not turn it back. Last of the Storm Kings, last of the Durrandon, Argilac did just that for a time . . . but near the end of his life, when he had grown old, King Argilac made a clumsy attempt to use House Targaryen of Dragonstone as a shield against the growing might of the ironmen and their king, Harren the Black. Never grasp a dragon by the tail, the old proverb says. Argilac the Arrogant did just that, and succeeded only in turning the eyes of Aegon Targaryen and his sisters westward.

When they came ashore at the mouth of the Blackwater Rush to begin their conquest of the Seven Kingdoms, with them came a black-eyed, black-haired bastard named Orys Baratheon.

HOUSE BARATHEON

House Baratheon was born amidst the rain and mud of the battle known to history as the Last Storm, when Orys Baratheon thrice turned back the charge of the knights of Storm's End and slew their king Argilac the Arrogant in single combat. Storm's End, long thought to be impregnable, yielded to Orys without a battle (wisely, given the fate of Harrenhal). Afterward Orys took King Argilac's daughter to wife and adopted the Durrandon arms and words as his own to honor Argilac's valor.

The favor that Aegon the Conqueror showered upon Orys Baratheon made many credit the rumors that he was Aegon's bastard half brother. Though never proved, that tale is widely believed to this very day. Others suggest that Orys rose so high because of his prowess at arms and his fierce loyalty to House Targaryen. Even before the Conquest, he served as Aegon's champion and sworn shield, and his defeat of King Argilac only added further luster to his name. When King Aegon granted Storm's End to House Baratheon in perpetuity, and named Orys Lord Paramount of the Stormlands and the Hand of the King, none dared suggest that he was unworthy of these honors.

During Aegon's invasion of Dorne in 4 AC, however, Lord Orys was taken captive whilst attempting to bring his forces through the Boneway. His captor was the Wyl of Wyl, known as the Widow-lover, who struck off Orys's sword hand.

Afterward, all accounts say that Lord Orys became crabbed and bitter. Resigning his office as King's Hand, he turned his attention to Dorne, obsessed with the idea of revenge. His chance came during the reign of King Aenys I, when he shattered part of the Vulture King's host and Lord Walter Wyl, the Widow-lover's son, fell into his hands.

The Baratheons remained closely connected to House Targaryen and played a significant role in the troubled reigns of Aegon the Conqueror's successors. Lord Orys Baratheon's grandson, Lord Robar, was the first great lord to openly proclaim for Prince Jaehaerys against his uncle, Maegor the Cruel. For his loyalty and courage, he was named Protector of the Realm and Hand of the King following Maegor's strange death upon the Iron Throne. During the remainder of King Jaehaerys's minority, Lord Robar shared the rule of the realm with the king's mother, the Dowager Queen Alyssa. Half a year later the two wed.

From their union sprang the Lady Jocelyn, who married the eldest of the Old King's sons and became mother to the Princess Rhaenys—"the Queen Who Never Was" as the glib jester Mushroom called her—and Boremund Baratheon,

---

FROM THE HISTORY OF ARCHMAESTER GYLDAYN

Orys Baratheon, known now as Orys One-Hand, rode forth from Storm's End one last time, to smash the Dornish beneath the walls of Stonehelm. When Walter Wyl was delivered into his hand, wounded but alive, Lord Orys said, "Your father took my hand. I claim yours as repayment." So saying, he hacked off Lord Walter's sword hand. Then he took his other hand, and both his feet as well, calling them his "usury." Strange to say, Lord Baratheon died on the march back to Storm's End, of the wounds he himself had taken during the battle, but his son Davos always said he died content, smiling at the rotting hands and feet that dangled in his tent like a string of onions.

LEFT | *Seven-pointed star carved in stone.*   ABOVE | *The arms of House Baratheon (center) and some of its vassals (clockwise from top): Buckler, Caron, Connington, Dondarrion, Estermont, Penrose, Seaworth, Selmy, Staedmon, Swann, and Tarth.*

who succeeded his father as Lord of Storm's End. At the Great Council of 101 AC, convened by King Jaehaerys I to debate the matter of succession, Lord Boremund was outspoken in supporting the claim of his niece, Princess Rhaenys, and her son, Prince Laenor of House Velaryon, but found himself on the losing side of the argument.

The power of Storm's End and its close proximity to King's Landing and the Iron Throne made the Baratheons the first of the great houses of Westeros whose support was sought by Princess Rhaenyra and King Aegon II after the death of their father, King Viserys I Targaryen. By that time, however, Lord Boremund had passed and it was his son Borros who ruled, and Borros was a different kind of man entirely.

Where Lord Boremund had been staunch in support of Rhaenyra's late husband Laenor, Lord Borros scented opportunity and proved reticent when courted by Lucerys Velaryon, Rhaenyra's second son by Prince Laenor. When Lucerys flew his dragon to Storm's End, seeking support, he found that his cousin Prince Aemond Targaryen had arrived before him and was busily arranging his marriage to one of Borros's daughters.

Lord Borros was infuriated at the message Lucerys carried—wherein Princess Rhaenyra betrayed an unseemly arrogance in assuming Storm's End would support her cause—and by Prince Lucerys's refusal to take one of his lordship's daughters for his bride (the prince was betrothed to another). He angrily ejected the young Velaryon from his hall and did nothing to prevent Prince Aemond from following him to take revenge for the eye he had lost to Lucerys years earlier, so long as said revenge was not enacted within the walls of Storm's End.

Prince Lucerys tried to flee on his young dragon, Arrax, but Aemond pursued him upon his great dragon, Vhagar. Had a storm not been howling through Shipbreaker Bay, Lucerys might have escaped, but it was not to be; the boy and his dragon both died, tumbling into the sea within sight of Storm's End as Vhagar roared triumphantly. It was the first royal bloodshed in the Dance of the Dragons, though much more was to follow.

In the early part of the war, Lord Borros proved reluctant to face the dragons personally. But toward the end of the Dance, he and his stormlanders seized King's Landing during the Moon of the Three Kings, restoring the city to order and winning promises that his eldest daughter would become the new queen of the widowed King Aegon II. Then he boldly led the last of the royalist host against the approaching riverlanders, who were commanded by the young Lord Kermit Tully, the even-younger Benjicot Blackwood, and Blackwood's sister Alysanne. When the Lord of Storm's End learned that the host was led by boys and women, he grew confident in his victory, but Bloody Ben Blackwood, as he was remembered after, broke his flank, while Black Aly Blackwood led the archers who brought down his knights. Lord Borros was defiant to the end, and the accounts claim he killed a dozen knights and slew Lords Darry and Mallister before he himself was slain by Kermit Tully.

With his death and the defeat of his stormlanders, the Dance of the Dragons was all but over. House Baratheon had gambled greatly in supporting King Aegon II, and it was a choice that brought them nothing but ill during the reign of King Aegon III (the Dragonbane) and the regency preceding it.

As the years passed, and king followed king upon the Iron Throne, these old rifts were forgotten, and the Baratheons came to serve the crown faithfully once more . . . until the Targaryens themselves put that loyalty to the test. This occurred during the reign of King Aegon V Targaryen (known to history as Aegon the Unlikely), when the Lord of Storm's End was Lyonel Baratheon, a swaggering giant of a man known as the Laughing Storm, one of the greatest fighters of his day.

Lord Lyonel had always been amongst King Aegon's most leal supporters; so firm was their friendship that His Grace gladly agreed to betroth his eldest son and heir to Lord Lyonel's daughter. All was well until Prince Duncan met and became smitten with the mysterious woman known only as Jenny of Oldstones (a witch, some say), and took her for his wife in defiance of his father the king.

OF LORD BORROS, SEPTON EUSTACE WRITES

Lord Boremund was stone, hard and strong and unmoving. Lord Borros was the wind, which rages and howls and blows this way and that.

RIGHT | *Ser Duncan the Tall of the Kingsguard facing Lord Lyonel Baratheon in single combat.*

The love between Jenny of Oldstones ("with flowers in her hair") and Duncan, Prince of Dragonflies, is beloved of singers, storytellers, and young maids even to this day, but it caused great grief to Lord Lyonel's daughter and brought shame and dishonor to House Baratheon. So great was the wroth of the Laughing Storm that he swore a bloody oath of vengeance, renounced allegiance to the Iron Throne, and had himself crowned as a new Storm King. Peace was restored only after the Kingsguard knight Ser Duncan the Tall faced Lord Lyonel in a trial by battle, Prince Duncan renounced his claim to crown and throne, and King Aegon V agreed that his youngest daughter, the Princess Rhaelle, would wed Lord Lyonel's heir.

As the Seven in their wisdom would have it, it was the match that King Aegon V agreed to in order to appease the Laughing Storm that ultimately led to the end of Targaryen rule in the Seven Kingdoms. In 245 AC Princess Rhaelle fulfilled her father's promise and wed Ormund Baratheon, young Lord of Storm's End. The following year she gave him a son, Steffon, who served as a page and a squire at King's Landing and became a close companion of Prince Aerys, eldest son of King Jaehaerys II and heir to the Iron Throne.

Sadly, Lord Steffon drowned in Shipbreaker Bay whilst returning from a mission to Volantis, where King Aerys II had sent him to seek a wife for his son Rhaegar . . . but Steffon's own firstborn son, Robert, succeeded him as Lord of Storm's End and grew to be one of the finest knights in the Seven Kingdoms—a warrior so strong and fearless that many hailed him as the Laughing Storm reborn.

When the madness of King Aerys II became too much to be borne, it was to Lord Robert that the lords of the

Many other Baratheons have won renown over the centuries, following in the footsteps of Orys One-Hand and the Storm Kings before him. Ser Raymont Baratheon, a younger son of Lord Baratheon, served in the Kingsguard when Aenys I was forced to war against the Faith, and saved the life of his king when the Poor Fellows attempted to murder him in his bed. Knights such as the Stormbreaker and the Laughing Storm brought glory onto the house, whilst Lord Ormund Baratheon fought and died beneath the Targaryen banner on the Stepstones during the War of the Ninepenny Kings.

realm turned. In 282 AC, at the ford of the Trident, Robert Baratheon slew Rhaegar Targaryen, Prince of Dragonstone, and shattered his host, effectively ending three centuries of rule by the House of the Dragon. Soon thereafter he ascended the Iron Throne himself as Robert I Baratheon, the progenitor of a glorious new dynasty.

THE MEN OF THE STORMLANDS

As King Robert proved upon the Trident—and as the lords and kings before him showed likewise—the men of the stormlands are as hardy and fierce and skilled in war as any in the Seven Kingdoms. The longbows of the Marchers are especially famed, and many of the most famous bowmen of song and history are said to hail from the Dornish Marches. Fletcher Dick, the notorious outlaw of the Kingswood Brotherhood, was born in a village near the Marcher castle of Stonehelm, and is held by many to be the finest archer who ever drew bow.

The stormlands have also produced their share of great seamen and sailors. Storm's End itself, looming over the great cliffs of Durran's Point and the treacherous rocks of Shipbreaker Bay, offers no safe anchorage for either warship or merchant craft, but in the time of the Storm Kings, war fleets were oft maintained on Massey's Hook, Estermont,

Many of the folk of Tarth, highborn and low alike, claim descent from a legendary hero, Ser Galladon of Morne, who was said to wield a sword called the Just Maid given to him by the Seven themselves. Given the role that the Just Maid plays in Ser Galladon's tale, Maester Hubert, in his *Kin of the Stag*, has suggested that Galladon of Morne was no rude warrior of the Age of Heroes turned into a knight by singers a thousand years later, but an actual historic figure of more recent times. Hubert also notes that Morne was a royal seat of petty kings on the eastern coast of Tarth until the Storm Kings made them submit, but that its ruins indicate that the site was made by Andals, not First Men.

and in the towns and fishing villages along the Sea of Dorne. Later, other monarchs preferred to dock their fleets on the western shore of Tarth, where that great island's mountains helped to shelter them from the storms that often raged through the narrow sea. The Sapphire Isle, as some call it, is ruled by House Tarth of Evenfall Hall—an old family of Andal descent that boasts of ties to the Durrandons, the Baratheons, and more recently to House Targaryen. Once kings in their own right, the Lords of Tarth still style themselves "the Evenstar," a title that they claim goes back unto the dawn of days.

The fiercest fighters in the stormlands, and perhaps in all of Westeros, are undoubtedly the men of the marches, who are said to be born with sword in hand and oft boast of learning to fight even before they learn to walk. Theirs is the task of protecting the realm of the Storm Kings from the ancient enemies to the west and, especially, the south.

The castles of the Dornish Marches are among the strongest of the realm, and for good reason, for seldom has a generation passed when they have not faced some new attack. They were established to create a bulwark against incursions from the Dornish and the Kings of the Reach. The Marcher lords are duly proud of their history as key defenders of the realm of the Storm Kings, and many are the ballads and tales of their valor.

Among the sternest of the Marcher seats are Stonehelm, the ancient seat of House Swann, with its watchtowers of black and white stone, which stands above the waters of the river Slayne with its rapids, pools, and waterfalls; Blackhaven, home to House Dondarrion, with its forbidding black basalt walls and bottomless dry moat; and Nightsong of the Singing Towers, where House Caron has held sway for many centuries. Though styled as lords of the marches, the Carons hold no dominion over the other Marcher lords; they count themselves the oldest of the Marcher houses,

Famous for their warriors and singers alike, House Caron has a storied history that stretches back to the Age of Heroes. The Carons are wont to say that the nightingales of their house have been seen on a thousand battlefields, and the histories show that Nightsong has been besieged no less than thirty-seven times in the last thousand years.

however (a claim the Swanns dispute), and have always been prominent in leading the defense of the stormlands.

As the marches are famed for their strong castles and their ballads, the rainwood is known for its rain, its silences, and a wealth in fur and wood and amber. Here the trees rule, it is said, and the castles oft seem as if they have grown from the earth instead of being built. But the knights and lords of the rainwood have roots as deep as the trees that shelter them, and have oft proved themselves steadfast in battle, strong and stubborn and immovable.

STORM'S END

The history of the building of Storm's End is known to us only through songs and stories—the tales of Durran Godsgrief and fair Elenei, daughter of two gods. Supposedly it was the seventh of the castles that Durran raised

During Robert's Rebellion, Lord Tyrell of Highgarden laid siege to Storm's End for a year, without result. If the garrison's supplies had been sufficient to the task, the castle might have held out indefinitely, but the war had come

S torm's End is surely an old castle, but when compared to the ruined ringforts of the First Men or even the First Keep of Winterfell (which a past maester in service to the Starks examined and found to have been rebuilt so many times that a precise dating could not be made), the great tower and perfectly joined stones of the Storm's End curtain wall seem much beyond what the First Men were capable of for many thousands of years. The great effort involved in raising the Wall was one thing, but that was more a brute effort than the high art needed to make a wall where even the wind cannot find purchase. Archmaester Vyron, in his *Triumphs and Defeats*, speculates that the tale's claim that the final form of Storm's End was the seventh castle shows a clear Andal influence, and if true, this suggests the possibility that the final form of the castle was only achieved in Andal times. Mayhaps the castle was rebuilt on the site of earlier castles, but if so, it was long after Durran Godsgrief and his fair Elenei had passed from this earth.

in that spot (though that number may well be a later interpolation of the Faith).

Maesters who have served at the castle testify to its vast strength and ingenious construction. Whether designed by Brandon the Builder or not, its great curtain wall, with its stones so cunningly fitted that the wind cannot get a grip on them, is justly famed. So, too, is the great central keep that thrusts up into the sky to overlook Shipbreaker Bay.

Storm's End has never fallen to storm or siege, the histories tell us. Well can it be believed.

quickly and the storehouses and granaries were only half-full. By year's end, the garrison under Lord Robert's brother Stannis was sorely tested by hunger and want, only to be saved by a common smuggler who slipped through the Redwyne blockade one night carrying a load of onions and salt fish to Storm's End. Thus, the castle was able to stand unbroken until Robert defeated Rhaegar on the Trident and Lord Eddard Stark arrived to end the siege.

I t is said that, every seventy-seven years, a storm greater than all others comes howling down upon Storm's End, as the old gods of sea and sky try once more to blow Durran's seat into the sea. It is a pretty tale . . . but a tale is all it is. The records of the maesters of Storm's End show that there are fierce storms nearly every year, especially in autumn, and whilst some are greater than others, there are no records that show unusually powerful storms seventy-seven years apart. The greatest storm in living memory was in 221 AC, in the last year of the reign of Aerys I, and the greatest before that was the storm of 166 AC, fifty-five years earlier.

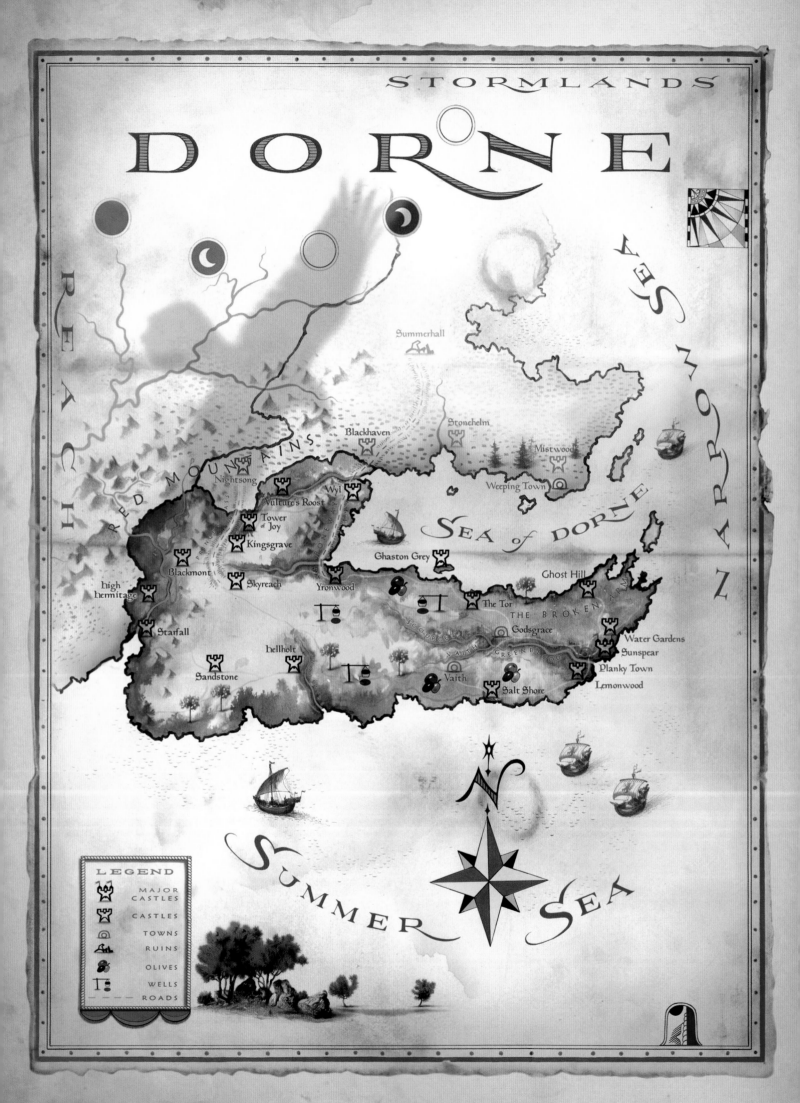

DORNE

ONLY A DORNISHMAN can ever truly know Dorne, it is said.

The southernmost of the Seven Kingdoms is also the most inhospitable . . . and the strangest, to the eyes of any man raised in the Reach or the westerlands or King's Landing. For Dorne is different, in more ways than can be told.

Vast deserts of red and white sand, forbidding mountains where treacherous passes are guarded by treacherous peoples, sweltering heat, sandstorms, scorpions, fiery food, poison, castles made of mud, dates and figs and blood oranges—these things comprise most of what the smallfolk of the Seven Kingdoms know of Dorne. And all these things exist, to be sure, but there is far more to this ancient principality than that, for it has a history that stretches back to the Dawn Age.

The Red Mountains that compose its western and northern boundaries have kept Dorne separate from the rest of the realm for thousands of years, though the deserts have played a role as well. Behind that wall of mountains, more than three-quarters of the land is an arid wasteland. Nor is the long southern coast of Dorne more hospitable, being for the most part a snarl of reefs and rocks, with few protected anchorages. Those ships that do put ashore there, whether by choice or chance, find little to sustain them; there are no forests along the coast to provide timber for repairs, a scarcity of game, few farms, and fewer villages where provisions might be obtained. Even freshwater is hard to come by, and the seas south of Dorne are rife with whirlpools and infested with sharks and kraken.

There are no cities in Dorne, though the so-called shadow city that clings to the walls of Sunspear is large enough to be counted as a town (a town built of mud and straw, it must be admitted). Larger and more populous, the Planky Town at the mouth of the river Greenblood is mayhaps the nearest thing the Dornish have to a true city, though a city with planks instead of streets, where the houses and halls and shops are made from poleboats, barges, and merchant ships, lashed together with hempen rope and floating on the tide.

Archmaester Brude, who was born and raised in the shadow city that huddles beneath the crumbling walls of Sunspear, once famously observed that Dorne has more in common with the distant North than either does with the realms that lie between them. "One is hot and one is cold, yet these ancient kingdoms of sand and snow are set apart from the rest of Westeros by history, culture, and tradition. Both are thinly peopled, compared to the lands betwixt. Both cling stubbornly to their own laws and their own traditions. Neither was ever truly conquered by the dragons. The King in the North accepted Aegon Targaryen as his overlord peaceably, whilst Dorne resisted the might of the Targaryens valiantly for almost two hundred years, before finally submitting to the Iron Throne through marriage. Dornishmen and Northmen alike are derided as savages by the ignorant of the five 'civilized' kingdoms, and celebrated for their valor by those who have crossed swords with them."

The Dornishmen boast that theirs is the oldest of the Seven Kingdoms of Westeros. This is true, after a fashion. Unlike the Andals, who came later, the First Men were not seafarers. They came to Westeros not on longships but afoot, over the land bridge from Essos—the remnants of which exist today only as the Stepstones and the Broken Arm of Dorne. Walking or riding, the eastern shores of Dorne would inevitably have been where they first set foot upon Westerosi soil.

Few, however, chose to remain there, for the lands they encountered were far from welcoming. The children of the forest called Dorne the Empty Land, and for good reason. The eastern half of Dorne is largely barren scrub, its dry, stony soil yielding little, even when irrigated. And once beyond Vaith, western Dorne is naught but a vast sea of restless dunes where the sun beats down relentlessly, giving rise from time to time to savage sandstorms that can strip the flesh from a man's bones within minutes. Even Garth Greenhand could not make flowers bloom in an environment so harsh and unforgiving if the tales told in the Reach can be believed. (Dorne's own legends make no mention of Garth.) Instead he led his people through the mountains to the fertile Reach beyond. Most of the First Men who came after him took one look at Dorne and followed.

Yet not all. Some there were who saw a beauty in that stark, hot, cruel land and chose to make their homes there. Most of them settled along the banks of the river they named the Greenblood. Though meager when compared to the Mander, the Trident, or the Blackwater Rush, the waters of the Greenblood are truly the lifeblood of Dorne.

Most of the First Men who chose to remain in Dorne, instead of wandering north in search of sweeter lands, settled close to the banks of the Greenblood, digging canals and

Most Dornish rivers are in full flood only after the rare (and dangerous) rainstorms. The rest of the year they are dry gullies. In all of Dorne, only three rivers flow day and night, winter and summer, without ever going dry. The Torrentine, arising high in the western mountains, plunges down to the sea in a series of rapids and waterfalls, howling through canyons and crevasses with a sound like the roar of some great beast. Rising from mountain springs, its waters are sweet and pure, but dangerous to cross, save by bridge, and impossible to navigate. The Brimstone is a far more placid stream, but its cloudy yellow waters stink of sulfur, and the plants that grow along its banks are strange and stunted things. (Of the men who live along those selfsame banks, we shall not speak). But the Greenblood's waters, if sometimes muddy, are healthful for plant and animal alike, and farms and orchards crowd the river's banks for hundreds of leagues. Moreover, the Greenblood and its vassals, the Vaith and the Scourge, are navigable by boat almost to their source (if shallow and plagued by sandbars in places), and therefore serve as the principality's chief artery for trade.

ditches to bring its life-giving waters to the trees and crops they planted. Others preferred to dwell beside the narrow sea; the eastern shores of Dorne are more forgiving than the southern, and soon many small villages arose, sustaining themselves on fish and crabs. The more restless of the First Men pushed onward and made homes for themselves in the foothills south of the Red Mountains, where storms moving north were wont to drop their moisture, creating a fertile green belt. Those who climbed farther took refuge amongst the peaks, in hidden valleys and high mountain meadows where the grass was green and sweet. Only the bravest and the maddest dared to strike out inland across the deep sands. A few of these found water amongst the dunes and raised holdfasts and castles on those oasis; their descendants, centuries later, became the Lords of the Wells. But for every man who stumbled on a well, a hundred must surely have died of thirst beneath the blazing Dornish sun.

From such origins did the three distinct types of Dornishmen we know today arise. The Young Dragon, King Daeron I Targaryen, gave them the names we know them by in his book, *The Conquest of Dorne*. Stony Dornishmen, sandy Dornishmen, and salty Dornishmen, he named them. The stony Dornishmen were the mountain folk, fair of hair and skin, mostly descended from the First Men and the Andals; the sandy Dornishmen dwell in the deserts and river valleys, with their skin burned brown beneath the blazing Dornish sun; the salty Dornishmen of the coasts, dark-haired and lithe and olive-skinned, have the queerest customs and the most Rhoynish blood. (When Princess Nymeria came ashore in Dorne, most of her Rhoynar preferred to remain close to the sea that had been their home for so long, even after Nymeria burned their ships.)

THE BREAKING

The single most important event in Dornish history, and mayhaps the history of all Westeros, is one about which, to our frustration, we know far too little.

Most of what we do believe of the Breaking comes to us through song and legend. The First Men crossed from Essos to Westeros by land, all agree, walking or riding across through the hills and forest of the great land bridge that connected the two continents in the Dawn Age. Dorne was the first land that they entered, but few remained, as we have chronicled; many and more pressed on northward, through the mountains and mayhaps across the salt marshes that once existed where the Sea of Dorne is now. As the centuries passed, they came in ever-increasing numbers, claiming the stormlands and the Reach and the riverlands for their own, eventually reaching even the Vale and the North. They drove the elder races before them, slaughtering giants wherever they found them, hewing down weirwood trees with their bronze axes, making bloody war against the children of the forest.

The children fought back as best they could, but the First Men were larger and stronger. Riding their horses, clad and armed in bronze, the First Men overwhelmed the elder race wherever they met, for the weapons of the children were made of bone and wood and dragonglass. Finally, driven by desperation, the little people turned to sorcery and beseeched their greenseers to stem the tide of these invaders.

And so they did, gathering in their hundreds (some say on the Isle of Faces), and calling on their old gods with song and prayer and grisly sacrifice (a thousand captive men were fed to the weirwood, one version of the tale goes, whilst another claims the children used the blood of their own young). And the old gods stirred, and giants awoke in the earth, and all of Westeros shook and trembled. Great cracks appeared in the earth, and hills and mountains collapsed and were swallowed up. And then the seas came rushing in, and the Arm of Dorne was broken and shattered by the force of water, until only a few bare rocky islands remained above the waves. The Summer Sea joined the narrow sea, and the bridge between Essos and Westeros vanished for all time.

Or so the legend says.

Most scholars do agree that Essos and Westeros were once joined; a thousand tales and runic records tell of the crossing of the First Men. Today the seas divide them, so plainly some version of the event the Dornish call the Breaking must have occurred. Did it happen in the space of a single day, however, as the songs would have it? Was it the work of the children of the forest and the sorcery of their greenseers? These things are less certain. Archmaester Cassander suggests elsewise in his *Song of the Sea: How the Lands Were Severed,* arguing that it was not the singing of greenseers that parted Westeros from Essos but rather what he calls the Song of the Sea—a slow rising of the waters that took place over centuries, not in a single day, and was caused by a series of long, hot summers and short, warm winters that melted the ice in the frozen lands beyond the Shivering Sea, causing the oceans to rise.

Many maesters find Cassander's arguments plausible and have come to accept his views. But whether the Breaking took place in a single night, or over the course of centuries, there can be no doubt that it occurred; the Stepstones and the Broken Arm of Dorne give mute but eloquent testimony to its effects. There is also much to suggest that the Sea of Dorne was once an inland freshwater sea, fed by mountain streams and much smaller than it is today, until the narrow sea burst its bounds and drowned the salt marshes that lay between.

Even if we accept that the old gods broke the Arm of Dorne with the Hammer of the Waters, as the legends claim, the greenseers sang their song too late.

No more wanderers crossed to Westeros after the Breaking, it is true, for the First Men were no seafarers . . . but so many of their forebears had already made the crossing that they outnumbered the dwindling elder races almost three to one by the time the lands were severed, and that disparity only grew in the centuries that followed, for the women of the First Men brought forth sons and daughters with much greater frequency than the females of the elder races. And thus the children and the giants faded, whilst the race of men spread and multiplied and claimed the fields and forests for their own, raising villages and forts and kingdoms.

LEFT | *The three kinds of Dornishmen—the stony, the sandy, and the salty.*

KINGDOMS OF THE FIRST MEN

The disunity of the Dornish is apparent even from our oldest sources. The great distances between each pocket of settlement and the difficulties of travel across burning sands and rugged mountains helped to isolate each small community from all the others and led to the rise of many petty lords, more than half of whom in time began to style themselves kings. Petty kings existed throughout all of Westeros, to be sure, but seldom so many (nor so petty) as the Dornish kings under the First Men.

We shall not attempt to speak of all of these. Most ruled over domains so small, or conquests so short-lived, that they are scarce worthy of note. A few of the greatest do warrant mention, however: those whose lines put down deep roots and endured for thousands of years to come.

At the mouth of the Torrentine, House Dayne raised its castle on an island where that roaring, tumultuous river broadens to meet the sea. Legend says the first Dayne was led to the site when he followed the track of a falling star and there found a stone of magical powers. His descendants ruled over the western mountains for centuries thereafter as Kings of the Torrentine and Lords of Starfall.

North and east, beyond a great gap in the mountains that provided the shortest and easiest passage from Dorne to the Reach, House Fowler carved its own seat into the stony slopes overlooking the pass. Skyreach, that seat became known, for its lofty perch and soaring stone towers. At the time, the pass it brooded over was commonly known as the Wide Way (today we name it the Prince's Pass), so the Fowlers took for themselves the grandiose titles of Lords of Skyreach, Lords of the Wide Way, and Kings of Stone and Sky.

In a similar vein, far to the east where the mountains ran down to the Sea of Dorne, House Yronwood established itself in the high valleys and green foothills below the peaks and seized control of the Stone Way, the second of the two great passes into Dorne (one far steeper, narrower, and more treacherous than the Wide Way of the west). Well protected and comparably fertile, their lands were also well timbered and possessed of valuable deposits of iron, tin, and silver as well, making the Yronwoods the richest and most powerful of the Dornish kings. Styling themselves the Bloodroyals, Lords of the Stone Way, Masters of the Green Hills, and High Kings of Dorne, the lords of House Yronwood in time ruled northern Dorne, from the mountain domains of House Wyl to the headwaters of the Greenblood . . . though their efforts to bend the other Dornish kings to their will were seldom successful.

A second, rival High King of Dorne also existed during the times of the First Men, ruling from a great wooden motte-and-bailey castle on the south bank of Greenwood near Lemonwood, where the river flows into the Summer Sea. This was a curious kingship, for whenever a king died, his successor was chosen by election from amongst a dozen noble families that had settled along the river or the eastern shores. The Wades, Shells, Holts, Brooks, Hulls, Lakes, Brownhills, and Briars all threw up kings who ruled from the high hall amongst the lemon trees, but in the end this curious system broke down when a disputed election set the royal houses to warring against one another. After a generation of conflict, three of the old houses were wiped from the earth, and the once-powerful river realm had shattered into a dozen quarrelsome petty kingdoms.

Other small kingdoms existed elsewhere in Dorne, in the deep sands, amongst the high peaks, along the salt shore, and on the isles and the Broken Arm, but few of these ever approached the power and prestige of the Daynes of Starfall, the Fowlers of Skyreach and the Wide Way, and the Yronwoods of Yronwood.

THE ANDALS ARRIVE

The Andals made their mark on Dorne, as they did on all Westeros south of the Neck. Yet most historians agree that their impact was less here than in any of the other southron kingdoms. Unlike the First Men, the Andals were seafarers, and the more adventurous of their captains knew the Dornish coasts well and were wont to say that there was naught to be found there but snakes, scorpions, and sand. Small wonder then that comparatively few of the invaders bent their oars southward when there were richer, greener lands far closer at hand, just across the narrow sea from Andalos itself.

Yet there are always a few who walk the roads that others shun, seeking after fortunes in the bleaker corners of the world. And so it was with the Andals who made their way to Dorne. Some contested with the First Men

RIGHT | *A Sword of the Morning carrying Dawn.*

Sword of the Morning

The Daynes of Starfall are one of the most ancient houses in the Seven Kingdoms, though their fame largely rests on their ancestral sword, called Dawn, and the men who wielded it. Its origins are lost to legend, but it seems likely that the Daynes have carried it for thousands of years. Those who have had the honor of examining it say it looks like no Valyrian steel they know, being pale as milkglass but in all other respects it seems to share the properties of Valyrian blades, being incredibly strong and sharp.

Though many houses have their heirloom swords, they mostly pass the blades down from lord to lord. Some, such as the Corbrays have done, may lend the blade to a son or brother for his lifetime, only to have it return to the lord. But that is not the way of House Dayne. The wielder of Dawn is always given the title of Sword of the Morning, and only a knight of House Dayne who is deemed worthy can carry it.

For this reason, the Swords of the Morning are all famous throughout the Seven Kingdoms. There are boys who secretly dream of being a son of Starfall so they might claim that storied sword and its title. Most famous of all was Ser Arthur Dayne, the deadliest of King Aerys II's Kingsguard, who defeated the Kingswood Brotherhood and won renown in every tourney and mêlée. He died nobly with his sworn brothers at the end of Robert's Rebellion, after Lord Eddard Stark was said to have killed him in single combat. Lord Stark then returned Dawn to Starfall, and to Ser Arthur's kin, as a sign of respect.

who had come before them for the choice lands along the Greenblood and the coasts, or ventured into the mountains. Others established themselves in places where no man had gone before them.

Amongst those were the Ullers and the Qorgyles; the former raised a grim, stinking seat beside the sulfurous yellow waters of the Brimstone, whilst the latter established themselves amidst the dunes and deep sands, fortifying the only well for fifty leagues around. Farther east, the Vaiths raised a tall, pale castle in the hills, at the juncture of the two streams that formed the river that soon bore their name. Elsewhere in the realm, the Allyrions, the Jordaynes, and the Santagars carved out holdings for themselves.

And on the eastern shore, between the Broken Arm and the Greenblood, an Andal adventurer named Morgan Martell and his kin descended on lands loosely held by House Wade and House Shell, defeated them in battle, seized their villages, burned their castles, and established dominion over a strip of stony coastlands fifty leagues long and ten leagues wide.

Over the centuries that followed, their strength grew . . . but slowly, for then and now the lords of House Martell were renowned for their caution. Until the coming of Nymeria, no Dornishman would ever have counted them amongst the great powers of the country. Indeed, though surrounded by kings on every side, the Martells themselves never presumed to claim that title, and at certain points in their history, they willingly bent the knees to the Jordayne kings of the Tor, the pious Allyrions of Godsgrace, the many petty kings of the Greenblood, and the mighty Yronwoods of Yronwood.

THE COMING OF THE RHOYNAR

The Martells ruled their modest domains for hundreds of years before Princess Nymeria and her ten thousand ships made landfall on the coast of Dorne, near to the place where the castle Sunspear and its shadow city now stand.

The story of how Nymeria took Mors Martell as her lord husband, burning her ships and binding her Rhoynar to his house, heart and hand and honor, has been told elsewhere. We need not tell it again here. Nor will we repeat the old familiar tales of battles won and lost, alliances made and broken.

Suffice it to say that the wealth and the knowledge that the Rhoynar brought with them to Westeros, together with the ambition of Lord Mors and the indomitable will of Nymeria of the Rhoyne, enabled the Martells to greatly expand their power, as they defeated one lord and petty king after another, until at last they toppled even the Yronwoods and united all of Dorne . . . not as a kingdom, but as a principality, for Mors and Nymeria never named themselves as king and queen, preferring the titles prince and princess, after the fashion of the fallen city-states of the Rhoyne. Their descendants continued that tradition until the present day, even whilst defeating many a rival and proving themselves against the Storm Kings and the Kings of the Reach alike.

In the songs, Nymeria is said to have been a witch and a warrior; neither of these claims is true. Though she did not bear arms in battle, she led her soldiers on many battlefields, commanding them with cunning and skill. It was a wisdom she passed along to her heirs, who would themselves command the hosts when she grew too aged and infirm. And though none matched Nymeria's feat of sending six captive kings in golden fetters to the Wall, her heirs succeeded in keeping Dorne independent against the rival kings north of the mountains and keeping it whole against the rancorous, hot-tempered lords of mountain and desert whom they ruled.

House Martell has guided Dorne for seven hundred years, raising its great towers at Sunspear, seeing the shadow city and the Planky Town rise, and defeating all those who threatened its dominion.

ABOVE | *The arms of House Martell (center) and some of its vassals (clockwise from top), Dayne, Fowler, Jordayne, Qorgyle, Toland, Uller, Vaith, Wyl, Yronwood, Allyrion, and Blackmont.*

THE NAMES OF THE SIX KINGS SENT BY NYMERIA TO THE WALL, AS RELATED IN THE HISTORIES

YORICK OF HOUSE YRONWOOD, the Bloodroyal, the richest and most powerful of the Dornish kings deposed by House Martell.

VORIAN OF HOUSE DAYNE, Sword of the Evening, renowned as the greatest knight in all of Dorne.

GARRISON OF HOUSE FOWLER, the Blind King, aged and sightless, yet still feared for his cunning.

LUCIFER OF HOUSE DRYLAND, Last of His Ilk, King of the Brimstone, Lord of Hellgate Hall.

BENEDICT OF HOUSE BLACKMONT, who worshipped a dark god and was said to have the power to transform himself into a vulture of enormous size.

ALBIN OF HOUSE MANWOODY, a troublesome madman who claimed dominion over the Red Mountains.

QUEER CUSTOMS OF THE SOUTH

Separate as they have been—and then a thousand years ago joined with the Rhoynar—the Dornish have their own proud, fraught history and their own ways.

The stony Dornish have the most in common with those north of the mountains and are the least touched by Rhoynish custom. This has not made them close allies with the Marcher lords or the Lords of the Reach, however; on the contrary, it has been said that the mountain lords have a history as savage as that of the mountain clans of the Vale, having for thousands of years warred with the Reach and the stormlands, as well as with each other. If the ballads tell of brave skirmishes with cruel Dornishmen in the marches, it is largely to do with the lords of Blackmont and Kingsgrave, of Wyl and Skyreach. And of Yronwood, as well. The

Wardens of the Stone Way remain the proudest and most powerful of House Martell's vassals, and theirs has been an uneasy relationship at best.

The sandy Dornishmen are more Rhoynish and are used to the harsh way of life in the desert. The rivers of Dorne are paltry when compared to the Mander or the Trident, but they bring water enough to irrigate fields and sustain villages and towns. Outside of them, however, men live in different fashion: moving from desert oasis to desert oasis, crossing the sands with the aid of what wells they know of in the midst of the wastes, raising their children along with their goats and their horses. It is the sandy Dornish who are the chief breeders of the famed sand steeds, considered the most beautiful horses in the Seven Kingdoms. Though

ABOVE | *Princess Nymeria and Mors Martell enthroned in Sunspear.*

Before Nymeria came, the Kings of Yronwood were the most powerful house in all of Dorne—far greater than the Martells of the time. They ruled half of Dorne—a fact that, to this day, the Yronwoods let no one forget. In the centuries after House Martell rose to the rule of Dorne, the Yronwoods have been the house likeliest to rebel, and have done so several times. Even after Prince Maron Martell united Dorne with the Iron Throne, this habit remained. Lords of Yronwood rode for the black dragon in no less than three of the five Blackfyre Rebellions.

light-boned and unable to easily bear the weight of a knight in armor, they are swift and tireless, able to run through a day and a night with no more than a few drinks of water. The Dornish love their sand steeds almost as much as they love their children, and King Daeron would remark in the *Conquest of Dorne* that the Knight of Spottswood stabled his sand steeds in his own hall.

The salty Dornish, the scions of the Rhoynar, lost their mother tongue over the centuries, though that tongue still marks the way the Dornish speak the Common Tongue— stretching some sounds, rolling others, and lilting still others in odd places. Dornish speech has been described by some as charming, and by others (the marchers, chiefly and unfairly) as incomprehensible. But more than that, the Rhoynar brought with them their customs and their laws, which the Martells then spread throughout Dorne. So in Dorne, alone among the Seven Kingdoms, it is the eldest child—man or woman—who will inherit, and not just the eldest son. Great ladies and famous princesses abound, and are the subject of songs and tales as much as the great knights and princes.

There are other customs besides that mark the Dornish as different. They are not greatly concerned if a child is born in wedlock or out of it, especially if the child is born to a paramour. Many lords—and even some ladies—have paramours,

chosen for love and lust rather than for breeding or alliance. And when it comes to matters of love, that a man might lie with another man, or a woman with another woman, is likewise not cause for concern; while the septons have often wished to shepherd the Dornishmen to the righteous path, they have had little effect. Even the fashions are different in Dorne, where the climate favors loose, layered robes and the food is richly spiced, ready to burn the mouth with dragon peppers mixed with drops of snake venom.

Standing apart from the rest of the Dornish—salty or sandy or stony alike—are the orphans of the Greenblood, who wept when Nymeria burned their ships. From their ruins they made their poleboats, to ply the Greenblood and dream of the day that they could return to Mother Rhoyne. Of pure Rhoynish blood, they still speak their tongue amongst themselves, it is said—though in secret after the three successors of Nymeria's grandson, Prince Mors II, attempted to forbid it.

These successors were also known as the Red Princes (though two were princesses), and their reigns were marked by wars both within and without Dorne. They created the Planky Town as a gathering place, lashing together the poleboats and ferries. It grew from there, and in time the princes raised a citadel nearby to guard it as more and more ships from the Free Cities found it a convenient harbor.

An example of the differing Dornish laws and attitudes due to the influence of the Rhoynar may be found, curiously, in the last days of the Dance of the Dragons. From Archmaester Gyldayn's history concerning Gaemon Palehair's brief reign:

One decree after another came down from the House of Kisses, where the child king had his seat, each more outrageous than the last. Gaemon decreed that girls should henceforth be equal with boys in matter of inheritance, that the poor be given bread and beer in times of famine, and that men who had lost limbs in war must afterward be fed and housed by whichever lord they had been fighting for when the loss took place. Gaemon decreed that husbands who beat their wives should themselves be beaten, irrespective of what the wives had done to warrant such chastisement. These edicts were almost certainly the work of a Dornish whore named Sylvenna Sand, reputedly the paramour of the king's mother Essie, if Mushroom is to be believed.

RIGHT | *Aegon I unleashing Balerion's flames during the time of the Dragon's Wroth.*

DORNE AGAINST THE DRAGONS

Of all the challenges the Dornishmen have faced, none have loomed so large as that posed by Aegon the Conqueror and his sisters. Great was the valor the Dornish showed in battle, and great the grief at the losses they suffered, for the price of freedom was steep. Yet alone of all the Seven Kingdoms, Dorne remained independent of House Targaryen, resisting attempt after attempt by Aegon, his sisters, and their successors to make the Dornish bend their knees before the Iron Throne.

The Dornishmen fought no great battles against the Targaryens, nor did they seek to defend their castles against the dragons when they came, for Meria Martell, Princess of Dorne at the time of Aegon's Conquest, had learned much from the Last Storm and the Field of Fire, and from the fate of Harrenhal. Instead, when Aegon turned his eye to Dorne in 4 AC, the Dornish simply vanished before the dragons.

Queen Rhaenys led the first assault on Dorne, moving swiftly to seize Dornish seats as she approached Sunspear and burning the Planky Town on Meraxes, whilst Aegon and Lord Tyrell warred in the Prince's Pass against the mountain lords. The Dornish defenders harried and ambushed the Targaryen forces, then would scamper beneath their rocks as soon as they saw the dragons take flight. Many of Lord Tyrell's men died of sun and thirst as they marched on Hellholt. Those who survived to reach the castle found it empty, the Ullers all fled.

Aegon had more success, but other than the brief siege at Yronwood, where he was opposed by a handful of old men, boys, and women, he found little opposition. Even Skyreach, the great seat of the Fowlers, was abandoned. At Ghost Hill, the seat of House Toland atop the white chalk hill that overlooks the Sea of Dorne, Aegon saw the banner bearing the Toland ghost flying above the walls and received word that Lord Toland had sent out his champion to face him. Aegon slew the man with his sword, Blackfyre, only to learn that he was Lord Toland's mad fool and that Lord Toland himself was gone with his household from the castle. In later days, the Tolands would take a new banner, showing a dragon biting its own tail, green on gold in memory of the motley of their brave fool.

Elsewhere, Lord Orys Baratheon's assault up the Boneway proved a disaster. The canny Dornishmen rained rocks and

FROM THE HISTORY OF ARCHMAESTER GYLDAYN, ON THE DEFENESTRATION OF SUNSPEAR

Lord Rosby, Castellan of Sunspear and Warden of the Sands, had a kinder end than most. After the Dornishmen swarmed in from the shadow city to retake the castle, he was bound hand and foot, dragged to the top of the Spear Tower, and thrown from a window by none other than the aged Princess Meria herself.

arrows and spears from the heights, murdered men in the night, and in the end blocked the Boneway both before and behind. Lord Orys was captured by Lord Wyl, and many of his bannermen and knights besides. They remained captive for years before finally being ransomed for their weight in gold in 7 AC. And even then, each and every one of them returned lacking a sword hand, so that they might never take up arms against Dorne again.

Still, save for the assault in the Boneway, the Dornish simply yielded up their seats, the lords refusing to defend them or bend the knee. The same was the case when the Targaryens at last came to Sunspear, where Princess Meria (mocked by her foes as the Yellow Toad of Dorne but to this day a hero to the Dornish) had herself vanished into the sands. There Queen Rhaenys and King Aegon gathered what courtiers and functionaries remained and declared themselves the victors, placing Dorne under the rule of the Iron Throne. Leaving Lord Rosby to hold Sunspear and Lord Tyrell in charge of a host to put down any revolts, the Targaryens returned to King's Landing on the backs of their dragons. Yet they had hardly set foot in the royal city than Dorne rebelled against them and did so with shocking rapidity. Garrisons were put to the sword, and the knights who led them were tortured. In truth, it became a game among the Dornish lords, to see which knight would live the longest as bit after bit of him was removed.

Setting out with his garrison at Hellholt to conquer Vaith and retake Sunspear, Lord Harlan Tyrell and his entire army vanished in the sands, never to be heard from again. The reports of travelers in the area claim that occasionally the winds shift the sands to reveal bones and pieces of armor, but the sandy Dornishmen who wander the deep desert say that the sands are the burial grounds of thousands of years of battles, and the bones might be from any time.

The war against the Dornish entered a different phase after the release of Orys One-hand and the other handless lords, for King Aegon was by that time intent on revenge. The Targaryens unleashed their dragons, burning the defiant castles again and again. In return, the Dornish responded with fire of their own, sending a force to Cape Wrath in 8 AC that left half the rainwood ablaze and sacked half a dozen towns and villages. Matters escalated, and more Dornish seats fell to dragonfire in 9 AC. The Dornish responded a year later by sending a host under Lord Fowler that seized and burned the great Marcher castle of Nightsong and carried off its lords and defenders as hostages, whilst another army under Ser Joffrey Dayne marched to the very walls of Oldtown, razing the fields and villages outside it.

So again the Targaryens turned to their dragons, unleashing their fury upon Starfall and Skyreach and Hellholt. It was at Hellholt where the Dornish had their greatest success against the Targaryens. A bolt from a scorpion pierced the eye of Meraxes, and the great dragon and the queen who rode upon it fell from the sky. In her death throes, the dragon destroyed the castle's highest tower and part of the curtain wall. Queen Rhaenys's body was never returned to King's Landing.

FROM THE HISTORY OF ARCHMAESTER GYLDAYN

Whether Rhaenys Targaryen outlived her dragon remains a matter of dispute. Some say that she lost her seat and fell to her death, others that she was crushed beneath Meraxes in the castle yard. A few accounts claim the queen survived her dragon's fall, only to die a slow death by torment in the dungeons of the Ullers. The true circumstances of her demise will likely never be known, but the histories record that Rhaenys Targaryen, sister and wife to King Aegon I, perished at the Hellholt in Dorne in the tenth year After the Conquest.

RIGHT | *The death of Meraxes.*

The two years that followed were later called the years of the Dragon's Wroth. Grief-stricken at the death of their beloved sister, King Aegon and Queen Visenya set ablaze every castle, keep, and holdfast in Dorne at least once . . . save for Sunspear and the shadow city. Why this is so remains a matter of conjecture. In Dorne, it was said the Targaryens feared that Princess Meria had some cunning means of slaying dragons, something she had purchased from Lys. Likelier, however, is Archmaester Timotty's suggestion in his *Conjectures* that the Targaryens hoped to turn the rest of the Dornish, who suffered so much destruction, against the Martells, who were spared. If this is true, it may explain the letters dispatched from the marches to the Dornish houses, urging them to surrender and claiming that the Martells had betrayed them by buying their safety from the Targaryens at the expense of the rest of Dorne.

Regardless, the last and least glorious phase of the First Dornish War then began. The Targaryens placed prices on the heads of the Dornish lords, and half a dozen and more were killed by assassins—though only two of the killers ever lived to collect their reward. The Dornish responded in kind, and many were the pitiless deaths that followed. Even in the heart of King's Landing, no one was safe. Lord Fell was smothered in a brothel, and King Aegon himself was attacked on three separate occasions. When Queen Visenya and an escort were set upon, two of her guards died before she cut down the last villain herself with Dark Sister. Worse occurred at the hands of the Wyl of Wyl, whose deeds we need not recount; they are infamous enough and still remembered, especially in Fawnton and Old Oak.

Dorne was a blighted, burning ruin by this time, and still the Dornish hid and fought from the shadows, refusing to surrender. Even the smallfolk refused to yield, and the toll in lives was uncountable. When Princess Meria at last passed away in 13 AC, her throne passed to her son, the aged and failing Prince Nymor. He had had enough of war and sent a delegation led by his daughter, Princess Deria, to King's Landing. This delegation carried the skull of Meraxes with them, as a gift for the king. It was ill received by many— Queen Visenya and Orys Baratheon among them—and Lord Oakheart urged that Deria be sent to the meanest of brothels to service any man who would have her. But King Aegon Targaryen would not countenance such an act and instead listened to her words.

Dorne wanted peace, according to Deria—but the peace of two kingdoms no longer at war, not the peace between a vassal and a lord. Many urged His Grace against this, and the phrase "no peace without submission" was often heard in the halls of the Aegonfort. It was claimed that the king would look weak should he agree to such a demand and that the lords of the Reach and stormlands who had suffered so much for his cause would be angered.

Swayed by such considerations, it is said, King Aegon was determined to refuse the offer until Princess Deria placed in his hands a private letter from her father, Prince Nymor. Aegon read it upon the Iron Throne, and men say that when he rose, his hand was bleeding, so hard had he clenched it. He burned the letter and departed immediately on Balerion's back for Dragonstone. When he returned the next morning, he agreed to the peace and signed a treaty to that effect.

What the letter contained, none know to this day, though many have speculated. Did Nymor reveal that Rhaenys lived still, broken and mutilated, and that he would end her suffering if Aegon ended hostilities? Was the letter ensorceled? Did he threaten to take all the wealth of Dorne to hire the Faceless Men to kill Aegon's young son and heir, Aenys? These questions shall never be answered, it seems.

The result, however, was a peace that lasted through the troubles of the Vulture King and beyond. There were other Dornish Wars, to be sure, and even during times of peace, raiders out of Dorne continued to descend from the Red Mountains in search of plunder in the richer, greener lands to the north and west.

Prince Qoren Martell did lead the Dornish to fight in support of the Triarchy when they warred with Prince Daemon Targaryen and the Sea Snake over the Stepstones. During the Dance of the Dragons, both sides courted the Dornishmen, but Prince Qoren refused to take part: "Dorne has danced with dragons before," he was reported to have said in response to Ser Otto Hightower's letter. "I would sooner sleep with scorpions."

It was not until the ascent of King Daeron I that the treaty of eternal peace proved to be less than eternal, and we know the cost of that. The Young Dragon's conquest of Dorne was a glorious feat, rightly celebrated in song and story, but it lasted less than a summer and cost many thousands of lives, including that of the bold young king himself. It was left to Daeron's brother and successor, King Baelor I the Blessed, to make the peace, and the cost of that was grievous as well.

The later attempt by King Aegon IV the Unworthy to invade Dorne with "dragons" of his own design is hardly

worthy of discussion; it was a mad folly, start to finish, and ended in humiliation. It was Aegon's son, King Daeron II the Good, who finally brought Dorne into the realm . . . not with iron and fire but with soft swords and smiles and a pair of well-considered marriages, and a solemn treaty that granted the Dornish princes their style and their privileges and guaranteed that their own laws and customs should always prevail in Dorne.

Dorne continued to be closely allied with House Targaryen in the years that followed, with the Martells supporting the Targaryens against the Blackfyre Pretenders and sending spears to fight the Ninepenny Kings on the Stepstones. Their loyal service was rewarded when Rhaegar Targaryen, Prince of Dragonstone and heir to the Iron Throne, took to wife Princess Elia Martell of Sunspear, and sired two children by her. But for the madness of Rhaegar's father, Aerys II, a prince of Dornish blood might very well have one day ruled the realm, but the upheavals of Robert's Rebellion brought about the end of Prince Rhaegar, his wife, and his children.

Prince Qoren's daughter would be of a different mind. Princess Aliandra came young to her seat and thought herself a new Nymeria. A fiery young woman, she encouraged her lords and knights to prove themselves worthy of her favors by raiding in the marches, but also showed great favor to Lord Alyn Velaryon when his first great journey took him to Sunspear, and again when he returned from the Sunset Sea.

ABOVE | *Aegon the Conqueror reading the Prince of Dorne's missive.*

SUNSPEAR

Sunspear's history is a curious one. Having been little more than the squat, ugly keep called the Sandship in early days under the Martells, beautiful towers bearing all the hallmarks of Rhoynish fashion would eventually spring up around it. It became known as Sunspear when the sun of the Rhoyne was wedded to the spear of the Martells. In time, the Tower of the Sun and the Spear Tower were both constructed—the great golden dome of the one, and the slender, high spire of the other becoming the first things that visitors beheld by land or by sea.

The castle sits on a spur of land, surrounded on three sides by water . . . and on the fourth side by the shadow city. Though the Dornish may call it a city, it remains no more than a town, and a queer, dusty, ugly town at that. The Dornish built up against the walls of the Sunspear, then built up against the walls of their neighbors' homes, and so on out, until the shadow city took on its current form. Today, it is a warren of narrow alleys, bazaars filled with the spices of Dorne and the east, and the homes of the Dornish built of mud brick that remains cool even in the height of the burning summer.

The Winding Walls were raised some seven hundred years ago, wrapping Sunspear and winding throughout the shadow city in a snaking, defensive curtain that would force even the boldest enemy to lose their way. Only the Threefold Gate provides a straight path to the castle, cutting through the Winding Walls, and these gates are heavily defended at need.

ABOVE | *A lady of House Martell in the Dornish desert.* RIGHT | *Sunspear.*

Beyond the Sunset Kingdom

OTHER LANDS

WESTEROS FORMS BUT one small part of our world, the far reaches of which yet remain unknown even to the wisest of men. Though our purpose here was to chronicle the history of the Seven Kingdoms, it would be remiss of us to ignore the other lands beyond the seas—at least in brief—for each has its own character and contributes its own colors and patterns to the vast tapestry that we call the known world.

Sadly, the Citadel's knowledge grows thinner the farther we travel from the lands that the men of the east call the Sunset Kingdoms, for congress with the more distant realms of Essos has ever been sparse. We know even less about the southern reaches of Sothoryos and far Ulthos, and nothing at all about whatever lands may lie beyond the Last Light and across the Sunset Sea.

And the same strictures, of course, apply to time as well as distance. As we have shown with Westeros itself, the more ancient the civilization, the less that can truly be

known of it. Thus, I will neglect entirely the vanished civilizations of Valyria and Old Ghis and whatever remnants of those cultures remain—whose known particulars I have already touched upon elsewhere in this volume. While as for mysterious Qarth, I can point to no better source than Colloquo Votar's *Jade Compendium*, the foremost work on the lands around the Jade Sea.

Yet still there are kernels of knowledge to impart, even from the most exotic of locales . . . though much and more of what we know of these far places derives from travelers' tales and legends and should be viewed as such.

For now, let us begin with our closest and best-known neighbors, the Free Cities. Their histories are known to us from the records their own scholars and magisters have made over centuries, reaching to the earliest times of their establishment as freeholds. It is thanks to these same records that something of the histories of the peoples who preceded the Valyrians are known to us.

O
ne issue that plagues all studies of the ancient records is how differently the varied cultures reckon days and seasons and years. Archmaester Walgram's great work, *The Reckoning of Time*, delves deeply into this problem, but there is little consensus on what the dates we have actually mean in our own reckoning.

PREVIOUS PAGES | *The mist-enshrouded ruins of Chroyane, the festival city of the Rhoynar.*   ABOVE | *The coins of the Free Cities (top l. to r.) Braavos, Pentos, Lys, Myr, Tyrosh; (bottom l. to r.) Volantis (front and back), Norvos, Qohor, Lorath.*

THE FREE CITIES

ESSOS, THE VAST continent across the narrow sea, teems with strange, exotic, and ancient civilizations, some still extant and striving, others long fallen and lost to legend. Most of these are far too distant to be of any concern to the people of the Seven Kingdoms, save mayhaps for those seafarers bold enough to sail strange waters in search of gold and glory.

The Nine Free Cities, however, are our closest neighbors and chief partners in trade, and their histories are much entwined with our own. For centuries, trading galleys have sailed up and down the narrow sea, delivering fine tapestries, polished lenses, delicate lace, exotic fruits, strange spices, and myriad other goods, in return for gold and wool and other such products. In Oldtown, King's Landing, Lannisport, and every port from Eastwatch to the Planky Town, sailors, bankers, and merchants from the Free Cities can be found, buying and selling and telling their tales.

Each of the Free Cities has its own history and character, and each has come to have its own tongue. These are all corruptions of the original, pure form of High Valyrian, dialects that drift further from their origin with each new century since the Doom befell the Freehold.

Eight of the Nine Free Cities are proud daughters of Valyria that was, still ruled by the descendants of the original colonists who established themselves there hundreds or thousands of years ago. In these cities, Valyrian blood is still greatly prized. The ninth stands as an exception, for

Braavos of the Hundred Isles was founded by escaped slaves fleeing their Valyrian masters. Those first Braavosi came from every land beneath the sun, it is said, but as centuries passed, they bred with one another regardless of race or creed or language to form a new mongrel people.

We speak of Nine Free Cities, though across the width of Essos one may find many other Valyrian towns, settlements, and outposts, some larger and more populous than Gulltown, White Harbor, or even Lannisport. The distinction that sets the Nine apart is not their size but their origins. At their height before the Doom, other cities, such as Mantarys, Volon Therys, Oros, Tyria, Draconys, Elyria, Mhysa Faer, Rhyos, and Aquos Dhaen were grand and glorious and rich, yet for all their pride and power, none ever ruled itself. They were governed by men and women sent out from Valyria to govern in the name of the Freehold.

Such was never true of Volantis and the rest of the Nine. Though born of Valyria, each was independent of its mother from birth. All but Braavos were dutiful daughters, neither making war upon Valyria nor defying the dragon lords in any matter of significance; they remained willing allies and trading partners of their mother and looked to the Lands of the Long Summer for leadership in times of crisis. In lesser matters, however, the Nine Free Cities went their own ways, under the rule of their own priests and princes and archons and triarchs.

LORATH

The Free City of Lorath stands upon the western end of the largest in a cluster of low, stony islands in the Shivering Sea north of Essos, near the mouth of Lorath Bay. The city's domains include the three principal islands of the archipelago, a score of smaller isles and outcrops (almost all uninhabited save for seals and seabirds), and a thickly forested peninsula south of the isles. The Lorathi also claim dominion over the waters of Lorath Bay, but fishing fleets from Braavos and whalers and sealers out of Ib often venture into the bay, for Lorath does not have sufficient strength to make good its claim.

In former days Lorath's rule extended as far east as the Axe, but the city's power has dwindled over the centuries, and today the Lorathi exercise effective control over only

the southern and eastern shores of Lorath Bay; the western shore of the bay is part of the domains of Braavos.

Lorath is the smallest, poorest, and least populous of the Nine Free Cities. Save for Braavos, it is also the northernmost. Its location, far from the trade routes, has helped to make it the most isolated of the "daughters of Valyria that was." Though the Lorathi isles themselves are bleak and stony, the surrounding waters teem with shoals of cod, whales, and grey leviathans that gather and breed in the bay, and the outlying rocks and sea stacks are home to great colonies of walrus and seal. Salt cod, walrus tusks, sealskins, and whale oil form the greater part of the city's trade.

In ancient days, the isles were home to the mysterious race of men known as the mazemakers, who vanished long before the dawn of true history, leaving no trace of themselves save for their bones and the mazes they built.

Others followed the mazemakers on Lorath in the centuries that followed. For a time the isles were home to a small, dark, hairy people, akin to the men of Ib. Fisherfolk, they lived along the coasts and shunned the great mazes of their predecessors. They in turn were displaced by Andals, pushing north from Andalos to the shores of Lorath Bay

Sprawling constructs of bewildering complexity, made from blocks of hewn stone, the mazemakers' constructions are scattered across the isles—and one, badly overgrown and sunk deep into the earth, has been found on Essos proper, on the peninsula south of Lorath. Lorassyon, the second largest of the Lorath isles, is home to a vast maze that fills more than three-quarters of the surface area of the island and includes four levels beneath the ground, with some passages descending five hundred feet.

Scholars still debate the purpose of these mazes. Were they fortifications, temples, towns? Or did they serve some other, stranger purpose? The mazemakers left no written records, so we shall never know. Their bones tell us that they were massively built and larger than men, though not so large as giants. Some have suggested that mayhaps the maze-makers were born of interbreeding between human men and giant women. We do not known why they disappeared, though Lorathi legend suggests they were destroyed by an enemy from the sea: merlings in some versions of the tale, selkies and walrus-men in others.

and across the bay in longships. Clad in mail and wielding iron swords and axes, the Andals swept across the islands, slaughtering the hairy men in the name of their seven-faced god and taking their women and children as slaves.

Soon each island had its own king, whilst the largest boasted four. Ever a quarrelsome people, the Andals spent the next thousand years warring one upon the other, but at last a warrior styling himself Qarlon the Great brought all the islands under his sway. The histories, such as they are, claim he raised a great wooden keep at the center of Lorassyon's vast, haunted maze and decorated his halls with the heads of his slain foes.

It was Qarlon's dream to make himself King of All Andals, and to that end he went forth time and time again against the petty kings of Andalos. After twenty years and as many wars, the writ of Qarlon the Great extended from the lagoon where Braavos would one day rise all the way east to the Axe, and as far south as the headwaters of the Upper Rhoyne and Noyne.

But his southward expansion brought him into conflict not only with other Andal kings but also the Free City of Norvos on the Noyne. When the Norvoshi closed the river against him, he left his hall in the maze to lead the attack against them, defeating them in two pitched battles in the hills. Unwisely, he took these victories too much to heart and marched against Norvos itself. The Norvoshi sent to Valyria for help, and the Freehold rose to the defense of its distant daughter, though all the lands of the Andals and the Rhoynar lay between them.

Distances meant little and less to the dragonlords in the summer of their power, however. It is written in *The Fires of the Freehold* that a hundred dragons took to the skies, following the great river north to descend upon the Andals as they lay siege to Norvos. Qarlon the Great burned with his army, and afterward the dragonlords flew onward, bringing blood and fire to the isles of Lorath. Qarlon's great keep went up in flames, as did the towns and fishing villages along his shores. Even the great stones of the mazes were scorched and blackened by the firestorms that swept across the islands. It is said that not a man, woman, or child survived the Scouring of Lorath, so hot did those fires burn.

Thereafter the Lorathi isles remained uninhabited for more than a century. Seals and walrus returned in great numbers, and crabs scuttled through the scorched and silent mazes. Whalers from the Port of Ibben put ashore to mend their hulls or find freshwater, but they never ventured inland, for the islands were said to be haunted, and the Ibbenese believed any man accursed who went beyond the sound of the sea.

When men at last returned to the isles to live, they were men from Valyria itself. Thirteen hundred and twenty-two years before the Doom, a sect of religious dissidents left the Freehold to establish a temple upon Lorath's main isle.

These new Lorathi were worshippers of Boash, the Blind God. Rejecting all other deities, the followers of Boash ate no flesh, drank no wine, and walked barefoot through the world, clad only in hair shirts and hides. Their eunuch priests wore eyeless hoods in honor of their god;

only in darkness, they believed, would their third eye open, allowing them to see the "higher truths" of creation that lay concealed behind the world's illusions. The worshippers of Boash believed that all life was sacred and eternal; that men and women were equal; that lords and peasants, rich and poor, slave and master, man and beast were all alike, all equally worthy, all creatures of god.

An essential part of their doctrine was an extreme abnegation of self; only by freeing themselves of human vanity could men hope to become one with the godhood. Accordingly, the Boash'i put aside even their own names, and spoke of themselves as "a man" or "a woman" rather than say "I" or "me" or "mine." Though the cult of the Blind God withered and died out more than a thousand years ago, certain of these habits of speech endure even now in Lorath, where men and women of the noble classes regard it as inutterably vulgar to speak of one's self directly.

The Blind God and his followers made the ancient mazes of the first Lorathi their towns, temples, and tombs, and dominated the islands for three-quarters of a century. But as the years passed, other men, who did not share their faith, began to cross the bay to hunt seal and walrus or fish for cod. Some chose to stay. Huts and hovels sprang up anew along the shores and became villages. Men came from Ib and Andalos and other, stranger lands, and the islands became a refuge for freedmen and escaped slaves from Valyria and its proud daughters, for the priests of the Blind God taught that every man was the equal of every other. Three fishing villages on the western end of the largest isle waxed so populous and prosperous that they grew together into a town, and with the passage of years stone houses grew where daub-and-wattle hovels once stood, and the town became a city.

These new Lorathi were at first subservient to the followers of Boash who had come before them, and for many years the priests of the Blind God continued to rule the islands. In time, however, the numbers of newcomers swelled whilst the ranks of the faithful dwindled. The worship of Boash fell away, as the priests who remained became more worldly and corrupt, forsaking their hair shirts, hoods, and piety and growing fat and rich off the taxes they extracted from those they ruled. Finally the fishermen, farmers, and other smallfolk rose in rebellion, throwing off the shackles of Boash. The remaining acolytes of the Blind God were slaughtered—all save a small handful who fled to the great temple maze on Lorassyon, where they remained for the best part of a century, until the last of them died.

After the fall of the blind priests, Lorath became a freehold after the manner of Valyria, ruled over by a council of three princes. The Harvest Prince was chosen by a vote of all those who owned land upon the islands, the Fisher Prince by all those who owned ships, the Prince of the Streets by the acclamation of the free men of the city. Once chosen, each prince served for life.

These three princes continue to sit today, though the titles have become purely ceremonial. The true authority resides with a council of magisters made up of nobles, priests, and merchants. Its isolation meant that the Lorathi were little involved in the events of the Century of Blood, save for those few who sold their swords to Braavos or Norvos.

Today Lorath is generally accounted the least of the Nine Free Cities; the poorest, the most isolated, the most backward. Though possessed of large fleets of fishing vessels, the Lorathi build few warships and have little in the way of military power. Few Lorathi ever leave their islands, and fewer still ever make their way to Westeros. They prefer to trade with their nearer neighbors, Norvos, Braavos, and Ib.

NORVOS

The Free City of Norvos stands upon the eastern banks of the river Noyne, one of the greatest of the vassal streams of the Rhoyne. The high city, ringed about by mighty stone walls, looms above high, stony bluffs. Three hundred feet below, the lower city spreads along the muddy shores, defended by moats, ditches, and a timber palisade much overgrown with moss. The ancient nobility of Norvos lives in the upper city, dominated by the great fortress-temple of the bearded priests; the poor huddle below amongst the wharves, brothels, and beer halls that line the riverfront. The two parts of the city are joined only by a massive stone stair, called the Sinner's Steps.

Great Norvos, as the Norvoshi name their city, is surrounded by rugged limestone hills and dense, dark forests of oak and pine and beech, home to bears and boars and wolves, and game of all sorts. The city's domains stretch as far as the western bank of the Darkwash to the east and the Upper Rhoyne to the west. Norvoshi river galleys rule the

PREVIOUS PAGES | *The priests of the Blind God among the mazes of Lorath.*

Noyne as far south as the ruins of Ny Sar, where she joins the Rhoyne. Great Norvos even claims dominion over the Axe upon the Shivering Sea, though this claim is disputed, often bloodily, by the Ibbenese.

Close by the city walls, the Norvoshi work the land on the terraced farms. Farther out, men gather behind stout timber palisades in holdfasts and walled villages. The streams here are swift-running and stony, and caverns honeycomb the endless hills. Many of the caves are home to the brown bears common to these northern lands, others to packs of red or grey wolves. In some can be found the bones of giants

Like her sister cities Lorath and Qohor, the Free City of Norvos as we know her today was originally founded by religious dissidents from Valyria. At the height of her power, the Freehold was home to a hundred temples; some had tens of thousands of worshippers, some precious few, but no faith was forbidden in Valyria, nor were any exalted above the others.

Many Valyrians worshipped more than one god, turning to different deities according to their needs; more, it is said, worshipped none at all. Most regarded freedom of faith as a hallmark of any truly advanced civilization. Yet

---

*S*ome scholars have suggested that the dragonlords regarded all faiths as equally false, believing themselves to be more powerful than any god or goddess. They looked upon priests and temples as relics of a more primitive time, though useful for placating "slaves, savages, and the poor" with promises of a better life to come. Moreover, a multiplicity of gods helped to keep their subjects divided and lessened the chances of their uniting under the banner of a single faith to overthrow their overlords. Religious tolerance was to them a means of keeping the peace in the Lands of the Long Summer.

---

and painted walls that speak of men's dwelling here in ages past. One cavern system, some hundred leagues northwest of Norvos, is so vast and deep that legend claims it is the entrance to the underworld; Lomas Longstrider visited it once and counted it as one of the world's seven natural wonders in his book *Wonders*.

Though Great Norvos dominates the headwaters of the Rhoyne today, the Norvoshi are not descended from the Rhoynar who ruled that mighty river of old. Like the other Free Cities, Norvos is a daughter of Valyria. Yet before the Valyrians another people dwelt along the Noyne where Norvos stands today, raising rude villages of their own.

Who were these predecessors? Some believe them to have been kin to the mazemakers of Lorath, but that seems unlikely, for they built in wood, not stone, and left no mazes to confound us. Others suggest that they were cousins of the men of Ib. Most, however, believe them to have been Andals.

Whoever these first Norvoshi might have been, their towns did not survive. Legend tells us they were driven from the Noyne by an onslaught of hairy men out of the east, surely some close kin of the Ibbenese. These invaders in turn were expelled by the fabled prince of Ny Sar, Garris the Grey, but the Rhoynar did not linger, preferring the more temperate climes of the lower river to the dark skies and cold winds of the hills.

to some, this plethora of gods was a source of continuing grievance. "The man who honors all the gods honors none at all," a prophet of the Lord of Light, R'hllor the Red, once famously declared. And even at the height of its glory, the Freehold was home to many who believed fiercely in their own particular god or goddess and regarded all others as false idols, frauds, or demons, bent on deceiving mankind.

Dozens of such sects flourished in Valyria, sometimes quarreling violently with one another. Inevitably, some found the tolerance of the Freehold to be intolerable and set out into the wilderness to found cities of their own, godly cities where only the "true faith" would be practiced. We have already spoken of the followers of the Blind God Boash who founded Lorath and what befell them there. Qohor was settled by worshippers of that grim deity known only as the Black Goat, as shall be related shortly. But the sect that settled Norvos is as strange, or stranger, than either of these, and far more secretive. Even the very name of their god is revealed only to initiates. That he is a stern deity cannot be doubted, for his priests wear hair shirts and untanned hides and practice ritual flagellation as part of their worship. Once initiated, they are forbidden to shave or cut their hair.

From the founding to the present, Great Norvos has been a theocracy, ruled by its bearded priests, who are

Only Norvoshi priests are permitted beards; freeborn Norvoshi of both high and low birth favor long, unswept mustachios, whilst slaves and women are shaved bare. Norvoshi women, indeed, shave off all their body hair, though the ladies of the nobility will don wigs, especially when thrust into the company of men from other lands and cities.

themselves ruled by their god, who speaks his commands to them from the depths of their fortress-temple, which only true believers may enter and live. Though the city has a council of magisters, its members are selected by the god, speaking through his priests. To enforce obedience and keep the peace, the bearded priests keep a holy guard of slave soldiers, fierce fighters who bear the brand of a double-bladed axe upon their breasts and ritually marry the longaxes they fight with.

Travelers paint upper Norvos as a grim grey place of sweltering summers, bitter cold winters, harsh winds, and unending prayer. The lower city, with its riverman's haunts, brothels, and taverns, is said to be much livelier. There, out of the sight of priests and nobles alike, lowborn Norvoshi feast on red meat and river pike, washed down with strong black beer and fermented goat's milk, whilst bears dance for their amusement and (it is whispered) slave women mate with wolves in torchlit cellars.

Archmaester Perestan notes the importance the Norvoshi give to the axe as a symbol of power and might and proposes that this is proof that the Andals were the first to settle Norvos, suggesting the bearded priests took the emblem from ruins they found as they established Great Norvos. As he argues, next to the carvings of seven-pointed stars, carvings of a double-bladed axe appeared to have been the next most favored symbol of the holy warriors who conquered the old Seven Kingdoms.

Etched in Stone by Archmaester Harmune contains a catalog of such carvings found throughout the Vale. Stars and axes are found from the Fingers into the Mountains of the Moon, and even as far into the Vale of Arryn as the base of the Giant's Lance. Harmune supposes that, with time, the Andals became more devoted to the symbol of the seven-pointed star and so the axe fell by the wayside as an emblem of the Faith.

It should be said, however, that not all agree that these carvings represent axes. In his refutation, Maester Evlyn argues that what Harmune calls axes are in fact hammers, the sign of the Smith. He explains the irregularity of the depictions of these hammers as the result of the Andals' being warriors, not artisans.

No account of Great Norvos is complete without a mention of the city's three bells, whose peals govern every aspect of city life, telling the Norvoshi when to rise, when to sleep, when to work, when to rest, when to take arms, when to pray (often), and even when they are permitted to have carnal relations (rather less often, if the tales be true). Each of the bells has its own distinctive "voice," whose sound is known to all true Norvoshi. The bells bear the names Noom, Narrah, and Nyel; Lomas Longstrider was so taken by them that he named them one of his nine *Wonders Made by Man*.

QOHOR

EVEN MORE MYSTERIOUS than Norvos and Lorath is their sinister sister, the Free City of Qohor, easternmost of all the daughters of Valyria. Qohor stands on the river Qhoyne on the western edge of the vast, dark, primordial forest to which she gives her name, the greatest wood in all of Essos.

In folklore, even as far as Westeros, Qohor is sometimes known as the City of Sorcerers, for it is widely believed that the dark arts are practiced here even to this day. Divination, bloodmagic, and necromancy are whispered of, though such reports can seldom be proved. One truth remains undisputed, however: The dark god of Qohor, the deity known as the

Lake and the markets of Selhorys, Valysar, Volon Therys, and Old Volantis.

The Forest of Qohor also yields up furs and pelts of all kinds, many rare and fine and highly prized, as well as silver, tin, and amber. The vast forest has never been fully explored, according to the maps and scrolls at the Citadel, and it likely conceals many mysteries and wonders at its heart. Like many northerly forests, it contains elk and deer in great numbers, along with wolves, tree cats, boars of truly monstrous size, spotted bears, and even a species of lemur—a creature known from the Summer Isles and Sothoryos, but otherwise rarely seen farther north. These lemurs are said

A preserved example of a lemur from the Forest of Qohor can be found stuffed and mounted in the Citadel, though so many hands have patted it for luck in their examinations that its fur has long since fallen out.

Black Goat, demands daily blood sacrifice. Calves, bullocks, and horses are the animals most often brought before the Black Goat's altars, but on holy days condemned criminals go beneath the knives of his cowled priests, and in times of danger and crisis it is written that the high nobles of the city offer up their own children to placate the god, that he might defend the city.

The woods that surround Qohor are the principal source of the city's wealth. The earliest settlement here was a lumber camp, the city's histories reveal. Even to this day, it is as hunters and foresters the Qohorik are most famed. The shining cities and sprawling towns of the lower Rhoyne hunger for wood, and their own forests have long ago been depleted, cut down and plowed under for fields and farms. Huge barges heavy with timber depart the docks of Qohor every day for the long voyage down the Qhoyne to Dagger

to have silver-white fur and purple eyes, and are sometimes called Little Valyrians.

The artisans of Qohor are far famed. Qohorik tapestries, woven primarily by the women and children of the city, are just as fine as those woven in Myr, though less costly. Exquisite (if somewhat disturbing) wood carvings can be bought in Qohor's market, and the city's forges have no peer. Qohorik swords, knives, and armor are superior to even the best castle-forged steel of Westeros, and the city's smiths have perfected the art of infusing deep color into the metals of their work, producing armor and weaponry of lasting beauty. Only here, in all the world, has the art of reworking Valyrian steel been preserved, its secrets jealously guarded.

Qohor is also famed as the gateway to the east, where trading caravans bound for Vaes Dothrak and the fabled lands beyond the Bones are outfitted and provisioned before heading into the gloom of the forest, the desolation that was

LEFT | *A procession honoring the sacred god of Norvos.*

Maester Pol's treatise on Qohorik metalworking, written during several years of residence in the Free City, reveals just how jealously the secrets are guarded: He was thrice publicly whipped and cast out from the city for making too many inquiries. The final time, his hand was also removed following the allegation that he stole a Valyrian steel blade. According to Pol, the true reason for his final exile was his discovery of blood sacrifices—including the killing of slaves as young as infants—which the Qohorik smiths used in their efforts to produce a steel to equal that of the Freehold.

refresh themselves after the crossing and sell and trade the treasures they have acquired. This trade has helped to make Qohor one of the richest of the Free Cities and surely the most exotic (though it is said the city was ten times richer still before the destruction of Sarnor).

Strong stone walls protect Qohor, but the people of the city are not of a martial bent. The Qohorik are merchants, not fighters. Apart from a small city watch, the defense of the city is entrusted to slaves—the eunuch infantry known as the Unsullied, bred and trained in the ancient Ghiscari city Astapor upon the shores of Slaver's Bay. During the Century of Blood that followed the Doom of Valyria, Qohor and Norvos made common cause against Old Volantis when the Volantenes attempted to bring all the Free Cities under their heel. Since that time, those two Free Cities have been more often allies than enemies, though it is known that the bearded priests of Norvos regard the Black Goat of Qohor as a demon, with an especially vile and treacherous nature.

Four hundred years ago, when a Dothraki *khal* named Temmo rode out of the east with fifty thousand savage horsemen at his back, three thousand Unsullied turned him back at the gates of Qohor, withstanding no fewer than eighteen charges before Khal Temmo died and his successor bid his men cut off their braids and toss them at the feet of the surviving eunuchs. From that time to this, the Qohorik have relied upon the Unsullied to protect their city (though they have been known to hire free companies as well in time of peril and to offer lavish gifts to Dothraki *khals* to persuade them to pass on).

ABOVE | *A sacrificial altar dedicated to the Black Goat.*

THE QUARRELSOME DAUGHTERS: MYR, LYS, AND TYROSH

The easternmost of the Free Cities—Lorath, Norvos, and Qohor—have little commerce with Westeros. For the rest, it is a different matter. Braavos, Pentos, and Volantis are all coastal cities blessed with great harbors. Trade is their life's blood, and their ships travel to the far ends of the earth, from Yi Ti and Leng and Asshai-by-the-Shadow in the far east, to Lannisport and Oldtown on Westeros. Each city has its own customs and histories. Each has its own gods, too—although the red priesthood of R'hllor holds sway in all of them and often wields considerable power. Over the centuries, their rivalries have been many, and the squabbles and wars between them could—and do—fill volumes.

All this is also true of Myr, Lys, and Tyrosh, those three quarrelsome daughters whose endless feuds and struggles for dominion have so often managed to embroil the kings and knights of Westeros. These three cities surround the large, fertile "heel" of Essos, the promontory that divides the Summer Sea from the narrow sea and was once part of the land bridge that joined that continent to Westeros. The fortress city of Tyrosh stands upon the northernmost and easternmost of the Stepstones, the chain of islands that remained when the Arm of Dorne fell into the sea. Myr rises on the mainland, where an ancient Valyrian dragonroad meets the tranquil waters of a vast gulf known as the Sea of Myrth. Lys is to the south, on a small archipelago of islands in the Summer Sea. All three cities have claimed part (or all) of the lands between them, which we know today as the Disputed Lands, for all attempts to fix borders between the domains of Tyrosh, Myr, and Lys have failed, and countless wars have been fought for their possession.

In history, culture, custom, language, and religion, these three cities have more in common with one another than with any of the other Free Cities. They are mercantile cities, protected by high walls and hired sellswords, dominated by wealth rather than birth, cities where trade is considered a more honorable profession than arms. Lys and Myr are ruled by conclaves of magisters, chosen from amongst the wealthiest and noblest men of the city; Tyrosh is governed by an archon, selected from amongst the members of a similar conclave. All three are slave cities, where bondsmen outnumber the freeborn three to one. All are ports, and the salt sea is their life's blood. Like Valyria, their mother, these three daughters have no established faith. Temples and shrines to many different gods line their streets and crowd their waterfronts.

Yet the rivalries between them are long-rooted, giving rise to deep-seated enmities that have kept them divided, and oft at war with one another, for centuries—to the undoubted benefit of the lords and kings of Westeros, for these three rich and powerful cities, if united, would make for a formidable and dangerous neighbor.

Lys, the most beautiful of the Free Cities, enjoys what is perhaps the most salubrious climate in all the known world. Bathed by cool breezes, warmed by the sun, on a fertile island where palms and fruit trees grow in profusion, surrounded by blue-green waters teeming with fish, "Lys the Lovely" was founded as a retreat by the dragonlords of old Valyria, a paradise where they might refresh themselves with fine wines and sweet maids and soothing musics before returning to the fires of the Freehold. To this day, Lys remains "a feast for the senses, a balm for the soul." Its pillow

ABOVE | *A Myrish tradeswoman.*

The truth of the combined strength of Myr, Lys, and Tyrosh was proved when these three cities did in fact unite, albeit briefly, in the aftermath of their victory over Volantis at the Battle of the Borderland. Pledging eternal friendship with one another, they came together in 96 AC as the Triarchy, though in Westeros their union was best known as the Kingdom of the Three Daughters. The Triarchy began with the stated aim of cleansing the Stepstones of pirates and corsairs. This was welcomed in the Seven Kingdoms and elsewhere at first, for the pirates greatly stifled trade. The Three Daughters won a swift victory over the pirates, only to begin to demand increasingly exorbitant tolls of passing swifts after gaining control of the islands and the channels between. Soon their rapaciousness surpassed that of the pirates they replaced—especially when the Lyseni started demanding handsome youths and beautiful maidens as their toll.

For a time, the Triarchy found itself overmatched by the power of Corlys Velaryon and Daemon Targaryen and lost much of the Stepstones, but the men of Westeros were soon distracted by their own quarrels, and the Three Daughters reasserted their power—only to be brought down by internal conflicts following the murder of a Lyseni admiral by a rival for the affections of the famous courtesan called the Black Swan (the niece of Lord Swann, she in time came to rule Lys in all but name). The rival alliance of Braavos, Pentos, and Lorath helped bring about the end of the Kingdom of the Three Daughters.

houses are famed through all the world, and sunsets here are said to be more beautiful than anywhere else on earth. The Lyseni themselves are beautiful as well, for here more than anywhere else in the known world the old Valyrian bloodlines still run strong.

Tyrosh, an altogether harder city, began as a military outpost, as its inner walls of fused black dragonstone testify. Valryian records tell us the fort was raised initially to control shipping passing through the Stepstones. Not long after the city's founding, however, a unique variety of sea snail was

discovered in the waters off the bleak, stony island where the fortress stood. These snails secreted a substance that, when properly treated, yielded a deep dark reddish dye that soon became wildly fashionable amongst the nobility of Valyria. As the snails were found nowhere else, merchants came to Tyrosh by the thousands, and the outpost grew into a major city in the space of a generation. Tyroshi dyers soon learned to produce scarlet, crimson, and deep indigo dyes as well by varying the diet of the snails. Later centuries saw them devise dyes of a hundred other shades and hues, some naturally and some through alchemy. Brightly colored garments won the favor of lords and princes the world over, and the dyes that produced them all came from Tyrosh. The city grew rich, and with wealth came ostentation. Tyroshi delight in flamboyant display, and men and women both delight in dyeing their hair in garish and unnatural colors.

The origins of Myr are murkier. The Myrmen are believed by certain maesters to be akin to the Rhoynar, as many of them share the same olive skin and dark hair as the river people, but this supposed link is likely spurious. There are certain signs that a city stood where Myr now stands even during the Dawn Age and the Long Night, raised by some ancient, vanished people, but the Myr we know was founded by a group of Valyrian merchant adventurers on the site of a walled Andal town whose inhabitants they butchered or enslaved. Trade has been the life of Myr ever since, and Myrish ships have plied the waters of the narrow sea for centuries. The artisans of Myr, many of slave birth, are also greatly renowned; Myrish lace and Myrish tapestries are said to be worth their weight in gold and spice, and Myrish lenses have no equal in all the world.

Whereas Lorath, Norvos, and Qohor were founded for religious reasons, the interests of Lys, Tyrosh, and Myr have always been mercantile. All three cities have large merchant fleets, and their traders sail all the world's seas. All three cities are deeply involved in the slave trade as well. Tyroshi slavers are especially aggressive, even going so far as to sail north beyond the Wall in search of wildling slaves, whilst the Lyseni are famously voracious in seeking out comely young boys and fair maids for their city's famous pillow houses.

The wife of King Viserys II Targaryen, who gave birth to both King Aegon IV (the Unworthy) and Prince Aemon the Dragonknight, was the Lady Larra Rogare of Lys. She was a great beauty of Valyrian descent, and seven years the prince's elder when she wed him at nine-and-ten. Her father, Lysandro Rogare, was the head of a wealthy banking family whose power waxed even greater following the alliance to the Targaryens. Lysandro assumed the style of First Magister for Life, and men spoke of him as Lysandro the Magnificent. But he and his brother Drazenko, the Prince Consort of Dorne, died within a day of one another, beginning the precipitous fall of the Rogares both in Lys and the Seven Kingdoms.

Lysandro's heir, Lysaro, spent vast sums in pursuit of power and fell afoul of the other magisters, even as his siblings became embroiled in plots to control the Iron Throne. After his fall, Lysaro Rogare was scourged to death at the Temple of Trade by those he had wronged. His siblings received less fatal punishments, and one among them—Moredo Rogare, the soldier who carried the Valyrian sword Truth—eventually led an army against Lys.

The Lyseni are also great breeders of slaves, mating beauty with beauty in hopes of producing ever more refined and lovely courtesans and bedslaves. The blood of Valyria still runs strong in Lys, where even the smallfolk oft boast pale skin, silver-gold hair, and the purple, lilac, and pale blue eyes of the dragonlords of old. The Lysene nobility values purity of blood above all and have produced many famous (and infamous) beauties. Even the Targaryen kings and princes of old sometimes turned to Lys in search of wives and paramours, for their blood as for their beauty. Aptly, many Lyseni worship a love goddess whose naked, wanton figure graces their coinage.

The wars, truces, alliances, and betrayals betwixt and between Lys, Myr, and Tyrosh are far too numerous to recount here. Many of their conflicts are so-called trade wars, fought entirely at sea, wherein the ships of the combatants are granted licenses to prey upon those of the foes—a practice that Grand Maester Merion once termed "piracy with a wax seal." During the trade war, only the crews of the warring ships faced death or piracy; the cities themselves were never threatened, and no battles were fought on land.

Far bloodier, though less frequent, were the land wars fought over the Disputed Lands—a formerly rich region that had been so devastated during the Century of Blood and afterward that today it is largely a wasteland of bone and ash and salted fields. Yet even in these conflicts, Tyrosh, Myr, and Lys seldom risked the lives of their own citizens, preferring instead to hire sellswords to fight for them.

The Disputed Lands has been the birthplace of more of these so-called free companies than any other place in the known world, beginning during the Century of Blood. Even today, there are twoscore free companies in the region;

PREVIOUS PAGES | *A council of the Triarchy.* ABOVE | *A Lyseni noblewoman.*

Among the oldest of the free companies is the Second Sons, founded by twoscore younger sons of noble houses who found themselves dispossessed and without prospects. Ever since, it has been a place where landless lords and exiled knights and adventurers could find a home. Many famous names from the Seven Kingdoms have served in the Second Sons at one time or another. Prince Oberyn Martell rode with them before founding his own company; Rodrik Stark, the Wandering Wolf, was counted one of them as well. The most famous Second Son was Ser Aegor Rivers, that bastard son of King Aegon IV known to history as Bittersteel, who fought with them in the first years of his exile before forming the Golden Company, which remains to this day the most powerful and celebrated of these sellsword bands, as well as (some claim) the most honorable.

Other companies of note include the Bright Banners, the Stormcrows, the Long Lances, and the Company of the Cat. Other companies besides the Golden Company have been formed by men from the Seven Kingdoms, such as the Stormbreakers, which was founded in the aftermath of the Dance of the Dragons, or the Company of the Rose, formed by wild men (and, according to some accounts, women) from the North who refused to bend the knee, after Torrhen Stark gave up his crown, and instead chose exile across the narrow sea.

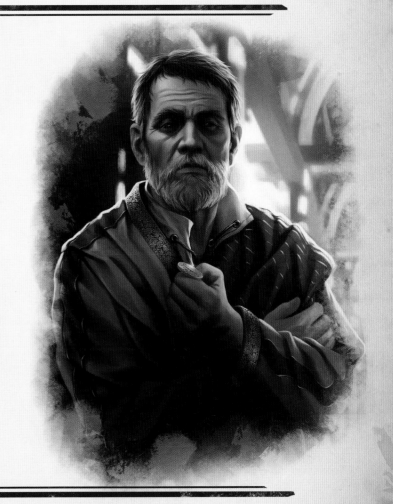

when not employed by the three quarrelsome daughters, the sellswords oft seek to carve out conquests of their own. Some have also been known to seek employment for their blades in the Seven Kingdoms, both before the Conquest and after.

The wars amongst Tyrosh, Lys, and Myr have not only fueled the births of the free companies in the Disputed Lands but have brought about the formation of fleets of pirates and seaborne mercenaries as well, sellsails ready to fight for whoever will pay. Most are based in the Stepstones, the isles that dot the narrow sea between the Broken Arm and the eastern coast.

These pirate fleets make any journey through the Stepstones treacherous. It is said that the swan-ships of the Summer Isles sometimes avoid the Stepstones entirely, risking the deep sea rather than chancing an attack by corsairs. Others with less skill at sea, and vessels less fit for the deep ocean, have no choice. These pirate dens, when they grow too volatile and numerous, are sometimes swept clean by the fleets of the archons of Tyrosh or the triarchs of Volantis or even the Sealords of Braavos. But they always manage to return.

In times past, the pirates have caused enough turmoil that royal fleets have been sent from King's Landing and Dragonstone to deal with them. Lord Oakenfist himself spent more than one season hunting pirates, to great acclaim, and the Young Dragon intended to wed a sister to the Sealord of Braavos to seal an alliance with him, with the aim of removing the pirates that were hindering trade with the newly conquered Dorne. Grand Maester Kaeth discusses this at length in *Lives of Four Kings*, arguing that here King Daeron erred, for talk of a marriage alliance with Braavos, which was at that time at war with Pentos and Lys, emboldened the other Free Cities to lend crucial aid to the Dornish rebels.

ABOVE | *A Tyroshi merchant.*

PENTOS

Pentos is the nearest of the Free Cities to King's Landing, and trading ships pass back and forth between the two cities on an almost daily basis. Founded by Valyrians as a trading outpost, Pentos soon absorbed the hinterlands surrounding it, from the Velvet Hills and the Little Rhoyne to the sea, including almost the whole of the ancient realm of Andalos, the original homeland of the Andals. The first Pentoshi were merchants, traders, seafarers, and farmers, with few of high birth amongst them; perhaps for this reason, they were less protective of their Valyrian blood and more willing to breed with the original inhabitants of the lands they ruled. As a consequence there is considerable Andal blood amongst the men of Pentos, making them perhaps our closest cousins.

Despite this, the Pentoshi hold to customs very different from those of the Seven Kingdoms. Pentos counts itself a daughter of Valyria—and the old blood can indeed be found there. In elder days, the city was ruled by a prince of high and noble birth, chosen from amongst the adult males of the so-called forty families. Once chosen, the Prince of Pentos ruled for life; when one prince died, another would be chosen, almost always from a different family.

Over the centuries, however, the power of the prince steadily eroded, whilst that of the city magisters who chose him grew. Today it is the council of magisters that rules Pentos, for all practical purposes; the prince's power is largely nominal, his duties almost entirely ceremonial. In the main, he presides over feasts and balls, carried from place to place in a rich palanquin with a handsome guard. Each new year, the prince must deflower two maidens, the maid of the sea and the maid of the fields. This ancient ritual—perhaps arising from the mysterious origins of pre-Valyrian Pentos—is meant to ensure the continued prosperity of Pentos on land and at sea. Yet, if there is famine or if a war is lost, the prince becomes not a ruler

Given the risks attendant to the office, not all the nobles of Pentos are eager to be chosen to wear the city's crown. Indeed, some have been known to refuse this ancient but perilous honor. The most recent and famous of these is the notorious sellsword captain called the Tattered Prince. As a youth, he was elected by the magisters of Pentos after a long drought and the execution of the previous prince in the year 262 AC. Rather than accept the honor, he fled the city, never to return. He sold his sword, taking part in battles in the Disputed Lands, then founded one of the newer free companies of the East, the Windblown.

but a sacrifice; his throat is slit so that the gods might be appeased. And then a new prince is chosen who might bring more fortune to the city.

For most of its history, slavery was widely practiced in Pentos, and Pentoshi ships played an active role in the slave trade. Several centuries ago, however, this practice brought the city into conflict with her northern neighbor, Braavos, the "bastard daughter of Valyria," founded by a fleet of escaped slaves. Over the course of the last two hundred years, no less than six wars have been fought between the two cities over this issue (and, it must be pointed out, for control of the rich lands and waters that lie between them).

Four of these ended in Braavosi victory and Pentoshi submission. The last of them, concluded one-and-ninety years ago, went so poorly for Pentos that no fewer than four princes were chosen and sacrificed within the span of a single year. The fifth man in this bloody succession, Prince Nevio Narratys, convinced the magisters to sue for peace after a rare victory—one, it was rumored, that Nevio purchased by means of bribes. In the peace accords, Pentos was forced to make certain concessions—most notably the abolition of slavery and a withdrawal from the slave trade.

These provisions remain the law in Pentos to this day though certain observers have noted that many Pentoshi ships evade the prohibition against the slave trade by running Lysene or Myrish banners up their masts when challenged,

whilst in the city itself there are tens of thousands of "free bond servants" who seem to be slaves in all but name, for they are collared and branded much like their counterparts in Lys, Myr, and Tyrosh, and subject to similar savage disciplines. In law, these bond servants are free men and women, with the right to refuse service as they will . . . provided they are not in debt to their masters. Almost all of them are, however, since the value of their labor is oft less than the costs of the food, clothing, and shelter provided them by those they serve, so that their debt grows rather than diminishes over time.

A further provision of the peace accords between Braavos and Pentos limits the Pentoshi to no more than twenty warships and prohibits them from hiring sellswords, entering into contracts with free companies, or maintaining any army beyond the city watch. Undoubtedly these are among the reasons that the Pentoshi are now notably less belligerent than the people of Tyrosh, Myr, and Lys. Despite its massive walls, Pentos is oft seen as the most vulnerable of the Free Cities.

For this reason, its magisters have adopted a conciliatory attitude not only toward the other Free Cities but also with the Dothraki horselords, cultivating a precarious friendship with a series of strong *khals* over the years, and showering lavish gifts and chests of gold upon any who brought their *khalasars* east of the Rhoyne.

VOLANTIS

The greatest, richest, and most powerful of the Nine Free cities are Braavos and Volantis. And there is a curious connection between the two, for in many ways they stand in opposition to one another. Braavos lies in the far north of Essos, and Volantis to the far south; Volantis is the oldest of the Free Cities, and Braavos the youngest; Braavos was founded by slaves, whilst Volantis is built upon their bones;

Braavos's greatest might is at sea, whilst that of Volantis is upon the land. Yet both remain formidable powers, their histories deeply marked by the Freehold of Valyria.

Ancient and glorious, Old Volantis—as the city is oft named—sprawls across one of the four mouths of the Rhoyne, where that mighty river flows into the Summer Sea. The older districts of the city lie upon the eastern banks, the newer on the west, but even the newest areas of Volantis are many centuries old. The two halves of the city are linked by the Long Bridge.

The heart of Old Volantis is the city-within-the-city—an immense labyrinth of ancient palaces, courtyards, towers, temples, cloisters, bridges, and cellars, all contained within the great oval of the Black Walls raised by the Freehold of Valyria in the first flush of its youthful expansion. Two hundred feet tall, and so thick that six four-horse chariots can race along their battlements side by side (as they do each year to celebrate the founding of the city), these seamless walls of fused black dragonstone, harder than steel or diamond, stand in mute testimony to Volantis's origins as a military outpost.

Only those who can trace their ancestry back to Old Valyria are allowed to dwell within the Black Walls; no slave, freedman, or foreigner is permitted to set foot within without the express invitation of a scion of the Old Blood.

For the first century of its existence, Volantis was little more than a military outpost established to protect the borders of the Valyrian empire, with no inhabitants save the soldiers of its garrison. From time to time dragonlords descended to take refreshment or meet with envoys from

and murder held sway, and eunuchs, pirates, cutpurses, and necromancers mingled freely.

In time the lawless city on the west bank became such a cesspit of crime and depravity that the triarchs had no choice but to send their slave soldiers across the Rhoyne to restore order and some semblance of decency. Strong tides and treacherous shifting currents made the crossings difficult, however, so after some years, the triarch Vhalaso the Munificent commanded that a bridge be built across the Rhoyne.

Those same tides and currents, and the river's width, made the building an epic task, requiring more than forty years and many millions of honors. Triarch Vhalaso did not live to see what he had wrought . . . but once completed, the Long Bridge had no rivals save for the Bridge of Dream in the Rhoynar festival city of Chroyane. Strong enough to support the weight of a thousand elephants (or so it is claimed), the Long Bridge of Volantis stands today as the longest bridge in all the known world. Lomas Longstrider named it one of the nine wonders made by man in his book of that title.

For much of its early history, Volantis benefited from the trade between Valyria and the Rhoynar, waxing ever more prosperous and powerful . . . whilst Sarhoy, the ancient

---

Many of the Old Blood of Volantis still keep the old gods of Valyria, but their faith is found primarily within the Black Walls. Without, the red god R'hllor is favored by many, especially among the slaves and freedmen of the city. The Temple of the Lord of Light in Volantis is said to be the greatest in all the world; in *Remnants of the Dragonlords*, Archmaester Gramyon claims that it is fully three times larger than the Great Sept of Baelor. All who serve within this mighty temple are slaves, bought as children and trained to become priests, temple prostitutes, or warriors; these wear the flames of their fiery god as tattoos upon their faces. Of the warriors, little enough is said, though they are called the Fiery Hand, and they never number more or less than one thousand members.

---

the Rhoynar cities upriver. Over time, however, taverns and brothels and stables began to sprout up outside the Black Walls, and merchant ships began to call as well.

Blessed with a magnificent natural harbor and an ideal location at the mouth of the Rhoyne, Volantis began to grow rapidly. Homes and shops and inns spread up the east bank of the river and into the hills beyond the Black Walls, whilst across the Rhoyne on the west bank the foreigners, freedmen, sellswords, criminals, and other less savory elements threw up their own shadow city, where fornication, drunkenness,

and beautiful Rhoynish city that had previously dominated that commerce, suffered a corresponding decline. Inevitably, this led the two cities into conflict. The long series of wars that followed, the details of which have been recounted elsewhere, culminated with the utter destruction of the cities of the Rhoyne and the flight of Nymeria and her ten thousand ships. Though the dragonlords of Valyria won the victory, it is rightly said that Volantis was the principal beneficiary. Sarhoy remains in ruins to this day, a desolate and haunted place, whilst Volantis, with its Long Bridge and Black

Walls and huge harbor, ranks amongst the great cities of the world.

Inside the Black Walls, Volantenes of the Old Blood still keep court in ancient palaces, attended by armies of slaves. Outside, the foreigners, freedmen, and lowborn of a hundred nations may be found. Seafarers and traders swarm the city's markets and harbors, together with slaves almost beyond count. It is said that in Volantis, there are five slaves for every free man—a disproportion in numbers matched only by the ancient Ghiscari cities of Slaver's Bay.

The custom in Volantis is that the faces of all slaves are to be tattooed—marked for life to show their status, and carrying that burden of the past even if they are freed. The styles of tattooing are many, and are sometimes disfiguring. The slave soldiers of Volantis wear green tiger stripes upon their faces, which denote their rank; prostitutes are marked by a single tear beneath their right eye; the slaves that collect the dung of horses and elephants are marked with flies; fools and jesters wear motley; the drivers of the *hathays,* the carts pulled by the small elephants of Volantis, are marked with wheels; and so on.

Volantis is a freehold, and all freeborn landholders have a voice in the governance of the city. Three triarchs are elected annually to administer her laws, command her fleets and armies, and share in the day-to-day rule of the city. The election of the triarchs occurs over the course of ten days, in a process that is both festive and tumultuous. In recent centuries, the office has been dominated by two competing factions, unofficially known as the tigers and the elephants.

Partisans of various candidates—and of the two factions—rally on behalf of their chosen leaders, dispensing favors to the populace. All freeborn landholders—even women—are granted a vote. Though the process strikes many outsiders as chaotic to the point of madness, power passes peacefully enough on most occasions.

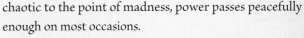

After the Doom engulfed Valyria and the Lands of the Long Summer, Volantis asserted its right to rule over all the other Valyrian colonies throughout the world. Such was the might of the "First Daughter" that for a time she succeeded in establishing hegemony over several of the other Free Cities during the Century of Blood. Eventually,

Many Volantenes regard themselves as the natural and rightful successors to the dragonlords of old Valyria and desire to achieve dominance over the other Free Cities and, in time, the world. The tigers advocate achieving this dominance through war and conquest, whereas the elephants prefer a policy of trade and growing wealth.

ABOVE | *Slave markings of Volantis.*

the Volantene empire collapsed of its own weight, brought down by an alliance of those sister cities that still remained free and the rebellion of those that had been subdued.

Since that time, the elephants—the more peaceable of the Volantene factions—have dominated the annual choosing and the office of triarch. Yet years of expansion under the tigers gave Volantis control over several lesser cities, most notable amongst them the great river "towns" of Volon Therys, Valysar, and Selhorys (each larger and more populous than King's Landing or Oldtown). The Volantenes also control the Rhoyne as far as the tributary river Selhoru, and hold sway over the Orange Coast to the west. These lands are protected by slave soldiers against the Dothraki horselords, who sometimes test the Volantene defenses, and the other Free Cities, who attempt to grow stronger at the expense of their sister city.

While Volantene elections are mostly peaceful, there have been significant exceptions. Nysseos Qoheros's *Journals* contain a report of the Triarch Horonno, who had been returned as triarch for forty years running, for he was a great hero during the Century of Blood. After his fortieth election, he declared himself triarch for life, and though the Volantenes loved him, they did not love him so much as to see their ancient customs and laws usurped for his ease. He was seized by rioters not long after, stripped of rank and title, and torn apart by war elephants.

BRAAVOS

At the far northwestern corner of Essos, where the Shivering Sea and the narrow sea come together, the Free City of Braavos stands upon its famed "hundred isles" amidst the shallow brackish waters of a fog-shrouded lagoon.

The youngest of the Nine Free Cities, Braavos is also the wealthiest, and in all likelihood the most powerful. Originally founded by escaped slaves, its humble beginnings were rooted in nothing more than a desire to be free. For a great part of its early history, its secret status made it of little consequence in the wider world. But in time it grew, eventually emerging as a power almost without rival.

Neither prince nor king commands in Braavos, where the rule belongs to the Sealord, chosen by the city's magisters and keyholders from amongst the citizenry by a process as convoluted as it is arcane. From his vast waterside palace, the Sealord commands a fleet of warships second to none and a mercantile fleet whose purple hulls and purple sails have become a common sight throughout the known world.

Braavos was founded by fugitives from a large convoy of slave ships on its way from Valyria to a newly established colony in Sothoryos, who rose in a bloody rebellion, seized control of the ships on which they were being transported, and fled to "the far ends of the earth" to escape their erstwhile masters. Knowing they would be hunted, the slaves turned away from their intended destination and sailed north instead of south, seeking a refuge as far from Valyria and her vengeance as could be found. Braavosi histories claim that a group of slave women from the distant lands of the Jogos Nhai prophesied where they would find shelter: in a distant lagoon behind a wall of pine-clad hills and sea stones, where the frequent fogs would help to hide the refugees from the eyes of dragonriders passing overhead. And so it proved. These women were priestesses, called moonsingers, and to this day the Temple of the Moonsingers is the greatest in Braavos.

Since the escaped slaves came from many lands and held many faiths, the founders of Braavos created a place where all gods were given their due and decreed that none would ever be made paramount over another. They were a diverse people, whose numbers included Andals, Summer Islanders, Ghiscari, Naathi, Rhoynar, Ibbenese, Sarnori, even debtors and criminals of pure Valyrian blood. Some had been trained in arms to serve as guardsmen and slave soldiers; others were bedslaves, whose art was the giving of pleasure. There were many sorts of household slaves amongst them: tutors, nursemaids, cooks, grooms, and stewards. Others were skilled craftsmen: carpenters, armorers, masons, and weavers. Some were fishermen, some field hands, some galley slaves, many common laborers. The new freedmen spoke many tongues, so the tongue of their late masters—Valyrian—became their common language.

And because they had risked their lives in the name of freedom, the mothers and fathers of the new city vowed that no man, woman, or child in Braavos should ever be a slave, a thrall, or a bondsman. This is the First Law of Braavos, engraved in stone on the arch that spans the Long Canal. From that day to this, the Sealords of Braavos have opposed slavery in all its forms and have fought many a war against slavers and their allies.

The lagoon where the fugitives found refuge seemed a drear and uninviting place of mudflats, tidal shallows, and salt marshes at first glance, but it was well hidden behind outlying islands and sea stacks, and oft cloaked even from above by fog. Moreover, its brackish waters were rich with fish and shellfish of all sorts, the sheltering islands were thickly forested, and iron, tin, lead, slate, and other useful materials could be found nearby on mainland Essos. More crucially, the lagoon was remote and little visited; though the escaped slaves were weary of flight, most of all they feared recapture.

Undiscovered, Braavos grew and prospered. Farms, homes, and temples sprouted across the low-lying islands, whilst fishermen harvested the bounty of the great lagoon and the seas beyond. Amongst the other shellfish the Braavosi discovered was a certain sea snail, akin to those that had made Tyrosh and its dyes rich and famous. The snail yielded a dark purple dye. To change the look of their stolen ships, Braavosi captains dyed their sails this color whenever they sailed beyond the lagoon. Taking care to avoid Valyrian ships and cities wherever possible, the Braavosi began to trade with Ib, and later with the Seven Kingdoms. For a long while, however, Braavosi merchant ships carried false charts and practiced an artful deceit when questioned about their home port. Thus, for more than a century, Braavos was known as the Secret City.

Sealord Uthero Zalyne put an end to that secrecy, sending forth his ships to every corner of the world to proclaim the existence and location of Braavos, and invite men of all nations to celebrate the 111th festival of the city's founding. By that time all of the original escaped slaves were dead, along with all of their former masters. Even so, Uthero had

LEFT | *The execution of the Triarch Horonno.*

sent envoys from the Iron Bank to Valyria several years prior, to clear the way for what became known as the Uncloaking or the Unmasking of Uthero. The dragonlords proved to have little interest in the descendants of slaves who had escaped a century before, and the Iron Bank paid handsome settlements to the grandchildren of the men whose ships the founders had seized and sailed away (whilst refusing to pay for the value of the slaves themselves).

Thus was accord achieved. The anniversary of the Uncloaking is celebrated every year in Braavos with ten days of feasting and masked revelry—a festival like none other in all the known world, culminating at midnight on the tenth day, when the Titan roars and tens of thousands of revelers and celebrants remove their masks as one.

Despite its humble origins, Braavos has not only become the wealthiest of the Free Cities, but also one of the most impregnable. Volantis may have its Black Walls, but Braavos has a wall of ships such as no other city in the world possesses. Lomas Longstrider marveled at the Titan of Braavos—the great fortress of stone and bronze in the shape of a warrior that bestrides the main entrance into the lagoon—but the true wonder is the Arsenal. There, one of the purple-hulled war galleys of Braavos can be built in a day. All the vessels are constructed following the same design, so that all the many parts can be prepared in advance, and skilled shipbuilders work upon different sections of the vessel simultaneously to hasten the labor. To organize such a feat of engineering is unprecedented; one need only look at the raucous, confused construction in the shipyards of Oldtown to see the truth of this.

It would be folly, however, not to give the Titan its due. With his proud head and fiery eyes looming close to four hundred feet above the sea, the Titan is a fortress of a type never seen before or since, cast in the form of a huge giant straddling two seamounts. The Titan's legs and lower torso are black granite, originally a natural stone archway, carved and shaped by three generations of sculptors and stonemasons and wrapped in a pleated bronze skirt; above the waist, the colossus is bronze, with green-dyed hemp for hair. When seen from the sea for the first time, the Titan is a sight terrifying to behold. His eyes are huge beacon fires, lighting the way for returning ships back inside the lagoon. Within his bronze body are halls and chambers, murder holes and arrow slits, such that any vessel that dared to force the passage would surely be destroyed. Enemy ships can easily be steered onto the rocks by the watchmen inside the Titan, and stones and pots of burning pitch can be dropped onto the decks of any that attempt to pass between the Titan's legs without leave. This has seldom been necessary, however; not since the Century of Blood has any enemy been so rash as to attempt to provoke the Titan's wrath.

Today Braavos is one of the world's greatest ports and welcomes trading ships of all nations (save for slavers). Within the vast lagoon, Braavosi ships dock at the splendid Purple Harbor, located near the Sealord's Palace. Other vessels must use the port called the Ragman's Harbor, a poorer and rougher port by all accounts. Still, there is so much wealth to be had in Braavos that ships come from as far as Qarth and the Summer Isles to trade there.

Braavos is also home to one of the most powerful banks in the world, whose roots stretch back to the beginnings of the city, when a few of the fugitives took to hiding such valuables as they had in an abandoned iron mine to keep them safe from thieves and pirates. As the city grew and prospered, the shafts and chambers of the mine began to fill. Rather than let their treasure sit idle in the earth, the wealthier Braavosi began to make loans to their less fortunate brethren.

Thus was born the Iron Bank of Braavos, whose renown (or infamy, to hear some tell it) now extends to every corner of the known world. Kings, princes, archons, triarchs, and merchants beyond count travel from the ends of the earth to seek loans from the heavily guarded vaults of the Iron Bank.

The Iron Bank will have its due, it is said. Those who borrow from the Braavosi and fail to repay their debts oft have cause to rue such folly, for the Bank has been known to topple lords and princes and has also been rumored to send assassins against those it cannot remove (though this has never been conclusively proved).

Braavos is a city built on mud and sand, where a man is never more than a few feet from the water. Some say the city has more canals than streets. This is an exaggeration, yet it cannot be denied that the swiftest way to move about the city is over water, in one of the myriad serpent boats that ply the canals, rather than by foot through the maze of streets, alleyways, and arched bridges. Pools and fountains are seen everywhere in Braavos, celebrating the city's ties to the sea and the "wooden walls" that defend her. The brackish waters of the lagoon that surrounds the "hundred isles" were the source of much of the city's early wealth, yielding up oysters, eels, crabs, crawfish, clams, rays, and many sorts of fish.

Yet the waters that nourish and protect Braavos also imperil her, for during the past two centuries it has become apparent that some of the city's islands are sinking under the weight of the buildings that now cover them. The old-

PREVIOUS PAGES | *The Titan of Braavos.* ABOVE | *The Iron Bank of Braavos*

Archmaester Matthar's *The Origins of the Iron Bank and Braavos* provides one of the more detailed accounts of the bank's history and dealings, so far as they can be discovered; the bank is famous for its discretion and its secrecy. Matthar recounts that the founders of the Iron Bank numbered three-and-twenty; sixteen men and seven women, each of whom possessed a key to bank's great subterranean vaults. Their descendants, whose numbers now exceed one thousand, are known as keyholders to this day, though the keys they display proudly on formal occasions are now entirely ceremonial. Certain of the founding families of Braavos have declined over the centuries, and a few have lost their wealth entirely, yet even the meanest still cling to their keys and the honors that go with them.

The Iron Bank is not ruled by the keyholders alone, however. Some of the wealthiest and most powerful families in Braavos today are of more recent vintage, yet the heads of these houses own shares in the bank, sit on its secret councils, and have a voice in selecting the men who lead it. In Braavos, as many an outsider has observed, golden coins count for more than iron keys. The bank's envoys cross the world, oft upon the bank's own ships, and merchants, lords, and even kings treat with them almost as equals.

est part of the city, just north of the Ragman's Habor, has in fact already sunk, and is now known as the Drowned Town. Even so, there are still some Braavosi, of the poorest sort, who dwell in the towers and upper floors of its half-submerged buildings.

Braavos is a city renowned for its architecture: the sprawling Sealord's Palace, with its magnificent menagerie of queer beasts and birds from all around the world; the imposing Palace of Justice; the huge Temple of the Moonsingers; the aqueduct that the Braavosi named the sweetwater river, carrying much-needed freshwater from the mainland of Essos (for the water in the canals is brackish, muddy, and too foul to drink because of the refuse thrown into it by the city's inhabitants); the towers of the keyholders and noble families; and the House of Red Hands, a great hospice and center of healing. In and amongst these noble structures are countless shops, brothels, inns, alehouses, guildhalls, and merchants' exchanges. Along the streets and bridges stand statues of past Sealords, lawgivers, sailors, warriors, even poets, singers, and courtesans.

The temples of Braavos are far famed as well, and some are truly wonders to behold. The Temple of the Moonsingers is the foremost of these, for the Braavosi have a particular reverence for that deity, as previously recounted. The Father of Waters is almost as venerated; his watery temple is built anew each year for his feast days. The Lord of Light, red R'hllor, has a great temple on Braavos as well, for his worshippers have grown ever more numerous in the past hundred years.

Descended from a hundred different peoples, the Braavosi honor a hundred different gods. The greatest of these have temples, but deep in the heart of the city can be found the Isle of the Gods, where even the least of the gods have temples. The Sept-Beyond-the-Sea and its septons and septas offer worship to the Seven every day for sailors off the ships from the Seven Kingdoms that come to Braavos to trade.

In Braavos men and women from far-flung corners of the world may sit together, as they have done for hundreds of years, eating and drinking and telling tales. All are welcome in the Secret City, it is said.

ABOVE | *The temple district of Braavos.*

Many of the courtesans of Braavos are celebrated in song and story, and a few have even been immortalized in bronze or marble. In the Seven Kingdoms, the most storied and infamous of these are the Black Pearls. The first woman to bear that name was the captain and pirate queen Bellegere Otherys, who reigned briefly as one of the nine paramours of King Aegon IV Targaryen, and bore him a bastard daughter, Bellenora, the second Black Pearl, a famous courtesan acclaimed by the singers of her day as the most beautiful woman in all the world. Her descendants became courtesans as well, each in turn known as the Black Pearl, and each having in her veins some measure of the blood of the dragon to this very day.

It must also be said that the courtesans of Braavos are renowned throughout the world, yet are all free women, unlike the more famous beauties of the pleasure gardens of Lys or the brothels of Volantis. Their art is not only for the bedchamber; their wit and their bearing make them much sought after by the richest merchants, the boldest captains, the most distinguished visitors. Keyholders, lords, and princes seek their favors. The most famous courtesans take poetic names that add to their allure and mystery. Singers vie for their patronage, whilst the bravos with their slender swords oft duel to the death in the name of a courtesan.

The swordsmanship of the bravos of the Secret City is as famed as the beauty of her courtesans. Largely unarmored, and wielding slender pointed blades far lighter than the longswords of the Seven Kingdoms, these warriors of the streets practice a swift, deadly style of fighting. The greatest bravos call themselves water dancers, given the custom of dueling upon the Moon Pool near the Sealord's Palace; it is

Pilman of Lannisport, a ship's captain, provided an account of a water-dancer duel to the Citadel. The water dancers, he tells us, do seem to barely skim upon the surface, but it is an illusion caused by the darkness, for they always duel at night. The captain insisted he never saw anything like it for grace or skill, however.

claimed that true water dancers can fight and kill upon the pool's surface without disturbing the water itself.

Though many a deadly swordsman can be found amongst the bravos and water dancers, by tradition the greatest of them all is the First Sword, who commands the personal guard of the Sealord and protects his person at all public events. Once chosen, Sealords serve for life. Inevitably, there are always those who wish to cut that life short to effect some change in policy. Through the centuries, the First Swords have fought many famous duels, taken part in a dozen wars, and saved the lives of scores of Sealords, for good and ill.

No discussion of Braavos would be complete without a mention of the Faceless Men. Shrouded in mystery and rumor, this secretive society of assassins is said to be older than Braavos itself, with roots that go back to Valyria at the height of its glory. Little is known for certain about these killers, however.

ABOVE | *The coins of the Faceless Men of Braavos (front and back).* RIGHT | *The Summer Isles*

BEYOND THE FREE CITIES

DO WE KNOW all of the lands and peoples who exist in the world? Surely we do not. Our maps have their limits, and even the finest of them raise as many questions as they answer about the far lands to the east, featuring all-too-frequent blank spaces where we have no knowledge. Yet it may profit us much to discuss something of those places we do know, even if their commerce with the Seven Kingdoms is small at best compared to that of the Free Cities.

THE SUMMER ISLES

South of Westeros, cradled in the deep blue waters of the Summer Sea, the Summer Isles bask in the warm southern sun. More than fifty islands make up this verdant archipelago. Many are so small a man could walk across them in an hour, but Jhala, largest of the isles, stretches two hundred leagues from tip to tip. Beneath its towering green mountains are vast forests, steaming jungles, beaches of green and black sand, mighty rivers teeming with monstrous crocodiles, and fertile vales. Walano and Omboru, though less than half the size of Jhala, are each larger than all the Stepstones combined. These three islands are home to more than nine-tenths of the peoples of the isles.

Flowers of a thousand different sorts bloom in profusion on the Summer Isles, filling the air with their perfume. The trees are heavy with exotic fruits, and a myriad of brightly colored birds flitter through the skies. From their plumage the Summer Islanders make their fabulous feathered cloaks. Beneath the green canopies of the rain forests prowl spotted panthers larger than any lion and packs of lean red wolves. Tribes of monkeys swing through the branches of the trees

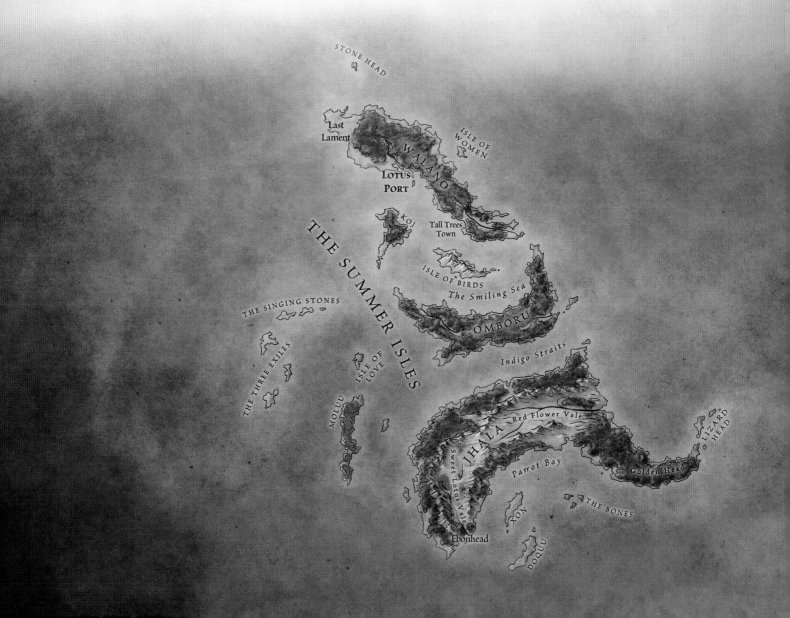

above. Apes abound as well: the "old red men" of Omboru, silver pelts in the mountains of Jhala, night stalkers on Walano.

The Summer Islanders are a dark people, black of hair and eye, with skins as brown as teak or as black as polished jet. For much of their recorded history, they lived in isolation from the rest of mankind. Their earliest maps, as carved into the famous Talking Trees of Tall Trees Town, show no lands but the isles themselves, surrounded by a vast world-spanning ocean. As islanders, they took to the seas in the dawn of days, first in oared coracles, then in larger, swifter ships with sails of woven hemp, yet few ever ventured be-

and stronger ships, capable of carrying sufficient provisions to cross long stretches of ocean whilst withstanding even the fiercest storms at sea. Malthar Xaq, a prince of the small island of Koj, was the greatest of these shipbuilders, and is remembered today as Malthar the Windrider and Malthar the Mapmaker.

A new era of exploration and trade began as the great ships struck out across the waters, dispatched by Malthar and his fellow princes. Many did not return. More did. Naath, the Basilisk Isles, the northern coasts of Sothoryos, and the southern coasts of both Westeros and Essos were

Lomas Longstrider, who visited the Summer Isles in his search for wonders, recorded that the sages of the isles claimed that their ancestors once reached the western shores of Sothoryos and founded cities there, only to have them overwhelmed and destroyed by the same forces that wiped out later Ghiscari and Valyrian settlements on that perilous continent. The Citadel's archives hold a few ancient chronicles of Valyria, but none speak of these supposed cities, and there are maesters who cast doubts on the truth of these claims.

yond the sight of their own shores . . . and those who sailed beyond the horizons did not always return.

The first recorded contact between the Summer Isles and the wider world occurred at the height of the Old Empire of Ghis. A Ghiscari merchant ship made landfall on Walano after being blown off course by a storm, only to flee in terror at the first sight of the local inhabitants, whom the Ghiscari took for demons with skins burned black by the fires of hell. Thereafter, Ghiscari sailors took care to stay well away from the Demon Isle, as they named Walano on their charts; they had no inkling of the existence of Omboru, Jhala, or the lesser islands.

This contact had a profound effect upon the Summer Islanders themselves, for it proved that other peoples lived in the lands beyond the waves. Their curiosity (and avarice) thus awakened, the princes of the isles began to build larger

all visited, and within less than half a century, a thriving trade had grown up between the Summer Isles and the Freehold of Valyria. The islands lacked iron, tin, and other metals, but were rich in gemstones (emeralds, rubies, and sapphires, and pearls of many sorts), spice (nutmeg, cinnamon, pepper), and hardwoods. A fashion developed amongst the dragonlords for monkeys, apes, panther cubs, and parrots. Bloodwood, ebony, mahogany, purpleheart, blue mahoe, burl, tigerwood, goldenheart, pink ivory, and other rare and precious woods were also much in demand, along with palm wine, fruit, and feathers.

The Valyrians offered gold for slaves as well. Then as now, the Summer Islanders were a handsome people, tall, strong, graceful, and quick to learn. These qualities drew pirates and slavers from Valyria, the Basilisk Isles, and Old Ghis. Much woe ensued as these raiders descended on

Maester Gallard's *Children of Summer* remains a chief source on the history of the Summer Isles. Much of the history—which was once obscured by the fact that so many of the Summer Isles histories were recorded in highly complicated, formal verse—have been rendered quite clear by his exhaustive efforts. Though certain controversies remain—Mollos's questioning of Gallard's chronology of the early princes of Walano being one example—no better work on the subject has appeared.

peaceful villages to carry their inhabitants into bondage. For a time, the princes of the isles abetted this trade by selling captured foes and rivals to the slavers.

The histories carved into the Talking Trees tell us that these "Years of Shame" endured for the better part of two centuries, until a warrior woman named Xanda Qo, Princess of Sweet Lotus Vale (who had herself been enslaved for a time), united all the islands under her rule and made an end to it.

As iron was scarce and costly in the isles, armor was little known, and the long thrusting spears and short stab-

To give her archers a solid platform from which to draw and loose, Xanda Qo built ships larger than any previously seen in the Summer Sea—tall graceful ships cunningly fit together without so much as a single nail, many walled with rare hardwoods of the isles made harder still with magics, so the rams of slaver ships cracked and splintered against their sides. As swift as they were strong, her ships oft sported tall, curved prows carved into the shapes of birds and beasts. These "swan necks" won them the sobriquet of "swan ships."

Though it took the best part of a generation, the Summer Islanders, led by Princess Xanda's daughter (and eventual

bing spears traditional amongst the Summer Islanders had proved of little worth against the steel swords and axes of the slavers, so Xanda Qo armed her sailors with tall bows of goldenheart, a wood found only on Jhala and Omboru. These great bows far outranged the recurved bows of horn and sinew the slavers carried, and could throw a yard-long shaft hard enough to pierce through mail and boiled leather and even good steel plate.

successor) Chatana Qo, the Arrow of Jhahar, ultimately prevailed in what came to be known as the Slavers' Wars. Though the unity of the isles did not survive her own reign (for the Arrow wed unwisely and did not rule as well as she had fought) slavers even now will flee at the sight of a swan ship, for each of these proud vessels is known to carry a complement of deadly archers armed with goldenheart bows. To this day, the bowmen (and women) of the Summer

ABOVE | *A swan ship of the Summer Isles.*

Isles are esteemed the finest in the world. Nor can their bows be matched by common bows, for the princes of the isles have forbidden the export of goldenheart wood since the Slavers' Wars; only bows of dragonbone are known to surpass them, and those are exceedingly rare.

Certain Summer Islanders with a desire to see the wider world have been known to take up service abroad as mercenary bowmen and sellsails. Others have joined the pirates of the Basilisk Isles; some became captains of dark renown whose deeds are spoken of with dread in ports as distant as Qarth and Oldtown. Summer Islanders have risen high amongst the free companies of the Disputed Lands, as guardsmen in the retinues of the merchant princes of the Free Cities, or as pit fighters in the slave cities of Astapor, Yunkai, and Meereen . . . but despite the undoubted prowess and skill at arms they display as individuals, the islanders are not a warlike people.

The Summer Islanders have never once invaded any lands beyond their own shores nor attempted the conquest of any foreign people. Their great swan ships sail farther and faster than the vessels of any other nation, to the very ends of the earth, yet the princes of the Summer Islands have no warships as such and seem to prefer trade and exploration to conquest.

Throughout their long history, the Summer Islands have been united under a single ruler no more than half a

dozen times, and never for long. Today, each of the smaller islands has its own ruler, styled as a prince or princess in the Common Tongue; the larger islands (Jhala, Omboru, and Walano) oft have several rival princes.

Nonetheless, the isles are by and large a peaceful place. Such wars as are fought there are highly ritualized, with battles that resemble tourney mêlées, wherein bands of warriors meet on battlefields chosen and consecrated in advance, at times deemed auspicious by their priests. They fight with spears and slings and wooden shields, just as their forebears did five thousand years ago; the goldenheart bows and yard-long shafts carried by their archers into battle against foes from across the sea are never used against their own people, for their gods have forbidden this.

Wars on the Summer Isles seldom last longer than a day, and do no harm to any but the warriors themselves. No crops are destroyed, no homes are put to the torch, no cities are sacked, no children are harmed, no women are raped (though warrior women oft fight beside their men in the line of battle). Even the defeated princes suffer neither death nor disfigurement though they must leave their homes and palaces to spend the remainder of their days in exile.

Though Jhala is the largest of the Summer Isles, Walano is the most populous. There can be found Last Lament, with its great harbor, sleepy Lotus Point, and sun-dappled Tall Trees Town, where priestesses in feathered robes carve

THE OTHER SUMMER ISLES

Whilst Jhala, Walano, and Omboru dominate the archipelago, a number of the smaller isles are worthy of mention:

THE SINGING STONES, west of the main isles, have jagged peaks so riddled with holes and airways that they make a strange music when the wind blows. The people of the Stones can tell which way the wind is blowing from the sound of their song. Whether gods or men taught the stones to sing, no one can say.

STONE HEAD, the northernmost island in the chain, is plainly the work of men; the north face of this sea-girt rock has been carved in the stern likeness of some forgotten god, glowering out across the sea. His is the last visage that Summer Islanders see as they sail north to Westeros.

KOJ, once home to Malthar the Mapmaker, still boasts the finest shipyards in the archipelago. Three-

quarters of the islanders' famed swan ships are built on Koj, and the Pearl Palace, seat of the Princes of Koj, is renowned for its collection of charts and maps.

ABULU, a small desolate isle northeast of Walano, served for more than two years as home to Nymeria and her followers. The princes of the isles refused to allow her to settle on the larger islands, for fear of waking the wroth of Valyria. As most of Nymeria's people were female, Abulu became known as the Isle of Women, a name it still bears today. Disease, hunger, and slave raids took a steady toll of the Rhoynar there, until finally Nymeria led her ten thousand ships back to sea in search of a new refuge. A few thousand of her followers chose to remain behind, however, and their descendants remain on the Isle of Women to this day.

RIGHT | *Worship at a Summer Island temple of love.*

songs and stories into the trunks of the enormous tower trees that shade the town. On these Talking Trees can be read the whole history of the Summer Islanders, together with the commandments of their many gods and the laws by which they live their lives.

Though a score of gods both great and small are honored on the Summer Isles, a special reverence is shown to the god and goddess of love, beauty, and fertility. The union of male and female is sacred to these deities; by joining together in this act of worship, the islanders believe, men and women give honor to the gods who made them. Be they rich or poor, male or female, of high birth or low, all Summer Islanders are expected to dwell for a time in the temples of love that dot the islands, sharing their bodies with any who might desire them.

Most serve the gods for no more than a year, but those deemed the most beautiful, the most compassionate, and the most skilled remain. In Braavos they might be called courtesans, whilst in King's Landing they were thought no more than whores, but on Jhala, Walano, Omboru, and the other isles these priests and priestesses are much esteemed, for here the giving of carnal pleasure is regarded as an art as worthy of respect as music, sculpture, or dance.

Today the Summer Islanders are a common sight in Oldtown and King's Landing, and the swan ships with their billowing clouds of sails traverse all the seas of earth. Bold mariners, their captains scorn to hug the coasts like other seafarers but instead strike out fearlessly across the ocean deeps, far from the sight of land. There are certain indications that explorers from Koj may well have mapped the western coasts of Sothoryos to the very bottom of the world and discovered strange lands and stranger peoples far to the south, or across the endless waters of the Sunset Sea . . . but the truth of these tales is known only to the princes of the isles and the captains who serve them.

NAATH

Northwest of Sothoryos, in the Summer Sea, lies the mysterious island of Naath, known to the ancients as the Isle of Butterflies. The people native to the island are a beautiful and gentle race, with round flat faces, dusky skin, and large, soft amber eyes, oft flecked with gold. The Peaceful People, the Naathi are called by seafarers, for they will not fight even in defense of their homes and persons. The Naathi do not kill, not even beasts of the field and wood; they eat fruit, not flesh, and make music, not war.

The god of Naath is called the Lord of Harmony, oft shown as a laughing giant, bearded and naked, always attended by swarms of slender maidens with butterfly wings. A hundred varieties of butterflies flitter about the island; the Naathi revere them as messengers of the Lord, charged with the protection of his people. Mayhaps there is some truth to these legends, for whilst the docile nature of the Naathi seem to make their island ripe for conquest, strangers from beyond the sea do not live long upon the Isle of Butterflies.

The Ghiscari seized the island thrice in the days of the Old Empire; the Valyrians erected a fort there whose walls of fused dragonstone can still be seen; a company of Volantene adventurers once built a trade town, complete with timber palisades and slave pens; corsairs from the Basilisk Isles have landed on Naath countless times. Yet none of these invaders survived, and the Naathi claim that none lasted more than a year, for some evil humor lurks in the very air of this fair isle, and all those who linger too long on Naath soon succumb. Fever is the first sign of this plague, followed by painful spasms that make it seem as if victims are dancing wildly and uncontrollably. In the last stage, the afflicted sweat blood, and their flesh sloughs from their bones.

The Naathi themselves are seemingly untroubled by the illness.

Archmaester Ebrose, who has made a study of all known accounts of the affliction, believes that it is spread by the butterflies that the Peaceful People revere. For this reason, the disease is oft called butterfly fever. Some believe the fever is carried only by one particular sort of butterfly (a large black-and-white variety with wings as big as a man's hand is favored by Ebrose), but this remains conjecture.

Whether the butterflies of Naath are true handmaids of the Lord of Harmony, or no more than common insects like their cousins in the Seven Kingdoms, it may well be that the Naathi are not wrong in regarding them as guardians.

Sad to say, the corsairs who prowl the seas around Naath long ago learned that the chances of dying of butterfly fever were low so long as they did not remain upon the island for more than a few hours . . . and lower still if they only came ashore at night, for butterflies are creatures of the day and love the morning dew and the afternoon sun. Thus it is that slavers from the Basilisk Isles oft descend upon Naath during the dark of night, to carry off whole villages into bondage. The Peaceful People always bring good prices, it is said, for they are as clever as they are gentle, fair to look upon, and quick to learn obedience. It is reported that one pillow house on Lys is famed for its Naathi girls, who are clad in diaphanous silken gowns and adorned with gaily painted butterfly wings.

Such raids have become so frequent since the Century of Blood that the Peaceful People have largely abandoned their own shores, moving inland to the hills and forests, where it is harder for the slavers to find them. Thus the fine handicrafts, shimmering silks, and delicate spiced wines of the Isle of Butterflies are seen less and less in the markets of the Seven Kingdoms and the Nine Free Cities.

THE BASILISK ISLES

East of Naath, the long chain of islands known as the Basilisk Isles could not be more different. Named for the fierce beasts that once infested them, the Basilisks have for long centuries been the festering sore of the Summer Sea, inhabited only by corsairs, pirates, slavers, sellswords, murderers, and monsters, the worst of humanity. They come from every

land beneath the sun, it is said, for only here can such men hope to find others of their own ilk.

Life on the Basilisks is nasty, brutal, and oft short. Hot, humid, and swarming with stinging flies, sand fleas, and bloodworms, these islands have always proved singularly unhealthy for man and beast alike. Ruins found upon the

Isle of Tears, the Isle of Toads, and Ax Island hint at some ancient civilization, but little is now known of these vanished men of the Dawn Age. If any still survived when the first corsairs settled on the islands, they were soon put to the sword, so no trace of them now remains . . . save perhaps upon the Isle of Toads, as we shall discuss shortly.

The largest of the Basilisks is the Isle of Tears, where steep-sided valleys and black bogs hide amongst rugged flint hills and twisted, windswept rocks. On its southern coasts stand the broken ruins of a city. Founded by the Old Empire of Ghis, it was known as Gorgai for close on two centuries (or perhaps four; there is some dispute), until the dragonlords of Valyria captured it during the Third Ghiscari War and renamed it Gogossos.

By any name, it was an evil place. The dragonlords sent their worst criminals to the Isle of Tears to live out their lives in hard labor. In the dungeons of Gogossos, torturers devised new torments. In the flesh pits, blood sorcery of the darkest sort was practiced, as beasts were mated to slave women to bring forth twisted half-human children.

The infamy of Gogossos outlived even the Doom. During the Century of Blood, this dark city waxed rich and powerful. Some called her the Tenth Free City, but her wealth was built on slaves and sorcery. Her slave markets became as notorious as those of the old Ghiscari cities on Slaver's Bay. Seven-and-seventy years after the Doom of Valyria, however, it is said their stink reached even the nostrils of the gods, and a terrible plague emerged from the slave pens of Gogossos. The Red Death swept across the Isle of Tears, then the rest of the Basilisk Isles. Nine men of every ten died screaming, bleeding copiously from every orifice, their skin shredding like wet parchment.

For a century thereafter, the Basilisks were shunned. It was not until the coming of the corsairs that men returned to the isles once again. The Qartheen pirate Xandarro Xhore was the first to raise his banner there, using the stones he found on Ax Isle to erect a grim black fort above his anchorage. The men of the Brotherhood of Bones soon followed, settling at the western end of the chain upon the Isle of Flies. From these bases, Xandarro and the Brotherhood were perfectly placed to prey upon merchantmen rounding the shattered, smoking remnants of the Valyrian peninsula. Within half a century, almost every one of the Basilisks was home to a nest of corsairs.

In our present day, the Brotherhood of Bones is long forgotten, and all that remains of Xandarro Xhore is the fort he left on Ax Isle, but the corsairs still haunt the Basilisks. Once every generation, it seems, fleets are sent to the islands to clear out these vermin of the seas. The Volantenes have been especially assiduous in this regard, often in alliance with one or more of the other Free Cities. Some of these raids have ended in failure when the corsairs fled, forewarned. Others, more ably led, have seen hundreds hanged and scores of ships seized or sunk or put to the torch. One ended in infamy, when the Lysene captain Saathos Saan, commanding the fleet sent to destroy the corsair strongholds, himself turned pirate and reigned as King of the Basilisk Isles for thirty years.

No matter the outcome of such efforts, the corsairs always seem to resume their depredations after a time. Their

A few of the Basilisk Isles have certain unique aspects that warrant further mention:

Talon, a large claw-shaped island north of the Isle of Tears, is honeycombed with deep caves, most of them inhabited and fortified. This island serves as the slave mart for the corsairs, where captives are held until they can be sold or (less often) ransomed. It is also home to Barter Beach, where the pirates trade with one another.

On the Isle of Toads can be found an ancient idol, a greasy black stone crudely carved into the semblance of a gigantic toad of malignant aspect, some forty feet high. The people of this isle are believed by some to be descended from those who carved the Toad Stone, for there is an unpleasant fishlike aspect to their faces, and many have webbed hands and feet. If so, they are the sole surviving remnant of this forgotten race.

Many of the corsairs cling to the gruesome custom of festooning the hulls and masts of their ships with severed heads, to strike fear into their foes. The heads dangle from hempen rope until all the flesh has rotted off them, whereupon they are replaced with fresh ones. Rather than consign the skulls to the sea, however, the corsairs will deliver them to Skull Isle, as an offering to some dark god. Thus it is that great piles of yellowed skulls can be seen lining the shores of this small, windswept, uninhabited rock.

towns sprout up like toadstools, only to be abandoned the next year, or the year after, left to rot away and sink back into the mud and slime from which they rose. Port Plunder, the most famous of them, is celebrated in many a song and story, yet cannot be found on any map . . . for the good and sufficient reason that there have been at least a dozen Port Plunders, on as many islands. Whenever one is destroyed, another is founded, only to be abandoned in turn. The same is true of Sty, Whore's Gash, Black Pudding, and the other pirate lairs, each viler and more infamous than the last.

In summary, the Basilisk Isles are best avoided, for no good has ever come to those who journey hence.

SOTHORYOS

Men have known of the existence of the vast, savage land to the south since the first of them took to the sea in ships, for only the width of the Summer Sea separates Sothoryos from the ancient civilizations and great cities of Essos and Westeros. The Ghiscari established outposts on its northern shores in the days of the Old Empire. They raised the walled city Zamettar at the mouth of the river Zamoyos, and built the grim penal colony Gorosh on Wyvern Point. Qartheen adventurers hungry for profit sought gold, gems, and ivory along the eastern coasts of Sothoryos. Summer Islanders did the same in the west. The Freehold of Valyria thrice established colonies on Basilisk Point: the first was destroyed by the Brindled Men, the second lost to plague, and the third was abandoned when the dragonlords captured Zamettar in the Fourth Ghiscari War.

Yet we cannot claim to know Sothoryos well. Its interior remains a mystery to us, covered by impenetrable jungle, where ancient cities full of ghosts lie in ruins beside great, sluggish rivers. Only a few days' sail south of Basilisk Point, even the shape of its coasts remains unknown (it may be that the Summer Islanders have explored and mapped these

ABOVE | *Corsairs: the plague of the Basilisk Isles.*

shorelines, but they guard their charts jealously and do not share such knowledge).

Colonies planted here wither and die; only Zamettar endured for more than a generation, and today even that once-great city is a haunted ruin, slowly being reclaimed by the jungle. Slavers, traders, and treasure hunters have visited Sothoryos over the centuries, but only the boldest ever venture far from their coastal garrisons and enclaves to explore the mysteries of the continent's vast interior. Those that dare more oft than not set forth into the green never to be seen again.

We do not even know the true size of Sothoryos. Qartheen maps once showed it as an island, twice the size of Great Moraq, but their trading ships, venturing farther and farther down the eastern coats, were never able to find the bottom of it. The Ghiscari who settled Zamettar and Gorosh believed Sothoryos to be as large as Westeros. Jaenara Belaerys flew her dragon, Terrax, farther south than any man or woman had ever gone before, seeking the boiling seas and steaming rivers of legend, but found only endless jungle, deserts, and mountains. She returned to the Freehold after three years to declare that Sothoryos was as large as Essos, "a land without end."

Whatever its true extent, the southern continent is an unhealthy place, its very air full of foul humors and miasmas. We have already seen how Nymeria fared on its shores, when she attempted to settle her people there. Blood boils, green fever, sweetrot, bronze pate, the Red Death, greyscale, brownleg, wormbone, sailor's bane, pus-eye, and yellowgum are only a few of the diseases found here, many so virulent that they have been known to wipe out whole settlements. Archmaester Ebrose's study of centuries of travelers' accounts suggests that nine of every ten men visiting Sothoryos from Westeros will suffer one or more of these afflictions, and that almost half will die.

Nor is disease the only danger that those who seek to know this wet, green land must face. Huge crocodiles lurk beneath the surface of the Zamoyos and have been known to overturn boats, swimming up from below so they might devour their occupants as they struggle in the water. Other streams are infested by swarms of carnivorous fish capable of stripping the flesh from a man's bones in minutes. There are stinging flies, venomous snakes, wasps and worms that lay their eggs beneath the skins of horses, hogs, and men alike. Basilisks both great and small are found in great numbers on Basilisk Point, some twice the size of lions. In the forests south of Yeen, there are said to be apes that dwarf the largest giants, so powerful they can slay elephants with a single blow.

Farther south lie the regions known as the Green Hell, where beasts even more fearsome are said to dwell. There, if the tales are to be trusted, are caverns full of pale white vampire bats who can drain the blood from a man in minutes. Tattooed lizards stalk the jungles, running down their prey and ripping them apart with the long curved claws on their powerful hind legs. Snakes fifty feet long slither through the underbrush, and spotted spiders weave their webs amongst the great trees.

Most terrible of all are the wyverns, those tyrants of the southern skies, with their great leathery wings, cruel beaks, and insatiable hunger. Close kin to dragons, wyverns cannot breathe fire, but they exceed their cousins in ferocity and are a match for them in all other respects save size.

Brindled wyverns, with their distinctive jade-and-white scales, grow up to thirty feet long. Swamp wyverns have been known to attain even greater size, though they are sluggish by nature and seldom fly far from their lairs. Brownbellies, no larger than monkeys, are even more dangerous than their larger kin, for they hunt in packs of a hundred or more. But most dreaded of all is the shadow-wing, a nocturnal monster whose black scales and wings make him all but invisible . . . until he descends out of the darkness to tear apart his prey.

Unsurprisingly, Sothoryos is thinly peopled when compared to Westeros or Essos. A score of small trade towns cling to the northern coast—towns of mud and blood, as

---

In Septon Barth's *Dragons, Wyrms, and Wyverns*, he speculated that the bloodmages of Valyria used wyvern stock to create dragons. Though the bloodmages were alleged to have experimented mightily with their unnatural arts, this claim is considered far-fetched by most maesters, among them Maester Vanyon's *Against the Unnatural* contains certain proofs of dragons having existed in Westeros even in the earliest of days, before Valyria rose to be a power.

some say: wet and humid and full of misery, where adventurers, rogues, exiles, and whores from the Free Cities and the Seven Kingdoms come to make their fortunes.

There are riches hidden amongst the jungles and swamps and sullen, sun-baked rivers of the south, beyond a doubt, but for every man who finds gold or pearls or precious spices, there are a hundred who find only death. The corsairs of the Basilisk Isles prey upon these settlements, carrying off captives to holding pens on Talon and the Isle of Tears before selling them to the flesh markets of Slaver's Bay, or the pillow houses and pleasure gardens of Lys. And the native races grow ever more savage and primitive the farther one travels from the coasts.

The Sothoryi are big-boned creatures, massively muscled, with long arms, sloped foreheads, huge square teeth, heavy jaws, and coarse black hair. Their broad, flat noses suggest snouts, and their thick skins are brindled in patterns of brown and white that seem more hoglike than human. Sothoryi women cannot breed with any save their own males; when mated with men from Essos or Westeros, they bring forth only stillbirths, many hideously malformed.

The Sothoryi that dwell closest to the sea have learned to speak the trade talk. The Ghiscari consider them too slow of wit to make good slaves, but they are fierce fighters. Farther south, the trappings of civilization fall away, and the Brindled Men become ever more savage and barbaric. These Sothoryi worship dark gods with obscene rites. Many are cannibals, and more are ghouls; when they cannot feast upon the flesh of foes and strangers, they eat their own dead.

Some say that there were other races here once—forgotten peoples destroyed, devoured, or driven out by the Brindled Men. Tales of lizard men, lost cities, and eyeless cave-dwellers are commonplace. No proof exists for any of these.

Maesters and other scholars alike have puzzled over the greatest of the engimas of Sothoryos, the ancient city of Yeen. A ruin older than time, built of oily black stone, in massive blocks so heavy that it would require a dozen elephants to move them, Yeen has remained a desolation for many thousands of years, yet the jungle that surrounds it on every side has scarce touched it. ("A city so evil that even the jungle will not enter," Nymeria is supposed to have said when she laid eyes on it, if the tales are true). Every attempt to rebuild or resettle Yeen has ended in horror.

THE GRASSLANDS

Beyond the Forest of Qohor, Essos opens up upon a vast expanse of windswept plains, gentle rolling hills, fertile river valleys, great blue lakes, and endless steppes where the grass grows as high as a horse's head. From the Forest of Qohor in the west to the towering mountains known as the Bones, the grasslands stretch more than seven hundred leagues.

It was here amidst these grasses that civilization was born in the Dawn Age. Ten thousand years ago or more, when Westeros was yet a howling wilderness inhabited only by the giants and children of the forest, the first true towns arose beside the banks of the river Sarne and beside the myriad vassal streams that fed her on her meandering course northward to the Shivering Sea.

The histories of those days are lost to us, sad to say, for the kingdoms of the grass came and went in large measure before the race of man became literate. Only the legends persist. From such we know of the Fisher Queens, who ruled the lands adjoining the Silver Sea—the great inland sea at the heart of the grasslands—from a floating palace that made its way endlessly around its shores.

in the fertile fields south of the Silver Sea. Tales are told of the Hairy Men, a race of shaggy savage warriors, who rode to battle on unicorns. Though larger than the Ibbenese of the present, they may well have been their forebears. We hear as well of the lost city Lyber, where acolytes of a spider goddess and a serpent god fought an endless, bloody war. East of them stood the kingdoms of the centaurs, half man and half horse.

In the southeast the proud city-states of the Qaathi arose; in the forests to the north, along the shores of the Shivering Sea, were the domains of the woods walkers, a diminutive folk whom many maesters believe to have been kin to the children of the forest; between them could be found the hill kingdoms of the Cymmeri, the long-legged Gipps with their wicker shields and lime-stiffened hair, and the brown-skinned pale-haired Zoqora, who rode to war in chariots.

Most of these peoples are gone now, their cities burned and buried, their gods and heroes all but forgotten. Of the Qaathi cities, only Qarth remains, dreaming of past glories

---

Sufficient tales survive to convince most maesters of the past existence of the Silver Sea, though because of diminishing rainfall over the centuries, it has shrunk so severely that today only three great lakes remain where once its waters glistened in the sun.

The Fisher Queens were wise and benevolent and favored of the gods, we are told, and kings and lords and wise men sought the floating palace for their counsel. Beyond their domains, however, other peoples rose and fell and fought, struggling for a place in the sun. Some maesters believe that the First Men originated here before beginning the long westward migration that took them across the Arm of Dorne to Westeros. The Andals, too, may have arisen

beside the jealously guarded Jade Gates, which link the Summer and Jade seas. The others were extinguished, driven into exile, or conquered and assimilated by the people who succeeded them.

Westeros remembers their conquerors as the Sarnori, for at its height their great kingdom included all the lands watered by the Sarne and its vassals, and the three great lakes that were all that remained of the shrinking Silver Sea. They

---

Archmaester Hagedorn has put forth the theory that the centaurs were no more than mounted warriors, as perceived by neighboring tribes who had not yet learned to tame and ride horses. His views have become widely accepted at the Citadel, despite the purported "centaur skeletons" that turn up in grotesqueries from time to time.

LEFT | *Ruins on Sothoryos.*

called themselves the Tall Men (in their own tongue the *Tagaez Fen*). Long of limb and brown of skin they were, like the Zoqora, though their hair and eyes were black as night. Warriors, sorcerers, and scholars, they traced their descent to the hero king they called Huzhor Amai (the Amazing), born of the last of the Fisher Queens, who took to wife the daughters of the greatest lords and kings of the Gipps, the Cymmeri, and the Zoqora, binding all three peoples to his rule. His Zoqora wife drove his chariot, it is said, his Cymer wife made his armor (for her people were the first to work iron), and he wore about his shoulders a great cloak made from the pelt of a king of the Hairy Men.

Such a man may or may not ever have existed, but none can doubt the glory of the Tall Men at their height. A proud and quarrelsome people, they were seldom ever united under a single ruler, but their kingdoms dominated the western grasslands, from the forest of Qohor to the eastern shores of the vanished Silver Sea, and fifty leagues beyond. Their gleaming cities were strewn across the grasslands like jewels across a green velvet mantle, shining beneath the light of sun and stars.

The greatest of these cities was Sarnath of the Tall Towers, where the High King dwelt in his fabled Palace With a Thousand Rooms.

Annals, and records of them from Qarth, Slaver's Bay, and the Free Cities. Sarnori traders traveled to Valyria and Yi Ti, to Leng and Asshai. Sarnori ships sailed the Shivering Sea to Ib and the Thousand Islands and Far Mossovy. Sarnori kings warred against the Qaathi and the Old Empire of Ghis, and led many a foray against the bands of nomadic horsemen who roamed the steppes to their east.

Their riders wore steel and spider silk and rode coal-black mares, whilst the greatest of their warriors went to battle in scythed chariots pulled by teams of bloodred horses (oft driven by their wives or daughters, for it was the custom amongst the Sarnori for men and women to make war together).

Even in the Seven Kingdoms, the glory of Sarnath of the Tall Towers was celebrated, and Lomas Longstrider included the Palace With a Thousand Rooms amongst his nine *Wonders Made by Man*.

Today, however, the Kingdom of Sarnor is largely forgotten, and there are many and more in Westeros, even students at the Citadel, who know little and less of its long, proud history. Their towers are all fallen, their cities ruined and abandoned, and noxious weeds and tall grasses grow where once their farms and fields and towns were found. The lands that they once ruled are but thinly peopled and

---

By law and custom all the lesser Sarnori kings were subject to the High King, but in truth very few of the High Kings ever exercised any real power.

Eastward rose Kasath, City of Caravans; Sathar, the Waterfall City, at the juncture of two branches of the Sarne; Gornath by the Lake, with its canals; Sallosh by the Silver Shore, City of Scholars, with its vast library and Painted Walls. Downstream, where the Sarne turned north, the prosperous river cities Rathylar, Hornoth, and Kyth served the ships that plied her deep blue waters. Here, too, stood Mardosh, the City of Soldiers, renowned as Mardosh the Unconquerable. At the delta, where the Sarne splintered and flowed into the Shivering Sea, could be found the port cities Saath (to the west) and Sarys (to the east).

The Kingdom of Sarnor (so called, though it boasted twoscore rival kings) was amongst the known world's great civilizations for more than two thousand years, yet much of what we know of them comes only from fragments of their otherwise lost histories, most notably the *Summer and Winter*

traversed only by the wandering *khalasars* of the Dothraki horselords and such caravans as the *khals* permit to make the long, slow crossing from the Free Cities to Vaes Dothrak and the Mother of Mountains.

Travelers name these the Haunted Lands for the many ruined cities that dot them, or the Great Desolation for their emptiness, but it is as the Dothraki sea that these grasslands are best known today. That usage is comparatively recent, however, for the Dothraki are a young race, and it was only since the Doom destroyed Valyria that their *khalasars* came to dominate these lands, sweeping out of the east with fire and steel to conquer and destroy the ancient cities that once thrived here and carrying off their peoples into bondage.

The fall of the great Sarnori kingdoms took less than a century. Even as the Free Cities of the west became locked in a savage struggle for domination during what became known

The Old Empire of Ghis fought five wars against the rising Freehold of Valyria, history tells us. In the Second and Third Ghiscari Wars, the Tall Men took up their swords as allies of Valyria. In the Fourth War, rival kings took opposite sides, some joining the Ghiscari and others the Valyrians. Lomas Longstrider wrote of a fallen obelisk carved about with the figures of Ghis's allies in that fourth war, and noted that the tallest warriors depicted—made taller by high helms—were the Sarnori. The obelisk was raised by Ghis, but the carvings were Valyrian, for all the warriors were captured and enslaved.

as the Century of Blood, the grasslands, too, exploded into war. During the years that followed the Doom, the riders of the eastern steppes, hitherto divided into threescore quarrelsome tribes at perpetual war with one another, had finally been united under a single leader, a Dothraki *khal* called Mengo. Counseled by his mother, the purported witch queen Doshi, Khal Mengo compelled the other nomads to accept his rule, extinguishing or enslaving those who refused.

Then, in his old age, he turned his eyes westward.

Contemptuous of the horselords, who had been no more than a nuisance to them for centuries, the Tall Men ignored the threat from the east for far too long, even as the *khalasars* began to raid across their eastern marches. Some of their kings even sought to use the Dothraki in their own wars, offering them gold and slaves and other gifts to fight against their rivals. Khal Mengo took these gifts gladly . . . then took the conquered lands as well, burning fields and farms and towns to return the grasslands to their wild state (for the Dothraki consider the earth to be their mother and think it sinful to cut her flesh with plows and spades and axes).

Not until Mengo's son Khal Moro brought his *khalasar* to the very gates of Sathar, the fabled Waterfall City, did the Tall Men seem to realize their peril. Broken in battle, the men of Sathar were put to the sword, their women and children carried off as slaves; three-quarters of them died on the grueling march south to slave marts at the Ghiscari hill city Hazdahn Mo. Sathar, loveliest of the cities of the grasslands, was burned to ash and rubble. It is written that it was Khal Moro himself who gave the ruins their new name: Yalli Qamayi, the place of Wailing Children.

Even then, the kings of Sarnor proved unable to unite. As Sathar burned, the kings of Kasath to the west and Gornath to the north sent forth their armies, not to aid their neighbors but to lay claim to a share of the plunder. In their greed for land, Kasath and Gornath even came into conflict with one another and fought a pitched battle

three days' ride west of Sathar, as plumes of black smoke rose in the eastern sky.

This is not the place to chronicle the events of the years and wars that followed, as the great cities of the Kingdoms of Sarnor fell piecemeal to the Dothraki. Those who wish a more detailed account are directed to Bello's *The End of the Tall Men*, Maester Illister's *Horse Tribes, Being a Study of the Nomads of the Eastern Plains of Essos***,** the eastern chapters and appendices of Maester Joseth's *Battles and Sieges of the Century of Blood,* and Vaggoro's definitive *Ruined Cities, Stolen Gods.*

Let it suffice to say that of all the proud Sarnori cities, only Saath remains unruined today, and that port city is a sad place, much diminished from what it once was, surviving largely because of support from Ib and Lorath (whose colony of Morosh is nearby). Only in Saath do men still name themselves *Tagaez Fen*; fewer than twenty thousand remain, when once the Tall Men numbered in the millions. Only there are the hundred gods of the Kingdom of Sarnor still worshipped. The bronze and marble likenesses that once adorned the streets and temples of the Tall Men now lean crookedly, overgrown by weeds, along the grassy ways of Vaes Dothrak, the sacred city of the horselords.

Sathar was the first of the cities of the grasslands to fall to the Dothraki, but by no means the last. Six years later, Khal Moro razed Kasath as well. In this attack his riders were aided, incredibly, by Gornath, whose king had made common cause with the Dothraki and taken one of Moro's daughters to wife. Yet Gornath itself fell next, a dozen years afterward. Khal Horro had by that time slain Khal Moro, ending the line of the mighty Khal Mengo. The King of Gornath died at the hand of his own Dothraki wife, who despised him for his weakness, we are told. Afterward, Khal Horro took her for his own, as rats devoured the corpse of her late husband.

Horro was the last of the great *khals* to command the allegiance of all Dothraki. When he was slain by a rival, only three years after the destruction of Gornath, his great *khalasar* splintered into a dozen lesser hordes, and the riders once again resumed their quarrelsome ways. Yet the reprieve this provided the Kingdom of Sarnor proved short-lived, for the Tall Men had shown their weakness, and the *khals* who followed Horro shared his taste for conquest. In the years that followed, they strove to outdo one another by conquering ever wider territories, destroying the cities of the grasslands, enslaving their peoples, and carrying their broken gods back to Vaes Dothrak to testify to their victories.

One by one, the remaining cities of the Tall Men were overwhelmed and destroyed, leaving only ruins and ashes to mark where their proud towers once stood. For scholars and students of history, the fall of Sallosh by the Silver Shore was especially tragic, for when that City of Scholars burned, its great library was not spared, and most of the history of the Tall Men and the peoples who had gone before them were lost for all time.

Kyth and Hornoth soon followed, destroyed by rival *khals*, each of whom sought to outdo the other in savagery.

The fortress city Mardosh the Unconquerable defied the horselands the longest. For close unto six years the city endured, cut off from its hinterlands, encircled by a succession of *khalasars*. Driven to starvation, the Mardoshi devoured their dogs and horses, then rats and mice and other vermin, and finally began to eat their own dead. When they could endure no longer, the surviving warriors of the city garrison slew their own wives and children to keep them from the *khals*, then opened the city gates and rushed forth for one final attack. They were cut down to a man. Afterward, the Dothraki named the ruins of Mardosh Vaes Gorqoyi, the City of the Blood Charge.

The fall of Mardosh finally awakened the remaining Sarnori kings to the depth of their peril. Putting aside their own quarrels and rivalries at last, the Tall Men gathered from up and down the Sarne, assembling a great army beneath the walls of Sarnath, intent on breaking the power of the *khals* for good and all. Led by Mazor Alexi, last of the High Kings, they struck out boldly to the east. In the tall grass halfway between Sarnath and the ruins of Kasath, they met

the assembled power of four *khalasars* on what forever after was known as the Field of Crows.

Khal Haro, Khal Qano, Khal Loso (the Lame), and Khal Zhako commanded almost eighty thousand horsemen between them, we are told. The great host of the High King of Sarnor was led by six thousand scythed chariots, with ten thousand armored riders behind them, and another ten thousand light horsemen (many of them women) on the flanks. Behind them marched the Sarnori foot, close to a hundred thousand spearmen and slingers, giving the Tall Men a great advantage in numbers. On this all chroniclers agree.

As battle was joined, the Sarnori chariots threatened to carry all before them. Their earth-shattering advance smashed through the center of the Dothraki horde, the spinning blades on the wheels of their chariots slicing through the legs of the Dothraki horses. When Khal Haro himself went down before them, cut to pieces and trampled, his *khalasar* broke and fled. As the chariots thundered after the fleeing horsemen, the High King and his armored riders plunged in after them, followed by the Sarnori foot, waving their spears and screaming victory.

Their elation was short-lived. The rout was feigned. When they had drawn the Tall Men deep into the trap, the fleeing Dothraki turned suddenly and unleashed a storm of arrows from their great bows. The *khalasars* of Khal Qano and Khal Zhako swept in from north and south, while Loso the Lame and his screamers circled round and attacked the Sarnori from the rear, cutting off their retreat. Completely encircled, the High King and his mighty host were cut to pieces. Some say a hundred thousand men died that day, amongst them Mazor Alexi, six lesser kings, and more than threescore lords and heroes. As the crows feasted on their corpses, the riders of the *khalasars* walked amongst the dead and squabbled over their valuables.

Bereft of defenders, Sarnath of the Tall Towers fell to Loso the Lame less than a fortnight later. Not even the Palace With a Thousand Rooms was spared when Khal Loso put the city to the torch.

The remaining cities of the grasslands followed one by one, as the Century of Blood drew to its close. Sarys, at the mouth of the Sarne, was the last to fall but yielded little in the way of slaves or plunder, for the people of the city had largely fled by the time that Khal Zeggo descended upon it.

It must not be thought that the Kingdom of Sarnor was the only victim of the horselords. The Valyrian colony Essaria, sometimes remembered as the Lost Free City, was similarly overwhelmed. Today its ruins are known to the Dothraki as Vaes Khadokh, the City of Corpses. In the north, Khal Dhako sacked and burned Ibbish, reclaiming most of the small foothold the men of Ib had carved out on the northern coast of Essos (a much smaller Ibbenese colony survives in the dense forests beside the Shivering Sea, huddled around the town they have named New Ibbish). In the south, other *khals* led their hordes into the Red Waste, destroying the Qaathi towns and cities that once dotted that desert, until only the great city of Qarth remained, protected by its towering triple wall.

again under some great *khal* and turn west once more in search of new conquests.

The Dothraki have oft attempted to extend their power eastward as well, but there they have found the Bone Mountains to be an almost insurmountable obstacle. Those bleak, inhospitable peaks form an immense stone wall between the horselords and the riches of the Further East. Only three passes exist large enough to bring an army through, and athwart those stand the mighty fortress cities Bayasabhad, Samyriana, and Kayakayanaya, defended by tens of thousands of redoubtable female warriors, the last remnants of the great kingdom of Hyrkoon, which once flourished beyond the Bones in what is now known as the Great Sand Sea. Many a *khal* has died beneath their walls, and still those walls stand inviolate.

West of the Bones, however, from the Shivering Sea in the north to the Painted Mountains and Skahazadhan in the south, the vast expanse of grass where civilization first flowered remains a windswept desolation where no man

---

Despite their long history, little can be said with any certainty of the Qaathi—a people now gone from the world save for a remnant in Qarth.

What can be said is that the Qaathi arose in the grasslands and established towns there, coming into contact and occasional conflict with the Sarnori. They would oft have the worse of these wars, and so began to drift farther south, creating new city-states. One such, Qarth, was founded on the coast of the Summer Sea. Yet the lands in the south of Essos proved more inhospitable than those the Qaathi had vacated, turning to desert even as they established their foothold there. The Qaathi people were already well on their way to collapse when the Doom struck, and any hopes of using the chaos in the Summer Sea to their advantage vanished when the Dothraki attacked, destroying all the remaining Qaathi cities save for Qarth itself.

Yet in a way, the Dothraki destruction led to a resurgence for Qarth. Forced to look instead to the sea, the Pureborn who ruled Qarth swiftly constructed a fleet and took control of the Jade Gates—the strait between Qarth and Great Moraq, which joins the Summer Sea to the Jade Sea. With the Valyrian fleet destroyed, and Volantis's attention turned west, there were none to oppose them as they established control over the most direct route between east and west, and so gained immeasurably in both trade and levied tolls for safe passage.

Many in the Free Cities believe that the westward thrust of the horselords was turned back at Qohor, when Khal Temmo's attempt to take that city was defeated by the valor of three thousand Unsullied slave soldiers who stood fast against eighteen charges of his screamers. To believe that the stand of the Three Thousand of Qohor put an end to Dothraki dreams of conquest, however, suggests a complacency akin to that of the High King of Sarnor's when the horselords first came boiling out of the east. Wiser men know that it is only a matter of time until the *khalasars* unite

dares plow a furrow, plant a seed, or raise a house for fear of the *khalasars* that wander freely there to this very day, exacting gifts from any man who seeks to cross their lands and making war upon each other.

The Dothraki remain nomads still, a savage and wild people who prefer tents to palaces. Seldom still, the *khals* drive their great herds of horses and goats endlessly across their "sea," fighting one another when they meet and occasionally moving beyond the borders of their own lands for slaves and plunder, or to claim the "gifts" that the magisters

It is said that the fortress cities of Bayasabhad, Samyriana, and Kayakayanaya are defended by women out of the belief that those who give birth are the only ones permitted to take life at will. The *True Account of Addam of Duskendale's Journeys*, a merchant's account of his alleged travels in eastern Essos, provides little further insight into these matters, or any others that scholars are interested in, and instead spends most of its time finding ways to remind readers that the warrior women walk about bare-breasted and decorate their cheeks and nipples with ruby studs and iron rings.

and triarchs of the Free Cities bestow upon them whenever they chance to wander too far west.

The horselords have only one permanent settlement: the "city" they call Vaes Dothrak, which stands beneath the shadow of the lonely peak they call the Mother of Mountains, beside a bottomless lake they name the Womb of the World. It is here that the Dothraki believe their race was born. No true city, Vaes Dothrak has neither walls nor streets. Its grassy thoroughfares are lined with stolen gods, its palaces made of woven grass.

This hollow shell of a city is ruled by women: the crones of the *dosh khaleen,* all widows of dead *khals.* The Dothraki esteem Vaes Dothrak as the holiest of cities. No blood may be shed there, for the riders believe this to be a place of peace and power, where one day all the *khalasars* shall gather together once more beneath the banners of the great *khal* who will conquer all, the "stallion who mounts the world."

For us, however, the only true importance of Vaes Dothrak is the trading that takes place there. The Dothraki themselves will neither buy nor sell, deeming it unmanly, but in their sacred city, by leave of the *dosh khaleen,* merchants and traders from beyond the Bones and the Free Cities come together, to haggle and exchange goods and gold. The caravans that feed the great Eastern and Western Markets of Vaes Dothrak give handsome gifts to the *khals* they meet crossing the Dothraki sea, and in return receive protection.

So, strange to say, this empty "city" of the nomads has become the gateway between east and west (for those who travel by land). Many distant peoples who might not otherwise meet, or even know of one another, gather here in this queer bazaar beneath the Mother of Mountains, and trade in safety.

The Shivering Sea is bounded to the west by Westeros, to the south by Essos, to the north by the vast frozen wilderness of ice and snow that seafarers call the White Waste, and to the east by lands and seas unknown.

The true extent of this vast, chilly, inhospitable ocean may never be known, for no man of the Seven Kingdoms has ever sailed farther east than the Thousand Islands, whilst those who venture too far north encounter howling winds, frozen seas, and mountains of ice that can crush even the strongest ship. Beyond them, sailors tell us, blizzards rage eternally and the very mountains themselves scream like madmen in the night.

It has long been accepted amongst the wise that our world is round. If this is true, it ought to be possible to sail over the top of the world and down its far side, and there discover lands and seas undreamed of. Over the centuries, many a bold mariner has sought to find a way through the ice to whatever lies beyond. Most, alas, have perished in the attempt, or returned south again half-frozen and much chastened. Whilst it is true that the White Waste recedes during summer and expands again in winter, its very shorelines ever changing, no seafarer has succeeded in finding this fabled northern passage, nor the warm summer sea that Maester Heriston of White Harbor once suggested might lie hidden and entombed behind the icy cliffs of the far north.

Sailors, by nature a gullible and superstitious lot, as fond of their fancies as singers, tell many tales of these frigid northern waters. They speak of queer lights shimmering in the sky, where the demon mother of the ice giants dances eternally through the night, seeking to lure men northward to their doom. They whisper of Cannibal Bay, where ships enter at their peril only to find themselves trapped forever when the sea freezes hard behind them.

They tell of pale blue mists that move across the waters, mists so cold that any ship they pass over is frozen instantly; of drowned spirits who rise at night to drag the living down into the grey-green depths; of mermaids pale of flesh with black-scaled tails, far more malign than their sisters of the south.

Of all the queer and fabulous denizens of the Shivering Sea, however, the greatest are the ice dragons. These colossal beasts, many times larger than the dragons of Valyria, are said to be made of living ice, with eyes of pale blue crystal and vast translucent wings through which the moon and stars can be glimpsed as they wheel across the sky. Whereas common dragons (if any dragon can truly be said to be common) breathe flame, ice dragons supposedly breathe cold, a chill so terrible that it can freeze a man solid in half a heartbeat.

Sailors from half a hundred nations have glimpsed these great beasts over the centuries, so mayhaps there is some truth behind the tales. Archmaester Margate has suggested that many legends of the north—freezing mists, ice ships, Cannibal Bay, and the like—can be explained as distorted reports of ice-dragon activity. Though an amusing notion, and not without a certain elegance, this remains the purest conjecture. As ice dragons supposedly melt when slain, no actual proof of their existence has ever been found.

Let us put aside such fancies and return to fact. Despite the sinister legends that have grown up around its northernly reaches, the waters of the Shivering Sea teem with life. Hundreds of varieties of fish swim through its depths, including salmon, wolf fish, sand lances, grey skates, lampreys and other eels, whitefish, char, shark, herring, mackerel, and cod. Crabs and lobsters (some of truly monstrous size) are found everywhere along its shores, whilst seals, narwhals, walruses, and sea lions have their rookeries and breeding grounds on and around the countless rocky islands and sea stacks.

Ice dragons notwithstanding, the true kings of these northern waters are the whales. Half a dozen types of these great beasts make their homes in the Shivering Sea, amongst them grey whales, white whales, humpbacks, savage spotted whales with their hunting packs (which many call the wolves of the wild sea), and the mighty leviathans, the oldest and largest of all the living creatures of the earth.

The westernmost reaches of the Shivering Sea, from Skagos and the Grey Cliffs to the delta of the Sarne, are

Legend claims a thousand ships lie entombed in Cannibal Bay, some still inhabited by the children and grandchildren of their original crews, who survive by feasting upon the flesh of sailors newly caught by the ice.

the richest fishing grounds in the known world. Cod and herring are especially abundant here. Fisherfolk from lands as distant as the Three Sisters (in the west) and Morosh (in the east) have been known to work these waters . . . but they do so at the sufferance of the Free City of Braavos, whose fleets dominate the seas northwest of Essos, protected by their Sealord's warships. Together with banking and trade, fishing is one of the "three pillars" upon which the wealth and prosperity of Braavos is founded.

Sailing eastward, an intrepid seafarer will eventually pass from Braavosi waters to those where the Free City of Lorath holds sway, albeit with a feebler grip, and thence past the Axe, where many different peoples have lived and died and perished over the millennia in wars beyond count. East of the Axe are the deep blue waters of Bitterweed Bay, where ships from Ib and Lorath have so oft contested for supremacy, and the last great war fleet of the Kingdom of Sarnor was sent to the bottom by the Sealord of Braavos. On Ib these waters are known as Battle Bay, whilst the Lorathi named them Bloody Bay. By any name, a thousand sunken ships and the bones of fifty thousand drowned sailors are said to be strewn across the bay's bottom, home to the crabs for which Bitterweed is renowned.

Beyond Bitterweed Bay lies the delta of the Sarne, the great north-flowing river whose many vassal streams drain much of central Essos. Here stands Saath with its white walls, the last (and least, many say) of the great cities of the fallen Kingdom of Sarnor. The ruins of Saath's sister city Sarys, sacked and destroyed by a Dothraki *khal* centuries ago, can be found across the width of the delta. Between them, at another mouth of the great river, rises the Lorathi mining and fishing colony Morosh.

Those bold enough to continue still farther east will next pass the shores of the small, pastoral Kingdom of Omber, whose craven kings and feeble princes are best known for the grain, gems, and girls they pay the Dothraki horselords each year to be left unmolested. East of Omber our sailor will reach the Bay of Tusks, famed as the breeding grounds of walrus. And soon thereafter, the intrepid seafarer will find himself crossing the heart of the Shivering Sea, where every rock and wave is ruled by the hairy men from the great island of Ib.

IB

Through the centuries many different peoples have made their homes upon the shores and islands of the Shivering Sea and sent their mariners across its chilly grey-green waters. The most enduring and significant of these are the Ibbenese, an ancient and taciturn race of islanders who have fished the northern seas since the dawn of days from their homes upon the Ibbish isles.

The Ibbenese stand apart from the other races of mankind. They are a heavy people, broad about the chest and shoulders, but seldom standing more than five and a half feet in height, with thick, short legs and long arms. Though short and squat, they are ferociously strong; at wrestling, their favorite sport, no man of the Seven Kingdoms can hope to equal them.

Their faces, characterized by sloping brows with heavy ridges, small sunken eyes, great square teeth, and massive jaws, seem brutish and ugly to Westerosi eyes, an impression heightened by their guttural, grunting tongue; but in truth the men of Ib are a cunning folk—skilled craftsmen, able hunters and trackers, and doughty warriors. They are the most hirsute people in the known world. Though their flesh is pale, with dark blue veins beneath the skin, their hair is dark and wiry. Ibbenese men are heavily bearded; wiry body hair covers their arms, legs, chests, and backs. Coarse dark hair is common amongst their women, even on the upper lip. (The persistent myth that Ibbenese females have six breasts has no truth to it, however.)

ABOVE | *The ice of the White Waste.*

Though the men of Ib can father children upon the women of Westeros and other lands, the products of such unions are often malformed and inevitably sterile, in the manner of mules. Ibbenese females, when mated with men from other races, bring forth naught but stillbirths and monstrosities.

Such matings are uncommon; though ships from the Port of Ibben are a common sight in harbors up and down the narrow sea, and even as far away as the Summer Isles and Old Volantis, the sailors who crew them keep to their own kind even when ashore and display a deep suspicion of all strangers. On Ib itself, men of other lands and races are restricted by law and custom to the harbor precincts of the Port of Ibben and forbidden to venture beyond the city save in the company of an Ibbenese host. Such invitations are exceedingly rare.

Ib is the second largest island in the known world; only Great Moraq, between the Jade and Summer Seas, is larger. Stony and mountainous, Ib is a land of great grey mountains, ancient forests, and rushing rivers, its dark interior a haunt of bears and wolves. Giants once dwelt on Ib, we are told, but none remain—though mammoths still roam the island's plains and hills, and in the higher mountains, some claim unicorns can be found.

The Ibbenese of the woods and mountains have even less love of strangers than their cousins by the sea and seldom speak any tongue but their own. Foresters, goatherds, and miners, they make their homes in caves or houses of grey stone dug into the earth and roofed with slate or thatch. Towns and villages are rare; the Ibbenese of the interior prefer to dwell apart from their fellows, in solitary compounds, gathering only for weddings, burials, and worship. Gold, iron, and tin can be found in abundance in the mountains of Ib, as well as timber, amber, and a hundred sorts of pelts in the island's forests.

The Ibbenese of the shore are a more venturesome folk than their cousins from the woods and mountains. Bold fishermen, they travel the northern seas widely in search of cod, herring, whitefish, and eel, but it is as whalers that they are best known in the wider world. Their great-bellied whaling ships are a common sight in ports up and down the narrow sea and beyond. Though seldom pleasing to the eye (or nose), Ibbenese ships are renowned for their strength for they are built to weather any storm and withstand the assaults of even the largest leviathans. The bone, blubber, and oil of the whales they hunt are Ib's chief stock-in-trade,

and have made the Port of Ibben the largest and richest city of the Shivering Sea.

Grey and gloomy, the Port of Ibben has ruled over Ib and the lesser isles since the dawn of days. A city of cobbled alleys, steep hills, and teeming docks and shipyards, lit by hundreds of whale-oil lamps suspended over its streets on iron chains, the Port is dominated by the ruins of the God-King's castle, a colossal structure of rough-hewn stone that was home to a hundred Ibbenese kings. The last such king was thrown down in the aftermath of the Doom of Valyria, however. Today, Ib and the lesser isles are governed by the Shadow Council, whose members are chosen by the Thousand, an assembly of wealthy guildsmen, ancient nobles, priests, and priestesses not unlike the magisters' councils of the Free Cities.

Far Ib, second largest of the Ibbenese islands, lies more than a hundred leagues southeast of Ib itself and is altogether a bleaker and poorer place. Ib Sar, its only town, was originally a place of exile and punishment where the Ibbenese of old sent their most notorious criminals, often after mutilating them so they might never return to Ib itself. Though that practice ended with the fall of the God-Kings, Ib Sar retains an unsavory reputation to this very day.

The men of Ib have not always confined themselves to their islands. There is abundant evidence of Ibbenese settlements on the Axe, on the Lorathi isles, and along the shores of the Bitterweed Bay and the Bay of Tusks (in the west) and Leviathan Sound and the Thousand Islands (in the east), and history tells of several Ibbenese attempts to seize control of the mouth of the Sarne, attempts that brought the hairy men into bloody conflict with the Sarnori sister cities Saath and Sarys.

The God-Kings of Ib, before their fall, did succeed in conquering and colonizing a huge swathe of northern Essos immediately south of Ib itself, a densely wooded region that had formerly been the home of a small, shy forest folk. Some say that the Ibbenese extinguished this gentle race, whilst others believe they went into hiding in the deeper woods or fled to other lands. The Dothraki still call the great forest along the northern coast the Kingdom of the Ifequevron, the name by which they knew the vanished forest-dwellers.

The fabled Sea Snake, Corlys Velaryon, Lord of the Tides, was the first Westerosi to visit these woods. After his return from the Thousand Islands, he wrote of carved trees, haunted grottoes, and strange silences. A later traveler, the merchant-adventurer Bryan of Oldtown, captain of the cog *Spearshaker*, provided an account of his own journey across the Shivering Sea. He reported that the Dothraki name for the lost people meant "those who walk in the woods." None of the Ibbenese that Bryan of Oldtown met could say they had ever seen a woods walker, but claimed that the little people blessed a household that left offerings of leaf and stone and water overnight.

At its greatest extent, the Ibbenese foothold on Essos was as large as Ib itself and far richer. More and more of the hairy men crossed over from the islands to make their fortunes there, cutting down the trees to put the land under the plow, damming the rivers and streams, mining the hills. Ruling over these domains was Ibbish, a fishing village that swelled to become a thriving port and the second city of the Ibbenese, with a deep harbor and high white walls.

All that ended two hundred years ago with the coming of the Dothraki. The horselords had hitherto shunned the forests of the northern coasts; some say this was because of their reverence for the vanished wood walkers, others because they feared their powers. Whatever the truth, the Dothraki did not fear the men of Ib. *Khal* after *khal* began to make incursions into Ibbenese territories, overrunning the farms and fields and holdfasts of the hairy men with fire and steel, putting the males to the sword whilst carrying off their wives into slavery.

The Ibbenese, a notoriously avaricious and, yea, even niggardly people, refused to pay the tribute the *khals* demanded, choosing to fight instead. Though the men of Ib won several notable victories, famously destroying the huge *khalasar* of the fearsome Khal Onqo in one epic battle, the Dothraki only came in greater numbers, as each new *khal* sought to eclipse the conquests of the last. The *khalasars* pushed the Ibbenese farther and farther back, until at last they overwhelmed even the great city of Ibbish. Khal Scoro was the first to take the city, breaking through the Whalebone Gates to loot the temples and treasuries and carry off the city's gods to Vaes Dothrak. The Ibbenese rebuilt, but a generation later Ibbish was sacked again by Khal Rogo, who put half the city to the torch and marched ten thousand women to slavery.

Today only ruins remain where Ibbish once stood, a place the Dothraki name Vaes Aresak, or City of Cowards . . . for when the *khalasar* of Onqo's grandson, Khal Dhako, approached to sack the city once again, the remaining inhabitants took to their ships and fled back across the sea to Ib. In his wroth, Dhako not only put the abandoned city to the torch but burned so much of the surrounding countryside that he was thereafter known as the Dragon of the North.

Ib retains a modest foothold on Essos even to this day, on a small peninsula surrounded by the sea and defended by a wooden wall almost as long as the ice Wall of the Night's Watch, if not a third as high, a towering earth-and-timber palisade bristling with defensive towers and protected by a deep ditch. Behind the earthworks, the men of Ib have built the town of New Ibbish to rule over their much-diminished domains, but sailors say that the new town is a sad and squalid place, more akin to Ib Sar than to the thriving city that the horselords reduced to ruins.

EAST OF IB

Beyond the Ibbish coastlands and forests of the Ifequevron, the foothills of the Bones rise up out of the grasslands, and farther east the mountains themselves march down to meet the sea. Even from miles out into the Shivering Sea, the great northern peaks, with their icy crowns and jagged spires, seem to split the very sky. Krazaaj Zasqa, the Dothraki call the northernmost of the Bones: the White Mountains.

Beyond them lies another world, one that very few Westerosi have ever visited. Those who have come this far, like Lomas Longstrider, have come by land through the mountain passes or by the way of the warm southern waters and the Jade Gates.

Though the eastern waters of the Shivering Sea are as rich as those of the west, few come to fish them save the Ibbenese themselves, for beyond the Bones are found the lands of the nomadic Jogos Nhai, a savage race of mounted warriors with no ships and no interest in the sea. Whalers from the Port of Ibben regularly hunt Leviathan Sound, where those great beasts come to mate and birth their young, and Ibbenese fishermen speak of vast schools of cod in the deeper waters, seals and walrus on the rocky islands to the north, and spider crabs and emperor crabs everywhere, but elsewise these eastern seas are empty.

Still farther east lie the so-called Thousand Islands (Ibbenese chartmakers tell us that there are in truth fewer than three hundred), a sea-girt scatter of bleak windswept rocks believed by some to be the last remnants of a drowned kingdom whose towns and towers were submerged beneath

the rising seas many thousands of years ago. Only the boldest or the most desperate mariners ever make landfall here, for the people of these islands, though few in number, are a queer folk, inimical to strangers, a hairless people with green-tinged skin who file the teeth of their females into sharp points and slice the foreskins from the members of their males. They speak no known tongue and are said to sacrifice sailors to their squamous, fish-headed gods, likenesses of whom rise from their stony shores, visible only when the tide recedes. Though surrounded by water on all sides, these islanders fear the sea so much that they will not set foot in the water even under threat of death.

Even Corlys Velaryon dared sail no farther east than the Thousand Islands; this was where the Sea Snake turned back on his great northern voyage. In truth, there was no reason for him to continue, save for his hunger to learn what lay beyond the next horizon. Even the fish taken from these eastern seas are oddly misshapen, with a bitter, unpleasant taste, it is said.

Only one port of note is to be found on the Shivering Sea east of the Bones: Nefer, chief city of the kingdom of N'ghai, hemmed in by towering chalk cliffs and perpetually shrouded in fog. When seen from the harbor, Nefer appears to be no more than a small town, but it is said that nine-tenths of the city is beneath the ground. For that reason, travelers call Nefer the Secret City. By any name, the city enjoys a sinister reputation as a haunt of necromancers and torturers.

Beyond N'ghai are the forests of Mossovy, a cold dark land of shapechangers and demon hunters. Beyond Mossovy . . .

No man of Westeros can truly say. Certain septons have claimed that the world ends east of Mossovy, giving way to a realm of mists, then a realm of darkness, and finally a realm of storm and chaos where sea and sky become as one. Sailors and singers and other dreamers prefer to believe that the Shivering Sea goes on and on, unending, past the easternmost coasts of Essos, past islands and continents unknown, uncharted, and undreamed of, where strange peoples worship strange gods beneath stranger stars. Wiser men suggest that somewhere beyond the waters we know, east becomes west, and the Shivering Sea must surely join the Sunset Sea, if indeed the world is round.

It may be so. Or not. Until some new Sea Snake arises to sail beyond the sunrise, no man can know for certain.

THE BONES AND BEYOND

EAST, BEYOND VAES DOTHRAK and the Mother of Mountains, the grasslands give way to rolling plains and woods, and the earth beneath the traveler's feet turns hard and stony and begins to climb upward, ever upward. The hills grow wilder and steeper, and soon enough the mountains appear in the far distance, their great peaks seeming to float against the eastern sky, blue-grey giants so huge and jagged and menacing that even Lomas Longstrider, that dauntless wanderer (if his tales be true), lost heart at the sight of them, believing that he had at last reached the ends of the earth.

The ancestors of the Dothraki and the other horse peoples of the grasslands knew better, for some remembered crossing those mountains from the lands that lay beyond. Did they come west in hopes of fairer fields and plenty or in search of conquest, or were they fleeing before some savage foe? Their tales do not agree, so we may never know, but of their travails we may be certain, for they left their bones behind to mark their passing. The bones of men, the bones of horses, the bones of giants and camels and oxen, of every sort of beast and bird and monster, all can be found amongst these savage peaks.

From them the mountains take their name: the Bones. Tallest of all the mountain ranges in the known world from the Sunset Sea to Asshai-by-the-Shadow, the Bones extend from the Shivering Sea to the Jade Sea, a wall of twisted rock and sharp stone stretching more than five hundred leagues from north to south and a hundred leagues from east to west.

Deep snows crown the northern Bones, whilst sandstorms oft scour the peaks and valleys of their southern sisters, carving them into strange shapes. In the long leagues between, thundering rivers roar through deep canyons, and small caves open onto vast caverns and sunless seas. Yet however inimical the Bones might seem to those who do not know them, they have been home to men and stranger things over the centuries. Even the snowcapped northernmost peaks (known as Krazaaj Zasqa or White Mountains in the Dothraki tongue), where the cold winds come howling off the Shivering Sea winter and summer, were once home to the Jhogwin, the stone giants, massive creatures said to have been twice as large as the giants of Westeros. Alas, the last of the Jhogwin disappeared a

thousand years ago; only their massive bones remain to mark where they once roamed.

"A thousand roads lead into the Bones," wise men say from Qarth to Qohor, "but only three lead out." As impassable as the Bones appear from afar, there are indeed hundreds of footpaths, goat tracks, game trails, streambeds, and slopes by which travelers, traders, and adventurers may find their way into the heart of the mountains. In certain places, ancient carved steps and hidden tunnels and passages exist for those who know how to find them. Yet many of these paths are treacherous, and others are dead ends or traps for the unwary.

Small parties, well armed and well provisioned, may make their way through the Bones by myriad ways when led by a guide who knows the dangers. Armies, trading caravans, and men alone, however, are well advised to stay to the main routes, the three great mountain passes that bridge the worlds of east and west: the Steel Road, the Stone Road, and the Sand Road.

The Steel Road (so named for all the battles it has seen) and the Stone Road both originate in Vaes Dothrak, the former running almost due east beneath the highest peaks, the latter curving southeast to join the old Silk Road at the ruins of Yinishar (called Vaes Jini by the horselords) before beginning its climb. Far south of these, the Sand Road passes through the southern Bones (sometimes called the Dry Bones, for water is scarce there) and surrounding deserts, connecting the great port city of Qarth with the market city Tiqui, the gateway to the east.

Even along these well-traveled routes, crossing the Bones remains grueling and hazardous . . . and safe passage comes at a price, for on the far side of the mountains stand three mighty fortress cities, last remnants of the once-great Patrimony of Hyrkoon. Bayasabhad, the City of Serpents, guards the eastern end of the Sand Road and exacts tribute from all those who seek to pass. The Stone Road, with its deep defiles and endless, narrow switchbacks, passes beneath the walls of Samyriana, a grey stone city carved into the very rock of the mountains it defends. In the north, fur-clad warriors ride the Steel Road over swaying bridges and through underground passageways, escorting caravans to and from Kayakayanaya, whose walls are black basalt, black iron, and yellow bone.

LEFT | *A woman of the Thousand Islands.*

Many accounts inform us that the mountain warriors of Kayakayanaya, Samyriana, and Bayasabhad are all women, daughters of the Great Fathers who rule these cities, where girls learn to ride and climb before they learn to walk, and are schooled in the arts of the bow, the spear, the knife, and the sling from earliest childhood. Lomas Longstrider himself tells us that there are no fiercer fighters on all the earth. As for their brothers, the sons of the Great Fathers, ninety-nine of every hundred are gelded when they reach the age of manhood and live out their lives as eunuchs, serving their cities as scribes, priests, scholars, servants, cooks, farmers, and craftsmen. Only the most promising males, the largest and strongest and most comely, are permitted to mature and breed and become Great Fathers themselves in their turns. Maester Naylin's *Rubies and Iron*—named for the penchant of the warrior women to wear iron rings in their nipples and rubies in their cheeks—speculates on the circumstances that led to such strange customs.

The three fortress cities began as true forts, outposts and garrisons raised up by the Patriarchs of Hyrkoon to guard the western marches of their realm against the brigands, outlaws, and wild men of the Bones, and the savages who dwelt beyond them. Over the centuries, however, the citadels grew into cities, whilst Hyrkoon itself withered into dust, as its lakes and rivers dried away and its once-fertile fields turned to desert. Today the heartland of Hyrkoon is the Great Sand Sea, a vast wasteland of restless dunes, dry riverbeds, and ruined forts and towns baking beneath the sun. Water is said to boil away, it is so hot in the deep, southern portions of the sea.

Beyond the Great Sand Sea another world awaits: the Further East, a vast land of plains and hills and river valleys that seems to have no end, where strange gods rule over stranger peoples. Many great cities and proud kingdoms have risen and flourished and fallen here since the dawn of days; most of these are little known in the west, even their very names long forgotten. Only the broadest outlines of the histories of the Further East are known to the Citadel, and even in those tales that have come west to us, over long leagues of mountains and deserts, there are many omissions, gaps, and contradictions, making it all but impossible to say with any certainty what portion is true and what portion has arisen from the fevered imaginings of singers, storytellers, and wet nurses.

Yet the oldest and greatest of the eastern civilizations endures to our present day: the Ancient, Glorious, Golden Empire of Yi Ti.

YI TI

A fabled land even in the Seven Kingdoms, Yi Ti is a large and diverse country, a realm of windswept plains and rolling hills, jungles and rain forests, deep lakes and rushing rivers and shrinking inland seas. Its legendary wealth is such as to allow its princes to live in houses of solid gold and dine on sweetmeats powdered with pearls and jade. Lomas Longstrider, awestruck by its marvels, called Yi Ti "the land of a thousand gods and a hundred princes, ruled by one god-emperor."

Those who have visited Yi Ti as it is today tell us that the thousand gods and hundred princes yet remain . . . but there are three god-emperors, each claiming the right to don the gowns of cloth-of-gold, green pearls, and jade that tradition allows to the emperor alone. None wields true power; though millions may worship the azure emperor in Yin and prostrate themselves before him whenever he appears, his imperial writ extends no farther than the walls of his own city. The hundred princes of whom Lomas Longstrider wrote rule their own realms as they please, as do the brigands, priest-kings, sorcerers, warlords, and imperial generals and tax collectors outside their domains.

This was not always so, we know. In ancient days, the god-emperors of Yi Ti were as powerful as any ruler on earth, with wealth that exceeded even that of Valyria at its height and armies of almost unimaginable size.

In the beginning, the priestly scribes of Yin declare, all the land between the Bones and the freezing desert called the Grey Waste, from the Shivering Sea to the Jade Sea (including even the great and holy isle of Leng), formed a single realm ruled by the God-on-Earth, the only begotten

RIGHT | *Hyrkoon the Hero with Lightbringer in hand, leading the virtuous into battle.*

son of the Lion of Night and Maiden-Made-of-Light, who traveled about his domains in a palanquin carved from a single pearl and carried by a hundred queens, his wives. For ten thousand years the Great Empire of the Dawn flourished in peace and plenty under the God-on-Earth, until at last he ascended to the stars to join his forebears.

Dominion over mankind then passed to his eldest son, who was known as the Pearl Emperor and ruled for a thousand years. The Jade Emperor, the Tourmaline Emperor, the Onyx Emperor, the Topaz Emperor, and the Opal Emperor followed in turn, each reigning for centuries . . . yet every reign was shorter and more troubled than the one preceding it, for wild men and baleful beasts pressed at the borders of the Great Empire, lesser kings grew prideful and rebellious, and the common people gave themselves over to avarice, envy, lust, murder, incest, gluttony, and sloth.

When the daughter of the Opal Emperor succeeded him as the Amethyst Empress, her envious younger brother cast her down and slew her, proclaiming himself the Bloodstone Emperor and beginning a reign of terror. He practiced dark arts, torture, and necromancy, enslaved his people, took

a tiger-woman for his bride, feasted on human flesh, and cast down the true gods to worship a black stone that had fallen from the sky. (Many scholars count the Bloodstone Emperor as the first High Priest of the sinister Church of Starry Wisdom, which persists to this day in many port cities throughout the known world).

In the annals of the Further East, it was the Blood Betrayal, as his usurpation is named, that ushered in the age of darkness called the Long Night. Despairing of the evil that had been unleashed on earth, the Maiden-Made-of-Light turned her back upon the world, and the Lion of Night came forth in all his wroth to punish the wickedness of men.

How long the darkness endured no man can say, but all agree that it was only when a great warrior—known variously as Hyrkoon the Hero, Azor Ahai, Yin Tar, Neferion, and Eldric Shadowchaser—arose to give courage to the race of men and lead the virtuous into battle with his blazing sword Lightbringer that the darkness was put to rout, and light and love returned once more to the world.

Yet the Great Empire of the Dawn was not reborn, for the restored world was a broken place where every tribe of

men went its own way, fearful of all the others, and war and lust and murder endured, even to our present day. Or so the men and women of the Further East believe.

At the Citadel of Oldtown and other centers of learning in the west, maesters regard these tales of the Great Empire and its fall as legend, not history, yet none doubt that the YiTish civilization is ancient, mayhap even contemporary with the realms of the Fisher Queens beside the Silver Sea. In Yi Ti itself, the priests insist that mankind's first towns and cities arose along the shores of the Jade Sea and dismiss the rival claims of Sarnor and Ghis as the boasts of savages and children.

Whatever the truth, Yi Ti was beyond question one of the places where men first climbed from the pit of savagery to civilization . . . and literacy, for the wise men of the east have been reading and writing for many thousands of years. Their most ancient records are cherished, almost venerated, but are also jealously guarded by their scholars. Such accounts as we have are pieced together from hearsay from travelers and scattered texts that have escaped Yi Ti to find their way across the seas to the Citadel.

To tell the tale of Yi Ti is far beyond our scope here, comprising as it does hundreds of emperors and myriad wars and conquests and rebellions. Let it suffice to say that the Golden Empire has known golden ages and dark ages, that it has waxed and waned and waxed again throughout the centuries, that it has weathered floods and droughts and sandstorms and quaking of the earth so violent as to swallow entire cities, that thousands of heroes and cravens and concubines and wizards and scholars have passed across the pages of its histories.

Since the Further East emerged from the Long Night and the centuries of chaos that followed, eleven dynasties have held sway over the lands we now call Yi Ti. Some lasted no more than a half century; the longest endured for seven hundred years. Some dynasties gave way to others peacefully, others with blood and steel. On four occasions, the end of a dynasty was followed by a period of anarchy and lawlessness when warlords and petty kings warred with one another for supremacy; the longest of these interregnums lasted more than a century.

THE GOD-EMPERORS OF YI TI

To recount even the most important events of this long history would require more words than we have, yet we would be remiss if we did not at least mention a few of the more fabled of the god-emperors of Yi Ti:

HAR LOI, the first of the grey emperors, whose throne was said to be a saddle, for he spent his entire reign at war, riding from one battle to another.

CHOQ CHOQ, the humpbacked, fifteenth and last of the indigo emperors, who kept a hundred wives and a thousand concubines and sired daughters beyond count but was never able to produce a son.

MENGO QUEN, the Glittering God, third of the jade-green emperors, who ruled from a palace where the floors and walls and columns were covered in gold leaf, and all the furnishings were made of gold, even to the chamber pots.

LO THO, called Lo Longspoon and Lo the Terrible, the twenty-second scarlet emperor, a reputed sorcerer and cannibal, who is said to have supped upon the living brains of his enemies with a long, pearl-handled spoon, after the tops of their skulls had been removed.

LO DOQ, called Lo Lackwit, the thirty-fourth scarlet emperor, a seeming simpleton cursed with an affliction that made him jerk and stagger when he walked, and drool when he tried to speak, who nonetheless ruled wisely for more than thirty years (though some suggest that the true ruler was his wife, the formidable Empress Bathi Ma Lo).

THE NINE EUNUCHS, the pearl-white emperors who gave Yi Ti 130 years of peace and prosperity. As young men and princes, they lived as other men, taking wives and concubines and siring heirs, but upon their ascent each surrendered his manhood root and stem, so that he might devote himself entirely to the empire.

JAR HAR, and his sons Jar Joq and Jar Han, the sixth, seventh, and eighth of the sea-green emperors, under whose rule the empire reached the apex of its power. Jar Har conquered Leng, Jar Joq took Great Morag, Jar Han exacted tribute from Qarth, Old Ghis, Asshai, and other far-flung lands, and traded with Valyria.

CHAI DUQ, the fourth yellow emperor, who took to wife a noblewoman of Valyria and kept a dragon at his court.

Though Yi Ti is a vast land, much of it covered by dense forest and sweltering jungles, travel from one end of the empire to the other is swift and safe, for the great web of stone roads built by the Eunuch Emperors of old have no equal in all the world, save for the dragonroads of the Valyrians.

The cities of Yi Ti are far-famed as well, for no other land can boast so many. If Lomas Longstrider can be believed, none of the cities of the west can compare to those of Yi Ti in size and splendor. "Even their ruins put ours to shame," the Longstrider said . . . and ruins are everywhere in Yi Ti. In his *Jade Compendium,* Colloquo Votar—the best source available in Westeros on the lands of the Jade Sea—wrote that beneath every YiTish city, three older cities lie buried.

Over the centuries, the capital of the Golden Empire has moved here and there and back again a score of times, as rival warlords contended and dynasties rose and fell. The grey emperors, indigo emperors, and pearl-white emperors

with the rude, sprawling garrison city called Trader Town as his capital. Which of these three emperors will prevail is a question best left for the historians of the years to come.

No discussion of Yi Ti would be complete without a mention of the Five Forts, a line of hulking ancient citadels that stand along the far northeastern frontiers of the Golden Empire, between the Bleeding Sea (named for the characteristic hue of its deep waters, supposedly a result of a plant that grows only there) and the Mountains of the Morn. The Five Forts are very old, older than the Golden Empire itself; some claim they were raised by the Pearl Emperor during the morning of the Great Empire to keep the Lion of Night and his demons from the realms of men . . . and indeed, there is something godlike, or demonic, about the monstrous size of the forts, for each of the five is large enough to house ten thousand men, and their massive walls stand almost a thousand feet high.

Certain scholars from the west have suggested Valyrian involvement in the construction of the Five Forts, for the great walls are single slabs of fused black stone that resemble certain Valyrian citadels in the west . . . but this seems unlikely, for the Forts predate the Freehold's rise, and there is no record of any dragonlords ever coming so far east.

Thus the Five Forts must remain a mystery. They still stand today, unmarked by time, guarding the marches of the Golden Empire against raiders out of the Grey Waste.

ruled from Yin on the shores of the Jade Sea, first and most glorious of the YiTish cities, but the scarlet emperors raised up a new city in the heart of the jungle and named it Si Qo the Glorious (long fallen and overgrown, its glory lives now only in legend), whilst the purple emperors preferred Tiqui, the many-towered city in the western hills, and the maroon emperors kept their martial court in Jinqi, the better to guard the frontiers of the empire against reavers from the Shadow Lands.

Today Yin is once more the capital of Yi Ti. There the seventeenth azure emperor Bu Gai sits in splendor in a palace larger than all King's Landing. Yet far to the east, well beyond the borders of the Golden Empire proper, past the legendary Mountains of the Morn, in the city Carcosa on the Hidden Sea, dwells in exile a sorcerer lord who claims to be the sixty-ninth yellow emperor, from a dynasty fallen for a thousand years. And more recently, a general named Pol Qo, Hammer of the Jogos Nhai, has given himself imperial honors, naming himself the first of the orange emperors,

Of the lands that lie beyond the Five Forts, we know even less. Legends and lies and traveler's tales are all that ever reach us of these far places. We hear of cities where the men soar like eagles on leathern wings, of towns made of bones, of a race of bloodless men who dwell between the deep valley called the Dry Deep and the mountains. Whispers reach us of the Grey Waste and its cannibal sands, and of the Shrykes who live there, half-human creatures with green-scaled skin and venomous bites. Are these truly lizard-men, or (more likely) men clad in the skins of lizards? Or are they no more than fables, the grumkins and snarks of the eastern deserts? And even the Shrykes supposedly live in terror of K'dath in the Grey Waste, a city said to be older than time, where unspeakable rites are performed to slake the hunger of mad gods. Does such a city truly exist? If so, what is its nature?

On such matters, even Lomas Longstrider is silent. Perhaps the priests of Yi Ti know, but if so, these are not truths they care to share with us.

THE PLAINS OF THE JOGOS NHAI

North of Yi Ti, the windswept plains and rolling hills that stretch from the Golden Empire's frontiers to the desolate shores of the Shivering Sea are dominated by a race of mounted warriors called the Jogos Nhai. Like the Dothraki of the western grasslands, they are a nomadic people who live their lives in yurts, tents, and saddles, a proud, restless, warlike race who prize their freedoms above all and are never content to remain in one place for long.

Yet in many ways these riders of the Further East are very different from the horselords of the west. The Jogos Nhai are as a rule a head shorter than their counterparts and less comely to western eyes—squat, bowlegged, and swarthy, with large heads, small faces, and a sallow cast of skin. Men and women both have pointed skulls, a result of their curious custom of binding the heads of their newborn during their first two years of life. Where Dothraki warriors pride themselves on the length of their braid, the men of the Jogos Nhai shave their heads but for a single strip of hair down the center of the skull, whilst their women go wholly bald and are said to scrape all the hair from their female parts as well.

The mounts of the Jogos Nhai are smaller than the fiery steeds of the Dothraki, for the plains east of the Bones are drier and less fertile than the Dothraki sea, their grasses sparser, offering meager sustenance to horses. And so these easterners ride zorses, hardy beasts originally made by breeding horses with certain strange, horselike creatures from the southern regions of Yi Ti and the island of Leng. Foul-tempered beasts, their hides marked with black and white stripes, the zorses of the Jogos Nhai are renowned for their toughness and can supposedly survive on weeds and devil grass for many turns of the moon and travel long distances without water or fodder.

Unlike the Dothraki, whose *khals* lead huge *khalasars* across the grasslands, the Jogos Nhai travel in small bands, closely connected by blood. Each band is commanded by a *jhat*, or war chief, and a moonsinger, who combines the roles of priestess, healer, and judge. The *jhat* leads in war and battle and raid, whilst other matters are ruled by the band's moonsinger.

Dothraki *khals* make endless war on one another once beyond the sacred precincts of Vaes Dothrak, their holy city, but the gods of the Jogos Nhai forbid them to shed the blood of their own people (young men do ride out to steal goats, dogs, and zorses from other bands, whilst their sisters go forth to abduct husbands, but these are rituals hallowed by the gods of the plains, during which no blood may be shed).

The face the zorse-riders show outsiders is very different, however, for they live in a state of perpetual war against all the neighboring peoples. Their attacks upon N'ghai, the ancient land to the northeast of their domains, has reduced that once-proud kingdom to a single city (Nefer) and its hinterlands. Legend claims that it was the Jogos Nhai, led by the *jhattar*—the *jhat* of *jhats* and war leader of the whole people—Gharak Squint-Eye, who slew the last of the stone giants of Jhogwin at the Battle in the Howling Hills.

Before the Dry Times and the coming of the Great Sand Sea, the Jogos Nhai fought many a bloody border war against the Patrimony of Hyrkoon as well, poisoning rivers and wells, burning towns and cities, and carrying off thousands into slavery on the plains, whilst the Hyrkoon for their part were sacrificing tens of thousands of the zorse-riders to their dark and hungry gods. The enmity between the nomads and the warrior women of the Bones runs deep and bitter to this very day, and over the centuries a dozen *jhattars* have led armies up the Steel Road. Thus far all these assaults have broken against the walls of Kayakayanaya, yet the moonsingers still sing of the glorious day to come when the Jogos Nhai shall prevail and spill over the mountains to claim the fertile lands beyond.

Even the mighty Golden Empire of Yi Ti is not exempt from the depredations of the Jogos Nhai, as many a YiTish lord and princeling has learned to his grief. Raids and incursions into the empire are a way of life amongst the nomads,

Amongst the Jogos Nhai, *jhats* are usually men and moonsingers women, but female *jhats* and male moonsingers are not unknown. This is not always obvious to strangers, however, for a girl who chooses the warrior's way is expected to dress and live as a man, whilst a boy who wishes to be a moonsinger must dress and live as a woman.

RIGHT | *The Jogos Nhai riding upon zorses.*

the source of the gold and gems that drape the arms and necks of their moonsingers and *jhats*, and of the slaves that serve them and their herds. Over the past two thousand years, the zorse-riders of the northern plains have reduced to ruins a dozen YiTish cities, a hundred towns, and farms and fields beyond counting.

During that time, many an imperial general and three god-emperors have led armies across the plains in turn, to bring the nomads to heel. History tells us that such attempts seldom end well. The invaders may slaughter the herds of the nomads, burn their tents and yurts, collect tribute in the form of gold, goods, and slaves from the bands they chance to encounter, and even compel a handful of *jhats* to vow eternal fealty to the god-emperor and forswear raiding forever . . . but most Jogos Nhai flee before the imperial hosts, refusing to give battle, and sooner or later the general or emperor loses patience and turns back, whereupon life resumes as before.

During the long reign of Lo Han, forty-second scarlet emperor, three such invasions of the plains ended as described, yet the end of his days found the Jogos Nhai bolder and more rapacious than they had been when first he donned the imperial regalia. Upon his death, therefore, his young and valiant son Lo Bu determined to end the threat posed by the nomads for all time. Assembling a mighty host, said to be three hundred thousand strong, this bold young emperor crossed the frontiers with slaughter as his only purpose. Tribute could not sway him, nor hostages, nor oaths of fealty and offerings of peace; his vast army swept across the plains like a scythe, destroying all, leaving a burning wasteland behind it.

When the Jogos Nhai resorted to their traditional tactics, melting away at his approach, Lo Bu divided his huge army into thirteen smaller hosts and sent them forth in all directions to hunt down the nomads wherever they might go. It is written that a million Jogos Nhai died at their hands.

At last the nomads, facing the extinction of their race, did what they had never done before. A thousand rival clans joined together and raised up a *jhattar*, a woman in man's mail named Zhea. Known as Zhea the Barren, Zhea Zorseface, and Zhea the Cruel, and famed even then for her cunning, she is remembered to this day in the Golden Empire of Yi Ti, where mothers whisper her name to frighten unruly children into obedience.

In courage, valor, and skill at arms, Lo Bu had no peer, but in cunning he proved to be no match for Zhea. The war between the young emperor and the wizened *jhattar* lasted less than two years. Zhea isolated each of Lo Bu's thirteen armies, slew their scouts and foragers, starved them, denied them water, led them into wastelands and traps, and destroyed them each in turn. Finally her swift riders descended upon Lo Bu's own host, in a night of carnage and slaughter so terrible that every stream for twenty leagues around was choked with blood.

Amongst the slain was Lo Bu himself, the forty-third and last of the scarlet emperors. When his severed head was presented to Zhea, she commanded that the flesh be stripped from the bone, so that his skull might be dipped in gold and made into her drinking cup. From that time to this, every *jhattar* of the Jogos Nhai has drunk fermented zorse milk from the gilded skull of the Boy Too Bold By Half, as Lo Bu is remembered.

LENG

Southeast of Yin, surrounded by the warm green waters of the Jade Sea, the verdant isle of Leng is home to "ten thousand tigers and ten million monkeys," or so Lomas Longstrider once claimed. The great apes of Leng are also far-famed; amongst them are spotted humpback apes said to be almost as clever as men, and hooded apes as large as giants, so strong that they can pull the arms and legs off a man as easily as a boy might pull the wings off a fly.

Leng's history goes back almost as far as that of Yi Ti itself, but little and less of it is known west of the Jade Straits. There are queer ruins in the depths of the island's jungle: massive buildings, long fallen, and so overgrown that rubble remains above the surface . . . but underground, we are told, endless labyrinths of tunnels lead to vast chambers, and carved steps descend hundreds of feet into the earth. No man can say who might have built these cities, or when. They remain perhaps the only remnant of some vanished people.

The present inhabitants of Leng are of two sorts, so utterly different from one another that we must regard them as entirely separate peoples.

For much of its recent history, Leng has been a part of the Golden Empire of Yi Ti, ruled from Yin or Jinqi. During these epochs, tens of thousands of soldiers, merchants, adventurers, and sellswords made the migration from the empire to the island, seeking their fortunes. Though Leng broke free of Yi Ti four hundred years ago, the northern two-thirds of the island are still dominated by the descendants of these YiTish invaders.

OTHER ISLANDS OF NOTE IN THE JADE SEA, AS RECORDED BY CORLYS VELARYON IN HIS LETTERS

THE ISLE OF ELEPHANTS, whose *shan* rules from a palace made of ivory.

MARAHAI, the paradise isle, a verdant crescent attended by twin fire islands, where burning mountains belch plumes of molten stone day and night.

THE ISLE OF WHIPS, a bleak and barren way station where slavers from half a dozen lands buy, sell, breed, break, and brand their chattel before sending them onward.

To the traveler, they remain indistinguishable from the people of the Golden Empire; they speak a dialect of the same language, pray to the same gods, eat the same foods, follow the same customs, and even reverence the azure emperor in Yin . . . though they worship only their own god-empress. Their principal towns, Leng Yi and Leng Ma, resemble Yin and Jinqi far more than they do Turrani, the city to the south.

On the southern third of Leng dwell the descendants of those displaced by the invaders from the Golden Empire. The native Lengii are perhaps the tallest of all the known races of mankind, with many men amongst them reaching seven feet in height, and some as tall as eight. Long-legged and slender, with flesh the color of oiled teak, they have large golden eyes and can supposedly see farther and better than other men, especially at night. Though formidably tall, the women of the Lengii are famously lithe and lovely, of surpassing beauty.

For much of its history, Leng has been an isle of mystery, for the native Lengii seldom sailed beyond sight of their own shores, and such seafarers who chanced to glimpse their coasts whilst crossing the Jade Sea met a cold reception should they dare to come ashore. The Lengii had no interest in foreign gods, foreign goods, foreign food or dress or customs; nor did they allow outsiders to mine their gold, harvest their trees,

gather their fruit, or fish their seas. Those who attemped to do so met a swift and bloody end. Leng became known as a haunt of demons and sorcerers, a place to be avoided, a closed island. And so it remained for many centuries.

It was mariners from the Golden Empire who opened Leng to trade, yet even then the island remained a perilous place for outsiders, for the Empress of Leng was known to have congress with the Old Ones, gods who lived deep below the ruined subterranean cities, and from time to time the Old Ones told her to put all the strangers on the island to death. This is known to have happened at least four times in the island's history if Colloquo Votar's *Jade Compendium* can be believed.

Not until Jar Har, sixth of the sea-green emperors, conquered Leng with fire and steel and took it into his empire did these slaughters cease for good and all.

In the four centuries since Leng threw off the yoke of Yi Ti, the island has flourished under the rule of a long line of god-empresses. The first of the current dynasty, still revered in the east as Khiara the Great, was of pure Lengii descent; to please her subjects, she took two husbands, one Lengii and one YiTish. This custom was continued by her daughters and their daughters in turn. By tradition the first of the imperial consorts commands the empress's armies, the second her fleets.

Legends persist that the Old Ones still live beneath the jungle of Leng. So many of the warriors that Jar Har sent down below the ruins returned mad or not at all that the god-emperor finally decreed the vast underground cities' ruins should be sealed up and forgotten. Even today, it is forbidden to enter such places, under penalty of torture and death.

LEFT | *A YiTish male and a Lengii female.*

ASSHAI-BY-THE-SHADOW

And so we come, nearly, to the end of the world.

Or, at least, the end of our knowledge.

Easternmost and southernmost of the great cities of the known world, the ancient port of Asshai stands at the end of a long wedge of land, on the point where the Jade Sea meets the Saffron Straits. Its origins are lost in the mists of time. Even the Asshai'i do not claim to know who built their city; they will say only that a city has stood here since the world began and will stand here until it ends.

Few places in the known world are as remote as Asshai, and fewer are as forbidding. Travelers tell us that the city is built entirely of black stone: halls, hovels, temples, palaces, streets, walls, bazaars, all. Some say as well that the stone of Asshai has a greasy, unpleasant feel to it, that it seems to drink the light, dimming tapers and torches and hearth fires alike. The nights are very black in Asshai, all agree, and even the brightest days of summer are somehow grey and gloomy.

Asshai is a large city, sprawling out for leagues on both banks of the black river Ash. Behind its enormous land walls is ground enough for Volantis, Qarth, and King's Landing to stand side by side and still have room for Oldtown.

from all over the known world come to trade, crossing vast and stormy seas. Most arrive laden with foodstuffs and wine, for beyond the walls of Asshai little grows save ghost grass, whose glassy, glowing stalks are inedible. If not for the food brought in from across the sea, the Asshai'i would have starved.

The ships bring casks of freshwater too. The waters of the Ash glisten black beneath the noonday sun and glimmer with a pale green phosphorescence by night, and such fish as swim in the river are blind and twisted, so deformed and hideous to look upon that only fools and shadowbinders will eat of their flesh.

Every land beneath the sun has need of fruits and grains and vegetables, so one might ask why any mariner would sail to the ends of the earth when he might more easily sell his cargo to markets closer to home. The answer is gold. Beyond the walls of Asshai, food is scarce, but gold and gems are common . . . though some will say that the gold of the Shadow Lands is as unhealthy in its own way as the fruits that grow there.

The ships come nonetheless. For gold, for gems, and

An account by Archmaester Marwyn confirms reports that no man rides in Asshai, be he warrior, merchant, or prince. There are no horses in Asshai, no elephants, no mules, no donkeys, no zorses, no camels, no dogs. Such beasts, when brought there by ship, soon die. The malign influence of the Ash and its polluted waters have been implicated, as it is well understood from Harmon's *On Miasmas* that animals are more sensitive to the foulness exuded by such waters, even without drinking them. Septon Barth's writings speculate more wildly, referring to the higher mysteries with little evidence.

Yet the population of Asshai is no greater than that of a good-sized market town. By night the streets are deserted, and only one building in ten shows a light. Even at the height of day, there are no crowds to be seen, no tradesmen shouting their wares in noisy markets, no women gossiping at a well. Those who walk the streets of Asshai are masked and veiled, and have a furtive air about them. Oft as not, they walk alone, or ride in palanquins of ebony and iron, hidden behind dark curtains and borne through the dark streets upon the backs of slaves.

And there are no children in Asshai.

Despite its forbidding aspects, Asshai-by-the-Shadow has for many centuries been a thriving port, where ships

for other treasures, for certain things spoken of only in whispers, things that cannot be found anywhere upon the earth save in the black bazaars of Asshai.

The dark city by the Shadow is a city steeped in sorcery. Warlocks, wizards, alchemists, moonsingers, red priests, black alchemists, necromancers, aeromancers, pyromancers, bloodmages, torturers, inquisitors, poisoners, godswives, night-walkers, shapechangers, worshippers of the Black Goat and the Pale Child and the Lion of Night, all find welcome in Asshai-by-the-Shadow, where nothing is forbidden. Here they are free to practice their spells without restraint or censure, conduct their obscene rites, and fornicate with demons if that is their desire.

RIGHT | *Asshai-by-the-Shadow.*

Most sinister of all the sorcerers of Asshai are the shadowbinders, whose lacquered masks hide their faces from the eyes of gods and men. They alone dare to go upriver past the walls of Asshai, into the heart of darkness.

On its way from the Mountains of the Morn to the sea, the Ash runs howling through a narrow cleft in the mountains, between towering cliffs so steep and close that the river is perpetually in shadow, save for a few moments at midday when the sun is at its zenith. In the caves that pockmark the cliffs, demons and dragons and worse make their lairs. The farther from the city one goes, the more hideous and twisted these creatures become . . . until at last one stands before the doors of the Stygai, the corpse city at the Shadow's heart, where even the shadowbinders fear to tread. Or so the stories say.

Is there any truth to these grim fables brought back from the end of the earth by singers and sailors and dabblers in sorcery? Who can say? Lomas Longstrider never saw Asshai-by-the-Shadow. Even the Sea Snake never sailed so far. Those who did have not returned to tell us their tales.

Until they do, Asshai and the Shadow Lands and whatever lands and seas might lie beyond them must remain a closed book to wise men and kings alike. There is always more to know, more to see, more to learn. The world is vast and wondrous strange, and there are more things beneath the stars than even the archmaesters of the Citadel can dream.

Afterword

In the years since I first set pen to parchment, much has changed both in Westeros and beyond. Readers must understand that such a work as this is not the labor of a mere few weeks . . . or even years. I first set the framework for this history during the peaceful years at the height of good King Robert's reign, intending to dedicate the volume to Robert and his heirs as a history of the land and the world that they had inherited.

But such was not to be. The death of the noble Hand, Jon Arryn, has unleashed a madness on the land, a madness of pride and violence. The madness has robbed the realm of Robert, and of his fair son and heir Joffrey. Pretenders strive to steal the Iron Throne, and disturbing rumors of dragons reborn trickle in from the east.

In such times of trouble, we must all pray that good King Tommen shall see a long reign, and a just one, to usher us again out of the darkness and into the light.

LEFT | *Dragons reborn?*

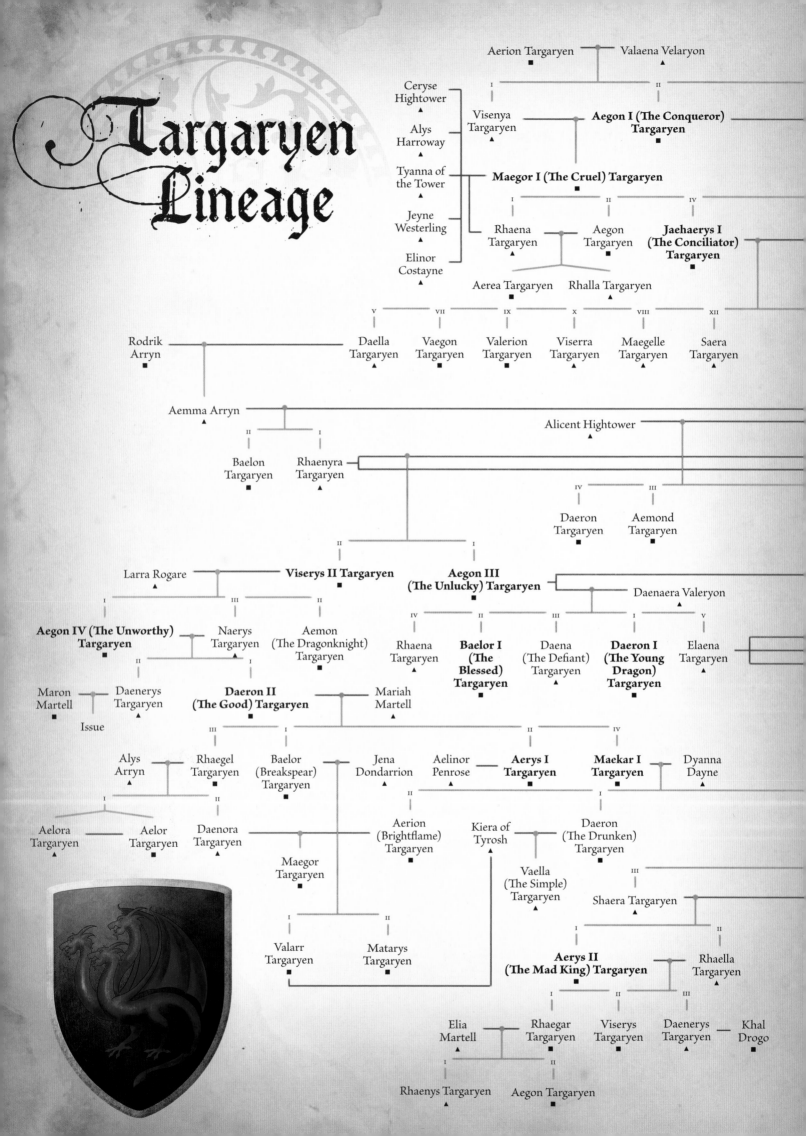

Targaryen Lineage

Aerion Targaryen ■ — ● — Valaena Velaryon ▲

I · II

Ceryse Hightower ▲

Visenya Targaryen ▲ — ● — Aegon I (The Conqueror) Targaryen ■

Alys Harroway ▲

Tyanna of the Tower ▲ — Maegor I (The Cruel) Targaryen ■

I · II · IV

Jeyne Westerling ▲

Rhaena Targaryen ▲ — ● — Aegon Targaryen ■ · Jaehaerys I (The Conciliator) Targaryen ■

Elinor Costayne ▲

Aerea Targaryen ▲ · Rhalla Targaryen ▲

V · VII · IX · X · VIII · XII

Rodrik Arryn ■ — ● — Daella Targaryen ▲ · Vaegon Targaryen ■ · Valerion Targaryen ■ · Viserra Targaryen ▲ · Maegelle Targaryen ▲ · Saera Targaryen ▲

Aemma Arryn ▲ — ● — Alicent Hightower ▲ — ●

II · I

Baelon Targaryen ■ · Rhaenyra Targaryen ▲ —

IV · III

Daeron Targaryen ■ · Aemond Targaryen ■

II · I

Larra Rogare ▲ — ● — Viserys II Targaryen ■ · Aegon III (The Unlucky) Targaryen — Daenaera Valeryon ▲

I · III · II · IV · II · III · I · V

Aegon IV (The Unworthy) Targaryen ■ · Naerys Targaryen ▲ · Aemon (The Dragonknight) Targaryen ■ · Rhaena Targaryen ▲ · Baelor I (The Blessed) Targaryen ■ · Daena (The Defiant) Targaryen ▲ · Daeron I (The Young Dragon) Targaryen ■ · Elaena Targaryen ▲

II · I

Maron Martell ■ — ● — Daenerys Targaryen ▲ · Daeron II (The Good) Targaryen ■ — ● — Mariah Martell ■

Issue

III · I · II · IV

Alys Arryn ▲ — ● — Rhaegel Targaryen ■ · Baelor (Breakspear) Targaryen ■ · Jena Dondarrion ▲ · Aelinor Penrose — Aerys I Targaryen · Maekar I Targaryen — Dyanna Dayne ▲

I · II · II · I

Aelora Targaryen ▲ — Aelor Targaryen ■ · Daenora Targaryen ▲ · Aerion (Brightflame) Targaryen ■ · Kiera of Tyrosh — ● · Daeron (The Drunken) Targaryen ■

Maegor Targaryen ■

Vaella (The Simple) Targaryen ▲ · Shaera Targaryen ▲ — ●

I · II · III

Valarr Targaryen ■ · Matarys Targaryen ■ · Aerys II (The Mad King) Targaryen ■ — Rhaella Targaryen ▲

I · II · III

Elia Martell ▲ — ● — Rhaegar Targaryen ■ · Viserys Targaryen ■ · Daenerys Targaryen ▲ — Khal Drogo ■

I · II

Rhaenys Targaryen ▲ · Aegon Targaryen ■

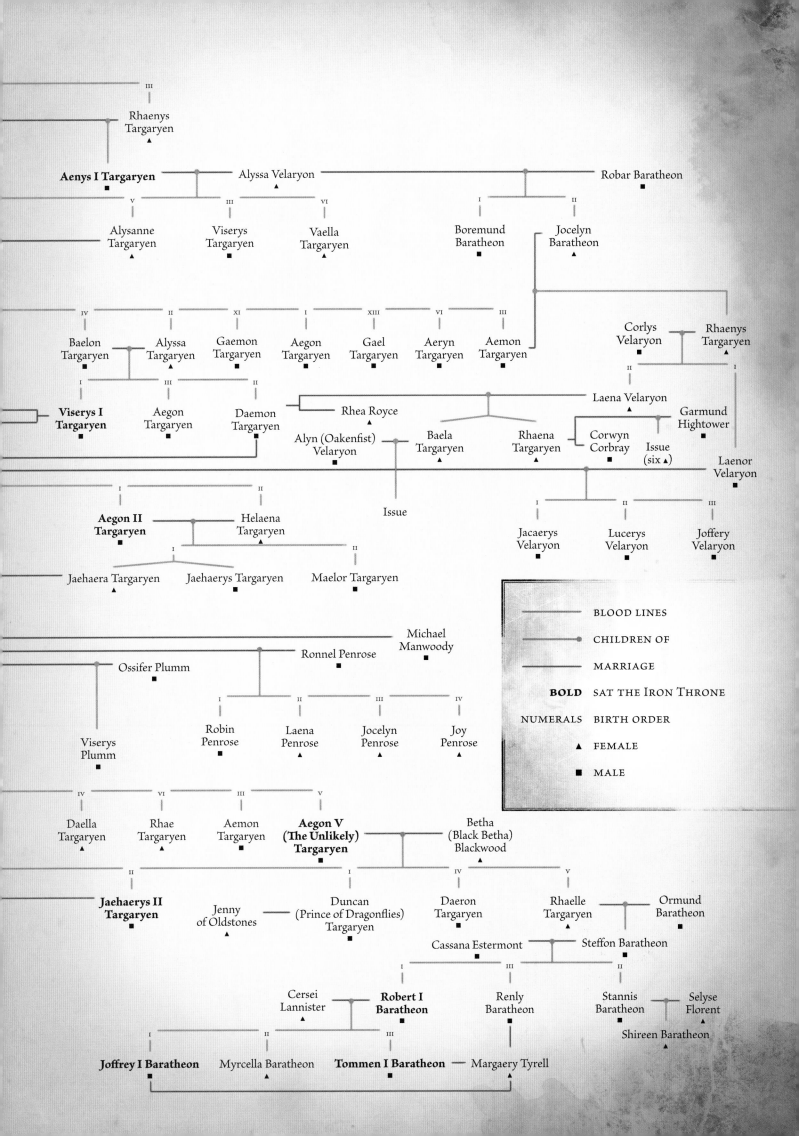

Stark Lineage

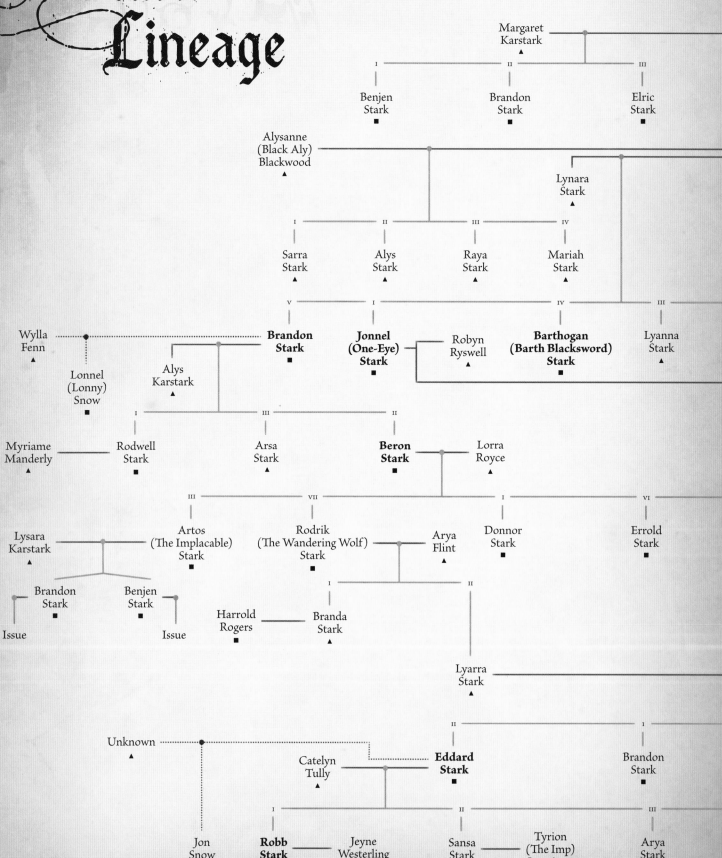

Margaret Karstark

I — Benjen Stark ■

II — Brandon Stark ■

III — Elric Stark ■

Alysanne (Black Aly) Blackwood ▲

Lynara Stark ▲

I — Sarra Stark ▲

II — Alys Stark ▲

III — Raya Stark ▲

IV — Mariah Stark ▲

V — **Brandon Stark** ■

Wylla Fenn ▲

Lonnel (Lonny) Snow ■

Alys Karstark ▲

I — **Jonnel (One-Eye) Stark** ■

Robyn Ryswell ▲

IV — **Barthogan (Barth Blacksword) Stark** ■

III — Lyanna Stark ▲

Myriame Manderly ▲ — Rodwell Stark ■

Arsa Stark ▲

I — Rodwell Stark ■ (I) ... Arsa Stark ▲ (III) ... **Beron Stark** ■ (II)

Lorra Royce ▲

III — Lysara Karstark ▲

VII — Artos (The Implacable) Stark ■

Rodrik (The Wandering Wolf) Stark ■

Arya Flint ▲

I — Donnor Stark ■

VI — Errold Stark ■

Brandon Stark ■ — Issue

Benjen Stark ■ — Issue

Harrold Rogers ■ — Branda Stark ▲

Lyarra Stark ▲

Unknown ▲

Catelyn Tully ▲

II — **Eddard Stark** ■

I — Brandon Stark ■

I — Jon Snow ■

Robb Stark ■ — Jeyne Westerling ▲

II — Sansa Stark ▲ — Tyrion (The Imp) Lannister ■

III — Arya Stark ■

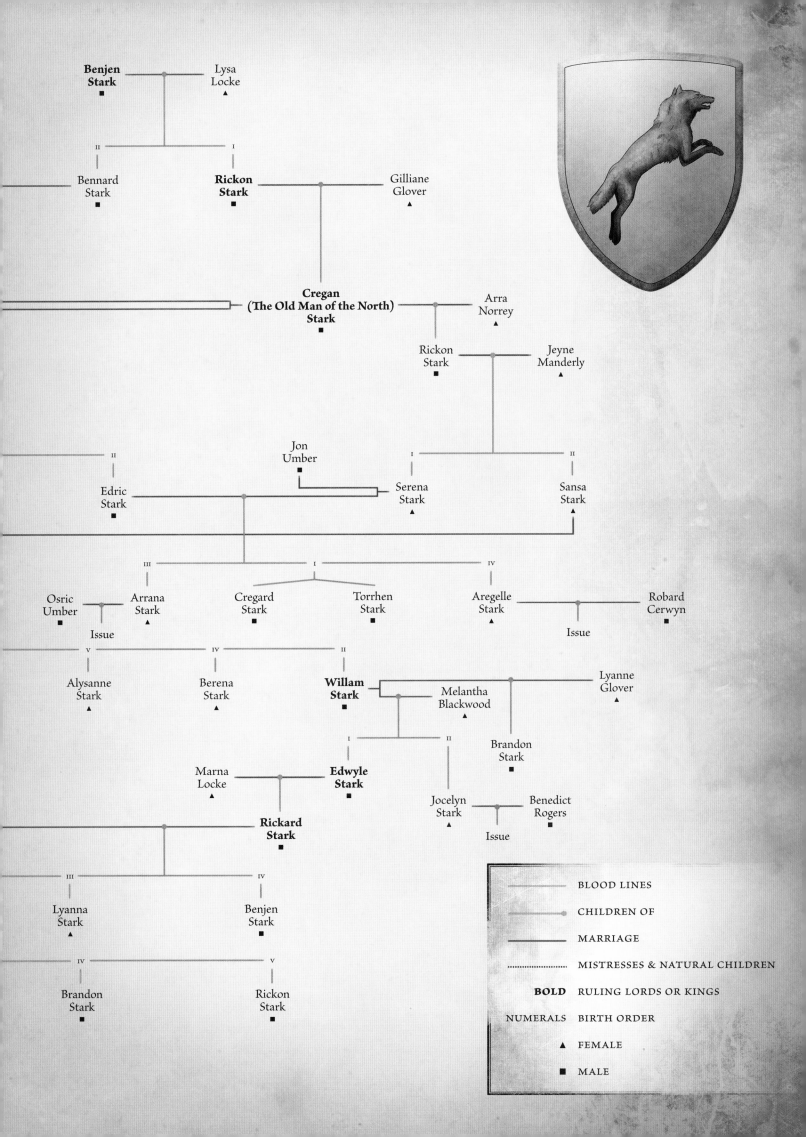

Benjen Stark ■ — Lysa Locke ▲

II — Bennard Stark ■

I — **Rickon Stark** ■ — Gilliane Glover ▲

Cregan (The Old Man of the North) Stark ■ — Arra Norrey ▲

Rickon Stark ■ — Jeyne Manderly ▲

II — Edric Stark ■

Jon Umber ■

I — Serena Stark ▲

II — Sansa Stark ▲

III — Osric Umber ■ — Arrana Stark ▲
Issue

I — Cregard Stark ■ — Torrhen Stark ■

IV — Aregelle Stark ▲ — Robard Cerwyn ■
Issue

V — Alysanne Stark ▲

IV — Berena Stark ▲

II — **Willam Stark** ■ — Melantha Blackwood ▲ — Lyanne Glover ▲

I — Marna Locke ▲ — **Edwyle Stark** ■

II — Jocelyn Stark ▲ — Benedict Rogers ■
Issue

Brandon Stark ■

Rickard Stark ■

III — Lyanna Stark ▲

IV — Benjen Stark ■

IV — Brandon Stark ■

V — Rickon Stark ■

BLOOD LINES

● CHILDREN OF

MARRIAGE

.... MISTRESSES & NATURAL CHILDREN

BOLD RULING LORDS OR KINGS

NUMERALS BIRTH ORDER

▲ FEMALE

■ MALE

Lannister Lineage

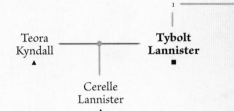

Teora
Kyndall
▲

**Tybolt
Lannister**
■

I

Cerelle
Lannister
▲

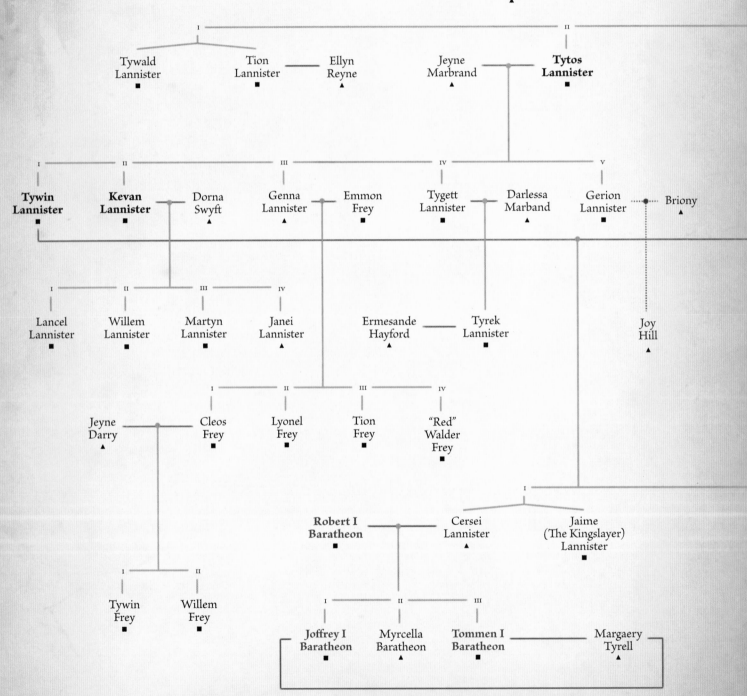

I

Tywald
Lannister
■

Tion
Lannister
■

Ellyn
Reyne
▲

Jeyne
Marbrand
▲

**Tytos
Lannister**
■

II

I **Tywin
Lannister**
■

II **Kevan
Lannister**
■

Dorna
Swyft
▲

III Genna
Lannister
▲

Emmon
Frey
■

IV Tygett
Lannister
■

Darlessa
Marband
▲

V Gerion
Lannister
■

Briony
▲

I Lancel
Lannister
■

II Willem
Lannister
■

III Martyn
Lannister
■

IV Janei
Lannister
▲

Ermesande
Hayford
▲

Tyrek
Lannister
■

Joy
Hill
▲

I Jeyne
Darry
▲

Cleos
Frey
■

II Lyonel
Frey
■

III Tion
Frey
■

IV "Red"
Walder
Frey
■

**Robert I
Baratheon**
■

Cersei
Lannister
▲

Jaime
(The Kingslayer)
Lannister
■

I

I Tywin
Frey
■

II Willem
Frey
■

I **Joffrey I
Baratheon**
■

II Myrcella
Baratheon
▲

III **Tommen I
Baratheon**
■

Margaery
Tyrell
▲

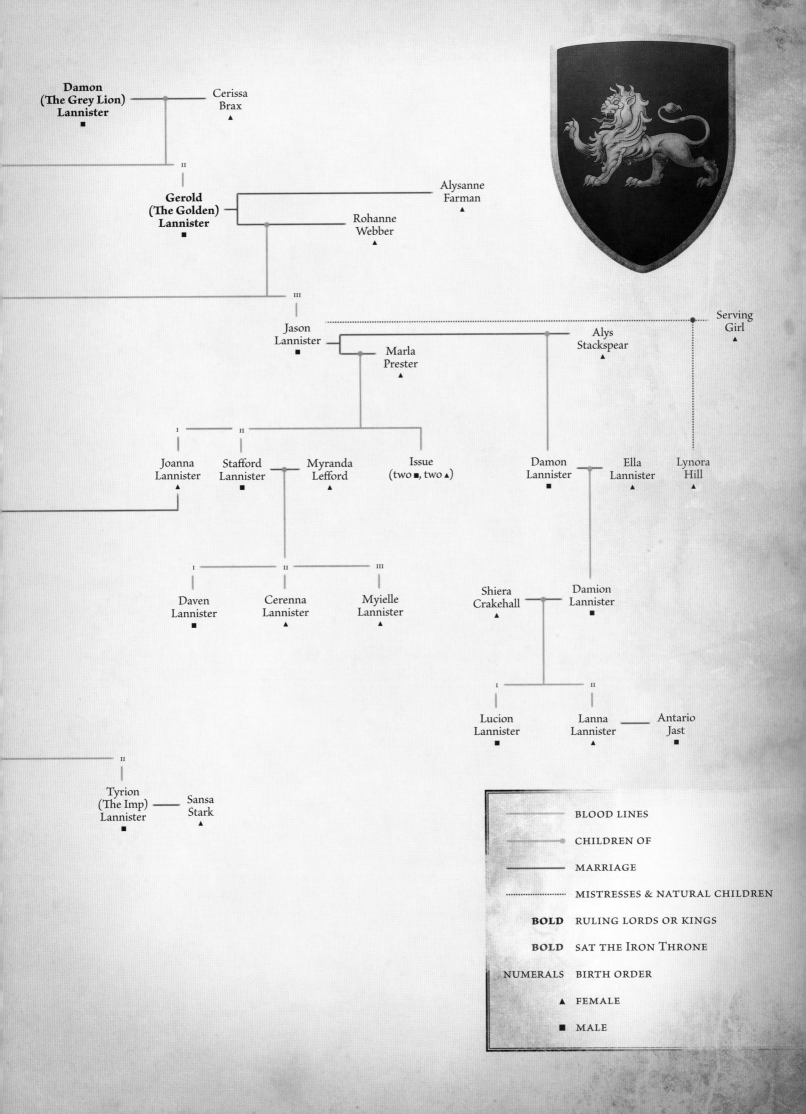

**Damon
(The Grey Lion)
Lannister** ■

Cerissa
Brax ▲

II

**Gerold
(The Golden)
Lannister** ■

Alysanne
Farman ▲

Rohanne
Webber ▲

III

Jason
Lannister ■

Marla
Prester ▲

Alys
Stackspear ▲

Serving
Girl ▲

I

Joanna
Lannister ▲

II

Stafford
Lannister ■

Myranda
Lefford ▲

Issue
(two ■, two ▲)

Damon
Lannister ■

Ella
Lannister ▲

Lynora
Hill ▲

I

Daven
Lannister ■

II

Cerenna
Lannister ▲

III

Myielle
Lannister ▲

Shiera
Crakehall ▲

Damion
Lannister ■

I

Lucion
Lannister ■

II

Lanna
Lannister ▲

Antario
Jast ■

II

Tyrion
(The Imp)
Lannister ■

Sansa
Stark ▲

BLOOD LINES

● CHILDREN OF

MARRIAGE

⋯⋯ MISTRESSES & NATURAL CHILDREN

BOLD RULING LORDS OR KINGS

BOLD SAT THE IRON THRONE

NUMERALS BIRTH ORDER

▲ FEMALE

■ MALE

CROWNLANDS

RIVERLANDS

REACH

harrenhal

Wickenden

BAY of CRABS

CRACKCLAW POINT

Claw Isle

Maidenpool

Rook's Rest

Dragonstone

Antlers

Driftmark

THE GULLET

Duskendale

Sharp Point

Rosby

KING'S LANDING

ROSBY ROAD

BLACKWATER BAY

Stonedance

MASSEY'S HOOK

GOLDROAD

The Red Keep

BLACKWATER RUSH

ROSE ROAD

Tumbleton

WENDWATER

Haystack hall

Felwood

Bronzegate

KINGSROAD

Evenfall hall

Storm's End

NARROW SEA

LEGEND

♜	MAJOR CASTLE
♜	CASTLES
⌂	CITIES
◉	TOWNS
🌾	GRAIN
– – –	ROAD

STORMLANDS

Targaryen Reign

BC
1 AC

Aegon I (The Conqueror)

37 AC — Aenys I
42 AC — Maegor I (The Cruel)
48 AC

Jaehaerys I
(The Conciliator)

103 AC

Viserys I

129 AC — Aegon II
131 AC

Aegon III

157 AC — Baelor I (The Blessed)
161 AC — Daeron I (The Young Dragon)
171 AC — Viserys II
172 AC — Aegon IV (The Unworthy)
184 AC

Daeron II (The Good)

209 AC — Aerys I

221 AC — Maekar I

233 AC

Aegon V
(The Unlikely)

259 AC — Jaehaerys II
262 AC

Aerys II
(The Mad King)

283 AC

Baratheon Reign

283 AC

Robert i

298 AC — Joffrey I
299 AC — Tommen I
present

INDEX

Page numbers of illustrations appear in italics.

Adarys, Alequo (Silvertongue), 111, 112
Addam of Hull (Velaryon), 76, 77, 78, 81
Aegon I Targaryen (the Conqueror), 10, 27, 31–45, *48*, 49, 51, 76, 155, 186, 188, 216, 217, 227, 243–47
    the Conquest and, 34–45, *34*, *38*
    crown of, *51*, *52*, 55, 106
    dragon of, Balerion (*see* dragons)
    Iron Throne of, 45, *46*, 51
    letter of Prince Nymor, 246, *247*
    progresses of, 51
    reign after The Conquest, 49–51
    sword of, 35
    word sent to the Seven Kingdoms, 34, *35*
Aegon II Targaryen, 71, 72, *72*, 73–81, *77*, 82, 160, 170, 189, 190, 198, 228
Aegon III Targaryen, *72*, 78, 79, 80, 81, *82*, 82–86, *85*, 87, 170, 190, 198, 228
    Regents of, 83
Aegon IV Targaryen (the Unworthy), 91, 94, 95, 95–99, *97*, 100, 101, 158, 246–47
    Great Bastards of, *97*, 98, 101
    nine mistresses of, *98*, 98–99, *99*, 276
Aegon V Targaryen (the Unlikely or "Egg"), 31, 106, *107*, 107–10, 199, 201, 228, 230
Aegonfort, 35, 39, 45, 49, 50, 246
Aegon's High Hill, 35, 49, 55, 56
Aenar the Exile Targaryen, 26, 32–33
Aenys I Targaryen, 51, *52*, 52–54, 57, 157, 188, 224, 230
Aerys I Targaryen, 104–5, 190
Aerys II Targaryen (the Mad King), 113–21, *114*, *121*, 124–29, *125*, 142, 160, 170, 203, 204, 218, 230, 239, 247
Age of Heroes, 10–17, 145, 169, 181, 195, 196, 207, 221, 232
Allyrion, House and nobles, 44
Alyn of Hull (Velaryon and Oakenfist), 76, 77, 83–84, 87, 88, 91, 247, 265
Andalos, 17, 18, 138, 163, 167, 169, 238, 254, 255, 256, 266
Andals, 5, 17–20, *18*, *19*, 137, 138, 143, 151, 156, 163, 164, 165, 166, 168, 169, 170, 175, 182, 183, 184, 195, 196, 211–13, 216, *223*, 238, 240, 254–55, 257, 258, 266, 287
    seven-pointed star of, 19, *226*, 258
Argos Sevenstar, 138
Arryn, Artys (the Falcon Knight) 19, 165, 166, 167, 169, 170
Arryn, House and nobles, 19, 33, 52, 67, 167, 169–70, 172
    kings of, 167, 168
Arryn, Jeyne, 83
Arryn, Jon, 127, 160, 170, 191, 311
Arryn, Rodrik, 65, 169–70
Arryn, Ronnel, 36, 40, 43, 52–53, 169
Arryn, Sharra, Queen of the Vale, 36, 40, 43
Asshai-by-the-Shadow, 5, 11, 63, 110, 197, 261, 299, 308–9, *309*
Astapor, 14, 260, 280, 297
Axe, 17, 18, 255, 257, 295, 296
Ax Isle, 24, 283
Azor Ahai, 11, 301

Baelor I Targaryen, *89*, 89–93, *90*, *93*, 246
    sisters of, *91*, 91
Ball, Quentyn (Fireball), 95, 199
Band of Nine, 109, 111
Baratheon, Boremund, 65, 227–28
Baratheon, Borros, 78, 80, 228
Baratheon, House and nobles, 60, 111, 131, 221, 227–30, *229*, *230*, 311
Baratheon, Lyonel, 108, 228, *229*, 230
Baratheon, Orys, 33–36, 39, *40*, 40, 53, 87, 226, 227, 230, 243–44
Baratheon, Robert. *See* Robert I Baratheon
Baratheon, Steffon, 111, 113, 120, 230
Bar Emmon, Lord of Sharp Point, 34, 65
Bar Emmon, Togarion (the Terrible), 225
Barrow Kings, 135, 138, 145
Barth, Septon, 7, 11, 13, 26, 60, 62, 65, 75, 93, 94, 143, 198, 214, 285, 308
Basilisk Isles, 24, 169, 185, 186, 278, 280, 282–84, *284*, 286
Basilisk Point, 24, 284, 285
Battle Above the Gods Eye, 78
Battle Beneath the Gods Eye, 56, 59, *157*, 198
Battle of the Kingsroad, 78, 80, 82
Battle of Seven Stars, *164–65*, 166–67, 169, 170
Battle at Stonebridge, 56, *56–57*
Battle of Wendwater Bridge, 107–8, 200
battles, various, 12, 25, 33, 36, 56, 78, 84, 128, 138, 151, 154, 197, 211, 218, 224, 226, 262, 304. *See also* Conquest, The; Dance of the Dragons
Beesbury, Lord, 73
Belaerys, Jaenara, 285
Beldecar, 22, 23, 24

Belgrave, Gyles, 82
Bernarr II, 153
Bite, 168
Bitterbridge, 56, 75, 207
Blackfyre, Aenys, 106
Blackfyre, Daemon (Daemon Waters), 93, 95–96, *97*, 100, 101, *103*, 107, 170
Blackfyre, Daemon II, *104–5*, 104–5
Blackfyre, Daemon III, 105, 107, 199
Blackfyre, Haegon, 105, 107
Blackfyre, Maelys the Monstrous, 103, 109, 111, 112, *112*
Blackfyre Rebellions, 101–5, *103*, 107, 160, 170, 199–200, 218, 242
Blackmont, House and nobles, 25, *240*, 241
Black Pearls, 98, *98*, 276
Black Swan, 262
Blackwater Bay, 26, 32, 36, 107
    ports of trade on, 65, 117
Blackwater Rush, 31, 33, 34, 35, 36, 40, 45, 49, 56, 64, 100, 113, 127, 138, 151, 152, 153, 155, 221, 224, 225, 226, 235
Blackwood, Black Aly, 82, 228
Blackwood, Melissa, 98, 99
Blackwoods of Raventree Hall, 108, 116, 151, 152, 153, 154, *156*, 156, 157, 228
Blood and Cheese, 74–75
Bloody Gate, 19, 167
Bolling, Theo, 59
Bolton, House and nobles, 137, 138, 145
Bones (Bone Mountains), 259, 287, 292, 293, 298, 299–300, 304
    Brotherhood of, 283
Braavos, 15, 17, 27, 114, 168, 186, *252*, 253, 255, 256, 261, 262, 265, 267, 271–77, *272–73*, *274*, *275*, 276, 295, 297
Bracken, Barba, 98, 99, 101
Bracken, House and nobles, 116, 151, 152, 154, 155, 156, 157
Brandon the Breaker, 145
Brandon the Builder, 5–6, 10, 142, 169, 207, 209, 215, 224, 233
Bridge of Dream, 23, 268
Brightstone, Jon, 163
Broken Arm of Dorne, 8, 222, 235, 237, 238, 240, 261, 265
Bronze Kings of Runestone, 163, 164
Broome, Alfred, 80
Butcher's Ball, 78
Butterwell, Lord, 95, 104, 105

Cannibal Bay, 294
Cargyll, Arryk, 70, 75
Cargyll, Erryk, 72, 75
Caron, House and nobles, 83, 232
Castamere Castle, 203
Casterly Rock, 10, 36, 70, 113, 114, 115, 117, 121, 129, 172, 180, 184, 185, 187, 197, 198, 202, 203, 204–5, *205*
Casterlys of the Rock, 195–96
Castle Black, 5, 7, 62, 141, *145*, 146
Celtigar, Crispian, 35
Celtigar, Edwell, 59
Celtigars of Claw Isle, 32, 34, 65
centaurs, 287
Century of Blood, 32, 68, 260, 264, 269, 270, 273, 282, 283, 288–89, 292
Charlton, Theo, 155
Chatana Qo, the Arrow of Jhahar, 279
Chelsted, Qarlton, 124, 125, 126, 129
children of the forest, 5–6, 7, *7*, 8–10, 12, 19, 19, 145, 175, 195, 204, 211, 222–23, *226*, 235, 237
Chroyane, 11, 21, 22, 23, 268
Citadel of the Maesters, ix, 5, 8, 17, 26, 31, 45, 65, 93, 105, 106, 124, 145, 151, 207, 216, 223, 278, 287, 302
Cockshaw, Lord, 105
Cole, Criston, 67, 70, 71, 73, 75, 78
Connington, Jon, 125, 128
Conquest, The, 31–45
    AC or BC dating and, 31
    battles, 34–41
Corbray, Corwyn, 83, 163
Corbrays of Heart's Home, 165, 166, 170
Correy, Qarl, 71
Costayne, Elinor, *59*, 59
Costayne, Leo, 190
Crabb, Clement, 60
Crag Castle, 83, 195
Crakehall, House and nobles, 185, *199*
Crakehall Castle, 54
Crannogmen, *140*, 140–41
Cymmeri, 287, 288

Daenys the Dreamer, 26, 32
Daeron I Targaryen (the Young Dragon), 85, 87, *87–88*, 89, 91, 217–18, 221, 246, 265
Daeron II Targaryen, 96, *100*, 100–103, 247
Dagger Lake, 22, 27, 259

Dance of the Dragons, 66, 73–81, 141, 159, 189, 190, 198, 217, 228, 246
    battles, 75, *76*, 76, 77, 77–78, 80, 81, 160
    greens and blacks, 68, 77, 78
    Two Betrayers, 76, 77
Darklyn, Denys, 117–19
Darklyn, Robin (Darkrobin), 51
Darklyn, House and nobles, 34–35, 118, 224
Darry, Jonothor, 128, 129
Dawn Age, 5–9, 10, 163, 169, 195, 263
Dayne, Arthur, 121, 125, 239
Dayne, Joffrey, 244
Daynes of Starfall, 25, 238, 239, *240*, 241
Deep Lake Castle, 60
Deep Ones, 214
Defiance of Duskendale, 117–19, *119*, 129
demon road, 27
direwolves, 6, *7*, 8
Disputed Lands, 27, 103, 108, 109, 111, 112, 185, 186, 261, 264–65, 267, 280
Doggett, Joffrey (Red Dog of the Hills), 58
Doom of Valyria, 17, 26–27, *28*, 32, 68, 131, 288, 289, 296
Dorne, 8, 25, 33, 36, 43–45, 49, 52, 53, 68, 87–88, *88*, 89, 90, 96–97, 100, 114, 128, 151, 217–18, 221, 222, 226, 227, 235–49
    bed of scorpions and Lord Tyrell, 88, 218
    the Breaking, 237
    map, 234
    petty kings of, 240
    Rhoynar and, 23–25, 236, 240, 242, 268
    Targaryens and, 43–45, 44, 88, 221, 235, 242, 243–47
    types of Dornishmen, *236*, 236
Dornish Wars, 49, 51, 217, 227, 246
Dothraki, 14, 17, 27, 260, 267, 288–93, *290–91*, 295, 296, 297, 298, 299, 304
    dosh khaleen, 293
    khal and *khalasars* of, 14, 260, 267, 288, 289, 297, 304
Dragonpit, 57, 78, 79, *79*, 81
dragons, 13, 15, 23, 26, 27, 32, 33, 60, *61*, 66, 75, 76, 77, 78, 81, 96–97, 109–10, 120, 285, 294, 302
    Arrax, 228
    Balerion, the Black Dread, 27, *28–29*, 33, 35, 36, *38*, 38, 41, 42, 45, 53, 55, 56, 57, 60, 63, 81, *86*, 187, 216, 243, 246
    Cannibal, 75, 81, 86
    Caraxes, 68, 78, 81
    Dreamfyre, 58, 81
    Grey Ghost, 75, 81
    last Targaryen dragon dies, *86*, 86, 173
    Meleys (the Red Queen), 75, 76, 77, 81
    Meraxes, 33, 34, 35, 36, 39–40, 44, 244, *245*, 246
    Moondancer, 80, 81
    Morghul, 81
    Morning Light, 81, 86
    Nagga, the sea dragon, 178–79
    Quicksilver, 52, 56, *157*
    Seasmoke, 63, 75, 76, 78, 81
    Sheepstealer, 75, 76, 81, 86
    Shrykos, 81
    Silverwing, 75, 76, 81, 86
    Stormcloud, 78, 81, 84
    Sunfyre, 75, 77, 79, *80*, 80, 81
    Syrax, 78, 81
    Terrax, 285
    Tessarion, 78, 81
    Vermax, Arrax, and Tyraxes, 71, 78, 81, 143
    Vermithor, 60, 75, 76, 78, 81
    Vhagar, 33, 36, *37*, 43, 55, 71, 72, 75, 78, 81, 216, 228
Dragonstone, 26, 27, *30*, 31, 32, 33, 34, 51, 55, 72, 75, 120, 143, 214, *231*, 246
Dragon's Wroth, 49, *243*, 246
Drahar, Craghas (Crabfeeder), 68
Driftmark Castle, 32, 34, 65, 67, 71, 72, 77
Drowned God, 20, 175, 178, 179, 182, 183, 184, 187
Dryland, Lucifer, 241
Dun Fort, 118, 119
Durrandon, Argella, 39–40
Durrandon, Argilac the Arrogant, 27, 33–34, *34*, 36, 39, 226, 227
Durrandon, Arlan III, 153–54, 155, 221, 226
Durrandon, Arlan V, 155
Durrandon, Arrec, 33, 151, 154–55, *155*, 186
Durrandon, House and nobles, 33, 40, 153, 156, 221, 223–24, 225, 226
Durrandon, Qarlton, 225–26
Durran Godsgrief, 10, 207, 221, 223, 224, 233
Durran the Third, the Storm King, 25
Duskendale, 34, 49, 117–19, *119*, 152, 221
Dustin, House and nobles, 78, 82, 135, 137
dwarves, 68, 116, 121. *See also* Mushroom

Elyria, 27, 253
Erastes, Terrio, 297
Erreg the Kinslayer, *19*, 19, 152
Essos, 4, 13, 15, 22–23, 26, 103, 109, 111, 235, 237, 253. *See also* Valyria
eunuchs, 14, 120, 124, 255, 260, 268, 300, 302, 303. *See also* Unsullied
Evenfall Hall, *232*, 232
Eyrie, 40, 43, 52–53, 167, 168, 170, *171*, 172–73, 218

Faceless Men, 277
Faith, the, 20, 31, 34, 45, 49, 53–54, 55, 62, 151–52, 163, 175, 178, 184, 207, 211, 216, 230, 233
    Seven gods of, 17, 18, 51, 89, 90, 94, 151, 153, 163, 168, 175, 184, 211, 216, 218, 255
Faith Militant, 45, 54, 55–58, 62, 153, 216
False Dawn, 81, 82
Farman, House and nobles, 59, 180, 190, 195, 196, 197, *199*
Farwynds, House and nobles, 176
Field of Fire, 41, 42, 205, 219
First Men, 6, 7, 8–9, *10*, 10, 11, 12, 19–20, 108, 135, 136, 143, 145, 147, 151, 156, 163, 164–65, 167, 170, 175, 177, 180, 195, 196, 204, 209, 212, 214, 222–23, 235, 237, 238, 287
Fisher Queens, 287, 288, 302
Fishers, 152, 156
Flowers, Mervyn, 84, 85
Fossoway, Derrick (Bad Apple), 111
Fourteen Flames, 13, 15, 17, 26, 27, 143
Fowler, House and nobles, 25, 210, 238, 240, 241, 244
Free Cities, 15, 18, 26–27, 49, 83, 109, 111, 114, 116, 177, 198, 221, 252, 253–76, 280, 288–89, 292, 293
Free Companies, 27, 83, 111, 260, 264, 280
    noteworthy, 265, 267
Frey, Forrest, 159, *159*

Gaemon Palehair, 79, 84, 242
Galladon of Morne, 231
Gardener, Garse VII, 33
Gardener, Garth VII (Goldenhand), 182, *210*, 210–11, 212
Gardener, Garth IX, 211, 212
Gardener, Garth X (Greybeard), 212, 218
Gardener, Garth XI, 213
Gardener, Gwayne V, 211, 212, 217
Gardener, Gyles III, 212, 217
Gardener, Merle I (the Meek), 211
Gardener, House and nobles, 33, 40, 41, 45, 197, 207, 209–11, 215, *217*, 217, 218
Gargon, Lord (the Guest), 52, 157, 158
Garin of Chroyane (the Great), 22–23, 26
Garris the Grey, 257
Garth Greenhand, 10, 207–9, *208*, 218, 235
    celebrated children of, 208
Garth the Gardener, 209
Gates of the Moon (castle), 170, 172, 173
Gaunt, Gwayne, 118
Ghiscari, 5, 13, 14, 15, 22, 27, 260, 269, 278, 282, 284, 286, 289, 302
Ghost Hill, 25, 243
ghouls, 24, 286
giants, 5, 6, 7, 145, 169, 175, 195, 204, 222, 237, 257, 296
Gipps, 287, 288
Gods Eye, 8, 33, 36, 40, 78, 81, 104, 124, 126. *See also* battles
godswoods, 20, 143
Golden Company, *102*, 103, 105, 107, 108, 109, 199, 202, 265
Goode, Glendon, 78
Goode, Gregor, 51
Goode, Griffith, 51

Grafton, House and nobles, 163–64
Grandison, Lorent, 83
Grasslands, 287–93, *290–91*
Grazdan the Great, 13, 14
Great Council of 101 AC, *62–63*, 63, 65, 66, 68, 94, 159, 170, 228
Great Council of 233 AC, 106
Great Sand Sea, 292, 300, 304
Great Spring Sickness, 103, 104, 170
Greenblood, 25, 44, 87, 235–36, 238, 240
    orphans of, 25, 242
Greenfield Castle, 195
green men, 9, 9, 19
greenseers, 6–7, 8, 211
Grey, Garibald, 78
Greydon of the Reach, 25
Greyiron, House and nobles, 176, 179, 181–82
Greyjoy, Balon, 131, 191, 193
Greyjoy, Dagon, 104, 141
Greyjoy, Dalton (Red Kraken), 188–90
Greyjoy, Goren, 53, 74, 187–88
Greyjoy, Loren (Old Kraken), 138
Greyjoy, Quellon, 190–91
Greyjoys of Pyke, 175, 176, 177, 180, *187*, 187–88, 190, 191, 214
Grey King, *176*, 178–82
greyscale, 23, 64, 186, 285
Grey Waste, 300, 303
Gulltown, 36, 43, 49, 83, 128, 163–64, 165, 168, 253

Hairy Men, 17, 255, 257, 287
Hardhome, 148
Harmund, House and nobles, 184–85
Harren the Black, 33, 34, 36–37, 151, 155, 156, 157, 186
Harrenhal, 33, 34, 36, 37, 52, 62–63, 63, 72, 77, 98, 155, 156, 157, 158, *159*, 186
    destruction of, 38, *38*, 42, 227
    lords of (list), 158
    tourney at, 121, *122–23*, 124–26
Harren the Red, 52, 53, 157, 158
Harroway, Alys, 53, 59, *59*, 158
Harroway, House and nobles, 53, 59, 158
Hastwyck, Morgil, 96
Hellholt, 25, 243, 244
Highgarden, 41, 109, 184, 207, 212, 213, 218–19, *219*
High Heart, 19, 152
High Septons, 31, 45, *48*, 49, 51, 52, 53, 55–58, 59, 62–63, 93, 100, 216
High Tide Castle, 65
Hightower, Alicent, 65, 67, 68, 70, 71, 72, 72, 73, 77
Hightower, Ceryse, 53, 59, *59*
Hightower, Gerold, 111–12, 126
Hightower, House and nobles, 45, 53, 59, 78, 146, 210, 214–16, *217*
Hightower, Lymond, 180, 210, 215
Hightower, Otto, 65, 67, 68, 70, 77, 246
Hill, Addison, Bastard of Cornfield, 51
Hoare, Harwyn (Hardhand), 33, 151, 154, 155, 156, *185*, 185–86, 187, 226
Hoare, House and nobles, 33, 36–37, 38, 138, 156, 183–84, 186
Hoare, Qhored I (the Cruel), 153, 180, 210
Hollard, Dontos, 119
Hollard, Symon, 119
Honeywine river, 78, 207, 213, 215, 216
Horro (Dothraki *khal*), 289–90
Hugh the Hammer, 76, 77, 78, 81
Hugor of the Hill, 17, 163, 169

Hukko (Hugor), 18
Humfred the Mummer, 51
Hundred Kingdoms, 34
Hyrkoon, Patrimony of, 299, 300, 304
Hyrkoon the Hero, *301*, 301

Ib and the Ibbenese, 17, 254, 255, 256, 257, 271, 287, 289, 292, 295–97, 298
    east of, 298
    lesser isles of, 296
ice dragons, 294
ice spiders, 11, *11*
Iron Bank, 91, 113, 273, 274, *274*, 275
ironborn, 7, 20, 33, 36, 104, 138, 139, 141, 151, 153, 154–55, 156, 169, 175, *181*, 182, 185, 188, 197, 210
Iron Islands, 7, 20, 52, 53, 93, 104, 138, 157, 174, 175–93, 197, 210, 226
    "the black line," 183–86, 187
    driftwood crowns, 178–82, 187
    main grouping of seven, 175, 176
    noble houses of, 187
    the Red Kraken, 188–90, *189*
Iron Throne, 45, 46, 51, 58, 72, 94, 105, 107, 111, 170, 198, 201, 230, 242, 246, 247
Isle of Faces, 19, 223, 237
Isle of Tears, 283, 286
Isle of Toads, 24, 283

Jade Gates, 287, 292
Jade Sea, 13, 292, 299, 300, 302, 306, 308
    islands of note in, 307
Jaehaerys I Targaryen, 51, 53, 58, 59, 60–65, *61*, *62–63*, 64, 158, 159, 170, 198, 219, 227, 228
Jaehaerys II Targaryen, 108, 111–12, 113, 201, 203
Jar Har, 307
Jenny of Oldstones, 108–9, 228, 230
Jhogwin, the stone giants, 299
Jogos Nhai, 271, 298, 303, 304–5, *305*
Joramun, 145, 147–48
Joron I Blacktyde, 181–82
Justman, Benedict, 152, *153*
Justman, House and nobles, 152–53, 154, *156*, 156, 180

Kingsguard, 10, 49–50, 54, 58, 59, 67, 70, 75, 94, 107, 117, 126, 128, *229*
King's Hand (various reigns), 36, 53, 56, 60, 65, 67, 68, 72, 82, 83, 84, 87, 89, 90, 95, 98, 99, 106, 107, 111, 113, 120, 121, 129, 157, 158, 170, 198, 204, 227
King's Landing, 36, 45, 49, 50, 51, 62, 72, 77, 79, 113, 114, 116, *130*, 190, 198, 204, 228, 253, 266. *See also* Dragonpit
    Great Sept, 92, *92*, 120, 218
    House of Kisses, 79
    Rhaenys's Hill, 49, 54, 57
    Sept of Remembrance, 49, 54, 54, 55
    Visenya's Hill, 49, 55, 79, 92
kingsroad, 62, 78, 80, 82, 128
Kingswood Brotherhood, 121, 231, 239
Knight of the Laughing Tree, 126

Lands of Always Winter, 5, 7, 10
Lands of the Long Summer, 26
Lannisport, 33, 49, 114, 115, 117, 124, 172, 190, 196, 253, 261
Lannister, Cersei, 116, 117, 121, 131, 204
Lannister, Damon (Grey Lion), 199
Lannister, Gerion, 115, 117, 201
Lannister, Gerold I, 180, 199–200
Lannister, House and nobles, 33, 36, 40–41, 70, 115, 116, 121, 180, 184–85, 196, 197
    arms of, 199
    early nobles, 196–97, 198, 199
    Lineage, 316–17
    Targaryen rule and, 198–204
Lannister, Jaime, 116, 117, 121, 125–26, 128, 129, 204
Lannister, Jason, 78, 189–90, 198, 201, 204
Lannister, Joanna, 115, 116, 190, 203–4
Lannister, Lelia, 184–85
Lannister, Tybolt (Thunderbolt), 196, 199
Lannister, Tygett, 115, 116, 117
Lannister, Tyland, 83, 198
Lannister, Tyrion (dwarf), 116, 121
Lannister, Tytos, 114–15, 200–201, 202, 204
Lannister, Tywin, 113, 114–15, 116, 116–17, 118, 119, 120, 121, 124, 125, 126, 129, 200, 201, 202, 204
Lann the Clever, 10, 195–96, 207, 209
Lashare, Liomond, 111
Last Light, 252
Leng, 65, 261, 300, 304, 306, 306–7
Lo Bu, 305
Long Night, 11–12, 131, 137, 145, 222, 263, 301, 302
Longstrider, Lomas, 11, 23, 197, 257, 259, 273, 278, 288, 299, 300, 303, 306, 309
Lonmouth, Joffrey (Knight of Kisses), 71
Lonmouth, Richard, 125
Lorath, 15, 253–56, 252, 254–55, 257, 261, 262, 263, 289, 295, 296
Lothston, Danelle, 158
Lothston, House and nobles, 98, 99, 158
Lothston, Jeyne, 99, 99
Lys, 15, 25, 26, 27, 68, 84, 85, 94, 186, 246, 252, 261–65, 264, 267, 276
Lyseni Spring, 84

Maegor I Targaryen (the Cruel), 51, 52, 53, 54, 55–58, 58, 59, 157, 158, 159, 198, 216, 227
    brides of, 53, 59, 59
Maekar I Targaryen, 101, 102–3, 104, 105, 106, 158, 199
    crown of, 106, 106
magic, 21, 22, 25, 26, 59, 127, 158, 198, 259, 283, 285, 301, 308–9
Maidenpool, 34, 41, 49, 67, 83, 125, 151, 152, 153, 221, 224
Malthar Xaq (Windrider, Mapmaker), 278
Manderly, Torrhen of White Harbor, 83, 85
Manderly, House and nobles, 138
Mander river, 207, 209, 210, 211, 218, 235
Mantarys, 27, 253
Manwoody, House and nobles, 91, 241
Marbrand, Jeyne, 200, 200, 201
Marbrands of Ashemark, 199, 199
Marcher Lords, 53, 221, 231, 232
Marilda of Hull, 76
Marsh Kings, 140–41
Martell, Doran, 120, 128
Martell, Elia, 120, 125, 126, 127, 128, 129, 247
Martell, House and nobles, 25, 33, 44–45, 53, 240, 240, 241, 242, 246, 247, 248, 265
Martell, Lewyn, 125, 128, 129
Martell, Mariah, 89, 91, 100
Martell, Maron, 100, 100, 101, 242
Martell, Meria, 44, 44–45, 53, 243, 244, 246
Martell, Mors, 25, 240, 241
Massey, Maldon, 224
Massey, Triston, Lord of Stonedance, 34, 35
Massey's Hook, 34, 107, 199, 221, 222, 224, 225, 231
mazemakers, 214, 253–54, 254–55, 256
Meereen, 14, 297
Megette (Merry Meg), 98, 99
Mengo (Dothraki khal), 289
merlings, 65, 164, 169, 214
Mern, King of the Reach, 36, 40–41
Merryweather, House and nobles, 217
Merryweather, Marq, 83
Merryweather, Owen, 121, 125, 128
Moat Cailin, 8, 20, 136, 138
Moon of the Three Kings, 79
moonsingers, 15, 271, 275, 304
Mooton, Jon, 35, 41
Mooton, House and nobles, 34, 156, 224
Mooton, Manfryd, 83
Mooton, Myles, 125, 128
Moro (Dothraki khal), 289
Mossovy (Far Mossovy), 288, 298
Mountains of the Moon, 18, 19, 33, 163, 167, 168, 172, 309
    notable clans (list), 167
Mudd, House and nobles, 34, 152, 156, 156
Mudd, Marq (the Mad Bard), 154

Mudd, Tristifer IV, 19, 152, 156, 172
Mudd, Tristifer V, 19, 152
Murmison, Septon, 53
Musgood, Jack, 149
Mushroom (dwarf), 68, 71, 73, 75, 91, 93, 143, 159, 242
Myr, 27, 68, 116, 252, 261, 261–65, 267
Mysaria, the White Worm, 67, 74

Naath, the Isle of Butterflies, 24, 278, 282
Neck, 8, 19, 20, 41, 135, 138, 140–41, 141, 152
Nettles, 76, 81
New Gift, 60, 135, 141
New Keep, 138
Nightfort, 145
Nightsong Castle, 232, 244
Night's Watch, 5, 6, 12, 50, 60, 105, 107, 131, 135, 138, 140, 141, 145–46, 147, 149
    castles of, 145, 146, 146
Norridge, Jeremy, 109
North, 8, 12, 20, 33, 42, 82, 93, 107, 134, 135–43, 139, 140, 168, 207
Norvos, 15, 17, 27, 252, 255, 256–59, 258, 261, 263
Noyne river, 17, 255, 256–57
Nymeria, Princess of Ny Sar, 22, 23–25, 24, 236, 240, 241, 268, 280, 285, 286
Ny Sar, 21, 23, 257

Old Ghis, 11, 13–14, 14, 18, 214, 252, 278, 283, 288. See also Ghiscari
Old Mother (pirate queen), 111
Oldstones Castle, 108, 152, 156, 172
Old Tongue, 135, 139, 177
Oldtown, 31, 33, 34, 45, 82, 114, 116, 172, 180, 184, 198, 207, 211, 212–16, 213, 253, 261, 280. See also Citadel
    Hightower, 172, 204, 207, 214–15, 215
    Starry Sept, 45, 51, 53, 207, 216, 218
Oros, 27, 253
Osgood III Shett, 163
Others, 11, 11, 12, 146
Otherys, Bellegere, 98, 98, 276

Pact, the, 8–9, 10, 19
Pate of Longleaf (Lionslayer), 78
Peake, Gormon, 104, 105
Peake, Lorimar, 138
Peake, Unwin, 83, 84
Peake Uprising, 199
Pentos, 15, 17, 18, 27, 55, 59, 252, 261, 262, 265, 266, 266–67
pirates, 36, 49, 68, 83, 109, 111, 168, 169, 225, 262, 265, 280, 282, 283–84, 284, 286
Planky Town, 88, 235, 240, 242, 243, 253
Plumm, Ossifer, 91, 95
Poor Fellows, 54, 55, 56, 57, 62, 77, 230
Prince's Pass, 43, 87, 210, 218, 238
Pyke Castle, 8, 192, 193
pyromancers, 103, 110, 120, 127

Qaathi, 287, 288, 292
Qarlon the Great, 255
Qarth and the Qartheen, 13, 252, 280, 283, 284, 285, 287, 288, 292, 299
Qhoqua, Xhobar, 111
Qhorwyn the Cunning, 185, 186
Qoheros, Nysseos, 270
Qoherys, House and nobles, 157, 158
Qohor, 15, 26, 27, 252, 257, 259–60, 260, 261, 263, 288, 292, 299
Qorgyle, House and nobles, 25, 88, 240, 240

rainwood, 114, 212, 221, 222, 224, 226, 233, 244
Rat, Hawk, and Pig, 105, 109
Rat Cook, 136
ravens, 7, 34, 35, 55, 191, 202, 203
Raventree Hall, 154
Rayder, Mance, 131
Reach, 10, 12, 33, 36, 41, 100, 128, 138, 182, 206, 207–19, 213, 240
    Gardener kings, 209–11, 212
    noble houses of, 217, 217–18
    the Oakenseat, 211, 212, 212
reavers, 176–78, 179, 180, 184, 185, 186, 188, 188–89, 190, 210
Redbeard, Raymun, 141, 149
Redfort, House and nobles, 19, 169
Red Keep, 49, 56, 60, 65, 74, 90, 94, 100, 105, 106, 116, 119, 120–21, 129, 130, 158, 204
    Maidenvault, 90, 92, 94
Red Kings, 137, 138
Red Mountains, 36, 43, 87, 207, 213, 217, 221, 222, 235, 236
Redwyne, House and nobles, 33, 60, 65, 128, 217
religions and lesser gods, 6, 8, 11, 15, 17, 18, 20, 147, 151–52, 167, 224, 237, 257, 268, 271, 275, 281, 282, 287, 289, 300, 304. See also Faith, the; specific gods
    Black Goat, 257–58, 258, 259, 260
    Borash, 254–55, 255–56, 257
    Church of Starry Wisdom, 301
    green god, 207 (see also Garth Greenhand)
    Storm God, 175
Reyne, Ellyn, 199–200, 200, 201, 202, 203

Reynes of Castamere, House and nobles, 195, 196, 199, 200, 201, 202, 203
R'hllor, 11, 26, 257, 261, 268, 275
Rhoynar, 11, 17, 18, 20–21, 21–25, 22, 236, 240, 257, 263, 268, 280
Rhoyne (Mother Rohyne), 11, 17, 18, 21, 22, 23, 27, 242, 255, 256, 267–68, 270
Riverlands, 150, 151–61
    ruling houses (list), 156
Riverrun, 52, 58, 109, 154, 156, 157, 159, 160, 161
Rivers, Aegor (Bittersteel), 99, 101–2, 102, 103, 105, 108, 199, 265
Rivers, Benedict the Bold, 152
Rivers, Brynden (Bloodraven), 99, 101–2, 104, 105, 106, 107
Rivers, Samwell, 154
Robar II of Runestone, 164–65, 166–67, 169
Robert I Baratheon, ix, 113, 127–29, 128, 131, 160, 170, 191, 193, 204, 230–31, 311
Robert's Rebellion, 127–29, 170, 191, 204, 218, 233, 239, 247
Rogare, House and nobles, 264
Rogare, Larra, 84, 94, 95, 264
Rohanne of Tyrosh, 100, 101
Roote, Richard, 51
Rosby, 33, 34, 75, 152
Rosby, Lord, 75, 77, 244
Rossart, Wisdom, 120, 124–25, 129
Rowan, Thaddeus, 83, 84
Roxton, Bold Jon, 76
Royces of Runestone, House and nobles, 19, 52, 78, 163, 164, 167, 170
Royce, Rhea, 66–67, 70, 71
Ruby Ford, 128, 129

Saan, Samaro, 111
Sandship, The, 25, 248
Sarhoy, 21, 22, 268
Sar Mell, 21, 22, 23
Sarnath, 288, 290–91, 290–91
Sarne, 287, 288, 290, 292, 294, 295, 296
Sarnor and Sarnori, 17, 287–88, 289, 290, 296, 302
Seastone Chair, 7, 175, 187, 188, 189, 190, 191, 214
Selhorys, 23, 259, 270
sellswords, 27, 108, 109, 111, 198, 264–65, 267, 282. See also Free Companies
Selmy, Barristan, 112, 112, 119, 126, 128, 129
Selmys, House and nobles, 221
Serala of Myr (Lace Serpent), 118, 119
Sereni of Lys, 97, 98, 99
Seven Kingdoms, 10, 15, 18, 26, 31, 33, 112. See also specific kingdoms
Seven-Pointed Star, The, 17, 163
shadowbinders, 309
shadowcats, 7
Shell, Dywen, 163
Shepherd, 77, 78
Shield Islands, 182, 191, 207, 208, 210, 211
Shiera Seastar, 97, 99
Shipbreaker Bay, 81, 120, 221, 230, 231, 233
Shivering Sea, 17, 26, 168, 214, 253, 257, 271, 287, 292, 294–95, 296, 298, 299, 300, 304
Shrike, 184–85
Shrykes, 303
Silver Sea, 287, 288
skinchangers (or beastlings), 6, 137
Skyreach, 25, 238, 243, 244
Slaver's Bay, 13, 14, 26, 27, 269, 283, 288
slavery and slaves, 13, 14, 15, 17, 18, 22, 24, 25, 26, 177, 258, 263, 264, 267, 278, 279–80, 282, 286, 297. See also Braavos
    Volantis and, 268–69, 269, 270
Sloane, Edgar, 113
Smoking Sea, 27
Snow, Brandon, 42
Snowbeard, Edrick, 143
snowbears, 8
Sothoryos, 24, 252, 271, 278, 281, 284–86, 286
Spotted Tom the Butcher, 111
Stackspear, William, 83
Starfall, 25, 238, 244
Stark, Brandon, 113, 127
Stark, Cregan, 5, 82–83, 141
Stark, Eddard, 113, 127, 129, 160, 170, 191, 233, 239
Stark, Ellard, 65, 141
Stark, Lyanna, 126–27, 142
Stark, Rickard, 113, 138, 141, 142
Stark, Torrhen (the King Who Knelt), 36, 40, 41–42, 43, 141, 169, 265
Starks of Winterfell, 5, 12, 33, 51, 135, 138, 139, 140, 141–43, 149, 168, 169, 265
    as Kings of Winter, 137, 137–38
    Lineage, 314–15
Staunton, Symond, 124, 125, 126
Stepstones, 25, 36, 70, 71, 83, 84, 103, 111, 112, 113, 138, 153, 169, 185, 186, 188, 189, 230, 235, 237, 246, 247, 262, 265, 277
Stokeworth, Alyn, 53, 75, 77
Stokeworth, Falena, 98, 98, 158
Stokeworth, Maia, 93
Stoneborn of Skagos, 139, 139–40
Stonedance Castle, 224, 225

RIGHT | *The Twins.*

Stone Hedge, 151, 155
Stonehelm, 232
Storm Kings, 33, 151, 153–54, 224, 225–26, 230, 231, 240
Stormlands, 39, 40, 62, 96, 100, 128, 186, 211, 212, 220, 221–33, 223
  castles of, 232, 232
  petty kings of, 224
Storm's End, 33, 34, 36, 39–40, 90, 108, 113, 120, 128, 142, 153, 154, 155, 212, 221, 222, 224, 227, 232, 233
Strong, Harwin (Breakbones), 70, 71, 72, 158
Strong, House and nobles, 49, 68, 72, 158
Strong, Larys Clubfoot, 72, 77, 79, 82, 158
Summerhall, 31, 100, 104, 110, 111, 113, 128, 201
Summer Isles, 24, 49, 214, 265, 277, 277–81, 279, 281, 296
Summer Sea, 5, 7, 10, 22, 24, 26, 188, 237, 261, 277, 282, 292
Sunderland, Marla, 36, 168
Sunset Kingdoms, 18, 252
Sunset Sea, 175, 176, 177, 190, 204, 207, 210, 281, 299
Sunspear, 88, 89, 114, 141, 235, 240, 243, 244, 247, 248, 249
Swann, House and nobles, 232, 233, 262
swan ships, 265, 279, 279, 280, 281
swords
  Blackfyre, 35, 55, 58, 59, 88, 96, 96, 243
  Brightroar, 197, 197
  Dark Sister, 35, 50, 57, 66, 78, 246
  Dawn (Sword of the Morning), 239, 239
  Just Maid, 231
  Lady Forlorn, 165, 166
  Lamentation, 78
  Lightbringer, 301, 301
  Nightfall, 189
  Orphan-Maker, 76
  Truth, 264

Tagaros, Marqelo, 197
Talking Trees, 278, 279, 281
Tall Men, 287–88, 289, 290, 291
Tall Trees Town, 49, 278
Talon, 24, 283, 286
Tarbeck, House and nobles, 59, 198, 199, 200, 201, 202–3
Targaryen, Aegon. See Aegon the Conqueror
Targaryen, Aegon, Prince of Dragonstone (son of Aenys I), 53, 56, 157, 198
Targaryen, Aegon the Elder. See Aegon II
Targaryen, Aegon the Younger. See Aegon III
Targaryen, Aelora and Aelor, 105
Targaryen, Aemon (son of Jaehaerys I), 64, 88, 89, 90, 90
Targaryen, Aemon (son of Viserys II), 94, 96
Targaryen, Aemond (One-eye), 68, 71–72, 72, 75, 77–78, 81, 228
Targaryen, Aerion (Brightflame), 105, 106
Targaryen, Alysanne, 53, 60, 64, 65, 81, 170
Targaryen, Alyssa, 63, 65, 227
Targaryen, Baela (twin), 71, 80, 81, 82, 84
Targaryen, Baelon the Brave, 60, 62, 63, 65
Targaryen, Baelor Breakspear, 101, 102–3
Targaryen, Daella, 65, 170
Targaryen, Daemon, 66–68, 67, 70, 71, 72, 73–81, 159, 246, 262
Targaryen, Daena, 90, 91, 91, 93, 94, 95
Targaryen, Daenerys, 98, 100, 101
Targaryen, Daeron. See Daeron I Targaryen
Targaryen, Daeron (son of Aegon IV). See Daeron II Targaryen
Targaryen, Daeron (son of Aegon V), 109
Targaryen, Daeron the Daring, 71, 72, 78, 81, 85–86
Targaryen, Duncan, 108, 109, 111, 230
Targaryen, Elaena, 32
Targaryen, Elaena (sister of Baelor I), 90, 91
Targaryen, Gaemon the Glorious, 53
Targaryen, Helaena, 68, 72, 74–75, 78, 81
Targaryen, House and nobles, 13, 31–129, 90. See also specific rulers
  allies of, 32, 33, 34, 36, 37
  banner of, 36, 68, 76
  end of rule by, 113
  Kings of (chart), 319
  Lannisters and, 198–204
  Lineage, 312–13
  peak of power, 66
  sibling marriage of, 33, 52, 53, 108, 109
  Valyrian blood of, 31
Targaryen, Jaehaera, 81, 83, 84, 190
Targaryen, Jaehaerys, 72, 73, 74, 81
Targaryen, Maekar. See Maekar I Targaryen
Targaryen, Maelor, 74–75
Targaryen, Naerys, 94, 95, 96, 98–99
Targaryen, Rhaegar, 113, 115, 117, 119, 120–21, 124, 125, 126–27, 127, 128–29, 191, 218, 230, 231, 233, 247
Targaryen, Rhaella, 110, 113, 115, 117, 120, 121, 126, 129
Targaryen, Rhaelle, 108, 230
Targaryen, Rhaena, 53, 56, 58, 59, 59, 198
Targaryen, Rhaena (sister of Baelor I), 90, 91, 91
Targaryen, Rhaena (twin), 71, 81, 82, 84
Targaryen, Rhaenyra, 67, 68, 70, 70–71, 72, 73–81, 159, 160, 170, 189, 190, 198
  death of, 80, 80

sons of, 71, 72, 72, 73
Targaryen, Rhaenys, 33, 34, 35, 36, 49, 51, 52, 169, 244
  attack on Storm's End, 39–40
  battle with Mern IX and Loren I, 40–41
  Dorne and, 43–45, 44, 243, 244
  "rule of six" and, 51
Targaryen, Rhaenys (the Queen Who Never Was), 60, 63, 68, 70, 71, 227, 228
  dragon and battle, 75, 76, 77, 77, 81
Targaryen, Shaera, 108, 109
Targaryen, Vaegon (the Dragonless), 65
Targaryen, Visenya, 33, 35, 36, 37, 43, 49–50, 54, 57, 173, 205, 246
  battle with Mern IX and Loren I, 40–41
  dragon, 33, 36, 37, 43, 55
  son Maegor, 51, 52, 53, 54, 55, 57
  sword, 35, 50, 57
Targaryen, Viserys (son of Aerys II), 117, 120, 125, 126, 129
Targaryen, Viserys (son of Alyssa), 57
Targaryen, Viserys (son of Rhaenyra). See Viserys II Targaryen
Tarly, Savage Sam, 53
Tarth, House and nobles, 232
Teague, House and nobles, 153–54, 156
Temmo, 260, 292, 297
Thorne, Rickard, 75
Thousand Islands, 288, 294, 296, 298, 298
thralldom, 177, 271
Three Sisters, 36, 138, 153, 168, 169
Toland, House and nobles, 25, 243
Tollett, Torgold the Grim, 166
Tourney of the Field of Roses, 219
Towers, House and nobles, 158
Triarchy (Kingdom of the Three Daughters), 68, 78, 83, 246, 262, 262–63
Trident, 19, 151, 153, 154, 155, 191, 231, 235
Truefyre, Trystane, 79
Tully, Celia, 109
Tully, Edmyn, 37, 39, 155, 157
Tully, Elmo, 160, 160
Tully, Kermit, 160, 228
Tullys of Riverrun, 52, 78, 153, 154, 156, 156, 159, 160, 187
Tyanna of the Tower, 59, 59
Tyrell, Harlan, 41, 217, 244
Tyrell, Luthor, 109
Tyrell, Lyonel, 88, 217–18
Tyrells, House and nobles, of, 87, 88, 198, 207, 211, 213, 217, 217–18, 233, 243
Tyria, 27, 253
Tyrosh, 25, 26, 27, 68, 111, 112, 116, 186, 252, 261–65, 265, 267

Ulf the Sot (Ulf the White), 76, 77, 78, 81
Uller, House and nobles, 25, 240, 240, 244
Ulthos, 13, 252
Umber, Harmond (Drunken Giant), 149
unicorns, 140, 287, 296
Unsullied, 14, 260, 292
Upcliff, Ursula, 164
Urron Redhand, 20

Vaes Dothrak, 288, 290, 293, 293, 299, 304
Vaith, Cassella, 98, 99
Vale of Arryn, 18, 19, 20, 33, 36, 37, 40, 43, 43, 52, 66–67, 163–73
  coastal islands, 168
  the Fingers, 19, 33, 138, 163, 164, 165, 166, 168, 258
  map, 162
Valyria and Valyrians, 5, 6, 8, 11, 12, 12, 13–27, 17, 31, 197, 198, 213, 214, 252, 253, 255, 267. See also Free Cities
  appearance of people, 13, 94, 264
  cities, 15, 17, 18, 22, 23, 243–76
  conquests by, 15, 17, 18, 22, 26
  the Doom, 17, 26–27, 28, 32, 68, 214, 288, 289, 296
  dragonlords, 12, 17, 18, 21, 22, 23, 26, 32, 214, 257, 261, 268, 273, 283, 303
  Five Forts and, 303
  marriage of siblings, 33, 53
  religions of, 257, 261, 268
  slavery and, 15, 18, 278
  survivors of the Doom, 26
Valyrian steel, 7, 15, 26, 166, 188, 239, 260
Valysar, 23, 259, 270
Vance, Armistead, 156
Varys (the Spider), 120, 124–25
Velaryon, Alyssa, 53, 57, 60
Velaryon, Corlys (Sea Snake), 65, 66, 67–68, 71, 72, 76, 77–78, 80–81, 82, 83, 189, 246, 262, 296–97, 298, 307, 309
Velaryon, Daemon, 36, 56, 58
Velaryon, House and nobles, 32, 34, 51, 65, 67, 68, 71, 72, 77, 84, 189
  Driftwood Throne of, 65
Velaryon, Jacaerys, 71, 72, 72, 75, 78, 81
Velaryon, Joffrey, 71, 72, 72, 78
Velaryon, Laenor, 63, 70–71, 228
  bastards of, 76
  dragon of, 63

murder of, 71
Velaryon, Lucerys, 71, 72, 72, 81, 124, 228
  dragon of, 228
  murder of, 73–74
Velvet Hills, 17, 18, 21
Vhalaso the Munificent, 268
Viserys I Targaryen, 53, 63, 65, 66, 66–72, 158, 170
  death of, 72, 73
  marriages, 67, 68, 73, 170
  tourney of 111 AC, 68, 68–69
  Year of the Red Spring (120 AC), 71
Viserys II Targaryen, 72, 84, 85, 86, 87, 89, 90, 92, 93, 94, 95
Volantis, 15, 18, 22, 26–27, 116, 120, 169, 186, 230, 252, 253, 260, 261, 265, 267–70, 270, 276, 292, 296
  elephants and tigers, 26, 27, 33, 269, 270
  slave tattoos, 268, 269
Volon Therys, 22, 23, 259, 270
Vulture Hunt, 53
Vulture King of Dorne, 52, 53, 227, 246
Vypren, House of, 159

Walano, 24, 277, 278, 280, 281
Wall, 5–6, 12, 62, 107, 138, 142, 145–49
  captured kings sent to, 25, 240, 241
  constructing of, 2–3, 145
wargs, 6, 137
War of the Ninepenny Kings, 111–12, 112, 113, 121, 201, 230, 247
War of Three Princes, 22
War on Dagger Lake, 22
Warrior's Sons, 45, 54, 55, 56, 57, 62, 216
water dancers, 276
Waters, Jon and Jeyne, 91
Waters, Marston, 80, 84–85
Weeping Town, 221
Weirwood Alliance, 226
weirwoods, 6, 8–9, 8, 19, 20, 152, 175, 218
Westerlands, 12, 33, 40, 56, 62, 74, 84, 102, 113, 115, 126, 153, 169, 176, 180, 182, 189, 195–204
  castles of, 195
  great houses of, 195
  map, 194
Westerling, Jeyne, 59, 59
Westerling, Roland of the Crag, 83
Westerlings, House and nobles, 70, 195, 199
Westeros, 10, 13, 15, 33, 53, 135. See also Seven Kingdoms; specific rulers
  Aegon the Conqueror's reign, 49–51
  ancient peoples of, 5, 8
  Andals arrive and conquer, 18–20
  breaking of land bridge to Essos, 237
  Conquest, 31–45
  governance, 51, 62 (see also Iron Throne)
  Kings (chart), 319
  legal code, 51, 62
  map, in ancient days, 4
  as Rhaesh Andahli, 18
  Targaryen rule ends, 113
  ten thousand ships and, 23–25
Whent, House and nobles, 121, 124, 158
White Harbor, 135, 138
White Knife river, 138, 168
White Mountains (Krazaaj Zasqa), 298, 299
white walkers, 12, 222
Whitewalls, 104, 105
wildlings, 5, 6, 12, 19, 135, 141, 146, 147, 147–49, 148, 149, 263
  Gendel and Gorne, 7, 148, 149
Winterfell, 5, 10, 113, 126, 135, 142, 142–43, 168
Winter Fever, 198
Winter Wolves, 78, 82
Wolf's Den, 138, 168
Wyl, House and nobles, 25, 89, 90, 224, 227, 238, 241, 244
Wylde, Jasper (Ironrod), 77
wyverns, 285

Xanda Qo, 279

Year of the False Spring (281 AC), 124
Yeen, 24, 285, 286
Yi Ti, 11, 13, 65, 261, 300–305, 306
  Five Forts, 303
  God-Emperors of, 302
Yronwood, House and nobles, 25, 238, 240, 240, 241, 242, 243
Yunkai (the yellow city), 14

Zalyne, Uthero, 271, 273
Zamettar, 24, 284, 285
Zamoyos, 24, 284, 285
Zhea the Barren, 305
Zoqora, 287, 288
zorses, 304, 305

RIGHT | *Jon Snow and Ghost.*

ART CREDITS

RENÉ AIGNER: pages 185, 298, 309

RYAN BARGER (Fantasy Flight): page 38

ARTHUR BOZONNET (Studio Hive): pages 8, 18, 19, 23, 80, 89, 90, 106, 125, 139, 176, 226, 260, 274, 276, 282

JOSÉ DANIEL CABRERA PEÑA: pages 85, 103, 112, 148–149, 239

JENNIFER SOL CAI (Velvet Engine): inside end papers, pages viii, 51, 78, 88, 96, 187, 137, 156, 169, 187, 199, 217, 227, 240, 312, 315, 317, 319

THOMAS DENMARK (Fantasy Flight): page 136

JENNIFER DRUMMOND: pages 24, 114

JORDI GONZÁLEZ ESCAMILLA: pages ii, iii, x, 10, 28–29, 54, 76–77, 178, 225, 232, 254–255, 262–263, 270, 301

MICHAEL GELLATLY: pages 4, 134, 150, 162, 174, 194, 206, 220, 234, 318

TOMASZ JEDRUSZEK (Fantasy Flight): pages 181, 188–189, 230–231, 248, 293

MICHAEL KOMARCK: pages 48, 58, 116 (Fantasy Flight), 118, 157, 243, 247

JOHN McCAMBRIDGE: pages 37, 164–165, 213, 258, 284

MOGRI (Velvet Engine): inside end papers, pages viii, 137, 169, 227, 240, 315

TED NASMITH: pages v, 16, 30, 50, 130, 132–133, 142, 144, 158, 161, 171, 192, 205, 215, 219, 249, 323

KARLA ORTIZ: pages 66, 87, 107, 127, 241

RAHEDIE YUDHA PRADITO (Velvet Engine): pages 51, 78, 88, 96

DHIAN PRASETYA: pages 85, 103, 112, 148–149, 239

PAOLO PUGGIONI: pages 79, 122–123, 173, 222–223, 272–273, 290–291

JONATHAN ROBERTS: pages 146, 275, 277, 284, 294–295

THOMAS SIAGIAN (Velvet Engine): inside end papers, pages viii, 156, 187, 199, 312, 317, 319

MARC SIMONETTI: pages 11, 14, 27, 35, 46–47, 56–57, 61, 62–63, 67, 92 (Fantasy Flight), 97, 102, 104–105, 110, 121, 155, 183, 266, 279, 281, 304–305

CHASE STONE: pages 2–3, 20–21, 42–43, 68–69, 74, 229, 245

PHILIP STRAUB: front end papers, pages 250–251

JUSTIN SWEET: pages 86, 310, 325, back end papers

NUTCHAPOL THITINUNTHAKORN (Studio Hive): pages 197, 212, 236, 252, 286

MAGALI VILLENEUVE: pages 9, 12, 32, 44, 52, 59, 64, 70, 82, 91, 95, 98–99, 100, 128, 153, 159, 160, 200, 202, 210, 261, 264, 265

DOUGLAS WHEATLEY: pages vi, vii, 6, 7, 34, 40, 72, 81, 140, 147, 208, 269, 306, 320–321

END PAPER | *Rhaegar Targaryen and Lord Robert Baratheon meeting at the Ruby Ford during the Battle of the Trident.*